PRAISE FOR DEBBIE MACOMBER
AND HER FAVORITE ANGELS

"Three heartwarming angels to spend Christmas with."
—Sandra Canfield

"Debbie Macomber is one of our premier storytellers."
—Anne Stuart

"*A Season of Angles* is a delightful, heartwarming read.
Shirley, Mercy, and Goodness will touch the lives of every
reader. I loved it!"
—Lori Copeland

"Charming and touching by turns. It would take a real
Scrooge not to enjoy this story of three ditsy angels and
answered prayers."
—Elizabeth Lowell

Books by Debbie Macomber

Touched by Angels

Someday Soon

The Trouble with Angels

One Night

A Season of Angels

Morning Comes Softly

Purrfect Love

Sooner or Later

Christmas Angels: Three Heavenly Romances

Published by HarperPaperbacks

Christmas Angels
Three Heavenly Romances

Debbie Macomber

HarperPaperbacks
A Division of HarperCollins*Publishers*

HarperPaperbacks

A Division of HarperCollins*Publishers*

10 East 53rd Street, New York, N.Y. 10022-5299

A Season of Angels. Copyright © 1993 by Debbie Macomber
The Trouble with Angels. Copyright © 1994 by Debbie Macomber
Touched by Angels. Copyright © 1995 by Debbie Macomber

ISBN: 0-06-108690-8

HarperCollins®, HarperMonogram, and HarperPaperbacks™ are trademarks of HarperCollins*Publishers* Inc.

HarperPaperbacks may be purchased for educational, business, or sales promotional use. For information, please write:
Special Markets Department, HarperCollins*Publishers,*
10 East 53rd Street, New York, N.Y. 10022-5299.

Printed in the United States of America

First HarperPaperbacks printing: November 1996

Back cover illustration by Jim Griffin

Designed by Anthony Ramondo

Library of Congress Cataloging-in-Publication Data is available upon request from the publisher.

Visit HarperPaperbacks on the World Wide Web at
http://www.harpercollins.com/paperbacks

❖ 10 9 8 7 6 5 4 3 2 1

A Season of Angels

To Kevin and Marcia Hestead
for the shining example of God's love

Chapter

★ ☆ ★

1

The manger was empty. Leah Lundberg walked past the nativity scene Providence Hospital put out every year, stopped, and stared. The north wind cut through her like a boning knife as Leah studied the ramshackle stable, her heart heavy, her life more so.

The blue of Mary's gown had long since faded, she noted. Joseph, leaning heavily against his staff, was slightly off-balance, and looked as if he'd topple in a stiff wind. There seemed to be one less lamb this year and one of the donkey's ears was missing. It was a small wonder the structure remained upright with the weight of the angel, yellow now instead of golden, nailed to the top. Triumphantly, she blew her chipped horn proclaiming the glorious news of the Savior's birth.

The hospital had reconstructed the Christmas scene every Advent for the last fifty years, long before Leah was born, long before she realized an entire lifetime of tears could be stored within a single tattered soul.

It was ironic that a woman who toiled as a nurse day after day on a maternity ward would be childless herself. Her work with laboring mothers was her gift, they said, her special talent. Women specifically requested that she be with them for the birthing of their children.

For whatever reason, Leah had been granted the touch, a gentle hand, and a sympathetic heart. Birthing mothers claimed she was inspiring, encouraging, and supportive. Labor didn't seem nearly as difficult when Leah was with a patient. She'd heard it all before, countless times, the praise, the gratitude. What most of Leah's patients didn't know was that she, who was an expert at labor and delivery, had never given birth herself.

Her patients left the hospital with their arms and their lives full. Each afternoon, Leah walked out of Providence alone. And empty.

3

Tears crowded her eyes and spilled unheeded down her cheeks. She bowed her head and closed her eyes in prayer. "Dear God," she whispered, choking down the emotion, "please give me a child." It was a plea she'd whispered innumerable times over the last ten years. So often that she was convinced God had long since given up hearing. Or caring.

Wiping the moisture from her face, she gathered her coat more closely around her thin shoulders and headed for the staff parking lot. She forced herself to smile. It upset Andrew that she continued to dwell on their inability to have children, and she didn't want him to know she'd been crying.

Her husband had accepted the news with little more than a shrug. He felt bad, knowing how desperately she longed for a baby, but it wasn't nearly as earth-shattering to him. If God saw fit to send children into their lives, then fine, if not, that was fine too.

It wasn't all right with Leah and she doubted that it ever would be.

Leah's prayer whistled in the breeze, up through the bare spindly arms of a lanky birch tree, winging its way higher and higher until it had ascended the clouds and drifted into the warm winds of heaven. It arrived fresh with the salt of her tears at the desk of the Archangel Gabriel. The very angel who'd announced the news of the virgin birth to Mary nearly two thousand years earlier. His responsibilities had been wide and varied through time, but he felt a certain tenderness for humans and their multiple problems. He found earth's population to be a curious lot. They were stubborn, rebellious, and arrogant. Their antics were a constant source of amusement to those behind the pearly gates. Who could help laughing at a group of people who heatedly declared that God was dead and clung to the belief that Elvis was alive?

"Leah Lundberg," Gabriel repeated softly, frowning. The name was vaguely familiar. He flipped the pages of a cumbersome book until he'd found what he was seeking. Sighing, he relaxed against the back of his chair and slowly shook his head. Leah was one of his most persistent cases. He'd heard her prayer often, had ushered it himself to the very feet of God.

Gabriel had sent countless couriers to intercede on Leah's behalf, but their efforts had been met with repeated failure. Time after time, their reports came back virtually the same. It was a familiar problem that blocked the answer to Leah's prayer. Herself.

It would have been much easier if Gabriel could sit down with Leah and talk out this matter face-to-face. Circumstances arose now and again when doing exactly what was required, but generally not when it came to answering prayer. Humans tended to believe all that was required of them was a few mumbled words, then they were utterly content to leave the matter in the hands of God.

Through the ages humans had yet to discover what should have been obvious. The answers to prayer required participation. The people of earth expected God to do it all. Only a shocking few realized they had their own role to perform.

A good example was a request that had come in earlier from Monica Fischer, a preacher's daughter. Monica had asked for a husband. Normally this wouldn't be a problem; she was twenty-five and strikingly attractive, or would be if she didn't choose to disguise her natural beauty. The whole process of attracting a young man was complicated by her self-righteous attitude. Few men, even devout servants of God, were willing to marry sanctimonious prudes.

Gabriel hadn't decided how he would handle Monica's request or the prayer that had come in the unusual form of a letter from Timmy Potter. Gabriel had a soft spot when it came to children's prayers. Timmy was nine, and had requested a father.

Gabriel shook his head, needing to clear his thoughts. He'd deal with one prayer at a time. For the moment Leah's request was the most pressing, and the most challenging. He'd figure out something for Monica and Timmy later.

He stood and walked around his desk. Gabriel thought best while on his feet. It didn't help matters that Leah chose Christmastime to issue her fervent prayer. The busiest time of year, no less. His best prayer ambassadors were already out on assignment and those who were left were young angels lacking in experience.

Of course there was always Mercy. She possessed a heart of pure gold and was especially patient with humans. But there was a small problem with this particular angel.

Mercy was enthralled with earthly things. Mechanical things. She seemed particularly fond of escalators and motor scooters and not even heaven knew what else. Reports of her escapades circulated in both spheres.

An angel, especially one under Gabriel's command, simply did not hijack meter maids' carts. That business with the forklift on the San Francisco waterfront . . . well, that didn't bear thinking about.

Gabriel's musings were interrupted by the whisper of rustling wings. Mercy appeared bright-eyed and hopeful before him, her hands clasped in prayerlike fashion. She was a dainty thing, petite in stature when compared to several of the other prayer ambassadors.

"You wanted to see me."

Gabriel grinned. He hadn't sent for Mercy, but apparently God had.

"I'd be happy to volunteer my services in any way I can," Mercy offered brightly, her wings fluttering slightly with anticipation. "I want to prove myself."

"Can you stay away from motor scooters?"

Mercy nodded eagerly. "And jet skis."

Jet skis. He hadn't heard about that one and it was best that he didn't, not now, at least. "I can't have you intercepting any more Boeing 747s."

"I've learned my lesson, Gabriel," she murmured, and smiled innocently, as if to suggest that these incidents were a series of minor misunderstandings. "I promise I won't get into any of the trouble I have before."

"I'm sure you won't," Gabriel muttered.

"Then you'll give me the assignment?"

Gabriel stood. His seven-foot stature was intimidating, he knew. Each time the heavenly Father had sent him on a mission to earth he'd been required to calm a multitude of fears before relaying his message.

"The prayer is from Leah Lundberg," Gabriel explained with a thoughtful frown. "For the past ten years she's been in constant communication with heaven. She longs for a child."

Compassion filled Mercy's deep blue eyes. "Her arms must feel empty."

"When Leah first married Andrew Lundberg the prayer request came now and again, but when she didn't become pregnant after repeated failure, well, let me put it like this. Leah had us in a tizzy for a good long while. At one point we had five angels assigned full-time to her prayers. A year later we reduced it to one, and now her prayers are infrequent, and her faith is weak."

Mercy blinked several times. "This is a problem case, isn't it?"

Gabriel nodded. Mercy had achieved some success in answering prayer, but her experience was limited. To assign her to Leah was an extreme measure. Gabriel regretted that, but he didn't have much choice.

"How often does she pray now?" Mercy asked, and her wings stilled.

"Once or twice a year. She's given up believing God listens to the concerns of his children. Unfortunately she's given up on her faith too," Gabriel explained with regret. "If that isn't tragic enough, she's walking straight toward the pit of despair."

"But that's not true about her prayers going unheard," Mercy cried. "Someone should tell her, give her a message, offer her hope. Why, all that poor, dear woman needs is a bit of reassurance." Agitated, the petite angel paced the area in front of Gabriel's desk. "Send me, please, Gabriel, I promise to stay out of trouble."

The archangel hesitated. He had the sinking feeling that Mercy's promise would quickly become famous last words.

He noticed that the tips of her wings feathered out and fluttered gently when he nodded. "I'll go with you and explain the circumstances. I can't afford to spare you much past Christmas."

"Just until Christmas," Mercy protested. "That doesn't give me much time."

"Do whatever you feel is necessary to help her," he said, granting her unprecedented powers.

Gabriel didn't want to say it, but when it came to Leah Lundberg, he felt her prayer had little likelihood of being answered. Over the last ten years the human had been given countless chances. Mercy was one of the least experienced angels in his task force. He didn't hold out much hope that she'd succeed when so many other far more accomplished ambassadors had failed.

"We should start right away, then, don't you think?" Mercy pressed, eager to begin.

Gabriel glanced at the stack of unanswered prayers piling up on his desk and nodded. "I can only spare a few moments."

"I'd appreciate whatever help you can give me."

Gabriel grumbled under his breath. This could be a waste of precious time, then again, it might well be the answer to a long-standing request. He'd witnessed far greater miracles.

"Come with me," the archangel instructed, and Mercy followed obediently behind him. He was fond of this prayer ambassador although he wasn't keen on admitting as much.

"I hope I can help her."

"I hope so too," Gabriel murmured. "Look with me and I'll introduce you to Leah and Andrew Lundberg."

Slowly he raised his massive arms and with one swift motion the thick white clouds parted into a gentle mist that slowly dissipated. The scene unfolded like the opening pages of a pop-up book as the majesty that surrounded Mercy evaporated into the midst of the mundane world. The archangel and Mercy stood on the sidelines as Leah Lundberg opened the front door of her house and walked inside.

*   *   *

"I'm home," Leah called out to her husband, removing her thick winter coat and hanging it in the hall closet. As always her house was spotless. Her furniture was polished, the latest in contemporary styling. The black-lacquer-on-silver dining table shone back at her like a mirror. Her gaze rested on a white lambskin sofa that had cost nearly four thousand dollars. Her home was expensive and ultramodern. A child would wreak havoc in her pristine domain.

Leah's friends envied her home. Their own were often a minefield of toys and other traps children left scattered about. Her friends' lives centered around feeding schedules, soccer practices, and flute lessons. Leah would gladly relinquish her grand piano for a crib and the Persian rug for a playpen. She would gladly trade her tidy existence for the chaos and joy a child would bring into her life and marriage.

"I've got dinner cooking," her husband announced from inside the kitchen. "How does marinated flank steak, new red potatoes, and fresh asparagus sound?"

"Excellent." She moved into the kitchen and wrapped her arms around Andrew's waist.

Their massive kitchen included every modern convenience imaginable. A large room for two people who dined out more often than they ate at home. Andrew, an architect, had designed her kitchen when they believed their future included children. She'd clung to the thread of that hope, but it had grown impossibly thin as the fiber of her dreams had worn away.

Leah's eyes rested on her shiny, clean cupboards and her waxed, spotless floor. Her heart moved into her throat with a sharp stab of unexpected pain. She longed for a refrigerator door smudged with jelly-coated fingerprints, and linoleum scuffed with marks made from walking shoes and toy trucks.

"Did you have a long day?" Andrew asked.

Leah nodded. She deeply loved her husband. Without him, she didn't know how she would have endured the last several years. "We delivered three babies before noon. Two boys and a girl." Leah had long since lost count of the number of births she'd assisted. Hundreds, she guessed. But it didn't matter how often or how commonplace it seemed, the miracle of birth hadn't lost its impact.

"What about you?" she asked.

"Same old grind as always," Andrew mumbled, preoccupied with their dinner preparations.

"We should have ordered out."

"I don't mind," he told her, and she could hear the warmth in his voice. "I talked to the decorator about a tree," he said, and turned to face Leah. He buried his face in her hair and breathed in deeply. "I thought we'd have the tree done in angels this year."

"Angels," Leah repeated softly. "That sounds nice."

"Mom phoned earlier," he continued. "She invited us over for Christmas Eve."

Leah nodded. Christmas was meant for children. Instead of stringing popcorn and cranberries on the tree with her toddlers, she was working with a decorator who would shape their Christmas tree into a work of art. She would have much preferred a work of love.

When, Leah asked herself, when, oh, when, would the raw edges of her pain go away? She'd be a good mother. Andrew would be a doting, loving father. That God in his almighty wisdom had not seen fit to give her a child was the cruelest of fates. Tears filled her eyes and she looked away, not wanting Andrew to see. He knew her so well it was difficult to hide anything from him.

"Leah?"

She snuggled closer in his arms, needing the warm security of his love.

"It's worse at Christmastime, isn't it?" he asked gently.

They'd had this same conversation a hundred times over the years. With nothing new to add, with nothing new to share, it was best shelved.

"When will dinner be ready?" she asked, easing herself from the comfort of Andrew's embrace. She managed a watery smile. "I'm starved."

"Have you seen enough?" Gabriel asked, standing directly behind Mercy.

She'd seen more than she wanted. Slowly, thoughtfully, Mercy dragged her gaze away from the scene below. Compassion swelled and throbbed within her. "Leah's hurting so terribly."

"She hasn't stopped and won't until . . ."

"Until when?" Mercy prompted.

"Until she's found her peace."

"Peace," Mercy cried, folding back her wings. "The poor dear's at war with herself."

Gabriel looked surprised by her insight. "Leah must fully accept her inability to bear a child before the invisible threads that bind her fall away," Gabriel explained. "Then and only then will she be ready."

"This is my mission, to show Leah the way to peace?" The tentacles of dread gripped Mercy's tender heart. Gabriel was seeking the impossible. She longed to help this woman of the earth, longed to ease the pain of her loneliness and the desolation of her soul. Slowly Mercy shook her head, wondering how she, an inexperienced prayer ambassador, would break through the barrier of Leah's misery and lead her to the warm, sandy shores of serenity.

"You may choose to refuse," Gabriel announced formally.

"I would never do that," Mercy said, surprising herself with the strength of her fervor. She didn't know how she'd manage but somehow, some way, she'd find a means of accomplishing her mission. One thing she'd learned since her appointment as a prayer ambassador. With God's help she could forge a path where there hadn't been one before. With God's help she would make a way where there was none.

"I can't spare you any longer than three weeks, earth time," Gabriel reminded her. "Not with the New Year coming on. You know what it's like around here when people start making resolutions. By the middle of January, earthlings decide to take one last-ditch effort and try prayer."

"Only three weeks," Mercy repeated slowly. Even now she was having a difficult time pulling her gaze away from the scene between Leah and her husband.

"You'll contact me with any problems?" Gabriel asked.

Mercy bristled. The archangel's offer insinuated that she'd encounter more than her share, which was an unfair assumption. It was true she'd had trouble with the last assignment, had gotten sidetracked a time or two, but she successfully managed to complete her mission.

"There's no physical reason why Leah can't become pregnant?" Mercy asked, wanting to be certain she had her facts straight. The last thing she wanted was to walk into the middle of a prayer request without adequate information.

"None whatsoever," Gabriel stated matter-of-factly. "Leah and Andrew have been to see every fertility specialist on the West Coast."

"What about adoption?"

"They applied five years ago, but the waiting list is several years long. They were chosen by a birth mother and then bitterly disappointed when she changed her mind at the last minute. They withdrew their name shortly afterward."

"How very sad," Mercy said softly.

"The Lundbergs are deeply in love."

"That helps."

Gabriel's chuckle caught Mercy off guard. She swiveled her attention to the archangel, who was clearly amused.

"What's so funny?" Mercy demanded, irritated and not taking time to censure the thought. Gabriel, after all, was an archangel and she was in no position to be questioning him.

"Nothing," he said, smiling broadly.

Gabriel wasn't one to smile. He did so only rarely. Mercy wasn't convinced it was even in his personality profile.

"I'll give this prayer request my best effort," Mercy said, thinking it was important that Gabriel know that.

"I trust you will. Just promise me one thing."

Here it came, the long list of offenses she'd managed to rack up in the short while she'd been serving as a prayer ambassador. "Yes?" she said, straightening for the coming lecture.

"Stay away from scooters and escalators this time."

Mercy grinned. "I will."

Chapter

★ ✦ ★

2

It was a disgrace, a downright disgrace the way Providence Hospital continued to use the same weatherworn figures in their nativity scene, Monica Fischer mused. The colors had faded and the animals, why, it was a travesty how dilapidated they'd become. If the hospital insisted upon decorating the grounds for Christmas, then they should do so properly.

"Did you see the nativity scene at Providence Hospital?" she asked her father as she joined him and the other choir members outside Nordstrom's department store, downtown Seattle.

"I adore the crèche," Lloyd Fischer said with a beaming smile. "Mary's seen better years, I know, but I can't help thinking that battered stable must be much closer to the way it actually was that night in Bethlehem than we realize."

Her father was right, Monica knew. He generally was. She tried to be as charitable in thought and deed as he was, but it seemed beyond her. That was the crux of her problem, Monica realized. Every man she met was measured against her father's goodness and none had withstood the evaluation. Not even Patrick, whom she'd dated off and on for the last two years. Apparently their relationship was more off than she realized. He'd phoned two weeks earlier to tell her he was engaged to someone else.

That hurt and it hurt deeply. Monica had been dating Patrick all this time and assumed they'd enjoyed each other's company. She hadn't a clue he was seeing anyone else. True, they hadn't spoken of love or commitment, but they'd shared something special, at least Monica had thought it was special.

To make matters worse Patrick had finished by saying he would always think of Monica as a special friend. Monica had wanted much more than his friendship. It was time for her to marry and start her own family, and she'd foolishly set her sights on the wrong man. Now she'd need to make up for lost time, but by heaven, she vowed she'd marry and soon. There was a man for her, she was convinced of that, and she fully intended to find him.

"Are you ready?" her father asked, cupping her elbow.

Monica nodded. She enjoyed these Christmas performances the church choir gave each December in the busy downtown streets. The harried shoppers would pause and listen to the joyous music, enjoying the short respite from the hectic holiday rush. For a few short moments peace would descend like a warm blanket upon the milling crowd.

Monica climbed to the soprano section on the back row of the risers. She was tall, nearly five-nine, and stood a full head above the majority of the sopranos. Unlike the others, she opted for sensible flats with her dark blue suit. Her hair, although shoulder length, was tucked into a tight bun at the base of her neck. She wore no cosmetics and frowned upon women who did.

This was the first year their music was provided by their own church band. To Monica's way of thinking they should have made a point of practicing more often. The band's mistakes stuck out in an otherwise flawless program.

She played the piano, and as a favor to the choir director, Michael Simpson, sat in for a couple of weeks in their practice sessions. She hoped her dedication and example would inspire the small group. Her plan hadn't worked and no one seemed to appreciate the rigorous practice schedule she set for herself and the others. Eventually she'd gone back to the choir, and was pleased she had. Michael, as a means of making amends, asked that she sing a short solo in one of her all-time favorite Christmas carols, "Silent Night."

When everyone was positioned on the risers, Michael raised his baton. The choir snapped to attention. Monica was proud of the professionalism of their small ensemble. Their voices rose in melodic harmony, blending smoothly. Monica's clear, high soprano voice escalated gloriously with the others. When she sang, she felt closer to heaven than at any other time, even when she prayed, which was something she'd been doing a good deal of lately. She needed a husband.

"Monica's the tall one on the top riser," Gabriel said, pointing out the earthling to Goodness. Like Mercy, Gabriel held a special fondness for this prayer ambassador, who, again like Mercy, possessed certain character traits that left him with misgivings. If it weren't for the business of the Christmas season, he wouldn't have assigned Goodness such a difficult case.

Unfortunately he had little choice and of those ambassadors left, Goodness was his best chance of seeing this prayer to fruition. If only he could guarantee that Goodness would stay away from television and movie screens. The incident of her showing up on an in-flight movie and using John Wayne's voice to warn everyone of approaching turbulence continued to rankle. He'd counseled her on a number of occasions, but to no avail.

"I know what you're thinking," Goodness said, looking up at him with eyes filled with innocent promise. "I won't pull any more stunts with humans. I've learned my lesson."

"You're sure this time?"

Goodness glanced toward Monica and nodded eagerly.

Gabriel wished he shared her confidence. His own gaze drifted toward Monica Fischer. Her name was a familiar one as her father, a man after God's own heart, often included her in his prayers. Monica came from a strong religious background. With her father serving as the pastor, Monica had been raised in the church. It was ironic that what the young woman lacked was faith when she was surrounded on all sides by it. Instead Monica was deeply religious and had yet to distinguish the differences between faith and religion.

"She's lovely," Goodness claimed, locking her wings together. "Finding Monica a husband won't be the least bit difficult, not when she's so outwardly beautiful. God must have a special man in mind for her."

"He does," Gabriel agreed with some reluctance, wondering just how much he should explain to this inexperienced ambassador. Goodness would learn everything she needed to know soon enough, he decided. The information he had would overwhelm her now. Soon enough Goodness would recognize exactly what God had planned for Monica Fischer.

The angel focused her attention on him, her eyes wide and questioning, awaiting an explanation. "What is it I must teach her?"

Gabriel drew in a deep breath and explained. "I fear Monica's steeped in the juices of her own self-righteousness. She struggles to be good under her own power and ignores all the help made available to her through faith."

Goodness sighed with heartfelt sympathy. "She must be miserable."

"No," Gabriel returned without hesitation, "she just makes everyone else feel that way. Monica's complicated her life with a long list of rights and wrongs and dos and don'ts. Her head's so clouded with matters unrelated to faith that she's lost sight of what it means to be a child of God. Her struggles are useless when everything has already been done for her. All she need do is ask." But Gabriel wasn't telling Goodness anything new. The earth was populated with those who looked for redemption through religion.

"The poor dear."

Gabriel didn't view Monica in those terms. It was her type that caused him the greatest concern. While Monica struggled to lead people to God, her sanctimonious ways often steered them in the opposite direction.

"She sings very well," Goodness commented.

Gabriel nodded. "She's gifted in several areas."

"I shouldn't have any trouble teaching what she needs to know before Christmas."

How confident Goodness sounded, Gabriel noticed. He sighed inwardly, wondering once more how much he should explain, then decided it would be best not to discourage Goodness's enthusiasm. She'd discover everything she needed to know soon enough.

"The man God has for her is ready for a wife?"

Gabriel was beginning to feel a twinge of guilt. "Yes, and eager. Very eager. Only he doesn't know it yet, but you won't have to worry about him. Monica's the one who needs you."

"Then I'll do everything within my power to help her."

"You're ready?" Gabriel asked, thinking he'd best send her soon before he said too much. This request would be a learning experience for this young prayer ambassador as well as for her charge. All he could do was hope for the best.

"Let's go," Goodness said, impatient to leave the splendor of heaven and walk incognito into a dull, sin-cloaked world.

Gabriel watched as Goodness floated down from heaven, thinking humans were right about one thing. God often did work in mysterious ways and never more so than in this instance. Gabriel was confident of one thing. Neither Goodness nor Monica Fischer would ever be the same again.

Monica looked out over the gathering crowd and was pleased at the attention their small choir had garnered. Shoppers stopped, their arms folded around packages and some of the tiredness left their eyes. A few joined in and sang themselves. Children were lifted in their fathers' arms for a better look. The transformation the singing group produced brought a small, satisfied smile in Monica's heart.

Then she noticed a man who stood head and shoulders above the others. He seemed to be trapped by the people around him, and was impatiently edging his way around the gathering.

Being on the top riser gave her an excellent view and she frowned at this intruder. He needed both a shave and a haircut. Even from this distance she noted his eyes, which were a cutting shade of cobalt blue. He seemed to need to get somewhere and was impatiently making his way through the crowd, scooting around one and then another with nary a word of pardon. He wore a beige trench coat and looked as if he'd slept in the bedraggled thing.

Monica's gaze followed him as long as she could, but he soon moved out of her peripheral vision. What an unpleasant man, she decided, annoyed at his intrusion into their performance. No doubt he was a modern-day Scrooge who resented every moment wasted on the celebration of the Savior's birth.

The small church band struck up the first chords of the next carol, "Silent Night." The highest notes were well within Monica's vocal range and her voice was strong enough to ring out loud and clear. When the moment arrived for her short solo performance she allowed her soul to soak up the music and fly free. Then unexpectedly, from out of nowhere, another voice joined and blended with hers.

Quickly Monica looked in both directions to see who had been so bold as to disrupt her one moment of glory. She knew she shouldn't be so concerned, but it bothered her, and yet as far as she could tell none of the other sopranos were singing.

She raised her voice a full octave, straining her vocal chords. The second voice followed her lead, angelic in its purity and so strong it all but drowned out her own. What perplexed Monica most was that no one else around her seemed to notice anything was amiss. Faces from the audience gazed on approvingly and even the choir director smiled, delighted by her performance.

As she drew to a close, the last of the notes fading into nothingness, the small crowd cheered and she was enthusiastically applauded. Annoyed that her one and only solo had been interrupted by an intruder, Monica twisted around to see if she could find the second voice.

She must have been more energetic in her efforts than she realized because she lost her balance. Her arms flew out in an effort to catch herself, but before she could alert anyone to her plight, she tumbled backward off the top step of the riser.

Crying out, her arms flapping in empty space, she was surprised to land in the unexpected cushion of a man's waiting arms.

"Well, well, what do we have here?"

It was him. The very man she'd noticed earlier, the one who'd cut his way through the crowd with such impatience.

"Ah . . ." For the life of her Monica couldn't make herself speak. All she could do was stare into his handsome features. On closer inspection his eyes were a deeper shade, a metallic blue, amused now, but dispassionate. The thick lines that fanned out from his eyes weren't from smiling. They spoke of experience, most of it harsh, and disenchantment, most of it warranted, she guessed. Lines bracketed his mouth as well, they deepened as he studied her with the same curiosity with which she regarded him.

"No need to take such a chance," he chided. "If you wanted an introduction all you needed to do was ask."

Gasping and breathless, Monica struggled until he slowly, reluctantly lowered her feet to the ground. He waited until she'd found her balance before he released her completely.

"You might want to thank me," he suggested lazily.

Flustered, Monica blinked several times, seldom at a loss for words as she was now. "Thank you," she managed, the words as stiff as starch, stuck in her dry throat. "I'm not sure what happened, but apparently I lost my balance."

His brazen grin broadened. "Was that you singing just now?"

She nodded, and the curiosity got the better of her. "Did you hear two voices or one?"

"One."

"But there were two. That's what flustered me so. Another voice blended with mine. A strong soprano. Surely you heard the other voice?"

"Listen, lady, all I heard was you and I'm not much for religious music, but from where I was standing you sounded real good."

She blushed with pleasure. Her voice was adequate and she did love to sing, but she didn't possess any great talent. To assume she did would have been vain on her part, and vanity was a greased track straight to the arms of the devil as far as Monica was concerned. "Thank you again."

"You need some help joining the others?"

Monica glanced toward the riser and shook her head. The ensemble was almost finished with their program and it would only disrupt the group to have her climb back into position now.

"Then I'll be on my way," he said. "I can hardly wait to tell Lou. It isn't often a beautiful woman throws herself into my arms."

"I didn't throw myself into your arms," she informed him primly, straightening the sleeves of her dark suit jacket.

"Not technically perhaps, but there you were, pretty as a picture gazing up at me, asking for a kiss."

Monica bristled. "I most certainly was not."

"It felt good to be in my arms too, didn't it?"

"I beg your pardon?" Monica stared at him in numb disbelief. Was the man so arrogant he actually assumed she'd hurl herself into open space on the off chance a man would catch her? He was being ridiculous and she took delight in telling him as much.

He was smiling when she finished, a cocky off-center smile that lifted the edges at one side of his mouth. "I'd say, from the look of you, having a man hold and kiss you is exactly what you need."

This sounded like a threat to Monica, and she pinched her lips together and retreated a step. "You're disgusting!"

He raised his hands, palms up. "I'm just an innocent bystander. I was minding my own business, looking for nothing better than to drown my sorrows in a cold beer when you catapulted into my arms. The way I look at it, you should be thanking your lucky stars I was here to catch you."

"You were headed toward the Blue Goose?" she asked, realizing now why he'd been so determined to cut through the crowd. He wanted a drink.

"Lady, after the day I've had, you'd need a beer, too."

"Don't," she pleaded, urgently taking a step toward him.

He glared at her, and his beige trench coat fanned out at his sides. The cold cut through Monica, but it didn't seem to bother him. "Don't what?" he demanded impatiently.

"Drink. There are better ways of dealing with problems other than alcohol."

"Lady . . ."

"My name's Monica. Monica Fischer," she said, holding out her hand to him. He looked at it for a moment as if he were going to ignore it before reluctantly exchanging handshakes.

"And you're . . ."

"Sorry I ever met you," he muttered.

"Please, let my friends and me help you," she said, gesturing toward the ensemble standing on the risers, singing the last of the songs.

"Listen, all I want is a cold beer and some peace and quiet. I've been on a stakeout for the past twenty hours and I . . ."

"You're with the police?"

He hesitated, and it was evident by the way he glanced longingly toward the Blue Goose that he had other matters on his mind. "I'm a private detective," he admitted. "There, does that satisfy you?"

"You must be tired," she tried again, thinking fast, hoping to convince him of the error of his ways.

"And getting more so every minute. Good-bye, Marcia."

"Monica," she corrected. She hurried after him, convinced she owed him this much for having saved her from certain injury.

"Whatever," he said, without looking her way. "Have a good day."

"Has anyone ever talked to you about the direction your life is headed?" she asked, scurrying to keep pace with him. She was tall, but he was taller and it took two of her strides to equal one of his.

"Are you going to preach at me next? Trust me, the last thing I need now is a sermon."

"Not if you promise me you won't drink."

"Listen," he said, stopping abruptly, "I'm trying to be as polite as I can, but my patience for this malarkey is long gone. I'm a responsible adult and I don't have a problem with alcohol, so if you don't mind, I'd prefer to be left alone."

"You're drinking beer, aren't you, and it's barely afternoon," Monica insisted. "Anyone who needs alcohol this early in the day must be addicted."

"Fine, then, to satisfy you, I'll order coffee. There, are you happy?"

Monica knew a lie when she heard one. "Don't try to appease me with lies," she said, glaring at him.

They'd crossed the street by this time and he continued to ignore her as much as possible, but Monica was making that difficult. She didn't know what was driving her to behave so uncharacteristically. Normally she wasn't nearly as aggressive; she was weak on evangelism, but this man desperately needed help and she was returning a favor. He'd saved her and now it was her turn to do him a good deed and rescue him, although it was clear he didn't appreciate or welcome her efforts.

They'd reached the Blue Goose and Monica hurled herself against the thick wood door, flinging out her arms until she stood spread-eagled across the entrance.

"What the hell do you think you're doing?" he demanded, glaring at her.

"I'm saving you from yourself."

"Go save someone else, would you?" His eyes were formidable, cold and cutting, but Monica refused to back away.

"I'm doing this for your own good."

He clamped his mouth closed and appeared to be counting to ten. His head nodded with each number and by the time he reached eight, his patience had evaporated. "Either you move or I'll be forced to move you myself and I guarantee you won't approve of my methods."

Monica was saved from having to make a decision when the door opened and she was momentarily pushed to one side. By the time she'd turned around and recovered, her reluctant hero had disappeared. It didn't take her two seconds to know where he'd gone. For half a heartbeat she toyed with the notion of going inside the Blue Goose after him.

Defeated and mildly discouraged, Monica trudged her way across the street. The other choir members were mingling with the crowd, passing out invitations for the Christmas Eve service. The idea had been her father's and although Monica feared they might attract riffraff from the streets, she hadn't said as much. It wouldn't do any good to argue with her father, not when he had such a soft spot in his heart for street people.

"Monica." Michael Simpson, the director, edged his way around two altos and moved toward her. "What happened?"

"I lost my balance and fell off the riser," she explained.

His eyes widened. "Are you all right?"

She nodded. "A . . . someone caught me."

"I'm glad you weren't hurt." His smile was shy as he gently patted her hand. "I wanted to congratulate you on your solo."

"But . . ."

"Your voice was never more pure."

Monica gestured weakly. To accept the credit would have been wrong. "But another voice joined mine. Didn't you hear it? I swear it came out of nowhere."

"Another voice," Michael asked, frowning. "I only heard you, and you were magnificent. You really outdid yourself."

"Monica, Monica." The Reverend Fischer hurried to his daughter's side and clasped her hand between his. His eyes shone bright with tears. "I've never heard you sing more beautifully. You sounded so much like your mother. I'd almost forgotten what a stunning voice she had. This is God's gift to you, this voice."

"But, Dad . . ." She stopped, not knowing how to explain. There had been another voice that merged with hers. One that didn't happen to belong to anyone in the choir. It didn't belong to anyone she knew.

*   *   *

"Goodness, Goodness, Goodness," Mercy said in that small chiding tone Gabriel had used with her so often in the past. "You were the one singing, weren't you?"

Goodness did not attempt to deny it. "I couldn't help it. 'Silent Night' is one of my personal favorites."

"But she heard you."

"I know." That part had been unintentional. Simply put, Goodness had gotten carried away with herself. But she had used considerable restraint. No one, however, seemed to appreciate that part. She could have used Barbra Streisand's voice. Barbra could really belt out "Silent Night," or Judy Garland. Now, that would have caused a whole lot of comment. To her credit, Goodness had resisted, although on second thought, she did an excellent Carol Burnett.

"What if Gabriel hears about this?"

"Don't worry about it." The archangel would eventually find out, Goodness knew. There would be no keeping it from him, but even that hadn't been enough for her to resist singing with Monica.

"He might take you off the assignment."

"Not a chance. Gabriel's shorthanded as it is. If he was going to pull me off this prayer request it would be for something a whole lot more troublesome than singing." The prayer ambassador was far more concerned by the consequences of her folly. Monica had fallen into the arms of that hard-nosed, disgruntled private investigator. If anything unsavory had happened, Goodness would have held herself personally responsible.

Chapter

★ ☆ ★

3

"*Timmy,*" *Jody Potter* called from the compact kitchen. "Dinner's ready."

"In a minute." The nine-year-old kept his gaze level with the television as he worked the controls of the Sega game. "I'm just about to save the world."

"Timmy, please, we go through this every night." Jody's nerves were on edge and had been ever since she'd found the letter. The folded sheet of paper had slipped from Timmy's school binder when she'd set it on the kitchen counter the night before.

A letter to God, but this wasn't any ordinary letter. Timmy had asked for a father. Jody's first instinct had been to sit him down and explain that he already had a father. Only Timmy had no recollection of Jeff, who'd died when Timmy was barely ten months old.

Timmy had no way of knowing how proud Jeff had been of his son. How he'd insisted holding him each night when he returned from the office and feeding him his last bottle. Timmy didn't remember that it was his father who'd sung him to sleep and then stood by his crib, gently patting his back. Her son couldn't possibly remember that Jeff had burst into tears of joy the night Timmy had been born.

What Timmy wanted now was a father who was alive. Someone who could throw a ball and catch better than she could, according to his letter. Someone who understood and enjoyed football. Someone who would be a friend.

What Timmy accepted far better than she did herself, Jody realized, was that Jeff was forever lost to them. Her son was looking for a replacement.

"I won," Timmy cried, leaping to his feet, holding his hands high above his head while he danced around the living room.

"I'm relieved to know the world is safe at last," Jody muttered, carrying the meat loaf over to the round oak table. "Can we eat now?"

"I guess." From habit, Timmy hurried into the bathroom and washed his hands, drying them against his thighs as he joined his mother moments later.

They sat down at the table together and Jody passed the vegetables.

Timmy stared down at the bowl and frowned. "I hate green beans."

"Take three." Jody didn't know why she chose three, but it seemed a reasonable number and she was hoping to have a heart-to-heart talk with her son. A confrontation over green beans would be detrimental to her plan.

Timmy judiciously sorted through the vegetables until he'd located three stubby green beans. Then he carefully placed them on the edge of his plate where they were in danger of slipping unnoticed onto the tablecloth. He paused and glanced up at Jody, who pretended not to notice.

She waited until he'd drowned his slice of meat loaf in catsup and loaded his plate with fruit salad and mashed potatoes before she broached the subject of his letter.

"We were supposed to write someone for Christmas," Timmy explained after she mentioned having found it. "I'm too old for this Santa Claus stuff so I went straight to the source. It was silly anyway, the post office won't mail a letter to God. The teacher made a fuss about it and now you are too. What's the big deal?"

"Nothing," Jody was quick to assure him. "It's just that I hadn't realized you wanted a father so badly."

"Every kid does," he said. "Don't they?"

"I guess." Jody's own father had died a year earlier and she missed him still. It had been a crushing emotional blow she hadn't expected. Her father's heart attack had taken the family by surprise. Just a week earlier, he'd been in for his yearly physical and was given a clean bill of health. Both Jody and her mother had been rocked by shock and grief. She'd assumed because her father had lived a long, full life that death would be easier to accept. That hadn't been the case any more than it had been with Jeff, whose death had come without warning.

"I don't mean to be rude, Mom," Timmy continued, burying a green bean deep in his pile of mashed potatoes, "but you can't throw a ball worth a darn and I need to practice. Mr. Dillard said I had a chance of being a really good player someday."

"I see."

"You're not ugly either. I bet there's some man out there who'd be willing to marry you."

Jody had to stop and think about that one. Her son wasn't intentionally insulting her. In his eyes, he'd paid her a high compliment. "I'm sure there is someone who'd be willing to take a chance and marry me," she said after a moment.

"You think so?" How eager he sounded. He scooted to the edge of his seat, propped his elbows against the table, and looked solidly at her. "Could you find and marry him before Christmas?"

"Timmy, be serious, Christmas is less than a month away."

"You mean it'll take longer than that to get me a dad?"

"Yes, I'm sure it will."

"How much longer?"

Jody shrugged, not knowing how to answer. "I . . . I don't know if I'm ready to be married again."

"Why not?" Timmy asked, his eyes wide and innocent. "Rick Trenton told me his mom's been married three times. You've only been married once. I was thinking about that and it doesn't seem right. You're a lot prettier than Rick's mom and she's already had two more husbands than you."

"It doesn't have to do with how pretty a woman is."

"Then what does it have to do with?" He cocked his head to one side, awaiting her answer.

Jody wished she knew. "Marriage is a complicated business." Much more complex than she could adequately explain to a nine-year-old boy who seemed to think she could find a husband on a grocery store shelf. She was about to suggest signing him up for Big Brothers when Timmy buried his fork in his meat and added, "Besides, I was thinking about you having a baby. I've decided I wouldn't mind if I had to share my bedroom. Rick's mom just had another baby and she let me hold him, and you know what, I kinda liked it."

"How does Rick feel about having a little brother?"

"He thinks it's cool, especially since he's got two little sisters. Rick said you don't get a choice if it's a boy or a girl when babies are born. I don't know how I'll feel about a sister instead of a brother, but I decided I'd do what Rick does."

"And what's that?"

"Take what he gets."

Jody set her fork aside, her appetite gone. "That's a mature attitude," she murmured, wondering what she was going to do next. Timmy was serious. He wanted a father. Now he was talking about a brother or sister, too.

"Then you'll start looking for a new dad for me?" His big brown eyes studied her carefully as if her decision was a momentous one.

"I'll think about it," Jody said thoughtfully. "Now eat your green beans."

"I already did."

"They're buried in your mashed potatoes," she said, waving her fork at him. "Now eat."

"Aw, Mom."

It wasn't until after nine that night, when Timmy was sound asleep in his bed, that Jody walked over to the bookcase and took out the bulky photo album. She sat in the overstuffed chair that had been Jeff's favorite and held the book against her breast in the dim light.

For several moments she closed her eyes. It had been almost a year since she'd last looked at the pictures. Twelve long months since she'd tortured herself with the memories. Timmy was right. It was way past the time for her to pick up the pieces of her life instead of dwelling in the past. A sob swelled in her throat as she tried to figure out how she was ever going to give up loving Jeff.

"That's Timmy's mother," Gabriel said in quiet, somber tones.

Shirley looked down upon the young mother and her heart ached. "She seems to be crying. What's happened to make her so sad?"

"She's thinking about Jeff, her husband who died," the archangel explained.

"Why does she torture herself this way?" It made no sense to Shirley that this young woman would continue to torment herself with memories.

"Jody is the problem," Gabriel continued. "She continues to hold on to her husband. Before you can answer Timmy's prayer you've got to deal with Jody. She must learn to trust enough to willingly let go of the past and reach toward the future. If she doesn't, she'll never be ready for the man God has for her."

"But it's been over eight years, doesn't she realize what she's doing to herself and to her son?"

"No, all she knows is the pain. Your assignment is to gently guide her toward the joy that awaits her and Timmy."

"And you expect me to accomplish this before Christmas?"

Gabriel didn't look any more pleased about this time restraint than Shirley. "I can't spare you any longer."

Shirley's wings stretched to their full reach, then folded over themselves once more. She'd assumed this would be a cushy assignment. After all, she'd only been serving as a prayer ambassador for a short while. The other cases she'd been given had been far less complicated.

"I . . . might not be able to help her," Shirley murmured.

"Apparently God the Father feels otherwise, or he wouldn't have personally requested you for Timmy's prayer."

"But how can I reach Jody when others have failed? How can I show her she doesn't have to stop loving Jeff, only open up her heart and her life to the love God has ready and waiting for her?"

"You'll think of something, only . . ." Gabriel hesitated and leveled his strict gaze on her. "You're not to pull the tricks you have in the past, understand?"

"Yes," Shirley agreed. "I won't misplace a single thing," she promised.

"That's what Goodness and Mercy told me earlier. I don't know what it is about you three, but you worry me more than all the other prayer ambassadors combined." He wiped his hand across his face, and briefly closed his eyes. "Just do your level best to stay out of trouble."

Chet Costello sat down at the bar in the Blue Goose and ordered a cold draft beer. He glanced over his shoulder to be sure that pesky little missionary hadn't decided to follow him inside. Seldom had he met a more aggravating woman.

"What's plaguing you?" Lou asked from the other side of the bar. He polished the mahogany surface with a clean rag, his hand making wide circular movements as he studied Chet. "You look like you've lost your best friend."

"You would too if you'd sat up all night in the cold."

"You were on a case?"

"No," Chet returned sarcastically, "I enjoy spending my nights in a freezing car peeking at a couple through binoculars. These infidelity cases have always thrilled me."

"No need to bite my head off."

"Then don't ask stupid questions." His little run-in with the do-gooder hadn't done anything to improve his mood. He'd encountered a hundred pious souls just like her over the years, each one convinced he needed to be saved from himself. He'd had it with that religious garbage years ago, and hadn't darkened the door of a church since his mother had died ten years earlier. He had no intention of changing his ways now.

He laughed out loud, the sound echoing like a sonic boom around the almost empty bar.

"What's so funny?" Lou asked, eager to share in the humor.

Chet paused, the beer bottle poised in front of his mouth. "She said there were better ways of settling problems than booze."

"Who?" Lou asked, bracing both hands against the edge of the bar and grinning, waiting for an explanation.

"Never mind." Chet wasn't in the mood to talk. She'd gotten under his skin, he realized, somewhat surprised. What was her name again? Marcia, no Monica. With her clear, dark eyes and her prim and proper ways, she was desperate to save him from the clutches of demon alcohol.

Part of the problem was how good she'd felt in his arms, all soft and feminine. The last time he'd held a woman had been . . . longer than he cared to think about, Chet realized. It was this job, he decided, that soured him on relationships. No one was faithful anymore, not according to the statistics he'd collected. The child custody cases were the worst and he'd sworn off those. After he'd left the police department years earlier, he'd floundered for a bit before deciding to work as a private investigator. What a crock of bull this had turned out to be. The time was fast approaching when he'd need to find something else. He wouldn't go back to the force, not after Tom's death. He didn't trust himself, not anymore. His partner had gotten killed, and Chet had accepted responsibility for the loss of his friend. The incident continued to haunt him. There were certain things in life a man didn't put behind him, and this was one.

For reasons he couldn't explain, the erstwhile missionary drifted back into his mind, with her warm, pleading gaze and her soft, sweet mouth.

"You know, what she really needs is to be kissed," he said aloud. "None of this pansy stuff of holding hands and gazing longingly into each other's eyes either."

Lou glanced his way and without comment continued to polish the sleek wooden surface of the bar. After a moment, he paused and scratched his head. "You looking to talk?" he asked.

"Hell, no."

"That's what I thought." The bartender resumed his task.

Remembering the way she'd flung herself against the tavern door produced another burst of laughter. The buttons of her jacket had strained with the effort until she resembled a martyr tied to the stake. She had nice, full breasts, although heaven knew she did everything she could to disguise the fact that she was a woman. If he ever did have the opportunity to kiss her, which was highly unlikely, the first thing he'd do was pull the pins from her hair. It was a travesty to keep it twisted away from her face that way. She'd have thick, luxuriant hair and he'd run his fingers through it. He imagined she'd put up a fuss at that. Anything remotely related to sensual pleasure was sure to be sin, pure, unadulterated sin.

Chet knew her type. The mission house down the street from his office was filled with do-gooders thinking their efforts with the derelicts and vagrants was going to make a difference. Chet felt sorry for them more than he did the street people they struggled to reach with their message.

Then why couldn't he stop thinking about her? The hell if he knew. The hell if he cared. One consolation, he wasn't likely to run into her again.

"Of course I remember you, Mr. Lundberg," Mrs. Burchell, the caseworker from New Life Adoption Agency, assured him over the telephone. "It's good to hear from you again."

Andrew rolled the mechanical pencil between his palms, praying he was doing the right thing. "I'd like to know how difficult it would be for my wife and me to resubmit our application." He leaned against the back of his chair. Leah had been on his mind all day and he was worried about her.

It was so damn unfair that they couldn't have children. What troubled him most was that there didn't seem to be any physical reason. They'd spent years, and thousands of dollars, working with fertility specialists. Leah's life was governed by that ridiculous book she kept. He swore she'd documented her temperature every morning for the last seven years.

Perhaps if they'd been able to pinpoint the problem as his, Leah might have been able to accept their situation.

"I have your file right here," the caseworker went on to say. "I know you and your wife were terribly disappointed when Melinda Phillips decided to rescind the adoption of her infant son. It doesn't happen often, but unfortunately these girls do change their minds."

"I understand," Andrew said, not wanting to rehash the details. Having the birth mother change her mind had been much harder on Leah than it had him. They'd gone to the hospital, their hearts filled with joy, only to return empty-handed an hour later. Afterward Leah had sat for hours alone in the nursery they'd so lovingly prepared. Nothing Andrew could say reached her. He'd been disappointed too and for a while there'd been a strain between them. Then one day he returned home from the office and discovered that Leah had dismantled the nursery. She calmly announced that she'd withdrawn their application from New Life and that they'd simply wait for her to become pregnant and bear a child of their own. She refused to subject them to that kind of torment again.

"I'll be happy to resubmit your names," Mrs. Burchell said, "but I must warn you there are fewer babies available for adoption now than before."

"How long would you predict?"

The caseworker hesitated. "I can't really say. It's different with every couple."

"What about the Watcombs?" Andrew asked. "We went through the orientation classes with them three years ago."

"Ah, yes, the Watcombs. Jessie and Ken, am I right?"

"Yes. Has their adoption gone through?"

"Not yet, but we're hopeful we'll have an infant for them soon."

Andrew's hopes plummeted. The Watcombs were special people and he couldn't imagine any young mother not choosing them to rear her child.

"You were in the same orientation class as the Sterlings, weren't you?"

Andrew allowed the name to filter through his mind. "He was a fireman as I recall."

"That's the couple. They adopted a baby girl last October."

"That's wonderful."

"I thought you'd be pleased."

He was, of course, but a small part of him couldn't help being envious. Leah desperately wanted a child, and in an effort to reassure her he'd downplayed his own desire for a family. He loved his wife and would give anything for them to have a child.

"Do you still want me to resubmit your name?" Mrs. Burchell asked after a moment's silence.

"Please," he said, his hand tightening around the receiver. If it took another five years or more, then that was just how long they'd need to wait. That he was doing this behind Leah's back didn't sit well with him, but some action needed to be taken, and this seemed the most logical choice. If they were chosen by a birth mother again, then they'd make the necessary adjustments. A child was welcome into their lives at any time. Love guaranteed.

For the life of her, Monica hadn't been able to forget the private investigator. Heaven knew she'd tried. He was little better than an alcoholic, drinking beer in the middle of the day. Not only that, he'd been arrogant, rude, and curt with her. He'd treated her as if she were a senseless child when she'd tried to help him.

Monica didn't understand what it was about this one man that intrigued her so. She'd gone to bed that night and dreamed of him. She'd woken breathless, her heart pounding double time. A woman had no control over her dreams, Monica assured herself. If she had, Monica certainly wouldn't have allowed that . . . man to touch her. The very idea was appalling. No, Monica corrected, closing her eyes and shaking her head, that wasn't the truth. It was the problem. She had thought about him touching her, kissing her. Her untamed imagination had taken over and she'd allowed it to happen in her dreams.

"There you are," her father said, strolling into the living room. "I've been looking for you." He settled down in the leather chair by the fireplace and reached for the evening paper. "I'm afraid I'm going to need you tomorrow afternoon."

"For what?" He seemed to forget she had a job and even if she did work as the church secretary it was a demanding position. Her father would cover for her if necessary, but she would rather he asked first instead of volunteering her services, which was something he often did.

"Mrs. Ferdnand just phoned and she can't be a bell ringer for the shift she signed up to take last Sunday."

"But, Dad." Standing on a cold street corner and collecting charitable donations was the last way Monica wished to spend an afternoon. An hour never lasted so long and by the end of her shift she'd be frozen solid.

"I wouldn't ask if it wasn't necessary."

"I know." It was useless to argue with him. The man had the patience of Job and an answer for every argument.

"It's downtown so you'll be sure to get plenty of traffic," her father added, reaching for the sports section of the newspaper and folding it open.

"Great." She stabbed the needle into the fabric and set aside her needlepoint. After working on this Ten Commandment project for weeks she was only on the fourth commandment, which meant she hadn't a prayer of finishing before Christmas. She studied the tiny stitches. Ironically the one she was currently stitching stated Honor Thy Father and Thy Mother. God must have worked it out that way, sealing any argument she might have given.

"Are you all right?" her father asked her unexpectedly, momentarily setting the paper aside.

"I'm fine," she said, then amended, "a little tired perhaps."

"I thought as much. You don't seem to be yourself lately."

"Oh?"

"I know this thing with Patrick hurt you and . . ."

"Patrick is a friend, Dad. He was never anything more. I don't know why you insist upon dragging his name into every conversation." It was a white lie to suggest she hadn't cared about Patrick, but sometimes she found those necessary, although she was never comfortable stretching the truth.

"I noticed Michael talking to you the other day. He's a very nice young man." He eyed her speculatively as if waiting for her to comment.

"Very nice," she agreed. But Michael didn't stir her blood, he didn't make her heart throb and the thought of him kissing her produced not so must as a whit of excitement.

Her father was right, there was definitely something wrong with her.

The following afternoon, Monica was dressed in her dark blue suit, standing on the corner of Fifth and University, ringing her little heart out. Surely there was a reward awaiting her in heaven for this.

A man dressed in leather and wearing enough gold to strangle himself stopped and inserted a ten-dollar bill in the bright red pot. When Monica thanked him, he insisted upon "giving her five." It took her a good three minutes to realize what he intended. He was simply looking to slap her hand. He ambled away, suggesting she get with it, whatever or whomever "it" was.

Okay, so she wasn't cool, if that was the current vernacular. Nor was she hip or groovy or several other words that came to mind. She was God's willing servant. All right, she wasn't so willing just then, but she was doing her part and that was all that mattered.

Her ears were cold and her fingers had lost their feeling and she had another half hour to go when it happened.

It was him.

The man who'd caught her in his arms three days earlier, the one she'd attempted to restrain from entering the Blue Goose. He was standing on the other side of the street waiting for the traffic to pass so he could cross. Everyone else would wait for the green light and the walk sign, but not him. Oh, no, he was too impatient for that.

She stopped ringing the bell, then started again with a vengeance, closing her eyes, hoping with everything in her that he'd simply walk past and not notice it was her.

Monica should have realized that would have been asking too much.

"Well, well, well," he said, strolling all the way around her. "And who do we have here? Monica, am I right?"

She ignored him and stared straight ahead, jerking the small bell back and forth for all she was worth, her shoulders so stiff they ached.

"It's mighty cold to be standing outside for any length of time, isn't it?"

Monica didn't deign to answer him. A lady in a fur coat walked past and dropped a few coins into the red kettle. "Merry Christmas," Monica said from pure habit.

"The same to you," the private investigator answered.

"Please leave me alone," she whispered.

"It seems to me I asked the same thing of you recently and did it help? Oh, no, you were convinced I needed to be saved." He flung his hands into the air. "Hallelujah, brother."

"Please." She tried again.

"Not on your life, sister," he responded.

"If you continue to pester me you'll leave me no choice but to contact the police and have you forcibly removed."

"Threats?" He folded his arms over his broad chest and arched both brows in mock terror. "So you want to involve the authorities. Fine. Good luck finding a cop walking his beat. In case you weren't aware, the city's seriously understaffed, and this time of year is busier than most."

Monica knew God was looking out for her when a city cop turned the corner just then, casually sauntering down the sidewalk. "Officer, Officer," she called, wasting no time. "This man is bothering me."

The policeman, who was tall and burly beneath his thick coat and cap, was casually swinging his billy club. "You troubling this young lady, Chet?"

It was just her luck that they knew each other.

"Bothering this woman? Me? You know me better than that," Chet answered, beaming Monica a cocky smile. "I've got more important things to do."

"That's what I thought."

"He refuses to leave," Monica supplied huffily.

"Now, listen, miss, I know Chet's a sorry-looking alley cat, but he's harmless. Let me assure you, you're in no danger from him."

"Thanks, Dennis," Chet said and dipped his head slightly.

"That's simply not true," Monica tried again, more adamantly this time. "I politely asked him to leave and he refused."

Dennis bounced the billy club against his open palm a couple of times. "Chet, stop pestering this pretty young lady."

"Sure thing."

Dennis touched the tip of his hat. "He'll leave you alone now, miss." With that he strolled away.

"You aren't going to leave, are you?"

"Trust me, sweetheart, he's got better things to do than listen to you making a fuss over nothing. This is a public sidewalk, there's nothing Dennis can do but ask me to move on, which he's already done."

"Why do you insist upon doing this?" Monica demanded, straightening her shoulders. She forced herself to look directly ahead of her and away from him, because looking at Chet caused her stomach to flutter as if she were coming down with the flu.

"Hey," he said, raising both hands, "I'm paying you back for what you did the other day."

"I was trying to help you."

"You were a major pest. Now you know how it feels."

"If you're looking for me to apologize, then—"

"No, thanks." He walked all the way around her once more, then stood directly in front of her, hands on his hips. "You know, you might really be something in the looks department if you ever decided to wear makeup."

Monica ignored the comment.

"A little blush and eyeliner aren't tools of the devil, you know."

She pursed her lips to restrain herself for chastising him the way he deserved.

"My, oh, my, look at that sour puss. I was right the first time."

"About what?" she demanded before she could stop herself.

"What you really need is to be kissed, and sweetheart, I'm the man to do it."

Chapter

★ ☆ ★

4

Chet never intended to kiss Monica. He'd taken delight in teasing her and she was easy game. Her face flushed with color, brightening her cheeks, and her eyes snapped with outrage, challenging him. Chet was ready to laugh and walk away when a Metro bus came rushing down the street, the thick tires spraying the sidewalk with a shower of icy, muddy water.

Monica, standing as close to the curb as she was, would receive the brunt of the spray. Thinking quickly, Chet caught her by the shoulders and whirled her around. The bus passed and the muddy water sprayed him against the back of his legs. He grimaced as the icy liquid soaked through his trousers at his calves.

"What are you doing?" Monica demanded.

Her back was against the brick building and she was breathing hard. Her breasts rose up and down and her hands clenched at the lapels of his trench coat as though to push him away. When she moistened her lips as if she fully expected him to follow through with his threat, it was his undoing. He felt as if a fist had been plowed into his gut. He didn't want to kiss her any longer, he *needed* to.

"No, please," she blurted out, sounding as if she were near panic.

"Relax," he whispered coaxingly. "This isn't going to hurt in the least."

She jerked her head to one side but he caught her by the chin. By all that was right he should have released her then, but the temptation was too strong, too sweet and piercing to ignore.

Slowly he lowered his mouth to hers with the confidence of years of experience. His lips cut off her gasp of protest, and the strong pressure of his mouth opened hers to him. She tasted good, damn good, a hell of a lot better than he expected. When his tongue entered her mouth, her nails dug into his coat, and then she amazed him and quite possibly herself with a soft, womanly sigh of pleasure. Under his tutelage her mouth opened further, and unwilling to let this opportunity slip past him, Chet slanted his head and kissed her with months of pent-up passion.

He didn't mean to be so demanding, but he couldn't stop himself.

With effort, Chet forced himself to break off the intensity of the kiss and wean himself away from her with a series of short, nibbling ones. With a reluctance he didn't dare question, he lifted his mouth from hers. He would have enjoyed continuing this experiment and given the opportunity, a hell of a lot more.

Monica's chest was heaving and her eyes were closed. Her head was slightly lowered but not enough to disguise the soft, feminine look about her. He noticed that half the pins were missing from her hair so that it fell haphazardly over one shoulder. Hell, he didn't even remember doing anything more than plowing his hands into the thick fullness and positioning her head so he could kiss her properly.

Her eyes slowly opened and she looked slightly dazed and definitely pale. She gazed at him steadily for just a moment and then quickly lowered her eyes. Her slender throat moved up and down as she swallowed and it seemed that she was getting ready to speak.

"I . . . wish you hadn't done that."

"No, you don't," he returned, sounding far more cocky than he intended. Insolence was part and parcel of his job. He didn't like it in himself, but he didn't know how to stop.

"Please, will you leave me alone now?"

"Is that what you really want?"

She nodded, but refused to meet his eyes.

He stepped away from her and she immediately went about tucking her hair back into place, her hands trembling so badly that Chet had to resist offering to help.

"It was just a kiss," he said in a weak effort to comfort her, although he was beginning to feel he was the one who needed reassurance. This woman was completely unaware of what a powerful punch she packed. She'd felt good in his arms, damn good, as if that was where she was supposed to be. The thought didn't sit well with Chet. Nor was he keen on admitting how difficult it was to walk away from her.

"I . . . think it would be best if you left," she said, struggling valiantly to compose herself. She refused to look up at him.

Chet's mind was sluggish and his pulse still hadn't returned to normal. He nodded, unable to think of anything more to say. As he moved away from her, he found the small, silver bell she'd dropped on the sidewalk. Stooping, he retrieved it for her.

"Thank you," she whispered.

"You're sure you're all right?"

She nodded and Chet stepped away from her, walking backward. He bumped into a lamppost, his shoulder hitting it hard enough against the steel column to jar him. Sucking in a deep breath, he rubbed his hand over the tender spot, turned, and walked away.

He didn't want to think about what had just happened. He'd kissed a woman who, for all intents and purposes, was living the life of a nun. It shouldn't have been this good. One taste should have been enough to cure him of ever thinking about her again. He could tell right now that it wasn't going to happen that way.

By the time Chet returned to his office, he discovered he was shaking like a leaf. He'd faced danger a dozen times, hell, more than that, but no encounter with life or death had left him so jittery that he needed to sit down. It took a morally uptight missionary intent on saving the world to reduce him to this.

"Oh, Leah, look," Pam Hewitt said, holding up a thick cable-knit sweater the color of winter wheat. "Doug would love this." She checked the price tag and then slowly shook her head. "Unfortunately I can't afford a hundred bucks for a sweater."

"I thought we were shopping for a party dress for you," Leah reminded her friend. They'd known each other since university days and kept in close contact although they weren't able to get together often. Pam had temporarily traded in her nurse's uniform to be a full-time housewife and mother to her three youngsters. Leah loved each one, but Scotty, the just-turned three-year-old, held a special place in her heart. The baby Andrew and she were to have adopted had been born around the same time. Somehow Leah had transferred to Scotty all the love she had for the child that was to have been hers. She gave Pam's three children gifts every Christmas and invented excuses for outings with them, but it was Scotty who ruled her heart.

"I hate Christmas parties," Pam muttered, folding the sweater and setting it back on the table. She ran her hand over the top and sighed expressively. "I was thinking I'd cut down the fancy maternity dress I wore a couple of years ago and—"

"Absolutely not," Leah insisted. "We're going to find you a dress that will make you feel like a queen for Doug's Christmas party."

"That will take some doing," Pam muttered. "Two years at home with the kids and I'm afraid I've lost it."

"Lost what?"

"I don't know how to explain it," Pam admitted slowly. "I think a part of the brain starts to deteriorate after so many years of dealing with diapers, bottles, and potty training. It's like you're on the children's level for so much of the day that you lose the ability to communicate with other adults."

"All this tells me is that you need to get away more often."

"That's probably true," Pam agreed, "but you wouldn't believe the trouble it is to find a baby-sitter, especially on weekdays."

"What about taking some time for yourself while the kids go down for their naps?"

Pam laughed softly as they headed toward the escalator. "Nap time is like an oasis in the middle of the day. I treasure every moment of that hour, but lately even that time's been robbed from me. I'm sewing Scotty and Jason Batman pajamas and that's the only free time I have to do it."

"Batman pajamas?"

"They're crazy about him and Spiderman."

"Why don't you sew in the evenings?" Leah suggested. It made perfect sense to her since the three were generally in bed by eight.

Pam laughed and shook her head. "Because, my dear friend, I'm too pooped. Honestly, I head for bed no more than an hour after the kids. I never dreamed I'd be in bed before nine. Remember me, the original night owl? Trust me, kids will do that to you."

A pang of envy struck Leah at the thought of her life being dominated by the demands of a houseful of children. Then again, the grass always appeared greener on the other side of the fence. More than once, Pam had said how much she envied Leah her freedom.

Freedom. True, she often had time on her hands, but for what?

"I'm on a budget, you know," Pam complained when they reached Nordstrom's second floor.

"Would you stop?" Leah demanded, laughing. "We haven't even gotten to the woman's section yet and already you're convinced you aren't going to find anything."

"My old maternity dress isn't all that bad."

"Pam!" Leah braced her hands against her hips and glared at her friend. "Now I understand why Doug insisted I go shopping with you. He knew darn good and well that you'd end up buying something for everyone else and nothing for yourself."

"Did you see that darling pinafore," Pam said, pointing toward the children's section. "Diane would look like an angel dressed in that."

Leah looped her arm through Pam's and steered her in the opposite direction. "I'll tell you what I'm going to do."

"What? Hog-tie me and force me to try on several dresses?"

"Close. I'm taking you directly to the dressing room and bringing the party dresses in to you."

Pam's shoulders sagged with defeat as they entered the dressing room area. "All right, just try to find something reasonably priced, will you?" Leah opened the white louvered door and gently pushed her friend inside.

Pam stuck out her hand and waved her index finger. "Check on the sale rack first. I'll feel better about spending so much money on myself if the dress is discounted."

"Never you mind," Leah argued. "I'm not even going to let you look at the price tag."

"But, Leah—"

"Don't even try to argue with me. I'd have thought you'd know better by now." Smiling to herself, Leah left the dressing room.

"My hips aren't nearly as slender as they used to be either," Pam called after her. "You'd better start with a size twelve instead of a ten . . . better make that a fourteen."

Leah stopped long enough to roll her eyes, then headed for a rack of newly arrived fashions. It took less than five minutes to find a wide selection that would suit her friend.

"Mercy, where are you?" Goodness called, frantically circling Nordstrom's like the second hand of a clock gone berserk.

Mercy turned around to find Goodness, her wings all aflutter, breezing six feet off the ground, close to a state of panic.

"I need to talk to you right away," Goodness said breathlessly.

"Over here," Mercy called, wondering what could possibly have gone wrong so quickly. "I'm on the light fixture."

Goodness soared to her side, rustling the dress display and toppling a mannequin. Apparently feeling guilty, she scooped up the lifeless form and set it back into place to the horror of a sales clerk who gasped and placed her hand over her heart to watch a lifeless form right itself.

"Goodness," Mercy shouted. "Would you stop before you get us both into trouble?"

"I need help," Goodness blurted out for the second time, joining Mercy who was dangling from the light fixture.

"So soon? You just received the assignment. What could have possibly gone wrong?"

Goodness, who was easily flustered, looked helpless and confused. She cast a pleading look at Mercy. "I knew I was in way over my head when Gabriel first gave me this assignment, but I wanted to help Monica Fischer. You know I'm a sucker for romance, and finding her a husband didn't sound as if it would be the least bit difficult." She stopped long enough to draw in another deep breath. "Now the poor girl's more confused than ever and I'm afraid it's all my fault."

"What happened?"

"Nothing . . . well, obviously it's something, but . . . oh, dear, I'm afraid I've made a terrible mistake."

"I take it this has something to do with finding Monica a husband?"

Goodness nodded energetically. "I found the most suitable young man who has a wonderful heart for God. He directs the choir and he's half in love with her already."

"Then what's the problem?"

"Monica isn't the least bit excited about him. She has this dangerous attraction for that . . . that private eye. They're completely incompatible. Why, a union between the two of them will never do, and I fear I'm the one responsible for them meeting."

Mercy frowned. "Goodness, when will you ever learn?"

"Me!" Flustered, she wrung her hands and eyed her fellow angel. "You don't think I know that was you riding up and down the escalator just now?"

"You couldn't have known that was me."

"Let's just say I made an educated guess," Goodness said confidently. "A woman's being treated with smelling salts and two kids are telling everyone what they saw, and it sounds to me as if they were describing you. Who else do you know with long, blond hair, deep blue eyes, and magnificent wings? You know better than most that children's spiritual eyes have yet to close. You were taking a terrible chance."

"Ah . . ."

"Just as I thought. Mercy, what are you going to do if Gabriel hears about this? You know he will eventually. Why, he could pull you off of this assignment in nothing flat and with good reason."

"But he won't," Mercy said with utter confidence.

"How can you be so sure?"

"Because he'd never have assigned me to this prayer request if he had anyone else to send. We both know that."

"But he might never give you another assignment if you continue to do crazy stunts like that."

"Sure he will. Gabriel has a soft spot in his heart for the three of us. I venture to say we're his favorites, although he'd never let us know that."

Goodness stared at her with round, disbelieving eyes.

"He'll forgive me just about anything," Mercy continued, undaunted, "because I'm going to find a way to teach Leah what she must learn and as soon as she does, she'll become pregnant."

"Mercy, have you been sniffing the eggnog again?"

"Don't be ridiculous."

"But you've got the most difficult assignment by far. How can you be so confident Leah's ever going to learn what she must when so many others have failed?"

"Simple," Mercy said with a cocky tilt to her head, "I'm going to teach her. Now stop worrying about me. Let's concentrate on what's happening with you and Monica Fischer."

Goodness adjusted her wings around the troublesome light fixture. "I hate to admit it, but I'm worried. She really likes this Chet fellow."

"Chet who?"

"Chet Costello. He's a private investigator and from what I've managed to learn of him . . . let me just say this, Gabriel would need to assign a legion of angels to work with him."

"You're sure Monica's infatuated with him?"

Goodness nodded. "I read her journal this morning and it was full of all the things she felt while he kissed her. She said she never knew that kissing could be this good or that a woman felt those kinds of things when a man touched her."

"Oh, my." Mercy waved her hand in front of her heated face.

"And that's not the half of it."

"You mean there's more?"

"She wrote that she felt herself responding to him even when she promised herself she wouldn't and how disappointed she was when he stopped."

"Do you think Michael knows about Chet?"

"No one knows, not even her father. She raced home afterward and went directly to her room where she wrote everything down. When her father came to ask if she wanted dinner, Monica claimed she wasn't hungry."

"Kissing is better than food?" This was a whole new thought to Mercy.

"Apparently so."

Goodness wrung her hands once more, then blurted out, "Say something. Anything. I need help."

Mercy slowly shook her head back and forth. "You've got trouble."

"I know that, otherwise I wouldn't be here. What do you suggest?"

Mercy thought long and hard. "We both need to talk to Shirley. She's much better at deciphering these matters than we are."

"Let's meet at Reverend Fischer's church at midnight in the choir loft," Goodness suggested as she elegantly slid off the dangling fixture. "I'll see you then."

Mercy nodded.

Goodness fully intended to leave the shopping mall right then and return to Monica, who was sitting in the church office typing up the bulletin for the Sunday morning worship service. But when she shot past a video store, she skidded to a stop. Mercy seemed confident that Gabriel would leave them on their assignments because he was so shorthanded. Maybe she should test her friend's theory, and have a little fun herself.

Row upon row of television screens faced her. There must have been over fifty in various sizes and shapes, all tuned to the same channel. The temptation was too much to resist.

She hesitated and laughed silently at the thought of her face showing up on all fifty screens at once. The mere suggestion was her downfall. If Mercy could ride up and down the escalator then she should be able to enjoy a few short moments of notoriety.

"This is our best model," the salesman was saying, stepping over to the wide twenty-five-inch screen. The salesman was busily showing an older couple the capabilities of the remote control when Goodness popped onto the screen.

"What's that?" The grandmotherly woman pointed to the television.

"It seems to be a . . . woman with wings," the man with her added.

"Wings?" The salesman quickly adjusted the buttons. "We had it tuned to a game show earlier. It's nothing to worry about, folks, this happens sometimes. I'll just change the channel."

"The same woman appears to be on that channel as well," the woman said. "If I didn't know better I'd say it was an . . . angel. Do you think she's trying to tell us something, Delbert?"

"She sure is," the man grumbled. "She's saying we shouldn't be buying this fancy new television when the one we've got is perfectly fine."

"Don't be ridiculous. This is the punishment you get for skipping mass last Sunday. God's sent this angel to show you the error of your ways. Then again"—she hesitated while Goodness adjusted her wings for show—"she might be telling us we should pick up some lottery tickets on our way home."

The salesman was becoming more and more agitated as he punched a variety of buttons on the remote control. "I'm sure there's been some mistake." He looked around and shouted, "Harry! I think it might be a good idea if I have the manager took a look at this."

"I've seen enough," the older man said, reaching for his wife's arm. "Let's get out of here."

"It has to do with you missing church, I'm sure of it."

"Don't be ridiculous," her husband said with annoyance.

"We are going to stop for lottery tickets on the way home, aren't we?"

"We don't do this nearly often enough." Jody's mother set the pot of tea on the oak kitchen table.

"I agree," Jody said, slipping into the chair across from her mother. She didn't drop by to visit her mother as often as she had before her father's death earlier in the year. Her childhood home stirred far too many memories. Privately Jody wondered how her mother managed. Perhaps it wasn't so difficult to understand. Jody continued to live in the tiny two-bedroom house she and Jeff had purchased when she'd first learned she was pregnant with Timmy. Giving up even this small part of her life with her late husband was more than she could have borne.

"Where's Timmy this evening?" Helen Chandler wanted to know.

Jody smiled although she knew her mother didn't understand her amusement. "He's spending the night with his good friend, Rick Trenton."

"I thought it was Ricky."

"They're in the fourth grade this year and suddenly Ricky is Rick. Timmy is Tim to all his friends now too. He's growing up more and more."

"I didn't think that sort of thing happened until junior high."

Jody had been amazed herself. "Kids mature much faster these days. Generally Rick spends the night with us, but his mother just had a baby and Timmy's enthralled with the little tyke. He . . . he went so far as to suggest that I remarry so he could have a brother."

"He said that, did he?"

"I don't mind telling you, Mom, it threw me for a loop. I found a letter in Timmy's binder. His class was assigned to write a letter and he opted to address his to God."

"That grandson of mine is one smart cookie. What did he have to say?"

Jody stirred a spoonful of sugar into her tea with enough energy for some to slosh over the rim of the delicate china cup. "He wrote about needing a dad."

Helen Chandler grew quiet at that. Jody expected her mother to laugh or perhaps lecture, but she hadn't expected her to say nothing.

"You don't have any comment to make?" she asked, eyeing her mother speculatively.

"Of course I do, but I'm not so sure you want to hear it."

At this point Jody was more than willing to listen to words of wisdom. She'd thought of little else but the letter from the moment it had slipped from Timmy's binder. The conversation with her son had served to disconcert her even more. This hadn't been an impulse; he'd been serious.

"Go ahead, Mom, say what you want and I'll listen."

Her mother smiled and reached for Jody's hand, squeezing it gently. "I don't think I fully appreciated your grief when Jeff died. I ached for you and would have given anything to bring Jeff back, but the depth of your pain escaped me until . . . until this past year." She paused as if she needed to steel herself. "After Ralph died I knew what you'd endured. The death of a loved one is the sharpest pain a human can experience. I felt like a piece of myself had died with your father."

"Oh, Mom." Jody's grip on her mother's hand tightened, to let the gesture say what she couldn't because of the huge constriction blocking her throat. They were close, had always been close. Jody had been an only child and the bond had been firm and strong between her and her parents.

"I can appreciate far more the agony you endured when you lost Jeff. I understand why your grief has lingered all these years, but I also know Timmy is right. The time is long past due for you to get on with your life."

"But—"

"Listen, please, and when I've finished you can say what you wish.

"Take the love you and Jeff shared and place it in the most tender part of your heart. Treasure the few short years you had together as a precious gift God gave you and then offer it back to Him in gratitude that you found such a special man to love."

Tears rolled unchecked down Jody's cheeks. She'd assumed the well was dry after spending the night looking through the photo album, but they returned fresh and hot, streaming down her face.

"In my heart I know Jeff wouldn't have wanted you to grieve this way."

"I know that too," Jody whispered, struggling to check the emotion. She'd wanted to be strong when she spoke to her mother, but it took only a few words for her to realize how weak she actually was.

"Meeting other men, even marrying again, doesn't mean you have to stop loving Jeff," her mother continued.

"I don't think I could ever stop loving him."

"I understand that. It would be impossible for me to stop loving your father."

"It is time for me to start dating again, isn't it?" Even as Jody made the suggestion, she couldn't help wondering if she was doing the right thing. It didn't feel right, but then nothing had from the moment she'd received word Jeff was gone. It seemed as if her world had been knocked off its orbit and would never right itself. Now her mother and her son were saying different. There was a new life waiting for her and the possibility of finding love again, if she were willing to put the past behind her and march forward.

"It's past time," her mother told her gently. "I'm sure you've been asked out over the years. You're a beautiful young woman."

Jody nodded, twisting a tissue with her hands. "Glen Richardson surprised me last week with an invitation to dinner. I was so shocked I didn't know what to tell him."

"I don't believe I've heard you mention his name before."

"He's one of the attorneys at the firm. I don't work directly with him, but it seems we continually bump into each other at the copy machine. It's become something of a joke."

"What did you tell him?"

"Heavens, Mother, I don't remember. I made up some ridiculous excuse, but he said he'd ask again and he probably will."

"And when he does?" her mother prompted.

"When he does," Jody said, clenching the tissue in both hands, "I'll . . . I'll promise to think about it."

"Jody Marie Potter!"

Jody laughed and relaxed against the back of her chair. "Oh, all right. One date, just to test the waters."

Her mother smiled broadly, looking downright pleased with herself.

The phone was ringing when Jody let herself into her house later that same night. Setting down her purse, she hurried into the kitchen and caught it on the fourth ring, just before the answering machine took over.

"Hello," she said, her voice shaking with breathlessness.

"Jody?"

The voice was strangely familiar. "Yes?"

"This is Glen . . . Glen Richardson. I hope I didn't catch you at an inconvenient time."

Jody's shoulders sagged against the wall. "No. I just unlocked the door and had to run to catch the phone."

"The funniest thing just happened. I was thinking of calling you and for the life of me, I couldn't find your number. Then I walked into the kitchen and found it attached to the phone. Heaven only knows how it got there. It seemed fate was telling me to give you a jingle," Glen said, sounding confused even now. "And to think I caught you just as you walked in the door."

"I just got back from visiting my mother."

"I suppose you've already had dinner."

"I'm sorry, Glen, but we ordered Chinese takeout." He sounded so bewildered that she almost felt sorry for him. "What are you doing, sitting home alone on a Friday night?"

"My best gal turned me down for a date."

It took Jody a moment to realize he was talking about her, leading her to wonder what excuse she'd given him earlier.

"I was thinking I should suggest a deli sandwich and a couple of sodas for the next time we meet at the copy machine. Larry Williams warned me that you don't date often."

Often. The last time she'd gone out with a man, she'd ended up marrying him. Jeff had been persistent too, she remembered, unwilling to take no for an answer. He'd wooed her carefully and when they'd fallen in love, it was the kind of love that was meant to last a lifetime. She might marry again, even give birth to another child, but she'd never stop loving Jeff. This was her vow, to his memory and to the extraordinary love they shared.

"Jody?" Glen said, interrupting her thoughts.

"I'm sorry, I got distracted."

"I know it's short notice and all, but how about a movie? I understand there're several good ones playing. How would you feel about that? I could meet you at the theater if that'd make you more comfortable," he added, rushing the words together in his eagerness.

So soon. It was happening so fast, much faster than she'd expected. Much too soon, long before she was ready. Then she remembered her mother's words about placing the love she shared with Jeff in the most tender part of her heart. She didn't know what to make of him finding her number pasted on his telephone.

"A movie," she repeated. There was a six-plex less than a mile from her house. "Ah, all right."

"Great," Glen said, sounding a little like Timmy when she'd given in on something he'd really wanted. "This is just great. I promise you, you won't be sorry. Just you wait and see."

Jody wondered if that were possible.

Chapter

★ ✮ ★

5

Shirley loved old white churches with tall steeples and huge bells. In the Reverend Lloyd Fischer's church she felt a certain kinship with this righteous man of God. She was waiting for her two compatriots in the choir loft, which was situated up the winding stairway in the back of the old church. The freshly polished pews gleamed in the moonlight and the scent of lemon oil wafted toward her.

She frowned as she viewed the magnificent old organ. It would take a minor miracle to keep Mercy away from this. The public address system didn't bear thinking about.

"Shirley?" Goodness arrived first, agitated and impatient, racing up and down the center aisle.

"Up here."

Goodness joined her, hurling herself over the wooden railing of the choir loft. "Where's Mercy? She should have been here by now."

"I'm sure she will be soon."

No sooner had Shirley spoken than Mercy appeared. "I'm up here. No one bothered to tell me Leah Lundberg's a night owl." She sagged into one of the choir chairs and tilted back her head. "I'm bushed. Leah had me running from one end of the shopping mall to the next. After she found her friend an absolutely delightful party dress, she took off on her own and shopped for hours. I didn't know a single human being possessed so much energy."

"We're all learning lessons about earthlings," Shirley maintained. Her own experiences had been exhausting as well.

"You're telling me," Goodness joined in. "All Monica's done since Chet kissed her is stew in the juices of her self-righteousness. She's convinced God never intended a good Christian woman to experience desire. I think it must be the first time she was ever kissed, I mean really kissed. I don't mind telling you, this whole situation has got me plenty worried."

"You?" Mercy cried, and a look of frustration and bewilderment marked her face. "How am I supposed to help Leah when she crams every spare minute of the day with mindless activity? It isn't any wonder the woman has no peace. She doesn't take time to listen to herself, let alone anyone else."

"This must be a common trait with humans," Shirley added thoughtfully. "Have you seen Jody's yard? Why, it's meticulous. The woman must spend every available minute maintaining those flower beds."

"I'd hoped to make a real difference in Leah's life," Mercy continued, "and now I wonder if that's possible."

Shirley surveyed the small group of prayer ambassadors. She was new at this and uncertain herself, but then they were all relatively inexperienced and it made sense that they help each other.

"What about you, Shirley?" Mercy asked, her gaze skittering past the organ and then drifting lazily toward the huge pipes. Shirley could all but see Mercy's mind feverishly devising ways of getting at that organ.

"As it happens, things are developing nicely with Jody and her son, Timmy," Shirley said, walking directly in front of the organ, cutting off Mercy's view. "Jody went out on her first date in years this evening and afterward Glen asked her out for dinner and she agreed."

"Glen? Who's Glen?"

"An attorney. They work for the same law firm. Glen's hardworking and sincere. From what I was able to learn about him, he's interested in settling down and starting a family. I'm sure once Timmy meets him everything will fall neatly into place."

Goodness slapped one disgruntled wing against her side. "I'm going to do my very best to remain angelic here, but it seems to me you received a cushy assignment while Mercy and I are at our wits end."

Mercy chimed in in agreement. "In case you haven't guessed, Goodness and I are experiencing some minor difficulties."

"It might help," Shirley said in gentle, forgiving tones, "if you stayed away from escalators and television screens."

"You heard?" Goodness ventured.

Shirley nodded. "And so has Gabriel."

Mercy closed her eyes. "Is he furious?"

"He hasn't pulled you off the assignment, has he?" Shirley asked. "I heard what you said this afternoon, and you're right. Gabriel doesn't have the angel-power to replace you just now and I'm sure all will be forgiven if, and it's a big if, Mercy is able to help Leah find her peace. Goodness, you've got to help Monica find a decent husband."

"I thought it'd be easier than it is," Goodness confessed in a small voice.

Mercy joined her friend, sagging defeatedly into a chair. "We could both do with some suggestions. This prayer business is difficult work."

Goodness agreed with a sharp nod. "Being around humans for any length of time is enough to make any angel go stir-crazy."

Shirley did a poor job of containing a smile. How well she understood her friends' frustrations. Most of her career had been spent working with humans. "Just don't ever volunteer to work as a guardian then," she suggested. The stories she could tell!

"Can you help us, Shirley?" Mercy asked.

Her friends' faces were both tired and gloomy, and Shirley didn't know if she had any words of wisdom to offer them. "I can try. Tell me what's happening."

Mercy and Goodness exchanged glances. "You go first," Goodness suggested.

"I've already told you about Leah's day. I've spent most of my time observing her, and frankly, I haven't gained a lot of insight into her personality. She holds her pain deep inside herself, unwilling to give up even the smallest portion of it, as if it were something of value."

Shirley thoughtfully mulled over this information. "If that's the case, it seems to me she must find joy before she finds peace."

Stubbornly Mercy folded her arms and frowned and her chest lifted with a gigantic sigh. "Gabriel didn't say anything about joy. All he mentioned was peace. Who exactly does he think I am, St. Peter?"

"Perhaps that was the problem with the other prayer ambassadors. They were looking for shortcuts as well."

"Oh, all right," Mercy said ungraciously. "But how am I supposed to teach her about joy? Joy, peace, what's the difference?"

"What are Leah's favorite things?"

Mercy frowned. "It's difficult to tell. She enjoys her home, but she'd gladly relinquish it for the chance to be a mother. While she was with her friend this afternoon, they talked quite a bit about Pam's kids. A spark shone from Leah as they discussed the children, especially her friend's three-year-old. I think she said his name was Scotty."

"Children," Shirley repeated, her thoughts deep and grave.

"But that's the crux of the problem, don't you see," Mercy said, and the expression in her eyes changed, becoming more intent. "She doesn't have a child so she holds fast to her disappointment. The child will bring her the true joy, and I doubt that anything else will."

Goodness had grown especially quiet. "What if you brought a child into her life for a short time, like a weekend or something? You could manage that, couldn't you?"

"I suppose." But Mercy didn't sound overly enthusiastic.

"If she had a taste of deep inner happiness, she might be willing to release a portion of her pain," Goodness added. "It seems to me what Shirley's saying is that what Leah really needs isn't an absence of sorrow, or a feeling of gladness. Earthly joy wouldn't accomplish your purpose. Leah needs a connection with heaven."

"Yes," Shirley shouted with her excitement. She couldn't have said it better herself. "That's exactly what I mean."

"In other words," Mercy said slowly, thoughtfully, "if Leah would be willing to take hold of a . . . higher level of joy, then she might be willing to release her disappointments and frustrations."

"Exactly," Shirley said and Goodness echoed, "Exactly."

Shirley realized they made it sound simple, but she didn't envy Mercy her task. It was little wonder so many other prayer ambassadors had been defeated by Leah's problem.

Mercy stood and was pacing in front of the huge church organ, sending longing looks toward the antique instrument. "Anyone have any other suggestions how I'm supposed to accomplish this?"

Shirley was silent and so was Goodness.

"Don't worry, I'll think of something," she offered brightly. "I always do."

"Let me tell you what's going on with Monica," Goodness said next, looping her legs over the arm of the chair and tilting her head back with a dramatic flair. She sighed and placed the back of her hand against her brow. "She's enthralled with this . . . this private investigator. The choir director might as well not exist, and Michael's perfect for her, just perfect."

"What about Chet?" Mercy asked. "He might not be as bad as you think."

"He's not for Monica," Goodness said firmly, brooking no argument. "I was able to check into his past and believe me, it isn't a pretty picture. He's lied, he's stolen and been in trouble with the law, although he once worked for them. He's not exactly what I'd call an upstanding prospective husband for a minister's daughter."

"Oh, my," Mercy mumbled.

Shirley mulled over the situation, tapping her fingers against the top of the railing, her thoughts moving in several different directions at once.

"Furthermore," Goodness added seriously, "he's egotistical, chauvinistic, and he hasn't darkened the door of a church in more than ten years. The last time he prayed he was in his early teens."

"He doesn't sound like the man for Monica," Mercy agreed.

Shirley hesitated, then decided she might as well speak her mind. "I don't think we should be so hasty here. Isn't your mission to teach Monica to be more flexible and accepting of others? From what I understand she's caught in a trap of following a list of rules and regulations."

"Yes, but any lessons I have to teach her don't include Chet."

Shirley wasn't convinced of that. "From what you've told me, she views everything as black and white, with little room for compromise."

"True," Goodness was willing to admit, "but don't you see? The two are completely incompatible. Gabriel wanted me to get her feet wet, not throw her off the Freemont Bridge."

"All I can suggest is that you be patient with Monica."

"One thing's in my favor," Goodness said, sounding encouraged. "They aren't likely to meet again."

"Then there's nothing to worry about," Mercy said, slipping onto the bench in front of the massive organ.

"Mercy," Shirley warned, knowing her friend well enough to recognize the movement was anything but casual. The organ was too big a challenge to ignore.

"Don't worry," Mercy reassured her, "I'm going to be good."

Shirley wasn't the least bit convinced, and she was right. As she winged her way out of the church and back to her charge, a blast of organ music crescendoed into the night. Groaning aloud, Shirley recognized the opening bars from *Phantom of the Opera* and knew exactly where they'd come from.

"Dinner was lovely," Jody said, slipping out of the rich velvet booth in the luxurious downtown restaurant. Glen had been a wonderful dinner companion. Although Jody had been nervous when he'd come to pick her up at the house, he'd quickly put her at ease.

"It's still early," Glen was saying as he helped her on with her full-length wool coat. "I can take you back to the house, if you want, but I was hoping you'd consider taking a ferry ride with me."

It had been a year or more since Jody had last been on any of the Washington State ferries. After she'd received the word of Jeff's death, she'd come down to the waterfront often. She found a peace, a solace here that escaped her otherwise. On more than one occasion she'd whiled away an hour or more riding the ferry, standing on the deck facing the wind, letting it batter her. She'd close her eyes and pretend Jeff was with her. She'd breathe in the scent of sea and salt while the birds screeched overhead. Each time she came away rejuvenated.

"Where do you want to go?" she asked, reluctant for reasons she didn't care to explain. The ferry ride had been her own private haven, and she wasn't entirely sure she wanted to share this.

"Anywhere you like. The Bainbridge run is a half hour each way. We could get a caffé latte and look at the city lights. The Bremerton run is an hour each way."

"All right," Jody surprised herself by saying. It was easy to be with Glen. He was friendly and undemanding, allowing her to set the course of their evening, deciding even if there was to be a relationship. Jody found the lack of pressure necessary and reassuring.

He kept his hand at her elbow as they walked along the waterfront. The scent of Puget Sound mingled with that of fried fish from the take-out booths was in the crisp night air. The cold nipped at Jody's cheeks and she buried her hands deep within the silk lining of her coat pockets.

"Here," Glen said, wrapping the muffler her mother had knit for her around her face, covering her mouth and ears. "I can't have you catching a chill."

How thoughtful he was, she noted. This was exactly the type of thing Jeff would have done. Jody forced all thoughts of her dead husband from her mind. It was time to let go, time to put the past behind her and look forward, not back.

Remember Lot's wife.

Jody didn't know where the thought came from, it was as if someone had whispered it into her ear. Lot's wife? Why she would even think of the biblical character was beyond her. All Jody could remember was that Lot's wife had turned into a pillar of salt when she fled Sodom and Gomorrah. Against the angels' command, she'd stopped and looked back.

That was it, Jody realized with a sudden burst of insight. Instead setting her course for the future, Lot's wife had looked back over the life that she'd once had. In many ways Jody had been doing the same thing, and in the process she'd become frozen, unable to move forward to whatever awaited her.

They arrived at the ferry terminal minutes before the ferry pulled away from the huge dock, headed toward Bainbridge Island. Holding hands and laughing, Jody and Glen raced through the terminal and onto the ferry, their steps echoing like ricocheting bullets in the stillness of the night.

While Jody found them a table in the small cafeteria section, Glen ordered their caffé lattes. She was lucky enough to find a booth by the window. Surprisingly, there didn't seem to be many passengers. The majority of the commuters remained in their cars for the short crossing.

"Here we go," Glen said, slipping into the seat across from her and handing her the thick paper cup.

Jody trained her gaze out of the window, watching the city lights grow smaller as the huge boat effortlessly glided its way across Puget Sound. She lowered her gaze to the hot drink cradled in her hands. The time had come for her to be forthright with Glen.

"You mentioned the other night that you'd learned I don't date much."

"That's the scuttlebutt," Glen agreed.

"I'm a widow."

"I know that too, with a nine-year-old son. I was sorry to have missed meeting him."

"Timmy and my mother went to McDonald's for dinner. I'm sure he'll still be awake when we get back." She didn't mention that he'd probably give Glen the third degree, asking him about baseball and other sports. To be fair she should warn Glen about her son's inquisitiveness, but before she could he spoke again.

"No one seems to know much more about you."

"I . . . generally don't combine my home life with business."

"I understand," Glen was quick to assure her. "If you'd rather not talk about yourself, that's fine. I don't want you to think I'm pressuring you."

"You aren't," she said, touched by his gentleness and how hard he worked to please her. "It's only fair that I tell you about Jeff . . . he was my husband."

"Only if you want," he said and sipped from his coffee. As he did, Jody noticed what nice hands he had. Large, but gentle. They were the kind of hands that comforted a child, that shook on fair deals, and were rarely clenched in anger.

"I met Jeff shortly after he graduated from college," Jody continued. "I was going into my junior year and we fell deeply in love. We dated for several months and talked about marriage. The next thing I knew Jeff had sold his car so he could buy me an engagement ring." She paused as she remembered how she'd wept with joy the night he'd given it to her. For weeks afterward he took a bus to job interviews. "To make a long story short," she continued when she could, "he got a job with Boeing and shortly after that we were married. Timmy wasn't a planned pregnancy, but I've thanked God for my son every night since I lost Jeff. I . . . I don't know what I would have done if it hadn't been for Timmy. He . . . he gave me a reason to live."

She paused, needing a moment to collect herself.

"Jeff's job entailed a lot of traveling. He was always very good about keeping in touch with me. Timmy was only ten months old when Jeff was sent on assignment to Berlin. We set a convenient time for him to phone me each day. When he didn't call one evening I knew immediately that something was dreadfully wrong. I tried his hotel room several times, but there wasn't any answer."

Her voice wobbled and Glen reached for her hand.

"A week passed with no word. Nothing. I was frantic and so was Jeff's mother. Together we traveled to Germany. We stayed there nearly a month, in an effort to learn what we could."

"You mean he just disappeared into thin air?" Glen asked as they pulled into Winslow, the dock on Bainbridge Island. The sound of the cars driving off the ferry was followed by those boarding. The activity in the cafeteria increased.

"It seemed that way. We did everything we could, pulled every string, made a nuisance of ourselves at the police station and the American embassy. The best we could figure then was that Jeff had gone for a walk along the Spree River, which was close to the hotel. There'd been a string of muggings and beatings that year. The only scenario the authorities could give was that Jeff had been the victim of such a crime and either been thrown or had fallen into the river. I toured every hospital in the city. Gloria, Jeff's mother, did as well. She insisted Jeff was alive, and refused to give up hope."

"And you?"

"I held on to the belief as well because the alternative didn't bear thinking about. Soon there was nowhere else for us to look, no one for us to see. We didn't have anywhere else to turn, and had no choice but to return to the States. Gloria lives on the East Coast and after I returned to Seattle, she continued to pressure the powers that be."

"Did she learn anything?"

"Nothing . . . but I did." Those early months had been a living nightmare to Jody. "As much as I believed in Jeff's love for me and Timmy, I couldn't help wondering if this disappearance was planned. I know it sounds ridiculous now, but you have to understand my mental state at the time. I . . . had him investigated. If there was another woman in his life, I needed to know about her. I had to find out if this was some kind of cruel hoax."

"What did you learn?"

Jody focused her gaze on the caffé latte. "Very little. The only remote possibility came from a background check and I discovered Jeff had been approached by a government agency, the CIA, I believe—one of those—while he was in college. He turned down the offer. My father had a good friend in government who did some discreet checking and they reported back that what I'd found out was true. Jeff had been recruited, but declined, and that was the end of it."

"How'd you manage to live?"

"It wasn't easy because I wasn't working at the time. Within a few months my finances were a nightmare. My parents helped me out as much as they could, but I didn't want to live off their generosity. I couldn't. Jeff had disappeared, but because there wasn't a body I couldn't collect his insurance or any of the other benefits that would normally be available to a widow. Somehow I managed to hold on for nine months, with the help of my family and a few good friends. Eventually I was forced into filing for a divorce in order to sell some property. That gave me income to return to school and live on until I could get a job."

"They never found a body?"

Jody looked out the window, the night was inky and thick, and her heart felt more so. "Yes, eventually they did, but it took nearly three years."

"My God, what happened?"

A tingling sensation roved up and down her spine even now, after all this time. "I . . . received word from the German police that they'd found a body caught in the cable beneath a bridge. They believed it was Jeff. They needed me to provide dental X rays and claim the body."

"It must have come as a terrible shock."

Jody managed a nod. "It was. As best the authorities could figure, Jeff was mugged, beaten, and knocked into the river and left for dead. The body was so badly decomposed that there wasn't any real way of telling us much more than that. The news came at a bad time. Timmy had the chicken pox and I don't think I could have borne returning to Germany. Those weeks in Berlin three years earlier had been the most painful of my life. I thought to ask Jeff's mother to go, but she was always a bit eccentric and after Jeff's death she became more so."

"How do you mean?"

"She continually insisted Jeff was alive and was furious with me when I divorced him. Our relationship was strained afterward. She claimed she'd talked to spirits in a séance, and Jeff had sent a message to her. He wanted Gloria to tell me how terribly disappointed he was in me because I'd divorced him. I didn't talk to her much after that."

"She insisted he was alive and that she'd been able to talk to him in a séance? It sounds like she had a rough time of it."

"She has. I don't know that she'll ever fully recover." Then again, Jody didn't know if she would either. "My father, bless his heart, volunteered to make the trip. The dental X rays matched and that's the end of it. That was nearly five years ago now. Jeff's been gone a total of eight years."

"I'm sorry, Jody, I really am. Jeff must have loved you and Timmy very much."

"I know he did. I get angry with myself that I doubted him even for that little bit."

"Anyone would have." Glen took their empty cups and deposited them in the garbage. He slipped into the seat and seemed unnaturally quiet. "I don't pretend to understand the grief you experienced, but I was in a relationship that lasted for three years. Breaking it off was one of the most emotionally difficult times of my life."

"Would you think I was prying if I asked you what went wrong?"

His mouth moved into a half smile. "Not at all. You were frank with me and deserve the same consideration. I loved Maryann and wanted to marry her, but she's a successful attorney and, well, I'll simplify it by explaining that her career is more important to her than marriage. Somehow or another we got involved in a game of ultimatums. I wanted a wife and children. Maryann claimed she wasn't ready for either. In the end she suggested a compromise. She thought it was a good idea for us to move in together. I wasn't willing to fall into that trap, and that was more or less the end of it."

"You still love her, don't you?"

Glen lowered his gaze. "I think it's very much like you and Jeff, I don't think I'll ever stop loving her. It's been several months now and nothing's going to change. I've accepted that and apparently so has she. We still bump into each other in court occasionally, and it's awkward, but there's nothing left for either of us to say."

"Then it doesn't bother you that I have a child?"

Glen straightened in his seat. "Bother me? I consider your son a bonus."

"Don't say that until you meet him. He's quite a character."

"I'm looking forward to doing exactly that."

They were nearing the Seattle dock and Glen stood, eager for them to be on their way. He glanced at the gold watch on his wrist. "You think Timmy might still be awake?"

Jody laughed and nodded. "I'm sure of it. He's anxious to meet you too and please don't hold it against me if he asks you a lot of personal questions."

"Does Timmy like sports?"

"He loves them. According to his coach, he's going to be a dynamite pitcher someday."

"Really." Glen actually beamed. "I was the pitcher for our high school team."

"You were?" This was like a match made in heaven. Almost too good to be true. "If you mention that to my son, he'll be your friend for life."

Their pace was fast as they headed toward the car. Glen's hand was at Jody's elbow and although they were walking up a steep hill, it didn't seem to thwart their enthusiasm.

As Jody suspected, Timmy was dressed in his pajamas waiting for her return. The instant he heard the front door open, he raced from the family room like pistons firing awake an engine. He stopped abruptly in front of Glen and threw back his head to look up at him.

"How tall are you?"

"Six-two. Is that tall enough?" Glen asked, crouching down so that they met eye to eye.

"That depends."

"Timmy, where are your manners?" Jody reminded her son.

"I've got to check him out, don't I?"

"Let me introduce you before you bombard him with questions," she said.

Timmy held out his hand. "I'm Timothy Jeffery Potter."

Glen stuck out his much larger hand. "Glen Francis Richardson, but don't tell anyone my middle name's Francis, all right?" The two exchanged enthusiastic handshakes.

"I won't tell a soul." Timmy spit on his two fingers and crossed his heart. "I promise and you can zap me with a laser gun if you find out that I have."

Just then Helen Chandler came out of the family room, which was situated off the kitchen, and Jody made the introductions. "If you don't mind, I'm heading home. My favorite television program's about to start and I don't want to miss it."

"I'll see you to the door," Jody said. She needn't have worried about Glen. Timmy led him back into the family room, insisting that he show Glen his baseball card collection. At this rate her dinner date would be there for hours.

"How'd it go?" her mother whispered loud enough to be heard into the next county and certainly the family room.

"Very well," Jody said, opening the door. She didn't want to stand in the doorway and carry on a conversation when it was likely Glen could hear every word they were saying.

"Do you like him?"

"Mother."

"Well, do you?" Helen pressed.

"Yes."

Her mother threw back her head and shocked Jody out of five years of her life by shouting, "Hallelujah!"

"Mom," Timmy called from the other room. "Are you coming? Did you know Glen has a signed Ken Griffey, Jr., baseball card?"

"I have to go," Jody said, grateful to her son for the convenient excuse. This was neither the time nor the place for this intimate conversation with her mother. "I promise I'll call you after church tomorrow morning."

"Mom," Timmy shouted again, "can Glen go to church with us?"

"Ah . . ." Jody glanced from her mother to the other room, not knowing which way to turn.

"Go and talk to Glen and Timmy. We can chat later." Before Jody could turn away, her mother impulsively reached for her and hugged her. "Everything's going to be just fine. I can feel it. I've waited a good long time for this," she said and kissed Jody on the cheek with a loud smack.

"Mom." Timmy raced into the room and grabbed her by the hand, dragging her into the other room. "If Glen comes to church with us, you'll cook breakfast for him, won't you? Make something really good, though, okay, because I told him you're a really fabulous cook." He lowered his voice substantially, to a soft whisper. "Just don't serve that liver sausage stuff you did at Christmas, it was yucky."

"All right, all right," Jody said, walking into the room. It amazed her how easily Timmy had accepted Glen. Her eyes met Glen's and he smiled at her. "You've got yourself quite a son, Jody. He's everything you said and more."

"I like Glen, too," Timmy announced. "I bet he'd make me a great dad."

Chapter

★✩★

6

"You're up bright and early," Lloyd Fischer said when Monica came down the stairs early Sunday morning. It was still pitch-dark and although Monica had tried countless times, she hadn't been able to get back to sleep. Every time she closed her eyes, Chet Costello drifted, unbidden and unwelcome, into her thoughts, planting himself in her mind and refusing to go away.

If that wasn't bad enough, Monica was scheduled to sing with the choir that afternoon in downtown Seattle. She'd be near the Westlake Mall where she'd first met Chet. The tantalizing threat of bumping into him a third time had plagued her like an overdue mortgage payment.

"I couldn't sleep," Monica mumbled, helping herself to a cup of coffee. She kept her back to her father, letting him know she wasn't interested in conversation. She didn't mean to be rude, but she didn't feel up to her usual cheerful chatter.

Her father generally woke around four on Sunday mornings, enthusiastic and eager to review his sermon and make any last-minute changes. He was the first one at the church, turning on the furnace so the building would be warm when the congregation arrived. He was a gentle spirit, her father, a man who brought joy to God's heart. His tendency to look at the bright side of an issue was often a source of contention between them, but it was a minor fault.

One of them had to maintain a realistic outlook on life and it was the role she'd chosen. Because of this, others tended to view her in a less than favorable light. Her father, on the other hand, was loved by all. He was a good shepherd to his flock, sensitive and gentle, steering them toward a deeper understanding of God's word.

Monica sluggishly stirred a teaspoon of sugar into the coffee. She wasn't looking forward to the outing with the choir, and had toyed with the idea of digging up a plausible excuse not to go. Knowing it would have caused a hardship for the others was her only hesitation.

No, she corrected, striving for honesty, that wasn't entirely true.

Some small, dark part of herself hungered to see Chet again. It pained and troubled her to admit that. The man had taken advantage of her, threatened her, and then, against her will, had blatantly kissed her. The mere thought of their last encounter brought a flash of heated color to her cheeks.

It mortified her to recall the way she'd responded to him, the way she encouraged his advance, the way her body had reacted to his. No decent woman would feel the things she had, Monica was convinced of that. Patrick had kissed her several times early on in their relationship, and what she'd experienced with him had been a small spark of tenderness. When Chet had kissed her, she'd felt as if she were standing in the middle of a forest fire.

"Are you feeling all right?" her father asked, studying her closely as she sat down at the kitchen table across from him.

Now was the perfect time to say she wasn't up to par. *That* was all she need do. Her father would be the one to suggest she not participate in the choir's performance that afternoon. Naturally she'd put up a token fuss, but he'd be adamant, insisting her health was more important, and the choir could make do without her.

"I'm fine, Dad," she murmured. She braced her elbows against the edge of the table and sipped from the thick ceramic cup, wondering what it was about Chet that caused her to be so weak willed. It was unlikely that she would run into him, although, as luck would have it—not that she believed in such matters—she'd encountered Chet twice now within the same week.

Her father left and returned to the kitchen a moment later, dressed in his thick winter coat. He wrapped a wool scarf around his neck, slipped his hands into leather gloves, and announced, "I'm going over to the church."

She acknowledged him with a nod, grateful she'd be alone for the next several minutes. Instead of worrying about the possibility of seeing Chet, she should be praying for him. The man was clearly in need of divine intervention. One look at him told her everything she needed to know about his shabby life and immoral habits. Their all-too-brief conversations had reinforced her suspicions. He was cynical, irrational, stubborn, and only heaven knew what else.

"Then why won't he leave me alone?" she asked out loud, surprising herself with the shrill sound of her own voice.

She leaped from her chair and paced the compact kitchen.

Absorbed in her thoughts, Monica continued walking about the room, circling the wooden table a number of times. She'd prayed long and hard for God to send a man into her life, but she hadn't asked how she was supposed to recognize him.

How she wished her mother were alive. Esther Fischer had always seemed to know what to do even in the most awkward of situations.

Her father looked surprised to see her when he returned fifteen minutes later. His nose was red and his cheeks bright with color from the short walk from the church to the parsonage.

"It's a beautiful morning," he announced cheerfully, removing his gloves, one finger at a time.

It could be blizzard conditions and her father would say the same thing. Sundays were beautiful to him no matter what the weather, because he was leading his flock in worship.

"Dad," Monica said, walking over to the refrigerator and taking out a carton of eggs and a package of bacon. She set them on the counter and then purposely turned around to face him. "When you met Mom, how did you feel? I mean did you have an inkling that this was the woman you'd eventually love and marry?"

If her father thought her question was out of the ordinary, he gave no indication. "I saw your mother for the first time in church."

"I know." She loved the story of how her parents had met while in the college-age Sunday school class. Her mother's family had recently moved into the area and Esther had felt shy and awkward that first Sunday.

Her father had been captivated by the beautiful young woman and had wanted to claim the empty seat beside her. Unfortunately several of the other young men had shared the same idea. While they were arguing about it, Esther had quietly stood and moved over to the chair and sat next to Lloyd. It wasn't a wildly romantic story, but Monica had enjoyed hearing it again and again as a young girl. It had deeply impressed her that her mother, although she was only nineteen at the time, had the presence of mind to choose such a wonderful man as Monica's father.

Monica doubted that she had such finely tuned discrimination herself, and after meeting Chet she was convinced of it.

"Did I know that first Sunday I was going to love your mother?" her father repeated her question slowly, his look thoughtful. "It's funny you should ask about her. I was just thinking about her myself and how she loved cold, crisp mornings such as this."

"How soon after you met did you realize you were going to love her?" Monica pressed, anxious now.

Her father poured himself a fresh cup of coffee. "It would sound romantic if I said I did that first Sunday, wouldn't it? Don't get me wrong, I was attracted to Esther from the moment I laid eyes on her. Any young man with a lick of sense would have been. She was lovely then and more so as the years progressed."

"You dated for several years, didn't you?"

"Yes, those were difficult times. We weren't married until four years later, after I'd completed seminary."

"I know that. What I want to know is when you realized you were in love with her."

He sat down at the table and rubbed his hand over his face.

Monica laughed. "It shouldn't be this hard, Daddy."

He nodded, his dark eyes intense. "I was trying to think back and it's been more years than I care to count. As best as I can remember, falling in love was a gradual process for me. Your mother and I saw a good deal of each other and I always enjoyed her company. It just seemed to me that she'd make a good pastor's wife and so I asked her to marry me."

"I see." Monica didn't bother to hide her disappointment. She'd been looking for something that hadn't been there. Her parents, while deeply in love, hadn't shared any great passion for each other. To the best of her memory she couldn't remember them doing more than holding hands in public.

Her disappointment must have shown because her father looked at her and asked, "This troubles you?"

"Oh, no. I . . . I was just wondering, is all. It isn't important." Only it was.

Even when they were young and in love her parents had been sensible and prudent when it came to choosing their life's partners. There hadn't been any explosion of—she hated to even say the word—*passion* between them. They'd drifted into marriage as a natural conclusion to a long-standing relationship.

It was the way her romance had started with Patrick, but their relationship had fizzled out and died without Monica even realizing what had happened. What she'd hoped to hear had been a confirmation of the feelings she'd experienced since meeting Chet. Not that she'd ever consider marrying anyone like him.

"I deeply loved your mother."

"I know that, Dad."

"I understand you're impatient to be a wife yourself, and all I can say is that God will bring a man into your life in His own time."

Monica nodded and, returning to the stove, placed an iron skillet on the stove. "I'm in no rush," she said, and even as she spoke, Monica knew that wasn't true.

"Remember what happened when Sarah decided to take matters into her own hands by giving Abraham her servant girl?"

"I remember."

"Don't make this a do-it-yourself project."

Monica laughed. "I won't."

Her father was silent for a moment, then asked, "Michael's certainly a nice-looking young man, don't you think?"

Monica resisted the urge to laugh outright. Her father couldn't have been less subtle. The choir director was a couple of years younger than Monica, not that it mattered. He was reserved and quiet, and frankly, she couldn't imagine spending the rest of her life with him. She liked Michael, and appreciated his efforts with the choir, but when she looked at him there wasn't any spark, any sizzling attraction. She felt nothing.

How she wished she could say the same for Chet. What she felt for him had to be immoral. It *was* immoral. Only that morning when she was trying desperately to sleep, her thoughts had been full of Chet and the kiss they'd shared. The mere memory had turned her body into a traitor. Monica was convinced those feelings were ones godly women were never meant to experience.

"Ah, yes," her father continued, blithely unaware of the route her unruly thoughts had taken. "Michael would make you a good husband. I'm an old man, and I don't know much about romance, but my guess is that he'd very much like to get to know you better."

"He's a good man," Monica agreed, unwilling to say anything more.

"You could do far worse."

Her father hadn't a clue how true those words were. He approved of Michael, but she had no doubts of what the good reverend would think should she introduce him to Chet. Monica could well imagine the look of alarm that would come into his eyes. Naturally, he'd be gentle with his concern, but his response would be impossible to conceal.

After she'd finished frying the bacon and eggs, Monica set the plate on the table and said, "I'm going upstairs to change."

Her father tossed a surprised look her way. "You're not eating?"

She shook her head.

"You're sure you're feeling all right?"

At the moment Monica wasn't sure of anything.

*   *   *

"Come sit with me," Andrew invited. Leah's husband was relaxing on the white leather sofa, his feet stretched out and propped against the end of the glass coffee table. He set aside the morning paper and held out his arms coaxingly to her.

"I was going to wash the breakfast dishes," Leah said, and hesitated.

"Do them later."

"Andrew!" Her husband had the look about him that was unmistakable. He wanted her the way a man wants his wife and he wasn't willing to wait much longer.

"Yes?" she asked, poising her hand against her hip and shifting her weight to one foot. "It's barely ten o'clock in the morning." She didn't know why she was making excuses, she was as eager for him as he was her. This was a good time of the month as well, her temperature would confirm that, but she hadn't taken it yet that morning.

"So? Who cares about the time?" he asked, holding his arm out to her. "Does the clock have to chime a certain number of times before I'm allowed to make love to my wife?"

"No." She walked toward him, her steps slow and provocative. When she was close, Andrew gripped hold of her waist, and gently lowered her onto his lap.

"Have I told you lately how beautiful you are?"

Leah smiled and shook her head. "Not since yesterday morning."

His hands stroked the length of her arms, his touch light and gentle. "Then I need to make up for lost time, don't I?"

"By all that's right, you should do penance."

"Oh?"

She looped her arms around his neck and pressed her forehead to his. Andrew's hands were busily working open the fastenings of her robe. After ten years of married life, Leah's body was well acquainted with that of her husband's. He was hard and eager, but she couldn't allow them to become so caught up in the urgency of the moment.

His hand found her breast and her heart began to pound, hard and steady. He kissed her neck, and she closed her eyes, sighing softly when his tongue explored the throbbing hollow, working his way upward over her chin toward her lips.

Their kiss was slow, sultry, and thorough. She was breathless and panting by the time Andrew dragged his mouth from hers.

"You taste good."

"So do you," she whispered, her eyes closed.

His hands left her breasts and eased aside the elastic of the silk bottoms of her pajamas to sensuously stroke her flat stomach.

Andrew groaned as she moved against him, and kissed her again and then again, each one growing more intense in length and need.

"You know what I want?" he whispered hoarsely close to her ear, panting.

"You haven't made any effort to disguise it." Her hand went on a mission of its own, worming its way between the folds of his pajama bottoms. His abdomen tightened when she encountered his skin.

"Leah," he warned.

She found her goal, not that there was any attempt to hide his desire from her. Her fingers closed around his engorged manhood. Andrew groaned and caught her by her shoulders, pushing her back onto the leather couch. Her pajama bottoms were stripped from her before she had a chance to catch her breath.

"Stop, Andrew," she whispered, caught in the urgency of his need, and struggling against her own. She braced her hands against his shoulders to maintain the distance between them.

"Stop?" He looked down on her as if in a daze, then shook his head as though he needed to clear it. "You've got to be kidding."

"Let's go in the bedroom."

"Why?" He kissed her neck and his hands sought her breasts. "You're my wife, I can make love to you any place I damn well please, can't I?"

"I should take my temperature first. This might not be the best time of the month for us to be doing this. If we're going to make love let's do it when there's a chance I could get pregnant."

The silence that followed her words was filled with tension. Leah didn't know what she'd said that was so terrible. Their lovemaking had always been arranged according to her menstrual cycle and her temperature, which signaled ovulation.

"Andrew?" she asked, not understanding.

He moved away from her and straightened his clothes. She noticed that his hands were shaking. The anger came off him in waves like heat shimmering off concrete in the hottest days of summer.

"It'll only take a moment," she promised.

He kept his back to her. Still not understanding what she'd said, Leah sat up herself and straightened her own pajamas.

"It . . . it only makes sense if we're going to make love to do it at a time when I could get pregnant."

At her words, Andrew vaulted off the sofa and stormed into their bedroom. It was rare for him to act this way and she instinctively followed, wanting to right the wrong.

"Don't you agree?" she asked softly, placing her hand on his arm.

He whirled on her then, eyes flashing with anger, his teeth clenched. "No, Leah, I don't agree."

The force of his anger took her by surprise and she gasped and automatically stepped away from him. She couldn't remember him ever looking at her this way.

"I . . . I assumed you want a baby too," she offered weakly.

"I do." The words were hurled at her like sharp knives. "But not at the expense of everything else. It might come as a shock to you, but I'd appreciate being treated more like a husband and less like a robot. Every time we make love, all you can think about is making a baby. Did you ever stop to consider why we make love less and less often? Have you?" he shouted.

Leah had backed all the way across the room. Her backside was flattened against the wall. "I . . . I didn't notice we made love less often."

"For the last seven years it's been sex on demand. Our entire love life is centered on what time of the month it is. If Mars is lined up with Jupiter or some such stuff."

"That's ridiculous," she said, wanting to defend herself.

"My thoughts exactly. We make love when you want, when you think there's a remote possibility you might become pregnant. It isn't love any longer, it's sex, and if that was all I wanted, I could get it on the street."

Leah felt the color drain from her face. "You . . . you don't mean that." It was a fear she'd lived with from the moment she realized she might never bear a child, that Andrew would eventually leave her. That he'd find another woman who could give him the family he wanted.

He tore out of his pajamas, dressing quickly. "I can't remember the last time we made love," he said, jerking a shirt from the closet. The hanger swung with the force of his action. "Really made love," he amended. "It isn't me you want, it's what I can give you, and if I can't, then I'm no use to you."

"That's not true."

Andrew didn't answer. He yanked on a pair of pants, then sat on the end of the mattress to pull on his socks and shoes. His shirt wasn't buttoned as he stalked past her, toward the door.

"Where are you going?" Leah asked, running after him. Tears blurred her eyes and it was difficult to speak normally.

"Out."

"Andrew," she cried, "please wait."

His hand was on the door, his back to her.

"Don't go. You're right. I'm sorry, so sorry. Please."

His shoulders rose and then relaxed. For the longest time he didn't move. She wasn't entirely sure he was breathing—she knew she wasn't. The only sound in the room was her soft whimper as she struggled not to weep.

"I won't be gone long," he said, opening the door and walking out.

Leah flinched when the door closed, the sound exploding in the otherwise quiet room. She pressed a hand to her flat stomach and for a moment she thought she was going to be physically sick.

How long she stood there, paralyzed with pain, she didn't know. She couldn't guess. After a while she turned and headed for their bedroom. Slumping onto the edge of her mattress, she opened the drawer of her nightstand, reached for the temperature chart she faithfully kept, and the thermometer. Staring at them, her eyes filled with tears. After a moment, she walked into the kitchen. Her feet felt heavy and made small scuffing sounds against the floor as she listlessly made her way across the other room.

She opened the garbage compactor and tossed both inside. Along with the spiral pad and the temperature gauge, Leah felt as if she were throwing away her dreams.

It took her a moment to compose herself before she drew in a deep, stabilizing breath and reached for a dirty plate from their breakfast. She rinsed it off and blindly stacked it into the dishwasher.

Chet wasn't anywhere in the audience, at least not where Monica could see him. Relief swept through her as she looked out over the crowd of Christmas shoppers from her stance on the top riser. She hadn't approved of this Sunday afternoon outing. To her way of thinking a performance on Sunday wasn't proper for Christians. The way she interpreted the Bible, the Sabbath was a day of rest. Those who opted to spend their time shopping were breaking the observance of the Lord's day. She'd tried to reason with her father and Michael when they'd first planned this performance weeks earlier, but her objection had been overridden. Her father had claimed their singing was a way of spreading the message of love and joy. As usual, Monica had no argument.

Now she was pleased it had been overridden because it gave her an opportunity to see Chet again—if she did. It didn't feel good to admit that, but Monica was tired of fooling herself. She needed to see him again, just once more, to banish him from her mind, to prove there could never be anything between them.

The performance went well, although Monica was preoccupied searching the sea of faces for Chet's. No doubt he was entertaining himself in the Blue Goose, the bar he chose to frequent. It would serve him right if she walked right in there and demanded to talk to him. She could embarrass him the way he had her.

Sneaking away from the others, however, proved to be more difficult than she anticipated.

"Are you coming?" Michael asked her. He was tall and so thin the first thing she thought of whenever they met was that someone should feed him.

Monica looked up at him, her mind a blank. She hadn't been listening to the conversation and hadn't a clue what he was talking about.

"To Sherry's," he elaborated when she didn't respond right away. "She's invited the ensemble over for hot cider and cookies."

"I . . ." Her gaze darted to the Blue Goose. "I have an errand to run first, but I'll be there shortly."

"An errand," Michael repeated. "Downtown?"

She said in a no-nonsense tone, grateful he didn't quiz her about what she was doing, especially in light of her earlier protests about abusing the Lord's day. "I won't be long . . . you go on ahead with the others. I'll be at Sherry's within the hour."

"You mean you aren't going back with everyone else?"

The man seemed to have a comprehension problem. "Yes," she said forcefully. "I already explained I have an errand I need to run." Then feeling mildly guilty for the outburst, she added, "I won't be long."

"Perhaps we should wait for you."

"No," she said quickly. She could well imagine what the others would think if they saw her walking into a tavern. "I appreciate the offer, but that isn't necessary."

Michael looked as if he weren't sure what he should do, which only served to irritate her further. "Perhaps I should stay with you."

"Michael, please, that isn't necessary." The man seemed intent on thwarting her, which aggravated her so much she was barely civil. "I'll see you within the hour." Not waiting for any further arguments, she turned and abruptly walked across the street to the Westlake Mall.

The crowds were thick and the moment she was free to leave, she escaped the shopping mall and hurried across the street. Making certain none of the other choir members had lingered, she walked purposefully toward the Blue Goose.

Her hand was on the door when she realized what she was doing. She was willing to walk into an establishment that practiced iniquity in the lowest form, in order to locate Chet. A man who plagued her thoughts from the moment they'd met. Something was dreadfully wrong with her.

She turned, practically running in her eagerness to escape, stopping only when she came to the street. She felt someone move behind her.

"I thought as much. You were looking for me, weren't you?"

There could be no mistaking the voice. It belonged to Chet Costello.

Chapter

★ ☆ ★

7

It must have taken Jody forty-five minutes to persuade Timmy to go to bed, and then only after Glen agreed to help her tuck him in.

"I'm not tired," Timmy insisted as Jody pulled back the sheets of his twin bed. "I want to talk to Glen."

"About what?" Jody knew the instant the words escaped her lips that she'd walked right into that with both feet.

"All kinds of stuff. I need to know what kind of dad he's going to be. After all, God sent him, didn't he?"

A gigantic hole for her to fall in would have been welcome just then. Her son had a knack of knowing exactly what to say that would embarrass her the most. "Timmy, please."

"I don't really need to be tucked in," Timmy told Glen, sounding mature for his years. "I just wanted to show you my stuff." Something that he'd spent every available moment doing since Glen had arrived. Timmy had dragged out his baseball mitt and bat and his beloved baseball card collection for Glen to inspect. The poor man hadn't had a moment's peace in over an hour.

"Good night, Tim," Jody said sternly, standing in the doorway, her hand on the light switch.

"'Night, Mom. 'Night, Glen."

Jody felt as though her cheeks were red enough to guide ships lost in the fog. She barely knew Glen and already her son was announcing what a great father he'd make. There was no help for it, she was forced to explain.

"I'll get you that coffee now," she said, leading the way into the compact kitchen and reaching for a mug. Her back ached from holding it so straight and stiff. She didn't know how she could possibly explain. "I apologize for what Timmy said earlier."

"About what?"

"You know, about you making him a great father. He's at the age now where he misses a man in his life."

"I imagine his friends talk about their dads."

Jody nodded. "Recently Timmy wrote a letter in school to God asking for a father. Apparently he looks at you as the answer to his prayer because . . . well, because you're the first man I've dated in a long while and . . ."

"That explains the comment about God sending me," Glen said as he carried the two steaming coffee mugs to the table.

"I suppose." Jody reluctantly admitted that much. "I didn't want you to feel pressure because of what he'd said and I certainly didn't want you to think that . . . that I'd put him up to it."

"I didn't." Glen sat down and crossed his legs, relaxing against the chair. He appeared more amused than concerned. "He's a wonderful boy. You've done a good job raising him."

"Thank you." His words made her proud, but at the same time she realized that she'd failed her son in some way, otherwise she would have recognized his need for a man in his life. Her father had served that purpose for Timmy until his death and the void had been deeply felt by her young son.

"I'm honored that Timmy thinks I'm good father material," Glen added between sips of coffee.

"It helped that you had a signed Ken Griffey, Jr., baseball card," Jody teased, then grew serious. "I thought I should explain why Timmy's so eager for us to get to know each other better."

The lines that fanned out from Glen's eyes relaxed as he set aside his mug and reached for her hand. "I'm just as eager to know you and Timmy better, but I'm an adult and it wouldn't be considered cool to let it show. I realize we've only been acquainted a short while, and it's much too soon to be thinking along the lines Timmy is, but . . ." He hesitated and his eyes studied hers, his look intense. He seemed to be weighing his words carefully, then shrugged and added, "Oh, what the hell, you can think what you want, but I like you, Jody, I like you a lot, and I think Timmy's a great kid. I haven't made it a secret that I'm strongly attracted to you.

"As far as I'm concerned the fact that you have a son who's looking for a father is an added bonus. I want a family, and have for some time. I'd be pleased if we both started thinking along those lines.

"There, I've said it and I've probably shocked you, but we're both mature adults, capable of handling the truth, don't you think?"

Jody didn't know what to say. She felt overwhelmed and

apprehensive. She stood abruptly, nearly toppling her chair in her haste. "I'm flattered, really flattered, but . . . it's too soon, much too soon for us to be thinking along those lines."

"Of course it is," Glen agreed patiently. "I'm sorry, Jody, I didn't mean to upset you. You're right, of course, I got caught up in Timmy's enthusiasm. Forgive me."

"There's nothing to forgive."

Glen hadn't done anything more than sample his coffee, but he stood and carried the mug to the sink. "I should be going."

Jody nodded, but immediately felt guilty. Glen looked a little like Timmy after she'd had to tell him no when it was something he really wanted.

"Would you be willing to see me again, or have I completely terrified you?" he asked when he reached the front door.

Jody couldn't see how she could refuse. "I'd enjoy going out with you again."

The defeated puppy-dog look was replaced with a wide smile. "I'll give you a call some time tomorrow, then."

"That'd be fine."

Glen opened the door and paused. "Would you be willing to see me if it weren't for Timmy?"

Jody laughed softly. "Probably."

She was rewarded with another warm grin that lit up his eyes. He took a small step toward her and then stopped abruptly and exhaled a long, deep breath. "I'd very much like to kiss you, but I'm afraid that might be pushing matters. We'll do this your way, Jody. I'm a patient man, especially when the prize is one of such value. Good night and thank you for one of the most enjoyable evenings of my life."

"'Night." She stood at the door and waited until he'd reached his car. Once he pulled away, his headlights illuminating the dark street, Jody closed the door and leaned against the heavy wood.

Glen had nice eyes, she decided. The eyes of a man she could trust, who wouldn't rush her into something she wasn't ready for. The eyes of a man who was well acquainted with pain and disappointment himself.

After a few moments she walked over to the mantel in the family room where Jeff's picture rested. She stared at his familiar features, the features she loved so dearly. Even after all these years, he had the power to stir her.

Reaching out, she traced her fingers over the outline of his jaw, waiting for the swell of emotion that generally accompanied such moments. To her surprise none came. Not guilt. Nor doubt. Jeff smiled benignly out at her and perhaps it was her imagination, she was sure it must be, but he seemed to approve of Glen, approve of the job she'd done raising Timmy. It seemed he was telling her that even in death he would always love her.

Leah heard the door shut. Andrew had returned after being away most of the day. She closed her eyes, and took a moment to compose herself before she faced her husband. He was right and she knew it. Having a child had become an obsession with her, so much so that she was systematically destroying the most important relationship in her life.

Stepping out of the kitchen, she watched as Andrew sat down in front of the television and reached for the remote control.

"I . . . I thought that must be you," she said, which sounded silly since it couldn't have been anyone else.

"As you can see, it's me." His words were as stark and cold as they had been earlier. It wasn't a good sign.

"Can we talk?" she asked, tentatively stepping into the room.

"I don't know that there's anything more to say."

The fact that they were having this conversation with his back to her said far more than any words they might have spoken.

"I'm sorry, Andrew," she whispered, struggling not to break into tears. She hated any kind of discord between them. They'd always been so close, she didn't think anything could destroy their love. She feared now that she might be wrong.

"You've already apologized, you don't need to do it again." The newsclips from the game between the Seattle Seahawks and the San Diego Chargers were playing and the noise of the game filled the room.

Leah, who was wearing jeans and a sweatshirt, wiped her hands against her thighs. "I was hoping we could talk," she said, lowering herself onto the far side of the sofa across from him.

"Leah, listen," Andrew said sharply, "I'm not good company at the moment. If we're going to talk it should be when we're both in the right frame of mind."

She could never remember Andrew being like this. They rarely disagreed and when they did, both were eager to resolve their differences.

"When do you think you'll be in the right frame of mind?" she asked, swallowing her pride.

"I don't know. I just need some time to put my thoughts together. I probably shouldn't have come back to the house, but it's damn cold and I wasn't keen about spending the rest of the day and evening sitting in my car."

"Of course you should have come back here. I'm glad you did. Do you want me to get you a cup of coffee? Some dinner?"

He shook his head. "What I'd appreciate more than anything is some time to myself."

"Sure," she said, scooting off the leather sofa, "whatever you want. Take all the time you need. I was thinking of going out anyway."

He acknowledged her with an abrupt nod and continued to stare at the television screen. "That sounds like a good idea."

So he wanted her to leave, was willing for her to go. Leah hadn't realized how deeply she'd injured Andrew's pride or how she'd weakened the foundation of their marriage. It came as a painful shock.

He didn't say anything more to her when she left. Leah went about gathering her coat and purse as if she were going on an outing she'd looked forward to for weeks. Humming softly she called out cheerfully, "I won't be late."

Not knowing where to go, Leah drove around for an hour before heading toward Pam's house. Her college friend knew there was something wrong the minute she opened the door. Not that Leah would have been able to hide it.

"Leah," Pam said, alarm filling her eyes. "What happened?"

Unable to speak, Leah shook her head from side to side.

"Come inside. I'm sure it's nothing a long talk and a strong cup of tea can't help."

This was what Leah loved about Pam—the ability to solve any problem with a cup of tea and a stiff upper lip. Now that she was here, she wasn't keen on talking. What she really needed was a friend, not a counselor.

"It's not all that bad," Leah said, making light of her troubles as she followed Pam into the kitchen. The sink was stacked with dirty dishes and the cupboards were smeared with miniature fingerprints, a stark contrast to her own spotless kitchen.

"Auntie Leah?" Scotty raced into the kitchen, clutching his stuffed dinosaur, the one she'd given him for his birthday a month earlier.

"Scotty, you're supposed to be asleep!" Pam said, hands on her hips.

Leah scooped the three-year-old into her arms and hugged him close while he pressed happy kisses over her face. He was a sweet boy with deep blue eyes and a froth of unmanageable curls and Leah loved him as much as if he were her own.

"How's my darling?" she asked, setting him on the countertop and brushing the curls away from his forehead.

"Look!" he said, proudly holding up his thumb.

"It's dry," Pam explained. "Scotty has given up sucking his thumb, isn't that right?"

Scotty nodded eagerly and Leah carried him back into the bedroom he shared with his younger brother. Thirteen-month-old Jason was sound asleep, his knees tucked under his stomach, his small buttocks thrust into the air.

"Shhh," Scotty said in a loud whisper as Leah set him back in his bed, after maneuvering around a stack of plastic building blocks and several wooden puzzles. Pieces were scattered all about the area.

"I'm very proud of you for not sucking your thumb," she whispered.

Scotty beamed with the praise. She kissed his forehead and tiptoed out of the room.

Pam had the tea brewed by the time Leah returned. "Where's Diane?" she asked about her friend's oldest child.

"Doug had to run an errand and she wanted to go with him. As you can see I haven't gotten around to the dinner dishes. Sit down and tell me what's upset you so much."

Leah didn't know where to start, or if she should. It wasn't easy to admit her failings. "Andrew and I had a spat, is all. We both needed some time to think matters through so I left."

"It's nothing serious, is it?"

Leah shook her head, discounting her concern. "I . . . I don't think so. We'll be fine."

Pam brought the china teapot to the table. "You're sure?"

"We rarely squabble and it upsets me when we do."

A series of short horn blasts interrupted their conversation. Although the sound was irritating there seemed to be a certain rhythm to it. Leah closed her eyes and listened carefully. If she hadn't known better she'd swear it sounded like someone was tapping out "Hit the Road, Jack."

Pam sent a curious look Leah's way. "Doug must need my help," she said, "he's certainly being clever about getting it."

"It sounds like . . ."

"'Hit the Road, Jack,'" Pam finished for her, snapping her fingers as she walked toward the door. She stopped abruptly and turned around, looking puzzled.

"Is it Doug?" Leah asked.

Pam shook her head. "It's coming from your car."

This had to be some kind of joke. She set aside her tea and followed Pam. "Are you telling me my car's making that weird sound?"

"It's your horn," Pam insisted. "Just listen."

"My horn!" She joined her friend at the doorway.

"This is the weirdest thing I've ever seen in my life."

"You?" Leah laughed. "I better find out what's going on here." She grabbed her car keys and hurried across the yard.

"Mercy, stop that right this minute."

Mercy whirled around to find Shirley hovering over the trunk of Leah's car, her hands braced against her hips. Knowing she'd overstepped her authority, Mercy reluctantly complied. No doubt she'd done it this time and the archangel had dispatched Shirley to send her home.

"Did Gabriel send you?" Mercy demanded defiantly. If she was going to crash, she was going down in flames.

"No, I'm here to stop you before you get yourself into even bigger trouble."

"I had to do something fast," Mercy cried. "Andrew's worried because he can't find Leah."

"What?"

Mercy should have known she'd need to explain. "Leah and Andrew argued this morning and now he feels terrible. He wants to talk to Leah but he doesn't know where she is."

"We're not to get involved in any human's life," Shirley chastised. "By the way, what's with that ridiculous song?"

"It was popular several years back, one Leah would recognize. I'm trying to tell her to hightail it home."

Shirley folded her arms over her chest and impatiently tapped her foot. "You're courting trouble with this one. By heaven, Gabriel's going to be furious. Secular music, no less. You couldn't have come up with something more . . . spiritual?"

"'Swing Low Sweet Chariot' just didn't hack it. I was desperate. It worked, didn't it? Look, Leah's leaving now and two to one she's headed home."

"You're placing bets now too?" Shirley said behind a smile. It wasn't unheard-of for a prayer ambassador on earth assignment to return home with a few minor bad habits. Some angels were known to have found gambling appealing.

"Are you with the God Squad Police Patrol or something?" Mercy blurted out impatiently. Shirley had the luxury of having everything falling neatly into place with her prayer assignment. The last she'd heard, Timmy's mother had agreed to date a fine, upstanding young man who'd make Timmy a great father.

She and Goodness should have it so easy. As for herself, Mercy was batting zero when it came to helping Leah, and from what she heard, Goodness wasn't in much better shape. If anything, matters had gotten progressively worse. In the last report from Goodness, Mercy had learned that Monica Fischer had stretched the truth in an effort to seek out Chet Costello. For a woman who prided herself on rigid honesty this was not an encouraging sign.

"I don't mean to sound so bossy," Shirley explained, looking apologetic, "but Gabriel could have your wings for this."

"My wings! I don't think so." It would take a whole lot more than tapping out "Hit the Road, Jack" on a car horn for that to happen.

"I'm only trying to help you."

"I know, but . . ."

A whoosh of warm wind accompanied Goodness, who arrived breathless and impatient, with her feathers ruffled with indignation. "What is going on with you two?" she demanded.

"Shirley decided to appoint herself as my guardian and—"

"I was watching out for your best interests."

"Stop! Both of you!" Goodness cried, tossing her arms in the air. "I had to leave Monica and Chet at the worst possible moment for this."

"Not really, we were—"

Goodness cut her off by stamping her foot. "Shall we all get back to our jobs? Humans are trouble enough without the three of us squabbling."

"I was only looking to help," Shirley offered with an injured look.

When Leah pulled into her driveway, she wasn't sure what to expect. The business with her horn had ceased the moment she started the engine. Since Andrew took care of the maintenance on their vehicles it was something she should tell him. But how could she explain her horn going all weird on her?

The front door to the house opened even before she had a chance to climb out of the car. Andrew's large frame filled the doorway as he rushed out to meet her.

"Where were you?" he asked, his face tight with concern. "I must have made a dozen phone calls and sounded like a complete idiot looking for my wife."

"I . . . I drove over to Pam and Doug's."

"Pam and Doug," Andrew repeated and stabbed his fingers into his hair as if to punish himself. "I should have tried them first—it makes perfect sense, the way you love those kids," he said, steering her toward the house. He closed the door, shutting out the cold.

"You weren't ready to talk, remember?" Leah said. "You were preoccupied with the sports news and needed time to sort through your feelings. Or so you said."

Andrew nodded. "I behaved like a fool. I'm sorry, Leah."

"You? I was the one who owed you an apology."

"You gave it," Andrew reminded her, and something she couldn't read flared in his eyes, "Hell, I don't know what was wrong with me."

"You needed your space," Leah supplied, removing her coat and hanging it in the hall closet. "We all do at one time or another. I understand."

"I should never have let you go. You wanted to settle matters then and there. I was the one who made everything so difficult." He brought her into the circle of his arms and sighed as she relaxed against him. "I love you so damn much," he said.

"I know," she whispered. His fingers lovingly worked through the tangles in her hair. "I love you too. You're right, Andrew, I realize that now and I'm so sorry for the way I've treated you—"

"Hush," he whispered, gently kissing her. "It's forgotten."

"You're the most important person in my life."

"I found the thermometer and record book in the garbage. Do you mean it, honey? Can we stop worrying about a pregnancy and concentrate on each other?"

Leah understood what he was asking. He wanted her to let go of the frantic need she had for a child, to stop looking for a pregnancy to fulfill her as a woman.

She'd cheated her husband out of far more than she realized. All these years she'd been subtly and not so subtly telling him his love wasn't enough. Every time she'd dragged him to another doctor, to another fertility clinic, through another series of tests, she in essence said she found him lacking and that she needed something more. She tagged a condition onto her happiness, insisting she needed a child, the child he should give her.

Wrapping her arms around Andrew's neck, Leah slowly nodded. The dream was dead. It had been from the moment she realized what she'd done to him.

*   *   *

"Mom." Timmy greeted Jody at the door the minute she walked into the house after work Monday morning. "A package came for me from Grandma Potter. Can I open it?" He was hopping up and down like a pogo stick, following her from one room to the next. "It's addressed to me."

"A package?"

"It's probably for Christmas. You're not going to make me wait, are you?"

Jody moved into the family room and stopped short. Timmy hadn't exaggerated, the package was huge. She was curious herself. Gloria was very good remembering Timmy on his birthday and Christmas, but she generally sent a check, claiming he should save for his college education.

"I don't think it'd do any harm to open it up," Jody said, curious herself.

"I've got the scissors all ready," Timmy said, racing into the kitchen.

"Don't run with scissors in your hand," she warned.

"I'm not a kid!" Timmy chided, walking back with exaggeratedly slow steps.

"Sorry," Jody said, smiling to herself.

The box had been carefully packaged, as if it contained something of exceptional value. Once the tape had been cut away they were able to peel back the cardboard lid. Timmy immediately starting digging when they discovered the box was filled with Styrofoam packing balls. The material flew in every direction. She laughed, watching her son virtually attack the present.

He bent over the top, his feet six inches off the ground. "There are a bunch of smaller boxes inside," he called, lifting out the first of what proved to be several.

Jody lined them up on the coffee table and Timmy opened the largest one first. "What's this?" he asked, bringing out a trophy.

Jody was puzzled herself.

"Look, there's a letter in here for you."

Jody took the envelope and ripped it open.

Dearest Jody and Timmy,

You're were right, Jody. Jeff is dead and it's time I accepted as much. Forgive an old woman who can't bear to believe that her only son is gone. The truth was too painful to accept. Painful for you and Timmy too, I realize.

It came to me the other day that now Timmy's growing up, he might be interested in having the things that once belonged to his father. Jeff's childhood treasures are his now and don't belong to a grieving mother. Take them, and treasure them, but most of all, remember Jeff.

"What's the trophy for?" Timmy asked, turning it upside down and examining the bottom. "This is weird, the way they put it together."

Jody could barely speak for the tears in her throat. "Your father won that when he was twelve," she said, holding on to the statue with both hands. "For soccer."

"My dad played soccer?"

Jody nodded.

"I didn't know that."

Jeff was wonderfully athletic, the same way Timmy was, but he'd concentrated on football and track in high school and college.

"Wow," Timmy said, "look at this. It's really old."

"It's your dad's report card from when he was in the first grade."

"He was smart, wasn't he?"

"Very smart."

"You were too, weren't you, Mom?"

She nodded.

Timmy was hurriedly opening one box and then the next. "This stuff is really neat. I can keep it, can't I, forever and ever?"

"Of course."

"I'm never going to forget my dad. Never," he vowed, sitting back on his legs and releasing a slow, uneven sigh. "You know, Mom, it might not be such a good idea for you to get me another dad. Not when I already have one. It was just that until now he was a face in a picture you keep by the fireplace. But he was really a neat guy, wasn't he?"

"Yes, sweetheart," she agreed, "he was someone very special."

Timmy's eyes grew serious. "Then it'd be wrong to look for another dad."

Chapter
★ ✦ ★
8

Monica was in a tizzy. Chet had seen her standing outside of the Blue Goose, and knew she'd sought him out. Her first thought was that she should adamantly deny everything. That, however, would be a lie and she prided herself on her honesty.

"Couldn't stay away, could you?" he said in that impertinent way of his.

"I'm sure you're mistaken," she snapped. The buzz of traffic zoomed past her as she stiffly stood on the curb, waiting for the light to change.

Chet laughed, the sound mingling with those from the street and the busy holiday shoppers. The signal changed and she remained frozen, unable to move with the others.

"I imagine that's as close to the truth as I'm likely to get from you," he said, and gripping hold of her elbow, escorted her across the street. He didn't tell her where he was taking her and she didn't ask. Although she had long legs, she had trouble keeping up with his brisk pace.

He steered her into Woolworth's and over to the lunch counter.

"What are we doing here?" she demanded, disliking the assumptions he was making.

He ignored her and slipped into a booth. She would have brought attention to herself if she'd continued standing so she uneasily claimed the seat across from him.

"You hungry?" he asked nonchalantly, reaching for the yellowed plastic-coated menu tucked behind the silver napkin dispenser.

"I . . . as a matter of fact I am, but . . . ."

"The steak sandwich is excellent and they don't do a bad chicken fried steak."

"I'll just have coffee," she told him. By all that was right she shouldn't be sitting with him. She barely knew the man and what she did know was a cause for a twenty-four-hour prayer vigil.

"Suit yourself."

The waitress came, an older woman with gray hair in a pale pink uniform. She chewed gum and looked more worn than the linoleum in Monica's kitchen.

"I'll have a BLT on wheat, with coffee," Chet ordered.

The waitress wrote down the order and looked to Monica expectantly.

"The same, only put mine on a separate ticket."

The woman left, jotting down Monica's order as she went.

"I saw you outside the Blue Goose," Chet announced casually.

It was all Monica could do not to cover her face with her hands. It mortified her to know he'd seen her standing outside the tavern, debating whether she should go inside or not.

"I know why you were there too."

"You do?" Her rebellious gaze shot to his. She was certain he could see her pulse beating in the vein in her neck, the sound echoing in her ear like thunder.

Chet set the menu back in place and waited for the waitress to finish pouring their coffee before he continued. "You're curious about the same thing as me."

"Which is?"

He smiled without humor. "I don't know if you have enough courage or honesty to admit it so I'll say it. We're both trying to figure out if what happened between us was real."

Monica had entertained a whole spectrum of possibilities of what had happened when Chet had kissed her. She blamed him, then herself, and eventually her upbringing. Having lived a sheltered, protected life hadn't prepared her for the sensual magnetism she experienced at his touch.

"I certainly don't have any intention of allowing you to kiss me again," she told him, the words ringing with disdain. It was important he understood this right now.

"Not to worry, I'm not exactly thrilled with the prospect myself. I'm curious, and you have to admit you are too, otherwise you wouldn't be here. Frankly, I can't figure out what it is about you that intrigues me so much."

"I . . . I was wondering the same thing myself. You won't leave me alone either."

Their sandwiches arrived and Chet tore into his as if he hadn't eaten in a week. Monica glared at him and pointedly reached for her napkin and spread it evenly across her lap. Bowing her head, she murmured a simple prayer of thanksgiving. When she'd finished, she lifted half the sandwich from her plate, holding it daintily in both hands. Chet had started on the second half of his before she'd taken the first bite.

When he finished, Chet reached inside his pocket and brought out a small spiral pad. He flipped through several pages until he found what he was looking for.

"Your father's name is Lloyd Fischer, the Reverend Lloyd Fischer. You're an only child and your mother died when you were in your teens. Currently the church employs you as a full-time secretary. You play the piano on Sunday mornings and teach a Sunday school class. Your two best friends are married and live in another state. It's said that you miss them dearly and write often."

Monica was so shocked it took an effort for her to disguise her distress. "How . . . how do you know all that?"

Chet grinned suspiciously. "I have my ways. I'm a private investigator, remember? Don't tell me you didn't find out what you could about me."

"I most certainly did not." She snapped her mouth closed before she added to the lie. She had looked up his name in the business directory and noted the address. His office was close to the Westlake Mall on First Avenue in a dingy part of town. The mission was situated on the same street and she'd mentally calculated which building was his. She'd looked his name up in the white pages as well and learned that his apartment was in the same building.

"So," he said, pushing the empty plate aside and reaching for his coffee. "Do you have any suggestions?"

"For what?" She wasn't sure where he was leading, but she had no intention of continuing with this farce. Having lunch with him was about as far as she intended to go.

"Figuring out what's going on between us," he said loudly, as if she were hard of hearing.

"Keep your voice down," she pleaded.

"The thing is," Chet continued, "I'm not sure I like you. You annoy the hell out of me and at the same time I can't help thinking you could be one hell of a woman if you'd let yourself go a little bit."

Monica jerked her shoulders back and scowled at him. "You haven't exactly endeared yourself to me either, Mr. Costello. You're everything I *don't* want in a man."

Instead of insulting him, her words appeared to do just the

opposite. He grinned as if she'd stroked his ego with compliments. "Ain't it a bitch?"

Her head snapped back at the use of vulgarity. "Kindly watch your language."

His grin was cocky in the extreme. "You want me so much you're practically frothing at the mouth."

Monica's hands were shaking so badly she could barely open her purse zipper. She removed her wallet and carefully extracted a five-dollar bill, which she set next to her plate.

"I don't believe there's anything more for us to say," she said crisply.

Chet held up his hand. "Don't be so hasty. We've got several matters to discuss."

Monica slipped out of the booth and dramatically tossed her purse strap over her shoulder. "I won't say it's been a pleasure," she said, taking her gloves from her coat pockets. "Good-bye, Mr. Costello."

She heard him swear and winced at his words as she walked away. His hurried footsteps sounded behind her before she left the store and reached the sidewalk.

"All right, I apologize," Chet murmured impatiently, "I shouldn't have said that."

The man was full of surprises. She certainly hadn't counted on him making amends any more than she'd expected him to chase after her. Monica wasn't sure how to react, or what she should do. She was more comfortable believing him to be a hopeless Neanderthal. His sincerity went against the assumptions she'd made about him.

"You want to go for a walk?" Chet asked before she had time to sort through her feelings. "It'll be a test of our control to see how long we can go without finding something to argue about."

"Where do you suggest we walk?" Monica asked, as if that were her only concern. She looked up at him and found his deep, blue eyes intently studying her.

"The waterfront's as good a place as any. There're always lots of things going on down there."

"All right." Her words were little more than wisps of sound. She hurriedly looked away because she found his gaze mesmerizing and buried her hands in her pockets. Chet followed suit, his own hands waist deep in the pockets of his beige coat.

"You seem to know a lot about me," she said as a means of opening the conversation, "it only seems fair for you to tell me something about yourself." She wasn't sure, but this sounded like a good place for them to start. Her only concern was in knowing exactly what they were starting. She didn't know if she could be friends with this man, and anything else was impossible.

"I'm thirty-three and have never been married," Chet said, cutting into her thoughts.

"Why not?"

"You're twenty-five and I didn't ask you that," he barked, then seemed to regret his tart remark. "I never found a woman who'd be willing to put up with me."

Monica smiled to herself. "I guess you could say the same thing about me. I don't seem to communicate very well with men. I thought I did, but I was wrong."

"That sounds like you're speaking from experience. I take it someone's hurt you."

She shook her head. "We're talking about you, remember?"

He frowned as if he found the subject boring and was much more interested in her. "What do you want to know about me?"

She shrugged, not knowing what to say. "Where'd you go to school, that sort of thing, and how you got into the detective business."

"All right," he said, releasing a beleaguered sigh. He seemed eager to get this part over so he could learn what he wanted to know about her. "I graduated from the University of Washington with a degree in criminology and took a job with the local police force. After a few years I decided I'd rather strike out on my own."

Monica speculated that there was a great deal missing in this story, but she didn't feel she should pressure him for details, not when she was unwilling to supply the missing pieces of her own story.

"Did you enjoy police work?"

"Yes and no. When I was shot—"

"You were shot?" Monica couldn't hide her alarm. She studied him for any evidence of permanent injury, and her heart raced at a furious pace.

"It was little more than a flesh wound, nothing to worry about physically, at any rate." He hesitated as if he'd said more than he intended, more than he wanted her to know.

"What do you mean?" she probed, not willing to drop the subject.

"Nothing. We'll leave it at that, all right?" The way he said it told her she wouldn't get any more information out of him. Knowing that he'd been physically injured had a curious effect on Monica. A strange sick feeling attacked her. Knowing he'd suffered terrible pain greatly distressed her.

They reached the waterfront, the day was cold and gray, and the angry sky reflected on the waters of Puget Sound. The sidewalks were crowded with the heavy tourist and Christmas traffic.

"What made you decide to become a private investigator?" she asked as they stood at the end of the pier. The wind buffeted her and she turned her back on its force. Chet, however, leaned against the rough wood railing, his hands clenched.

Chet glanced her way. "You aren't going to like the answer to this one."

"I asked the question, didn't I?" His attitude irked her.

"All right, since you asked, I'll tell you. A shapely blonde with loose morals and legs that reached all the way to her neck—"

"You're right," Monica cut him off, "I don't want to hear the rest."

"That's what I thought."

They strolled back to the sidewalk and turned into a small shop that specialized in seashells, tacky souvenirs, and gaudy jewelry. Curious, Monica moved to a crowded aisle, no particular destination in mind. She found a paper Japanese fan with a brightly painted dragon and spread it open, fluttering it in front of her face.

Chet grinned and she lowered the fan. Slowly the amusement drained from his eyes and darkened to a shade as deep and dark as a moonless night. His sudden enmity unnerved her and she quickly snapped the fan closed and returned it to the table, wondering what she'd done that had displeased him so.

His hand stopped her. "You're beautiful when you choose to be," he said.

His words confused her as much as his look.

She turned hurriedly up another aisle and paused at a rack of necklaces. Taking one, she slid the chain against the palm of her hand until she reached the pendant. A mustard seed was framed in a glass teardrop. The scripture verse about faith the size of a mustard seed leaped into her mind.

"Faith is an amazing thing," Chet surprised her by saying.

That he'd know the verse shocked her. "You've read the Bible."

He made a gallant effort not to laugh and failed. "I'm not a heathen, Monica, even if I've been known to frequent seedy bars and sleep with immoral women."

"I see." Embarrassed now by his honesty and her assumptions, she started to leave the shop. To her surprise, Chet took the necklace from her hand and carried it to the front of the store.

"What do you believe in?" she asked as they waited to make the purchase.

"Do I need to believe in anything?"

She could tell that the question made him uncomfortable. "Everyone has a belief system, whether he acknowledges it or not." She sounded far more versed in the subject than she was. Her own had been so clearly defined for her from the time she was a child.

He didn't answer her for a long, silent moment. "I believe life's a bitch," he said as he paid for the necklace.

Monica bristled, but then she'd asked and he'd told her.

He moved behind her and put the necklace around her neck. The glass teardrop felt cool against her skin. "Thank you," she whispered, touched that he'd bought it for her.

"Don't make a big deal out of a buck ninety-nine," he said as if he regretted the purchase.

When they came out of the store, Monica was surprised to find that it was snowing. She couldn't remember the weatherman mentioning snow. The fat flakes came down fast and furious and had already covered the sidewalk.

"I'd better hurry to the bus stop," she said, anxious to get home before the weather made it impossible. She was already an hour later than she said she'd be.

By the time they'd climbed the steep hill to the bus stop Monica was breathless. It seemed that everyone in town had decided to head for home at the same time. Within minutes it became clear she was in for a long wait.

"You go on," she urged Chet. "I'll be fine." But he refused to leave her and after waiting a half hour, Chet shook his head.

"This is ridiculous," he said, "I'll drive you home myself."

"But it's snowing, and the road conditions might make that impossible."

"We'll wait out the craziness and once everything settles down I'll get my car out of the parking garage."

He didn't leave room for her to argue, and she doubted he would have listened if she had. Chet steered her toward the exit and reached for her hand when it looked as if they might be separated in the crowd.

"Where are we going?" she asked while they were making their way down the street. The conditions were blizzardlike. They were bent nearly in half as they walked against the brunt of the storm.

Chet didn't bother to answer until they entered a red brick building. In the foyer, he stamped the snow from his shoes and led the way to the elevator.

"Where are we?" she asked, obediently following him.

"My building, and before you get that outraged virgin look I promise I won't so much as touch you."

"I'd better call my father or else he'll worry." Monica sincerely doubted that he'd ever dated a woman who needed to check in with her family. She was pleased she couldn't read his thoughts.

"No problem," Chet said. At his floor, he took her down a narrow, dark hallway. His office had his name painted on a milky white door. Chet inserted the key and opened it for her, letting her precede him.

The first thing Monica noticed was the calendar with a naked blond woman sprawled out on a blanket of black velvet. The year 1963 was printed in bold letters down the side. His desk looked as if it had weathered a war on the losing side. It was scarred and battered and so cluttered it was impossible to see any part of the surface. His chair came straight out of the 1920s. A row of antique slot machines lined one wall.

Chet made his way around her and Monica realized she'd been blocking the doorway. "This is my office," he explained.

"Your calendar's for the wrong year," she said, her voice little more than a whisper.

He laughed. "Only a woman would notice that." He walked over to the other door and opened it. "Home, sweet home," he said, gesturing for her to go before him.

Monica was just getting accustomed to the disarray in his office. She held her breath as she stepped into his living quarters, preparing herself for the worst.

She hesitated in the doorway. "It's not so bad," she said, then realized she'd verbalized the thought. There appeared to be some order to his studio apartment, compared to the chaos of his office.

Dishes were washed and stacked on the drainboard and the only food on the counter was a bowl with three overripe bananas. The sofa was a large overstuffed one with a stack of laundry—she couldn't tell if it was clean or dirty—piled in one corner.

"The phone's by the television," Chet said. "I'll make us some coffee."

"All right," she said, taking several tentative steps into the room and reaching for the phone. Her father answered on the second ring.

"I got caught in the snow," she explained.

"I don't understand why you didn't leave with the others." Her father was rarely angry, but he was close to being so now. "Just how do you propose to get home?"

"I'm an adult, Dad, I can take care of myself. Stop worrying. I'll call again if I run into any problems." Rather than get into discourse that required explanations, she quickly ended the conversation. When she'd finished, Chet brought her a steaming mug of coffee.

"It's instant," he said, and with one sweeping motion of his hand, he cleared the surface of the sofa.

Monica sat close to the edge of the cushions, cradling the mug with both hands, her back straight, her knees together. Rarely had she felt more out of place. She'd never been alone with a man in an apartment before and her sensibilities were badly shaken. Chet had promised to be a gentleman, and to her dismay she was sadly disappointed by his assurance.

"Relax," Chet said, sounding irritated. "You look like you're waiting for me to pounce on you. I said I wouldn't touch you."

She decided to ignore the comment. "Do you have any idea of how much snow is forecast?" she asked, looking for a means of light conversation. She wished now that she'd stayed and waited for a bus. No matter how tardy the transportation it would have saved them both this awkwardness.

"Sweetheart, the weatherman didn't know about this. You don't honestly expect me to figure it out, do you?"

She didn't like the way he said sweetheart. He made the term of affection sound like an insult. "I'd rather you didn't call me that."

"What?"

"Sweetheart."

"Why not?"

"Listen here, honeybunch," she murmured sarcastically, "I'm not your sweetheart or anything else."

"I didn't say you were. Let's just forget it, all right?" He stalked over to the sink and dumped what was left of his coffee. "I'll see about getting you home now."

One look out the window told her the snow hadn't let up in the least; if anything, it was coming down heavier. Chet wanted to be rid of her and she was just as eager to go. She didn't know what she was doing with a man who hung a picture of a naked woman in his office. She was out of her element and eager to get back where she belonged.

"I can take the bus." She felt obliged to volunteer, but it was doubtful how much longer the transit would continue to run in the heavy snow.

Chet cast her a look that told her what he thought of that idea. "Come on, this might take a while."

Monica bundled her coat around her and hurried after him. The wind was bitterly cold as it sliced through the open garage. Chet drove a battered Chevy Impala with a tailpipe that hung so low she wondered if he could make it over a speed bump. She couldn't imagine that the faded green was a factory color.

"My Mercedes is in the shop," he said, unlocking the passenger door for her.

Monica let herself inside and searched until she found the seat belt, clicking it into place. Chet started the engine, which came to life with the roar of a lion, and pulled out of the parking space.

The streets were terrible, and the traffic was a nightmare, but Chet was an excellent driver and managed to avoid the worst of it. Monica breathed a sigh of relief as they left the congested downtown area.

Both were quiet for several minutes, and as they neared her neighborhood, Monica tensed. "It might be a good idea if you dropped me off a block or so before the house."

"Why? You aren't wearing boots—your feet would be drenched within minutes."

"I know, it's just that . . ."

"It'll save you having to make explanations if your father happens to see me."

"Yes," she murmured, appreciating that he'd said it for her. He drove a few more blocks, before pulling over to the side of the road. The church and parsonage were within sight, but it wasn't likely that her father would notice her with Chet.

Now that she was near home, Monica wasn't eager for her time with Chet to end. She clenched her purse in her lap with both hands. "Thank you," she whispered, fingering the mustard-seed necklace. "For everything."

"Think nothing of it."

"I mean it," she said, more adamant this time. "You didn't need to do this and I appreciate everything you went through . . . even when it didn't seem like it." Only heaven knew how long it would take him to drive back into the city. The streets were difficult enough as it was.

Chet's hands were braced against the steering wheel, his gaze focused straight ahead. "I don't know that we solved anything."

"You're not the monster I assumed," she said, making light of her prejudices. Honesty, however, could be a burden. Now that she'd admitted as much, she wasn't sure where that left them. Monica didn't know and she doubted that Chet did either.

"You're not quite as prudish as I believed."

They looked toward each other and a smile blossomed between them, slow and sweet. Time stood perfectly still, but it seemed impatient as if waiting for them to act. The stillness swelled around them, cutting off sound except the silent wonder of the falling snow.

Monica didn't know who moved first. It didn't seem that either of them had, when she found her mouth inches from his. Chet was motionless. She could barely feel his breath, barely feel her own. She should move, should turn away from him and flee while she could, but she couldn't make herself do it. Enthralled, she raised her hands and placed them on his shoulders. He felt solid and strong. Her touch was all Chet needed. He bent forward and claimed her mouth in a slow, leisurely exercise.

This wasn't the way it was before. It was much better . . . much worse. She dragged her mouth from his, tears of frustration close to the surface, but she wasn't allowed to vent them or anything else. Before she could so much as draw in a stabilizing breath, Chet caught her face and brought her mouth back to his.

His need was urgent now and he kissed her again and again as waves of confusion assaulted her. A warm, dizzy feeling began to build within her, spreading throughout her body. The sensation flooded every cell. She was aware of everything about Chet, the taste, the feel, the masculine scent of him.

When they did finally ease away from each other, neither of them seemed to know what to say.

Slowly, Monica raised her eyes to his. His gaze revealed the extent of his confusion. The same bewilderment, the same questions, the same doubts.

Monica had no idea how long they stared. The air crackled with static electricity, with sexual tension.

"You better get inside," he said, and his voice sounded as if it were coming from the bottom of a deep well.

She nodded and turned away from him. Her hand was on the car door when he spoke again.

"Will the choir be downtown again any time soon?" he asked brusquely.

Monica wasn't so dense not to know what he wanted. He was asking to see her again. She shook her head and not daring to look at him, she said, "I was planning to do some Christmas shopping, though."

"When?"

The question shouldn't have been so difficult. Her plans had been nebulous at best. Sometime over the next weekend, but that seemed far too long to wait to see Chet again. A whole week was out of the question.

"Monday night," she said, still not looking at him. "Around six." Not waiting for a sign of confirmation from him, she hurriedly climbed out of the car. Walking as fast as she could, she rushed toward the house, not looking back until she reached her front porch. Only then did she chance a look over her shoulder.

Chet was parked in the same spot, she noted, waiting for her to make it safely inside the house.

Chapter

★ ✪ ★

9

Just when everything was straight in her mind, this had to happen, Jody mused as she drove home from work Tuesday afternoon. The snow that had taken Seattle by surprise on Sunday had melted away Monday morning to a dirty slush that filled the side streets.

Jody's route from the house to the office had been traveled so often she could almost do it blind. She avoided the busy intersections by taking a side street that led her past Providence Hospital.

For reasons she couldn't explain even to herself, she pulled into the hospital parking lot and climbed out of her car. Glen had asked to take Timmy and her out for pizza Thursday evening, and she'd put him off, claiming she had to check her schedule. He'd seemed surprised and disappointed, but he hadn't questioned her further.

Timmy claimed he didn't want another father, not now, not after he'd carefully gone through Jeff's items. For the first time his natural father was real to him. It didn't seem right to start another relationship now.

The nativity scene had been up for several days and she'd driven past it for the last seven years without ever stopping. Now seemed the perfect time. Now seemed the worst possible moment.

She walked over and stood before the manger scene, and breathed in the serenity.

"Jeff," she whispered, "help me." She didn't honestly expect him to hear her, nor did she believe it was possible for him to respond to her despondent prayer. Yet she reached out to him, because she wasn't sure which way to turn.

"You'd like Glen," she whispered. "He's the kind of man you would have called a friend."

The only sounds that returned to her were from the traffic in the streets.

This wasn't helping, Jody realized. Nor was it hurting. She took a few more minutes to soak in whatever comfort she could before returning to the car.

Timmy was waiting for her. Every day she called the baby-sitter when she left the office and Timmy walked down the block, unlocked the house, and was there when she arrived home a few minutes later. It made him feel less of a kid and more of a young adult. Less of a Timmy and more of a Tim.

The lights shone from the windows as she pulled into the driveway. Timmy was in the family room, the Sega football game blaring from the television screen.

"Glen called," he told her when she joined him.

"Did you bring in the mail?"

"It's on the counter. Nothing interesting, just bills."

Jody sorted through the small stack, disappointed not to receive so much as a single Christmas card. Her own had yet to be mailed.

"Are you going to call Glen back?" Timmy wanted to know as he expertly manipulated the game control.

"In a minute." She scooted the ottoman over to her son, who was kneeling on the floor, intent on his game. "Can we talk?"

"In a minute, Mom, I'm just to the good part."

"Are you ready to save the world again?"

He broke his concentration long enough to cast her a disgruntled look. "You can't do that with football."

"Oh."

Apparently having lost, he groaned and set aside the controller. "Okay," he said, looking at her expectantly. "I'm ready."

"Glen wanted to take us out to dinner one day this week. What do you think?"

Timmy's eyes brightened with enthusiasm before his gaze slid to the row of trophies he'd set out the night before on the fireplace mantel.

"I don't need another dad."

"I remember you said that earlier, I just wanted to be sure you meant it."

Although he looked disappointed, Timmy said, "I meant it. You'd better call Glen back and tell him no."

Timmy was unusually quiet during dinner, but Jody wasn't up to much conversation herself. After she'd finished the dishes, she phoned Glen, and was grateful when his answering machine came on. It was a cowardly thing to do, but she left a message on his recorder declining his offer to take Timmy and her to dinner.

Timmy was sound asleep when the doorbell chimed. Jody glanced at her watch, wondering who'd be dropping by unannounced at this late hour. She hesitated, then realized anyone who intended to do her harm wasn't likely to ring the doorbell first.

Glen stood on the other side of the door.

"Glen."

"I know it's late, but do you have a moment?"

"Of course," she said, stepping aside.

A blast of cold air accompanied him as he stepped into her house. He rubbed his hands together and cast her an apologetic look.

"Would you like a cup of coffee?"

"If you don't mind," he said, continuing to look uneasy. "I shouldn't have come."

Jody felt a twinge of guilt over the way she'd rejected his offer to take Timmy and her out for pizza. It had been a cowardly thing to do.

"Please, sit down," she said, motioning toward the kitchen table while she assembled a pot of coffee and waited for the liquid to drain through.

Glen stood until she'd finished with the coffee before he took a seat himself. Jody guessed that this didn't have anything to do with manners. He seemed preoccupied and nervous.

"I'm not exactly sure what I want to say," he began, stretching his arms across her tabletop. "I don't doubt that I'm making a fool of myself. I seem to do that when it comes to dealing with women."

"I'm sure that's not true." Jody's guilt was mounting until it was a palatable thing. Glen was one of the nicest men she'd ever known.

"I guess the real reason I'm here is to ask you what I did wrong."

"You didn't do anything wrong."

"I realize I was rushing you and if I haven't already apologized for that, then I am now. I . . . it's just that I think the world of you and Timmy, and knowing I'd done something—"

"Glen," she said, interrupting him. "Believe me, please, it isn't anything you said or did. Timmy received a package from his grandmother, Jeff's mother, with things that had been Jeff's as a boy, and now . . ."

"And now," Glen finished for her, "Timmy feels another man in his life would be betraying his father's memory." Glen grew silent for a moment, then slowly he leveled his gaze on her. "More important, so would you. I know how much you loved Jeff," he continued, his voice gaining conviction, "that was one of the things that attracted me to you the most. You're not the kind of woman who'd give her heart lightly, and when you do, it means something."

The compliment made her uncomfortable.

"That appeals to me, Jody, because I'm that kind of person myself. I didn't fall in love until recently and it's been hell getting over that relationship. Love means more to me than being sexually compatible. It means being an important part of your life as you'll be in mine. It means encouraging you to be everything you've ever wanted to be, sharing in your triumphs and comforting you in your failures. It means giving you the courage to try again. That's what love is all about."

Jody didn't know what to say. She wasn't likely to meet anyone like Glen in a good long time. A man who looked outside himself was a rarity. He'd spoken of his broken relationship and the pain it had brought him, and yet he was willing to trust again, willing to love again.

"I've been thinking about marriage for a long time," Glen went on. "And because of that I've put unnecessary pressure on you and Timmy. I want you to know how sorry I am."

"Please," she said, "don't apologize again. It isn't anything you've done."

He stood as if sitting had become intolerable. "I want you to know I don't plan on taking Jeff away from you and Timmy. It would be impossible. All I'm asking is that you give me a chance to prove myself to you. All I'm asking is that you make room in your life for me."

Jody recalled the way her son's eyes had lit up when she mentioned the outing with Glen and how that expression had gradually faded as he looked at the trophies that had once belonged to his father. Like her, Timmy had assumed having dinner with another man would betray Jeff's memory.

Glen plowed his hand through his hair. "I realize men aren't supposed to react to rejection like this. We're supposed to be flippant and to take it on the chin and all that. Forgive me, Jody, if I made you uncomfortable. I hope I haven't embarrassed you, but I wanted to speak my piece. I figured I'd better do it while I had the courage." He turned and walked out of her kitchen.

He was at the front door before she stopped him. "Glen?"

"Yes?"

"Thank you for stopping by. You've given me something to think about. I'll . . . probably see you at the copy machine soon."

He nodded and his soft, dark eyes held hers captive. "I can be patient, Jody, I just haven't proved it yet, but I promise you I will." With that, he turned and let himself out the door.

* * *

"Here they come." Bonnie Stewart stuck her head in the labor room door where Leah was stripping the sheets from the bed. Her patient had recently delivered a healthy eight-pound baby girl, her third child. The labor and delivery had gone smoothly and mother and father were delighted with their latest addition.

Leah's shift had been over half an hour earlier and she'd hoped to be long gone before the birthing-class tour group arrived. There was something about ten pregnant woman parading through the labor and delivery rooms that left a sour taste in her mouth.

She was being unfair, Leah realized, but meeting with these groups had always been a painful experience for her. Dealing with the mothers-to-be, one and often two or three at a time, was challenge enough. A roomful tested the very limits of her patience.

"I'll be out of here in nothing flat," Leah tossed over her shoulder. Bonnie didn't know the extent of Leah's dislike for these predelivery tours, but she was aware enough to warn her the little darlings were on their way.

"Leah, hello."

Once Leah had been asked to be a guest speaker for one of the birthing classes and she'd talked briefly about labor and delivery and answered an hour or more of questions. As luck would have it, the tour guide was Jo Ann Rossini who'd been the instructor for the class Leah had visited. Jo Ann walked into the room with ten or more women, all in varying stages of pregnancy.

"Ladies, this is the nurse I mentioned earlier. I sincerely hope one of you is lucky enough to go into labor during Leah's shift. Leah Lundberg is one of the most wonderful labor coaches you're likely to meet."

Leah appreciated Jo Ann's kind words, but she was eager to escape.

"I'll be out of your way in just a moment," Leah said, bundling up the sheets and stuffing them in the laundry basket.

"There's no need to hurry. You'd probably do a much better job of giving a tour around the labor room than me," Jo Ann insisted.

"Leah's shift was over a half hour ago," Bonnie said, coming in. Leah was so grateful she could have kissed her fellow nurse, not that staying beyond when they were scheduled was anything out of the ordinary. It was part and parcel of her job, which, despite everything, Leah loved.

"Would you mind if we asked you a couple of questions?" A timid voice rose from the back of the group. The girl didn't look to be any more than eighteen, with eyes the size of poker chips. Her hand rested on her protruding stomach, which she rubbed as if to reassure her unborn child.

"I've only got a few moments."

"My mother said only a woman who's been through labor and birth can fully appreciate what it's like for another woman," one of the other mothers-to-be added loudly. She was large and brusque and looked as if she wanted to punish her husband for getting her into this predicament. "Don't you think that's true?" she added on a brash note.

"Ah . . ." This definitely wasn't an area Leah wanted to address. "A doctor doesn't have to experience a festering cut to know how to treat one," she said, making sure no emotion bled into the words.

"How long can we expect the labor to last?" came another question. This one was less intrusive.

"It's different with every woman, as individual as we each are. I've seen women who suffer little more than a few twinges of pain, and others who feel like they're giving birth to a grand piano. Labor can last anywhere from a few minutes to days."

"That long?" It was the same timid voice that had spoken earlier.

"Just remember the vast majority are within the normal range."

"Thank you, Leah," Jo Ann said, stepping forward. "We appreciate your taking the time for this. I know you're on your way home so we won't keep you any longer. Remember Leah," Jo Ann said, speaking to her class. "Because once you've had her with you during labor you aren't likely to ever forget her."

"One last question." The same brassy woman who'd spoken earlier did so again. "Tell us how many children you've had yourself."

Leah looked at the other woman, her gaze connecting with hers. "None," she said, then turned and walked out of the room. Her steps gained speed as she hurried down the hallway, tears blurring her eyes.

"Bremerton," Shirley said, joining Mercy on the deserted flight deck of the aircraft carrier *Nimitz*. Bright stars dappled the crisp December night like beacons from home. "Why in the name of heaven did you decide we should meet here?"

"I like ships, especially navy ones."

Goodness shared a meaningful look with Shirley. "You haven't done anything, have you?"

Mercy's eyes widened, as if she were offended by the suggestion. "Good grief, I know better than to move ships around."

"Gabriel wouldn't ignore that," Shirley said, folding her arms and glancing approvingly toward Mercy as if to say she appreciated the maturity Mercy revealed.

"Gabriel, nothing," Mercy said, "I don't plan on tangling with the U.S. Navy. They can be real sticklers about that sort of thing, although it would be fun just once to—"

"Mercy!" both Goodness and Shirley cried simultaneously.

"Come on, you guys, don't you know a joke when you hear one?" The petite angel drifted effortlessly upward, resting on the bridge.

Goodness wasn't sure of anything these earth days. Humans had frustrated her in the past, but she'd never had to deal with one as obstinate and foolish as Monica Fischer. There was a soft spot in her heart for preachers' children. Goodness was convinced Gabriel was aware of her feelings and that was what had prompted him to give her this particular assignment.

"I don't mean to change the subject, but are those submarines over there?" Shirley asked. She was dangling from the top of the communication tower and pointed to a series of seven fast-attack black boats docked in the murky, moonless waters at the Puget Sound Naval Shipyard. "I don't believe I'll ever understand how the human mind works. Imagine designing a boat that's supposed to sink."

"Can we get back to the matters at hand?" Mercy asked. "I don't mind telling you I'm at my wit's end when it comes to helping Leah and Andrew."

"You!" Goodness cried.

Shirley cleared her throat. "To be honest, I should tell you matters aren't going all that well for me either."

"But I thought—"

"Weren't you saying—"

Shirley held up her hand, stopping them both. "Timmy's grandmother ruined everything for me. It's as bad now as it ever was. Jody turned down Glen's dinner invitation and Timmy believes if he becomes friends with Glen that he'll dishonor the memory of his father."

Goodness felt sorry for her friend. They should have realized nothing is ever as easy as it seems, but then Shirley had been so smug about her assignment.

"What are you going to do?"

"I don't know," Shirley admitted. "Glen's patient, but I wonder just how long he'll continue to invite Jody if she shows no signs of wanting to go out with him. Until the package arrived from his grandmother, Timmy was working with me, and we all know what an advantage it is to have a child on our side."

"How long is it until Christmas?" Earth time always served to confuse Goodness.

"Three weeks," Shirley mumbled, her wings sagging with discouragement.

"You've got plenty of time, just be patient and do what you can," Mercy suggested. "You'll find a way, I know you will."

Goodness didn't have any better ideas herself. Her own lack of success with answering Monica's prayer request was getting downright depressing. The preacher's daughter claimed she wanted a husband, yet she ignored the attention of the man most suitable. Instead she was flirting with disaster secretly meeting a private eye with an attitude problem.

"I'm doing worse than ever," Mercy admitted grudgingly, as if this were something new the others hadn't figured out yet. "Shirley had a great idea. She felt, and I'm in complete agreement, that if Leah could sample joy, then she might find the steps leading to serenity."

"What's the problem?"

"Everything," Mercy admitted, telling them about the scene in the hospital with the birthing class earlier that day. "I haven't figured out how to help her. Leah's more miserable now than when I first arrived."

"I thought you told me she seemed more accepting."

Mercy folded her arms. "Perhaps. It's difficult for me to tell. She's been overly burdened lately with work, the holidays, and the guilt of knowing how badly she's hurt her husband with her demands for a child. If anything, her grip on her pain has tightened—she holds it close to her heart so that it suffocates her happiness."

"Poor Leah," Shirley whispered, then turned her attention toward Goodness. "What about you? Are matters any better with Monica Fischer?"

"I'm growing more and more concerned about Monica," Goodness said, sharing her own disappointment. "She hasn't given Michael the time of day and he's such a dear young man."

"You sound as if you're attracted to him yourself."

"I am. Well, who wouldn't be? He's dedicated and caring and a prince of a guy, not that Monica's noticed."

"What about the private eye?"

Goodness tossed her hands into the air. "She continues to meet him on the sly. My guess is she's more attracted to him than ever."

"What about him?"

Goodness cringed. "The more I know about Chet Costello the less impressed I am. He's lived hard and loved hard and it shows."

"What does he want from Monica?"

Goodness didn't have the answer to that any more than she did the other questions. "As far as I can guess, she's everything he isn't. He doesn't share her faith, her interests, her values, yet he's attracted to those qualities. He carries the misery of his past with him, and as far as I can see he hasn't cared about anything or anyone for the last four or five years, himself included."

"You know, there might be hope for him yet," Shirley said. "Monica must think so too, otherwise she wouldn't continue seeing him."

"How can you suggest such a thing?" Goodness demanded. To her way of thinking, any relationship between the two was doomed from the start. If anyone was capable of teaching Monica the lessons she needed to know, it would be Michael, not Chet.

"I don't have any suggestions for you," Mercy told her. "I'm having enough trouble dealing with my own problems with Leah. I'm sorry I can't be of more help."

"Don't fret," Goodness said as means of encouragement to her friends.

"We've got three weeks yet," Shirley reminded them. "There's no need to panic. Anything can happen in that time, anything at all."

"Right," Mercy said, eyeing the aircraft carrier *Carl Vinson*. Goodness recognized that gleam in her friend's eye. It spelled trouble. She had to be honest, she found the radar system downright attractive. And feeling as disgruntled as she did with humans and romance, Goodness didn't think she should be held responsible for what might happen.

"You're both right," Shirley agreed, glancing toward the submarines. "Anything's possible."

Crews from all three Seattle television stations were at the Bremerton shipyard the following morning. The sky was filled with navy helicopters that circled overhead, and a no-fly zone had been declared.

The top navy brass converged on the area and the activity on Sinclair Inlet was unprecedented. No less than ten navy vessels circled the area. Three of the fast-attack submarines patrolled the waters.

"Can you tell us exactly what's happening here?" Brian Lewis asked Marilyn Brock, a reporter from Seattle's ABC television affiliate.

Marilyn Brock pressed the earphone to her head. "As best we've been able to learn, the aircraft carrier *Nimitz* and the *Carl Vinson* have traded places. You heard me right, Brian and Carol, traded places.

The *Nimitz* was docked at Pier 12 and is now in Pier 24, where the *Carl Vinson* was formerly docked.

"Also from what we've been able to find out, despite very tight security, an unidentified object showed on the radar screens this last evening. Reports are mixed. Some claim it was nothing more than a commercial flight off course, but others have said it was the silhouette of an angel."

"An angel?" Brian Lewis repeated.

"You heard me right. This is definitely one for the record books."

Chet had called himself every kind of fool. He'd waited around the area at the Westlake Mall for nearly thirty minutes and Monica had yet to show. After the tempestuous kisses they'd shared, she'd probably had her sensibilities so shaken she decided against seeing him again. It was just as well. Their relationship wasn't headed anywhere.

Monica Fischer was little more than a passing fancy to him, but even as he said the words, Chet wondered if they were true. What she was to him remained a deep, dark secret, even to himself.

Well, there wasn't any need to wait around here any longer. If she was going to meet him, she would have done so earlier. A cold beer would ease his disappointment, he decided, heading toward the Blue Goose.

"Chet, Chet Costello."

He caught the tail end of his name and whirled around, searching through a mob of empty faces, seeking Monica. His heart gladdened when he caught sight of her making her way through the crowds, weaving in and around those who were going too slow to suit her.

She wore her hair up and tightly pulled away from her face. The severe style sharpened her features, but Chet was too pleased to see her to worry about the way she wore her hair or the drab, lifeless colors that made up her wardrobe.

She was breathless by the time he reached her. He stopped himself just in time, otherwise he would have wrapped his arms around her and lifted her off the ground. As it was, his arms gripped hold of her elbows.

"I had trouble getting away," she explained, smiling up at him, her pretty eyes revealing her relief. "I wasn't sure you'd still be here."

"I was just about to give up," he admitted. They were causing something of a distraction and Chet turned, looping his arm over her shoulder and guiding her across the street. He hadn't a clue of how much time they'd have together, but he fully intended to make the most of it.

"Where are we going?" Monica asked.

Chet paused. "Do you have any place particular in mind?"

"No." She shook her head. "Do you?"

He wasn't sure she'd agree. "My apartment. You look half frozen and it's the only place I can think of where we'll have some privacy."

Her steps slowed. "I . . . don't think that's such a good idea."

"Why not?" he asked. He'd perfected his innocent look until it was practically an art form. "I was thinking we could talk, and get to know each other a little better." Sure he intended to talk, but there was a whole lot more on his agenda. Monica possessed a delectable body that she carefully disguised behind clothes that were at least one size too large for her. She needed to learn exactly what it meant to be a woman, and he was an able teacher. Ready and able. It had been a good long while since he'd been this strongly attracted to a woman. That worried him, but not enough to prevent him from seeing Monica. He'd sort through his feelings later once he'd coaxed her into his bed.

Generally Chet preferred to relieve his sexual frustrations with Trixie, a cocktail waitress who worked at the Blue Goose on weekends. They had a long-standing relationship, or better said, a long-standing understanding. They didn't pretend to be in love, pretense was beyond them both. A divorcée with two teenagers to raise on her own, the cocktail waitress wasn't looking for another long-term relationship, and God knew he wasn't either. They were comfortable with each other.

"I have to get back before nine, otherwise my father will ask a lot of questions and I refuse to lie to him."

"For the love of heaven, you're twenty-five years old."

"I know. You don't understand."

Pressuring her wasn't going to help his cause any. The way he figured it, after he'd made love to Monica he'd be over whatever it was that attracted him so strongly, and would exorcise her from his thoughts and his life.

"I was thinking we could have coffee and talk," she suggested.

"People might see us."

She blinked. Obviously that thought hadn't occurred to her, and being seen with him would surely be cause for talk. That might put her father and her in an embarrassing situation. Monica loved her father too much to do anything that would hurt him in any way.

"We could find a dark corner somewhere," she suggested next.

This wasn't going to be nearly as easy as he'd assumed. "All right," he agreed, "on one condition. I want you to take the pins out of your hair."

She looked at him as if he were daft. Her fingers tentatively investigated the back of her head. "You want me to let my hair down?"

It should have been clear, but he nodded.

"Why?"

"Do I need a reason?"

"I suppose not, it's just that it's such an unusual request." Already her fingers were working at the pins, unfolding the thick knot of hair, which streamed over her shoulders in a warm cascade of dark chestnut. She kept her gaze lowered as though she felt foolish.

He was right. Her looks were substantially softened by the effect. She was lovely, more so than he would have guessed. Her face was fresh and scrubbed clean. It didn't take much to imagine what a little makeup would do for her already appealing good looks.

"Great," he said, when it became apparent she was waiting for him to say something. "You don't look like you're waiting to be thrown to the lions now."

"I beg your pardon," she said, her eyes snapping.

Chet laughed boisterously and reached for her hand. "Come on, let's go have that coffee before we start arguing."

"I'll have you know I dress this way for a reason. I'm trying to promote a meek and humble spirit. With the world the way it is, with girls looking to Madonna as a role model, I feel I should do my part to promote purity."

"Sweetheart, listen, you shouldn't knock those gold-tip bras until you've tried one. Just promise me you'll let me be there when you do."

"I wish you wouldn't say things like that."

He probably shouldn't have. She was as skittish as a colt, as well he could understand. This was probably the most daring thing she'd ever done in her life, meeting him this way without her father knowing what she was up to.

"Do you want me to tell you how sorry I am?" he asked, as they made their way down First Street. A dingy cafe he frequented was about the only place he could think of where they'd have a bit of privacy.

"No."

Her response surprised him. He was thinking she'd demand an apology of him and then proceed to lecture him on the error of his ways. Perhaps there was hope for her after all.

The cafe was dreary, and he felt a bit embarrassed to be bringing Monica into such an establishment, but since she'd turned down the offer to visit his apartment, that didn't leave them with much choice.

He led her to a table in the back and called out his order for two coffees. The chef, Artie Williams, who was an old army cook, appeared from inside the kitchen. He wore a grease-smeared T-shirt and apron.

Artie glanced curiously toward Monica when he delivered two ceramic mugs. "You're out of your element with this girl, aren't you, Chet?" he said in his gravelly voice.

"Just pour the coffee and keep the commentary to yourself," Chet barked. He was having trouble enough breaking down Monica's barriers without his so-called friend's help.

Monica held the cup between both hands, as if she were looking to warm her palms. "What would you like to talk about?" she asked, her eyes nervously avoiding his.

"Why'd you come?" he asked. He'd feel he was making progress if he could get her to admit to their attraction.

"I . . . don't know. Michael asked me to stop by his house this evening and I had to make up this excuse and the whole time I was on the bus I kept thinking I must be crazy."

"Then we're both crazy," he muttered, and sipped his coffee. It was hot, black, and thick. Just the way he liked it.

Monica sipped hers too, made a face, then reached for the sugar bowl. She added three heaping teaspoons before she sampled the liquid again.

"Where does that leave us?" she asked.

"I was thinking you could tell me."

"I can't." She raised her eyes to his, then quickly lowered them. "No one's ever kissed me the way you have."

That didn't come as any surprise to Chet. "That's only the beginning."

"What do you mean?"

"Kissing is the tip of the iceberg. There are a dozen different directions we could go from there."

She looked at him as if she hadn't a clue what he was talking about and he realized what should have been obvious from the beginning. Monica Fischer, preacher's daughter, was a virgin. He didn't know there were any left in the world and damned if he hadn't stumbled onto the last living one.

"What's wrong?" she asked. "You look as if you just swallowed a basketball whole."

"I feel that way." He stood so abruptly that the chair shot two feet away from the table. Slapping a fistful of change on the table he reached for her arm, practically lifting her out of the chair. "Come on, we're out of here."

His grip was so tight, Monica's toes barely touched the ground.

"Chet," she cried, "what are you doing?"

"Getting you out of here."

"Where are we going?" she asked. The way her voice struggled to stay even revealed the extent of her surprise.

"I'm taking you back to the bus stop."

"Why?" She shook herself free of his hold and whirled around to face him.

"Because, sweetheart, I just realized something. You're a virgin and I'm the last person you should be around."

"Why?" she asked. Apparently she still hadn't caught on.

"Because," he said, having trouble keeping the anger out of his voice, although it was directed at himself, and not her. He was a bigger fool than he'd realized.

"*Because* doesn't tell me anything."

She was having trouble keeping pace with him, but Chet didn't care. The sooner he was rid of her the better.

"Tell me what's so terrible about being a virgin. Good grief, you make it sound like I've got a communicable disease or something."

"All right, since you want to know I'll tell you, but you aren't going to like it." Chet stopped in the middle of the sidewalk. Although it was well past seven the streets were busy. Several people were forced to walk around them. "I wanted you to go to my apartment tonight for one reason and one reason only. I planned to seduce you."

Monica went pale. "I see."

"Apparently you don't. Good-bye, Monica." Having said that he turned and walked away, leaving her standing alone in the middle of the sidewalk.

Chapter

★ ✯ ★

10

"*Mom, I need another quarter.*" Timmy raced up to the table at the pizza parlor, his face bright and his eyes sparkling with excitement. "I'm blowing the brains out of the Laser Man."

"I don't think this is the kind of video game I want you playing."

"Mom," he protested, "I was just kidding. I'm winning, or I was until just now, but I need another quarter. Hurry, I gotta get back before someone else gets the machine."

Luckily the pizza parlor wasn't overly crowded, although a handful of kids had gathered around a row of video games against the back wall. Jody didn't know how they could play at all with the lights so dim.

"Just a little while longer," Jody said, rummaging through her purse for yet another quarter. Timmy's easy acceptance of this outing with Glen had come as a welcome relief.

"Here." Glen held out a fistful of change to her son. "Take what you need."

"All these?" Coins spilled over Timmy's small hands. His eyes were round with disbelief as he hurriedly pocketed the change. "Gee, thanks."

"I want you to enjoy yourself."

"I will. Thanks, Glen," he said, walking backward. He turned abruptly, eager to get back to his prize machine.

"I don't know if that's such a good idea," Jody felt obliged to say. She didn't want Glen to spoil Timmy, especially if they were to continue seeing each other. Her son might come to look upon Glen as his own personal Santa Claus.

"I have an ulterior motive," Glen told her, his eyes brimming with a smile. "If Timmy's busy with the video machines, we'll have a chance to talk."

Jody already guessed as much, but was uncomfortable having him say it out loud. Agreeing to this outing had been an enormous decision for her.

She'd been afraid to accept, but more afraid not to. Afraid of what she was becoming, afraid of what she already was. She'd stood in one place for so long she feared she'd rooted there like the flower garden she so carefully tended. Bit by bit, Glen was urging her forward. Each step was agony. Each step momentous.

"It hasn't been so bad, now, has it?" Glen asked, coaxing her into admitting the truth. Even that didn't come easy.

"It has been fun," she agreed. Timmy had certainly enjoyed himself, downing an amazing five pieces of sausage and pepperoni pizza and a huge cola. Jody didn't know where he managed to put it all. Generally when they ordered a medium-size pizza it was enough for two meals.

"Would you feel comfortable enough to go out with me again?" Glen asked, and his eyes held hers steadily until she couldn't bear it any longer and looked away.

Glen was pressing his advantage and deliberately pushing her, forcing her to stretch her boundaries. This was only the beginning, she realized with a hundred forming regrets. From here on out it would only get more difficult, more threatening.

It certainly wasn't going to get any easier. Soon Glen would want to hold her and kiss her, and if she continued to date him, he'd consider it a natural conclusion to their spending time together.

He hadn't made any secret of what he was after. He wanted a wife and a family, and he'd said so from the first. Part of her attraction was her son. Glen and Timmy got along like gangbusters. Glen was literally the answer to her son's prayer. That was the crux of the problem. Jody wasn't dating Glen for herself, but for her son. Now she had to learn to do so for herself.

"I was able to get two tickets to *The Nutcracker.*"

"*The Nutcracker?*" Jody repeated, her voice no more than a breath of sound. The ballet was performed each December by the Pacific Northwest Ballet, and was said to be both charming and brilliant. For years Jody had heard how captivating the costumes and music were. Everyone she'd ever known who'd attended had come away filled with the Christmas spirit. Since Jeff's death, Christmas had been a season to endure, not one to enjoy. Something told her this year it would be different.

"They're for this Thursday night. I realize it's a weeknight, but I was lucky to get those."

"I . . ." The temptation was strong, stronger than she expected. "I'm honored that you'd ask me," she said, hedging, trying to decide if she should continue this relationship.

"Then you'll come?"

A full, tension-filled minute passed before she agreed with a short nod of her head.

Jody watched the play of glad emotions on Glen's face, watched how he struggled to disguise his excitement, and in that moment she realized she'd crossed the line.

This was the beginning for them.

Everything else that had led up to this moment had been a prelude of what was to come. The time was right. It had been for a good long while, but she'd been too stubborn to accept it. As odd as it sounded, she was too comfortable in her grief to recognize what was happening.

There was no turning back now. Any qualms she experienced would need to be met head-on, one at a time.

Glen must have realized how momentous her decision was because he reached across the table for her hand, squeezing her fingers. "You won't regret this," he whispered. "I promise."

"I don't know why you want to go out with me," she said, her voice small and trembling. She bit into her bottom lip in an effort to keep it still.

"You don't understand?" Glen frowned, as if dumbfounded by the question. "You're a beautiful woman, a woman of character and strength. Every time I'm with you I'm struck by your courage."

Jody laughed nervously. "Then why am I frightened out of my wits?"

"Because this is all so new, but I'm not going to push you into anything you don't want. Oh, I'll prod and poke and nudge you along from time to time, but you have my word, I won't rush you into anything you don't want."

"Mom." Timmy's voice echoed across the room sounding as though it came from the bottom of a tin drum. He raced back to the table, skidding to a stop. "When are we going to get our Christmas tree? I was talking to George, he's the kid who showed me how to beat Laser Man, and his family's already got theirs, and you know what? They went to this farm, but this isn't the kind with cows and pigs, this is a farm with Christmas trees. And guess what?" he asked, dragging in a deep breath. "They cut it down themselves. We could do that, couldn't we, Mom?"

"Ah . . ." Jody wasn't sure how she'd manage chopping down a tree, but she was up to the challenge. "I'll see if I can find out about the tree farm."

"I know where there's one," Glen volunteered. "It's a ways north, but if you wanted, the three of us could make a day of it. We'll leave early Saturday morning, get the tree, and then decorate it in the afternoon."

"That'd be great," Timmy said, so pleased he could barely stand still.

"How does that sound to you?" Glen asked, looking expectantly at her. What else could she say? Little by little Glen was easing his way into their lives. Jody was uneasy with that, and at the same time eager.

"It sounds like a lot of fun."

Glen's eyes met hers and a slow, satisfied smile started to form.

Monica's fingers bounced against the typewriter keys like clumps of hail hitting the sidewalk. Her hands kept pace with her thoughts, which sped at a record hundred words or more a minute.

She'd been stunned by what Chet had said to her. So shocked she hadn't had time to react. Not then. Reaction had set in later that evening as she rode the bus home. She'd tossed and turned most of the night, her indignation scaling previously unreached thresholds of fury.

Chet Costello was everything she'd originally assumed. He was much worse than she, in her innocence, had suspected. Egotistical, untrustworthy, why, the man was a blight on decency.

He'd planned to seduce her, to break down her defenses and use her body for his own selfish satisfaction. As if she'd have allowed such a thing! As soon as he realized she would have nothing more to do with him, he couldn't be rid of her fast enough. Without a qualm he'd cast her aside like so much dirty laundry.

The one glitch in his plan was that he hadn't expected her to be a virgin. As if she were the kind of woman who'd fall into bed with him! And to think she'd actually been—it pained her to admit this—attracted to that scoundrel.

Tears burned her eyes as she continued typing. Thank heaven her father was away for the morning. To think she'd actually toyed with the idea of introducing Chet to her father, of bringing him into their family home. That would have been a disaster. Her father had always been an excellent judge of character and he would have seen through Chet in an instant.

Monica drew in a deep, wobbly breath as her resentment flared bright and then slowly burned itself out. She covered her face with both hands and attempted to pull herself together, which was difficult when she was shaking so badly.

After several moments had passed, Monica straightened, and ripped the sheet of paper from the typewriter with a vengeance. Having vented her feelings, there was no need to mail the letter. Any further communication between them whatsoever was completely unnecessary. Her hand automatically reached for the mustard-seed necklace dangling from her neck, fingering it. She'd worn the piece every day since Chet had bought it for her, until it had become habit.

Chet had made his views on life plain. If anything she should be grateful that he'd put an end to this madness when he had. One small part of her, however, refused to conform. One small rebellious corner of her soul yearned for the discoveries he would have shown her.

The thought terrified Monica into accepting how far she'd slid toward sin.

Well, she was safe. He was out of her life now. Good riddance was all she could say.

A knock came softly from the outer door.

"Come in," she snapped, then realized she sounded like an old shrew, and said it again, softer this time. Church secretaries weren't supposed to be confrontational.

Michael opened the door and stepped inside. "Hello, Monica."

"Hello," she said, tossing the crumpled-up letter into the wastebasket.

"Your father said I'd find you here." He stepped into the office, his stance doubtful. His gaze hesitantly met hers, as if he were unsure of himself.

"What can I do for you?" she asked, working hard to keep the impatience out of her voice. All she needed now was for him to load her down with extra work. Having wasted a good portion of the morning writing Chet and telling him exactly what she thought of him left her with a backlog of unfinished church business.

"I realize it's short notice but I'd like to take you to lunch, that is, if you'd let me."

The invitation was so unexpected that she didn't know what to say. "Lunch?" She had to look at her watch to check the time. The morning had sped past on the wings of her aggravation. "I suppose that would be all right," she said without much enthusiasm.

"Great." His eyes lit up and she realized what nice eyes Michael had. He loved his music and had done wonders for the church choir. It was because of his efforts that the small band had formed. He'd volunteered several hours a week to church work.

Monica liked Michael. She'd always liked him—there wasn't anything to dislike about the young man. He was godly, principled, and sincere. Everything she should want in a man.

But didn't.

"If you have no objection I thought we'd go to the Pancake Palace. They serve a decent lunch."

"Sure." The Pancake Palace. That was the problem. Michael was a wonderful man, God's own servant. Humble, gentle, the perfect choice of a mate for a preacher's daughter, only . . . only she'd dined on pancakes most of her life and she was ready for some salsa.

There'd been a trace of hot sauce in Patrick. That was what attracted her to Chet, she realized now. He'd been daring and fun and he'd made her laugh. He'd also badly wounded her pride.

"I'll get your jacket for you," Michael offered. "I wouldn't want you to a catch a chill." He took her navy blue wool coat from the rack and held it open for her.

Michael was a gentleman and Chet was a rogue. If she had a lick of sense, she'd cultivate the relationship with Michael and thank God there were still men like him in this sick and decaying world.

Since the Pancake Palace was only two blocks away, they decided to walk. Monica buried her hands in her pockets and struggled to keep her attention on what Michael was saying. His voice was a low monotone and she had trouble concentrating.

A car drove past, the same sick green color of Chet's Impala, and she whirled around, wondering if it could possibly be him. Her heart leaped into double time at the prospect.

If it was Chet, it would do him good to see her with another man. If he'd come to apologize, as well he should, then she would accept nothing less than his pleading for forgiveness.

She held her head high, refusing to allow him to think he'd left her floundering in the wake of his crass behavior. But the sight of the car had been fleeting and she couldn't be entirely sure it was he. More than likely it wasn't. Men like Chet Costello didn't know how to apologize.

It was Andrew's night out with his friends, and Leah schlepped into the living room, carrying a book and a cup of coffee. The house was lonely without her husband. Empty. The contrast between her life and that of Pam who struggled to squeeze in a few moments for herself struck Leah once more.

What she needed was a hobby, Leah decided. Something that would take her mind off the fact that she didn't have a child. Something that would occupy her time so she didn't dwell on how hollow her life was. Perhaps she should do volunteer work. There were any number of worthy causes that would welcome her attention.

Maybe when the holidays were over, she decided.

She read the first chapter without much enthusiasm. Finally, she put the book down and wandered into the kitchen for a refill on her coffee and stopped abruptly in front of the sink. In the bay window she'd arranged a row of cacti she'd carefully nurtured over the years. Andrew teased her that if she forgot to water them, it wouldn't matter. Five thick pink-and-turquoise pots each held a different variety of cacti, and each one had sprouted a flower.

In the last hour.

A variety of pink, red, and white blossoms had appeared as if by some miracle from the time she'd finished the dishes and wandered into the living room, until now, no more than an hour later. It wasn't that she didn't notice. One might have gone undetected, but not five. She could have sworn not a single one had been blooming an hour earlier.

Unexpected tears pooled in her eyes, the moisture hot and unwelcome. She brushed them away from her cheeks with the back of her hand. "It seems everything in this house is fertile except me," she murmured aloud, and headed blindly toward the living room to await her husband's return.

Sitting on the kitchen counter, her knees crossed, her foot swaying like a too-fast pendulum, Mercy heaved a gigantic sigh. Getting those flowers to appear hadn't been an easy trick. She would have preferred African violets any day of the week over cacti!

Everything she'd done for Leah had backfired. The flowers were supposed to be a sign of hope. A way of telling her that all was not lost and that there was someone out there who'd heard her prayer and was working hard to see that it was answered. Well, it was back to the drawing board.

Perhaps what Shirley had suggested about Leah experiencing joy before she could find her peace was what it would take. First Mercy had to figure out a way to manage that, but if she could coax cacti into bloom, then anything was possible. Right?

*   *   *

"Shirley." Goodness shot across the darkened family room of Jody and Timmy Potter's house in a vapor of speed and excitement. "Give me five," she cried, holding up her right hand for the other angel to slap. What a difference a few earth hours could make. For the first time since Goodness had accepted this assignment she was making progress. Real progress. Monica and Michael had gone to lunch together. It wasn't much but it was a start in the right direction.

"Oh, do be quiet," Shirley whispered heatedly. "You know better than to be exuberant when there're children around. Timmy might very well hear you."

"But I've got great news. Monica and Michael had lunch together and I arranged the whole thing without them suspecting. I tell you it was a work of art the way I got Michael to show up at the church office."

"Please keep your voice down," Shirley pleaded a second time, placing her finger against her lips.

"All right. All right, I'll do my best, but this news is too good to keep to myself."

Shirley whirled around so unexpectedly that Goodness was caught by surprise. A sleepy Timmy Potter wandered into the room, rubbing his eyes. He was wearing flannel pajamas with silly-looking armed turtles.

Shirley moved behind him.

"Mom," Timmy called.

A moment later Jody Potter appeared in a long flannel nightgown that had seen better years. Shirley had her work cut out for her if she planned to find this woman a husband any time soon. Her charge looked downright frumpy.

"Timmy, what are you doing up?"

"I thought I heard something."

Jody turned on the light and searched the room. The minute her back was turned, Shirley and Goodness righted the floral arrangement and set the magazines in order. Both headed straight for the ceiling, hovering there.

Jody searched the room, finding nothing out of the ordinary. "There's no one here."

"I thought I heard something," Timmy said with a yawn. "But I guess not."

"I guess not, too," Jody said, placing her arm around her young son's shoulders and steering him back to his bedroom. "Unless, of course, it was God's own angels looking down and smiling on us."

"You think it might have been?" Timmy asked excitedly, looking up. He paused and blinked, rubbed his eyes again, then looked back.

"Who knows?" Jody said and turned out the light.

Monica's attitude toward Chet altered drastically over the next couple of days. He was still a scoundrel and a no-good rogue, but darned if she didn't miss him. There was no explaining it, no possible way of reasoning it out in her mind.

She tried to fill the emptiness that surrounded her with a flurry of activity. The night before, she'd dragged out the Christmas decorations and gone about setting them around the house and office. Her father, impressed by her initiative, assumed this burst of energy was somehow connected with her long lunch with Michael. Monica didn't correct him.

Monica knew she wouldn't see Chet again and wondered if he missed her. She wondered how he looked upon their time together or if he'd given her as much as a fleeting thought in the days since they'd last been together.

She wore her hair down that morning and when she walked into the kitchen her father lowered the morning paper and smiled gently at her.

"Monica," he said softly, "how nice you look."

"Thank you."

"Will you be seeing Michael again this afternoon."

"I . . . I don't know." How keen her father was on the young musician. He'd pegged Michael early on as the perfect husband for her. He was right. Her father generally was. How she wished she felt the same way about the earnest choir director. There was no question of what a fine man Michael was. Several of the eligible women at church would have gladly welcomed his notice. For now those attentions were sadly wasted on her.

"It seems to me I said something to Michael about coming over for dinner one night soon. You don't mind, do you?"

"Of course not, Michael is welcome anytime." So this was to be the way of it. Her father would chart her romance for her, making excuses for the two of them to be together again.

"I'm sure he'll approve of the way you've done your hair," he added, looking pleased.

She smiled weakly. "I'll see you in a few minutes," she said, anxious to escape their conversation.

"You're leaving for the office so soon?"

"I . . . have several things I need to do first thing this morning."

"I won't be in until later. I'm visiting Mrs. McWilliams," he reminded her, downing the last of his milk and setting the glass in the sink.

The woman was an old and faithful church member who'd recently broken her hip. Lloyd visited her at least twice a week.

"I'll see you later, then," Monica said, eager to make her escape. She walked across the yard to the old church building and let herself in by the side door that opened onto sanctuary area. She'd been raised in this building, lived the majority of her life in the same house with the same people.

Instead of heading directly to the office, which was situated in the room at the rear of the church off the foyer, Monica paused and looked toward the altar. An unspoken prayer rose in her throat and she found herself moving toward the altar rail.

Monica kelt there and slowly bowed her head. "Guide his life, Father," she whispered. The tears that filled her eyes came as a surprise and the remainder of the words were choked off in her throat. She wasn't sure how to pray for Chet. But God knew and she'd leave the man and the matter in his capable hands.

Several moments passed before she stood.

Her morning slipped past almost unnoticed. Typing was something of a chore with her hair continually falling in her face. It irritated her so much that she found two bobby pins in a desk drawer and clipped both sides behind her ears.

She was busy working on the bulletin for Sunday morning worship service when the door opened. Monica looked up from the typewriter and her pulse quickened. Quickened was a mild way of explaining what happened to her. Her heart was banging against her ribs with such force she wasn't able to do anything more than breathe.

"I see you took my advice about your hairstyle," Chet said, and sauntered into the office as if he were right at home.

"What are you doing here?" She glanced anxiously toward her father's office, forgetting he wasn't there.

"Don't worry, he's off visiting Mrs. McWilliams."

"How . . . how do you know that?"

Chet laughed lightly and rearranged the figurines that made up the nativity scene she'd set in a froth of angel hair, switching the camels and the mules. "I know just about everything there is to know about you."

Playing a game of cat and mouse with him was beyond her. Chet was much too clever for her. "Why are you here?"

"To see you. Why else? I'm not exactly the type of guy who frequents churches."

She was on her feet without knowing how she got there. Clenching her hands together in front of her, she drew in a steadying breath. "Why do you want to see me?"

"I figured I owed you an apology."

His willingness to admit it surprised her. "Then I accept your regrets," she informed him, sitting back down. "You don't need to trouble yourself further."

"I came for another reason," he said, easing himself onto the corner of her desk as if he had every right to do so.

"What's that?" Monica placed her hands on the keyboard, ready to resume her task although heaven knew she couldn't have typed had her life depended on it.

"You planning on seeing that milquetoast choir director again?"

"I . . . I don't believe that's any concern of yours."

"Perhaps not, but if you do, you're cheating him and you're hurting yourself."

Monica had taken about as much of his advice as she could tolerate. "What gives you the right to say those kinds of things to me?" she demanded.

"I know you, sweetheart."

She hated it when he called her that and he knew it. He was purposely trying to irritate her.

"You've got fire in your blood, not milk. You've sampled desire. Now that you know what it is to be weak with wanting a man, you won't be able to accept second best. Not anymore—it's too late for that."

"You have your nerve."

"You're right," he agreed readily enough, "I do." He stood and walked around to her side of the desk.

Monica watched him, not knowing what to expect. Every nerve was at full attention. A siren was blaring in her head, blocking out all sensible thought.

When he reached for her, she didn't offer the least bit of resistance. As it never failed to do, his touch rippled through her, snapping her senses to life. He roughly lowered his mouth to hers where he planted desperate, hungry kisses.

She resisted him at first, attempting to jerk her mouth from his, but he wouldn't allow it, trapping her face and plundering her mouth with his tongue. Her stand against him was pitifully weak, and soon she was as much a participant in the exchange as he was.

Slowly he eased himself away from her. "Dear God," he whispered, and Monica was convinced he didn't mean this as a prayer.

Something attracted his attention and he jerked his head around. "Someone's coming," he whispered.

Monica was too startled to do anything.

"Whoever it is, get rid of them," he instructed, slipping behind the door that led to her father's office.

Get rid of them, Monica thought in panic. She wasn't accustomed to playing these ridiculous cops-and-robbers games. She hadn't a clue of what to say or do.

The door opened just then and Michael strolled inside. He smiled at her warmly. "I hope I'm not catching you at a bad time."

"Bad time," she repeated with a phony laugh. "Of course not. Come on in, Michael."

Chapter

★ ✬ ★

11

"*You're sure you don't mind?*" Pam asked, leading Scotty by the hand into Leah's house. "After all the trouble I've gone through for this silly Christmas party of Doug's, who'd believe my baby-sitter would come down with the flu. At the last minute, no less. It was the oddest thing. One minute she was fine and the next she was sick."

"You should have brought over Diane and Jason too," Leah said.

Pam laughed outright at that. "Even my mother won't take all three at once." Flustered and in a rush, she set everything down on the sofa and started unpacking the items she'd brought along for her middle son. Sorting through the brown paper sack, Pam removed Scotty's pajamas, an extra set of clothes for the morning, his stuffed dinosaur, and a tattered yellow blanket. "He's mostly given up his blanky, but he might need a bit of security to sleep in an unfamiliar bed."

"I'll make sure he has it with him."

"I brought along some extra training pants," Pam said, setting out a stack of them.

"I don't wet," Scotty said, his fists braced against his small hips. "I'm a big boy."

"I forgot his potty seat," Pam cried. "Oh, well, you'll just have to hold him over the toilet."

"Don't worry, Scotty and I'll figure everything out as we go. Isn't that right, bud?"

"Right." She held out her hand for him to slap, which he did with enthusiasm, his arm making a high arch into the air.

Pam straightened and held back her hair with both hands. "I hope to heaven that's everything. Here's the number where Doug and I'll be," she said, pulling a slip of paper from her coat pocket. Getting down on her knees, she wrapped her arms around her three-year-old. "Promise me you'll be an extra good boy for Auntie Leah?"

Scotty clung to her neck and planted a wet kiss on her cheek.

"We're going to have a great time, aren't we, Scotty?" Leah urged, knowing how bad Pam felt to be leaving him in an unfamiliar setting.

Scotty nodded, but looked uncertain when his mother left. Pam was halfway out the front door when she turned back. "He probably needs to go now."

"Pam," Leah said, ushering her friend out of the house, "scoot, otherwise you'll miss your hair appointment."

"I'm hurrying—"

"Stop looking so worried. Everything's going to be just fine."

Scotty was standing at the window, his mouth pressed to the cold glass as he watched his mother pull out of the driveway. He looked at Leah and his bottom lip started to tremble.

"Scotty, how about helping me with lunch?" she asked, holding out her hand. "You can decide what to fix for Uncle Andrew, all right?"

The boy shook his head, smearing his lip prints from one pane to the next.

"Are you hungry?"

Once more Scotty shook his head. "I want my mommy."

"She's going out to dinner with your daddy and his friends from work."

"I want to go too."

"This dinner is only for mommies and daddies."

Apparently this wasn't what Scotty wanted to hear because the tears started in earnest. He was breaking her heart, standing with his back to the window, rubbing his eyes and sobbing softly. She couldn't bear to see her godson weeping so pitifully, so she lifted him into her arms to comfort him. Scotty buried his face in her shoulder, snuffling into her expensive cashmere sweater. Leah smiled to herself and shook her head. This was what it meant to be a mother, to be loved and needed. She'd treasure every moment of the time with this precious little boy.

It took Leah only a few moments to get Scotty interested in helping her assemble sandwiches. Andrew arrived about the time the boy was licking the jelly off the knife and sticking it back inside the jar.

"So we have company," he said, removing his jacket and hanging it on the peg just inside the door.

Scotty looked at her husband as an unknown entity, his big dark eyes following Andrew's movements around the kitchen as Leah explained Pam's sorry predicament.

"Peanut butter and jelly?" Andrew grumbled under his breath, eyeing their lunch.

"That was what Scotty wanted us to have."

"You sure he didn't suggest pastrami on rye?" Andrew mumbled out of the corner of his mouth.

"Scotty made the peanut butter and jelly all by himself," Leah said, urging her husband to compliment the boy on his efforts. There was more peanut butter on the countertop than the bread, but Scotty had done it himself and beamed with pride.

"So I noticed." Andrew skeptically lifted one corner of the bread. The peanut butter was spread so thin the white bread showed through. He looked at Leah and they both burst into laughter. It wasn't especially funny, but they seemed to find it so.

Scotty studied them as if he didn't know what to make of the two. Leah kissed his chubby cheek and set the sandwich and a small glass of milk down on the table. Moving out the chair, Scotty climbed onto the seat. He knelt on the cushion and leaned against the glass tabletop, his small hands circling the glass.

"Apparently lunch is served," Andrew said, bowing and gallantly gesturing for Leah to take her place at the table. He held out the chair for her, then seated himself.

After sampling the sandwich, Andrew eyed Leah. "Is Scotty choosing the dinner menu as well?"

"Hot dogs and macaroni and cheese," Scotty said with his mouth full of food.

Andrew looked at Leah and there was something so crestfallen in his eyes that she couldn't help it, she burst out laughing. Andrew didn't know what she found so funny, but soon he was laughing too. Scotty, who hadn't a clue of what was going on, joined in, milk dribbling out of the corner of his mouth.

Mercy looked down upon the scene from where she was lounging on top of the double-wide refrigerator. Her scheme had worked beautifully, although she did feel mildly guilty about inflicting Pam's babysitter with the virus.

Scotty's visit with Leah and Andrew was going much better than she'd anticipated. So well that it was all Mercy could do not to stand up and cheer. The sound of Leah and Andrew's laughter brightened the room like floodlights on an empty stage.

The kitchen radiated with the warmth of their happiness. The dim, dark pall of melancholy faded as the joy was slowly released, circling the room with tails of light. The gloom, discouragement, and despair that marked this house lifted like dissipating fog over the Golden Gate Bridge revealing the sound structure of this marriage, and the deep, profound love Leah and Andrew shared.

This was what Mercy had waited for so impatiently.

Joy.

Her gaze wandered closely over Leah and the emotion she read in the young woman's face deeply stirred her soul. At last they were making progress. The light was on, the mist had lifted.

It was a beginning.

The lunch was over and Leah lifted Scotty from the chair, washed his hands and face, and carried him into the guest bedroom. Knowing his penchant for amusing himself instead of napping, she sat in the rocking chair and held him in her lap. Scotty chose a book and she read to him until he dozed off.

For a long time after Scotty was asleep, Leah continued to hold him, enjoying these rare moments of peace and the ecstasy of having a child in her arms.

Kissing the top of his curly head, she was amazed at all Pam managed to do with a houseful of preschoolers. Scotty had only been with her a couple of hours and already she was emotionally and physically exhausted.

Andrew arrived just then, leaning indolently against the door frame, his face wide with a saucy grin. "It looks like you could use a nap yourself."

"No one ever told me toddlers could be so exhausting," Leah admitted.

"Here," Andrew whispered, gently lifting Scotty from her arms. "Let's put him to bed."

Moving around her husband, Leah turned back the sheets and Andrew carefully laid the sleeping child onto the mattress. Covering him with the quilt, Leah bent down and kissed her godson's forehead.

Neither Andrew nor Leah were in any hurry to leave the room. Standing next to her husband, she nestled in the warm security of Andrew's arms, her head resting against the solid wall of his chest.

"He's really something, isn't he?" Andrew said softly, so as not to disturb Scotty's sleep.

"He's a ball of energy."

Andrew kissed the side of her neck. "Come on, I think we could do with a nap ourselves."

From the way he made the suggestion, Leah knew resting was the last thing on her husband's mind. She caught his eye, and whispered regretfully, "Andrew, we can't."

"Why not?"

"Scotty might wake and—"

"Do you think Doug and Pam worry about that? Besides, I can be real quiet, and with some effort so can you," he whispered, steering her toward their bedroom.

Sometime later, Leah woke to the sounds of someone hopping up and down at the foot of her bed. She rolled onto her back to find Scotty doing a marvelous impression of a kangaroo.

"Hi, Scotty."

He was holding on to his front with both hands, his eyes wide and appealing.

"Scotty?" she asked, sitting up, clenching the sheets to her breasts. "Do you need to go potty?"

"That would be my guess," Andrew said, yawning. "Come on, fellow, I'll show you the way." Lifting the boy into his arms, Andrew carried him to the bathroom.

Leah grabbed her sweater and finished dressing. "How's everything going in there?" she called out.

"Not good. He seems to need something."

"What?"

Scotty apparently didn't trust Andrew to properly relay the message. "I need my blanky . . . I need my blanky . . . I need my blanky."

Leah retrieved the yellow monstrosity in record time and rushed back into the bathroom where Andrew was holding Scotty over the toilet seat. The boy grabbed the blanket, and held it against his face. As soon as the blanket was in position, he released a long, grateful sigh and relaxed.

When Scotty finished, Andrew sagged onto the side of the bathtub. "What was that all about?"

"Pam said something about forgetting his toilet seat. He must have been terrified of being perched up there."

Andrew looked at Leah and she looked at him and soon the two of them dissolved into giggles.

"I'm a big boy," Scotty insisted, looking downright proud of himself, his laughter mingling with theirs.

Monica was convinced Michael would guess that Chet was hiding behind the door in the other room. Why Chet felt he needed to disappear, she could only speculate.

The man was a fool to show up at the church this way. She'd wanted to shout at him, and throw the entire contents of her filing cabinet in his face. Heaven knew he deserved that and far worse. Why, she should have slapped him silly.

She would have, too, if she hadn't been so pleased to see him.

"Your hair looks especially nice today," Michael said with glowing approval.

"Thank you." Knowing Chet, it was probably all he could do to keep from leaping out from behind the door and commenting that he'd been the one to suggest the change.

"I'm playing the piano for the Methodists' church cantata this evening," Michael was saying. "Their regular pianist came down with the flu. I thought I'd stop by and see if you'd like to come along."

"Tonight?" Monica asked, stalling for time. In truth she was looking for an excuse, anything to get out of this date, but nothing readily presented itself.

"I mentioned this evening to your father and he said you didn't have anything planned," Michael pressed.

"No, I don't believe I do." So her father had put him up to this. She should have realized that sooner.

Michael hesitated, glancing at her as if he were waiting for her to say something more. Uncertain, Monica steadily met his look.

"Did Lloyd mention anything about dinner?"

"Dinner?" She knew she was beginning to sound like a parrot. "Why, yes. Dad did say something this morning about having you over for dinner some evening. We'd be more than happy to have you join us, if you'd like."

"Tonight?"

"Tonight . . . why, sure . . . tonight would be perfect, wouldn't it, since I'll be there for the Methodists' cantata."

"What time?"

"Six," she said automatically, willing to agree to anything that would convince him to leave faster. Knowing Chet was listening in on the conversation made matters ten times worse.

"Great," Michael said, looking well pleased with himself, "I'll see you around six, then. Would you like me to bring anything?"

"No. Everything's under control. Good-bye, Michael," she said, sitting back down at the typewriter, hoping he'd take the hint and kindly leave while her sanity was intact. She placed her hands on the keyboard until she noticed how badly she was trembling and immediately lowered them to her lap.

"I'll look forward to this evening," he said, reluctantly moving toward the door. He was looking for an excuse to stay, but she refused to give him one.

Despite her obvious signs of distress, she rolled a fresh sheet of paper into the typewriter.

"Your father claims you're a fabulous cook."

"I do a fair job," she muttered. This was getting worse every minute and she didn't know how much more she could bear.

"Good-bye for now."

"Good-bye, Michael," she said, closing her eyes in relief.

Michael left then and the door closed with a soft clicking sound. The instant he was gone, Monica leaped out of her chair, raced around her desk and into her father's study. By the time she arrived she was both breathless and furious.

"Why'd you hide?" she demanded. "Of all the crazy things you've said and done in the last few weeks, this takes the cake."

"It would have required awkward explanations," was all he'd say.

"Well, he's gone now."

"So I see." A frown darkened Chet's face and he glared at her. "So you're going to continue seeing him despite what I said."

"What choice did I have?" she cried, throwing her arms into the air. "I said what I had to get him to leave. Besides, what business is it of yours who I do or do not date?" How could he say such things to her when he was the one who'd put her in this predicament!

It took him a long time to answer. "You're right, it's none of my damn business."

Monica was pleased that Chet did care, but she didn't want him to know it.

"Michael's not so bad," he said after a moment, "it's plain as day that he's crazy about you."

The man was full of surprises. First he demanded that she stay away from Michael and now he was urging her to see the other man.

Chet's eyes were clouded, as if he carried the weight of the world on his shoulders. "I should never have come."

He strode past her and in her heart Monica knew if he walked out the door she'd never see him again. She had to do something.

He was all the way across the room, his hand on the doorknob, before she found the courage to speak. "Don't go." She advanced a single step toward him and stopped.

Chet turned around slowly, as if he wasn't sure he'd heard her correctly. Gradually a grin danced its way across his lips. "You don't want me to leave?"

Her tongue was trapped against the roof of her mouth and she shook her head, unable to say the words a second time. It had demanded every ounce of courage she possessed the first time.

His gaze narrowed into thin, disbelieving slits. "Why not?"

She shrugged.

"Come on, sweetheart, you can do better than that."

"Don't call me that." She backed away from him, as far as she could go, until her buttocks were pressed against the edge of her desk.

"What would you like me to call you?"

It was a mistake to have asked him to stay, a mistake to let him know how much of the time he dominated her thoughts. He made her weak where she'd once been strong, and she'd found no compensation for what she'd lost.

"I think you should go," she whispered.

He cocked his thick brows at that. "You don't seem to know what you want, do you? You want me to stay, yet you invite that mild-mannered choirboy for dinner."

"My father invited him."

"Ah, your father," Chet said thoughtfully. "Michael's the type of man he wants you to marry, isn't he? We both know what your daddy would think of the likes of me."

"That's not true. My father isn't like that."

"Sure," he scoffed. "He'd welcome me with open arms. Don't kid yourself, Monica, we both know better. Listen, sweetheart, forget I was ever here, all right?"

"No. No, I won't forget," she whispered heatedly. "I can't forget."

She read the questions etched in his eyes and realized they were a reflection of her own. She didn't have any of the answers and apparently neither did he.

Walking toward him was the boldest thing she'd ever done in her life. Flattening her palms against the hard expanse of his chest, she slowly, reluctantly raised her eyes to his.

He didn't give her a chance to speak. His mouth came down on hers in a kiss that was as hot as it was wild. With a low, guttural sound, he sent his tongue searching deep inside her mouth. Instinct dictated her actions as she raised her arms and looped them around his neck, giving herself completely to the mastery of his kiss.

His arms folded around her waist, greedily holding her against him as his mouth plundered hers. Her feet dangled several inches off the ground.

The kiss ended only when they were both desperate to breathe.

Monica was left stunned, her heart in a panic. It had always been like this between them, this craziness. Her head felt as if it were in its own orbit, spinning madly out of control. Emotionally she was a wreck, close to tears and trembling.

Chet's lips returned to hers in a series of long, slow kisses and her world righted itself. Everything slipped neatly back into place. Only when she lifted her head from his did outside influences overtake her.

For the love of heaven, they were in a church building, and yet she couldn't have left his arms in that moment for all the gold in the world.

"I've got to get out of here," Chet whispered against her neck. He drew in a deep breath, as if that would give him the necessary fortitude to ease her out of his arms.

"Not yet," she pleaded.

The sound of voices in the yard outside was all the incentive they needed. They broke apart, as if they'd been burned.

"That's my father," Monica said, her gaze flying to Chet's.

Chet jerked his head both ways. "I'll go out the window."

"That's crazy."

By the time she reached him in her father's office, he'd hoisted the window open and had one leg draped over the sill. "Meet me tonight," he said.

"When?" she pleaded, glancing over her shoulder. "Where?"

"Never mind."

"No," she whispered frantically. "Tell me when and where."

He smiled, and the look in his eyes was enough to cause spirals of heat to coil in her belly. He reached for her, kissed her once hard and fast and whispered, "I'll let you know." With that he vanished.

The door opened and her father casually strolled inside, humming softly to himself. He looked surprised to find her standing there.

"Monica."

"Yes, Dad?" she said, still trapped in a sensual daze.

"You might want to close the window. It's downright chilly in here."

"Oh, sorry," she said, lowering it as if it were nothing out of the ordinary to have it open in the middle of December.

"I'll open the door for you," Timmy cried, running toward the front porch, leaving Glen to untie the Christmas tree from the top of his car.

"Timmy has his own key," Jody explained, catching the rope that Glen tossed down to her as he untied the tree.

Glen looked toward the front of the house. "He enjoyed himself this afternoon, didn't he?"

Jody smiled and nodded. "I swear he was like a jackrabbit, leaping from one tree to the next, certain each time he'd found the perfect Christmas tree. It's a miracle we were able to convince him to choose just one."

"What about you, Jody?" Glen asked thoughtfully. "Did you have a good time too?"

It shouldn't be so difficult to admit to the truth, but it was.

"I had a very nice time," she said, keeping her eyes averted.

His laugh came unexpectedly. "Good girl," he praised. "I knew you could do it."

Jody laughed then too, because it was rather silly of her to hold out against the obvious.

Timmy returned breathless and excited. "The door's open," he announced, eager to help in any way he could.

Her son was a marvel, Jody mused. Rarely had she seen him more animated. He'd laughed and chatted incessantly, until she was convinced he was going to drive Glen nuts. For a man who wasn't accustomed to being around children, the attorney had been marvelous.

"Mom got the tree stand and all the decorations out last night," Timmy told Glen, for about the fifth time. Actually Jody had lost count of the number of times Timmy had felt it was necessary to clue Glen in to this information.

Together, the three of them carried the Christmas tree around to the backyard.

"We're going to need to cut off a couple of inches from the bottom," Glen said, once they'd got the tree to the patio and recovered. The trunk was too wide for the stand. "Think you might be able to help me saw it off?" he asked Timmy.

It was like asking the boy if he liked popcorn. Timmy beamed with pride as he solemnly nodded his head. "Sure, I can do it."

"I know you can," Glen said, affectionately patting his shoulder.

"While you're busy with that, I'll put on some hot chocolate," Jody said, pushing open the sliding glass door. The tears that stung her eyes were unexpected. She wasn't entirely sure what prompted them, nor was she sure she wanted to know.

The changes in Timmy had been revealing. Yes, it was Christmastime and yes, he was excited, but it made her realize how rare those times were. Generally Timmy involved himself in his video games and didn't show much enthusiasm for anything else—with the one exception being baseball, which he dearly loved.

Between sniffles, she brought the milk out of the refrigerator and set a pan on the stove, furious with herself for the weakness of tears.

Glen appeared unexpectedly and she twisted her head away, praying he wouldn't notice. "That's quite a boy you've got there," Glen said. "I swear he's another Paul Bunyan."

"He's certainly had the time of his life." She was grateful that the hot chocolate gave her an excuse to keep her back to him.

Glen moved behind her and gently placed his hands on her shoulders. Jody froze, unaccustomed to a man's touch.

He bent forward and kissed the side of her neck.

"Where's Timmy?" she asked, her voice trembling.

"Putting the saw away." Glen turned her so that they faced each other. He frowned when he saw her tear-bright eyes and slid his thumb across the high arch of her cheek. "Bad thoughts?" he asked.

She shook her head.

"Let me help." Then, before she could protest, he lowered his mouth to hers. It was hardly enough pressure to call it a real kiss. Gradually he increased the intensity, deepening the contact. Jody felt like a rag doll, limp and unresponsive. The kiss was sweet and undemanding, but Glen was the first man to touch her since Jeff. Doubts blew against her with hurricane force winds until she pressed her hands against his chest and broke the contact. Later she'd analyze her feelings toward Glen, but for now it was too new.

Glen sighed softly. "It would be very easy to fall in love with you." He continued to hold her until he heard Timmy's approach.

Once her son was back, Glen carried the tree into the house, and with a good deal of ceremony, set it in the living room. When it was in place in front of the large picture window, they sat back and sipped hot chocolate.

Unwilling to rest, Timmy sorted through the boxes of decorations. It seemed with every one, he found something he needed to show Glen. Each discovery involved a lengthy explanation.

Glen's patience surprised her, and she told him so.

"He's a great kid," Glen said. "Who wouldn't like him?"

"Can we decorate the tree now?" Timmy asked, standing in the middle of three strings of lights. Wires were wrapped around his feet and another strand was draped over his shoulder as he grinned broadly in their direction. "You aren't going to make me wait until Christmas morning to see my presents are you? I'm much too old to pretend I believe in Santa Claus."

"It's tradition," Jody said, as means of an argument.

"Oh, phooey. I still have to pretend I believe in that silly kid stuff for my grandma, but it's downright embarrassing. I just hope none of my friends finds out about it."

"Sometimes there are things a man has to do," Glen said, and Jody marveled that he kept a straight face.

"Can we decorate the tree now?"

"Sure," Glen agreed, setting aside his empty mug.

"It'll be our best tree yet, won't it, Mom?"

Jody was saved from answering by the phone. She left the pair to untangle the strings of lights and took the call in the kitchen.

"Hello."

"Jody, dear, it's so good to hear your voice."

"Hello, Gloria." It had been a year or longer since she'd last spoken to her former mother-in-law. "Did you get my letter?" Jody asked, glancing guiltily into the living room. There wasn't any reason for her to feel the least bit contrite for dating Glen or for kissing him, but she did, as if she'd been unfaithful to Jeff's memory.

"I have some very important news," Gloria said, ignoring the question.

"Who is it?" Timmy wanted to know.

"Just a minute, Gloria," Jody said, and placed her hand over the mouthpiece. "It's your Grandma Potter," she explained. "I'll let you talk to her when I'm finished. I'll call you in just a minute." When Timmy was gone, she replaced the receiver at her ear. "I'm sorry to interrupt you. You were telling me you had something important to tell me?"

"My dear, it's the most wonderful news. Brace yourself because what I'm about to tell you will come as a shock. Jeff's alive."

Chapter

★ ✬ ★

12

Monica paced her bedroom, wondering what, if anything, she should do now that she was home. Her evening with Michael had been miserable. Michael couldn't be blamed for that; he'd been sweet and considerate, wanting to please her.

When he'd arrived for dinner, he'd presented her with a potted pink poinsettia, which riddled her with guilt. Throughout the meal he'd praised her efforts while her father looked on approvingly. Monica was a fair cook, but the pot roast and mashed potatoes and gravy were nothing to brag about.

The cantata, while inspirational, had seemed to drag. Every note was torture and Monica knew why.

She was looking for Chet, half expecting him to slip into the pew next to her at the Methodist church. It was just like something he'd do. Monica had sat through the entire program with her stomach in knots wondering when and where Chet would show up.

After she returned home, she wondered if he'd come for her, as he'd said he would, but as the night ripened, she was further burdened with uncertainty.

Fortunately, her father had gone to bed early. She hadn't been fooled. Lloyd Fischer was hoping she'd invite Michael in for a cup of coffee and had afforded them the necessary privacy to talk. Monica, however, had made her excuses, thanked Michael for a lovely evening, and then quickly slipped inside the house.

Waiting for Chet was intolerable. The not knowing. Twice now she'd ventured through the house, turning lights on and off as she tiptoed from one room to the next, fearing she'd wake her father.

At ten, she sat on the end of her bed, depressed and miserable. She picked at her fingernails, which she kept square and neatly trimmed.

Although she'd often admired women with beautifully manicured nails, she personally thought of them as vain. The Bible has a good deal to say about vanity and a good many other things, including . . .

Her thoughts were interrupted by a soft knocking sound against her bedroom window. Monica flew off the bed and was breathless by the time she boosted open her window and stuck out her head.

"Chet?" she whispered as loud as she dared, leaning out. "Is that you?" She was eternally grateful that her father's room was at the front of the house, opposite her own.

"Are you expecting anyone else?"

She heard Chet, but couldn't see him. "Where are you?" she demanded, squinting into the inky black night. Shadows flickered here and there in what little light the moon offered. Still she couldn't locate him, and yet he sounded incredibly close.

He appeared then, like an apparition, and stood directly in front of her. For a moment they did nothing but stare at each other. Monica's heart was positioned somewhere between her chest and her throat and felt like a concrete ball.

Chet's look was unreadable. This private investigator was superbly talented at hiding his feelings.

Her own were as plain as a first-grade primer, she was sure of it. She was so pleased to see him it would have been impossible to disguise even a small part of her feelings.

His eyes darkened with intensity before he framed her face with his hands and gently pressed his mouth to hers. Monica sighed and wrapped her arms around his neck. The upper part of her body was thrust out the window so that her waist was pressed against the sill.

"I'm so pleased you came," she whispered again and again between frantic kisses. Her fingers were in his hair and her mouth was working against his, her need urgent.

The power Chet held over her was frightening. Each time they were together a little more of her restraint was stripped away. A little more of her control.

By the time they broke apart, Monica was gasping and trembling. She was aware of every part of her body his hands had touched. Her face, her shoulders, her neck. She felt a deep, physical hunger that shook her to the core.

"How was your date?" he asked.

She shook her head, not wanting to discuss Michael.

"Did you enjoy yourself?" he demanded, refusing to allow her to brush off the question. His hands held her face prisoner, and his eyes burned into hers.

"I was miserable."

His shoulders relaxed and he rewarded her with a shockingly thorough kiss. Before she had time to recover, he hoisted himself inside her bedroom.

Monica backed away from the window, and sank onto the edge of her mattress, her knees too weak to support her.

Chet glanced about the starkly furnished room and frowned. "Let's get out of here."

"Where would we go?"

"My place."

"I don't think that's such a good idea." Where she gathered the strength to refuse him she never knew. She folded her hands in her lap and concentrated on drawing in deep, even breaths. If ever she needed a clear head it was now.

Chet was pacing the room, restless and agitated. "We can't stay here."

"Why not?"

"Monica, be reasonable. Your father's—"

"On the other side of the house. He's a sound sleeper, he won't hear anything, and if he does, well, I'm twenty-five years old and if I care to invite a man into our house, then that's my business."

Chet's smile lacked amusement. "In case you haven't noticed, I'm in your bedroom, and inviting me to stay is a little like inviting the fox into the henhouse."

"Is your place any safer?"

He laughed softly at that. "No, but it'll ease my conscience. In the time it takes us to get there I just might find the strength to keep my hands off you. But I doubt it. You've got me so tied up in knots, its a wonder I'm able to do my job."

Monica wasn't in any better condition herself. Brushing the hair from her face, she forced herself to think rationally. That, she soon realized, was a mistake. "As far as I can see we have absolutely nothing in common," she mumbled under her breath, discouraged and depressed.

"Except we're so damn hot for each other we're both about to break out in a heat rash."

"A relationship built on physical attraction is doomed from the beginning."

Chet nodded. "I couldn't agree with you more."

"So," she said, straightening her spine, searching for the necessary resolve to do the right thing. "Where do we go from here?"

"The logical choice is to bed. It'd help matters tremendously, don't you think? It's what any other couple would do in like circumstances. We just might be able to put this damn foolishness behind us and get on with our lives."

His words felt like a cold slap in the face. "That's the most ridiculous thing you've ever said to me," Monica managed despite her outrage. "I'm not some bimbo you can use to satisfy your carnal cravings and then toss aside. Dear heaven." She moaned, covering her face with both hands. "I can't believe we're having this conversation."

"All right, all right," Chet whispered, kneeling down in front of her. He pried her hands away from her face, clasped them in his own, and kissed her knuckles. "You're right, it was a stupid thing to suggest. I shouldn't have spoken to you like that."

Leaning forward she rewarded his honesty with a lengthy kiss, one that gained in intensity and momentum until they were both sprawled across the top of her mattress, their arms and legs entwined.

"You shouldn't have done that," he whispered, his voice husky and low. He was struggling for control and for that matter so was she, but it felt so wonderfully good to be in his arms. Better than anything she'd experienced in all her twenty-five years.

"I better leave," he whispered.

"Not yet." She ran her tongue along the underside of his jaw, loving the taste of him; the scent of rum-and-spice aftershave enveloped her. She burrowed more completely into his embrace. For a moment she thought he intended to push her away, but instead he released a long, slow sigh and held her tightly against him.

"Monica . . ."

"Hmmm?" She felt the powerful strength of his erection and heaven help her, gloried in it. By slightly lifting her leg she was able to move ever so gently against the part of him that was uniquely male.

"Stop," he muttered between clenched teeth, "otherwise I won't be held responsible for what happens."

Monica smiled to herself, knowing he'd never do anything to hurt her. Where the assurance came from she couldn't be sure, but she felt it as strongly as she did his arms around her.

"I knew it would be a mistake to come," he mumbled, seemingly to himself.

Monica continued to move her mouth over his throat. Her tongue made small circular movements against his jaw and over his ear.

"You're playing with fire," he said, his voice stiff with resolve.

"I know," she assured him.

"A man can only take so much of this." The words were barely audible.

"I know that too."

His hands were busy with the fastenings of her blouse, which he peeled open with ease. Monica thought to stop him before he slipped it from her arms, but he was kissing her and the feelings were too incredible to interrupt. Her bra followed next and when the cold air hit her naked breasts, she squeezed her eyes closed, suddenly afraid.

Chet altered their positions so that she was straddled atop him.

"Open your eyes," Chet instructed after a moment.

Monica wildly shook her head. "I can't."

"You're very beautiful." The awe in his voice felt like a warm caress. The size of her breasts had been a constant source of embarrassment to Monica from the time she'd entered puberty. They were large and full. For most of her life she'd done what she could to mask them with the clothes she chose to wear.

She started when he touched her, lifting the fullness of her breasts in his palms, as though weighing them on a delicate scale. Monica bit into her lower lip and turned her head away.

The pad of his thumbs stroked her nipples, which immediately hardened and started to pulse as if they had taken on a life of their own. The ache intensified with each caress until she threw back her head and swallowed a moan.

His mouth closed over her nipple and he sucked once, hard and strong. Monica buckled at the bolt of sizzling-hot sensation. He calmed her with gentle words, caressing the length of her arms as he spoke.

Monica didn't know what caused her to relax, or when she opened her eyes, but suddenly everything went very still. Their gazes met and Chet raised his hand and brushed a stray tendril from her face. His hand lingered there and his eyes clouded with what she suspected was regret.

"I didn't mean for things to go so far," he whispered. He rolled away from her and changed their positions so that they were lying on their sides, facing each other.

Monica's head was cradled in his upper arm, their mouths separated by scant inches. Their breath merged and mingled. Her thigh met his. He was warm and hard and she was soft and happier than she could remember being in a good long while. Monica would have been utterly content to stay exactly like this for the next hundred years.

Being here with Chet like this forced her to acknowledge how incredibly lonely she'd been in the last few years. Her mother had died and her friends, the only two she considered good friends, had both married and moved away. Funny she hadn't realized how empty and pointless her life had become. Nor had she realized what poor company she was to herself and others.

"What are you thinking?" he asked.

Their eyes met and she found him openly studying her. She quickly averted her gaze. "I didn't realize how downright good a man could feel."

He laughed softly and kissed the tip of her nose. "That's very honest of you."

"I couldn't very well deny it."

"You could, and have," he said. His fingertips grazed her temple, softly caressing her face. "I'll be honest too. You feel damn good in my arms. Tonight," he whispered, "while you were with Michael, I was like a caged animal."

"He doesn't mean anything to me," she rushed to explain.

He closed his eyes and nodded. "I know, but it didn't make any difference. There was this band around my chest that tightened every time I thought about the two of you together. Yet I know in my heart Michael's a hell of a better man than I'll ever be."

"Don't say that," she pleaded, feeling the panic rising in her voice. His next suggestion might be that they not see each other again and she couldn't bear that.

"Monica, listen—"

"No. No, don't say it. I have an idea." The words rushed out on top of each other.

"An idea for us?"

She nodded and bent forward and kissed him, using her tongue in all the ways he'd taught her until they were both panting and clinging to each other.

"As you said," she whispered, her chest heaving, "we seem to get along fabulously well on the physical level."

He chuckled and buried his face in the lush fullness of her breasts, kissing each upturned nipple. "That, my dear, is putting it mildly."

"It seems to me that we could learn to communicate on other levels as well."

He went still and raised his gaze to hers. She swallowed and forced herself to smile. His eyes narrowed.

"I was thinking that, well, if we feel so strongly about each other then we should . . ."

"Should what?" he prodded.

Monica gathered her courage and blurted it all out at once. "That we should get married."

"Leah," Andrew whispered in the darkened theater.

Leah's gaze reluctantly left the screen, where a Walt Disney animation film was playing.

Her husband pointed to Scotty, who was curled up in his lap. The toddler was sound asleep. Husband and wife shared a meaningful smile. Andrew reached over and stole a handful of popcorn from her box.

"Do you want to leave?"

She shook her head, surprised he'd ask. "This is the very best part. Besides, Scotty will want to know what he missed."

The older grandmotherly type in the row in front of them turned around and glared pointedly at Andrew.

"My husband apologizes for disrupting the show," Leah whispered.

"So does my wife," Andrew added.

The woman huffily turned around and Leah smothered her laughter as best she could. Her husband certainly wasn't helping matters any. He was making faces at the old biddy, which caused Leah to giggle all the more.

The woman turned around once again and Leah nearly choked in her effort to keep from laughing outright. Once she'd composed herself, she scooted down in her seat and leaned her head against Andrew's shoulder. She hadn't laughed this much in one day since . . . she couldn't remember when. It didn't matter, she was laughing now and it felt incredible. When had she allowed her life to become so cheerless? Time had slipped between her fingers with barely a notice.

Scotty was a delight, and she loved him until her heart felt as if it would burst. He would be about the same age as the baby they'd wanted to adopt. In some unexplainable way, Leah had transferred to Scotty the love she had stored in her heart for the child taken from her. Pam must have understood that because she and Doug had asked Leah and her husband if they'd be Scotty's godparents.

In the last couple of years they'd done their duty and bought Scotty birthday and Christmas presents, but that had been the extent of their commitment. He held a special place in her heart, but Leah realized now that she'd cheated Andrew and herself out of the pleasure this child could bring into their lives.

Loving Scotty frightened her. She feared she might become overly attached to her friend's son. The pain of the lost adoption had cheated her out of enjoying Scotty the way she should. She'd feared that if she became overly attached, he'd be taken from her too.

The movie ended and the lights came up. Scotty yawned and, sitting up, rubbed his eyes.

"How you doing, big boy?" Andrew asked.

Scotty blinked several times, as if he'd forgotten where he was and who he was with. A look of panic came into his eyes as he glanced around the theater, and then to Leah.

"Remember, Mommy and Daddy went to dinner," Leah reminded him.

He nodded, but he didn't seem overly happy about it.

"I bet you're hungry," Andrew said, lifting him onto his shoulders. Andrew waited until the aisle was clear and then led the way out of the theater. It was dark by the time they reached the parking lot and the stars glittered like a splattering of diamond dust tossed across a bed of shiny black satin.

"Want to make a wish?" Leah asked.

Scotty looked to the heavens and nodded. He closed his eyes and drew in a deep breath, releasing it all at once. His eyes flew open and he grinned broadly.

"I bet he misses Diane and Jason," Andrew said, unlocking the car door.

"Nope," Scotty said. "I like you better."

"Don't get a big head," Leah warned her husband, under her breath. "He'd say the same thing to anyone who gave him horsey rides and took him to the movies."

"Maybe so," Andrew agreed, "but it's me he loves."

"Auntie Leah too."

Leah planted a kiss on his chubby cheek. "That's telling him, kiddo."

It wasn't until much later, hours after they'd finished the dinner dishes, long after they'd read Scotty a story and tucked him into the guest bed, that the emptiness surrounded her.

The night was dark and moonless as Leah slipped out of her bedroom and wandered into the room where Scotty slept. Standing over his sleeping figure, she gazed down on this perfect child who belonged to her friend, and held the pain of her loss tight within her soul.

She finally moved and walked over to the closet. Standing on her tiptoes, she brought down the baby book she'd hidden there.

Sitting in the silence and the dark, she held the book in her lap and turned each empty page until she'd made her way through the entire satin-covered book. From newborn to the space for the high school graduation photo. When she'd finished, she pressed the book against her heart and rocked back and forth, as if she were holding the long-awaited child in her arms.

Instead she clung to a hollow dream.

Jody gasped.

Jeff alive! It wasn't possible. She could hear her mother-in-law continue speaking but the words were unintelligible and seemed to come from a far-off distance. It was then that Jody realized she'd dropped the phone and had backed away.

"Jody." Glen was there and she turned and buried her face in his chest. "What is it?" he asked, his words as gentle as the arms that comforted her.

"Mom?" Timmy asked, picking up the receiver. Gloria continued talking, apparently not realizing anything was amiss. "Grandma says she needs to talk to you," her son said.

Jody shook her head. "No. No, I can't, not now."

"Tell your grandmother your mother will call her back later," Glen instructed. He encircled her shoulders and led her back to the living room. Gently he lowered her onto the sofa cushions. "What happened?"

Speaking was beyond her. Tears filled her eyes and spilled like burning acid against her cheeks, scalding her skin.

"Are you all right, Mom?" Timmy asked, racing to her side. "Grandma said she didn't mean to upset you. She told me to tell you to call her the minute you're feeling better."

"Did she say anything to you?" Jody demanded, gripping her son by the shoulders and making a careful study of his features. It was important that Gloria not say anything to Timmy. If her mother-in-law had made the outlandish claim to her son, Jody didn't know if she'd find it in her heart to forgive her.

"Say what?" Timmy wanted to know.

"I think your mother could do with a cold glass of water," Glen interrupted. "Would you get it for her?"

"Sure." Eager to help, Timmy hurried into the kitchen.

Glen's hands clasped Jody's. "What did Jeff's mother say to you?"

Speaking the words aloud was difficult. "She . . . claims Jeff's alive."

Glen released a troubled sigh. "Is there any chance it's true?"

Jody shook her head. "None. His body was positively identified by dental records. The same thing happened the first Christmas after we buried him. Gloria insisted Jeff wasn't dead. We argued and our relationship has been strained ever since. She's never understood that I had to divorce Jeff in order to sell the property, especially when she insisted she would continue to support Timmy and me, but I couldn't do that. I couldn't financially drain her or my own parents."

Glen sat next to her and gently patted her hand. "She sounds like a lonely old woman."

"I know. It shouldn't upset me when she does these things, but it does. I thought . . . I hoped she was making progress. I know she's trying, but it's hard for her. Jeff was her only child and she loved him very much."

"Here, Mom." Timmy vaulted into the room with a glass of water. The liquid sloshed over the rim as he presented it to her. "Is she all right?" Timmy asked Glen.

He nodded. "I think so."

"Grandma Potter's real nice," Timmy explained, "but she's a little weird sometimes. She visits old ladies who talk to the dead people and it doesn't have to be Halloween."

Jody, drinking the water, almost choked at Timmy's comment about Halloween. Leave it to a kid to put everything into the proper perspective.

"Your grandmother badly misses your father," Glen explained, kneeling down so his eyes were level with the nine-year-old. "And when you love someone so very much it eases the pain to pretend they're still with you."

"Grandma's been missing him a long time," Timmy said solemnly, then looked to Jody. "My mom has too. Until you came along all she ever thought about was my dad and her garden."

"How do you feel about that?" Glen asked.

"It bothered me a little because I'd like to have a dad who's alive and who can teach me the things a kid needs to know. I was kind of hoping you'd like me and my mom enough to stick around a while."

"I like you both a whole lot," Glen assured him.

"Enough to last through baseball season?"

Glen laughed and hugged the boy. "I'm sure I'll be around at least that long. Of course it's up to your mother if she wants to continue dating me."

"She does," Timmy said enthusiastically, "don't you, Mom?"

*   *   *

Jody knew she shouldn't allow her conversation with Jeff's mother to upset her, but it had. There'd been similar discussions over the years.

Jody remembered vividly every detail of every long-ago conversation. One had ruined her Christmas, but she refused to allow it to happen a second time. She'd met a good, kind man and she wasn't going to allow her ex-mother-in-law's grief to interfere in celebration of the holidays.

If that was the case, Jody reasoned, why couldn't she sleep? The house was dark and quiet, and she wandered from room to room, unable to quiet that deep inner part of herself.

The pain, she realized, was as fresh now as it had been when she'd been forced to accept that Jeff was dead.

Her father had phoned from Germany with the news. He explained that he'd be bringing Jeff's body home for burial. She had written down the flight details on a slip of paper and calmly thanked him for dealing with these agonizing details. It wasn't until after she'd hung up the phone that the full impact of what her father had said settled over her.

Jeff was dead. The years of not knowing had come to an end.

The intolerable waiting was over. The haunting questions had been answered, but the sharp edges of her grief were only beginning. The agony of the unknown felt almost comfortable compared to the brutal loss of hope she'd suffered in exchange.

Until Jeff's remains could be positively identified—until she could place her husband's body in the ground and stand at his tombstone, there had always been hope, however slim, that he was alive. Now that had been stripped away from her and she was left to bleed.

Jody remembered how she ripped the flight information from the pad and folded it over and over again until it was a tight square, clenching it in her fist. She needed something to hold on to. All there was for her was a folded slip of paper that listed the information on the flight that was bringing her husband's body home.

For a long time she'd done nothing but sit and stare into the silence. Her heart had felt as if it had stopped beating.

It was then, Jody realized, that a part of herself had died. No one could endure this kind of emotional torture and possibly survive.

She was dead to all the happy dreams they'd shared. Dead to whatever the future would hold, because she couldn't share her tomorrows with the man she'd loved so fiercely.

Helen Chandler had arrived shortly after the call came from Jody's father. She walked into the house and softly called Jody's name. Jody had stared up at her mother, her eyes dry, her heart shattered. At first she didn't acknowledge her presence. No one could comfort her. Not even her own mother.

"He's gone," Helen had whispered.

Jody nodded. She couldn't deny it any longer. The hope had been forever destroyed.

Her mother had attempted to console her, wrapping her arms around Jody's shoulders. But Jody held herself stiff and unyielding.

"Let him go," her mother pleaded. "Let him rest in peace."

"Peace?" Jody whispered. How could she possibly have peace now? She shook her head, refusing to release any part of her life with Jeff.

"He's been found, Jody. Jeff's coming home."

Perhaps Jeff's body had been located, Jody reasoned, but she was more lost now than ever. And she doubted that she would ever find her way again.

How much time had passed since that disastrous day, Jody wondered. Four years? Or was it five? Like so much else in her life, she'd lost track. She moved, one day into the next, dragging her pain with her, the weight almost more than she could bear.

It wasn't until Timmy had written the letter to God that she realized what she was doing to herself and to her boy. It had shocked her into taking action.

For the first time since Jeff's death, she was making a new life for herself and for her son, and she couldn't, wouldn't, let that be ruined. It had taken her this long to find her footing and she wasn't going to allow anyone to topple her again.

Chapter

★ ✯ ★

13

Angels rarely wept. It happened so seldom, and only while they were on earth duty. Mercy had heard tales of angel tears, but never experienced the phenomenon herself. It was an unpleasant experience. Now they came as a surprise, misting her gaze. She brushed them aside, feeling Leah's pain as deeply as if it were her own as the young nurse clenched the empty baby book against her bosom.

Mercy had done everything possible, but she hadn't been able to help. It was the most frustrating case she had ever encountered.

If only Mercy could sit down and talk to Leah, face-to-face. If only Mercy could explain to this woman of the earth that she must find serenity within herself before her prayer could be answered. But that was impossible.

And so they both wept.

Leah cried silent tears standing guard over her friend's child while Mercy wept openly, unable to contain her sorrow at this feeling of helplessness.

"Married." The word went through Chet like a bullet, with much the same effect. He bolted off the bed and stood, the sour taste of panic filling his mouth.

"It seems the logical thing to do," Monica said, her voice as sweet as chocolate-dipped caramels.

Chet rubbed his hand down his face, hoping that would set matters straight in his mind. It didn't. If anything, his thoughts filled with pure terror. "Sweetheart, in case you haven't figured it out, I'm not the marrying kind."

"That's the point," Monica continued softly, "I'm not either. It seems we're perfect for each other."

"You're not the marrying kind? Don't be ridiculous." She remained on the bed, so damn beautiful he had to force himself to look away. Otherwise he just might find himself considering her ridiculous suggestion. Much more of this sexual teasing they'd been exchanging and he'd find himself agreeing to just about anything.

"I'm twenty-five years old and have never been asked," she reminded him.

"Michael's chomping at the bit, waiting for the opportunity," Chet muttered. He couldn't believe he'd said that, not after the fretful evening he'd spent thinking about Monica cheek to cheek with the other man. He quickly glanced about the room, making sure he wasn't leaving anything behind, such as his heart and a good portion of common sense. He looped his leg over the windowsill, eager to make his escape before he found himself actually discussing the possibility of marriage. The mere thought sent cold chills down his spine.

"You're leaving?" Monica was kneeling on top of the mattress, holding her discarded blouse against her bare breasts. Her eyes were wide and pleading. "Don't go. Please."

The "please" had cost her a good deal, but Chet knew that if he didn't make his escape then and there, it would be too late. Before he knew what he was doing, he'd find himself agreeing to this asinine scheme of hers.

As it was, their ongoing relationship continued to confound him. He'd never meant to see her again after she'd lectured him on the misery brought on by the evils of alcohol. Little by little he'd knowingly allowed himself to be drawn to this preacher's daughter. They'd been a hair's breath from making love only moments earlier. She didn't seem to realize how close they'd come.

"I should have realized," she said in a small, pitiful voice, "that you wouldn't want to marry me."

Chet groaned inwardly. He was prepared to slip into the night as unnoticed as when he'd first arrived, but she'd managed to do it again. This woman knew exactly which cords to pull to reach him. It happened like this each and every time they met. Much more of this and she'd have the threads wrapped so securely around his heart there'd be no escape.

"It isn't that," he said, his back to her. Looking at her was dangerous, especially now with her lips swollen from his kisses and her hair all mussed up. He'd never known a woman who looked more beautiful when her hair wasn't combed.

"Then what is it?" she asked. From the nearness of her voice he knew she'd moved off the bed and was standing almost directly behind him.

Nothing but the truth would satisfy her, Chet realized, yet he hesitated, knowing she'd argue with the devil himself.

"Tell me exactly what it is then," she demanded, and he noticed she was regaining some of her natural pluck.

"Listen, sweetheart," he said, knowing she disliked the affectionate term, "I'm not good enough for you."

Until he'd met Monica his life had been reduced to wild weekends, blown paychecks, and cheap thrills with a cocktail waitress. He'd been shot, beaten, and chased down by a jealous husband. Not exactly pick-of-the-litter husband material for a minister's daughter, but there was no telling Monica anything. He'd learned that the hard way.

"Don't say that." Her arms came up under his and she looped her hands on his shoulders, then flattened the side of her face against his back. She felt so damn good and warm pressed to him that for an instant he was nearly swayed.

"Nothing could be further from the truth," she insisted. "Don't you realize how much you've taught me? I was a prude until we met and now I know what it means to be in love. You've made me proud to be a woman."

"Lessons rarely come cheap."

"What's that supposed to mean?" Her arms slipped away from him and Chet was eternally grateful. He slipped out of the window, landing with a thud on the hard ground below.

Turning around to face her was a mistake in what was proving to be a long line of tactical errors. Her eyes were bright with tears and her lower lip was trembling. Something sharp and painful twisted in his gut. He could deal far easier with her anger than he could her tears.

"I'm not going to marry you, Monica," he told her harshly. "So get that idea out of your head right now. It's just not going to happen."

She was silent for a moment, then nodded. "You can't get much clearer than that. Good night, Chet." Her voice was soft and a little broken.

Damn, but she had her hooks in him good and deep. The best thing for him to do was to get out while the getting was good. Working as a private investigator, Chet had developed a sixth sense for these things. The time to leave was about five minutes ago.

"I'll see you around," he tossed over his shoulder. He waited for her to close the window, but she didn't and he was left to wonder exactly how long she stood there watching him.

Fighting himself he made it all the way to his car, which he'd parked two streets over. He didn't want anyone to see his vehicle and connect Monica with him.

He unlocked the door and sat in the front seat and battled with himself until he accepted that he wasn't going to be able to leave matters unfinished between them.

He slammed his fist against the steering wheel, climbed out of the car, and retraced the same route he had taken only moments earlier. He came by the side of the darkened church and toward the back side of the house where Monica's bedroom was situated.

Her room was dark. He hesitated, then carefully made his way to the window, tapping lightly against the glass pane. He heard her climb out of the bed and pull up the sash.

Neither of them spoke right away. It was as if they were both unsure of what to say. After coming all the way back, Chet hadn't any more of a clue than when he left the car. Apparently Monica didn't either.

"I volunteered to be a bell ringer," she whispered. He couldn't see her face as clearly as he would have liked, but he could tell from the soft catch in her voice that she'd been crying.

Damn fool woman. She should have known better than to fall in love with the likes of him.

"When?" he found himself asking, already anxious to see her again. They were playing a no-win game, but for the life of him Chet couldn't make himself walk away from her.

"Tomorrow afternoon between two and three."

"Same street as before?"

"Yes." The last part was barely discernible. "Chet," she said more clearly, but he heard the hesitation in her voice. He heard the pain too, but ignored it as best he could, which was near impossible.

"Yeah?" he prompted when she didn't immediately continue.

She was kneeling, he noticed, her face only a short distance from his own. "Do you . . . are you in love with me?"

It didn't take him long to respond. "I don't know." It was the honest-to-God truth. What did someone like him know about love? Damn little to be sure.

"You can't be any more articulate than that?" The righteous ring was back in her voice and he found himself smiling.

"I like you," he said, realizing what an inadequate phrase that was.

"In other words I turn you on?"

He wasn't sure he liked her vernacular, but he wasn't in any position to be arguing since he was the one who'd taught her everything she knew about the sexual part of her nature. He never figured she'd be such a fast learner.

"It's more than that," was about all he was willing to admit.

"How much more?"

He should have known she wouldn't leave that alone. "I don't know," he said, raising his voice more than he'd intended. His words seemed to echo like thunder in the silence of the night. All they needed now was to wake her old man. "I just don't know," he repeated, softer this time. "Listen, Monica, it doesn't help to phrase the same question in different ways, the answer's going to be the same. I don't know about love. I've never been in love before, so how in the hell am I supposed to know if what I feel for you is any different than what I've felt in the past?"

"But surely you've had some experience with love."

His laugh was low and husky. "Experience I've got, lots of that, but mainly it's of the physical nature."

"In other words if . . . if we'd made love, then you might be able to tell me exactly what your feelings are toward me." The stiff indignation was back as inflexible as always.

"Not exactly." It did his heart good to hear the outrage in her voice, although he'd never known a woman who could irritate him faster. By the same token he'd never known a woman who did the other things to him she did either. The problem was, he still hadn't figured out whether he liked it or not. Mostly he liked it, he reasoned, otherwise he wouldn't keep coming back for more.

"I have my principles, Chet Costello, and I can tell you right now that I refuse to sleep with any man until after we're married."

Laughing was a gross error and he knew it, but he couldn't help himself. He could have had her any number of times. The only thing that had stopped him was knowing that neither one of them would be the same afterward.

Monica was innocent in the ways of men and he refused to take from her what rightly belonged to another. His thoughts were abruptly ended when Monica slammed the window shut, practically in his face.

Her eyes glared out at him accusingly.

He shouldn't have laughed and knew it even as the amusement escaped his throat. As means of an apology, he pressed his fingertips to his lips and then set his open hand against the cold windowpane.

Monica's angry gaze held his in what little light the moon afforded.

After a moment, she pantomimed his action and poised her hand on the other side of the glass against his.

Reluctantly, he dropped his hand and turned away from her while he had the strength. He didn't know where the relationship was leading and as far as he could see they were striding down a dead-end street, but for the life of him he couldn't make himself terminate it. Maybe he did love her. God almighty, he didn't ever want to think about the consequences of that.

"Young man."

The voice startled Chet. He was getting sloppy in his old age, otherwise he'd never have been heard cutting through her side yard. Chet whirled around to find a thin man standing on the front lawn, dressed in a robe and slippers, holding a flashlight. It could only be Monica's father.

Chet drew in his breath and waited.

"I'd like to know exactly what you're doing on my property this time of night?" Lloyd Fisher demanded, aiming the flashlight into his eyes, blinding him.

It was happening, Leah thought. She woke to the buzzing of the alarm and even before she opened her eyes she realized how queasy her stomach was. Was it possible? Could she be pregnant?

Mentally she tried to calculate the dates of her last menstrual cycle, and couldn't. Sometime the first part of November, she guessed. It would help if she hadn't tossed her notebook in the garbage.

It was wishful thinking, she finally decided. Or the flu. Probably a nasty virus, she mused, yawning.

"Morning," Andrew said, cuddling her. His hand automatically slipped over her abdomen as he scooted closer to her side. Leah savored his warmth. "Did you sleep well?"

"Hmmm."

"Me too."

Leah smiled. Their routine was the same every morning. It was these small things, these everyday habits that had become a part of the structure of their marriage.

After Andrew had gone to make the coffee, Leah decided to take her temperature for old times' sake, not that it would tell her anything.

Two minutes later she was studying the normal reading and calling herself a silly goose, grateful Andrew hadn't caught her with the thermometer in her mouth.

"I think I'll just have yogurt this morning," Leah said when she entered the kitchen.

Andrew studied her. "Are you feeling all right?"

"I'm fine," she assured him, taking a carton of blueberry-flavored nonfat yogurt out of the refrigerator. The bread popped up from the toaster and Andrew spread a thin layer of butter over the warm surface.

"You look a little pale," he commented, removing the lid from the strawberry jam. He smeared a thick coat over the toast and carried his plate and cup of coffee to the table.

"I do?" Her voice rose with a dash of excitement she couldn't hide. She brought her yogurt with her and joined him.

The toast was poised in front of Andrew's mouth and he slowly lowered it to his plate. He didn't say anything for several moments. "How late are you?"

"I don't know. I threw away my notebook, remember?"

"Surely you can figure it out."

"Can you?"

He shook his head. "I guess not. It doesn't matter though, does it? If you're pregnant we'll both be happy."

"And if I'm not?" she asked, watching him expectantly.

"Then you're not," he concluded, munching on the toast. He made it sound as if it didn't matter to him one way or another. Leah knew that wasn't true, not after having had Scotty with them for two days. Andrew was wonderful with children. He deserved to be a father. The familiar ache returned but the intensity wasn't as strong as it had been. The pain that had been so much a part of her all these years seemed to peel away and disappear.

She'd experienced this sensation only once before—the night she'd met Andrew.

She remembered the first time she saw him. They were both college students attending the University of Washington. Some friends had introduced them and the minute they'd exchanged greetings Leah felt a powerful emotional punch. She wished there was a word to describe the feeling that came over her. It was as if fate had given her a swift kick where she'd feel it.

From that moment on she knew this man was going to be an important part of her life. Afterward she discounted the feeling, chalking it up to the beer she'd had earlier. Andrew was steadily dating someone else at the time and she'd heard rumors that he was close to becoming engaged.

They ran into each other soon after that at the library. Leah was struggling with a chemistry class, certain she was going to fail. The library was the only place she could study and so she made the nightly trek across campus to hit the books.

Andrew had been grappling over a term paper and they'd sat at the same table for nearly two hours without speaking a word. Leah had wanted to get to know him better, but hadn't exchanged more than preliminary hello, good-to-see-you-again sort of chitchat.

Andrew left first, whispered something about being glad to see her again, and was gone. But when she'd walked out of the library he was waiting for her. A couple of friends had delayed him, he explained, and besides he didn't think it was a good idea for her to walk across the campus alone in the dark. So he escorted her back to her dorm.

They continued to meet nightly at the library long after his term paper had been turned in and graded. Later Andrew told her she was the only girl he'd ever dated who helped improve his GPA. He'd done more studying with her than any other woman he'd ever dated.

Leah didn't know when she realized she was in love with him. The night they'd met seemed a good choice. She just knew.

Just as she knew now, in the deepest most sheltered part of her heart, that she was going to have a child.

Leah didn't question where this knowledge came from. It wasn't intuition, or instinct, or anything psychic, but a deep abiding belief that her time of waiting had come to an end.

"I suppose you're going to buy one of those home pregnancy test kits," Andrew said, frowning, as he carried his empty plate to the sink. He rinsed it off and stuck it in the dishwasher.

They'd been through this procedure no less than a dozen times over the years. The minute she was a day late, Leah typically ran to the drugstore, needing to know the answer as soon as possible. For all the test kits she'd purchased over the years, she should be entitled to a discount.

"Not this time," she said.

"Why not?"

"Like you said, if I'm pregnant, great, and if not, well, then I'm not." She looped her arms around his neck and kissed him. "I love you."

He didn't answer her right away. Instead he carefully studied her upturned face. "Something's different."

"It is?" she asked, beaming him a smile.

"I don't know what, but it's there in your eyes."

Leah knew what it was. She was pregnant. Oh, heaven help her, she was diving into the deep end again and she hadn't meant for that to happen.

She knew she was pregnant. Felt it to the very marrow of her bones, but she'd believed the same thing a hundred times before.

Now was different. The feeling she had now was as powerful as the night she met Andrew, but she couldn't allow her sanity to rest on something as unmeasurable as a feeling.

"You're sure you're all right?" he asked, looking concerned.

"I feel wonderful," she said, tightly hugging her husband's waist. She closed her eyes, praying with all her heart that this wasn't a sick joke her mind was playing on her.

From the moment she'd received the call claiming Jeff was alive, Jody had dreaded contacting her mother-in-law. She carefully bided her time and waited until Timmy was down for the night. Even then it had taken Jody another half hour to fortify her courage enough to reach for the phone. She didn't know where she'd find the grit to face Jeff's mother when she was in one of these moods.

"Hello, Gloria," Jody said calmly, knowing she'd probably woken her mother-in-law from a sound sleep.

"Jody," she said groggily, "is that you?" Not giving her time to answer, she immediately continued. "I'm so pleased you called me back. I know this news is as much of a shock to you as it is me, but—"

"Gloria," Jody cut in calmly, unwilling to listen to any more. Her only chance of reaching Jeff's mother was when she sounded composed and confident. "Jeff is dead."

Someone had played the cruelest of hoaxes on them. "Who phoned you?" Jody demanded, and a telltale wobble came into her voice, betraying her slipping poise.

"I didn't get his name," Gloria explained. "You see, I was so excited that I wasn't thinking clearly, but he sounded very professional. He gave me details."

"What sort of details?" It was clear this line of questioning was flustering Jeff's mother all the more, but for the sake of them all Jody had to get to the bottom of this.

"I can't really tell you right this minute."

"Did he say where he was calling from?" Jody asked more calmly this time.

"Oh, yes, he was in Germany. Such a nice young man. You see, the call woke me in the middle of the night. I didn't believe him at first and then the more he talked the more I realized he was telling the truth. Jeff is alive. In my heart I always knew he was and now it's coming to pass."

"But wouldn't the authorities have contacted me?" Jody asked.

"I . . . don't know, dear. Maybe it has something to do with the divorce."

"But surely they'd want me to know. After all, Timmy is Jeff's son."

"I can't answer your questions, Jody. All I know is what they said."

"And what was that?"

"I should have written everything down, but I was too excited, and I'm on this new heart medication that makes my mind go all fuzzy at times."

Jody's grip on the phone relaxed. "Was this one of those times, Mom?" she asked softly.

"Oh, no, this was all very real. I thought to call you right away, but—"

"But you didn't," Jody concluded when the older woman hesitated.

"No," she admitted reluctantly.

"And why didn't you?"

"Because," Gloria said, following a heartfelt sigh, "I knew you wouldn't believe me, and I was afraid we would end up arguing and I do so hate the thought of us disagreeing. You and Timmy are the only family I have left."

Left. The details were quickly tallying in Jody's mind. Her mother-in-law was taking a new heart medication, one that, at times, confused her and she'd been woken abruptly from a sound sleep. The episode was probably a very lifelike dream. Not entirely sure the phone call had happened herself, Gloria had delayed contacting Jody until the following evening.

Because she'd been so desperate to believe her son was alive, Jeff's mother had clung to the dream, building it in her mind, until she'd convinced herself it was authentic.

"Have you heard from anyone since?" Jody asked softly.

"No. You think I should have, don't you?"

"It doesn't matter what I think. What do you believe?"

Speaking on the phone had always been an inadequate means of communication as far as Jody was concerned. She heard the faint intake of breath that came from her mother-in-law and knew Gloria was weeping softly. How Jody wished she could be there to wrap her arms around her and comfort her.

Jody had needed consolation herself the night before when Gloria had first phoned and there'd been a strong pair of arms to hold her. It had helped tremendously.

"How's Timmy?" her mother-in-law asked in an apparent effort to change the subject. "I bet he's getting excited for Christmas."

"Timmy's great." Jody couldn't talk about her rambunctious son and not smile. "We chopped down a Christmas tree this weekend."

"All by yourselves?"

Jody hesitated, unsure if she should mention Glen or not. This didn't seem to be the appropriate time to drop the news that she was dating again, although heaven knew it was well past the time she should.

"A friend went along and helped," she answered, being as diplomatic as she could.

"A friend," Gloria repeated slowly, thoughtfully. "Male or female?"

"Male." She couldn't leave it at that. She'd need to explain now. "Glen's an attorney who works at the same law firm I do."

"I see." Funny how much was visible in those two brief words. "Just how long have you been dating this . . . other man?"

"Mom, it isn't like that. We've only been out a couple of times, but it isn't anything . . ." She stopped herself in time from saying "serious." Glen was serious. He'd said as much from the first. He wanted a wife and family. Timmy wanted and needed a father figure. She needed a husband. One who would laugh with her, one who would hold her when she needed to be held. One who would fill the empty spaces of her heart.

"Everything's becoming clear to me now," Gloria said stiffly. "No wonder you don't want to hear about Jeff. You're involved with another man."

"Mother, that's not true." This was an impossible conversation, and growing more so every minute. The immediate sense of guilt she experienced was nearly crippling.

"The man who called from Germany knew that you'd divorced my son."

"Mother, we've been through this a thousand times or more. I didn't divorce Jeff because I didn't love him any longer. It was for financial reasons."

"I was never satisfied with that excuse and you know it. Both your parents and I were more than willing to support you."

"Mom, please—"

"The man who called asked me about you and Timmy."

"Mom, don't, please," Jody whispered, her small voice trembling. "It was a dream. It never happened."

"He did call." Gloria's high voice rattled from the telephone receiver. "Jeff's alive."

"I realize it's difficult for you to accept that I'm dating again, but it's time I got on with my life. Don't you think I've grieved long enough? Don't you think it's time?" Despite her resolve not to break down, she was crying. It happened like this nearly every time they spoke.

"I imagine you plan to marry this other man?" Gloria continued, her voice filled with disdain.

"I never said that."

"You can remarry, you know, there's nothing I can do to stop you."

"I don't know what I'm going to do," Jody said, bewildered and miserable, looking for a means of ending the conversation.

"That would make for a fine thing for my son to come home to, his wife married to another man."

"Mom, please don't say that."

"You know what I think?" Gloria said accusingly, knowing she had the upper hand. "You don't want Jeff to be alive. You've made such a fine life for yourself that it would be inconvenient for you if he did turn up alive."

"You know that's not true," Jody sobbed.

"Do I, now? You have your new boyfriend, you don't need Jeff anymore."

"Glen is a friend," she insisted.

"That isn't what you said earlier."

"I think it's time we ended this," Jody said, struggling for what little composure remained.

"That's just fine with me. But I think you should know, I'm going to tell Jeff myself just what kind of wife you turned out to be. He's going to call me soon, and then I'll tell him. Then he'll know the truth about you."

Chapter

★ ✪ ★

14

Leah walked into her house and was greeted with the fresh, pungent scent of evergreen. The decorator had arrived and set up the Christmas tree, and it was breathtakingly beautiful.

The flocked tree looked as if it belonged in the foyer of a classy hotel. Glossy gold bows were strung in one continuous ribbon from top to bottom. Bright red porcelain poinsettia flowers were symmetrically placed. And then there were the angels. Leah counted twelve. In gold gowns with massive white wings, each one playing a musical instrument. One had a guitar, the next a harp, another a saxophone, a tuba, and flute. A horn and trombone. It became a game to find each one hidden among the heavy white limbs.

"You're home," Andrew said, ambling into the living room from the kitchen. "Well," he said, his gaze following hers toward the Christmas tree, "what do you think?"

"It's beautiful."

"I thought so too."

She hung her coat in the closet.

"Debbi outdid herself this year," Andrew said, bending over and turning on the tree lights. Ten strings of miniature red globes glowed, casting warm shadows about the room.

The decorator was a friend of Andrew's mother. As part of her Christmas gift to Andrew and Leah, Shirley Lundberg had their Christmas tree decorated.

"I love the angels," Leah said, slipping her arm around her husband's waist and pressing her head to his shoulder.

"How'd your day go?"

There was far more to the question than what he was asking. What Andrew wanted to know was if she was feeling the same queasy sensation she had the last few days both in the mornings and late in the afternoons. He was asking if her period had started. In sum he wanted to know if she was pregnant.

"My day was great, how about yours?" she asked, smiling up at him.

His gaze skirted past hers. "Let's sit down," he suggested. With a flip of the switch, the gas fireplace roared to life and tongues of fire licked at the imitation logs.

Together they sank into the soft comfort of the leather sofa. Andrew's arm was tucked around her shoulders and he rested his chin on the crown of her head. "I've been thinking," he began.

"This sounds ominous."

He chuckled, but she noticed his laughter contained a dash of concern. "I'd feel a whole lot more comfortable if we got one of those pregnancy test kits," he continued.

"Why does it matter?" she asked, laughing off his request. "We'll know sooner or later, won't we?"

"You've been on this emotional high all week and I'm afraid if it continues much longer—"

"But I am pregnant," she said with supreme confidence. "I know it's finally happening for us. There's never been any physical reason why we can't have children. Dr. Benoit assured us of that countless times. How many times has he claimed all we need do is relax and that it'll happen when we least expect it? I don't know about you, Andrew, but I'm floored by this."

"Leah, please, listen to reason."

"Our time of waiting has passed," she insisted, unwilling to listen to his arguments.

"If you're so certain, then it won't matter if you take the test now or later, will it?" Andrew pressed.

"I'm not going to buy another one of those awful test kits. I hate them." She eased herself away from him and stiffly folded her arms. They'd been through this routine countless times and the result had always been devastatingly the same.

Negative.

No matter how long she studied the results she couldn't make them read what she yearned for so desperately. No, she wouldn't subject herself to that again.

"Leah, please. I just don't want you to get yourself worked up over this. You're a few days late and already—"

"I don't know that I'm late. You don't either. To my way of thinking, you're making more of this than necessary. As you said before, if I'm pregnant, great, if not, well, then I'm not pregnant."

He was uncharacteristically silent, but Leah knew her husband well enough to recognize how deceptive this calm could be.

"Let me do this my way," she asked, reaching for his hand and kissing his knuckles.

He didn't respond immediately. "I can't stand by and watch you do this to yourself. How many times have you gone through this?" he demanded. "It's always the same and each time your hopes go a little higher and you fall a little harder. Each time it takes you longer to recover."

Leah knew what he was saying was true, but this was different. This time she'd throw back her head and shout for joy. This time her heart and her soul would be left intact. How she wished there was some way to reassure Andrew.

"I don't want you to worry about me," she said.

"I am worried."

She leaned against him. "Don't, please."

"Does this mean you won't take the home pregnancy test?" The fire crackled in the distance adding punctuation to his request.

She hated to refuse him anything, but it was necessary. Those tests dredged up far too many unpleasant memories. That was all in the past, and her future, their future, was spilling over with promise.

"No, Andrew, I won't. Not this time." She threw her arms into the air and fell backward so that she was sprawled across his lap, smiling up into his face. "Now kiss me, you fool."

He closed his eyes as though to blot her out. "Leah, for the love of—"

She didn't allow him to finish, but gripped hold of his neck and levered herself upward until her mouth met his. As familiar as she was with her husband's body, Leah knew exactly what she needed to do to evoke a strong and positive response.

"Leah." Her name became a helpless plea.

"I have this incredible urge to ravish you," she whispered, opening the buttons of his neatly pressed dress shirt. He groaned when her hands met his warm skin.

"Dinner," he managed, between slow, deep kisses.

"What about it?" she asked, rotating her hands around to his back. His heart was pounding hard and fast, but then so was her own.

"Can wait," he told her brokenly.

Leah smiled softly to herself. "That's what I thought."

It wasn't until she was dressing for work the following morning that Leah found the pregnancy test kit. How long it had been sitting on the bathroom counter she could only speculate. Probably from the night before.

The night before. A small, satisfied smile lit up her eyes. They might be an old married couple, but the lovemaking couldn't get more incredible or more romantic than beneath a glowing Christmas tree in front of a flickering fire.

She carried the test kit into the kitchen with her and set it down on the kitchen table in front of her husband. "Is this a hint?"

"As broad as I can make it," he said, and finished his glass of orange juice. "For the love of heaven, let's get this agony over with."

It was then that Leah knew.

In the beginning she was afraid he was worried about her building her hopes upon a foundation of sand. But it was more than that. Andrew was suffering the torment of the unknown himself.

For years, Andrew had disguised his feelings, not allowing her to guess how very much he wanted children.

He was studying her now, his features sharp and anxious. "How much longer will you wait?"

She wanted to make some flippant reply, some casual remark that they could both laugh away, but it wouldn't work.

"If it'll ease your mind," she said, disliking even this small compromise, "I'll make an appointment with Dr. Benoit right away." The physician, however dear, produced a flood of unhappy memories. She couldn't think of him and not remember the months of hormone shots, the ultrasound, and everything else they'd attempted over the last seven years.

"All right, call your doctor friend," Andrew said, but he didn't sound especially pleased. He wanted to know. The sooner the better.

Not so with Leah. She'd already received all the confirmation she needed.

Monica had been standing in the cold, sounding the bell for charitable donations, for nearly forty-five minutes. She was cold, her feet hurt, and she was almost convinced Chet wouldn't show.

Not after her father had caught him walking out of their yard in the dead of night. Worse, she'd been left to speculate what had happened. Her father had remained uncharacteristically tight-lipped about the incident. She'd tried once to pry information from him, but to no avail. Any further questions and he'd guess that her interest was more than normal curiosity.

Monica felt Chet's presence several seconds before he came into view. Her body was developing a kind of sonar when it came to locating him. Her spirits lifted immediately and she drew in a deep breath and whispered a soft prayer of thankfulness.

"Hello," she whispered when he strolled up to the bright red pot and slipped a twenty-dollar bill inside.

"We need to talk," he murmured, not looking at her.

"I know."

"Can you meet me afterward?"

"Of course." She was in love and a woman in love would do whatever was necessary to be with her man. "Your apartment?" she asked, loving to tease him.

"No." The word was sharp and instant.

Monica couldn't help it, she laughed. "Where?"

"Pier Fifty-six. I'll be waiting for you at the restaurant. There's a table way in the back, closest to the water."

She nodded eagerly. "I shouldn't be much longer."

"I'll see you there," he murmured, and before she could say another word, he was gone. The man was like a magician. He could appear and disappear at the drop of a hat, or so it seemed.

Twenty minutes later, Monica was hurrying downhill, toward the Seattle waterfront. She raced across the street, promising herself she'd stop on her way to the bus stop and look at the Christmas display in Nordstrom's window. She'd heard it was angels this year, perched atop a train set that circled a frothy cloud. Stars shone bright from above. Another window was the traditional Santa's elves at the North Pole and Mrs. Claus baking sugar cookies.

Chet was sitting at the table, waiting for her. Puget Sound showed through the huge plate-glass window behind him. The sky was blue and clear and the ferry had just pulled away from the dock. The scene was lovely and for a moment she studied the tranquil waters.

"I'm so glad to see you," she said. She slipped out of her coat and waited a moment, wondering how long it would take Chet to notice her new dress, but he seemed preoccupied and said nothing. Monica was a bit hurt, but let it pass.

"I'm dying for a cup of coffee," she said.

Chet waved for the waitress, who carried the glass pot over to the table. "Do you want something to eat?" he asked Monica.

She shook her head. "Just coffee for me, thanks."

"Me too." The waitress refilled his cup and poured hers.

Chet smiled over at her and the same intense look was back, the one she'd noticed earlier. His frown deepened as if he'd become aware of a change.

"Something's different," he said, studying her.

Monica beamed proudly. He had noticed. "I'm wearing a little makeup," she whispered, leaning toward him. "Out of the blue I got a call from Donna Watkins, a lady from church. She invited me to lunch. Donna's wonderful with clothes and scarves and pretty pins. . . . I didn't always think so, but that doesn't matter now. She claimed she was getting dressed that morning and had the irrepressible urge to call me and invite me out.

"After lunch she took me shopping. I bought the dress and—" she tossed back her head to expose her earlobes "—these. They're lovely, aren't they?"

Chet's eyebrows shot toward his hairline at the sight of the small gold earrings. "I thought you claimed jewelry was a tool of the devil."

She might have thought that at one time, but would never have said so, at least not publicly. "Don't be ridiculous. I said that if a woman opted to wear jewels then whatever she chose should enhance a meek and gentle spirit."

"Earrings do all that?"

He was teasing her, but she didn't mind. "I think so. Donna did too, but then she had on these huge Christmas tree decorations. They're wild. As far as I can see, each woman is left to her own interpretation of this."

She took a sip of coffee, grateful for the warmth it offered her. "Do you like the dress?" She tried to make light of it, but her heart was dangling precariously on her sleeve. Everything she'd bought that afternoon had been with Chet in mind. Each time she stepped before the mirror, her first thought had been what he would think when he saw her.

"It's very pretty."

It wasn't much as compliments went, but enough. "It's the first thing I've had in years that isn't black, gray, or navy blue. Donna says I'm a summer, if you know what that means. I didn't until she explained, but basically I should be wearing pastels, pinks, pale blues, and the like."

Chet nodded, but looked distracted, as if this summer business were beyond him.

"I'm sorry," she said, setting her cup down hard in the saucer, "I didn't mean to get sidetracked. Tell me what happened with my dad?" She was breathless with anticipation. "He didn't say a word to me."

"Nothing happened."

Chet certainly seemed to be uncommunicative this afternoon.

"Nothing?" she demanded. There was more to this than met the eye.

"I explained I was a private investigator and had cut through his yard. I apologized for the intrusion. As far as I could tell he believed me. After he'd read over my license he went back into the house."

"That was it?" Surely there was something more. It wasn't her imagination, her father had been unnecessarily quiet all morning. He seemed preoccupied and absentminded. When she mentioned meeting Donna for an early lunch, he'd encouraged her, and even sounded pleased. He insisted she needn't come back to the office when she'd finished. Since she was volunteering downtown, she should go directly there.

"You seem so quiet," Monica said after several moments of silence. She'd never seen the serious side of Chet. She'd seen him angry and frustrated, aroused and flippant, but never serious.

He didn't seem to hear her. "I don't think I ever realized how truly beautiful you are."

Unaccustomed to compliments, Monica felt herself blush. Her heart was so full, it felt as if it were ready to burst. Love must do this to a woman, she decided, but she wouldn't change this incredible feeling for the world.

He leaned forward and reached for her hand, gripping her fingers hard with his own. "I've been doing some thinking."

"About us?" Her chest tightened as though she already knew what he was going to say. In that same moment she recognized that no amount of arguing would change his mind.

Chet nodded. "It has to end, Monica. I never intended matters to go this far. You're bright and beautiful and someday you'll meet a—"

She stopped him from saying anything more by pressing the tips of her fingers against his lips. She knew her eyes were wide and pleading. They stung with the effort to hold back a wall of tears.

"Don't say it," she pleaded softly.

His hand gripped her wrist and he closed his eyes, as if this were causing him as much pain as he was inflicting upon her. He kissed her fingers and slowly moved her hand away.

She lowered her gaze. "There's this song," she whispered in fractured tones, having trouble speaking. "Michael plays it on the piano. It's from some musical. I don't know which one . . . it's about two people who must end their affair, and the girl who's singing asks only one thing."

"What's that?"

"All she wants is to choose the time and place where he tells her good-bye. She wants it to be on a Sunday at the zoo. I don't know why she chose there, but she did." She forced herself to smile and realized a toddler would have seen through the effort. "I always thought that was the most ridiculous song. The only reason Michael played it was that he knew it irritated me, and now . . . now I think I understand."

Chet didn't say anything for several minutes. Monica couldn't.

"The time is now," he said. "It's over."

She nodded. "At least let me choose the place. Not here in some fancy restaurant with half the world looking on. Let's go outside to the end of the pier. Tell me there you don't love me. Tell me there you never want to see me again."

She didn't wait for him to agree or disagree, but stood, taking her coat. With her head held high, she walked out of the restaurant and down the long pier, stopping when she'd reached the farthest corner.

The wind blew hard against her as she stood at the railing looking out over the green, murky waters. It amazed her that she could be so outwardly calm and still hurt this badly.

For a moment she feared Chet would choose to leave her there alone, but she was wrong. Soon he joined her. Standing beside her, he braced his elbows against the railing, and looked out over the water. Dusk was setting, and a soft shade of pink brightened the horizon. The wind howled softly in the background.

"I can't say I don't love you, if that's what you're looking for." The words were almost accusing, tight with pain.

Monica's hands were buried deep in her coat pockets. She turned to study him. The wind slapped the loose tendrils of her hair about her face. "Why are you doing this?"

"Damn it, Monica, I don't want to argue. We both know all the reasons. We've been through all this. I'm not going to get involved in another debate with you. One of us has got to keep his head on straight. Do you think I'm enjoying this?"

"No."

"Accept it, then. It's over before either of us has more cause for regret."

So this was what it felt like to die, Monica mused. She closed her eyes as the pain worked through her heart, then slowly nodded.

"Michael's a good man."

"I don't love Michael," she said evenly. "I love you."

He ignored her. "I ran a background check on him for you and he's squeaky clean. You couldn't ask for better husband material."

"Don't, please," she whispered fervently. She knew what he was doing, but it wasn't helping.

"If you're not attracted to Michael, fine. He's not the only fish in the sea. For that matter I'm not either. You'll fall in love again. Within a couple of weeks, maybe less."

Monica's short laugh was filled with more tears than amusement. "Oh, Chet, don't you know me at all? Do you honestly believe I'm the kind of woman to walk from one relationship to another? Do you really think I'd ever marry a man I don't love?"

His lack of response was answer enough. "Just don't do anything stupid," he warned.

"Like what?"

"Hell, I don't know, join a convent or something."

"That's for Catholics."

"I realize that, but knowing you, you'd convert just to spite me. There's too much passion in you for that, understand? You've kept it buried for too damn long as it is. You'll do fine," he said starkly, turned, and started to walk away.

"Chet."

He stopped, and his back and his shoulders stiffened, but he didn't turn around.

"Would you hold me, please. One last time."

It looked as if he intended to keep on walking. He took one step, and then another. Monica bit down so hard on her lip to keep from calling for him that she tasted blood. Whatever it was that caused him to change his mind, she would never know.

Before another moment passed she was in his arms. His hold on her was hard and tight. Sobbing, she clung to him.

"You're a fool," she told him, weeping so hard, she doubted he could understand her.

"I've always been one. Why change now?"

"Because I love you."

"Yeah, well, that and two bits will buy you a cup of coffee." He broke away from her so abruptly that she nearly stumbled backward. Gripping her hands with his, he raised her fingers to his mouth. "Dear God, I can't believe . . ."

"What can't you believe?"

"Nothing." He closed his eyes and folded his fingers over hers. "There's so much I owe you."

"But, Chet," she pleaded, "don't you understand? I'm so grateful for you."

"This is my gift to you."

"What?" she sobbed, "breaking my heart?"

"No, letting you go before I screw up your life as much as I have my own." He dropped her hands, and without another word, turned and walked away.

It was highly uncommon to get a summons from Gabriel while on prayer assignment, and Goodness was convinced she was about to be pulled off the case. She had her arguments all lined up. Good ones too. Matters were going much better than they appeared at first glance. She intended to explain everything, if only he'd give her the opportunity.

At last Goodness had something positive to report. Monica had come to her senses. It was no small task dealing with this human either. The preacher's daughter had been a challenge from the first, but Goodness had made progress. With some effort, she'd arranged the phone call from Donna Watkins, although she was disappointed that Monica had chosen to impress Chet instead of Michael with her new outfit.

"Goodness." Gabriel greeted her upon her arrival. He was pacing, his massive hands clenched behind his back. "I'd like a progress report on Monica Fischer's prayer request."

"I was hoping you'd ask," Goodness said, eager to tell her side of the strange happenings. "There's a fine young man in her church by the name of Michael Simpson—"

Gabriel cut her off with a look. "I understand she's currently involved with Chet Costello. And from what I hear, you're responsible for the two of them meeting."

"Was involved," Goodness said quickly, steering the archangel away from the unfortunate incident of Monica literally falling into Chet's arms. "That's all behind her now."

"You're sure about this?"

"You needn't worry about Monica and that shoddy detective any longer," Goodness concluded, folding her hands and proudly flaunting her wings. "Michael Simpson has a good deal going for him. He's talented and dedicated. I'm sure that within a matter of days, Monica will—"

"Days?" Gabriel repeated.

"Perhaps it will take a week, but I'm confident Monica will come to her senses soon."

Gabriel continued his pacing. "From what I can see of matters, Monica Fischer is deeply in love, and it isn't with Michael Simpson."

"I'm sure this private detective was nothing more than a passing fancy."

"You think so, do you?" Gabriel asked calmly. "Look at this and then tell me what you think." With a wave of his arm, the walls of heaven slowly parted, followed by a rush of warm, humid winds. Mists swirled and Goodness squinted, having trouble locating Monica through the thick fog.

Soon the vista cleared. It took her a moment to recognize the stark interior of the old church. It was the very sanctuary where Goodness had met her friends—where Reverend Fischer tended his flock of faithful believers.

Monica was kneeling at the altar, her face buried in her arms as she openly sobbed. It was her tears and her prayers that had created the humid fog. The sounds of her pain rose pitifully toward heaven as if echoing from a sound chamber.

"She's changed," Gabriel said gently. "Her hair is different."

"Chet, he's the private detective—"

"I know him well."

"You do?"

Gabriel nodded. "Is he responsible for the other things as well? I notice she's wearing an attractive dress and gold earrings."

"Ah, I believe so." Now didn't seem the time to mention Monica's lunch with Donna Watkins.

Gabriel's nod was thoughtful. "I suspected as much. As I recall, the last time I saw Monica, she was trapped in the web of her own righteousness. Am I wrong, or is she a little more willing to accept the differences in us all?"

"I couldn't really say, but I must explain, I did a bit of research on this private detective and I don't mind telling you, he's had a sordid past."

"I see," Gabriel commented with a decided lack of appreciation. This wasn't a good sign. "How far back did you investigate him?"

"The last couple of years."

"Did you learn about his gunshot wound?"

"Ah, I wasn't aware he'd been wounded."

"He nearly died. As I understand it, he stepped in front of a bullet to save his friend. He was willing to sacrifice his own life for that of someone he loved. Unfortunately it wasn't enough, his friend died."

"Oh, dear." The picture Gabriel painted of Chet was becoming clearer. Goodness's gaze slowly returned to Monica, kneeling at the altar railing, pouring her heart out in prayer. It rose like a sweet-smelling mist toward heaven. "What's she saying?"

Gabriel stood behind Goodness. "She's thanking God for teaching her about love, for giving her the short time she had with Chet. Her heart is filled with gratitude."

Goodness frowned. "Gratitude comes with tears?"

"Very often it does," Gabriel admitted with a beleaguered sigh. "It seems to me you've taught Monica Fischer what she needed to learn."

"But I did nothing." Goodness was more confused than ever. Her efforts had all been geared toward Michael. "The changes are due to Chet Costello, not me."

"I know. Maybe we should look at him."

Goodness pressed her lips tightly together. "He's probably in a bar somewhere."

"He is." The picture of Monica faded and was replaced by one of Chet slouched atop a bar stool, nursing a shot glass. His shoulders were hunched forward and he ignored any attempts at conversation the bartender made.

"You notice he isn't in any church," Goodness felt obliged to point out.

"I realize that."

A cocktail waitress ambled to his side and whispered something. "That's Trixie." Goodness felt it was important that Gabriel know how well informed she was. She hadn't slouched in her duties.

"I know all about Trixie as well."

"Then you must be aware of their ongoing relationship," Goodness supplied.

"It's over and has been from the moment Chet met Monica," Gabriel said absently. "He's doing it again, you see."

"Drinking?"

Gabriel slowly shook his head. "No, he's sacrificing himself for another. He loves Monica, but he doesn't believe he's right for her. It seems to me that a man who's twice put the good of someone else before his own deserves something more than pain."

"He deserves love," Goodness whispered, watching Trixie.

Goodness thought she heard Gabriel groan. "Not Trixie," he said impatiently.

"Who, then?"

"Monica Fischer."

Goodness felt knocked off-balance. "You couldn't possibly mean that the good Lord intends to answer Monica's prayer for a husband with Chet Costello?"

Gabriel laughed, the rich and full sound echoing like a Chinese gong. "My dear Goodness, that's what he intended all along."

Chapter

★ ✬ ★

15

Jody swore she didn't sleep except in ten- or fifteen-minute snatches the entire night. It had been like this when Jeff had first disappeared. Mentally and physically exhausted, she'd fall into bed, immediately slip into a druglike sleep only to jerk awake minutes later. The pattern was back.

Jeff was alive.

Jeff was dead and buried. Buried and mourned.

Resurrected.

The next morning, when the alarm rang, Jody was tempted to call into work sick. The only thing that kept her from doing so was the idea of facing the day at home alone with her doubts—a day alone with her fears. Alone. It held no appeal.

Sensing her mood, Timmy was extra quiet. He dressed for school while she cooked his breakfast and drove him to the bus stop.

"Have a good day," she told him as he climbed out of the car.

"You too, Mom." With that he was gone, hurrying to meet his friends.

The traffic into the city was heavy, but Jody barely noticed. She drove by rote, her mind wandering from one inane topic to another. When she pulled into her assigned spot in the parking garage, she was surprised to realize where she was and had no memory of the commute.

At least while she was at the office she could occupy her thoughts with matters other than Jeff's mother. Despite everything, a small part of her—no, she corrected, a very large part of her—had been wounded by the things Gloria had said.

Why should it matter that her mother-in-law would tell her dead son what a terrible wife Jody was?

Somehow it did.

It unsettled her that Gloria's opinion of her was so important. Jody had been a good wife. No woman could have possibly loved Jeff more. No woman could have grieved harder, or longer—except, possibly, his mother.

Because of Timmy it was impossible for Jody to isolate her life the way Gloria had. Because of Timmy she was forced to deal with the present. She'd done a good job, or at least she assumed she had until her son had written his letter to God. Timmy needed her, not to look back and weep with her pain, but to stand tall and proud and to point the direction of their future.

Jody had no more than settled down at her desk, her thoughts more confused than ever, when Glen Richardson arrived. She looked up at the attorney's warm, concerned face, and felt an immediate sense of serenity.

He had a calming effect on her and had from the first. It hadn't taken long for him to become a good friend, and she'd never needed one more.

"How'd it go with your mother-in-law?" he asked, sitting on the edge of her desk.

Jody averted her gaze. "Not good."

"She's a lonely old woman."

"I know," Jody said, "but somehow that doesn't make this any easier."

Glen's eyes were sympathetic. "I'm sure it doesn't. How's Timmy?"

"Great. He's checking the water in the tree stand every morning just the way you said. I swear, he's brought every kid in the neighborhood home to show them the Christmas tree he cut down by himself."

"Hey, don't I get any credit?"

"Apparently not. He's got the neighborhood believing he's a regular lumberjack. He wanted to wear his plaid shirt and boots to school this morning. It seems he's got an image to live up to now."

Glen chuckled, but then his eyes grew serious. "I hope you don't mind, but I bought Timmy a baseball mitt for Christmas. I realize it was presumptuous of me to do something like that without talking to you first."

Jody wasn't sure how she felt about Glen giving them presents. It was thoughtful, yes, but baseball mitts were expensive and it seemed to imply that there was something more than mere friendship.

"The mitt he showed me is too small for his hand," Glen explained. "I'm surprised his coach let him play with it. If Timmy's going to pitch, and he certainly seems to have his heart set on that, then he'll need a properly fitting mitt."

"It was very kind of you, Glen."

"But?" He scooted off her desk, and seemed to be waiting for her to chastise him.

"Timmy will think he's in heaven." Jody couldn't make herself berate Glen. She wouldn't have known Timmy's mitt was too small if Glen hadn't told her. If anything, he'd proved Timmy's point. Her son needed a father's loving guidance.

Glen looked at his watch. "I better get back to my office. I have to be in court later this morning."

"Thanks for stopping by."

"No problem. How about dinner one night this week?"

Before Jody even thought about what she was doing, she nodded.

This was a pivotal moment for her.

She'd welcomed another man into her life, calmly accepted his companionship. She had taken for granted that she would see Glen again and soon. More earth-shattering was how much she was looking forward to spending more time with him.

Some of what she was feeling must have leaked into her eyes, because Glen didn't leave. Slowly, he walked around to her side of the desk, claimed a second chair, and sat down next to her.

"What just happened?" he asked, leaning forward and bracing his elbows on his knees. "Something clicked in your mind just now. I could see it as plain as day. Tell me what it was."

"I realized how pleased I was that we're dating."

He laughed, and Jody was certain he didn't understand the significance of what she was saying. For the last seven years she'd lived her life in limbo. The still, shadow-filled existence had become a shelter to her. It had protected her from exposing her heart to any additional pain. What she had missed in all those years, wrapped in a cocoon of safety, didn't bear thinking about.

Now here, out of the blue, like a miracle, was a man who'd gently pushed and prodded his way past the barriers of her resolve. A man who hadn't asked her to stop loving Jeff. He hadn't attempted to push her dead husband out of her life. All he'd asked was that she make room for him.

"Glen?"

"Yes." He reached for her hand, holding it lightly in his own.

Where she found the courage, she didn't know. Didn't question. All at once it was there, like the warming rays of dawn at the end of a long, cold night. "Would you like to marry me?"

At first her words were met with a shock-filled silence. Glen looked at her as if he suspected he hadn't heard her correctly. "Did you just say what I think you did?"

Jody had never been more embarrassed in her life. She hadn't a clue what had prompted her to ask such a thing. All at once the thought was there, and the words had tumbled from her lips like awkward chunks of ice over the edge of a pitcher. She wanted to reach out and jerk back the question, but before she had a chance to do or say anything more, Glen spoke.

"I would consider it the greatest honor of my life to be your husband and Timmy's stepfather."

"I shouldn't have—"

"You should have," Glen interrupted with feeling. "I just never dreamed this would happen so soon." He looked at his watch once more and she could see the regret work its way into his eyes.

"We'll talk about it later," she promised.

"Set the date, Jody. We can shop for an engagement ring this weekend." How eager he sounded, how pleased.

Maybe it wasn't such a crazy idea after all. She'd waited so long and here was an opportunity of a lifetime. Here was a chance of finding happiness and she was grabbing hold of it with both hands.

Yes, it was happening so fast, but that was the way she wanted it. If she had too much time to think about remarrying, she might find an excuse to change her mind.

"Let's get married in January, after the holidays," she blurted out as Glen headed for the door.

He turned around and flashed her a smile that rivaled the noonday sun. "January it is."

"Yes!" Shirley did a leap into the air off the filing cabinet, both hands raised in jubilation. A stack of papers went flying in all directions and Jody whirled around.

"What was that?" she asked as the papers fluttered to the ground.

Another woman in the office said, "It's that damn heating vent. It sends out a rush of hot air every now and again." She rolled her chair over to Jody. "Here, let me help you pick those up."

Jody looked up and frowned. The heating vent wasn't anywhere near the filing cabinet.

Shirley stayed plastered against the ceiling, her hands covering her mouth. "Oops," she whispered.

"Don't you think we should contact the maintenance man?"

"Naw," the other woman said. "It doesn't happen that often."

"Hey," Jody murmured, "look at this. It's a feather. How do you suppose a feather got in here?"

"I haven't got a clue," her friend said, handing her a stack of papers.

Shirley left before she caused any further damage and ascended directly toward the golden light of heaven, exhilarated with this unexpected turn of events.

To her delight Gabriel was waiting for her.

"Come in, come in," he greeted her. He was a magnificent angel, tall and regal looking, an impressive sight after a steady stream of men of the earth. For a fraction of a second Shirley admired the strength and power exuding from him.

"You're here to report about Timmy Potter?" Gabriel asked in a no-nonsense tone.

"That's right," Shirley said, nodding. "My mission's accomplished, Timmy's mother became engaged to Glen Richardson this morning."

"Glen Richardson," Gabriel repeated. He walked over to the desk where the cumbersome volume was stored and flipped open the thick book. He ran his finger down the page until he found Glen's name, then looked up at Shirley and frowned.

"He's a wonderful man and will make Timmy an excellent father," Shirley hurried to say. She strained her eyes to read what Gabriel seemed to question, but wasn't able to see anything beyond the archangel's massive hand.

"You need to return to earth right away," Gabriel continued. "There's been some misunderstanding. Jody and Timmy are going to need you. The winds of trouble are brewing."

"You can't tell me anything more than that?" Shirley asked. She should have known it wouldn't be this easy, especially since she was so new at this.

"There's nothing more I can tell you," Gabriel said, and she heard the regret in his voice.

"But . . ."

"Go," Gabriel said, spreading his massive wings. "You have work to do."

For years Leah had avoided the infant sections of department stores. Now she found herself drawn to them as if a magnet were luring her in their direction.

She was supposed to be Christmas shopping, instead she wandered about looking at beautifully crafted cribs, lovingly running her hand over the polished wood railings. The joy that blossomed in her heart was strong.

She was going to have a baby.

After all these years she was about to bear a child. Her waiting, her pain had come to pass.

Andrew's words of warning echoed harshly in the back of her mind. How she wished she could find some way to explain the deep certainty she experienced. She yearned to rub away his doubts and lend him the assurance she'd felt from that very first morning.

Soon she would be able to look him in the eye and tell him her body was nurturing his seed. For years she'd carried this dream with her, of watching her husband's expression when she told him he would soon be a father.

Nothing could have pleased her more than to purchase a complete layette right then and there, but she didn't want to risk another confrontation with Andrew. They had all the baby furniture they'd ever need in storage. Once Dr. Benoit had confirmed her pregnancy, there'd be plenty of time to set up a nursery.

Her appointment wasn't until the twenty-third, but she was fortunate to get one as quickly as that, so she wasn't complaining. Seeing the doctor that close to Christmas had its advantages. That way she wouldn't need to wait long to make the announcement to both sets of parents. If she saw Dr. Benoit any sooner, she'd never have been able to keep the happy news to herself.

Andrew's mother would be thrilled. Her own, too, of course, but her parents had plenty of grandchildren, while Shirley Lundberg impatiently waited for her first.

Leah had had names picked out for years. If they had a girl her name would be either Sarah, Hannah, or Elizabeth. A son would be named Isaac, Samuel, or John. Few understood the significance or what had prompted her decision.

The names were biblical. Leah shared a good deal in common with the three women. Sarah, Hannah, and Elizabeth had been barren too, but God had heard their prayers and answered them with the birth of their firstborn child. As it happened, all three were boys, and those were the names she'd chosen for her own child, should she bear a son.

Deep in her heart, Leah felt this child was a miracle. He was a testament to faith. Over the years her hope had grown weak and faltered, but God had listened. He'd heard her cries. Even when it seemed all that was returned to her was the echo of her own sobs, God had been faithful.

Unable to leave the infant department without purchasing one small item, Leah opted for a beautiful sterling silver Christmas tree ornament for Andrew with *Baby's First Christmas* beautifully inscribed in the silver. Technically she was a year early, but she was eager for Andrew's reaction when he opened this gift. By then he'd know for certain she was pregnant.

As she suspected, her husband was waiting for her when she arrived home from her Christmas shopping spree. He trailed behind her from the garage all the way into the guest bedroom, where she stored the unwrapped gifts.

"How'd the shopping go?" he asked, following close on her heels.

Leah set her purchases on the bed and tossed him a saucy smile over her shoulder. "Very well, thank you."

"Did you buy me anything?" One thing she'd always loved about Andrew was his childlike attitude toward Christmas. He was like a little kid about presents. He played silly guessing games with her, checked out the packages under the tree as often as he dared, and shook his gifts until they were in danger of being broken.

"I might have found you something," she answered cryptically, "and then again I might not."

"But you did," he said, sounding confident. He leaned against the doorway and cupped his hands behind his head, as if he had it all figured out. His pose suggested that she needn't wrap the gifts since he knew everything she'd bought anyway.

"You were gone a long time," he commented.

"Hmmm," she said, bringing the Christmas wrap out from the closet.

"Where'd you go?"

"Andrew, honestly!"

"Did you know the golf store was having a sale?"

"That does it," Leah said, throwing her arms in the air. "Scoot. I'm going to wrap these and I can't do it with you standing over my shoulder watching every move I make."

"Yes, but you have some great moves."

"Andrew, please, I'm serious. Scoot."

"Aha. So you did buy me something!"

"Good-bye, darling." She walked over to the door and closed it. The latch clicked softly into place.

Andrew stood stubbornly on the other side, refusing to leave. "You'll call me if you need anything, right?" he asked, sounding downright cordial.

"In a heartbeat."

A minute passed, perhaps two, but no longer. "Do you want something to drink?"

"No, thank you. Andrew, why don't you go in and watch television for a while?"

"Nothing good's on."

"What about football?"

"The game's over. How long is it going to take you to finish?"

"I can't rightly say." Was it any wonder family and friends made fun of her gift-wrapping efforts. She used more tape than any three people. She couldn't wrap a single gift without being hounded by her husband, who behaved more like a six-year-old than a mature adult.

A long, slow release of breath followed her announcement. "I'm going to make a cup of hot chocolate," he said, sounding as if he'd lost his last friend.

"Make two," she called out. She'd finish up later. By some miracle she'd managed to wrap everything she'd purchased for him, including a box of golf balls. The man had a sixth sense when it came to ferreting out his gifts.

Andrew was carrying steaming mugs of hot chocolate into the living room by the time she'd put everything away. They kicked off their shoes and snuggled up together on the sofa.

"When's your doctor's appointment?" Andrew asked, rubbing his chin along the side of her head. Leah was convinced she'd told him no less than three times. "The twenty-third."

He didn't say anything for a couple of moments. "How are you feeling?"

"Wonderful." Leah smiled to herself. He was becoming a believer. Bit by bit, little by little, as each day passed. Like her, he was afraid to believe. Like her, he couldn't make himself not do so.

"You know what I was thinking this afternoon?" she said, tilting back her head so their eyes could meet. "I'd like to start attending church services again."

"What brought this on?"

"I don't know. I realized it's been months since we last went to church. Far too long, and you know what? I miss it."

"I've always loved singing Christmas carols," Andrew said wistfully.

Leah nearly choked on her hot chocolate. "You can't sing."

"I know," he admitted readily, his eyes bright with silent laughter, "but that never stopped me."

"I noticed." She loved to tease him. It felt good to be together like this. "You wouldn't mind then if we went back to church?"

His eyes met hers. "Why should I? I think it's a good idea."

Leah nestled back into the warm security of his arms.

"It seems we have a good deal to be grateful for lately."

"Yes, it does," she agreed.

The moment was peaceful and serene and Leah happily traipsed along the meandering path of her thoughts. They led her on the same well-traveled road she'd traversed so often, trying to picture what Andrew's and her child would be like. She hoped, boy or girl, that their baby would inherit her husband's love of life, his excitement and joy for the little things.

"Leah," he said after a moment, "do you still believe you're pregnant?"

"I know I am. It's there—that confident feeling inside me. We're going to have a child, Andrew."

"You realize you've got me believing it now too, don't you?"

"Yes, and that's even better."

"This could be dangerous thinking for us both. We might be setting ourselves up for another major disappointment, and I don't think either one of us can take many more."

"We aren't," she assured him, not doubting, not even for an instant. "Here, feel," she said, taking the hot chocolate and setting it aside. Then, reaching for his hand, she pressed his palm against her stomach, holding it there, her fingers pressed over his. "Now tell me what you believe."

He was silent for what seemed like an eternity before he wrapped his arms around her and brought her tight against him, holding her as if he were suddenly afraid and needed someone to cling to.

"I love you," she whispered.

"I know," he whispered, and when they kissed she realized he was trembling.

"Monica," her father said, walking into the living room, his look contemplative. "Michael called again."

The needle was poised in her fingers, ready to pierce the linen fabric. "I don't feel much like talking, Dad. Would you make my excuses?"

"I explained you were a little under the weather."

She pulled the thread through the material. "Thank you." The needlepoint was a means of occupying her mind, but she doubted that she'd ever finish this project. The Ten Commandments were filled with Thou Shalt Not and that was the way she'd viewed life. Her views had subtly changed, thanks to knowing Chet.

Her father claimed his favorite chair across from her and reached for his Bible. He opened it and silently read for several moments before he gently closed the yellowed pages and set the leather-bound book aside.

"I've waited now for three days for you to tell me why you're so low. I don't know that I have the patience to hold out much longer."

Monica set aside the needlepoint, not knowing where to begin or how. The pain was too fresh yet, too raw. She lowered her gaze to her lap and clenched her hands together. Her father was a patient man, and she prayed he'd understand her hesitation.

He gave her a few moments, then leaned toward her and gently patted her knee. "It's at times like these that I wish your mother were alive. She'd be much better at understanding what's wrong than I am. Funny, isn't it," he said with a sad sort of laugh, "I counsel people from all walks of life and I can't help my own daughter."

"Dad, it's not that."

"I know, love. If it will make it easier, you don't need to tell me there's a man involved in all this. I have eyes in my head. In the beginning I believed it was Michael, but it's obvious he's not the one." He reached for his handkerchief and methodically cleaned his glasses. "I apologize for playing the role of the matchmaker with you two. I should have known better. I'm an old man who would like grandchildren someday."

Monica closed her eyes to a fresh wave of pain. Now there would be no children, because there was no Chet. It was melodramatic to think she would never fall in love again, never marry. But right then that was exactly how she felt.

"Whoever this young man is I'd like to thank him," her father continued after a lengthy silence.

"You don't know him, Dad."

"It doesn't matter."

She was forever grateful he didn't play a game of cat and mouse, attempting to guess Chet's identity.

"For the first time since you entered your twenties you've taken your eyes off yourself. You've worked so hard to do the right thing, to be the perfect example of God's love to others. Soon you focused all your efforts on yourself and how good you were. It was then that you started to notice the flaws in others. It became a vicious circle and I couldn't seem to reach you with the truth."

Monica raised her gaze to his. "I don't understand."

"Forgive me for sounding like the preacher I am. You're my only child and I love you more than words can say, but there've been times I wanted to take you by the shoulders and shake you good and hard."

"For what?" Although she asked the question, Monica was well aware of the answer.

"For standing in judgment of others instead of trying to look at them through God's eyes," her father continued.

"The man, his . . . his name is Chet," she whispered, feeling she owed her father some explanation. "I met him downtown, the first time the ensemble sang. He was going into a tavern and I tried to stop him by telling him how wrong it was for him to drink."

Her father smiled at that and settled back in his chair. "I suspect he didn't listen to you."

"No, quite the opposite. He laughed." She did too then, at the memory. Softly, sadly. "We met again by accident later and several times more by design.

"I couldn't understand what it was I found so intriguing about him. He's not like anyone I've ever known."

"You've been raised in the church. Your experience with the world has been limited."

She reached for a tissue and twisted it between her fingers. "He's a former policeman and has lived a hard life. He's done things neither of us would ever dream of doing. He's been shot and sometimes carries a gun, although he doesn't realize I know that."

"A gun?"

"At first glance he looks rough and mean," she hurried to explain, "but on the inside . . . I don't think I could have found a better man to love. He was honest when he didn't need to be, and gentle. There were any number of times he could have seduced me and didn't."

"I see."

The strain in her father's voice produced a small smile. She shouldn't have told him that part. Any father would have reacted the same.

"He's so damn noble I could cry . . . and have," she said, clenching her fists.

"I take it he's the one who insisted you not see each other again?"

Monica nodded. "He never said he loved me, but I know he does. He loves me so much he was willing to send me away rather than take the chance of hurting me."

"Monica," her father pleaded, "why didn't you bring him to meet me?"

It was a question that had plagued her as well. One she'd repeatedly asked herself the last few days. Chet had claimed he wanted it to end before there were more regrets, but she'd stewed in them for days. She feared Chet had assumed she was ashamed of him and that simply wasn't the case.

"I don't know why I didn't introduce you. I guess I was afraid you'd think ill of him, or me."

"But, Monica, you love this man. That would have been enough of a character endorsement for me. Your mother and I raised you and if you can't judge a man's worth by now then you wouldn't be our daughter."

"Oh, Dad, I wish I'd done so many things differently and now it's too late. Forgive me for not trusting you. I've been wrong about so much."

Her father patted her knee once more. "There's a special man for you. Remember how hurt you were when you learned Patrick was engaged."

Patrick. She'd nearly forgotten about him. It was laughable to think she'd been anything close to loving her former boyfriend. Her pride had been hurt at Patrick's surprise announcement. Far more than her ego was involved this time, and Monica sincerely doubted that she'd ever be the same again.

Chapter

★ ✯ ★

16

"*Hey, man, you don't look* so good," Lou, the Blue Goose bartender said as he poured Chet another shot glass of Kentucky bourbon.

"If you're looking for a pretty face," Chet muttered, "call Trixie."

"You got the flu?"

"Yeah," Chet said, thinking that would get Lou off his back. He wasn't interested in company or conversation.

"Then get the hell out of here," Lou continued. "No one wants to be sick for Christmas."

Christmas. It was just another day like all the others as far as Chet was concerned. Christmas was for families and he didn't have one. No one bought him gifts, and there certainly wasn't anyone he cared enough to buy one for other than . . . his thoughts came to a grinding halt.

Funny how a woman could mess up a man's mind. He'd known Monica what . . . two, three weeks? He'd lost count and within that short amount of time she'd managed to worm her way into his heart until she was like a virus that had spread to every part of his body.

He couldn't eat or sleep for want of her. He couldn't close his eyes without his head filling up with thoughts of her. Nor could he get the image of her out of his mind. The one of her standing at the end of the pier, the wind ruffling her hair, her beautiful eyes bright with tears . . . and love. A love so damn strong it was like a torchlight beaming directly at him.

That final picture of her would haunt him to the grave. He didn't know how he was going to get through the rest of his life without her.

The rest of his life. Chet nearly laughed out loud. What life? That was the real question. He was sick to death of the endless lies, the constant need for charades, flirting with disaster.

That's how it'd started with Monica. A game, because she irritated him. One diversion too many and this time he was paying the piper in spades.

The empty days stretched out before him, followed by cruel nights staked out in some dark alley or a cheap hotel room crawling with loneliness.

The rest of his life was reserved in hell. He was born there and had spent a good majority of his carelessly lived existence there, except for one brief furlough with a preacher's daughter. Just long enough for him to taste what could have been his, so he'd know exactly what it was he'd thrown away.

He emptied his drink, slapped the money down on the bar, and stood. The room spun and he shook his head, hoping that would help. It was too damn early in the afternoon to be drunk.

When he left the Blue Goose the cold hit him like a sharp claw. He squinted in the sunlight, cursing it as much as he cursed himself. The only person he had to blame for this was himself.

This was what he got for involving himself with a missionary. He'd known from the first time he kissed Monica that something like this would happen. It hadn't stopped him from seeing her again. It hadn't stopped him from caring. Nor had it stopped him from nearly screwing up her life.

The walk back to his office did him good. He was beginning to think he might be able to pull himself together and accomplish something by the end of the day, when he strolled past the department store window. Santa was there, and a long line of kids were waiting for him to listen to their wish lists. A little boy was squirming in his lap.

Something about the kid reached out and grabbed Chet by the gut. Perhaps it was the boy's eyes, maybe it was the color of the kid's hair, which was close to his own. It came to Chet then as unwelcome pain. If his life had been different, he might have had a son.

That fantasy along with everything else had been destroyed years ago when he'd been brash and naive enough to believe in justice and truth. Years ago before Tom was murdered, before he hadn't been able to save his partner.

He forced himself to keep walking until he reached his building. His office lacked welcome, but Chet had wasted enough time already. He had work to do.

He sorted through his mail and tossed it unopened into the garbage. Reaching over the top of his desk, he pushed the button for his answering machine. A series of impersonal beeps followed. No one wanted him, not even his clients.

What he needed, Chet decided, was a change of scene. He should have left this stinking city years ago. Now that he thought about it, he wasn't sure what it was that had prompted him to stay.

His mind made up, he pulled the phone from its jack, stuck it in the bottom desk drawer, and then searched through his filing cabinet for his lease, wishing he could remember the terms.

A knock sounded at his door.

"It's open," he shouted, shuffling though his papers. He made decent money, but had never gotten around to hiring himself a secretary. He wished now that he had.

"I'm looking for Chet Costello."

"You found him." He looked up and damn near swallowed his tongue. It was Monica's father.

Lloyd Fischer grinned in recognition. "So it was you? I was guessing, you see. Monica didn't give me your surname. Then again, I didn't ask."

"What can I do for you, Reverend Fischer?" Chet asked crisply. He wasn't going to put up with an interrogation. Fact was, he wasn't up to much more of anything.

"We're working at the Mission House," the older man explained, looking around the room. His eyes revealed neither approval nor disapproval, just mild curiosity.

"What can I do for you?" Chet pressed a second time.

The question seemed to take the reverend by surprise and he reverted his attention to Chet. "I'm not exactly sure. Would you mind if I sat down?"

"I was just on my way out." The last thing Chet wanted was a lengthy conversation with Monica's father.

"This won't take more than a couple of minutes," he said, and helped himself to a chair.

The reverend was being deliberately obtuse, and Chet gritted his teeth with impatience.

"When was the last time you saw my daughter?"

"Tuesday." Chet made a point of looking at his watch as if he needed to be someplace important soon. "If Monica didn't give you my name, how'd you find me?"

"I read your license, remember?"

He was losing it, Chet mused. He'd forgotten the old coot had caught him coming out of the side yard that night and had asked to see his identification.

"My daughter's badly hurt, you know."

For one wild second Chet assumed Monica had been injured and the fear that seared through him burned hotter than the bullet he'd taken years earlier.

"Life's tough and then you die," Chet stated unemotionally.

The man grinned as if he easily saw through Chet's ploy. The grin irritated Chet. "Listen, I have work to do."

"Monica claims you love her. Is that true?"

"No." The pain of the lie pricked his heart, but he ignored it. "Listen, if you're worried about what happened between us, let me assure you nothing did. Now, if you don't mind I've got an appointment."

"Yes, I suppose you do," the reverend said, slowly getting to his feet. He extended his hand. "It was a pleasure meeting you, young man. It's plain to see why Monica thinks so highly of you."

Chet's chest tightened with a crippling ache as they exchanged handshakes. "You should be beating the hell out of me for having ever touched your daughter."

The other man's eyes gentled as he slowly shook his head. "I was young once myself, you know, and deeply in love. Monica's a woman and old enough to know her own heart. I'm not here to judge you or my daughter. I came out of curiosity to meet you. And thank you."

"Thank me?" Lloyd Fischer was offering him gratitude when Chet had expected condemnation.

"Oh, yes, you've helped Monica tremendously." The minister looked older now than he had when Chet first saw him the fateful day he'd met Monica. Weary and burdened. "If there's ever anything I can do for you," he continued, "please don't hesitate to come see me."

"Sure," Chet said, but a man who'd lived the life he'd lived, and done the things he had, didn't make social calls to preachers.

He walked Monica's father to the door, and opened it for him, anxious for him to leave. If Lloyd Fischer stayed much longer, Chet just might start to believe in the impossible.

"She'll get over me," he said.

The older man nodded. "I suspect you're right. In due time. She loves you, and Monica's a good deal like her mother when it comes to love."

Chet hadn't a clue what that meant and furthermore he didn't want to know. His ladle of guilt was filled to capacity and overflowing.

"Good-bye, Chet. I appreciate you taking the time to talk to me." He patted Chet's upper arm as if he were little more than a schoolboy and then ambled out of the room.

Standing in the doorway, Chet watched as Monica's father absently walked down the hallway, strolling past the elevator. He turned around, looking confused, when he reached the end of the hall.

Chet shut the door, leaned against the thick white glass, and closed his eyes. He smelled of stale beer, hadn't shaved in two days, and as a general rule looked like shit, and this man of God had thanked him for damn near deflowering his daughter.

There was something screwy somewhere, and the hell if Chet could figure out where.

He was dizzy again and decided it was probably due to the fact that he hadn't eaten since the day before. The alcohol hadn't helped.

After showering and fixing himself something to eat he felt better. He'd finished his scrambled eggs when the thought subtly presented itself to him. Monica was at the Mission House. Hadn't her father said so himself?

"No," Chet said out loud. "I will not go down there." He reached for his television controller, his finger poised over the Power button.

"You're a fool," Chet muttered, already knowing there was no force on this earth that could keep him away.

He had no intention of talking to her. None. The picture windows in the place gave ample opportunity to view the inside without being noticed. He'd go down, check out what her father had said, and slip away without anyone being the wiser. It was something he'd done a thousand times before as part of his job. He was good at this sort of thing.

With purpose directing him, Chet locked up his office, and when the elevator didn't arrive fast enough to suit him, he took the stairs.

The mission was only a few doors away from his own building. It amazed Chet how easily he was able to find Monica in the crowd of workers. There seemed to be some sort of Christmas party going on. He spied Lloyd Fischer serving turkey with all the trimmings to a long line of derelicts.

Monica was in another part of the room with the children. Apparently she was telling them a story. A handful of kids were sitting on the floor looking up at the book she was holding. A toddler was fidgeting in her lap, reaching for her dangly earrings.

This was what hell must be like, Chet decided. To stand hidden in some corner and view the woman he loved so much it defied reason, and know he would never have her. Hell was watching her hold a child in her arms, and realizing she would never hold *their* child.

She was pale, Chet realized with regret, and dark circles shadowed her eyes. No wonder her father was concerned. Monica wasn't faring any better than Chet was himself. He wanted to shake some reason into her, but that was part of his hell too. He would never touch her again.

Coming here had not been one of his most brilliant ideas. He took a step back, and then another, and was ready to turn and walk away when Monica's gaze suddenly, unexplainably, locked with his.

Chet read her shock and watched the book she was holding tumble unnoticed from her fingers and fall to the floor.

Chet's heart faltered. He couldn't turn and walk away. Then she'd know his game. Then she'd know he'd purposely been spying on her. He had to do something and do it fast.

His shoes made harsh sounds against the sidewalk as he slammed into the Mission House door. He walked past the soup kitchen and moved directly to where Monica was sitting with the children. He braced his feet and glared down at her, sneering.

"Tell your father to stay away from me," he ordered coolly.

Monica's eyes widened with shock.

Not giving her a chance to recover, he turned and walked out, leaving the door to slam in his wake.

Jody let herself into the house that evening, same time as always. Timmy was sitting on the carpet in the family room, occupied with his video game.

"I'm home," she told him, walking into the kitchen.

"Hi, Mom," he called out. "Grandma called."

Jody's blood ran cold. "Grandma Potter?"

"Yes. She wants you to call her right away. She said—oh, darn—"

"What did she say?" Jody asked, hoping to hide her anxiety. It was times such as this that she regretted ever having purchased Timmy the video game system.

"Grandma said if you didn't call her right away that she would call you."

Jody wasn't up to another confrontation with Gloria.

"Glen's coming over for dinner," Jody announced, watching for her son's reaction, hoping to gain confidence in his enthusiasm to spend more time with the attorney. "I thought I'd make spaghetti."

"Sure. He'll like that." Timmy's gaze didn't waver from the television screen, his attention rapt.

Inviting Glen to dinner so they could talk to Timmy together about their engagement had been Glen's idea. Jody had immediately seen the wisdom of it, although now she wished she'd discussed the matter of her remarrying with her son much sooner.

Jody didn't doubt that Timmy would be thrilled. After all, this was what he wanted. His nine-year-old heart had yearned for a father, and his desire was what opened her eyes to the way she'd isolated her life.

"You want to help me set the table?" she asked, although it was an hour or longer before they'd eat.

"In a minute."

Jody rolled her eyes. She'd heard that phrase often enough to have it etched into the patio walkway.

Seeing that she wasn't going to get much conversation from her son, she fried the ground turkey and set the sauce to simmer. Once she'd finished, she reached for the phone and dialed her mother's number. If ever she needed emotional support it was now.

"Hi, Mom."

"Jody, how are you?"

"All right, I guess." She didn't want to unburden her soul, nor could she very well announce that she'd decided to marry Glen within earshot of Timmy. But she could tell her about Gloria's call.

"My guess is that Gloria wants to apologize, dear," her mother said, after Jody finished. "She was hurt and angry and said something she didn't mean, and now she's looking to make amends."

Jody was sure her mother was right, but needed confirmation before returning the call, and said as much.

"You need to remember," Helen continued, "you and Timmy are the only relatives she has left. I'm sure she regrets everything and would like to mend fences. The Christmas gifts you mailed probably arrived and they were the perfect excuse for her to contact you. She means well, sweetheart."

The doorbell sounded and Jody glanced at her watch. "That must be Glen," she explained.

"I do like that young man," her mother announced, and after a quick word in parting, Jody hung up the phone.

Her guess proved correct. Glen stood on the other side of the door, a bottle of wine in his hand and a bouquet of red rosebuds in the other. He kissed her on the cheek and handed her both.

"How's Timmy?" Glen asked as she arranged the roses in a crystal vase.

"Preoccupied," Jody whispered.

Glen's arm circled her waist as they returned to the kitchen. When Timmy noticed Glen had arrived, he turned off the game.

"Hi, Glen."

"How's it going, scout?"

"All right, I guess. Mom said you were coming over for dinner."

"Yeah, you don't mind, do you?"

"Oh, no," Timmy said, "I think it's great, but she made spaghetti and she makes me eat it with a spoon. She'll probably make you do the same thing."

"I think I can live with that, if you can."

"Yeah, I guess so," Timmy said.

"Son, Glen and I would like to have a talk with you before dinner." Rubbing her palms together as if warding off a chill, Jody looked at Glen for assistance. They hadn't talked about when they'd break the news to Timmy, and Jody worried their dinner would be a disaster with this hanging over their heads.

"Sure," Timmy said.

The three of them sat down together in the family room. Glen was next to Jody and Timmy sat across from them. Glen reached for Jody's hand.

"Your mother and I talked this afternoon and decided that we like each other very much," Glen explained.

"I kind of guessed that you did," Timmy said, "I saw you kissing her once."

"Did that trouble you?" Jody asked, watching her son for any tell-tale signs of jealousy. Although Timmy yearned for a father, he may not have understood that it would mean having to share his mother's attention with someone else.

"I don't know why people kiss on the lips," Timmy said. "It's seems silly when you're always warning me about germs, but adults seem to like it and even some kids. Rich told me he kissed a girl and it wasn't too bad."

"But how do you feel about me and your mother kissing?" Glen pressed.

Timmy frowned as if he didn't know how to answer. "All right, I guess."

Glen's hands tightened around Jody's. She noticed for the first time that he was nervous, which was something she suspected happened only rarely. Her gaze met his and he smiled weakly.

"Glen and I want to talk to you about us getting married," Jody said, surprised by how shallow her voice sounded. Saying the words aloud for the first time caused her heart to pound at a fast rate, as if she were walking up a steep hill. In many ways she was and the anticipation of this new path she'd chosen suddenly felt momentous.

"Does this mean we'd be a family?"

Jody nodded.

"I'd be your stepfather," Glen explained.

Timmy frowned at that. "But we'd still be a family?"

"Of course we would. Isn't that what you wanted?" Jody sensed Timmy's uncertainty and wanted to reassure him that there was nothing on this earth that would ever change her love for him.

"Would you have more babies like Rich's mom?"

Jody released her breath and looked at Glen. They hadn't discussed the prospect of having children.

"I'd like that very much," Glen answered for her. "But we'll leave the decision up to your mother."

"What do you think, Timmy, would you like it if Glen and I married?" Jody experienced the strongest need to break down and cry. It felt like a band around her chest that tightened more with each second.

"Sure, that would be great. Glen could help me be a better pitcher and then you wouldn't miss my dad so much. It'd be nice to be part of a real family."

Jody bit back the words that claimed they were already a *real* family, he and she together.

"It's settled, then," Glen said, "your mother and I are officially engaged. You know what this means now, don't you, Timmy? Another set of grandparents and aunts and uncles that you'll need to meet." He placed his arm around Jody's shoulder and squeezed gently.

The phone pealed just then and Jody knew in her heart that it was her mother-in-law. Bracing herself, she stood and reached for the phone.

Her guess was accurate.

"I want to apologize for our conversation the other night," Gloria said, sounding calm and collected. It was almost as if the fog in her mind had cleared.

"We both said things we regret," Jody assured her. "This is a difficult time for us."

"Oh, no," Gloria corrected, "you're wrong, my dear. Life couldn't be more beautiful. Christmas has always been my favorite time of year, and more so now than ever before."

"Mine too. Remember the year you joined Timmy and me. We wish your health was better so you could travel more."

"Jeff always enjoyed the holidays," she said.

Discussing her dead husband just then, minutes after she'd announced her engagement to another man, was more than Jody could bear.

"Mom, there's something you should know," she said quickly. "Something wonderful has happened and other than Timmy you're the first one to hear." She didn't mean to announce her engagement like this, but she couldn't think of any other way to divert Gloria from speaking about Jeff.

"You do sound excited and rightly so."

"I told you earlier I'd met another man."

Jody waited for some acknowledgment but none came. "We decided we want to be married," Jody said, "and have set the date for January."

"Married!" Gloria shrieked. "But you can't, you can't! What about Jeff?"

"If Jeff were alive why wouldn't he contact me or Timmy?" she asked reasonably.

"He's been very sick and weak. I haven't talked to him myself yet, but the German official told me he's recovering and asking about you and Timmy."

"Mom, give me the phone number of the person you're talking to and I'll contact him myself."

"I'm sorry, dear, I don't have it. But everything he's said is true, I swear it's true, Jeff's alive. You've got to believe me. You've got to break your engagement before Jeff learns you're involved with another man."

"Mom, this is a cruel hoax. We buried Jeff, remember?" Jody gently reminded her.

It was as if Gloria hadn't heard her. "What am I supposed to tell my son when he phones? I demand that you tell this other man you've changed your mind. No, no, I'll tell him for you. He'll listen to me."

"Mom, please," Jody pleaded, her voice low and trembling.

Glen was standing next to her then, his arm around his shoulder. Gently he took the receiver from her hand, and explained that he was the man Jody was marrying. Naturally she couldn't hear her former mother-in-law's response.

Jody turned into his arm and buried her face in his shoulder.

"Grandma thinks my dad's alive?" Timmy asked, when Glen had hung up the receiver.

Jody was trembling too hard to respond. Glen continued to hold her, patting her back. "Your grandmother wants it to be true so badly that she's convinced herself your father is still alive," Glen explained, when it was apparent Jody was in no condition to do so.

Somehow they made it through dinner, although the three of them took turns attempting to make a festive occasion of it. Glen tried the hardest. Timmy made an effort as well, and Jody too, however feeble. She was grateful when Glen claimed he was working on the brief for an important case and left shortly after they'd finished clearing the table.

Jody walked him to the door. "I'm sorry about Gloria."

"Don't worry," he said, pressing his forehead to hers. "We'll get through this." He wrapped his arms around her and kissed her gently.

Jody let him out the door and watched until Glen's car was out of sight. He was a good man, a decent man, but she didn't feel any great passion for him. She smiled sadly and realized she'd been lucky enough to know about love from Jeff. Love wasn't the reason she and Glen had decided to marry. They cared deeply for each other, shared the same goals, and were comfortable with each other. A lot of marriages had far less.

"I'm done with my homework," Timmy said some time later. Jody had finished the dishes and was busy writing out Christmas cards. She was later than usual this year.

"Are you telling everyone about Glen?" Timmy surprised her by asking. He reached for the top card and read her brief note.

"No."

"Why not?"

"I thought we'd send out announcements later. I've already mailed out half my cards and it doesn't seem fair that half my friends know and half don't."

Timmy nodded, as if her reasoning made perfect sense to him. He plopped his elbows on the table and tucked his chin in his hands as he watched her work.

"You know what I wish?"

"What?" she asked absently, thinking he was about to add another item to his detailed Christmas list.

"I wish what Grandma Potter said was true. I wish my dad was alive."

Jody's hand stilled as her fingers tightened around the pen. "I do too, sweetheart."

"Well, what do you think?" Shirley said, looking anxiously to Goodness. "Gabriel insists the winds of trouble are brewing, but I can't see it. Jody's engaged and from everything I can see Glen Richardson is a perfect match for her and Timmy."

Goodness, who was poised atop the Christmas tree, slowly shook her head. "You don't know very much about humans and love, do you?"

"Not really."

"After tracking Monica and Chet I could write a book."

"What's wrong with Jody and Glen?" Shirley asked impatiently. "They're great friends."

"I noticed, and that's a great place to *start* a relationship."

"If you're going to tell me Jody's still in love with Jeff, I'll agree with you. Good grief, I never dreamed this assignment would be so difficult. I do everything Gabriel wants and then he sends me hightailing it back to earth, claiming trouble's afoot. But he won't tell me where."

"It's obvious," Goodness said. "Glen doesn't love her either."

"Now, I sincerely doubt that. Glen's crazy about Jody."

"It's the little boy," Goodness said gently. "Glen's impatient for a family, and Jody has one ready-made for him."

"I disagree." Shirley might have been new at this business, but she didn't doubt Glen's honorable intentions for an instant.

"Why don't we check him out and see for ourselves," Goodness suggested. "I'll help you and then maybe you can help me. I'm having troubles of my own."

They left Timmy's house and had no problem locating Glen's. "He told her he was working on a brief," Shirley explained.

Glen was sitting at his desk, a pen poised in his hands, but he seemed to be having trouble. They watched for several moments while he did nothing more than stare into space.

"What's he doing?" Goodness whispered.

"I don't know. He seems to be thinking."

"Doesn't he know that will only get him into trouble?"

Shirley smiled. "I guess not. Look, he's opening a drawer."

Glen's shoulders heaved with a deep sigh as he removed a photograph from the bottom drawer. Goodness and Shirley looked over his shoulder. The photograph was that of a beautiful young woman with long black hair that cascaded over her shoulders.

"There's your trouble," Goodness whispered. "Glen's in love with another woman."

Chapter

★ ✯ ★

17

This wasn't going to be easy. Monica had carefully steeled herself for the coming confrontation with Chet. She stood outside his office door, her heart pounding hard and fast.

Fervently she prayed she was doing the right thing. All she knew was that she couldn't leave matters between them the way they were.

She could hear movement and knew Chet was there. She drew in a deep breath, knocked, turned the door handle, and stepped inside.

Chet was standing in front of his file cabinet, tossing one file after the other into a large cardboard container. Boxes were piled high on every bit of available space. His desk was clear, and the infamous calendar was down.

He was moving. Leaving Seattle. Leaving her.

"I won't be taking on any new—" He stopped abruptly when he saw it was Monica. For one all-too-brief moment tenderness flashed in his eyes, but that was quickly replaced with practiced hardness. His gaze became sharp and dangerous like that of a cornered animal that was prepared to lash out in order to protect itself.

"What are you doing here?" he said.

"My father wanted me to apologize," she began haltingly. "He never intended to offend you."

"You've apologized, now go."

What gave her the courage to stay, Monica would never know. "Why are you moving?"

He didn't answer, but continued working at a furious pace, lifting several thick folders at a time, carelessly tossing them into the box.

"Where are you going?" she asked, trying a different vein.

"Away. Monica," her name was little more than a frustrated sigh, "please, just go. Don't make this any more difficult than it already is."

190

"All right," she agreed and he visibly relaxed at her words. "If you answer one question."

"It's over," he said with sharp impatience. "Leave it at that."

"I can't." Monica had honestly tried to accept that he wanted her out of his life. But no matter how hard she struggled to find acceptance none would come.

"I'm not going to debate the issue with you."

"Just tell me why you don't want my love," she said forcefully. "Tell me what it is about me—"

"It has nothing to do with you. The problem is mine."

"Then tell me. I need to know." Despite her efforts to the contrary, her voice cracked with the strain of emotion.

Chet moved as if he were in pain, slowly and with difficulty. His back was to her as he stared out the window. Monica stayed where she was by the door, trembling and hating herself for subjecting them to this torment a second time.

The room seemed to spark with tension.

"I know you love me," she whispered. "You can't make me believe you don't. There has to be something more."

"I'm not good enough for you," he shouted. "Now for the love of God get out of here."

"No," she said softly. "Not until you tell me why you aren't good enough."

"Monica, please."

She walked over and stood next to him. He was so close she could feel his frustration. It seemed to come off him in waves.

"Why aren't you good enough?" she asked again.

Chet's hands were braced against the windowsill, his knuckles white. A war was being waged within him and the battle seemed to be a fierce one. When he turned to face her, his eyes were dull with pain.

"I murdered a man," he shouted. "There, you know, now leave." He pointed toward the door, his face growing red and angry. "Get out of my life, understand, before I ruin yours too."

The force of his anger rocked her, but Monica stood her ground. "I don't know the circumstances," she said shakily, "but if you killed him, then he must have deserved to die."

Chet jerked back as if she'd slapped him.

"It doesn't matter what you've done, I'll always love you."

"Damn you," Chet cried, and then reached for her, hauling her into his arms. The strength of his embrace all but crushed her, but Monica didn't care. There wasn't anyplace else she would rather be than with Chet. He seemed to be drinking in her softness, as if it were as vital to him in that moment as oxygen.

After a short while, he released a harsh shudder and relaxed his hold enough for her to breathe comfortably. He brushed the hair from her temple and kissed her there. "I'll always love you, too," he whispered brokenly.

It felt like heaven to be in his arms. For the first time in days Monica felt whole, as if the part of her that had been missing had been found.

"You're right when you say he deserved to die. He was a drug lord and brought misery to thousands all for the sake of money and power. An easy death was too good for him. He deserved to suffer."

"Are you wanted by the police?"

He shook his head and laughed shortly. "No, I was too smart for that. I goaded him into a fight and I knew, being the weasel he was, he'd go for his weapon. He did, but I was ready. After an investigation, it was decided that I acted in self-defense, but I knew the truth. I murdered him just as if I'd waited in a dark alley and shot him in the back. He didn't have a chance."

"The gunshot wound," she said, flattening her hand over the scar on Chet's shoulder. She could feel it even through the material of his shirt. "That was when you were shot, wasn't it?"

"No," Chet told her. "Not then."

"He scared you, though, didn't he? Tell me what he did to you."

"None of that matters." He released her then abruptly, as if he feared her touch, and backed away. "You got the answer you wanted, now go."

"But, Chet—"

"Go, damn you."

Monica flinched. "All right, but there's something you should know."

"How much more of this is there?"

"Not much, I promise you." Her voice wobbled a bit, but with the strength of her pride she managed to keep it under control. "There'll never be anyone who loves you more than I do."

"Monica." He groaned. "Stop, please. This isn't necessary."

"It is for me, so do me the courtesy of listening. Someday you're going to look back on your life and regret this moment."

"The only thing I regret is not moving sooner. Another twenty-four hours and I would have been out of here. You couldn't have waited one stinking day for this, could you?"

"No," she threw back at him. She didn't know when the tears

came, but she felt their moisture against her face and brushed them aside. "I'll haunt you . . . or rather, my love will. I swear that's what will happen. It doesn't matter if you travel to the other side of the world, I'll be there. It's my face you'll see when you look at another woman. And . . . and when you sleep, I'll be there each and every night. You won't be able to close your eyes without thinking of me, without knowing you walked away from the one woman in all this world who loves you."

"Damn it all to hell," Chet stormed, his hands knotted into tight fists. "Next you're going to tell me that you're going to sacrifice your life for me. Listen, Monica, I don't want you sitting here, believing that something's going to happen that will change my mind. It's over, understand? Over."

"Don't worry," she whispered and her shoulders quivered. "That's what I came to tell you. I won't be waiting for you, I can't, Chet. I've wasted too much of my life already."

"Good," he snapped. "That's just the way I want it."

Jody had dreaded the office Christmas party for days. She never had been one who enjoyed these types of social gatherings, and generally didn't stay beyond the first few minutes. Glen, however, thought the party the ideal time to announce their engagement to their peers.

He'd presented her with a lovely engagement ring, a solitaire diamond that was large enough to feel heavy and awkward on her finger. She'd removed Jeff's wedding ring years earlier, not because of any desire to put that part of her life behind her, but to satisfy her parents. Both were worried about her and although she'd hated it, she'd placed the simple gold band in her jewelry box to appease them.

She could tell from the sounds drifting from the reception area that the party was underway. There were enough goodies to feed a small Third World country. Everyone had contributed something. Jody was guilty of overdoing it herself, bringing a large homemade cheese roll and several dozen gingerbread cookies Timmy had helped her bake the night before.

Her mother was watching Timmy, and insisted Jody stay late and enjoy herself. Because she was with Glen, she was obligated to remain as long as her fiancé wanted.

Glen came looking for her, his smile gentle. "You ready?" he asked.

"Give me a moment to freshen up first, all right?"

"Sure," he said agreeably.

It seemed for a couple engaged to be married, neither of them revealed a high degree of enthusiasm. Glen looked tired. Jody knew he was working hard on a difficult case and put a lot of time and effort into his client's defense, but she strongly suspected his fatigue was something more than his workload.

The rest room was several doors down the hall. Jody walked past a number of offices and wondered how many other Christmas parties were going on in the building that night.

She'd just stepped into a cubicle in the ladies' room when she heard two women.

"You're sure he's engaged?" the first voice asked.

"Yes. Lily took a good deal of delight in relaying the details to me." The second woman sounded shaken and very close to tears.

Jody bit down on her lower lip. Lily was an attorney who worked with Glen. Was it possible the two were referring to Glen and her? She wondered what she should do, or if she should say something.

"Honestly, Maryann, what did you expect Glen to do? You told him in no uncertain terms that you weren't interested in marriage."

Maryann. This was the woman Glen had mentioned, the one he'd once loved. Jody squeezed her eyes closed and tried to remember the particulars of his and Maryann's romance. All she could recall was that Glen was convinced Maryann didn't love him. Breaking off the relationship had devastated him. It was this common ground of loss in which their own relationship had been rooted.

"I . . . I assumed we could live together," Maryann told her friend. "Couples do that these days, you know, test the waters to see if they're compatible. It seemed to be a reasonable thing to do in light of all the divorce cases I've handled over the years. Oh, damn," she said, "I hate it when I cry. Look what it's doing to my makeup."

"What are you going to do?"

"About what?"

Maryann's voice faded and Jody assumed that was because she was studying her reflection in the mirror.

"You aren't going to let him go ahead with the wedding, are you?"

"How can I stop him?" Maryann asked.

"Tell him the truth."

Maryann hesitated, and when she spoke Jody could hear her tears. "I don't even know what the truth is anymore."

"Tell him you're in love with him."

"It's too late for that. Oh, Shelly, honestly, you're too much of a romantic to realize love doesn't automatically fix everything."

"It does if you're both willing to work at it," Maryann's friend insisted.

Afraid of eavesdropping any longer, Jody walked out of the cubicle. It was then that the two women realized they weren't alone. Embarrassed, they both avoided looking in Jody's direction. Taking advantage of their surprise, Jody quietly slipped out of the rest room.

She returned to her office, walking past the merrymakers, needing some time alone to absorb what she'd learned. Sitting at her desk, she closed her eyes and tried to reason out what she should do.

The answer should have been far less complex than she was making it. Her sense of fairness said she needed to break off the engagement and explain what she'd heard to Glen. It was an ironic twist that in all the time she'd worked in the building she would meet Maryann now and overhear the conversation she had.

Yet there was a part of her that yearned to give her son the father he longed for, the man who would gently guide him through life. Timmy enjoyed Glen's company so very much. Her son had never been happier than the last few weeks when she'd been dating the attorney.

The real question was if Jody had it in her to grab hold of happiness, however limited, at the expense of another. Having placed the question in that frame, she knew instantly that she had no choice.

"I thought I saw you," Glen said, stepping into the small office. "What are you doing back here?"

Jody looked up from her desk and blinked, surprised to see him.

"What's wrong?" Glen asked. He was a gentle, sensitive man, Jody realized, and she was going to miss him dreadfully. But not nearly as much as Timmy would.

"Sit down," Jody said.

"Jody?" His eyes held hers as he sat.

She stared down at her hand and the beautiful diamond. Before she could find an excuse, she slipped the ring from her finger. "I should never have accepted this," she whispered.

"Why not?"

She held the ring out to Glen, but he didn't take it.

"We aren't in love," Jody said and her chest tightened with regret. "You're a special man and you deserve a woman who will love and treasure you with all her heart."

"You're that woman," Glen insisted.

"We both know that isn't true. If there was anything special about me, it was the fact that I have a son. Timmy was the real attraction. He represents the family you've always wanted. The son you long to have. I made a mistake too," she said, expelling her breath in a rush. "I hurried matters and all but proposed to you myself, long before either of us was ready for a committed relationship. I'm not exactly sure why I found it so urgent for us to marry so soon. Especially when I realized neither of us is anywhere near being ready."

"Let's not be hasty," Glen said, sounding very much like the attorney he was. "We can reason this out. There isn't anything that says we can't have a long engagement, get to know each other better. You're right, I am fond of Timmy, but don't discount what I feel toward you."

"There is a very good reason you shouldn't marry me," Jody whispered. "I'm deeply in love with another man."

"Jody, please, we've talked about this before. You don't need to worry about that. I'll never try to take Jeff's place in your life."

"And you," she continued undaunted, "are deeply in love with another woman." It wasn't until she said the words that she realized the depth of truth in them.

Glen didn't argue with her, and for that she was grateful. "I'd never be unfaithful to you," he assured her.

"But you're willing to do so with yourself."

Glen hesitated. "It's over, Jody, and has been for months. There isn't any hope of reviving the relationship. It's dead."

Jody smiled to herself and set the diamond ring on the desktop as she stood. "It may not be as dead as you think. I want you to wait here."

"Where are you going?"

"To find someone. I shouldn't be long."

Jody left him and hurried out the door. She wasn't entirely sure for which firm Maryann worked, but a quick inspection of the names on the outside of the doors on the floor helped. The receptionist directed her to Maryann's office.

"Hello," Jody said, letting herself inside. "I'm Jody Potter." She waited to see if the other woman recognized the name. "I was the one who overheard you speaking in the ladies' room a few minutes ago."

Maryann paled when she recognized Jody's name. "I had no idea you were there . . . we'd never met and . . ."

"Don't worry, I believe you. I'm here because I have an important question to ask you. Are you in love with Glen Richardson?"

The other woman folded her arms and looked out the window. "I don't mean to be rude, but this isn't any of your business. I understand you and Glen are engaged and—"

"It is my business now, don't you think?" Jody interrupted.

"I can imagine it was disconcerting for you to overhear my conversation with Shelly. It's just that . . . actually, I think it's best if I didn't say anything more." She drew in a steadying breath and then added graciously, "I want you to know that I wish you and Glen every happiness."

"Glen is a wonderful man."

"Yes, I know," Maryann whispered.

"It complicates matters considerably knowing how deeply he loves you," Jody said.

Maryann's head snapped up, her eyes wide with surprise. "I'm sure that's not true, not after the things that happened between us. I was such a fool. There's no hope, not anymore."

"Don't be so sure of that," Jody told her. "Glen's free."

"Free?"

"We're no longer engaged. He's waiting for you in my office now."

Jody had worked with attorneys for a number of years, but she rarely saw one speechless.

"Why . . . why are you doing this?"

Jody didn't feel particularly noble. "I've experienced that kind of love myself, and for a while was willing to take second best. Go to him, Maryann, and settle whatever it was that drove you two apart. But most of all, love him. He deserves to be happy and so do you."

Tears shone bright in the attorney's eyes. "Thank you," she whispered.

"Sure," Jody said, shrugging. "Anytime." She turned and walked out then, past the sounds of the Christmas party and into the cold, dark night the same way she had every evening since Jeff's death.

Alone.

Michelle Madison was alone and frightened, and desperately trying to disguise her fear. Leah had spent a good deal of the afternoon with her and the young woman's labor was progressing smoothly.

"How much longer?" Michelle asked, following an intense contraction. Her hands rested against her protruding stomach and she drew in a deep, calming breath.

"It shouldn't be much longer now," Leah assured her in gentle tones, although she was well aware it could be hours yet. She didn't want to discourage the young mother-to-be.

Michelle had come in earlier in the first stages of labor, before Leah had arrived for work. Because there was no one Michelle wanted to contact, she was alone. By the time Leah arrived for her shift, the labor had intensified and, frightened, Michelle had clung to Leah's hand, begging her to stay.

Since there weren't any other patients on the floor, Leah was able to linger at the young woman's bedside, guiding her step-by-step through the stages of labor and birth.

"I'm so pleased I'm having my baby with you," Michelle offered just before the next pain overtook her. She closed her eyes and drew in deep, even breaths while Leah softly encouraged her to relax and accept the pain.

"I was in the birthing class that visited the labor room when you were here."

Leah had thought the young woman looked vaguely familiar, but wasn't sure where she'd seen her.

"I don't expect you to remember me," Michelle continued. "Lots of people were asking you questions that day. Jo Ann Rossini claimed anyone who was lucky enough to have their babies on your shift should consider themselves blessed."

"As you might have guessed, Jo Ann's a longtime friend," Leah said, discounting the compliment. She wasn't a miracle worker and although she was gentle with the mothers, they were the ones who did the work. It was called labor for a reason.

"You said you don't have children yourself," Michelle murmured, her eyes closed as the lingering pain gradually faded.

There'd been a time when the careless comment would have felt like a body blow to Leah, but not now. A child nestled beneath her heart, nurtured by her body, one conceived in love.

"Not yet," Leah concurred. She carefully studied the fetal monitor, pleased that matters were progressing normally for Michelle.

"You want children, though?"

"Very much," Leah confirmed.

A smile, fragile and ever so slight, turned up the edges of Michelle's mouth. Leah guessed the girl was barely twenty, if that, but she didn't want to burden her with unnecessary questions.

Michelle massaged her belly and took in several calming breaths, bracing herself for the next pain. "I didn't expect to love this baby. I imagine that sounds odd to someone like you."

"Of course not," Leah said, wanting to reassure her.

"Lonny didn't want to have anything to do with me after he found out I was pregnant. I believed he loved me, and in his own way, I'm sure he did, but he wasn't ready for the responsibility of a wife and family."

"You don't sound bitter."

"I'm not. At first I was. Not until later did I realize Lonny was right. Getting married now would have been wrong for us both."

"You're very wise for your years." Leah greatly admired Michelle for looking past her pain and finding her peace. Women much older would have difficulty recognizing such deep truths.

"For a while I seriously considered getting an abortion. I never thought I was that kind of person. That's what my mother wanted and later when my dad found out, he did too."

"But you didn't."

"I'm pleased now that I decided to go through with the pregnancy. It hasn't been easy, especially toward the end when I looked like a blimp. My parents have had a difficult time dealing with me having this baby. They said they loved me, but if I wanted to do this, then I'd do it alone. That's why no one is here."

"You're a strong woman, Michelle."

"It was the right choice for me. What surprises me is how much I love this baby."

"You're going to be a good mother."

"I want to be the very best."

With this kind of attitude, Michelle had a chance, Leah decided. She stepped around to the end of the bed. "It's time we check you again." The last series of pains had gained in intensity and she suspected Michelle would soon be entering the third stage of labor.

Once the task was completed, Michelle relaxed. "Will you be in the delivery room with me?"

"I'm not sure," Leah said. "Normally I'd stay but I have a doctor's appointment this afternoon myself. Let's play this by ear and see how matters go. You're doing just great so I don't think there'll be any problem."

"Good," Michelle said faintly. "I want you to be there if you can. I need someone."

To have Michelle so alone at this important moment tore at Leah's heart. She longed to reassure her patient that she'd seen cases like hers often. "Your parents will come around soon enough," Leah said, gently patting her hand. "They're going to love this baby. They won't be able to help themselves."

"I think so too."

"Do you have any names picked out?"

Michelle shook her sweat-dampened head. "No, I didn't want to know if the baby was a girl or a boy. I thought I'd decide on a name later."

Another two hours passed before Michelle was ready for the delivery room. Leah went in with her, along with the anesthesiologist, Dr. Leon, and the gynecologist, Dr. Beecher. Leah had worked with the anesthesiologist on numerous occasions.

Michelle was a model patient and when the moment came for her baby to be born, she gave a shout of joy. "A girl, a girl." Leah weighed the squalling newborn, wrapped her in a warm blanket, and gently placed her in Michelle's arms.

"A girl," Michelle sobbed. "I'm so pleased I had a little girl. That was what I wanted, but I was so afraid to care."

"She's a beautiful baby," Leah said.

"Thank you. Thank you for your help."

After she carried the newborn into the nursery, Leah happened to glance up at the clock. She'd need to hurry if she was going to make it to Dr. Benoit's in time for her appointment. "I have to rush now, but I'll be by to see you in the morning," she told Michelle when she returned.

"Please don't forget," Michelle said.

"I won't," Leah promised. She started to leave, but Michelle grabbed hold of her hand. "I couldn't have done it without you. Thank you."

"I wasn't the one who worked so hard," Leah said, squeezing the young woman's hand. "Give yourself some credit."

Michelle beamed her a bright smile. "All right, I will." She closed her eyes and yawned. "I feel like I could sleep for a week."

" 'Bye for now." On her way out the door Leah realized Michelle was already asleep.

Leah felt wonderful. Her workday had been full and rewarding. She hurried into the parking lot and started her car, driving past the nativity scene on the hospital side yard. A sense of expectancy filled her. The way she felt, she didn't need Dr. Benoit to confirm what she already knew. There wasn't a doubt in her mind what he would tell her.

The housekeeper had instructions to place a bottle of fine champagne on ice, and there were two thick steaks in the refrigerator. This evening she and Andrew would celebrate. She'd call her parents and if possible wait until the following evening to let Andrew's mother know when they got together for Christmas Eve.

This would be the best Christmas ever, Leah was convinced of that.

Dr. Benoit was a kind older physician with a quick wit and a gentle heart. He'd been a comfort to her in those bleak years, reassuring and confident when Leah felt having a child was hopeless. It was only fitting that he be the one to tell her she was pregnant.

"Leah," he said, coming into the cubicle. His smile was warm and tender. "It's so good to see you again."

"You were right," she said, holding on to his hand with both of hers. "It's happened. Andrew and I are pregnant."

He said nothing, but then Leah gave him no opportunity.

"Kathy is thrilled for me." Kathy was the nurse who'd collected the urine sample from her.

"Let's sit down and talk," he said, directing her to the chair. "Leah, you don't know how deeply this pains me."

"Pains you?" she asked. "I'm going to have a baby. How could such wonderful news pain you?"

The doctor's eyes softened. He took her hand in his. "Leah, the test is negative."

"There must be some mistake," she said, leaping to her feet.

"I'd give anything to tell you otherwise."

"But I'm late and experienced all the symptoms," she argued. "It isn't possible for me not to be pregnant."

"The mind is very powerful. I don't believe science has a clue of its potential. When a woman wants a child as fervently as you do, she's sometimes able to convince her body she's pregnant. That's what I believe happened in your case."

It wasn't true. Leah refused to believe it, and yet she had no choice. Reaching for her purse, she walked toward the door.

"Are you all right?"

"Sure," she said, but she wasn't and she doubted that she ever would be again.

Chapter

★ ☆ ★

18

"*You're back early,*" Helen Chandler commented when Jody walked into the house after leaving the office party. She took off her coat and hung it in the hall closet.

"Jody, whatever is the matter?" her mother pressed. "You look as if you've been crying." Helen followed her into the kitchen where Jody poured herself a cup of coffee. She wasn't the least bit thirsty, but she needed something to hold on to while she steadied her nerves.

"Where's Timmy?" she asked, surprised not to find her son in front of the television screen, battling it out with alien warlords.

"In his room," Helen answered with a slight frown. "He's wrapping his gift for you. He wouldn't even show me what it is. Now tell me what's wrong. I can't remember seeing you like this in a good long while. You're as pale as a ghost."

"I broke off the engagement with Glen," Jody whispered, not wanting Timmy to hear. Not yet. She'd tell her son as soon as she'd composed herself and could do so without emotion. Her heart wasn't entangled with Glen's and yet she ached for all the might-have-beens.

"But why?" her mother asked, sinking into the chair.

"I don't love Glen."

"Love," her mother cried. "How could you *not* love someone like Glen? He's perfect for you and Timmy. Why, that man walks on water. You couldn't ask for a better husband."

"I'm not going to argue with you, Mom. Everything you say is true, but it was more than not loving him. I know what it's like to be deeply in love, but when it came right down to it, I realized I couldn't accept second best."

Her mother's shoulders sagged with defeat. "You might have grown to feel that way about him. Jody, for the love of heaven, you've got to let go of the past."

"There was one other minor complication with Glen," she said, holding the coffee mug tightly. "He's in love with someone else and I learned that she's still in love with him too."

Helen braced her elbows against the tabletop and hung her head. "And so you did the noble thing and stepped aside. Oh, Jody, what am I going to do with you?"

Jody laughed and impulsively squeezed her mother's arm. "This entire experience has been a valuable lesson to me. In my heart, I know I did the right thing. I just didn't expect it to hurt so much."

"Life's lessons aren't cheap."

Jody nodded. "Ever since Jeff disappeared, I've clung to the misty memories of our years together. The circumstances surrounding his death and all that followed caused me to build a cocoon around Timmy and me. I was so terribly frightened of being hurt again. Jeff was a good husband and I loved him more than I thought it was possible to love another human, but I've built up those years in my mind into a picture of paradise."

Her mother's head came up. "I've waited a good long while for you to realize this. It sounds like you've done some heavy-duty thinking these last few weeks."

"I have," Jody admitted, and a good deal of it had been enlightening. "More than anything I realize I've clung to a half-filled glass, afraid to let go of that small bit of happiness I'd found and reach for the quart jar that was sitting right in front of me."

Helen's frown deepened. "I'm afraid you've lost me with all this talk of glasses and quart jars. I thought we were talking about you and Jeff."

"I'm ready to get back to my life now," Jody said pensively, "ready to reach out in faith and trust God for Timmy's and my future. I'm going to squeeze every bit of joy I can out of what's left of my life. For the first time since Jeff's death I feel like I have one.

"I don't want to spend the rest of it alone, either. There's a man for me out there—someone who'll be a good father to Timmy, and a good husband for me. A man who'll be a friend, a partner, and a lover."

Helen bit into her lower lip. "I've waited years for you to tell me this. I don't know what happened to open your eyes to the truth, but I'm eternally grateful." She stood and hugged Jody. "I'll leave you to talk to Timmy now."

"Thanks, Mom."

"Any time," her mother said. "I love watching Timmy. He's a delight."

"For that, yes," Jody said with tears in her eyes. "But for everything else too, for being there when I needed you, for listening to me, and most of all for standing with me, loving me, giving me the emotional support I needed. You're the best mom in the world."

"You were like this as a little girl," her mother said with a smile, "buttering me up before Christmas."

Jody laughed and the two hugged.

"Mom," Timmy said, standing in the doorway. "Why are you and Grandma crying?"

They both started laughing then, which was sure to confuse him all the more.

"Where's Glen?" Timmy wanted to know next.

"I'll see you tomorrow," Helen said, reaching for her coat and purse.

Timmy watched his grandmother leave. "What's going on around here?"

Jody smiled and patted the top of his head. "I need to talk to you."

"Did I do something wrong?" His eyes grew round with concern, or perhaps guilt, Jody didn't know which.

"No," she assured him, placing her hand on his shoulder and bringing him close to her side. "This isn't about anything you did, I need to tell you something important about Glen and me."

"Mom," Timmy muttered dejectedly, leaning against the doorway in the bathroom as if his weight were too heavy to support, "are you sure we have to go to church? It isn't even Sunday."

"We've been through this before," Jody said, adding the finishing touches to her makeup. "It's Christmas Eve. After church we'll go to Grandma's house and open our gifts with her."

"Will she have hot chocolate and goodies like she did last year?"

"I'm sure she will. Is the car loaded?" Jody asked.

"I did that a long time ago. I wish you'd hurry."

"We have plenty of time." She knew what Timmy really wanted was for the minutes to go by fast so he could get to the gift-opening part of the evening. The Christmas Eve church service was just unnecessary nonsense as far as he was concerned.

"I'll only take a little bit longer," Jody promised. "Don't let me forget the cheese roll and the crackers. They're in the refrigerator."

"Ah . . ."

There was something in Timmy's voice that clued her in to the fact that there was a problem with the cheese roll.

"What?" she said, lowering the mascara brush and turning her head away from the mirror to study her son.

"About the cheese roll."

"What about it?" Jody returned the brush to the holder and tightened the top. Setting the cosmetic bag aside, she faced her son.

"I had a little party with my friends the day Grandma was watching me."

"Yes?" Jody prompted.

"Everyone had something yummy to bring and you took almost all the gingerbread cookies and besides I like the cheese roll better than cookies anyway."

"In other words there isn't any left."

Timmy nodded and hung his head. "I have the feeling this isn't going to be a very good Christmas anyway."

"Because of Glen?"

Timmy lifted one shoulder halfheartedly. "I understand why you aren't going to marry him and everything. But I was kinda thinking maybe he wouldn't mind coming by and seeing me every once in a while."

"We'll wait until after Christmas and ask, okay?" The real attraction for Glen had always been Timmy and she sincerely hoped the attorney would maintain contact with her son.

The doorbell chimed.

"Who could that be on Christmas Eve?" Jody wondered out loud.

"I'll see," Timmy said, running toward the front door.

"Timmy," Jody called out after him. "Let me answer that."

She was too late. Her son enthusiastically threw open the door as if he expected Santa Claus to be on the other side.

"Hi," he was saying cheerfully by the time Jody reached the door.

"Hello," Jody said automatically, then gasped as she recognized the man standing on the other side of the screen door. In that moment, she swore her heart stopped dead. She flattened her palm over it and the room started to sway. Staggering two steps, she reached for the door to keep herself from collapsing.

"Mom, what's wrong?"

"Timmy," she said on the tail end of a strangled sob, pulling her son protectively toward her. "This is your father."

*　　　*　　　*

Leah had shed so many tears over the last seven years that she discovered that her fountain was dry. A numb feeling attached itself to her as she walked toward her car. She was barren. There was no child to swell and stretch her womb. There never would be. And yet . . . . and yet she couldn't make her heart believe what surely was the truth.

The joy she'd felt these last two weeks, believing she was pregnant, was gone. All she could do was live day by day with the emptiness in her heart.

Now she must tell Andrew.

Naturally they'd both pretend it didn't matter, there was nothing else to do. They'd reassure each other and go on, one day into the next, through Christmas, pretending. All the family would be celebrating and she'd have no choice but to make believe all was well with her.

She drove home in a daze, parked her car in the driveway, and walked like a zombie into her house. She moved without direction or will, walking around the perfection of her home, stopping in front of their designer Christmas tree.

Her gaze rested on the beautifully wrapped gifts. Her one thought was to locate the Baby's First Christmas ornament she'd purchased for Andrew, remove it before he unwrapped it on Christmas morning.

Her search became frantic as she sorted through the presents. They'd both suffered enough.

Suddenly she was blinded by tears and couldn't locate the gift, couldn't recall which package contained the ornament. She tossed one gaily wrapped present after another aside, her chest heaving with sobs.

Collecting herself, her hands shaking almost uncontrollably, she methodically sorted the packages into two piles. Hers and Andrew's. Then one by one she tore open his presents until she'd located the silver ornament.

Taking it with her, she walked into the kitchen and threw it in the garbage. The champagne was on ice. She paused, picked it up, and with drops of water leaving a glistening trail across the floor, she carried that to the garbage as well.

The garage door sounded in the distance, signaling Andrew's return. His steps sounded eager as he approached the door leading to the house.

Leah was frozen with immobility.

Andrew walked into the kitchen and stopped when he saw her.

She didn't need to say a word. He came to her and wrapped her in his arms.

*   *   *

Leah woke the following morning, her throat dry and chest heavy. Her eyes stung. Andrew rolled over and tucked his arm over her side, scooting closer, cuddling her spoon fashion.

"Don't go to work today," he suggested. "I'll stay home with you."

"It's Christmas Eve. The hospital is already short-staffed."

"For once, think about yourself instead of that damned hospital."

The short fuse on his temper was the first indication he'd given her of his own bitter disappointment. In some ways having him release his frustration freed Leah.

"I'm all right now," she whispered.

"Call in sick," he pleaded.

"I need to work. It'll help." As if there was anything capable of easing this constant ache. It continued day after day, dull and constant, a steady, ever-present reminder that she was less of a wife, less of a woman.

Despite Andrew's protests, she dressed in her uniform, and even managed to down a cup of coffee before she left the house. Andrew walked her out to her car, looking weary and burdened. His hands were buried in his pockets.

"I'll meet you back at the house at four," he said. "I told mother we'd be at her place around four-thirty."

She raised questioning eyes to her husband.

"We're spending the evening with her, remember?"

"Of course." She'd momentarily forgotten.

"Do you want to cancel?" Andrew asked, tenderly brushing the hair from her forehead.

"No, I wouldn't want to disappoint her."

Andrew nodded and hugged Leah. They clung to each other for a moment extra and then reluctantly separated.

Leah drove to the hospital and for reasons she didn't understand, she walked over to the side yard where the faded nativity scene was displayed.

The manger was empty. As empty as her heart. As empty as her arms. She hung her head and closed her eyes. If this was a battle, she was surrendering. A prayer sailed straight from her heart.

"I don't know why you don't want me to have a child," she whispered, "but I can't hold on to this pain any longer. It hurts too damn much. I can't trust even myself." She'd given up trusting God years earlier, preferring to rely upon herself. Now that foundation had crumbled and she was left standing on the sharp rocks of her self-inflicted pain. In essence she was holding up a white flag to God, accepting whatever it was he had planned for her life. She was through fighting, through insisting she knew best, through being miserable.

Her prayer complete, she lifted her head. As she looked upward her gaze continued toward the faded yellow angel that adorned the rickety stable. Leah gasped as a breathless emotion clenched at her heart.

The angel was magnificent, golden and bright, her wings spanned out in elaborate display. She was so bright that Leah couldn't continue to look directly at her. She blinked, thinking this was some type of optical illusion. The sun bouncing off a mirror, or some such phenomenon. But when she opened her eyes, the angel was still there.

Glancing around, she wanted to point out this miracle to whomever she could find.

"Look," she cried out, spying an older woman walking along the sidewalk. Her head was bent against the wind. "It's an angel," Leah cried, attracting the other woman's attention.

The woman stopped and looked toward the nativity scene where Leah was standing.

"That angel's been there for years. Hospital ought to do something about replacing that old set. It's about to fall over."

"This is a real angel," Leah insisted, looking back, but when she did she realized God's messenger had vanished. Leah stared good and hard, wondering if God was attempting to tell her something. If so, the meaning was directed at her alone.

"If she's real, then heaven's in sorrier shape than I realized," the woman said with a deep-throated chuckle.

Leah's heart felt as light as an angel's feather as she walked into the hospital. Since she was a few minutes early, she stopped in the nursery to take a look at the baby girl Michelle had delivered the day before.

The infant, wrapped in a soft pink blanket, was sound asleep. A small red Christmas bow was taped to the side of her crib. Leah rarely visited the nursery. It had been a painful experience in the past, longing for a child so hopelessly herself, but she experienced none of the sharp edges of regret this time. It was as if the burden on her soul had been lifted.

"So here you are," Bonnie said when Leah stepped out of the nursery. "Your husband phoned, looking for you. He sounded anxious."

"Andrew?" He rarely contacted her at the hospital.

"I assumed you only had one husband," Bonnie teased. "You might want to call him yourself. From the sounds of it he's pacing the floor, waiting to hear from you."

Leah headed for the phone, but after four rings the answering machine kicked in. If it was that important, Andrew would call again soon.

He didn't. No more than ten minutes later, Leah was reading over the nurse's report at their station when Andrew came rushing down the corridor.

"Leah," he called breathlessly. He wrapped his arms around her waist and lifted her off the ground. His eyes were bright and his voice sounded as if he were about to burst into peals of laughter.

"What is it?" she pleaded.

He released her and his hands framed her face. "I love you, Leah, never more than I do this moment."

She stared up at him, wondering at his craziness.

"You were right about us having a child. That feeling you claimed you had. It's happening, sweetheart, just the way you said it would."

"But Dr. Benoit said—"

"Mrs. Burchell phoned not more than two minutes after you left the house."

The name was vaguely familiar to Leah, but she couldn't remember from where.

"The lady from New Life Adoption Agency," he filled in. "They have a child for us. She'll be ready to leave the hospital first thing tomorrow morning. The mother's already signed the adoption papers."

"But we withdrew our names," Leah cried, covering her mouth, unwilling to believe it was true.

"I asked that she reactivate our file weeks ago. We have a baby, Leah. A precious baby girl."

Monica was right, Chet realized. She'd announced her decision to torment him and by God she'd done it. He'd close his eyes and he'd be damned if she wasn't there like some ghost, pestering him until he ended up spending half the night dulling his mind with late-night television rather than attempt sleeping. The minute he tried, Monica was there, all sweet and soft, wrapping the tendrils of her love around his heart, reminding him of all he'd rejected.

He'd been trying to get hold of a moving company for the better part of the afternoon. Every one he called insisted on knowing his destination. That was the problem. They didn't have rates for "any place that wasn't Seattle."

The bartender ambled over to where Chet was sitting. He was new, Chet noted, young and wet behind the ears. He'd introduced himself as Billy. Appropriate enough since he looked more like a kid than an adult. If Chet were the one serving up the liquor he'd have carded the youth.

"You want another cup of coffee?" Billy asked.

"Please." Chet had given up on booze. The desired effect caused too many problems. True, he could drown his sorrows, as the saying went, but there was a heavy price to pay. Hangovers had never appealed to him.

"What do you think of the new big-screen television?" Billy asked. "The boss had it brought in this morning."

"Nice," Chet said, without looking. He wasn't interested in making conversation. He wasn't entirely sure why he'd stopped in at the Blue Goose. It was a damn sight better than hanging around his place, he decided. Everything he'd managed to accumulate in the last thirty-odd years was packed and ready to go. He just didn't know where he was headed yet.

The bar was deserted, Chet noticed, which was unusual this time of night. A couple was off in a dark corner and the two only had eyes for each other. Hands too, apparently. Other than the lovebirds and Billy, Chet was the only other customer. "Where is everyone?" he asked.

"Home, I guess. It's Christmas Eve."

"It is?" He'd lost track of the days. In the back of his mind he knew Christmas was close, but it was a day like any other as far as he was concerned.

"I don't expect we'll get much of a crowd this evening. Places like this generally don't over the Christmas holidays," Billy commented as if this were something he'd garnered in his vast experience tending bar.

"Guess not," Chet mumbled, unwilling to be drawn into a conversation, but he could tell from the way the kid was hanging around that he wasn't going to have much of a choice.

"You'd think Lou would close up shop," Billy said next.

Chet sipped from his coffee. It was dark, thick, and potent enough to satisfy a Cajun.

"Apparently you don't know Lou," Chet commented.

"Not very well," Billy agreed.

Thinking he might divert the kid's attention, Chet swiveled around in his chair and concentrated on the television. The national evening news was on, forecasting gloom and doom. Chet had heard enough of that.

"Mind if I change the channel?" he asked.

"Be my guest," Billy said, handing him the controller.

Chet worked his way through the stations. Nothing appealed to him, not even a rerun of a play-off football game telecast earlier that week.

"Hey, go back, would you?" Billy asked. "I have a friend who was picked up by the pros. He's a defensive lineman for the Redskins."

Disgusted, Chet handed the remote control back to the bartender. So much for that idea. Oblivious to Chet's ugly mood, Billy punched the controller until he found the play-off game.

The kid focused his attention on the screen, which suited Chet just fine as long as he left him alone.

Before he realized it, Chet had turned around on his bar stool and was watching the game himself. So this was what his life had boiled down to—sitting in some bar on Christmas Eve, talking to a kid he didn't know and didn't want to know and watching reruns of old football games on television.

At halftime Billy disappeared into the back storeroom. Chet cradled the coffee mug in his hands and studied the television screen. The commentator was the well-known former coach of the Los Angeles Raiders, John Madden.

"You should be ashamed of yourself, Chet Costello," the TV commentator said.

Chet's head snapped up. He was losing it. The television was actually talking to him.

"Yes, I'm talking to you," John Madden said again. "You're the biggest fool I've ever seen."

By that time Chet was on his feet. He stared down at his drink, thinking the kid had played a cruel joke on him and laced it with some mind-bending drug.

"Quit looking at your drink," the former coach told him. "It's only coffee."

Other men claimed to see pink elephants, but not Chet. Oh, no, that would have been too easy. He had to have some voice come out of a television to chastise him.

"You're in love with Monica Fischer, and she's in love with you. So what's the problem? You think you're being noble, don't you? Wrong. You're a fool."

Chet had had enough. He didn't need this. Slamming his cup down on the bar, he started out the door.

"Go ahead and run," the voice said, sounding so close he swore he could feel the breath against the back of his neck. "It's what you've been doing for most of your life."

"Shut up," Chet shouted.

The couple in the back of the room glared over at him, and Billy, who was hauling a box of pretzels to the front, stopped in his tracks.

"Something wrong?" the kid asked.

Chet shook his head and slammed out of the bar. "Damn," he muttered, running his hand down his face. It was worse than he imagined. Monica had decided ruining his sleep wasn't bad enough, now she'd taken on his waking hours as well.

He was putting an end to that right now. With purpose directing his steps, he walked to the parking garage and drove to her house.

The streets were full of parked cars. The Blue Goose might be less than busy, but Lloyd Fischer's church was doing a bumper business. Light spilled out of the church, and the parsonage was dark, all but one small light in the front of the house. Music filled the night, traditional Christmas carols played on an old-time pipe organ.

Chet found a place to park on the street, half a block down from the church. Several people were walking toward the building. There was a family with two small children in tow, and an older couple, holding hands, smiling up at each other.

Chet stayed where he was, hidden in the shadows. One thing he knew, he wasn't walking into that church. He was deciding what he was going to do when he spied Monica coming out of the parsonage. The porch light went on as the light in the living room was extinguished. Her silhouette was framed in the warm glow of the single bulb on the porch.

She seemed to be in something of a hurry, Chet noted. Rushing across the street, he met up with her on the sidewalk.

She stopped when she saw him. Surprise worked its way across her features, starting with her eyes and then her mouth. She opened it as if to say something, then closed it again. She hugged sheet music against her breast and seemed to be waiting.

Chet didn't know what he intended to say. It was too damn hard not to bring her directly into his arms, hold her against him, and breathe in her softness.

"Whatever you've done has got to stop," he said between clenched teeth.

"Done?" she echoed, and blinked as if she didn't understand what he was saying.

"Leave me alone," he ordered.

She nodded once and waited, apparently for an explanation.

"I can't eat or sleep, and now I'm hearing voices as well."

"Voices?" The edges of her mouth quivered with amusement. "And what did these voices say?"

"That I was a fool for walking away from you." Chet rammed his fingers into his hair.

Monica smiled boldly at that and Chet swore he'd never seen a woman more beautiful. He shouldn't have come, and now that he was here, God help him, he didn't know how he was ever going to leave.

"I wish I could claim credit for that, but I can't," she said softly. "Dad told me he suspected you were drinking heavily. My guess is that it was the liquor talking."

"Not this time," he argued. "I haven't had a drop all day."

"I can't help you, Chet," she said sadly and raised her fingers as if to touch his face. He meant to jerk away, but found he couldn't. As it never failed to do, her touch rippled through him like an electrical current. Her softness had branded his life and his heart. There was no escape. He could run to the far ends of the world and every breath he drew, every beat of his heart would be for her.

Capturing her wrist, he roughly drew her palm to his mouth where he planted a series of tender kisses.

"Dear God, Monica," he said, hauling her into his arms. He buried his face in the delicate curve of her neck and drew in several deep, uneven breaths. "I can't make myself leave you. I tried. God knows I tried."

The sheet music she'd been holding fell to the sidewalk as she clung to him. He felt her trembling, her tears moistening his face and her breath coming in soft gasps that fanned his throat.

He held her against him, his chin resting on the crown of her head. His eyes were tightly closed. "We'll get married, just the way you want, although I can't help but feel you're getting the bum end of this deal."

Chapter

★ ☆ ★

19

"You're my real-life dad?" Timmy asked, staring up at Jeff with wide, disbelieving eyes.

"Yes, son, I'm your father." Although Jeff answered Timmy, his gaze was leveled on Jody, his look expectant and filled with nervous anticipation.

Her pulse had yet to right itself, and the dizziness from the frantic beat of her heart continued. He was terribly thin, she noticed. His cheeks were hollow and his eyes seemed to sink back into his head. This was a man she didn't know and barely recognized as the one she'd loved.

Jeff seemed greedy for the sight of Timmy and her, staring at the two of them as if he couldn't quite believe this moment was real.

Timmy opened the screen door and Jeff walked inside the house, pausing in front of Jody.

Her eyes begged him to convince her this was happening and that he was as real as he seemed. She'd been under a good deal of stress and she feared that this was all a figment of her imagination. Some dream she'd wake from with a start. When Jeff had first disappeared she'd repeatedly dreamed of a moment like this when they'd be reunited. Then she'd wake with a heavy heart and the loneliness would close in and swallow her.

Her hand trembled as she worked up the necessary courage to touch him. She laid her fingers against his forearm. He felt solid and real. Warm and alive.

Alive. Jeff was alive.

"Where were you?" she asked in a sobbing breath, pressing her hands to her throat. "Why did you leave us? Why?" The questions crowded on top of each other, damming her mind and her tongue. The only one to escape was the least important.

"Do you mind if I sit down?" he asked, and Jody realized how terribly shaky he was. "I'm a bit weak yet," Jeff explained.

It was all Jody could do to nod.

Timmy took Jeff by the hand and led him to the sofa. "You don't look like my dad," he commented, carefully studying his father. "You're too old."

"I feel like I'm about a hundred," Jeff said, examining his son. He cupped Timmy's face and his eyes filled with tears. "Not a day passed that I didn't think about and pray for you. I carried the picture of you with me through the months. I swear it was what kept me alive. I could endure anything as long as I remembered my wife and my son."

"Where were you?" Timmy asked, sinking onto the cushion next to his father.

Trembling almost uncontrollably, Jody sat in the chair across from them both, her legs too numb to continue to support her.

"I was in a Russian prison," Jeff explained. "It's a miracle I was released."

"You were in Russia?" Jody repeated in a breathless whisper.

"I'd gone to Germany on business and on a fluke decided to visit East Berlin. I was curious about the other side of the wall, but doubted that I'd be able to make it through the border with an American passport. It was surprisingly easy to obtain fake identification."

"You went through all that trouble because you were curious about East Berlin?" Jody found the entire story unbelievable and a fermenting kind of anger took hold of her. He'd risked everything for some crazy need to look at life on the other side of the wall?

"I was young and stupid, so incredibly stupid," Jeff said, the regret weighing down his voice. "My German was passable, and all I intended to do was wander into a few shops and get a look around. I was heading back to the border when I stumbled upon two soldiers beating a teenager. They would have killed him. I couldn't stand by and do nothing and so I intervened. That proved to be a costly mistake."

Jody's anger dissipated. He'd paid a terrible price for his curiosity, and consequently so had she and Timmy.

"I was taken in for questioning and soon arrested," Jeff continued.

"Why didn't you contact the embassy?" Jody demanded. He could have saved them both this agony.

"I wasn't allowed. And when they discovered I was an American with a false passport my fate was sealed. I was a spy, and tried as one. I wasn't able to talk to an attorney, and the trial, such as it was, lasted all of two minutes. Before I fully understood what was happening to me, I was shipped off to a prison camp in Russia."

"Oh, dear God." Jody covered her mouth with both hands.

"I've been held there ever since."

"But how did you escape?"

"I didn't," Jeff explained. "I was freed. They dropped me off on a German street as if nothing had happened. The last two weeks I've been hospitalized and debriefed. From what I've been able to grasp this all has something to do with the breakup of the Soviet Union. There was a British man with an experience similar to mine who was released about the same time."

"Why wasn't I contacted right away?" Jody demanded.

"In the beginning I was too ill. Apparently the authorities communicated with my mother first. I learned that you'd divorced me."

"I had to do that for financial reasons," Jody told him. "It wasn't what I wanted."

A weak smile lit up his face.

"If you were well enough to travel, surely you could have made a phone call?" Jody wasn't satisfied, not yet.

"All I knew was that the woman I'd loved had divorced me. I talked to my mother only once and she insisted I get home right away because you were about to marry another man."

"Not anymore," Timmy told him. "They're only friends."

Once again, Jeff looked greatly relieved. "The doctors wanted to keep me longer, but I couldn't wait another minute. I had to reach you and talk to you face-to-face before it was too late.

"If getting out of Russia was miraculous, then finding an empty seat on a transatlantic flight was an even greater phenomenon. I was flying standby when some lady came running off the plane, claiming she was hearing voices over the headset that told her she shouldn't be on this flight. The funny thing was, she insisted it was Johnny Carson, speaking directly to her. Whatever her reason, I got her seat."

"But you were dead. My father took your dental records with him to Germany and your remains were positively identified. We buried you. This isn't possible, it just isn't possible."

"It wasn't me, Jody. I don't know why your father would do such a thing."

"Oh, Daddy," Jody whispered and briefly closed her eyes. "It was three years after you'd disappeared and I refused to give up hope. My life was in limbo. For financial reasons I'd had to divorce you. Your mother didn't understand and I felt so incredibly guilty. Dad must have assumed that if we buried a body, I'd be able to put the past behind me and get on with my life."

"Your father has a lot of explaining to do," Jeff said without rancor.

"He died a little more than a year ago. Unexpectedly. I'd like to believe that if he'd known he only had a short time to live, he'd have told me the truth."

"I believe he would."

Jeff was more generous than he need be.

"Your mother was telling me the truth," Jody whispered, remembering the calls she'd received from Gloria Potter.

"I don't blame you for not believing her. I was terribly ill and hadn't spoken to her myself. I want you to know that I love you, Jody. I've always loved you and Timmy. It was the memory of the two of you that got me through this hellish nightmare. I also realize a lot of things can change in eight years, and I won't stand in the way of your happiness. All I ask is that you allow me to have contact with my son."

"Oh, Jeff."

"Mom and Glen aren't engaged anymore," Timmy explained excitedly. "He was in love with someone else and Mom's still in love with you."

Jeff's eyes slowly sought out hers as if he were afraid to trust what he was hearing. "Is that true?"

She nodded. "I never stopped, not for an instant. I couldn't breathe and not love you."

Jeff held out his arms to her, Jody flew off the chair and inside a heartbeat was at his side. Jeff wrapped both Timmy and her in his embrace.

Tears rained down Jody's cheeks as she spread soft kisses over Jeff's face. The three of them were laughing and crying all at once.

"God answered my letter," Timmy said excitedly. "He gave me back my very own dad."

"A baby girl," Leah repeated, afraid there'd been some misunderstanding. "We should have been contacted by the adoption agency before now."

"Apparently the mother only made her decision yesterday afternoon. The crazy part is our daughter's right here in this very hospital. She's here, Leah. Here. Mrs. Burchell said she was born yesterday afternoon at Providence Hospital."

According to the records Leah had been reading when Andrew arrived, there'd only been one girl delivered on December twenty-third and that had been the birth she'd assisted. Michelle Madison's baby.

"Michelle," she whispered, closing her eyes. The frightened young woman who was so alone and had clung to Leah. The one Leah had spent her entire shift coaching through labor and birth.

"Andrew," she said, laughing and crying both at the same time. She took her husband by the hand. "Come, I'd like to introduce you to our daughter." Trembling, she led her husband toward the nursery. She had him remove his jacket and put on a sterile blue gown and set him in the rocking chair. Then with her heart so full it felt as though it would burst wide open, she gently lifted the sleeping infant from her crib and tenderly placed her in Andrew's arms.

"She's so tiny," her husband whispered, looking down on the plump pink face of their daughter.

"At eight pounds six ounces, her birth mother didn't think so," Leah said, smiling through her tears. "You two get acquainted and I'll be right back."

A look of panic came over Andrew. "Where are you going?"

"To talk to someone very special."

"What if she cries?"

"One of the nurses will help you, but don't look so worried. Everything will be all right." Including the rest of Leah's life.

Michelle was sitting up in bed when Leah came into the room. When she saw it was Leah, the young woman smiled and held out her hand, which Leah gripped. "Have you heard from the adoption agency yet?" Michelle asked.

Leah nodded. "My husband just told me." Now that she was here, Leah's heart was so full that she didn't know if it was possible to find the words to thank Michelle.

"When I decided against the abortion, I didn't know what I was going to do," Michelle started. "A friend suggested adoption and so I contacted New Life Adoption Agency. Their counselors were great, they didn't pressure me one way or the other. I met with them several times and they listened. You see, I assumed that in order to give up my baby, I had to keep myself from loving her, and I couldn't seem to make myself do that. In the beginning when Lonny left me, all the baby represented to me was heartache, and later as she started to grow and move, I discovered how very attached I was getting. I couldn't help being curious about adoptive parents, though, and for the first time, just a few weeks ago, I read over several profiles. Your letter stood out in my mind."

"Why?" Leah wanted to know. The letter had been written years earlier, and she couldn't remember any of what she'd said.

"You wrote about being a delivery-room nurse and how you felt about helping young women through labor and birth. It seemed to me you must be someone very special. Then by some kind of fluke the birthing class I was attending toured Providence Hospital and we met you. Naturally I didn't know your last name, but I remembered what you'd written. When I asked Jo Ann about you she told me you didn't have any children yourself and I figured you must be the Leah whose letter I'd read."

"That was why you chose to have your baby here at Providence Hospital?" Leah asked.

Michelle nodded. "It was pure chance that you could be with me. I still hadn't decided if I could give my baby up for adoption. Then yesterday after she was born, you said something that helped me make up my mind."

"I said something to help you decide?" Leah was incredulous.

Michelle nodded. "You told me I would be a good mother to my baby. I'm not giving her up because I don't love her. It's because I love her so very much that I can.

"Mrs. Burchell explained that you'd had one birth mother change her mind at the last minute. You needn't worry, that won't happen this time. I feel very strongly that God led me to you and your husband and you're exactly the right couple for my baby."

"How can I thank you?" Leah whispered through her tears.

"By loving her, guiding her through the years for me. When she's older and has questions about me, tell her how God brought the two of us together, tell her that he handpicked her family for me."

"I will," Leah promised, rubbing the moisture from her cheek.

The two women hugged and after she'd dried her eyes Leah returned to the nursery. Andrew was gently rocking back and forth staring down at the face of his newborn daughter. One tiny fist was clenched around his index finger. The newborn was holding on to her daddy's hand.

"It looks like the two of you are getting along nicely," Leah commented.

"I still can't believe she's really our daughter," Andrew said.

"I don't have a single doubt she belongs to us," Leah assured him.

"Have you decided on a name?"

"Yes," Leah said, her response automatic. "Angel." Some day she'd tell her husband and her daughter about seeing the special Christmas angel, but not now. The angel had been his sign to her, his confirmation. She would carry that very special gift with her through the years.

"Angel?" Andrew repeated slowly, glancing up. "But I thought you had three names already chosen and I don't recall any of them being Angel."

"It seems fitting to me. Do you object?"

"Angel Lundberg," he said again, as if testing it on his tongue. "It feels right. Angel Hannah Lundberg."

"My turn to hold her," Leah said.

Andrew stood and gently placed the sleeping baby in Leah's arms. Angel arched her back and stretched, yawning before she nestled comfortably in Leah's arms, as if this were exactly where she was supposed to be. With that Angel Lundberg immediately returned to sleep.

"You're willing to marry me?" Monica asked, unsure if she should trust what Chet was saying. "But why now?"

"Because I know you're right. I'll regret letting you go the rest of my life. I love you, Monica. I heard a voice telling me what a fool I was and if it wasn't the booze speaking, then . . . hell, I didn't think anyone up there cared about me."

"I love you, Chet Costello. I can't explain that voice, but whoever or whatever it was, I'm thanking God."

He smiled and gently kissed her. "Next thing I know we'll have a couple of kids and I'll be a regular churchgoer."

That sounded like heaven to Monica. "Would you kindly shut up and kiss me again?"

He pulled her to him as if she were the most precious thing he would ever touch, as if he cherished every moment spent with her.

Monica inched her mouth from his and stared up into his face. His eyes met hers and it seemed they were filled with a thousand regrets.

"I love you so much," she whispered.

"You must."

"Stop." She pressed her finger over his lips. "I don't pretend to know everything there is about the Bible and God, but I do know that he said he would forgive us when we ask. If it's peace of mind you're seeking, it's available."

"In church."

"No." She pressed her hand over his heart. "You won't find what you're seeking in any building."

"I killed a man," Chet reminded her. "He murdered my partner and attempted to kill me. That's a little more serious than jaywalking."

"Do you think you're the only one who's ever done something he wishes he hadn't? You say this man you murdered attempted to kill you first. What you don't seem to realize is that in some ways he succeeded. He's reached out from the grave and gotten a stranglehold on your heart and your life." Monica saw Chet as a man whose life had been shredded to ribbons with the ax of revenge and regret. "Your time of hate is over. You can stop punishing yourself now."

"My time of love is about to begin."

"Oh, yes," she said, winding her fingers into the hair at the base of his neck. "Now, what was it you were saying about the two of us getting married?"

"Soon, Monica, I'm not going to be able to wait for you much longer."

She could feel the heat coming into her cheeks. "I'm not going to be able to wait for you much longer either. I don't think there's ever been a woman more eager to give up her virginity than I am."

They kissed and the heat of their love and need was like a spontaneous combustion. Monica didn't know what would have happened if her father hadn't happened upon them just then.

It was the sound of Lloyd clearing his throat that broke them apart. "Dad," Monica said breathlessly. "Oh, Dad, you'll never guess what—"

"Reverend Fischer," Chet said, taking charge. He looped his arm around Monica's waist and held out his free hand to her father to shake.

"I take it congratulations are in order?" the reverend asked.

Chet nodded. "If you don't object, I'd like to marry your daughter."

"Object," her father said, laughing. He slapped Chet across the back. "I'm thrilled for you both. You don't mind if I announce it at this evening's service, do you?"

Chet looked at Monica, then back at her father. "I'd be more than pleased."

Together the three of them walked toward the church where the music swelled and teased the golden silence of the night with its lyrical melody.

Shirley, Goodness, and Mercy stood in the choir loft looking down on the congregation that had crowded into the church for Christmas Eve services.

"You should all be pleased with your efforts," Gabriel announced from behind them in a voice as light as yesterday's dreams.

The three prayer ambassadors whirled around. Gabriel hadn't meant to surprise them, but he was well pleased with their accomplishments. His trips to earth were few and far between, but this was a special night, one created for exceptions.

"Timmy has his father for Christmas," Shirley said proudly, "thanks to a bit of manipulation with the airlines and a certain passenger."

"We need to talk about that," Gabriel said sternly. Shirley was new to prayer assignments, and had much to learn. He noticed she'd picked up a number of bad habits from her friends.

"What's going to happen to Jeff and his family?"

The future could be read by only a chosen few. Gabriel was pleased to offer a view to his young charges. "Jeff and Jody will go on to have another child, but not for two years. They'll have a little girl. As you can imagine they have a fair amount of readjusting to do first."

"What about Timmy?" Shirley pressed. "He seems to be a very special young boy."

"He is. Timmy Potter will grow up to become a top-notch pitcher with his goals set on the major leagues. He has a strong faith that will sustain him all his life."

"What about Monica and Chet?" Goodness wanted to know next, her eyes eager for a look into the future.

Gabriel was tempted to comment about this last bit of trouble Goodness had gotten herself into with the television screen. He decided against it, however. Goodness's methods had been unorthodox, but had worked wonderfully well. Chet had gone directly from the Blue Goose to Monica.

"Now, there's an interesting couple," Gabriel said, studying the pair who sat in a pew in the front of the church, holding hands. "Chet will go back into police work. It's what suits him best and he's good at it. Monica will present him with four daughters and all four will be holy terrors. Their lives together are going to take a fair amount of adjustment as well. They're both strong-willed people, but their love for each other is much stronger."

"Leah and Andrew were able to bring Angel home this evening," Mercy told him, although Gabriel was well aware the couple's daughter was doing so well she was able to leave the hospital early.

"You might be surprised with what the future holds for them," Gabriel said. He wasn't overly pleased with Mercy's appearance atop the nativity scene, but at least this time she wasn't racing forklifts along a pier and frightening night watchmen out of ten years of their lives.

"Are they able to adopt another child?"

"No, but three earth years from now Leah will become pregnant with identical twin boys."

"Twins," Mercy echoed with delight. "That's wonderful."

"I'm proud of you three," Gabriel felt obligated to comment. Their success had delighted him. "You worked well together."

"'Surely goodness and mercy shall follow you all the days of your life,'" Goodness quoted the well-known Bible verse. "We make a great team."

"Can we do it again?" Shirley asked eagerly.

"Soon," Mercy insisted. "We help each other."

"I think we should all visit Los Angeles next," was Goodness's suggestion. "It seems to me that the City of Angels could do with our help."

The three looked expectantly toward Gabriel. "I'm not making any promises," he said, and with a sweep of his wings ushered the three ambassadors into the celestial realm of heaven where the Christmas celebration was just about to begin. All of heaven was awaiting their return.

The Trouble with Angels

To Ron and Linda Severns
Two of God's humble servants
Two wonderful friends

Chapter

★ ✦ ★

1

Karen Woods woke with a scream. Bolting upright in bed, she pressed her hand over her chest as she breathed deep and hard. Her pajamas were drenched with sweat, and her heart was pounding so fast that it felt as if it were about to race straight through her.

"Karen, Karen, what is it?" Grandma Shields flipped on the light and hurried into the guest bedroom.

The twelve-year-old sobbed once and held out her arms, needing comfort.

It was a dream she'd had before. Lots of times.

Her grandmother sat on the edge of the mattress, gathered Karen in her arms, and held her close. Karen knew she was too old to be cuddled this way, but just then she needed someone's arms around her.

"What is it, child?" Beverly Shields asked her softly, smoothing the damp hair away from Karen's brow. "You're trembling something terrible."

"I had a bad dream," Karen managed to say.

"The same bad dream you had the last time you stayed overnight?"

Karen nodded.

"Do you want to tell your grandma about this dream that frightens you so much?"

Karen shook her head. The nightmare was bad enough without having to tell anyone else about it. Some parts of it she didn't even remember, and one main part she did and wished she didn't. Every time she thought about the dream, she wanted to crawl under the blankets and not come out for a long time.

"Dreams can be real scary sometimes," her grandmother said gently, continuing to stroke Karen's brow.

"Don't leave, okay?" Karen asked. She felt like a wimp, needing her grandmother in bed with her, but she didn't care. She didn't want to be alone. In a few minutes she'd be okay, but not just yet.

Since her mom and dad's divorce, Karen had spent a lot of time by herself. She didn't mind that as much as she had when her parents used to fight. Before her father moved out of the house they'd done that almost all the time.

"Do you miss your mother?" Beverly asked. "Is that the trouble?"

Karen shrugged. Her mother's job as an auditor for one of the big Los Angeles banks often took her out of town. Karen didn't mind staying with her grandparents on the nights her mother was away. It was kind of fun.

"When I was a girl I sometimes had nightmares," Beverly told her.

Karen twisted around so she could see her grandmother's kind face. Even when she was only a little kid, she had liked her grandma Shields better than anyone.

"I dreamed a man with an ax was running after me, and no matter how fast I ran, he ran faster," Beverly Shields said, "and when he finally caught up with me, the ax would be rubber, and the murderer was my older brother. Then he'd laugh and laugh and laugh because it had been so easy to frighten me. That's when I'd wake up, shaking and afraid, and really mad."

"Did . . . did you go back to sleep?"

"Sometimes. I learned that if I closed my eyes and talked to God, I felt a whole lot better. I found talking to God works in a lot of situations."

"Do you do it often?" Karen asked.

"Oh, sure, all the time. Any time of the day or night I feel like it."

Karen studied her mother's mother once more. "No one suggested you see a counselor or anything like that?"

Her grandmother laughed outright. "Why would they suggest that?"

"Grandma, think about it. People don't exactly go around conversing with God, you know."

"Sure they do, but generally it's called prayer."

"Oh." Karen had pictured her grandmother carrying on a one-sided conversation with people listening in and thinking weird things about her. It was bad enough that Beverly put that fake hairpiece in her hair sometimes and stuck it there with bobby pins.

"I was thinking we might say a prayer together now, just the two of us," Beverly said softly.

"Mom and me used to go to church," Karen said, her voice dropping a bit, "but that was before the divorce and for a little while afterward. Then one Sunday Mom said she didn't want to go anymore."

"Yes, I know, but don't fret about that—you don't need to be a regular church attendee to pray."

Karen felt a little better knowing that. "Will you say the words, Grandma?"

"Some of them," Beverly Shields agreed. "But then you should say some of your own, too."

"Do we have to speak them out loud?"

"No, you can whisper them in your heart, too."

Karen closed her eyes and bowed her head. Then, remembering the pictures she'd seen in religious books, she gravely folded her hands. She wasn't entirely sure why people laced their fingers together when they prayed, probably so they wouldn't get distracted and wind their hair around their fingers or that kind of thing.

Her grandmother whispered a prayer, but Karen couldn't understand all the words. She did hear the part about asking God to "comfort Karen" and "calm Karen's fears." Grandma Shields went on for what seemed like a long time. After a while, Karen opened one eye and peeked and noticed her grandmother's lips were still moving.

Karen closed her eye again and waited. When the time seemed right she decided to pray, but she didn't trust God to hear her if she said the words inside her heart.

"Dear God," she prayed, whispering like her grandma had done, only louder. "It's me, Karen Woods. How are you? I'm fine. Well, sort of. I have bad dreams. Actually I don't mind the dreams so much, 'cause if you're listening, I'd rather ask for my mom. You see, she and my dad got a divorce. It was a messy one. But that was over two years ago, and my mother still hates my dad. And now my dad hates my mom. She's mad because, well, because my dad left us. Could you help Mom not hate my dad so much? And God," she said, speaking faster now, thinking she'd better cram in everything she could while she had his attention, "I'd really, really, really love it if you could see fit to give me a horse."

"A horse?" her grandmother echoed, sounding surprised.

Karen opened her eyes and nodded enthusiastically.

"What in the name of heaven would you do with a horse?"

"I want to learn to ride," Karen supplied eagerly. The answer should have been obvious, one would think. "Horses are the most beautiful creatures on earth. More than anything in this world, I want to ride like the wind."

"Does your mother know about this?"

Karen lifted one shoulder. "I talk about horses, but all she says is that we live in the city and there's no possible way for us to own so large an animal."

"That's true enough."

"But Mom's told me a thousand times that where there's a will there's a way."

"That's true, too," Beverly Shields agreed.

"Mom thinks if she gets me a cat, I'll forget about wanting to learn to ride, but she's wrong. I don't even like cats all that much." Karen yawned when she'd finished. "Well, I do, but I like horses a whole lot better."

"You'll sleep now?" Grandma Shields asked.

Karen thought she would. She scooted down into the thick blankets, and her grandmother covered her shoulders. After a moment, Karen closed her eyes. She did feel better. Maybe she ought to talk to God more often.

Karen's prayer intertwined with that of her grandmother and drifted effortlessly heavenward, steered by love, directed by divinity, toward the splendor of paradise, ushered into the very throne room of God. It arrived fresh with the sincerity of a child's heart, weighted with unspoken pain, and bright with honesty.

"Karen Woods," the Archangel Gabriel murmured, writing the twelve-year-old's name in the cumbersome Book of Prayer. He ran his finger down the brittle antique white pages until he found Beverly Shields's name, sighed heavily, and leaned back on the high-backed chair.

Beverly had prayed often for her daughter, Maureen Woods. The thirty-three-year-old woman had been trapped in a bog of bitterness since her divorce. Beverly's prayers had been stymied by Maureen's stubbornness and pride. The woman's resentment of her ex-husband had festered into a wound that had infected her entire life.

Gabriel was concerned about Karen and the girl's repeated nightmares. Setting aside the large quill pen, he closed his eyes in an effort to think of the best way to help Maureen Woods.

"I don't think we should disturb him." The soft, lilting voice belonged to Shirley, a prayer ambassador and former guardian angel.

"Don't be ridiculous. He's probably just resting, waiting for us."

Gabriel kept his eyes closed. This was Goodness. A delightful emissary and known troublemaker.

"I do hope he's considering sending us on another mission. It's been almost a year since our last one."

Mercy.

December was the busiest month of year. Gabriel should have anticipated meeting up with these three. If anything, he should have been surprised it took them this long to make their appearance.

"You did mention that we were most interested in working in Los Angeles this year, didn't you?"

"Ah, not exactly."

There was no help for it. Gabriel opened his eyes and looked up to find the trio standing on the opposite side of the table, their wings folded back neatly, looking as perfect as a Christmas card.

"We're back," Mercy said excitedly, flinging her arms enthusiastically into the air.

"So I see." Gabriel wasn't one to reveal much emotion. For one thing, he couldn't offer them prayer assignments. The truth was, he didn't trust the trio to stay out of trouble. What had happened the previous year was a prime example of the kind of mischief they got themselves into. Goodness didn't think Gabriel knew of her little shenanigans, but he did. The prayer ambassador had given in to her penchant for technical things. More than once.

He cringed every time he thought about Goodness giving advice to a human through the screen of a television set. That wasn't the worst of it, either.

Gabriel had heard plenty about Mercy on the escalators in Nordstrom's department store. And Shirley, the one he considered the most responsible, why, even the former guardian angel had become involved in a few escapades of her own.

"We understand you're shorthanded again this year." This was Goodness, excited as a child about the possibility of returning to earth.

"Things aren't as hectic as last year," Gabriel informed the trio, not allowing any emotion to steal into his voice. Despite all the hassles they'd given him, the archangel had a soft spot when it came to these three.

"That's not what we heard," Shirley said. "Rumor has it you're as overworked as ever and in need of a little help from your friends."

"We've come to volunteer our services." Mercy stepped forward eagerly, nearly colliding with the table.

"But we'd like to work in Los Angeles this time," Goodness informed him. "I'm right fond of California, and it seems to me the City of Angels could do with our help."

"But we must insist upon working together." Mercy crossed her arms, as if to say she was making her stand. "Remember what a great job we did last year? You can't let a golden opportunity like this slip through your fingers."

"Yes, I can." Gabriel didn't feel he could mince words. Weeks after their last venture to earth, he had been left to answer for their tomfoolery.

Goodness and Mercy bounced a shocked look off each other, then glared at him. "You can?"

"Karen Woods?" The softly spoken question came from Shirley, who was leaning over the Book of Prayer, her finger poised at Gabriel's most recent entry.

"She's a troubled young girl," Gabriel supplied, his heart heavy over the twelve-year-old's situation. It would take a prayer ambassador with far more experience than Shirley to work on this request.

"Her parents are divorced, right?"

Gabriel nodded.

"Karen loves them both very much," Shirley said under her breath. "Sometimes the girl feels like she's caught in a vicious tug-of-war between the two. From what I understand, she hasn't seen her father in over a year."

"That's true." Gabriel was beginning to understand. Shirley intuitively knew this information because an Authority much higher than his own had deemed it so. It seemed he was being overruled.

"Her father feels it's easier on everyone if he doesn't see Karen as often. He loves her, too, but he hates his ex-wife, and every time he picks up his daughter she finds an excuse to fight with him. Or a reason to report him to her attorney. Maureen Woods has worked overtime to make his life hell."

"Yes."

"I want to help," Shirley insisted. "Please let me."

"This isn't an easy request," Gabriel felt obliged to remind the prayer ambassador.

"I'm aware of that."

"We'll all help," Goodness and Mercy chimed in.

Gabriel was worried about the three of them doing exactly that and feared it wasn't help they'd be lending. "No, you won't," he said more heatedly than he intended.

The two leaped back a step at his sharp tone.

Gabriel could feel himself weakening. He was well aware that the oldest of the three angels was by far the most emotionally mature. Yet she had the least experience. But Goodness and Mercy? Again?

"I do wish you'd reconsider," Shirley pleaded softly.

"Oh, please do." Two pairs of blue eyes fluttered beguilingly at him. Goodness and Mercy folded their hands with a look as unsullied as grace itself.

Gabriel didn't know what it was about this trio that they wove such tight tentacles around his heart. He was an archangel and generally not given to flagrant displays of favoritism.

"Before either of us makes a decision, why don't we meet Karen's mother?"

"Excellent idea," Goodness said, hurrying to his side.

"I should have thought of that myself." Faster than a heartbeat, Mercy was there as well.

"I was referring to Shirley and me." Gabriel stared at the two, although in reality their enthusiasm amused him greatly.

"Of course we meant to include Shirley," Goodness said with a weak laugh.

"That was understood," Mercy added.

Gabriel freed himself of the two. "Shirley and me alone," he clarified, coughing in an effort to disguise a smile.

"Oh." Goodness's shoulders sagged with disappointment.

"Oh." Mercy slowly lowered herself onto a vacant chair.

"Go on without us," Goodness said as though Shirley were about to step into the last available place in a lifeboat leaving a sinking ship. "We'll wait here."

"Stay out of trouble," Gabriel advised.

"What could we possibly do to cause trouble?" Mercy questioned.

Gabriel didn't want to know the answer to that.

Maureen Woods lugged the heavy suitcase from the trunk of her car to the sidewalk. She stopped on her way into the small rental house to pick up the mail. After tucking a few bills and flyers under her arm, she pulled the newspaper free from its box and made her way to the front steps.

The door opened before she could fit the key into the lock, and Maureen brightened when she saw her daughter. "Hi, pumpkin face."

"Hi. How was the trip?" Karen held open the screen door for her mother.

"All right." Maureen stepped inside. She slipped out of her business suit jacket and laid it over the back of the couch before removing her shoes. It felt heavenly to be out of her pumps, which were still new enough to pinch her toes.

"I'll get your suitcase for you," Karen said eagerly.

Maureen appreciated the thought but knew it was too much for her daughter. "Thanks, honey, but it's too heavy."

"No, it isn't," Karen insisted. "See?" With both hands and all her might, the twelve-year-old managed to lift it a scant inch off the worn carpet.

"Karen, put it down, or you'll hurt yourself," Maureen insisted as she absently sorted through the mail. She paused when she saw the bill for her attorney, cringed, then tossed the mail on the counter without opening any of it. "How was your night with Grandma and Grandpa?"

"Fine."

"What did you have for dinner?"

Karen brightened a bit. "Swedish meatballs. My favorite."

"Grandma's going to spoil you," Maureen warned, grateful to her parents for keeping Karen for her when she traveled.

Karen laughed. "With apple strudel for dessert, and I ate three whole pieces."

Maureen gasped. "You'll get fat."

"I won't because I ran it off on Grandpa's treadmill. I can go faster than he can."

"Yes, but then you haven't had two open-heart surgeries, either."

"If you're worried about me not getting enough exercise, I have a solution."

Maureen knew from the sound of her daughter's voice that she wasn't going to like this. "Oh, what's that?"

"I could always take up horseback riding."

"Karen," Maureen groaned. It seemed her daughter brought the subject into every conversation. "We've been through this a hundred times. We can't afford a horse."

"That's where you're wrong." It was as though Karen had been waiting impatiently for this very argument. She disappeared into her bedroom and returned breathless a moment later. "This is the address I got from the library. Did you know you can get a horse free from the United States government?"

"Karen—"

"Mom, it's true. All you need to do is read this brochure. I wrote away to Utah for all the information. It should come any day now, but I had the lady at the library make me a copy of this pamphlet so you'd see I wasn't making this all up."

"Honey, think this through. Where would we possibly put a horse?"

"In a stable," Karen answered as if that much were obvious, or should have been.

"Where in the name of heaven would we find a stable?"

Karen elevated her hands until they were level with her shoulders. "Don't sweat the small stuff, Mom."

"The small stuff? I can barely feed the two of us on what I make. In addition to everything else, I can't afford to feed a horse."

"But I'd find a job, Mom. I'd do anything I could to earn money. I bet even Dad would be willing to help pay for my horse."

Maureen's face hardened at the mention of Brian. "No," she said sternly. "I won't allow you to bring your father into this. As for getting extra money from him, sweetheart, you're a dreamer. I've had to fight for every penny he's ever given us. He forgot about you the minute he walked out that door."

"That's not true."

"I don't want to argue with you about your father, Karen. If anyone should know how worthless that man is, it's me. Now enough about this stupid horse. I'm tired, and I don't want to argue."

Karen looked at her mother as if she'd been struck. "Will you read the pamphlet?" she asked in a tiny, hurt voice. "Please?"

"All right," Maureen agreed, already regretting her outburst. "I'm sorry, sweetheart. I didn't mean to blow up like that. It's just not a good idea to hit me with a bunch of stuff when I first get home."

"I'm sorry."

Maureen felt worse than ever. "It was my fault," she said, and hugged Karen. Then, deciding not to leave it sitting in the middle of the living room, she carried her suitcase into her bedroom. One of these days, when the lawyer was paid off, she was going to get herself a fancy suitcase with wheels so she could roll it from room to room.

Brian used to carry it for her. It had been about the only thing her son-of-a-bitch ex-husband had been good for.

"Do you see what I mean?" Gabriel asked, standing next to Shirley.

"Oh, poor Karen," the smaller angel said, and sighed deeply. "She loves both her parents. It's hurting her terribly to have her mother feel this way about her father."

"This is a complicated situation, involving many lives. Bitterness has eaten away at Maureen's heart until her life has become clouded with it."

"It's as if she were buried to her waist in sand and trying to walk," Shirley suggested.

"Exactly," Gabriel said, surprised by the prayer ambassador's insight. "She can't move forward in her life, weighted down as she is with hate."

"Emotionally, Maureen Woods is crippled."

"It doesn't help matters any that her ex-husband has remarried and seems happy."

"Is he? Happy, I mean?"

"He appears to be to Maureen, and it's like rubbing salt in her wounds. Karen's mother finds it grossly unfair that Brian should be living a new life with a wife and second family."

"But why?"

"Brian hurt her deeply. He mangled her self-esteem with his affairs. Maureen has a strong sense of justice, and it doesn't feel right to her that the man who broke his wedding vows should go merrily about his life, while she's left to raise their daughter alone."

"Does Maureen date?"

Gabriel gave a short, sharp laugh. "Hardly. A couple of men from the office asked her out, and she all but bit their heads off. She isn't interested in a new relationship. I believe I heard her tell a friend recently that all men are scum."

Shirley's eyebrows shot toward her hairline. "I see."

"According to Maureen, men are never to be trusted."

Shirley folded her wings and started to pace, apparently deep in thought. Pausing once, she turned to Gabriel and was about to ask something, then seemed to change her mind. Shortly afterward she resumed pacing.

"Can I help Karen?" she asked abruptly.

"That's not for me to know," Gabriel answered.

"The key is her mother."

"Yes," Gabriel agreed.

The prayer ambassador grinned then. "You know, I can't help thinking there's a horse in this somewhere."

"A horse," Gabriel repeated, thinking he'd rather not know how she intended to manage that.

Chapter

★ ✦ ★

2

"*His name's Paul Morris,*" Goodness said to Mercy, leaning over the Book of Prayer and studying the lengthy list of entries. "Reverend Paul Morris." She ran her finger down the narrow column. "According to what it says here, his wife died two years ago."

"How sad."

"His name's popped up at least six times in the last two pages."

"He must be deeply loved for that many people to be praying for him."

Goodness agreed. "What do you think could be wrong?"

Mercy raised her hands in a defeated gesture. "Your guess is as good as mine."

"He lives in Los Angeles, too."

"How'd you find his name?"

Goodness twisted around to look at her friend. "It just seemed to leap off the page at me."

"Goodness."

It was the Archangel Gabriel, just when Goodness least expected his return. She straightened quickly and noted that their cohort, Shirley, was no longer with him.

"Hi," she said, tense at being caught reading out of the Book of Prayer. She raised her right hand as if preparing to make a solemn vow.

"You were asking about Reverend Paul Morris?" Gabriel inquired.

"Yes," she said eagerly. "His name's listed several times in your book, and . . . well, it's just a matter of curiosity, you understand."

"Perhaps you'd care to drop in and visit him yourself?"

Goodness was convinced her ears had deceived her. She opened her mouth and flattened her palm over her breast. "Me? Really?" she managed in a squeaky, high-pitched voice. "I thought you said . . . I mean, I was under the impression . . ." She snapped her mouth closed before she talked herself out of meeting Paul Morris.

"It doesn't do any harm to look, now, does it?" Gabriel asked.

Goodness was almost giddy with delight.

"Go on ahead without me," Mercy said with a defeated sigh and with the dramatic flair of a stage actress. "I don't mind waiting here all by myself."

"I'm sure you won't," Gabriel said gruffly.

To be fair, Goodness did feel mildly guilty to be leaving her best friend behind. She'd gotten adept with guilt of late. She'd acquired the skill by hanging around with Catholics, who were proven experts.

"Let's take a look at Paul," Gabriel suggested, and raised his massive wings. With a wave of his huge arms, the clouds parted, and the scene that had once been inaccessible and unclear unfolded in vivid colors. The setting, appropriately so, was the church building itself.

Goodness scanned the polished wooden pews and saw no one. The area around the altar was empty as well.

"That's Paul at the organ," Gabriel explained.

Goodness found him in the choir loft. He must have sat down only recently because no music swelled through the church. No song of joy or triumph. Goodness heard only an empty silence.

"His wife played the organ for the church," Gabriel explained.

"Ah." Goodness wasn't sure she understood, but if Paul Morris found some whit of comfort sitting on a bench with his hands poised over the old ivory keys, she could find no harm in it.

"What you're hearing is a symphony of emotions," Gabriel explained. "A ballad of loneliness."

Goodness strained her ears and still heard nothing. She inserted her index finger into her ear and jerked it back and forth several times.

Gabriel's hand on her shoulder stopped her. "I didn't mean for you to take that literally. The music is coming from his grief. From the deepest, darkest corner of his heart."

"Oh." Goodness felt foolish now.

"Wait and watch," Gabriel instructed her. "I'll be back soon."

Goodness had a long list of questions, but apparently none of them was important because Gabriel was gone in the blink of an eye. The prayer ambassador was left alone, watching the lonely, hurting human below. Sadly, she was powerless to do anything more than observe.

*   *   *

Paul Morris slipped from the organ bench and headed for the church office. A glance at his watch told him he was already ten minutes late for his meeting with the worship committee. He hadn't meant for the time to slip away like that and, with renewed purpose, increased his pace.

Leta Johnson, his secretary, leaped from her chair the instant he walked into the office. "You're late," she announced, following him across the room.

"I know. I apologize."

"The committee's in the conference room," she said, and handed him a sheaf of papers. "I believe they've started without you."

In times past, Paul might have been offended that the committee would see fit to begin without him. But, frankly, he was relieved and hoped that they'd completed the business at hand. It would save him the burden of having to sit through yet another endless, boring meeting.

Unfortunately it didn't happen that way. An hour later the meeting adjourned and the two elders and three worship leaders were on their way out of the conference room. Paul stayed behind, gathering up the last of the paperwork. He looked up to find Steve Tenny watching him.

Paul offered the elder a warm smile. The two men had been good friends for a number of years. "How's it going, Steve?" he asked conversationally.

"Great. Is Joe coming home for Christmas?"

The ache in Paul's heart lightened at the mention of his son. "He'll be here next week sometime."

"It'll be good to see him."

Paul was counting the days. Joe's arrival from college and the three weeks he was scheduled to spend at home was the one bright spot in Paul's Christmas season.

"I imagine you'll be getting together with Bethany."

"She's sure to have us over two or three times," Paul agreed. His daughter was the apple of his eye. Now that she was married and living in Riverside, he didn't see her as often as he would have liked. Both Bethany and Eric worked, so they led busy lives and he didn't want to be a burden to them.

"I don't suppose I could talk you into taking a few days off and going hiking with me."

The thought tempted Paul, but with so many Christmas responsibilities, he hadn't the time. "Sorry, I can't now."

Steve mulled over his answer. "You're going to be fine," he stated matter-of-factly.

"Sure I am," Paul agreed automatically.

"It's been difficult the last couple of years without Barbara, but you've risen above all that now. You're doing great."

Paul wondered. "Yeah," he said, forcing a smile. "I'm doing great."

The two men walked out of the meeting room together. Steve patted Paul across the back before he headed out to the parking lot.

Paul watched the elder leave and wondered how it was that a man he'd counted his best friend for fifteen or more years didn't know him at all. Steve hadn't a clue to what Paul was feeling, didn't understand Paul's deep sense of loss.

His wife of twenty-four years had died, and it felt as if someone had chopped off his right arm. They had been partners not only in life, but in the ministry. Together they had slaved to build this church from the foundation to the very top of the steeple. Together they had held every position in the church. Over the years Barbara had been the Sunday school director, the nursery coordinator, in charge of missions, the choir director, and just about everything else, including janitor.

With a heavy heart weighing down his steps, Paul reluctantly returned to his office. Leta handed him a pink message slip when he walked in the door. "It's Madge Bartelli again," she said. "Bernard phoned and said she's in terrible pain."

"Madge," Paul repeated slowly. The parishioner was suffering from the same rare form of cancer that had claimed Barbara.

Why God would allow him to watch yet another woman suffer this way was beyond his comprehension. For the second time God had asked him to stand by helplessly, able to offer nothing more than a few trite words of comfort.

"I'm afraid Madge's taken a turn for the worse," Leta said sadly.

Paul nodded and entered his office, closing the door.

"You are going to phone her, aren't you?" Leta asked from the other side.

"Yes, of course," Paul assured her, and sat down at his desk.

"Bernard could use a few words of encouragement as well."

And just where was he supposed to find that? Paul asked himself. Encouragement? He felt devoid of the ability to help his friends. His deep well of hope and assurance had dried up when he'd lost Barbara. He had nothing to offer and damn little of himself left to give.

It seemed his secretary stood just outside his door until she heard him reach for the telephone. Paul flipped through his Rolodex until he found the Bartellis' listing and punched out the numbers.

Bernard answered on the second ring. "Pastor Paul, how good of you to phone."

"How's Madge?"

"Not good. Not good at all. She can't sleep. Even the pain medication the doctor prescribed doesn't help. I don't know what to do for her anymore."

"Have you tried reading to her?"

"Oh, yes. She tries to hide how bad it is, but I can see the pain in her eyes."

Barbara had tried to disguise her agony from Paul as well. He didn't think he would ever know the full range of suffering his saintly wife had endured. Bernard probably would never know, either.

"I realize it's a lot to ask of you," Bernard said, lowering his voice as if he wanted to be sure Madge couldn't hear him. "But if you could stop off at the house sometime later today and pray with Madge, I know it would help."

Paul closed his eyes. "Of course," he agreed. But he doubted that his prayers would matter.

He'd poured his heart out on Barbara's behalf. He'd laid himself down before God and pleaded with everything in him that his wife be healed. Paul had trusted and believed from the time he was a child. In all the years in the ministry, not once had he questioned God. Not even when he and Barbara had lost their unborn child. Not when his own parents had died within six months of each other.

Paul wasn't a man with a small faith. The Bible talked about mustard seed faith. His was larger than that. He recalled the day they'd first learned of Barbara's cancer. His faith hadn't been small then. He'd looked on this as a test, a challenge. He'd been so confident that God would miraculously heal his beloved wife.

Paul had given up looking for miracles. These days one would need a microscope to find his faith. It had been laid to rest in six feet of cold, wet clay along with his wife's casket.

"God bless you, Reverend," Bernard said softly, the once strong voice shaking with emotion, reminding Paul that cancer rarely claimed one victim.

"I'll be by later this afternoon," Paul promised.

He replaced the telephone receiver and buried his face in his hands. He was tired. The last time he'd taken time away had been . . . He paused, needing to think about it. Longer than it should have been, he decided. Steve had a good idea. Getting away for a couple of days held a lot of appeal.

Maybe when Joe arrived the two of them could take some time and go hiking. It would do Paul a world of good to escape the pressures of the church. That was all he really needed. Time away. Away from the stress and strain of the church. Away from the demands of the many who looked to him for answers when he had none to give.

Not anymore.

"Paul's a special man," Gabriel said, joining Goodness.

"He's warm and generous and loving," Goodness agreed.

"But . . ."

"But he's under a lot of pressure at the moment," the prayer ambassador surmised. "It seems to me his secretary is a bit more bossy than she needs to be."

"Perhaps," Gabriel agreed. His hands were linked behind his back, and he paced in front of Goodness like a drill sergeant with a raw recruit.

She had the feeling these questions were a test of some kind. Whether she received this assignment to earth or not depended on her answers.

"His friend doesn't seem to be much of a friend, either."

Gabriel's gaze narrowed on her. "How do you mean?"

"Well, it seems to me that a real friend would be willing to listen to Paul instead of making sweeping assumptions about his well-being."

Gabriel nodded several times. "Someone must realize all isn't right, otherwise there wouldn't be so many people praying for Paul Morris."

"Well." Goodness rubbed her palms back and forth several times. Her career as a prayer ambassador might rest on her response. "The trouble with Reverend Morris is much worse than most anyone suspects."

"Is that right?"

Goodness nodded, her movements emphatic. "People think he misses his wife."

"And he doesn't?" Gabriel's bushy eyebrows reached all the way to his hairline.

"Of course he does, but his troubles are much more complex than that. I'm afraid Reverend Paul Morris is one of the most desperate cases I've seen."

"Desperate?" Gabriel repeated.

"Yes." Goodness was less confident than earlier.

"What ails this man isn't going to be fixed by a voice through a television screen."

Goodness felt her pale cheeks fill with color. Yet she knew what the archangel said was true. "Why, that would be utterly . . ."

"Ridiculous," Gabriel supplied.

"It could work, but then I'd never attempt anything like that again," she said just to be on the safe side.

"What exactly is the problem with Reverend Morris?" Gabriel asked her outright.

Goodness blinked, surprised by his abruptness. "I thought you knew."

"You tell me."

"Paul Morris is infected with the most demanding of human maladies," Goodness murmured, saddened to speak the words aloud. "The dear man's deeply discouraged. He doesn't believe God heard his prayers, and now he wonders if He ever did."

Gabriel patted her shoulder gently. "You've judged his condition accurately."

Goodness brightened. "Does this mean I can work on this prayer request?"

Gabriel hesitated. "You said yourself that this was the most demanding of human troubles."

"Yes, but . . ."

"Unfortunately you lack the experience."

"But I can help him, I know I can," Goodness insisted.

"How do you propose to do that?"

"I haven't figured that out yet, but I'll think of something. I always do."

Gabriel frowned.

"Without tricks," she promised, folding her hands as if she were praying. She looked up at him with large, pleading blue eyes.

"I've heard that line before."

"This time I mean it."

"What about all those other times?" Gabriel pressed.

Goodness always meant to keep her promises. "This is different," she vowed.

"Answer me this," Gabriel said, ushering them both back to where Mercy sat waiting. When they appeared, Mercy, the third prayer ambassador, leaped to her feet as if she'd been sitting on a mattress spring.

"Yes?" Goodness said, following on Gabriel's heels.

"How did you know about Paul Morris?"

"Ah . . ." Goodness and Mercy exchanged knowing looks.

"She said his name jumped right off the page," Mercy supplied when Goodness's answer wasn't immediately forthcoming.

Gabriel ceased pacing. "Overruled again," he mumbled under his breath.

"What did he say?" Mercy whispered out of the side of her mouth.

"Something about being overdone."

"Overruled," Gabriel barked. His hands were clasped behind his back once more, and he didn't seem any too pleased.

"Is something wrong?" Again it was Mercy, curious to learn what she could.

"No," Gabriel snapped.

"I think there must be," Goodness whispered.

"Where's Shirley?"

"Earth, I think," Goodness suggested. Gabriel ignored them as best he could. He still hadn't stopped frowning.

"Los Angeles?"

Goodness nodded, and the two gleefully shot their arms into the air and gave each other a high five. The sound echoed like a Chinese gong in the stillness.

Gabriel whirled around to confront the two. "Where did you two learn about high fives?"

The archangel had a stare a rattlesnake would envy.

"Ah . . ."

"You see, Mercy's a Lakers fan."

"You are, too."

"I prefer the Seattle SuperSonics," Goodness insisted, "but will cheer for the Lakers in a pinch."

"Just exactly who are the Lakers?" Gabriel demanded.

"The Lakers," Goodness explained, shocked at the archangel's ignorance. "The Los Angeles professional basketball team. Does the name Magic mean anything to you, Gabe?"

Gabriel closed his eyes, and Goodness had the feeling he wasn't exactly praying.

"You've got assignments for us, don't you?" she asked triumphantly. She could think of no other reason for the archangel's look of complete frustration.

"It seems you'll to be working with Paul Morris after all," Gabriel informed Goodness, looking downright unhappy with the situation.

Goodness doubled up her fist and shot it into the air, leaping several inches from the floor. *"Yes!"*

"What about me?" Mercy wanted to know, trailing after Gabriel, who continued his marine drill-sergeant pace.

"In a minute." He turned and faced Goodness once more. "I'll tolerate none of the craziness you pulled last Christmas, understand?"

"Perfectly." Goodness snapped to attention.

"Can you tell me about my prayer assignment now?" Mercy pressed. "I don't mean to be a problem, but I do think I've been waiting long enough."

"Furthermore . . ." Gabriel paused when he felt Mercy tugging at his sleeve. "You wanted something?" he asked with a decided lack of patience.

"We need to talk."

"Talk?"

Mercy nodded. "I really do hate to be a nuisance, especially when you're in this frame of mind, but really, Gabriel, if you're going to send Shirley and Goodness to Los Angeles, it only seems fair—"

"You'll be assigned there as well."

Goodness was relieved. As far as she was concerned, there wasn't anything the three of them couldn't do once they put their minds to it. The three of them together. God willing, of course.

"Do you know who Catherine Goodwin is?" Gabriel asked Mercy.

The other angel blinked, then shook her head. "No, should I know her?"

For the first time in what seemed like a good long while, Gabriel smiled. "Come and meet a wonderful woman. You're going to like her very much."

Chapter

★ ✯ ★

3

Catherine Goodwin adjusted the clasp of her antique brooch as she pinned it to the neckline of her silk blouse. She squared her shoulders and studied her image in the mirror on the back of her bedroom door. Her hair was pinned in a soft bun, more white now than gray, she noted.

Her fingers lightly touched the cameo she wore at her neck. She felt the love it represented as strongly now as she had fifty years earlier when Earl Standish had presented it to her. The light wool skirt and ivory-colored blouse were her best—she saved them for special occasions. Like this afternoon.

"I look like an old woman," Catherine mumbled, then allowed her shoulders to relax before she smiled at her reflection. "But then, I am an old woman," she admitted softly.

Catherine moved into her tiny kitchen and checked to be sure the china cups and tray were ready for her guests. Her very special guests.

Not wanting her grandson, Ted, and his lady friend to wait needlessly for her to be called downstairs, Catherine took the elevator to the large reception room of the Wilshire Grove Retirement Center.

"Catherine." Joy Palmer, the resident service director for Wilshire Grove, joined her. Her eyes were warm and approving. "How lovely you look."

Catherine blushed at the praise. Joy was a personal favorite of hers among the staff members. The majority of the employees of Wilshire Grove were extraordinarily good people, but Joy held a special place in Catherine's heart.

Being around the service director every day was what kept Catherine thinking young. Although she was no more than twenty-five, Joy worked well with the retirees. She was patient and caring and, as far as Catherine was concerned, a rare jewel of a woman.

"Ted's stopping by this afternoon," Catherine explained.

"Well, no wonder you're all spiffed up," Joy said, and hugged Catherine's shoulders. "Your grandson's handsome enough to cause several hearts to flutter."

"He's certainly been good to me." One of the major advantages to having Ted's office in the downtown area of Los Angeles was that he was able to visit often. Generally he stopped in at the retirement center once or twice a week. Catherine looked forward to those times.

This visit, however, was different, because he was bringing along a young woman he wanted Catherine to meet. Ted had casually dropped Blythe's name into their conversations several times in the last few weeks. Catherine realized he must be getting serious about her and was seeking his grandmother's approval. Since Ted's parents lived in Portland, Oregon, Catherine was the only family he had in California.

"He's bringing a lady friend this time," Catherine explained, "and I do so want to make a good impression."

"You look divine," Joy assured her.

The resident service director had such a streak of sweetness that Catherine wondered if she dare believe her.

"The library committee met this afternoon," Catherine went on to say. She sat on the leather wing-backed chair, where she could easily see the front door.

"Were you able to hammer out a budget?" Joy asked, claiming the chair next to her.

"Yes, but it's difficult when there are so many books we'd like to buy. Several of the members think we should order the new audiotapes. It's getting hard for some of us to read these days, even with the books in larger print. Unfortunately there just aren't enough funds to purchase everything we'd like."

"It's hard, I know," Joy agreed. "Perhaps you should think of holding a fund-raiser. With only a few weeks to Christmas, you could make it a festive occasion and serve cookies and tea."

"Naturally we'd invite everyone to participate." Already Catherine could see the wisdom of such a plan. "We won't charge anything to attend our tea, but we could ask for donations."

"I'm sure the library committee would do an excellent job."

"I know they would," Catherine agreed. "What a great suggestion. Thank you, Joy. I'll speak with the committee members first thing tomorrow morning."

Ted appeared just then, holding open one side of the double glass doors. "Here's my grandson now," Catherine said.

"You haven't got a thing to worry about," Joy assured her softly, then stood and discreetly disappeared.

Catherine's eyes didn't waver from the front door. How eager she was to meet this woman who'd captured her grandson's attention! The woman who preceded him into the retirement center was sophisticated and professional looking. Catherine discovered she was holding her breath. Ted's lady friend was exceptionally lovely.

Catherine stood as her grandson approached. Ted's eyes met hers and were bright with laughter. He was tall and handsome and the joy of Catherine's life. How very proud she was of her grandson, of his accomplishments, of the distinguished young man he'd grown up to be. Seeing Ted was like looking at the very best of herself and Earl.

"Grandmother," Ted said, placing his arm around her thin shoulders, "it gives me a good deal of pleasure to introduce you to Blythe Holmes."

"Blythe," Catherine said, taking the other woman's hand between her own. "I couldn't be more honored."

Only a hint of warmth entered the younger woman's blue eyes. "The pleasure's all mine," Blythe said.

"I've arranged for us to have tea in my room," Catherine said nervously.

It seemed Blythe hadn't heard her. She looked around the room, studying the artwork on the walls. Catherine watched as the younger woman's gaze landed on Catherine's friends and then bounced away dismissively. Blythe frowned when she saw Charles, a retired army officer. Charles sometimes forgot who and where he was.

Catherine felt Blythe's aversion to Charles, although he was doing nothing more than staring sightlessly into the distance and mumbling nonsense to himself. She found herself wanting to defend the retiree, explain what a gentle, kind man he was, and tell Ted's friend that he'd once been a war hero. Of course, she could do none of that.

"This is very . . . nice," Blythe said with a lack of sincerity. It was as if she had to say something, and "nice" was the only word she could think to utter. Until that moment Catherine had never noticed how weak the word *nice* could be.

"Would you like a tour of Wilshire Grove?" Catherine asked, proud of her home and wanting to show it off.

"No," Blythe said, but thanked her for the invitation with a smile.

Catherine led the way to the elevator, chatting nervously as she escorted her guests inside. She watched as Ted reached for Blythe's hand and felt her heart warm.

"We each have our own apartment," Catherine explained for Blythe's benefit when they reached hers. "I have a small kitchen, although I rarely cook these days. However, I did manage to bake a batch of Ted's favorite cookies this morning."

"Chocolate chip?" Ted asked, his eyes as round and eager as a five-year-old's.

"Chocolate chip," Catherine said, and laughed softly. She motioned toward the overstuffed sofa. "You two make yourselves comfortable while I put on the water for tea."

"Let me help," Ted insisted, following Catherine into the kitchen. The moment they were out of earshot he snatched a cookie off the silver platter and leaned his hip against the counter. "Isn't she beautiful?" he asked, looking at Blythe as if he'd located buried treasure the day he'd met her.

"She's as lovely as a fashion model," Catherine agreed, delighted to see his dark eyes sparkle. Her grandson was in love. Catherine had been waiting years for this moment. Ted was thirty, and it was time he started thinking seriously about settling down.

Catherine looked across her compact living room to Blythe. She had crossed her long legs and leaned back against the sofa, but there was a restlessness about her. Of course she might be wrong, but Catherine sensed a sadness there.

With a shake of her head, Catherine pulled her gaze and her thoughts away from her female guest. It was too soon for her to make such sweeping judgments, she chided herself, wondering why she would think such thoughts about a woman she barely knew.

Ted carried the tray into the living room for her.

Sitting on the edge of her cushion, Catherine served them each a cup of tea. Ted helped himself to a second cookie.

"Should you really be eating that?" Blythe asked Ted.

"Eating what?" he asked innocently, and winked at Catherine.

"I thought you said you were watching your fat intake."

"I am." He reached for another and handed it to her. "No one makes chocolate chip cookies the way my grandmother does. When I was a kid I used to wonder how she could make them taste so good. I still don't know her secret. Perhaps she'll give you the recipe."

"I'd be happy to, Blythe," Catherine volunteered.

"I can't possibly eat that," Blythe said about the cookie.

"Ted," Catherine chastised, "leave the poor girl alone."

"I want her to try just one cookie. Then she'll know what I mean. Come on, Blythe, just one bite."

"No," she said sharply, and when Ted frowned she laughed. "Oh, all right, if you insist, but I really shouldn't."

"It's only a cookie," Ted reminded her.

Catherine agreed. She was health conscious herself and would never bake anything for her family she seriously believed would harm them. As it was, she generally baked the cookies for Ted only on his birthday.

Blythe nibbled on the cookie as if she suspected it were laced with arsenic, then placed it on the delicate china plate.

Originally Catherine had thought to send the rest of the small batch home with Ted. Now she decided against that, not wanting to cause a problem between her grandson and his lady friend. The literary tea would need cookies, she mused, and she'd save the leftovers for then.

"So tell me how you two met," Catherine asked, and sipped her tea.

"At work," Blythe said matter-of-factly.

"Are you an engineer as well?"

Blythe nodded. "With nuclear certification."

"Congratulations." Blythe sounded proud and pleased, and Catherine wanted her to know she was happy for her accomplishments.

"I'm hoping Ted will see fit to do what's necessary to acquire his certification as well."

Ted stiffened slightly. "Let's not talk about this now."

"You're right," Blythe said sweetly. Looking to Catherine, she continued, "It's just that there are so few engineers with nuclear certification that they're in demand all across the country. Ted could work anywhere he chose."

Personally, Catherine was hoping he'd stay in Los Angeles for the time being, but she didn't want to seem proprietorial. Ted, after all, was his own person. Catherine wouldn't dream of holding him back because of her own selfish wishes.

Blythe made a point of looking at her watch. "What time did you say the dinner reservation was for, Ted?"

Ted glanced at his own watch. "We have plenty of time."

"I was hoping to change out of these heels," Blythe said.

"Go on, you two," Catherine said hurriedly. "The evening's young yet. Enjoy yourselves."

Ted hesitated. "You're sure? We've barely spent any time with you."

"I'm positive," Catherine assured him, gathering up the china cups.

"It was a pleasure to meet you, Mrs. Goodwin."

"Please, you must call me Catherine."

Blythe smiled and stood, eager, it seemed, to be on her way. "All right, then, I will. Thank you for having Ted and me over."

"The pleasure was all mine." Catherine stood with Ted and walked the couple to her door. After a few short words of farewell, they were gone.

A bit dazed, Catherine returned to her favorite chair and sank onto it. This visit hadn't gone anything like she'd wanted. It was clear Ted was enthralled with Blythe. It also seemed clear, at least to Catherine, that her grandson's relationship with Blythe was becoming serious.

It wasn't like Catherine to make judgments about others, especially people she barely knew. But in her heart she couldn't picture her grandson married to Blythe Holmes. The two simply didn't seem right for each other.

She was an old woman, Catherine reminded herself, and knew little of romantic relationships these days. She could very well be wrong. One thing was certain: she refused to interfere in her grandson's life.

Her thoughts restless, Catherine stood. Whenever she needed to think over something important, she generally slipped into the chapel. Tucked in a back corner of the building, the chapel had been built many years earlier in memory of a valiant World War II chaplain who'd died on the beaches of Normandy.

Not wanting to meet anyone and be sidetracked, Catherine took the stairs and silently entered the empty room.

She sat in the back pew for several moments, gathering her thoughts. When she'd composed herself inwardly, she bowed her head.

The prayer came directly from her heart. She remembered the day her grandson had been born and what a special gift he was to her. That he should enter the service and become an Airborne Ranger seemed almost fitting in light of the grandfather who'd served as a Ranger before him.

"Father," she whispered, "my prayer is a simple one. All I ask is that Ted marry the right woman."

There was much more that she wished to add. Instructions. Advice. But she left those words unsaid. After a few moments, she stood and quietly returned to her room.

"That's Catherine," Gabriel said, staring down upon the earthly scene below.

Mercy was intrigued. The archangel had claimed she'd like Catherine, and Mercy had, immediately. "What a dear, sweet woman she is."

Gabriel nodded. "Catherine Goodwin has a heart after God's own."

"What about Blythe Holmes?" Mercy was anxious to learn what she could about the younger woman. "Is she the right wife for Ted?"

Gabriel folded his massive wings against his back. "I don't have the answer to that. But I'm sure within a short amount of time you'll discover that for yourself."

"You know who *I* think he should marry."

"Who?" Gabriel's head bent back with surprise.

"Well, we just met her for a moment or two, but I think Joy Palmer—"

"Joy Palmer?" Gabriel said loudly enough to ruffle Mercy's delicate feathers. Sometimes the archangel forgot how much larger he was than a mere prayer ambassador.

"I realize we only just met her, but didn't you notice how gentle and caring she is toward Catherine and the other residents at Wilshire Grove?"

Gabriel studied Mercy for a lengthy, uncomfortable moment. "Yes, but that doesn't mean she'd make Ted Griffin a good wife."

"Catherine likes her," Mercy felt obliged to remind him.

"She's also fond of Emily, Thelma, Lucille, and the other ladies on the library committee, but I don't see you matchmaking Ted with any of them."

"That would be ridiculous," Mercy said, not understanding Gabriel's lack of insight. All this should have been obvious to him. "Those women aren't anywhere close to Ted's age. Joy Palmer is a mere five years younger."

Gabriel crossed his arms, as if to say he'd like nothing better than to end their conversation.

"Furthermore, I saw the look that came into Joy's eyes when Ted first arrived. It's clear to me that you're simply not that well versed in the area of human romance."

"And you are?"

"I know a little about romance," Mercy admitted. "Enough to know *interested* when I see it, and Joy was definitely interested."

"I won't have you pulling any of your funny business. Understand?"

Mercy put on her most injured look. "I wouldn't dream of doing a—"

"Yes, you would," Gabriel interrupted testily. "I'm telling you right now, I won't put up with any of it."

"Haven't I given you my word of honor?"

"A lot of good that did me last year," Gabriel mumbled under his breath. Then, with little fanfare, he lifted his massive arms, parting the thick clouds, and ushered them back into the prayer room.

Both Shirley and Goodness were waiting for her.

"Well?" Goodness asked.

"Gabriel was right," Mercy said, almost breathless, she was so eager to tell her friends everything she'd found out about Catherine Goodwin. She could handle this prayer request with one wing tied behind her back! "I'm really pleased to work with such a wonderful older woman."

"Just wait until I tell you what I learned," Shirley said, slumping onto a chair and raising her feet onto the ottoman. Both her arms dangled over the sides as if it demanded too much energy to lift them. "I'm afraid I'm going to need help. Lots and lots of help."

"You've got it," Goodness assured her. "Really, Shirley, this is the beauty of the three of us working together."

"We're a team."

"A team," Gabriel repeated, as if the idea of the three of them assigned to the same city should have been outlawed.

"Lighten up, Gabe," Goodness said, and pressed her hand against her hip. "We're going to be so good you won't even know we're on assignment."

"Los Angeles could use a bit of our help," Mercy said, thinking about all she'd seen in those brief moments allotted her.

"I don't think California's prepared for the likes of you three," Gabriel grumbled.

"None of these prayer requests should take long," Mercy said, feeling confident. As far as she could see, all she had to do was subtly steer Ted Griffin's interest toward a certain service director and leave the rest up to the two of them. She'd do it, Mercy vowed, without causing Gabriel any grief, either. She was, after all, an angel of her word.

"I need all three of you back here soon," Gabriel reminded them.

"How soon?" This came from Shirley.

Mercy didn't know the full extent of her friend's assignment, but the case seemed to be troubling Shirley. When she'd finished with hers, which shouldn't take any more than two or three days, she'd give her friend a hand.

"Before Christmas," Gabriel told them sternly.

"Before Christmas?" Goodness repeated. "But that's impossible."

"Nothing is impossible with God," the archangel reminded them.

Shirley released a long sigh. "I wonder how long it's been since he visited L.A."

Chapter

★ ✯ ★

4

Maureen tossed a frozen entrée into her grocery cart with a decided lack of enthusiasm. One of these days, when her legal fees were paid in full, she was going to enjoy the sheer luxury of eating in a restaurant again. One with waiters and real plates.

"I can't tell you how much I appreciate your keeping Karen for me," Maureen told her mother, who pushed the cart next to her own.

Beverly Shields leaned over the frozen-food counter for a can of orange juice. "Any time, Maureen, you know that. The child's a delight."

"I don't dare ask Brian to keep her. Which reminds me," she said, craning her neck to look one aisle over, "I need antacid tablets."

"Why couldn't you ask Brian?" her mother asked, following her over to the next aisle.

Maureen was sorry she'd mentioned her ex-husband's name. "Because."

"That makes no sense," Beverly said. "He *is* Karen's father."

"Don't remind me." Karen was the only good thing to come out of her sick marriage. "Might I remind you he hasn't asked for his court-appointed visitation rights in over a year? I can just imagine what he'd say if I called him out of the blue and asked him to watch Karen for three days while I was away on a business trip."

"He just might surprise you."

Maureen snickered. "I've had about all the surprises I can take from that man. Trust me, Mother, the less I'm in contact with Brian, the better."

"Perhaps."

Beverly was quiet, too quiet. It had surprised Maureen when her

254

mother invited herself along on this grocery shopping expedition. Shopping wasn't Maureen's favorite task. Not when she was struggling to make ends meet. It didn't help matters any to have Karen constantly dragging how much she wanted a horse into every conversation, as if Maureen could afford such an extravagance. As it was, she could barely squeeze enough for Christmas out of their already tight budget.

"Karen had another one of her nightmares," Beverly said casually as they rounded the corner to the shelves of cereals.

"When?" Maureen asked, which was a good indication of how frazzled this information left her. Karen had awakened screaming the night Maureen arrived home from her Seattle trip. It had taken the better part of an hour to calm her daughter. The twelve-year-old had clung to her until Maureen was afraid the youngster had cut off the blood circulation in her arm.

"The second night she was with us," Beverly answered. "She shook something fierce."

"Did she tell you what the dream was about?"

"Not a word."

Maureen bit down on her lower lip. Karen refused to tell her, too. What she should have done from the first was schedule an appointment for Karen with a counselor. A phone call to her attorney would tell her if she could get Brian to share the expense. It wasn't fair that she should have to shoulder it alone, the way she did everything else. Brian did pay child support, when the mood struck him, which unfortunately hadn't been lately.

"Your father and I talked—"

"I know what you're going to say," Maureen interrupted, angry and defensive. "And before you ask, I'll tell you I'm taking care of it."

Her mother's eyes widened at the unfairness of the attack. "Taking care of what?"

"Counseling for Karen."

"I wasn't going to suggest any such thing," her mother said with an injured air. She reached for her favorite bran cereal and placed it in the cart, her spine as stiff as a metal lamppost.

Maureen felt duly chastised. "I'm sorry, Mom, it's just that I'm worried about her. I don't know why Karen's having these nightmares. I feel so helpless." She rolled her cart a bit closer to her mother's. "I didn't mean to snap at you. Now tell me what it was you and Dad discussed."

"We were thinking it might help if we picked Karen up after school and kept her with us until you got home from work. I don't think it's a good idea for her to be alone so much of the time."

The generosity of their offer brought tears to Maureen's eyes. Her parents were retired now and enjoyed their freedom. Maureen knew the recent move hadn't been easy on her daughter. She hadn't liked changing Karen's school, either, but it couldn't be helped. The rent was cheaper, the commute shorter, and the place closer to her parents' house.

"I can't thank you enough, Mom, but no. Karen's capable of looking after herself, and it's only for an hour." Now that she lived closer to her family, Maureen didn't want to get in the habit of relying upon them too heavily.

"You're sure?"

"Mom, really. I don't want you to fret about Karen and me. The two of us are doing just great."

"Great, huh?" Beverly reached into Maureen's cart and picked up the extra large bottle of antacid tablets. "Are you still having troubles with your stomach?"

"It's not as bad as it used to be," Maureen told her, although it was sometimes worse. She didn't need to be a rocket scientist to figure out where all the indigestion came from, either. Once again Maureen had her ex-husband to thank. Brian wasn't happy with ruining her life; he wanted to slowly kill her, too.

"All men aren't like Brian," her mother said.

Maureen disagreed. From what she'd seen in the last few years, there was damn little to persuade her to become involved in another relationship. The next time she felt like getting married, she'd find a man she didn't like, bear him a child, and live in poverty the rest of her life.

"See what I mean?" Shirley said to her two friends from the roof of the huge grocery complex. "Maureen's so twisted up with hate, it's eating away the lining of her stomach. What can I possibly do to help her forgive her ex-husband?"

Goodness and Mercy looked at each other helplessly.

"I haven't got a clue," Goodness admitted.

Mercy didn't look any more helpful. "It's as bad as you claimed. She really does hate the man."

"The one who really concerns me is Karen," Shirley continued, unable to stand in one place. It was as if the woman were blind to what she was doing to her daughter. "The nightmares are getting worse."

"The poor kid." Mercy sat on top of the duct for the air conditioner, her face cupped in her hands.

"If only I could find an easy way for her to have a horse."

"A horse," Goodness echoed.

"Karen's crazy about 'em."

"Then that's what we'll have to do," Goodness said, as if this were the solution to their problems. "All the poor kid needs is a little fun, and before you know it those nightmares will disappear."

"Just where are we supposed to find a horse?" Shirley asked with limited patience. "And even if we could, Karen's mother couldn't afford to feed it."

"There are ways," Mercy said with complete confidence.

"Yes, but are these *ways* of yours going to get us jerked back to heaven by our small feathers?"

Mercy gave her a look of gold-plated innocence. "Why, I'd never suggest anything that would give dear Gabriel a moment's worry."

Shirley was just beginning to think she might have misjudged her friend's intentions when Goodness giggled. "Yes, you would," she said. "We all would, and good old Gabe knows it, too."

"Do you mind if we discuss Karen?" Shirley suggested. These two younger prayer ambassadors flustered her. They were far more daring than she was. Frankly, Shirley believed Gabriel had teamed her up with Goodness and Mercy just so she could keep an eye on these two upstarts.

"Oh, yes. Karen."

"Of course. Karen."

Now that she had their attention, Shirley felt it was time to mention what she'd discovered, although she wasn't exactly sure what to do with the information. "Of course, there's always Thom Nichols."

"Thom Nichols?" Mercy pressed.

"He owns a riding stable in the valley, and it's—"

"But that's perfect." Goodness vaulted upright in her enthusiasm.

"For Karen, perhaps, but it doesn't do anything about Maureen's troubles. I did tell Gabriel that I was certain there was a horse in this somewhere," Shirley said, feeling downright proud of herself, "but it isn't as if I can swoop down and tell Maureen about the stables."

A slow, gradual smile spread over Goodness's face. "Why can't you?"

"You've got that gleam in your eye again." Shirley was beginning to get worried. She'd seen that look before, and it usually spelled trouble. "How could you even think such things, Goodness? We've just arrived. We don't dare jeopardize everything so soon."

"Don't get all bent out of shape," Goodness said with a total lack of concern. "I'm not going to do anything I shouldn't. Now, tell me what you know about Nichols's Riding Stables."

Shirley removed the brochure from inside her wide sleeve and spread it open for the others to read. "It says they have afternoon riding lessons with gentle, well-behaved horses and lots of riding trails. It's ideal for someone like Karen."

"Allow me," Goodness said, *whoosh*ing the brightly colored brochure out of Shirley's hand. Before the other prayer ambassador could protest further, Goodness disappeared over the outer edge of the building. Given no option, Shirley followed just in time to find her fellow angel dodging her way between metal grocery carts, headed straight toward Maureen Woods's car.

Shirley watched in dismay as Goodness lured a cart away from a long line of them near the front of the store. She set it rolling across the large parking lot until it stopped directly behind Maureen's car.

A little boy who was walking into the store with his mother watched the cart take off on its own and then come to an abrupt halt. He must have been about five, Shirley gauged.

The boy tugged on the strap of his mother's purse, which was draped over her arm.

"Mom. Mom!"

"Stevie, how many times have I asked you not to pull on my purse? . . . Answer me, son. How many times?"

"But, Mom—"

"How would you like it if I yanked on you?"

"But, Mom, I just saw a cart move and stop all on its own," he told her.

"Then don't pull on my arm, and I won't pull on yours," she said, completely ignoring what the youngster had told her. With that, she reached for his hand and led him inside the store.

Shirley swore she was about to melt into the asphalt. "What are you trying to do?" she asked Goodness between gritted teeth. "See how fast you can get the three of us sent back in disgrace? We promised no monkey business, remember?"

"What's so unnatural about gravity pulling a cart a certain distance?" Goodness inquired with a look as innocent as freshly fallen snow. "All we—"

"*We?*"

"I." At least she had the good grace to correct herself, Shirley noted.

"All I did," Goodness continued, as if burdened with the incompetence of the other two, "was make the brochure accessible to a certain person we know and love."

"Look at that!" Maureen said as she trudged toward her parked car, loaded down with two heavy bags of groceries. "Don't you just hate it when thoughtless people leave their carts out? I'll need to put it away before I can leave."

"Here," her mother said, "let me move it out of your way."

"You have your own load—I'll get it," Maureen insisted. She set the bags inside the cart and opened the car trunk. After placing her mother's bags inside the car, she retrieved her own. "I'll take the cart back," she said, unlocking the passenger door for her mother.

She raced back toward the store and left the cart in the appropriate slot. A colorful piece of paper flew out and slapped her across the chest. Impatiently Maureen tossed it aside and half trotted back to her vehicle.

A gust of wind came up, carrying dirt and bits of grit with it. Maureen raced toward her car and climbed inside, thankful to escape the unexpected blast.

Just then the wind flattened the brochure against her windshield. She couldn't see a blasted thing, let alone attempt to drive.

"Maureen, do you see that?"

"Don't worry, Mom, I'll get it in just a moment."

"No, I mean do you see what the brochure is for?"

"No, Mother, I haven't read it."

"It's about a riding stable."

"How nice." Maureen didn't mean to be short-tempered, but she had other errands to run, and she wanted to get home before the frozen foods began to thaw.

She opened her car door, climbed out, snatched the brochure from her windshield, and tossed it onto the backseat.

"Nichols's Riding Stables," her mother said. "It just might be something that would interest Karen."

"I'm sure it would," Maureen said, twisting around to make sure no cars were coming before she backed out of the space. "I'll read it later, Mom."

She had five other errands to run, and it took another hour and a half before she was able to drop her mother off. Karen was playing with a girl in the neighborhood, so Maureen left her at her parents' place. Actually she didn't mind an afternoon alone.

The phone rang as she was carrying the last bag of groceries in from the car.

"Hello," she said, stretching the long cord to the refrigerator and setting two half gallons of milk inside.

"Hello. This is Thom Nichols. Is this Maureen Woods?"

Nichols. Nichols. The name sounded vaguely familiar. "Yes, it is."

"You left a message on my answering machine. I understand you're interested in riding lessons for your daughter?"

Paul Morris wasn't looking forward to his visit with Madge Bartelli and her husband. He feared the couple were looking for him to supply something he simply didn't have.

Hope.

Courage.

Reassurances.

God's love.

Paul felt as if he'd lost all four in his first go-around with cancer when Barbara had been so ill. There was nothing left over to offer Madge. Nothing with which to comfort her husband.

He paused outside the front door, and his hand tightened around the soft leather-bound book he'd brought with him. It seemed an eternity passed before he found the strength to raise his hand and ring the doorbell.

Bernard opened the door, and the older man's sad, tired eyes brightened when he saw Paul.

"God bless you, Reverend, for stopping by." He held open the screen door for him. "Just knowing you were coming lifted Madge's spirits. She's sitting up in the living room, waiting for you. It's the first time she's been out of bed in almost a week."

Paul's sense of guilt increased tenfold. He shouldn't have stayed away so long. He moved into the living room and was surprised by how frail Madge looked. He shouldn't have been. He knew what cancer did and hated the disease with everything in him.

Madge leaned back on the recliner, swaddled in blankets. Her once bright eyes were dulled with medication and pain. How thin she'd become, he noted, and her skin was unnaturally pale and sickly. The house smelled of disease and struggle.

It had been two weeks or more since his last visit. Paul was angry with himself for his selfishness. These people were part of the flock he'd been assigned to minister.

"Pastor Paul," Madge whispered. Her weathered face brightened with a smile when she saw him. "How good of you to stop by."

"I apologize for not coming sooner. Time just seems to slip through my fingers."

"You're so busy."

"I'm never too busy for you."

Madge managed another weak smile.

"I'll get some tea," Bernard said. "Madge enjoys a cup of tea now and again." Her husband said this as though he held on desperately to this one small part of their lives that they continued to share.

"Sit down, please," Madge invited.

Paul claimed the chair next to her. He knew she was in pain, knew she struggled not to let others realize how very bad it was. He knew all this because of his own wife.

How he missed Barbara in that moment. It had been hell on earth to watch the ravages of cancer strip away first her health, then her looks. The end was the cruelest aspect of the disease. It had stolen Barbara's dignity.

"It's such a beautiful day," Madge said, gazing longingly out the window. "Bernard brought me a poinsettia. I'd forgotten how pretty and red they can be. I do so love flowers."

Bernard returned just then, awkwardly carrying a tray with mugs and a teapot.

"You should have used the china cups," Madge said.

"I prefer a mug," Paul said quickly, not wanting them to worry about serving him on their finest dishes.

"I'm not much good at this," Bernard apologized as he set the tray on the coffee table. "Madge was always the one who could do such a pretty tray with those fancy linen napkins and the like. I tried, sweetheart."

"You did just fine."

Paul intercepted a look the long-married couple shared. One that was laced with a love so strong, it had bridged nearly fifty years.

"I brought along something I thought might help," Paul said, handing the worn book to Madge. "It was Barbara's, and she read it often. I'd like you to have it, and pray you find the same solace Barbara did in the psalms."

Madge lovingly ran her gnarled hand over the top of the leather-bound book. "*Psalms and Proverbs.*"

"The words were a comfort to her, especially on the nights she couldn't sleep."

"What a beautiful thing, to bring us your own saintly wife's book," Bernard said. He reached inside his back pocket, brought out a wrinkled white handkerchief, and blew his large nose. Paul thought that the older man's eyes shone with unshed tears.

"I'll treasure this little book and be sure it's returned to you when the time comes."

Paul drank from his mug. He had nothing to offer these godly people, but Barbara had reached out from the grave and lent him a hand when he needed it.

"Now tell us about Joe," Madge said after taking one small sip of her tea. The mug wobbled as if it were too heavy for her to lift. Bernard gently removed it from her hand and set it aside.

"I came to ask about you," Paul said, barely able to watch the tender way in which these two cared for each other.

"Joe will be home from college soon now, won't he?"

"Soon." Paul was eager for his son's arrival. Joe's homecoming was the one bright spot in Paul's holiday. The two would be together, and it would almost be as it had been in years past when Barbara was alive.

His son was a subject he found easy to discuss. He told the Bartellis about Joe's classes. As he finished speaking, he realized Madge had fallen asleep, and he dropped his voice.

"Bless you, Reverend," Bernard said, his face revealing his gratitude. "I swear this is the first time Madge's slept in nearly two days."

"How are you holding up?" Paul asked the older man.

Bernard's gaze skittered away from Paul, and he seemed uncomfortable with the question. "I'm not the one suffering."

"But in many ways Madge's cancer is as demanding on you."

"I don't mind taking care of her," he said, and his voice was stiff with pride. "I do a better job than those people in the hospital. At least when I touch her, I do it with love. To those doctors and nurses Madge is just another old woman. To me she's the woman I fell in love with and married all those years ago."

"What about your children? Are they coming home for Christmas?"

Bernard set his mug back on the tray, being careful not to make the least bit of sound for fear of disturbing his wife's precious rest. "No. They're spread out all over the country, and we don't want them risking the drive or taking on the expense of a plane trip." He lowered his head and focused on his folded hands. "The doctors told me they weren't sure how much longer Madge would last. Maybe six months more, but it could be over as soon as three. The children will want to be here then."

"Of course." Paul glanced at his watch. "Perhaps it would be best if I left now."

Bernard nodded. "I can't thank you enough for stopping by."

"I'll come again," Paul promised. "Possibly in a couple of days."

"We'd both appreciate that." Bernard stood slowly, seeming to have some trouble. "We don't mean to be a burden to you."

"You're never that." Bernard and Madge had unselfishly volunteered their efforts over the years. Now it was Paul's turn to return a small portion of all they'd given him and his family.

Paul left, and not wanting to cook himself something for dinner, he stopped off at a fast-food restaurant and ordered something quick, easy, and tasteless.

When he arrived at the house, the first thing he noticed was that the kitchen lights were on. Had be been careless and left them on that morning? He really did need to be more attentive to details.

Letting himself in by the back door, he tossed the grease-smeared white bag on the kitchen table and hung up his sweater.

"Dad?"

Paul's heart raced with excitement. "Joe? Is that you?"

"Dad!" His son rushed into the kitchen and hugged him excitedly. "Dad, there's someone I want you to meet."

A lovely blue-eyed young woman stood across the kitchen. Joe crossed to her and placed his arm around her shoulders. "Dad, I'd like you to meet Annie," he said, smiling brightly at his father. "I've asked her to be my wife."

It shouldn't have surprised Joy Palmer that Ted Griffin was romantically involved. He was tall, dark, and good-looking, and her heart raced like a stock car every time she laid eyes on him.

She did admit to a certain curiosity about the type of woman he'd date, so she did what she generally did when he came around. She watched and waited and made sure she had an unobstructed view of him.

His girlfriend was sophisticated and beautiful, Joy noted, but she didn't study the woman long. No need to give herself a bigger complex than the one she already had. Catherine's grandson was a hunk. It made sense that he'd date a woman who qualified as a beauty queen.

Catherine had been so anxious about this meeting and had wanted to make a good impression. Joy hoped everything had gone well.

Just before dinner, when Joy was preparing to leave for the day, she found Catherine sitting in the library. An unopened book was balanced on her lap.

"Well, Catherine," Joy said, standing in the doorway, "you're certainly looking pensive."

"Joy." The older woman's eyes brightened. "I thought you'd left by now."

"I had a few odds and ends to clear up. How'd the meeting go with your grandson and his friend?"

"Just fine."

"I caught a glimpse of her, and she's a beautiful woman."

Catherine nodded. "She seems . . ."

"Yes?" Joy prompted. It wasn't like Catherine to let something fade. The woman was as spry as someone fifteen years her junior.

"It's nothing," Catherine murmured, and shook her head. "You have a nice evening now."

"I probably won't do anything more exciting than sit home and watch the Lakers take on the Chicago Bulls."

"You like basketball?"

"I love it," Joy confessed.

Catherine brightened considerably. "Ted's always talking about the Lakers. It seems he's a fan himself. You've met my grandson, haven't you?"

Joy could feel the heat rise up her neck. "Not formally."

"But, my dear, you must. I'll make a point of seeing to it the next time he stops by. You two have a lot in common."

"Ah, I guess I'd better go now," Joy said, anxious to make her get-away. She and Ted had a lot in common! It was all she could do not to laugh out loud. Sure, they both might enjoy professional basketball. But she couldn't picture Ted Griffin with his feet propped up on her coffee table, a big bowl of popcorn in his lap. She couldn't see him thrusting his arms in the air over a three-point play and shouting with joy. With Joy.

Not the Ted Griffin who dated the picture-perfect woman she'd seen an hour or so earlier. No, men like Catherine Goodwin's grandson wouldn't be interested in someone like her. Joy was too much her own person to worry about having every hair in place and what her makeup looked like after eight hours on the job. She didn't have the creams and eye shadows necessary to be counted among the truly lovely. Besides, she was much too spontaneous for the sophisticated crowd he probably favored.

The problem was Joy's romantic heart. She did so love to dream. That's what there was between her and Ted. A silly romantic dream.

Joy stopped in her office just long enough to pick up her sweater and her purse. She would have gone directly to the employee parking lot if she hadn't seen Charles sitting, staring longingly out the window.

She crossed the large room and sat next to the old man. "It's time for dinner," she told him softly.

It was as if she hadn't spoken.

"I was just heading home," Joy told him, as if they were carrying on a normal two-sided conversation. "The Lakers are playing tonight, and I've been saving my energy so I could cheer them on."

Then Charles smiled briefly, but his gaze didn't leave the large picture window that gave a panoramic view of Wilshire Boulevard.

Joy leaned in closer and gently squeezed his hand. "I'll see you in the morning."

She'd turned away before she heard him speak. His voice was low and scratchy, as if it had been a long time since he'd used it.

"'Night, Joy."

It was the little things like Charles wishing her a good evening that caused Joy to love her job so much. Whistling a favorite Christmas carol, she hurried out to the parking lot. If she didn't hurry, she'd be late for the opening tip-off.

After tossing her purse onto the backseat of Edith, her '57 Chevrolet, Joy started the cranky engine. She knew she should have traded in this car for something more modern years ago, but she really loved antiques.

"Come on, old girl," she said when the battery didn't immediately fire to life. "One more time for the Gipper," she encouraged.

Edith responded with a low whine.

"You were just fine this morning," Joy reminded her. "Remember, I fed you gas and oil and promised you a wax job this weekend."

Edith's only answer was another sick-sounding whine, followed by an even sicker choke.

"All right," Joy muttered, "be that way. I'll call triple A, and those big men with the large mean truck will come and want to know all about your private parts."

Disgruntled, Joy climbed out of her car. She couldn't imagine what could possibly be wrong. Her father, who happened to be the world's greatest mechanic, kept Edith in top running condition. Unfortunately her father had tickets to the basketball game that evening, and she'd be stuck calling for a tow truck.

Joy was walking back toward the retirement center when a flashy red sports car pulled up. The door opened, and Ted Griffin got out.

Joy hesitated, wondering what Catherine's grandson was doing back so soon.

"I'll only be a minute, sweetheart," he told the woman inside. He straightened and glanced casually at Joy. His eyes widened, and all at once he started running toward her.

Ted Griffin grabbed Joy around the waist and pulled her out of the path of her very own vehicle. Edith, apparently under her own power, merrily plowed into the side of his car, then sat there purring as if her engine were as finely tuned as an expensive European model's.

Chapter

★ ☆ ★

5

"*Oh, my goodness.* Oh, dear." Joy raced to Ted's fancy sports car to examine the damage. "Edith," she cried, angrily slapping her hand against her vehicle's shiny trunk, "what's gotten into you?"

"What the hell happened?" Blythe leaped out of the passenger side and glared indignantly at Joy.

"Darling." Ted dashed to her side. "Are you all right?"

"I've just been struck by a runaway vehicle," she raged. "How do you expect me to feel?"

"Would you like me to call a medic?" Joy asked, wanting to do what she could to help.

"Don't be ridiculous."

"I think maybe you should sit down a moment," Ted suggested, leading Blythe safely inside the retirement center. Once she was seated in the foyer, Ted knelt in front of her.

Blythe held herself stiff and stared angrily at Joy, as if Joy had intentionally rammed her car into Ted's. "Exactly what were you trying to do? Kill me?"

"No-o-o," Joy said quickly, stammering in her rush to reassure the woman. "I can't tell you how sorry I am. I don't know what came over Edith. I had the car keys in my hand. See?" She held them up for Blythe's inspection. "How Edith's engine could have started up on her own that way is beyond me."

"Do you always refer to your car as Edith?" Blythe made the practice sound juvenile and silly.

"She's like a friend, you see."

"Friend or not, you're going to have to pay for this," Blythe insisted, her voice high and hysterical.

"Of course. There was never any question of that," Joy was quick to assure her. She didn't want to think what this small accident would do to her insurance premiums, but she had no choice. Edith was responsible.

"That was my car you slammed into."

"Blythe," Ted said, his voice calm and reasonable, "settle down. The important thing is that no one was injured."

"What about my car?" Blythe screeched in a most unladylike fashion. "It's only been out of the showroom two months. I knew we should have taken your car."

Ted pinched his lips together. "I'll check the damage myself."

"I'm going with you," Joy said, and followed Ted, unwilling to be left alone with Blythe, who no doubt would find more reasons to lambaste her.

Outside, the two vehicles were parked perpendicular to each other. Edith's nose rested gently against the driver's side, as lightly as if she were giving the highly polished red door a peck on the cheek. Joy noticed her car's engine had stopped as mysteriously as it had started.

"I'll back Edith away from your vehicle," she volunteered, "but she wouldn't start earlier. That's why I was headed back to my office. I'm terribly sorry, but I can't explain what happened."

"Don't worry about it. These crazy things sometimes happen."

Joy hopped inside her car and inserted the key in the ignition. To her complete and utter puzzlement, the engine purred to life like a spoiled, cream-fed kitten.

As soon as she'd pulled away and parked her antique car, she hurried over to view the extent of the damage. Her chest was tight with anticipation.

Ted knelt in front of the driver's door and ran his fingertips over the sports car's slick finish. From what Joy could see, there didn't seem to be so much as a single scratch.

"That's amazing," she whispered, so relieved it took restraint not to leap off the ground and cheer. "I don't see any damage. Of course, you'll want to check it again when the light's better." She wrote down the pertinent information regarding her insurance company, plus her name and address, and gave these to Ted.

"I'll have my mechanic look at it as well," Blythe announced sternly from the sidewalk. "As well as a friend who owns a body shop."

"Of course," Joy said. "Please do. As I said earlier, I fully intend to pay for your trouble."

"You're damn right you will."

"Blythe," Ted said softly, "I know you're upset, but there's nothing to worry about. The car doesn't even seem scratched. Let it go for now, and I'll take care of everything in the morning."

Blythe nodded and sagged as though the weight of the world were pressed upon her delicate shoulders. "The crazy thing is I found my handbag. The trip back wasn't even necessary. It was in the backseat, but I was sure I left it in your grandmother's apartment."

"It doesn't matter." Ted placed his arm protectively around her shoulders and led her around to the passenger side of the car. He held the door open for her and helped her inside.

"You'll get back to me about any damage?" Joy asked.

Ted nodded. "You might have your car checked out as well. Clearly something's wrong for it to take off on its own like that."

Joy folded her arms. "Thank you for your help."

Ted hesitated. "Do I know you?"

"I don't believe we've formally met. I'm Joy Palmer, the resident service director."

"Joy Palmer." He repeated the name, as if that would jar his memory.

"I know your grandmother quite well. She might have mentioned me."

"Ted," Blythe called from inside the car, "are we going to dinner or not?"

Ted rubbed his hand along the side of his jaw, as if he would have liked nothing better than to forget the whole thing. "It's nice to meet you, Joy. I'm sorry it had to be under these circumstances."

"I'm sorry, too."

"Ted!"

"I'll let you know about the car as soon as possible."

"I'd appreciate that." She watched as he drove away, before returning to her own vehicle. Then she slipped onto the driver's seat and closed her hands around the steering wheel. It took a full minute for her to relax.

"Honestly, Edith, I should park you overnight in a bad neighborhood for that little trick. You couldn't have rammed someone else's car?" Muttering to herself, Joy put the car in reverse and pulled out of the space.

She shook her head in wonder. She couldn't remember a time Edith had run better.

"What am I going to do with you?" Shirley asked from the brick fence that ran along the property line of Wilshire Grove Retirement Center.

"Do with me about what?"

"You know darn good and well," Shirley insisted.

"Are you asking about that little trick with Joy's car?" Mercy said, grinning gleefully.

Shirley wore an injured, disappointed look. "You know Gabriel wants me to keep an eye on you two. I'm older and more mature, and I just don't know what I am going to tell him."

"You worry too much. I didn't have anything to do with Joy's car moving. Gravity did."

"Gravity?"

"Sure. If Goodness can whip shopping carts around parking lots and call it gravity, then a little thing like a slow-moving car shouldn't be any big concern."

"That's it," Shirley said with great finality. "I can't take it any longer. I simply can't put up with this kind of mischief from you and Goodness. As far as I'm concerned, from here on out, you two are on your own." She brushed her hands together to illustrate her point.

"You're leaving us?" Mercy couldn't believe what she was hearing. "But we're a team."

"Did you or did you not promise Gabriel you wouldn't pull any of your tricks?"

"I did, but this was such a little thing. I really didn't think anyone would care. Edith helped introduce Joy to Catherine's grandson, didn't she?"

"A car is not a person," Shirley reminded her with limitless patience.

"Not normally, but in this case it's as if the car has her own personality. Joy treats her like a friend, and if she's sensitive to inanimate objects, just imagine how caring she is toward real people."

"Yes, but . . ."

"Don't you understand, Shirl? Joy's the woman Ted Griffin should be marrying, not a cold fish like Blythe Holmes."

"Maybe," Shirley agreed reluctantly. "Is he going to see her again?"

Mercy grinned, feeling downright smug about the answer to that. "I wouldn't doubt it, especially since one of them is about to win two tickets to the next Lakers game."

"One of them?"

"Yup. I just haven't decided who."

"Mercy," Shirley muttered, "you're incorrigible."

"Yeah, I know, but you'll forgive me, won't you?"

"I don't know."

"Just think, you can tell Gabriel how good I've been. I haven't so much as stepped on a single escalator the way I did last year."

"Congratulations, Joe and Annie," Paul said, forcing a happiness he didn't feel into his voice. He walked over to the young woman standing next to his son and held out his hand. "Welcome to our family, Annie."

She was a pretty thing. Small, with dark hair and deep blue eyes. Paul could see she was nervous by the way her hand trembled in his.

"Thank you, Reverend Morris."

"Now tell me when all this happened," Paul said, leading the way into the living room so they could sit down. Vaguely he could remember Joe saying something now and again about another student he was dating, but he hadn't thought his son was this serious.

"Annie and I've known each other four years now."

"We met as freshmen," Annie explained shyly.

"In the last couple of years we've been dating each other exclusively," Joe went on to explain.

Now that his son mentioned it, Paul could remember Joe making a fair number of long-distance calls last summer to a certain Oregon phone number.

"With us both graduating this June, we decided it was time to make plans for our future together." Joe looked to Annie, and the two gazed longingly at each other.

It hadn't been so many years that Paul had forgotten what it was like to be deeply in love. When he'd first fallen for Barbara, every minute they were apart had been too much to bear.

"I realize we're springing the news on you," Annie said, glancing nervously in Paul's direction, "but Joe thought it best if we announced our engagement this way. I hope you don't mind my staying a few days."

"Of course I don't mind. You couldn't be more welcome."

"We wanted to spend time with you first," Joe explained, "then drive to Eugene and let Annie's family know."

Paul nodded, although he was fairly certain neither one sought his approval. "And Christmas?" The words had a difficult time leaving his lips. He knew the answer even before he asked the question. His son would spend the day with his fiancée and her family.

"We thought we'd spend the day with Annie's family," Joe said, studying his father. "You don't mind, do you? I mean, we'll be here for several days. I want you to get to know Annie, since she'll soon be your daughter-in-law."

"Then you've decided on your wedding date?"

"Oh, yes, that was one of the first things we did," Annie explained. "I guess I'm a fairly traditional bride because I want a summer wedding."

"We chose the first Saturday in August," Joe said. "The fourth."

"August," Paul repeated slowly. In less than a year his son would be a married man.

"I'm nearly twenty-two, Dad," Joe said, sounding a little defensive. "I've got a good line on a job with King County up in Seattle. I know you had your doubts when I decided to get my degree in environmental health, but I'm not going to have a problem finding a decent job."

"What about you, Annie?" Paul found it important to ask questions rather than analyze his feelings. He felt lost, as if he were in a dark room and didn't know where to locate the light switch. The darkness seemed to be closing in around him, pressing against his heart. This was supposed to be his time with his son.

"I'll need another year of school for my teaching degree," Annie explained in a small voice. "I've already inquired about doing my student teaching in the Seattle area, and it doesn't look like it'll be any problem."

"It seems you've got everything all figured out." Although he knew he was being selfish, Paul didn't want to share his son. Not this Christmas. Not when he'd been looking forward to this time with Joe.

Joe and Annie gazed wistfully into each other's eyes. Ah, young love. How well Paul remembered the days he was courting Barbara and how they'd struggled to make ends meet while he was in seminary. Each Sunday they'd traveled to a different outlying church. Barbara would play the piano and lead the congregational singing, and he'd preach a rousing sermon. God had smiled down on their efforts and blessed them abundantly—for a time. And then the blessings had been abruptly cut off.

"You don't mind my being gone for Christmas, do you, Dad?" Joe asked.

Paul shook his head. "Don't you worry about me, son, I'll be fine."

"You won't spend the day alone?"

Given that he couldn't be with Joe, Paul preferred his own company. It seemed people crowded him from all sides. He loved his daughter, but when he visited, he found himself making excuses to leave after only an hour.

"Bethany will have me over, I'm sure," he said in answer to his son's question.

"There are a dozen or more people in the church who would fight to have you spend Christmas Day with them."

"Of course," Paul assured Joe. What he didn't explain was that he wasn't interested in squandering Christmas with church friends. He'd looked forward to spending this precious holiday with his only son. He'd thought about various activities for the two of them. Hiking. Maybe they'd fish a while. A few panfried lake trout were sure to cure what ailed him.

"We'd like your blessing on our marriage," Annie said.

Paul smiled. She was such a pretty thing, he could well understand his son falling for her. He was being selfish to want to hold on to Joe himself.

"You have my heartfelt congratulations, my blessing," Paul offered. "And my love. This calls for a celebration. Grab a jacket, I'm taking everyone out to dinner."

Joe's and Annie's young faces brightened with wide smiles.

Several hours later Paul tossed and turned, unable to sleep. Sleeping was becoming more and more of a problem of late. He never had much trouble drifting off, but he'd soon jerk awake and spend fruitless hours fighting to go back to sleep.

He threw aside the blankets and reached for his robe, then climbed down the stairs to the kitchen. He took a glass from the cupboard and was pouring himself some milk when Joe joined him.

"Hi." Joe rubbed a hand down his face and yawned.

"Did I wake you?"

"No, I was up, thinking about, you know, life."

"Life?"

"Mine and Annie's."

"Ah." Paul scooted out a chair at the cluttered kitchen table, and Joe soon joined him.

"Was it like this with you and Mom?" Joe wanted to know. "Did you love her so much that you wondered why it took you so long to realize you were in love?"

"Yes," Paul said, and chuckled. "Your mother was the one who defined our relationship."

Joe straightened and pressed a hand over his pajama-clad chest. "It's the same way with Annie and me. I don't know what I was thinking we'd do after we finished school. I guess I wasn't thinking, because one day she asked me straight out what I was going to do after graduation. I told her and then she started to cry and for the life of me I couldn't make her tell me why.

"The next afternoon she returned everything I'd ever given her. I'm telling you, Dad, you could have knocked me over with a Popsicle stick. Here I thought we had a wonderful relationship, and for no reason I could understand, Annie wanted to break it off."

"That was when you decided to marry her?"

"No," Joe admitted. "First off I had to know what I'd done that was so terribly wrong. I don't lose my cool often, but she really ruffled my feathers. I met her in the library one evening and asked her point-blank what I'd done, and Dad, I swear her answer tied me up in knots so tight, I didn't think I'd ever get my head straight again."

"What did she say?"

"That's the crazy part. She assured me I hadn't done anything."

"But why did she break up with you?"

"That's what I insisted upon knowing. It was her answer that turned my life around. She looked at me with those big, beautiful eyes of hers and said she realized after our talk that she wasn't going to have a part in my future.

"I wanted to argue with her right then and there, wondering where she'd ever come up with anything so stupid, but she wouldn't let me. She was close to crying by then, so she asked that I let her finish. She said she realized when I told her about the job in Seattle that I had no intention of including her in the rest of my life."

"Did you?" It sounded to Paul as if his future daughter-in-law might be guilty of a little manipulation. He wondered if his son realized this.

"That's just it. Of course I did. I naturally assumed that Annie would be there with me. I can't imagine what my life would be like without Annie. She's a part of me now. That's why I took it so hard when she severed the relationship."

What Paul noticed, and what hurt more than he dared show, was that not once during this painful time had Joe sought him out for his advice. Not once had his son contacted him to talk about this special young woman he loved.

Paul didn't think his son was looking for him to comment, and if he had been, Paul wasn't sure what he would have said. He might have said something wholesome about the benefits of love, something he could have used in a sermon one day. Fortunately he was saved from having to say anything. The phone rang.

"Who'd be calling this time of night?" Joe asked.

Paul didn't wonder anymore. Calls this late almost always meant unwelcome news. He walked into his small office and reached for the receiver, not wanting to disturb Annie, whom he presumed was sleeping.

"Hello."

"Reverend Morris?" Bernard Bartelli's voice trembled from the other end of the line. "I'm sorry to wake you."

"I was up, don't worry about it, Bernard. Now tell me what's happened." A part of Paul prayed that Madge had been released from her physical agony, yet he understood better than some how devastating that would be to those she'd left behind.

"It's Madge," Bernard said, struggling to keep his voice even. "She felt so much better after your visit and was up and walking around. Then she fell. I'm at the hospital. The doctor thinks she might have broken her hip."

Paul closed his eyes in pain and frustration. "I'm so sorry."

"Why would this happen to Madge?" Bernard demanded. "Why would God ask her to suffer more? Hasn't she already suffered enough?"

"I assure you, Mr. Nichols, I didn't leave a message on your answering machine," Maureen said, and drew in a shaky breath, determined to settle this matter once and for all. "But I did intend to contact you." It just so happened that her mother had beaten her to the punch.

Her words were met with a brief silence. "In other words, you didn't call me, but you planned on doing so."

"That's right."

"Then who left the message?"

"Actually, I'm fairly certain it was my mother," she said. "But since I've got you on the line, I'd like to ask you about riding lessons for my daughter."

Thom Nichols rattled off the details as if he'd given them out a hundred times that same afternoon and could recite them backward if asked. Maureen wrote down the pertinent information.

"My daughter's twelve," she said.

"I have a twelve-year-old myself," came Thom's companionable reply. "They can be quite a handful, can't they?"

"Oh, yes."

Thom told her about a recent incident with his daughter and Maureen found herself doodling, drawing a series of looped circles. She'd recently read an article that claimed there was some deep sexual meaning in doodles. Frankly, she had never been one to talk on the phone and draw silly, nonsensical symbols. All at once it was as if she were another Georgia O'Keeffe. She didn't know if it was the man or the sorry state of her sex life.

Thom Nichols was the friendly sort, she noted, and he liked to talk. Maureen found herself smiling once or twice, and before she realized what she was doing, she'd agreed to drive out to Nichols's Riding Stables the following day and meet Thom and his daughter.

If everything met with Maureen's approval, she'd sign Karen up for riding classes. That was what Maureen had agreed to, but as she replaced the receiver she realized she barely knew one end of a horse from the other. What she could find to approve or disapprove would fit on the head of a thumbtack.

Karen arrived home an hour later. She burst into the front door and demanded, "What's for dinner?"

"What do you want?"

"Steak and lobster."

"Well, you're getting spaghetti."

"I like spaghetti."

"With green beans and a tossed salad."

Karen shook her head in a way that made Maureen want to laugh. "Mom, you're ruining a perfectly good dinner with all that green stuff again."

"I thought we'd take a drive tomorrow," she announced casually as Karen set the table.

"That sounds like fun. Where do you want to go?" Karen stuffed bread sticks into a water glass and carried it over to their place settings.

Maureen hesitated, wondering how much she should say. She had the funny feeling she was traipsing around a pool of quicksand—one wrong step and she'd be stuck for life.

"I don't want you to get your hopes up. We're just going to check out this place and see if we can fit riding lessons into our budget."

Karen went stock-still. "Riding lessons?" she whispered with such rapture, one would think she'd stepped through the gates of heaven to walk on streets of pure gold. "On a real, live horse?"

"Yes, but—" Maureen wasn't allowed to finish. Karen flew across the kitchen at breakneck speed and threw her arms around her mother's waist with such ferocity that it nearly toppled Maureen.

"Oh, Mom! You're the most wonderful mother in the whole world. Riding lessons! Do I get to pick which horse I get to ride? Where is this place? How did you find out about it?"

"Settle down, sweetheart. One question at a time."

Maureen couldn't remember when her daughter had been more animated. She asked a dozen questions at least that many times until Maureen was thoroughly sick of the subject.

Karen went to bed without an argument and was up the next morning at the crack of dawn.

"Mom, Mom, wake up!"

Maureen managed to raise one apathetic eyelid to find her daughter standing next to her mattress, fully dressed in jeans and a sweatshirt. Her hair was combed and her teeth brushed. The newspaper was tucked in one hand, and her other sported a steaming cup of coffee.

"What . . . time . . . is . . . it?" Maureen didn't lift her head from the pillow, and the question came out slurred and pathetic sounding.

"Five-thirty."

Maureen groaned. "Honey, even the horses are still asleep."

"But they won't be by the time we arrive. Come on, Mom, it's a beautiful day. Rise and shine." The twelve-year-old set the frightfully thick newspaper and coffee on the nightstand. Before Maureen had time to prepare herself, Karen leaped on the bed, buckling the mattress.

"How long have you been up?" Maureen wanted to know.

"Since three-thirty. I couldn't sleep," Karen explained, tossing her arms into the air. "I tried and tried, but every time I closed my eyes all I could think about was learning to ride, and sleeping was impossible."

"All right." Maureen could see she was fighting a losing battle, although she refused to show up on Thom Nichols's back step before the sun rose. "Give me a few minutes to wake up." She struggled into a sitting position and pulled the hair away from her face.

"I can cook us breakfast. What would you like?"

Maureen shook her head. "Just coffee for now, thanks."

That Karen managed to get her out of bed, dressed, and fed before seven on a Sunday morning was little short of a miracle as far as Maureen was concerned. The last time she'd been up this early on a weekend, she'd been nursing Karen.

By sheer force of will she was able to hold her daughter off until nine, but it demanded every trick she had up the sleeve of motherhood.

Using the detailed directions Thom had given her, Maureen easily found her way to Nichols's Riding Stables. The sprawling adobe building was set back from the corral, which housed five or six horses.

Karen was out of the car and racing toward the corral as fast as her legs would carry her by the time Maureen had parked. Before she could so much as object, Karen had stepped onto the bottom rung of the fence and had folded her arms over a post as if she were born to be a buckaroo. By the time Maureen caught up with her, Karen was rooted to the spot, a look of sheer bliss over her face.

"Mom, look. Aren't they the most beautiful creatures you've ever seen?"

"Sweetheart, I don't think it's a good idea for you to be standing up there like that."

"I'm fine. People do this in the movies all the time."

"Can I help you?" a deep, resonant male voice asked from behind her.

Maureen turned around, prepared to apologize for the way Karen had instantly made herself at home, but the words never made it to her lips. Before her stood the embodiment of every cowboy hero she'd ever dreamed about as a teenage girl. He was Gary Cooper, John Wayne, and Clint Eastwood all rolled into one hunk of a man. He stood at least six inches taller than Maureen, and his hat added an additional four or five to that. His face was as tanned as soft leather and marked with the most striking pair of blue eyes Maureen had even seen.

"I'm Maureen Woods," she said when she could manage to stop staring. Her business acumen rescued her, and she stepped forward and offered him her hand. "I believe we talked yesterday."

"Thom Nichols," he said, removing his glove in order to shake hands with her. His palms were covered with thick calluses. "You're the divorcée, right?"

"I didn't tell you that," Maureen said defensively.

"No, I don't suppose you did," he said. "No offense meant."

"How'd you know?"

He removed his hat and slapped it across his thigh. "Can't rightly say. It must have been something you said."

"What are the horses' names?" Karen asked, jumping down from the corral.

"First off, they aren't just horses. The black one out there is Midnight, and he's a gelding. The spotted one's a mare named Thunder. The one in the corner's a roan. These are all terms you'll be learning later as part of the class."

"How long have you been operating Nichols's Riding Stables?" Maureen asked.

"A year or so now."

"Dad." A girl raced from inside the barn and stopped abruptly when she saw her father with Karen and Maureen.

Thom placed his arm around the girl. "This is my daughter, Paula."

"Hello, Paula," Maureen said.

"Hi." Karen raised her right hand in greeting. From the look she gave the other girl, one would think Thom Nichols's daughter was the luckiest girl alive.

"Why don't you give Karen a quick tour while I talk to her mother?" Thom suggested.

"Sure. Come on," Paula said, immediately taking charge. "Our cat, Tinkerbell, just had a litter of kittens, and I found them in the barn."

"Really? I've never seen newborn kittens before."

"That should keep those two entertained for a few minutes," Thom said. "Why don't I pour us each a cup of coffee and describe the riding course to you, and then you can decide if you want to sign Karen up for lessons or not."

Actually a cup of coffee sounded wonderful. "I don't mean to interrupt your morning. It's just that Karen was so excited, she all but dragged me out of bed at five-thirty. I'm sure you and your wife have better things to do than entertain me."

"It's no bother," Thom assured her, leading her toward the house. "By the way, I'm a widower."

Chapter

★ ✹ ★

6

"*Why would such* a thing happen to Madge?" Bernard asked, leaning forward on the hard, plastic hospital chair and wringing his hands. "She was in so much pain already. Did God think she needed more?"

"I don't know why God allows anyone to suffer," Paul confessed to the older man. He felt bitterly inadequate to comfort the long-standing church member. All Paul had to offer Bernard was his presence, and frankly he wasn't sure he was doing anyone a favor. Least of all Madge and Bernard.

Paul checked his watch. It was close to four. He'd been at the hospital the better part of three hours. Most of that time had been spent waiting for word from the doctors. They'd come ten minutes earlier with the news that Madge was resting comfortably.

"She isn't, you know," Bernard murmured.

"Isn't?"

"Resting comfortably."

"I'm sure she's sedated," Paul said.

"Yes, but the pain's still there. Beneath all that medication the pain's there."

Paul understood. Pain was a fiend, ever present, ever ready to devour one's strength. One's peace of mind. One's serenity. It had eaten away at Barbara like a voracious monster, never satisfied, never content, until Paul couldn't bear to see the suffering in his wife's eyes any longer.

"She's sleeping now," Paul said gently. "Let her rest. Go home and rest yourself."

"I couldn't sleep."

Paul knew about that as well. He'd felt guilty about sleeping when he knew Barbara couldn't. Guilty about being healthy when she was so desperately ill. Guilty about being alive when she was dead.

He'd wanted to stay awake with her, wanted to spend every precious moment she had left at her side. Yet he slept. The sleep of the damned, he suspected. Those damned to grieve. Those damned to be left behind. Those damned to live the rest of their lives alone.

"I'll drive you home," Paul offered, patting the older man's shoulder.

Bernard clasped his hands together and nodded slowly, as if the effort drained him of every ounce of strength he possessed.

"Hello, Mrs. Johnson," Joe Morris said, sticking his head in the door of the church office. "Have you seen my father around?"

"Joe." The woman who'd served as his father's secretary for as long as Joe could remember stood up behind the desk, walked around, and hugged him. "When did you get home?"

"Late yesterday afternoon."

"My, my, but you're a sight for sore eyes," she said, sounding genuinely pleased to see him.

Joe buried his hands in his pants pockets. It embarrassed him to have the women of the church make a fuss over him. He liked Leta Johnson better than most. At least she didn't pinch his cheeks and tell him what a handsome boy he'd turned out to be. Boy indeed! Last summer he'd been forced to bite his tongue to keep from reminding the church ladies he was twenty-one. Soon he'd be married. That should set matters straight once and for all.

"Have you seen my dad?" Joe repeated. Annie was waiting for him at the house, and he didn't want to get involved in a lengthy conversation with Mrs. Johnson.

"Not this morning," the secretary said with a thoughtful look. "Could you come in and talk a minute, Joe?"

Joe looked at his watch. "I don't really have a lot of time."

"That's fine. I'll only keep you a few moments. It's rather important."

"Okay." He walked inside the office and pulled a chair up to the secretary's scarred mahogany desk.

For someone so keen on talking to him, Mrs. Johnson didn't seem overly eager to start. Nor could Joe imagine what could be the problem. "Have you noticed any changes in your dad over the last year or so?" she asked.

"Changes? What sort of changes?"

"He's lost weight, hasn't he?"

"Oh, that," Joe said, relieved. "I suppose he isn't eating properly since Mom died. He walked into the house last night with a hamburger and fries. I think he intended on having that for dinner."

"Yet he's turned down a dozen dinner invitations last month alone," Leta murmured under her breath. "There are a host of families who'd be delighted to have your father join them once a month or so. He could eat a home-cooked meal every night if he wanted."

Joe didn't blame his father for preferring his own cooking. "He doesn't want anyone else to cook for him. Dad's too independent for that."

Leta Johnson found it necessary to store a couple of pens in her top desk drawer. "He seems to have gotten forgetful of late. More often than not I have to remind him of church meetings, and even when I do, he arrives late. The finance and worship committees have decided to start without him, and frankly I don't blame them. It's frustrating to arrive on time and then be kept waiting a half hour or longer."

Joe frowned. He'd always known his father to be a tyrant about punctuality. This wasn't typical of the man who'd raised him.

"That doesn't sound like Dad."

"I've known your father a good many years, Joe, and I'm telling you right now, something isn't right. It's like . . . it's like he's given up."

"He misses Mom," Joe said, more to himself than Mrs. Johnson.

"But it's been two years now, and I'd have thought matters would get better. Instead they've gradually grown worse. My own Floyd's been gone seven years. I know how difficult it is to lose one's mate."

"I don't know what to tell you," Joe admitted.

"Frankly, I'm worried. There isn't anyone I can talk to about this. I thought to phone your sister, but this sort of thing is difficult to discuss without being able to look the person in the eye, if you know what I mean."

Joe wasn't sure he did, but he nodded anyway.

"With you coming home for the holidays and all, I decided to wait. I was hoping you might know something I don't."

"I wish there was something I could tell you," Joe said, at a loss.

"This morning is a perfect example," the secretary continued. "I don't have a clue where Pastor Morris might be. He hasn't even come into the office, and there's a meeting of the elders at two. What am I supposed to tell them if he doesn't show?"

Joe hadn't a clue. Leta Johnson looked at him with wide, beseeching eyes, and he felt he had to say something. "Let me think about this, Mrs. Johnson. I'll get back to you."

"Thank you, Joe," she said, and sounded relieved.

Joe left the church, his head buzzing. He returned to the house and found Annie in the kitchen, washing dishes. She'd wiped down the countertops and cleared the mess off the table. It seemed with his mother gone, his father used the tabletop and counters as a filing cabinet. Odds and ends of mail were tucked in every conceivable corner. This troubled Joe, since he'd always known his father to be neat and orderly.

"I can't find my dad," he told Annie.

"I heard him come back to the house early this morning. Maybe he's still in bed."

"No," Joe said, growing concerned, "I already checked."

"Just a minute," Annie said, gazing out the kitchen window. "I think that might be your dad outside. It looks like he's in the garage."

"The garage?" Joe asked. He gave Annie a puzzled look and wandered outside. Annie followed.

Sure enough, his father was busy sorting through a stack of cardboard boxes that had been in precisely that spot for fifteen or more years.

"Dad?"

"Howdy, Joe," Paul said cheerfully. "Annie." He pushed up the sleeves of his sweater.

"What are you doing?" Joe asked, not knowing what to think.

Paul laughed and braced his hands against his hips. "What does it look like? I'm cleaning out this mess. I've got more junk than some of those disposal centers. It's time to clear some of this garbage out of here."

"Today?"

"Why not? It seemed like a perfectly good day to do a little cleaning."

Joe looked over to where his father had set their fishing gear. "I put that aside for you," his dad said, pointing toward the two poles. "You should take that stuff with you."

"But why?"

His father gave him an odd look, then leaned over and sorted through another stack of boxes, lifting one and then another. "I hear there's good fishing in Seattle."

"Dad," Joe said, not understanding any of this. "Mrs. Johnson said you have an elders' meeting this afternoon."

Paul straightened and frowned. "The meeting's this afternoon?"

"That's what she said. You haven't been into the office yet."

Paul Morris rotated his shoulders. "I meant to get over there earlier, then got sidetracked. I'll wash up now and meet with the elders."

He walked past Joe on his way into the house.

"Joe." Annie pressed her hand to his forearm. "What's wrong with your father?"

"I don't know. But I think I'd better phone my sister. Maybe she'll know what to do."

"I can't believe I'm doing this," Maureen mumbled as she shifted papers outside of her briefcase and set them on the car seat next to her. It was no small exaggeration to say she'd practically rearranged her entire work schedule to fit Karen's riding lessons into her already full week.

For the next several weeks Tuesday and Thursday afternoons would be a nightmare for her. She had to leave the bank at two, which meant she had to arrive at six in the morning. She was forced into giving up half her usual lunch hour as well in order to make up for time away from her desk. In addition, she brought her work home with her.

No sane woman would do this. Only a mother would agree to a schedule like this. A desperate mother.

On the bright side, Karen hadn't woken once with a nightmare from the moment Maureen had casually mentioned Nichols's Riding Stables. If the remedy for Karen's bad dreams was a few riding lessons, then Maureen would gladly shorten her lunch hour for the rest of her life.

Uncomfortable working in her car, Maureen shifted her position numerous times. She managed to prop her calculator on the dashboard and shuffle papers around her steering wheel in order to make notes where needed.

Two minutes after their arrival, Karen had disappeared inside the barn, looking for Thom Nichols's daughter and the new kittens. Maureen would have followed her, but she didn't think it would be a good idea to go traipsing into unknown territory in two-inch heels. Apparently Karen knew where she was headed.

Maureen was just beginning to think it might do her good to get out of the car and stretch her legs when a knock sounded against the car window.

Thom Nichols stood outside, his profile silhouetted against the last of the sunlight. Her heart did an immediate somersault, and not because he'd frightened her. It wasn't that she was attracted to him, she told herself. The cowboy fantasy, along with everything else romantic, had died a slow, painful death with Brian's deceit.

"Hello," she said as she rolled down her car window. She made sure her voice revealed little of what she was feeling. She was friendly, but not overly so. Cool. Collected.

"There's no need for you to wait in the car by yourself," Thom said.

"That's all right," she returned hurriedly, wanting to avoid spending time alone with him. "I was just catching up on some paperwork."

Thom looked to the sky as if some message were written in the clouds. "Daylight's about gone. Might as well come inside my office and have a cup of coffee with me. I'd be happy for the company."

Maureen would have found an excuse if it hadn't been for the last part about welcoming her companionship. He was lonely, the same way she was lonely. Only he was willing to admit it, whereas she preferred to ignore the obvious.

At their first meeting, he'd explained that his wife had died three years earlier. After he'd told a little about himself, he seemed to want her to share something about herself. Maureen hadn't. She rarely discussed her personal life with anyone.

Her head was telling her one thing as she stored the papers inside her briefcase, and her heart was saying something entirely contradictory. Why shouldn't she enjoy a cup of coffee with a man? Thom Nichols, her head told her, was more than just a man. He was rugged and solid, and those piercing blue eyes of his seemed to look straight through her.

It was unnerving. She'd looked at him and had the uncontrollable urge to weep. Thus far she'd managed to control her emotions. Thank God. She didn't even want to imagine what he would think of her if she started weeping for absolutely no reason.

"Ken's giving the kids their lesson this afternoon," Thom explained as he led her into a small office just inside the barn door. He took two large mugs off a Peg-Board on the wall and poured them each coffee.

Maureen cradled the mug between her hands and stared into the dark depths. After being holed up inside her car for the better part of an hour, she was grateful to be up and about. However, she wasn't sure spending time with Thom was necessarily good for her peace of mind.

"It seems Karen and Paula have hit it off like gangbusters," he commented, rolling the lone chair her way and inclining his lean hips against the edge of his desk. He stretched out his legs and crossed them at the ankles.

Avoiding eye contact, Maureen nodded. "We've recently moved, and it's been hard on Karen. She hasn't made new friends as easily as I thought she would."

"Paula could use a friend. She's getting to the age where she misses her mother."

"How are the kittens?" Maureen asked, quickly changing the subject. This man made her nervous in ways she'd forgotten. It'd been so long since she'd been around a man that she didn't know how to behave. She'd been a college student when she'd first met Brian, which was more years ago than she wanted to remember.

"Those kittens are as cute as a bug's ear."

Maureen's smile waned, and she looked at her watch.

"Ken will have the kids back in about thirty minutes," he said, and Maureen swore the man read her thoughts. "Do I make you nervous?"

"Yes," she admitted defensively.

This appeared to amuse him. He crossed and recrossed his ankles. "Why's that?"

"I . . . I don't really know."

"Sure you do, but you're afraid to admit it. That's all right, I don't blame you. Fact is, I like you, Maureen Woods."

"You like me?" Maureen wondered exactly what that entailed.

"Well, you're as prickly as a cactus—"

"So you see me as a challenge," Maureen said, wishing now she'd stayed inside her car. "Listen, my ex-husband taught me everything I need to know about—"

"I'm not your ex-husband," he said gently, interrupting her. Then, as if they were carrying on a perfectly casual conversation, he sipped his coffee and announced, "I'd like to date you."

The words exploded like tiny firecrackers in her mind. They vibrated within her and echoed through the empty years she'd spent since her divorce.

"Maureen?"

"I don't think so." No one in her right mind would voluntarily set herself up for the kind of heartache Brian had inflicted upon her and Karen. The endless list of lies. The hurt. The infidelity.

"Why not?"

Maureen should have guessed this was a man who didn't take no easily. She didn't know how to tell him she was afraid. Afraid of falling in love again. Afraid of making herself vulnerable. Afraid of being afraid.

"Date again? You've got to be joking. I haven't got time for a relationship."

"Maureen," he said gently, softly, "there's no reason to be scared."

He knew. He hadn't listened to her words; instead he'd heard the underlying fear as no one ever had before. He straightened, set aside his mug, and walked over to where she was sitting. Maureen's heart felt like machine-gun firing inside her chest. It was all she could do to keep from bolting from the office.

"I'm not going to hurt you," he told her in the silkiest of tones, and pressed his callused palm against her cheek.

Maureen flinched involuntarily at the unexpectedness of his touch. His hand was cool against her flushed skin.

"No one's going to hurt you," he told her. "Not anymore."

Maureen nearly laughed out loud. Apparently Thom hadn't gotten the message. All at once there were tears in her eyes. She couldn't remember thinking she was about to break into tears. She knew she should leave before she embarrassed herself any further. How she managed to keep them from falling and from making a complete idiot of herself was something she couldn't answer.

"I'd better go now," she said, abruptly setting her mug aside. "Thanks for the coffee," she muttered on her way out the door.

The instant she was alone, she pressed both index fingers under her eyes and drew in several deep, stabilizing breaths.

Maybe she was coming down with a virus, she reasoned. Crazy as it seemed, she prayed that was exactly what was happening to her.

She made it back to her car just in time for Karen to come racing from the corral.

"Mom, guess what?"

"What, sweetheart?"

"I learned all about saddles and stirrups and blankets, and I learned about the different brands used. Ken calls it cowboy calligraphy." She stopped long enough to draw in a deep breath before starting again. Maureen swore her daughter talked nonstop for another five minutes, mentioning in detail everything she'd learned until she was nearly panting.

"And guess what else?"

"I can't imagine," Maureen said, struggling to hold in a smile.

"Paula said I could have a kitten if it's all right with you, and . . ."

"A kitten," Maureen mumbled. Good grief, she should have seen that coming. "I'll think about it," she promised, and for now that was the best she could do. Actually she wouldn't mind a pet, but she'd need to read over her lease first.

"Oh, and one thing more," Karen said, so excited she could barely hold still. "I asked Paula to spend Friday night with us, that's all right, isn't it? She's asking her dad now."

Coward that she was, Maureen was about to usher her daughter into the car and make a clean getaway when Thom's daughter raced out of the barn. Thom was directly behind her. Maureen was certain his grin stretched from one ear to the other.

"I understand Karen's invited Paula to spend Friday night," he said with a glint in his eye. "I have a great idea. Why don't I treat the four of us to western-style barbecue first? We'll pick you up around six, all right?"

"Oh, Mom," Karen said, gazing up at her mother hopefully. "Dinner in a restaurant? Can we? Oh, please, it would be so much fun."

"Ah . . ." Maureen wasn't sure what to do.

"Please," Thom coaxed, and leveled one of his daredevil smiles on her.

"Ted!" Catherine set aside her magazine, delighted to see her grandson, especially when she wasn't expecting him. "How nice of you to drop by."

Ted gave her a warm peck on the cheek and sat down next to her in the parlor, which was the social gathering place for the retirement center. "I should have let you know I was stopping by."

"Nonsense." Catherine had given a good deal of thought to her meeting with Blythe Holmes and was beginning to think she might have overreacted. She was an old woman, set in her ways, and it was only natural that she feel a certain amount of—she hated to use this word—resentment toward the woman who'd be marrying her precious grandson.

Ted scanned the area as though looking for someone. "Do you happen to know a woman named Joy Palmer?"

"But of course."

"I need to talk to her."

Catherine's spirits lifted automatically. "You need to speak to Joy?"

"You might say we had a minor run-in the other night, and I wanted to reassure her everything's fine. She doesn't have anything to worry about."

"Run-in?"

"It's nothing, Grandma," Ted said, and patted her hand. "Before I look for Joy, tell me what's been going on with you."

"Well, the library committee met, and we've decided to hold a literary tea in order to raise money for a number of very good projects."

"When will that be?"

"A few days before Christmas," Catherine told him, but again she had the impression his mind wasn't on their conversation. She patted his hand. "I think Joy must be in her office," she whispered conspiratorially. "It's the first door to the left, off the hallway."

Ted grinned and squeezed her hand. "I'll be back in a few minutes."

"Take your time," Catherine said as she reached for her magazine once more. "I insist. I've got all the time in the world."

Catherine watched her grandson leave and couldn't help wondering about that gleam in his eyes. It had been a good long time since she'd seen it. He was up to something. She'd stake a batch of chocolate chip cookies on that.

Ted didn't understand why he felt it necessary to personally relay to Joy the information about Blythe's car. His grandmother would have been happy to give her the message. The thing was, he hadn't been able to stop thinking about Joy Palmer since their little run-in.

She wasn't his type. That was a definite. He liked his women a little more sophisticated, a little more glamorous, a little more . . . like Blythe, he decided.

When he was with Blythe, heads turned. Ted liked that. His friends envied him because such a beautiful, distinguished woman loved him. Call him a male chauvinist or whatever the popular terminology was these days, but he didn't care.

Nevertheless, over the last few days he'd found himself smiling whenever he thought about the resident service director naming her car Edith. He chuckled when he remembered the way she'd gotten all feisty when it looked as if Blythe were going to insult her car.

That was the one problem he had with Blythe, Ted admitted. The woman just didn't seem to have much of a sense of humor. He hoped that would change in time.

Ted found Joy sitting at her desk, reading a letter, her brow furrowed.

"Hello again," he said, leaning against the doorjamb.

She glanced up in surprise. Her eyes were round and expressive, Ted noted. He liked that, too. One wouldn't need to guess what she was thinking; it was right there for him to read, plain as a page in a book.

"Hi." She stood and then seemed surprised to find herself on her feet. She sat down abruptly and stared up at him as if she weren't sure what to expect.

"May I come in?" Ted asked, enjoying her discomfort.

"Of course. I'm sorry." She motioned toward the only other chair in the room, as if he needed guidance.

Ted sat down, relaxed against the back of the chair, and crossed his legs. He hoped she'd take the hint. The woman was wired as tight as unwaxed dental floss. "I stopped by to let you know I had Blythe's car checked out with a body shop."

"Was there any damage?"

"None that he could see." Blythe hadn't believed it and had insisted on a second opinion, but there wasn't any need for Joy to know that.

"What about a mechanic?"

"Not yet, but I doubt there's anything to be concerned about."

"My dad runs a shop no more than three miles from here. If you want, he could look at the engine for you, and he'd do a good job."

Problem was, Ted would have a difficult time convincing Blythe of that.

"What about . . . your friend? I hope there weren't any lingering effects from the accident."

"No, she's fine." Blythe had complained of a headache, but it had disappeared by the following day—until he'd made the mistake of asking her about it. Then, all of a sudden, she'd seemed to be suffering from low back pains as well as an intense headache. Soon afterward, she'd mentioned contacting an attorney.

When Blythe had first hinted at a lawsuit, Ted had thought she was joking. Only later had he realized she was serious. It irritated him that she would try to make much more of the incident, and his aggravation must have showed. Keeping his anger in check, he'd pointed out that there hadn't been any damage to either vehicle and it would be difficult to prove personal injury. He hadn't mentioned anything about her making an appointment with a doctor. No need to give her more ideas.

"You say your father's a mechanic," Ted said. "Then I'd like to suggest he give Edith a thorough checkup."

"I talked to him about what happened, and he said it wasn't possible. The only feasible explanation was that I hadn't put on the emergency brake, but I know I did." She paused as if attempting to recall the events of that evening. "I could have sworn her engine was running at the time of the accident. I remember how frustrated I felt because I was going back to my office to phone Triple A.

"Then not only does Edith start up, but she does so without the key in the ignition, backs out of the parking space all on her own. It was as if she were aiming for your . . . Blythe's car. But that's impossible."

"Sounds like one for the textbooks to me," Ted agreed.

"Here's something else for the books," she said, holding up the letter she'd been reading when he'd first arrived. "It's from radio station KIWI. I don't even listen to that station, unless they're broadcasting the Lakers games."

"They wrote you a letter?"

"It's more than that. The letter says my name was a winner in their drawing for two courtside seats for Friday night's basketball game."

"That's fabulous." Frankly, Ted would give his eyeteeth for those tickets. Courtside, no less. The game was scheduled against the red-hot Seattle SuperSonics and was sure to be one of the best of the year. From what he understood, the Forum had been sold out for weeks.

"I know, but for the life of me I can't remember entering their contest."

"You can't?"

She shook her head.

"Maybe someone put your name in for you?"

"Who?"

"A friend. Your father." As far as he was concerned, she shouldn't be asking so many questions.

Joy frowned. "That's not likely. I was trying to decide what I was going to do."

Ted couldn't believe what he was hearing. "Going to do? What do you mean? You'd be crazy to ask questions. Didn't anyone ever tell you not to look a gift horse in the mouth?"

"I know, but—"

"Those are the hottest tickets in town."

"I know that, too. The Forum's been sold out for three weeks."

"Do you follow the Lakers?"

She stared at him as if that were the most ridiculous question she'd ever heard. "Doesn't everyone?"

Ted laughed. Blythe hated anything having to do with professional basketball, but she was a good sport about letting him watch the games when they were televised. But he hadn't been to a game all year, and his mouth was watering at the thought of attending this one, especially with courtside seats.

"If you're thinking about selling the tickets," he said casually, "I'd be interested in buying them."

She looked more confused than ever. "I don't think so."

"If you haven't thought of anyone you'd like to take with you, I'd like to make a suggestion."

"What?"

Ted grinned, and then surprised even himself. "Take me."

Chapter

★ ✪ ★

7

Maureen was convinced barbecue sauce was smeared from one side of her face to the other. No matter how many times she checked the mirror, she was certain she'd missed a spot. Or several.

She'd let Thom know he wouldn't find her so easy to manipulate a second time. He knew exactly how she felt about this outing, yet he'd purposely used the girls' friendship to orchestrate their evening together.

Maureen planned on giving him an earful the minute they were alone. That had been her intention, only it never happened. The girls were so pleased to be together, and Thom couldn't have been more charming. Early on, she decided she'd have dinner with him, but she was determined not to enjoy herself.

Her resolve lasted all of ten minutes.

Then, before she knew it, she was wearing a plastic bib, and the most delicious smoky-flavored sauce was dripping from her chin. The spareribs were the best she'd ever tasted.

Soon Thom and the girls had her laughing, and against her better judgment, against every dictate of her will, she had a wonderful time.

"I hope you plan to invite me in for coffee," Thom announced when they pulled up in front of her small rental house. He turned off the ignition before she could answer. Apparently she wasn't being given a choice.

"I'll carry in Paula's overnight bag for her," he volunteered, as if the backpack were so heavy, it required someone with great physical strength to lift it.

He climbed out of the car, and Maureen fiddled with her house keys while he opened up the trunk and brought out the lightweight bag.

Maureen gave him a sideways look. "This is another underhanded trick in what is fast becoming a long line."

"Would you have gone to dinner with me without the girls?" he asked under his breath.

"No," she admitted readily.

"My point exactly. You would have sent me off on a lonely ride back to the valley without so much as a cup of coffee. What's a man to do?"

Maureen smiled despite herself. She really had enjoyed herself, more than any time she could remember in a long while. It felt good to laugh again. Good to hear Karen laugh.

"All right." She relented with poor grace. "I'll brew you a cup of coffee."

"That's better." Thom gave her one of his bone-melting smiles and followed her to the front door. The girls were practically dancing with excitement over the prospect of spending the entire night in each other's company.

Karen and Paula disappeared inside Karen's bedroom an instant after Maureen unlocked the front door. For the first time that evening, she found herself alone with Thom. Without the girls as a buffer, she was more aware of him as a man, more aware of herself as a woman.

"I'll make you that cup of coffee," she said, brushing her open palms together. "If you'd like to wait here, I'll have it out in a jiffy."

"I'll help." He followed her to the kitchen.

Maureen felt like a insect beneath a microscope, the way Thom's eyes followed her every move. She brought out the coffee grounds and added them to the filter.

"Would you kindly stop?" she demanded when she could stand it no longer.

"What am I doing that's so terrible?"

"You're staring at me."

"Is that a crime?"

"Yes."

"You know, when you smile and your face relaxes, you're an attractive woman. You should do it more often."

Maureen wasn't fishing for compliments, backhanded or otherwise. "I don't know what kind of game you're playing, but I don't want any part of it."

"Game?"

"Yes, game." Her hand trembled as she filled up the glass pot with water and poured all of it into the coffeepot dispenser. "If you have the sudden urge to date again, I advise you to look elsewhere for companionship. I'm not interested."

It disconcerted her to have him laugh just then, a low, rumbling sound, as if her words amused him.

"Is that so funny?" she demanded. She took down a mug. It slammed against the counter with a bang, much louder than she'd intended.

"What's so funny? You, Maureen Woods. You claim you don't want to see me again, and we both know that's a lie." Truth flashed in his eyes like a distant light.

"You're so sure of yourself," she managed finally, her pride rescuing her. "You men are all alike, you think that—"

"Are you saying you don't want to see me again?"

Maureen was fast learning that Thom Nichols didn't ask questions unless he was damn sure of the answers. She could deny it, tell a bold-faced lie, but he'd know exactly what it was, and so would she.

This was what made dealing with this man so impossible. She couldn't hide from Thom behind insults. He saw through her fears. He saw through her pain. He recognized the truth as if it had been tattooed across her forehead.

"Aren't you going to answer the question?" he asked. His tone was gentle. Her heart melted a little then, knowing he could have mocked her and didn't.

"No."

He smiled broadly, apparently encouraged by her lack of response. Joining her at the kitchen counter, he lifted her hand and placed it on his shoulder. He felt solid and real beneath her fingertips. Then he leaned forward and pressed his mouth to hers. The kiss was slow and gentle and at the same time the most erotic one she'd ever experienced. It had been so *long* since she had been kissed. Really kissed. That was it, she told herself. Not the man, but the fact it had been years since a man had taken her in his arms.

When he broke away Maureen was shaking so badly she needed to sit down. Apparently Thom felt much the same way, because he claimed the seat next to her.

She noticed his breath was ragged. Neither of them spoke. For her part, Maureen couldn't. At that moment she was incapable of uttering anything more than weak, unintelligible sounds.

Thom scooted his chair close to hers, angled toward her, and dropped a row of soft, delicate kisses along the underside of her chin and up toward her ear. Slowly, in heart-stopping increments, he brought his lips back to hers.

"I . . . think . . . you . . . should . . . leave . . . now." Maureen swore it took five minutes for the words to untangle themselves from the end of her tongue.

"I haven't had my coffee."

"Coffee." She'd almost forgotten about it. Surely the pot was ready by now. All she need do was pour him a cup and usher him to the door. Then her duty would be complete.

"Coffee." She was about to stand but discovered, to her chagrin, that her arms were wrapped securely about him. She hadn't a clue when that had happened.

Leaving him proved to be far more difficult than it should have been. Her eyes fluttered open, and she stiffened immediately. There, standing just inside the kitchen, were Karen and Paula, staring at them with wide eyes, their young faces creased with approving smiles.

"Wow," Karen whispered as if she couldn't believe her eyes. "Your dad just kissed my mom."

"He did? Great. This is really, really great," Paula said in the same awe-filled voice.

"If they get married, does that mean we'd be sisters?" Karen wanted to know.

Apparently an answer wasn't necessary for the two to celebrate. With their arms wrapped around each other, they let out a whoop and did a little jig about the kitchen.

"We aren't getting married," Maureen said forcefully, bolting out of her chair. She wanted to blame Thom for this, but she'd been as much a partner in the kissing episode as he.

He touched her, and the emptiness inside her echoed like a shout down a dry well. The years hadn't lessened the pain of her marriage, and this evening with Thom left her to face the haunting self-doubts. Brian had turned to another woman. He'd found her lacking, found her inadequate. Another man eventually would, too. She dared not risk that again. She didn't know if she could live through it a second time.

"Great going, Dad." Paula gave her father the thumbs-up sign. Thom's thumb went up in response.

"It might be a good idea if you girls let us two adults talk."

"Sure," Paula said, scooting out a chair and sitting down. She propped her hands on her face and looked to her dad. Karen sat next to her friend, her eyes as bright as fireworks against a dark July sky.

"Privately," Thom whispered to the girls.

"They want to be alone." Paula said this, apparently for Karen's benefit.

As soon as the two left the kitchen, Maureen started pacing. "That shouldn't have happened."

"What? Us kissing or the girls seeing us?"

"Both."

"The kissing really bothers you?" he asked.

Maureen knew this was another one of those incidents where he was well aware of her answer. "As a matter of fact, it does. If you want my opinion, I think you should be concerned yourself."

"Well, to be honest, I'll admit your kiss packs quite a wallop." He rubbed his hand down the side of his face as if to say he'd been surprised by the impact she'd had on him.

Maureen ignored his comment. "We've had exactly one dinner together, not even a dinner date, and already our daughters are talking about becoming stepsisters. Frankly, I think this is a cause for concern."

She breathed in deeply in an effort to gain perspective. Everything seemed to be happening much too fast. She wasn't like other women who floated easily in and out of relationships.

Ever since her divorce she'd been living in a vacuum, living off her bitterness. Brian had taught her well, and she wasn't looking for a repeat of that experience. "I won't allow you to pressure me into a relationship," she announced, her back ramrod straight.

He opened his mouth as if he intended to argue with her, but the phone rang just then and he apparently changed his mind.

Maureen glared at the phone.

"Go ahead and answer it," Thom advised after the third ring.

She walked across the room and reached for the receiver. "Hello," she said, knowing she sounded nothing like herself.

"Maureen." Her name was followed by a slight hesitation. "It's Brian. We need to talk."

"I've been doing a lot of thinking about Paul Morris," Goodness told her fellow prayer ambassadors. They sat on the bench in front of the church organ in Paul Morris's church. "What he really needs is one big, dynamic miracle to snap him out of this lethargy," Goodness said. She'd thought long and hard about his problems and hadn't come up with a single brilliant idea.

"What kind of miracle?" Shirley asked, her look skeptical. Goodness knew the third member of their team would be the one she'd need to convince the most. But before she could talk Shirley into participating, she had to come up with a plan of action.

"That's just it. I don't know what to do for him. Something that will elevate his faith. Something that will prove that his prayers have been heard, and that he is loved."

"Something that will let him know that if he feels distant from God, God isn't the one who moved."

"Exactly." Mercy's insight surprised Goodness. "Paul seems to think that God closed the door in his face."

"And bolted it shut."

"Right again, Mercy." Once more her peer's assessment of the situation impressed her.

"Exactly what are you two planning?" Shirley did a good job of imitating Gabriel's stern, distrustful look.

"We aren't planning anything yet," Goodness assured her. "That's the reason I called you both here. I need ideas."

"All I can say," Shirley muttered in a righteous tone, "is that you better not think about talking to him through a television set. Gabriel will yank all three of us out of here so fast it'll make our heads spin."

"I agree." Goodness knew without being reminded that anything to do with the electronic media would be pushing her luck. She'd asked for this assignment but was only now beginning to fully appreciate the difficulty of her task.

For several days now she'd been watching Reverend Morris. His son's engagement had been an unexpected blow. He'd hidden his feelings from Joe and Annie well.

The poor man was torn. He remembered all too well what it was to be young and in love, yet at the same time he'd been looking forward to spending time alone with his son.

"Any ideas?" Goodness threw out the question, ready and willing to listen to suggestions.

"Sure." Shirley's enthusiasm for this project surprised Goodness. "We could rearrange the pews, and move the choir loft over there." She pointed to a row of stained-glass windows against the long side wall of church.

"That's not a miracle, that's a mess," Goodness objected.

"Reverend Morris will think the building was struck by vandals," Mercy said.

"Do you have any better ideas?" Shirley asked, eyeing the two of them.

"You could also talk to Reverend Morris," Mercy suggested. "Not through a television screen, but one on one."

"What would I say?"

Goodness's tender heart went out to the man of God. She sincerely did want to help Reverend Morris in a way that would prove to Gabriel and others that she had matured. With this new level of personal growth, she could then handle the more complicated assignments on a regular basis instead of these once-a-year jobs.

"A miracle," Mercy said, running her agile fingers silently along the organ's keyboard.

"And not the opening from *Phantom of the Opera,* either."

"But I love Andrew Lloyd Webber's music."

"I know, but resist."

"All right," Mercy said, and with a sigh placed her hands in her lap. "I'm not much help, am I?"

"Don't worry about it."

Mercy glanced over her shoulder and then lowered her voice. "I'm keeping a low profile these days. After the trick with Joy's car and then arranging for her to win the drawing at the radio station."

"How'd you manage that?"

"You don't want to know."

"She changed the writing on the winning ticket," Shirley said in what was apparently a guess.

"But it worked," Mercy said defensively. "Ted and Joy are attending the game together this evening. I think we should all be there. The Lakers against the Seattle SuperSonics. It's going to be a great game, and who knows, we just might be to able to lend a hand now and again."

"Mercy, you shock me." This came from Shirley.

"Go on ahead without me," Goodness told her friends. "I'll join you later."

The two looked uncertain, as if they weren't sure they should leave their cohort behind.

"I insist."

"Are you going to work your miracle?"

"Yes," Goodness said decisively. Her eye caught the nativity scene placed to the side of the altar. The life-size figures were arranged inside the stable. Mary, Joseph, the wise men, and the shepherds gathered around the manger bed. The star atop the wooden stable was what caught Goodness's attention.

An angel. Perhaps Goodness was overlooking the obvious. She need only be herself.

A noise at the far end of the church attracted Goodness's attention. With no time to waste, she rushed to the manger scene and positioned herself at the appropriate spot at the peak of the stable roof.

Pastor Morris walked into the sanctuary just then. Goodness closed her eyes and glowed until the glory of God's light shone through her. Heat radiated from her body. Her wings were spread to their full magnificent glory.

She waited and waited.

Certain now that she'd captured Reverend Morris's attention, she opened her eyes, to discover him tucking his sermon notes into the Bible situated at the podium.

Goodness glowed brighter. The light spilled into the church, illuminating the room like a thousand gleaming candles.

Nothing.

Paul Morris walked down the center aisle, pausing now and again to tuck a hymn book in the proper receptacle.

When Goodness couldn't stand it any longer, she called out to him in her most angelic voice. "Paul Morris."

The reverend hesitated.

"God loves you," she told him, certain hearing her say the words would revolutionize the minister's life.

Paul scratched the side of his head and turned around. It was as if he were blind. After a moment he walked over to the side door, opened it, and stuck out his head.

"Leta," he called, "did you want me for something?"

"No," came the faint reply.

Paul scratched the side of his head once more. "I could have sworn I heard my name." With that he walked out of the church.

Goodness couldn't believe it. She'd performed perhaps her greatest miracle. She'd risked Gabriel's wrath. And for what?

Paul Morris hadn't even noticed.

The doorbell chimed, and Joy Palmer sucked in a deep breath and headed across her tiny apartment. She was actually going out on a date with Ted Griffin. Technically, it was a date.

He had invited her to dinner before the basketball game. She wasn't fool enough to believe he'd been influenced by anything other than gratitude for the ticket.

So she, like any other red-blooded woman, had made a snap decision to take him up on his generous offer. She'd been admiring him for months, and she wasn't about to let a golden opportunity like this slip through her fingers.

"Hello again," he said when she opened the door. He wasn't wearing a suit but had dressed casually in slacks, a sweater, and loafers. She couldn't remember ever seeing him in anything but business attire. He looked relaxed. Different.

"Hi." This evening wouldn't go well if she couldn't manage to utter words longer than one syllable.

"I hope you like Mexican food."

"Yes." Maybe next time she might try more than one word at a time, she mused.

"Mexican food gives Blythe heartburn, so I don't get to indulge myself often."

"I love it." Better, she thought, forcing herself to relax.

"Great, then we're off."

Joy reached for her sweater and purse. She clung to her handbag as if it were a life preserver and prayed Ted wouldn't notice how nervous she was. It was ridiculous, really. He was just a man. Not unlike a dozen others she'd dated over the years. It just so happened that he'd asked her out because she had two tickets to the hottest game in town.

Ted drove to a chic Mexican restaurant where there were fancy linen napkins on the tables, and minstrels strolling between the tables, serenading couples.

"This is really nice," she commented while the hostess led them to a table.

"I figured if I was going to sit courtside, then I owed you a meal, but I got to hankering for chicken enchiladas, and hoped Mexican food agreed with your stomach."

"Chicken enchiladas are my favorite, too," she said, and smiled up at the hostess as she handed them huge menus. Joy read over the selections, made her choice, and set the menu aside.

Chips and salsa had already been delivered to the table, along with a container of bottled water.

Their waitress came for their orders and left soon afterward. "I want to apologize for throwing myself at your feet and begging you to take me to the game with you," Ted said, and sipped from a glass of iced tea.

Joy smiled. Little did he know. This night was one she would long remember, she suspected. It was a first date and prom night all rolled into one fantastic evening. He'd spend this time with her, but every night from here on out he'd be with Blythe. Joy would take what she could get.

"My grandmother was absolutely delighted when I told her we were going to dinner," Ted told her.

"So she said." Joy suspected Catherine Goodwin would enjoy the role of matchmaker. Unfortunately it wouldn't work with her and Ted, since Ted was already seeing someone else. From what she surmised, Catherine's grandson and Blythe were close to becoming engaged.

Their food arrived on huge ceramic plates. Joy dipped her fork into the beans and cheese.

"I hope I haven't caused you any problems," Ted surprised her by saying.

"Problems?"

"With any male friends."

"Why would you do that?" The question made no sense.

"Think about it, Joy. Another man, especially someone you were dating on a regular basis, might be offended that you opted to take me to this game and not him."

"Well, you needn't worry. There's no male friend lurking around the corner."

Ted frowned. "You're not dating?"

This was a subject Joy had hoped to avoid. "Not at the moment."

Ted set his fork beside his plate and stared at her as if he found the information puzzling. "You must be joking. You're young, attractive, and fun. Why aren't you dating?"

"Listen," she said, sorry now she'd even answered him, "I won't ask you questions about your personal life and you don't ask me, agreed?"

"Agreed," he responded after a moment, but he seemed taken back by her outburst.

Actually she was surprised, too. Usually she wasn't confrontational, but she was living out a fantasy, and she didn't want it ruined by him analyzing her sorry lack of a social life.

As it was, her two older brothers and her father were constantly foisting eligible friends off on her. There just wasn't anyone she wanted to date. Well, maybe Ted, but he was already involved with Blythe.

Now that she was on a date with him—albeit one and only one date—she didn't want him ruining it with a promise to fix her up with one of his good buddies.

"I apologize," she whispered, her eyes avoiding his. "I didn't mean to snap at you."

"No, no," he said quickly, "the fault was mine. I shouldn't have pried. It's just that—" He stopped abruptly. "Never mind."

"If you're going to suggest a friend you want me to meet, please don't."

"A friend? No, I wasn't thinking of introducing you to any of my colleagues."

It was absurd that she was so pleased to know that.

When they'd finished their dinner, they headed for the Forum. By the time they arrived, the facility was quickly filling up. Joy was amazed at the different perspective one got at the court level compared to sitting in the stands.

"This is fabulous," Ted said as they settled onto the folding chairs on the sidelines. He twisted around and looked into the row upon row of seats behind him.

"I can't believe I'm here. Promise me one thing," she said. It was a long shot, but she was covering her bases. "If you ever meet my dad or my brothers, which I realize is highly unlikely, whatever you do, don't mention this, all right?"

"Ah-ha!" Ted said, and laughed. "So there is someone who would have given his right arm for these tickets."

"Yes. But family. It would have only caused problems. Three men. Two tickets. Besides, I was the one who won that silly drawing. I don't know how, mind you, but it was my name they pulled out of that giant barrel, and I love basketball as much as my father and brothers."

Applause erupted when the two teams ran onto the polished wood floor. Soon the players were taking practice shots, tossing the ball back and forth to each other. Joy was close enough to hear the *whoosh* of the balls as they passed from one pair of hands to another.

She craned her neck back to watch the men who raced past her. "I don't think I ever realized how tall everyone is."

"Me either," Ted agreed.

Within a few minutes the game started, and the action was non-stop. Whatever inhibitions Joy had experienced at the beginning of their evening vanished as the Lakers took the floor. She cheered when they scored and argued with the referee over what she felt was an unfair foul.

It wasn't until the fourth quarter, when she was relatively sure the Lakers would win the game, that she relaxed enough to realize that Ted was studying her.

"What?" she murmured. She would have looked away, but his gaze held hers fast and hard.

"Nothing," he said.

"Then why are you looking at me like that?"

Ted grinned. "I'm not entirely sure what 'that' means, but I will tell you I've never seen anyone enjoy a basketball game as much as you."

"Oh."

Her enthusiasm did seem to runneth over. She honestly tried to sit still for what remained of the game, but it was impossible. Each time the Lakers scored, she leaped to her feet and applauded loudly. And when an official, the very one who'd given the unjust penalty, happened to walk past her seat, she suggested he might want to have his eyes checked.

If the referee heard her, he chose to ignore the comment.

The score was tied the last two minutes of the game when Seattle took a time-out.

"We have to win," Joy said, wringing her hands.

"Why?" Ted wanted to know. "Do you have a lot of money riding on the outcome?"

"No!" She wasn't into gambling. "It's just that if I'm going to cheer my heart out for these guys, the least they can do is win."

"They have enough incentive of their own."

"I'm sure they do."

The buzzer blared, and the two teams returned to the court. Joy's eyes followed the time clock. Seattle scored, putting them in the lead. There was time, almost a minute and forty-five seconds, for the Lakers to tie up the game.

The Lakers piled two points onto the scoreboard, and the game was even. The last minute of the quarter dragged on for twenty. Just before the buzzer, Stanley, a rookie player for the Lakers, threw the basketball at midcourt. The ball *swoosh*ed through the net, and the fans went wild.

Without thinking what she was doing, Joy cried out excitedly and hurled herself at Ted. His arms went around her waist, and he lifted her from the ground and whirled her around several times in their own private celebration.

People crushed in around them, but Joy didn't notice and she doubted that Ted did, either. All at once she realized that she was in Ted Griffin's arms, holding on to him as if she intended never to let go.

Enjoy it, she told herself. Consider it a bonus.

She closed her eyes and savored the feel of his arms around her, savored his strength.

He released her abruptly, as if he realized he'd held her far longer than he should have. Joy made busywork, gathering her sweater and her purse. The Forum was emptying, the crowd pleased with the results of the game.

"Great game," she said, the first to breach the silence.

"One of the year's best."

"Stanley's going to be an asset to the team," she said, burying her hands in her pockets and standing shoulder to shoulder with the slow-moving crowd.

"He already is."

She noticed Ted didn't sound his usual self and wondered what was wrong. When she could, she chanced a look at him, hoping she wasn't being obvious. His face was tight, his eyes brooding and thoughtful.

All they'd done was share in the celebration of the win. It didn't mean anything.

"Don't look so worried," she said when they reached his car. He stood on the driver's side and she on the passenger's, the vehicle between them.

"Worried?" He raised his eyes to hers.

"I don't expect anything more from you, if that's what you're thinking. I know you're not going to see me again. So stop worrying about the hug. It was a hug, nothing more. I'm not going to tell Blythe, if that's what's bothering you." Joy knew she sounded defensive, but she couldn't help that. Already he regretted their time together. Regretted holding her.

"Leave Blythe out of this," Ted snapped, and inserted the key into the lock.

Chapter

★ ☆ ★

8

Maureen had done everything humanly possible to get out of driving Karen to her riding lesson the following Tuesday afternoon. Her parents would have been happy to take Karen, but they were attending a Christmas party with their bridge club. If it wasn't such a long drive, Maureen would have opted to drop Karen off and return for her later. But the lesson was shorter than the drive.

By sheer luck, Maureen had been able to avoid Thom when he'd driven back into town Saturday afternoon to pick up Paula. But she didn't expect to be so fortunate a second time.

"Mom," Karen murmured.

"What is it, honey?" Her daughter had been unusually quiet all afternoon. After the personal sacrifices Maureen was making for these riding lessons, one would hope Karen would reveal the enthusiasm she had earlier.

"Dad phoned on Friday night, didn't he?"

Maureen's fingers tightened around the steering wheel. "Yes, he phoned."

"Did he want to talk to me?"

Maureen never thought she was capable of hating anyone as much as she did Brian for the way he'd hurt their daughter. "He didn't say."

"I didn't think he did." Karen's head drooped down so far, her chin was tucked against her chest.

"So that's what all this is about." Maureen reached over and squeezed Karen's hand. "Come on, sweetheart, it's you and me. It has been for a good long time. We're doing all right, aren't we?"

"What did he want?"

"To be fair, I didn't give your father much of a chance to say."

Karen looked over to Maureen. "Did you tell him if he wanted anything, he should talk to your attorney?"

The kid knew her all too well. "Something along those lines," Maureen admitted.

"Is he?"

"I don't have a clue what your father will or won't do." What Maureen did know was that the less she had to do with Brian, the better for everyone involved. Just hearing his voice was like ripping open a freshly healed wound.

But in her case the wound hadn't healed. It had festered and the poison had acted like a malignancy, spreading into every part of her life. She wasn't so blind not to know what was happening. Yet she felt powerless to stop it.

Karen continued to study her, until Maureen found her daughter's eyes disconcerting. "Why are you looking at me like that?"

"I'm trying to see if your face changes."

"Changes?"

"Your voice does. Whenever you talk about Dad your voice gets deep and a little scratchy."

"Really?" Maureen hadn't noticed. "What about my face?"

Karen centered her focus on her mother once more. "Say something about Dad."

"Say something about Dad," Maureen repeated. "Well, let me think. We were married right out of college and—"

"Not like that. Talk about him the way you do now."

"I don't understand." Maureen momentarily diverted her attention from the road.

Karen's voice deepened as she said, "The bastard I used to be married to always said"—she paused—"like that."

"I sound like that when I mention your father?" Hearing Karen echo the biting words she'd repeated countless times was like a cold slap in the face.

"Yup. Just like that."

Had she actually spoken those words in that tone of voice for Karen to hear over and over again? Maureen's stomach knotted with the thought of what had happened to her since the divorce. She'd turned cold and angry. Bitter and ugly.

When Brian had first asked for the divorce, Maureen hadn't shed a tear. It was as though she'd been waiting for that moment almost from the first.

Brian had always been the restless sort, full of energy. There were places to go, people to meet. Increasingly he spent more time away from home on a variety of different projects.

She remembered the feelings of profound sadness after he'd moved out, and a multitude of regrets. If only she'd been a spotless housekeeper, a better cook, a more imaginative lover. If only she'd been more understanding. If only she'd listened more often. If only she'd talked to him. If only . . . if only . . . if only.

Then one day she decided she wasn't willing to accept the blame for their failed marriage any longer.

She wasn't the one who'd violated the vows they'd spoken before God and their families.

She wasn't the one who couldn't hold down a decent job for longer than six months at a stretch.

She wasn't the one who'd walked out on the family he'd agreed to support. But then Brian never had been much for financial responsibilities.

Overnight, it seemed, the love she felt for her college sweetheart and the only lover she'd ever had turned to a fire-quenching hatred. After he'd left, she'd decided to make his life a living hell. The same hell he'd given her all the years they were married.

"Mom," Karen asked her, "are you all right?"

"I'm fine, sweetheart." They pulled onto the dirt road that led to Nichols's Riding Stables.

"Are you going to be in the barn with Mr. Nichols when I'm finished with my lesson?"

"Ah." Maureen needed to think. Thom confused her, and she'd already decided not to see him again, other than what was unavoidable. "I don't think so."

"Where do you want me to meet you?"

"I'll be by the car," Maureen told her. She parked in her usual spot, and with her hands braced against the steering wheel she smiled at her daughter. "I'm sorry I called your daddy a bastard, Karen."

"Don't worry, Mom, I know my dad." Having said that, the twelve-year-old climbed out of the car, slammed the door, and raced toward the barn.

Thom's daughter was waiting for her, and the girls wrapped their arms around each other as if it had been months since they'd last spent time together. Like long-lost friends, the two headed inside the barn.

Maureen climbed out of the car. If she was going to avoid Thom, she couldn't sit in her car, waiting like a sitting duck. She was prepared this time and had changed out of her heels into her tennis shoes.

She needed time and space to think about her conversation with Karen. A walk. Any place where she could escape. Anywhere she could drown out the echo of her daughter's voice as she repeated the word Maureen had said so often. Bastard. Bastard. Bastard.

A number of horse trails led away from the stables, and Maureen chose one, following the narrow, winding dirt pathway.

"Damn you, Brian," she muttered, fighting the blast of anger. Brian hadn't talked to his daughter in over a year, and when he'd phoned he hadn't so much as asked about her.

True, Maureen hadn't given him much of an opportunity. No doubt he'd called because he was angry over her latest attempt to get him to pay child support. He'd probably boosted his courage with a couple of beers. He'd been out of work—that was the usual excuse—but he was working now and would give her what he could in time. She'd heard that countless times before and would rather he dealt directly with her attorney.

Maureen didn't want to hear his hard-luck tales. They were all too familiar. She'd told him coolly and unemotionally exactly what he could do with his lame excuses. Then she'd hung up and sat, and shaking with anger.

Thom had made an excuse to leave soon afterward. Not that Maureen blamed him. It wasn't until he'd driven away that she'd noticed the untouched pot of coffee. She wanted to explain to Thom about Brian, but it wasn't possible to wrap it up with a pretty pink bow. It was better that he not know.

She enjoyed Thom's company, but he didn't understand what it was to have suffered through a divorce. He didn't know what it was like to have his trust ravaged, to have his heart violated to the point that the last lingering vestige of respect had long since died.

From the little he'd told her about Paula's mother, Maureen knew they'd shared a deep and personal commitment to each other. The kind her own mother and father shared now.

Maureen walked as fast as her feet would go, her anger carrying her over the uneven pathway. Tired and breathing heavily, she turned off the road and followed a shallow stream as it wound around a crop of boulders. The stream had a peaceful effect, and she watched it for several moments, then decided to sit down and rest before heading back to the stables.

She found a good-size rock and sat there with her arms tucked around her bunched-up knees. She could see herself through Karen's young eyes, and she didn't like the picture. Yet she didn't know what to do to change the image in her mind.

Heaven was aware she could do nothing to change Brian. She'd tried, God help her, with a zero success rate.

Defeated, Maureen looked up. Daylight was fast slipping away, and she needed to get back to the stables. She slid off the rock and started back toward the trail, or where she last remembered seeing the trail.

She hesitated.

This didn't seem to be the right way. She turned and started in the opposite direction, certain she remembered that bend in the stream.

Within minutes it was so dark, she couldn't see more than a few inches in front of her. Fighting panic, she knew that either someone would come and find her or she'd wait until morning and discover the way back on her own.

Cupping her hands around her mouth, she called out as loudly as she could, "Is anyone out there?"

Only an eerie, unnatural silence greeted her frantic question.

"Please," she whispered. "Thom? Anyone?"

"I don't know what's wrong with Edith," Joy said as her father carefully lifted the hood of her dated Chevy in his repair shop. "She's been acting strange lately."

Ray Palmer smiled at his daughter. "If you translate 'strange' as Edith starting up of her own accord, you need more than a mechanic." Her father leaned over the engine, out of Joy's view.

"Did you see the Lakers game last night?" he asked, his words muffled, aimed as they were at the garage floor.

"It was great." Or it had been until after the game, when Ted had gone quiet and brooding on her. He'd driven her home as if he couldn't be rid of her fast enough.

She hadn't invited him up for a drink. Really, what was the use? It was more than apparent that he was glad the evening was over and he could be done with her.

While her father checked Edith's innards, Joy wandered around his shop. It smelled of grease and tires and gasoline. These scents had been like perfume to her when she was a little girl. Her brothers came down to the garage often, but it was only on rare occasions that Joy was allowed in her father's domain.

A BMW similar to Ted's pulled up out front, catching Joy's eye. A door slammed, and she watched in shocked disbelief as Ted Griffin nonchalantly walked into her father's shop.

"What are you doing here?" she asked, looking past him, certain Blythe would be with him, too. That he would bring his fancy girlfriend to her father's shop infuriated her. Blythe was sure to wrinkle her nose at the very thing Joy loved about this old shop. She waited, but apparently Blythe wasn't with him.

"As I recall, you were the one who mentioned that your father's a mechanic. It's time for an oil change, and I thought I'd give him the business. Unless you have any objections."

Eating her own words had never appealed to Joy. She suspected they tasted a good deal like crow. "Of course I don't object," she said, stepping down from her high horse. "I do remember mentioning Dad's shop."

Her father straightened, closed Edith's hood, and wiped his hand clean on the pink cotton rag. He studied Ted briefly and then looked to his daughter. "You know this young man, Joy?"

"Dad, this is Ted Griffin," she said, making a half-flopping motion with her hand. "Ted, my father, Ray Palmer."

"Hello, Mr. Palmer," Ted said, and stepped forward to offer his hand.

The two men exchanged robust handshakes. "Have you been having any problems with your car, son?"

A grin teased the corners of Ted's mouth. "None to mention. But I'd prefer to be on Edith's good side in light of what happened to my friend's car. I'd be grateful if you had the time for an oil change."

"So you were around the other night when Edith pulled her little trick. " Ray chuckled and stuffed the pink rag into the hip pocket of his gray-striped coveralls. "I always said it's never a good idea to turn your back on a frustrated woman."

"Daddy."

"Sorry, sweetheart, but it's true."

Joy noticed that Ted was doing an inadequate job of hiding a smile.

"Pull your car in here and I'll be finished with her in a jiffy." He walked over to the large garage doors and raised them so Ted could ease his car into the slot next to Joy's infamous Edith.

Her father directed Ted into the spot and then suggested, "Help yourself to the coffee. This shouldn't take more than fifteen minutes."

"How fresh is it, Dad?" Joy asked, knowing her father's penchant for strong coffee.

"It's fresh," Ray insisted. "I made it myself yesterday morning."

"Thanks anyway," Ted managed to say around a smile.

"If you two want to make yourselves useful," her father said as he raised the hood to Ted's car.

"Sure, what do you need?"

"Lunch," Ray told them. "There's a deli two blocks down. Get me something to hold me until dinner, will you?" The question was directed to them both.

"A sandwich," Joy offered.

"Anything."

Ted followed her out of the garage. They walked side by side for about half a block. "You don't need to come," she said stiffly. After all, she was perfectly capable of walking two blocks without an escort, especially him.

"I want to come."

"Why?" she asked, and briefly closed her eyes. Clearly he was looking for ways to make her miserable.

"Do I need a reason?"

Joy pinched her lips together. "Yes. I want to know why you're here."

"You know why."

"Okay, so I told you about my dad's shop, but did you have to come this morning? Did it have to be while I was here, too?"

"Yes," he murmured as though he were admitting to a fault. "I followed you here."

He couldn't have shocked her more had he confessed to a crime. "You did what? That's crazy!"

"I had to talk to you."

"About what?"

Ted's shoulders compressed with a sigh. "Last night."

"Why?" Joy asked in a small voice. "So you can tell me how bad you felt about going out with me when you're practically engaged to another woman? That's what I tried to explain. You don't need to come to me with a list of excuses. I don't need any explanations."

"Maybe I do," Ted said, his voice hard and loud. "I want to know why I can't stop thinking about you. What is it you do to me?" he demanded. "Because whatever it is, stop, because I don't like it. I had a perfectly wonderful life until your lunatic car—"

"Don't you dare talk about Edith that way!"

He raised his hands and drew in a steadying breath. "Sorry. The lunatic in this situation is me. I don't know you, I'm not even sure I want to know you, and yet I spent the vast majority of the night wishing like hell I'd kissed you."

The man said the most shocking things. To complicate everything, he was serious. His eyes were as dark as a moonless night. One thing was certain: he wasn't happy about any of this.

"I like you, Joy," he continued. "I like the way your eyes light up when you're happy. I like the way you have no compunction about giving advice to an official in a basketball game. And most of all, I like the way you wind melting cheese around your fork and then lift it to your mouth."

She smiled and looked down at the sidewalk. "But you wish to hell you didn't like me."

He was silent for a moment. "Something like that."

"So," she said, when suggestions weren't immediately forthcoming, "what do you intend to do about it?"

"That's just it. I don't know."

They strolled past a small neighborhood park and by tacit agreement turned into it. Joy walked over to the swing set she'd played on as a young girl. She recalled the summer days she'd sat on those very swings, arched her back, and aimed her feet for the sky. She'd been a dreamer then. She still was.

"I used to play here as a little girl," she told him. "My mother would bring my brothers and me. I'll never forget those Saturday afternoons in Lion's Park."

They sat on a bench, and Ted reached for her hand. "I want to kiss you," he said, his words soft and coaxing.

"Here?" She looked around, certain any number of people would be watching them. "Now?"

"I know it's crazy. Do you mind?"

Did she mind? The question was ludicrous enough to make her want to laugh out loud.

"I suppose it would be all right," she told him, and closed her eyes. Nothing happened for the longest time. Her eyes fluttered open. "You changed your mind?"

"Not exactly." He continued to look down on her.

"What?"

"Relax," he suggested "You look like a virgin sacrifice about to be offered up to the gods."

She ignored the latter part of his comment. "Relax," she echoed, and sagged her shoulders, slouching forward. "Is that better?"

"A little." He sounded as if he were lying.

"Why do you want to kiss me, anyway?" She had a right to know that much, especially if he was going to insult her in the process. Virgin sacrifice indeed!

"It's a test."

Frankly, Joy didn't like the sound of this. Tests had never excited her, whereas the thought of Ted kissing her did.

He lifted one of her hands and balanced it atop his shoulder.

Two could play this game. She reached for his arm and tucked it around the curve of her waist.

He inclined his head approvingly. He claimed her free hand and set it on the opposite shoulder, then joined his at the small of her back.

Neither moved, content for the moment to hold each other loosely. Time swelled and throbbed between them, and after a moment or two Joy could no longer feel her breath. Ted didn't seem to be breathing, either.

She half expected him to pull away and laugh the whole thing off, but neither of them was laughing at the moment. They weren't doing much of anything except waiting, wondering. It was as though they were both afraid of what lay beyond this first kiss.

Slowly, as if he expected her to stop him, he lowered his mouth to hers. Joy sighed softly when his lips settled over hers. The kiss was a leisurely exercise in introducing himself to her, in learning the shape and feel of her mouth, of acquainting his to her.

The kiss changed gradually, subtly, almost without notice, until it became something deep and urgent. Urgent on both their parts. The intensity of it took Joy's breath away and sent her pulse into double time.

She dragged her mouth from his, needing time to think this through, needing time to analyze what she was allowing to happen. Needing time to gauge the wisdom of it all.

Ted directed her mouth back to his and kissed her again with a need and depth that rocked her senses. He stopped abruptly and laid his forehead against hers.

"That answers that," he whispered.

"It does?" As far as Joy was concerned, it resurrected far more questions than answers.

"I want to see you again. Dinner, dancing, whatever you want."

"I'm free most any night." She should call for a counseling appointment right then and there. Something was drastically wrong with her to agree to date a man already involved with someone else.

"Monday. I'll pick you up on my way home from work."

With her eyes closed, she nodded. She had the distinct impression she was going to regret this.

"What do you mean, there's something wrong with Dad?" Bethany demanded, her voice sounding shrill and disbelieving through the telephone wire.

Joe raised his eyes to the ceiling. Having this conversation over the phone wasn't ideal, but he needed to discuss the problem with his sister, and he didn't want to spring it on her when she arrived for dinner. "Listen to me, Bethany, Dad just isn't himself."

"You mean physically?"

"No and yes. He's lost weight."

"Let me put you on hold," she said impatiently.

Elevator music hummed over the wire while his sister caught the second call. She was back almost immediately. "Sorry to keep you waiting," she mumbled. "Now what was it you were saying?"

"It's about Dad. I found him cleaning the garage in the middle of the day. Mrs. Johnson told me he hadn't even come into the office, and he had an elders' meeting that afternoon. If I hadn't found him when I did, he would have completely missed the meeting."

"Dad miss an elders' meeting?"

"Yes, Dad."

"But he's always been so conscientious about his leadership role in the church."

"That's not the half of it. Mrs. Johnson says he's consistently late for meetings. He isn't eating right, and to tell you the truth, he doesn't look good." Joe brushed the hair off his forehead. "On top of everything else, the house is a mess. I've never known Dad to be so untidy. There's mail all over the kitchen. Annie found a notice from the electric company that said if he didn't pay the bill in five days, they are going to cut off his electricity."

"My heavens. Has it been paid?"

"No. I showed it to him and he mumbled something about taking care of it right away. I told him I'd do it for him, and Annie and I went down personally and paid it."

"He's beginning to sound like an absentminded professor," Bethany commented.

"I think it's more than that."

"What do you mean?"

"He's not the same, Beth. When was the last time you saw him?"

Bethany paused. "Longer than it should have been. I know we're only an hour or so away, but we're so busy and—"

"I know, we all are. Dad could come see you, too."

"I've invited him over countless times, but he always has an excuse." Beth heaved a deep sigh, and Joe could almost picture his sister biting her lower lip, mulling over the situation. "He misses Mom."

"We all miss Mom."

"Maybe he needs a housekeeper. Somebody to come in a couple of times a week to clean up, keep him organized so there's not another one of those electric bill incidents."

"A housekeeper." That sounded like a workable solution to Joe, something positive they could do to help their father. Maybe matters weren't as bad as he thought.

"When are you and Annie heading north?" Bethany wanted to know.

"Not until the twenty-third, but to be honest, I don't feel good about leaving Dad like this. He likes Annie and everything. I mean, it'd be impossible not to love her, she's wonderful, but I wish we'd thought our plans through more carefully."

"Here comes another call," Beth said impatiently. "Damn."

Her impatience was cut off by a violin concerto as Joe was placed on hold. He mentally twiddled his thumbs until his sister came back on the line.

"Sorry," she mumbled. "Listen, Eric and I'll be over tomorrow evening for dinner. Go ahead and approach Dad about this house-keeper thing. Don't be obvious about it, just sound him out and then we can talk about it later, all right?"

"Great." Already Joe felt better. His big sister had a way of making matters right. He was grateful he had her to bounce his concerns off, otherwise he wouldn't have known what to do.

Paul Morris sat in his den. Books littered the floor, and he sighed as he set aside one volume and reached for another. He treasured his books and had spent many an evening in this very room, reading over thoughts of great minds and forming his own.

It was time to think about scheduling another series of sermons. He generally planned them up to six months in advance. One year he'd spent nearly nine months in the Gospel of John alone. Steve Tenny had suggested he write up his sermon notes and submit them for publication.

Paul had toyed with the idea for a time, but that was right before Barbara had been diagnosed with cancer; afterward, both their lives had become a crazed circus ride.

Those notes were in a binder on the shelf. Paul stood and reached for the binder and read through the first few pages. How proud he'd been of his insights, of the applications he'd made. As he read over the first few pages, he didn't see what all the fuss had been about. This wasn't any better or any worse than what he'd been preaching for the last twenty years.

Discouraged, he set the binder aside, determined to forget the project. Better yet, he'd throw the whole thing away.

He picked up his detailed notes and tossed them into the wastepaper basket.

A knock sounded against the door. "Come in," he said without much enthusiasm. Sometimes Mrs. Johnson came looking for him at the house, and he wished to avoid her as much as he could. The woman who'd served as his secretary all these years had become something of a pest lately.

He smiled when Joe entered the den. "Joe. I thought you and Annie were going grocery shopping for our dinner with your sister and Eric."

Joe frowned. "We finished that hours ago."

Paul looked at his watch. The time had slipped past without him noticing. That seemed to be happening more often of late.

"We were thinking about buying you a Christmas tree."

"A tree?" Paul repeated. "Don't bother, son. It's just going to be me this year, and heaven knows it'd probably become a fire hazard before I find the time to take it down."

Joe wore a hurt, little-boy look. "We've always had a tree, Dad."

It was all Paul could do to keep from reminding his son that Joe had always spent Christmas with him. "If you insist, buy me one of those small trees the grocery store sells in the flower pots. The ones that are already decorated. That would suit me just fine."

"All right," Joe agreed easily enough, and Paul was grateful. "By the way," Joe said, helping himself to a chair, "how's Mrs. Bartelli doing?"

Paul looked away. He didn't want to think about Madge and Bernard. "About as well as can be expected," he murmured. "I doubt she'll be home again."

"Then she's going to die soon?"

"Probably." Once again God would turn his back on a grieving family and yank away a loved one who had prayed desperately for healing, the way Paul had prayed for Barbara.

"That's too bad." Joe raised his feet and set them on the ottoman. "Say, Dad, since Annie's doing the cooking for tomorrow night's dinner, I thought I'd help straighten up the place a bit."

Paul looked around. True, books were stacked here and there, but it wasn't so bad. "Do you think it needs it?"

"Kind of," Joe said.

His son always had been the diplomatic one in the family.

"Fact is, I was thinking you could use someone who came in once or twice a week to clean for you."

Paul laughed. His own voice sounded rusty and odd to him. It must have been longer than he realized since he'd really laughed.

"What's that mean?" Joe asked, smiling himself.

"I don't need any housekeeper. Good grief, what would they do?"

"We could find someone who'd fix your dinner now and again."

"Why would I want anyone to do that?" Paul asked, seriously wanting to know. "I'm a good cook." He stood and slapped his son across the shoulders. "It's a nice thought, and I appreciate it, but no thanks."

Chapter

★ ☆ ★

9

The night closed in around Maureen with thick, dark hands. She shivered with cold and rubbed the length of her arms in an effort to keep her blood circulating. It seemed hours since she'd wandered away from the stables, but it couldn't possibly have been that long, could it?

"Help," she called out, forcing the panic from her voice. Her throat felt raw from calling. It was useless. No one knew where she was. No one was going to find her.

"Maureen."

Her name came faintly, like a warm whisper from the distance.

She bolted upright and stood on top of the rock. "Here," she shouted, cupping her mouth. "I'm over here!"

"Keep talking." The whisper became a tad stronger.

"This way," she shouted a second time, louder. A beam of light appeared, and Maureen carefully scooted down the rock and headed toward it.

"Maureen?"

"Here." The beacon was much brighter now and the voice recognizable. Thom. She should have known he'd be the one to find her. Her treacherous heart reacted with a solid jolt of happiness.

As she approached, he lowered the flashlight to the ground. "Are you hurt?" he asked, his voice gentle with concern.

"No, no, I'm fine." She longed to rush into his arms, bury herself in his warmth, but she managed to restrain herself. Instead she waited for the well-deserved lecture about wandering off without telling anyone where she was going.

It never came.

"I'm sorry for the trouble I caused you," she said, genuinely apologetic. It had been foolish and risky. She should have known better.

"If you're going to apologize to anyone, try Karen. She's nearly frantic."

"Oh, no." Maureen had warned her daughter against doing this very thing countless times. Her own actions had been stupid and irresponsible.

"I had to leave Midnight back on the trail." He shucked off his lambskin-lined jacket and draped it over her shoulders. It felt warm against her chilled skin. His scent circled her like the smoke from a lazy fire, and it felt as if his arms were around her, comforting her.

Taking his time, his fingers holding hers, Thom carefully guided her over the rocky path toward the trail. She held on to him firmly, afraid to let go. With her hand in his she felt secure and safe.

"Aren't you angry with me?" she asked when the silence grew too much for her. Heaven knew he had every right.

"Should I be?"

"Yes," she said crossly. "I was reckless and foolish, and it seems to me—"

"It seems to me," he interrupted, "you're angry enough with yourself. You don't need me lecturing you when you're doing such a fine job of it."

They reached the narrow trail. Midnight, his dark gelding, was tied to a tree, waiting impatiently. Thom smoothed his hand down the horse's long, sleek neck and spoke soothingly to the gelding. Maureen recognized the same calming, comforting voice. It rankled her pride that he spoke to his horse in the same gentle tones as he did her!

With an ease and grace she envied, he lifted himself onto the saddle. The leather creaked as it accepted his weight, and Midnight sidestepped twice, seemingly eager to head back to the barn.

Maureen wondered exactly what she was supposed to do when Thom slipped his foot free of the stirrup, leaned forward, and offered her his assistance.

She studied his extended hand for a moment. "You want me to climb on behind you?" she asked, and grimaced at the squeaky, nervous way her voice reverberated into the night. She'd never ridden horseback in her life.

"Yes." She noticed he didn't offer her any advice or instructions.

Luckily she had on a pants suit. She lifted her left foot and placed it inside the stirrup, but it was so high off the ground that it would have taken a forklift to heave her all the way up to where Thom was.

With one foot trapped three feet off the ground, she hopped around on her good foot in an effort to gain her balance. "Don't you dare laugh," she admonished.

"I wouldn't dream of it."

But she could already hear the amusement in his voice.

"Give me your hand," he instructed, and when she pressed her smooth palm in his callused one, he hoisted her upward. Her one foot flailed in midair for a moment or two before she was able to boost it over Midnight's back.

Thom sat forward in his saddle, giving her just enough space to rest her buttocks.

"Comfortable?" he asked.

"No problem," she assured him, gripping the saddle behind her in an effort to keep from wrapping her arms around his waist. Their positions were intimate enough. She wore his jacket, and that alone felt as if she were in his arms. If she touched him, she might have to deal with the emotions his kisses had roused. To the best of her ability, she pushed every thought of his kiss from her mind and settled as far back in the saddle as was possible.

Thom pulled on the reins. "You might want to hold on to my waist."

"I'm fine," she said confidently. Her fingers bit into the hard leather saddle.

Midnight took off in an easy trot. Within the first few seconds Maureen recognized it was either hold on to Thom or else slip straight off Midnight's back. As it was, she felt as if she were sitting on a trampoline. Her buttocks lifted several inches off the saddle and slammed down repeatedly.

Immediately her arms shot out and went around Thom in an octopus grip. Her head jerked up and down until her teeth felt as if they were about to fall out.

Thom patted her hands, which were joined at his stomach. "That isn't so bad, now, is it?"

He'd nearly unsaddled her on purpose in an effort to get her to hold him. Maureen was sure of it. She noticed that Midnight's gait was much more relaxed now, and she sat relatively comfortably behind him.

Maureen would have chastised Thom, but just then they trotted into the yard and Karen came racing toward them.

"Mom," she cried, "where were you?"

"Lost," she muttered. "I did something none of us should ever do. I went for a walk without telling anyone where I was going."

"You're restricted for a week," Karen said, sounding dead serious, then ruined her feigned outrage by giggling. "I was worried until Mr. Nichols decided to look for you. Paula told me he wouldn't come back until he'd found you."

A man of his word. Maureen didn't know there were any left in this world. She'd been married to a man who'd often bartered with the truth, a man who'd traded away his integrity and destroyed their marriage for a few moments' pleasure with another woman.

"Come inside the house," Thom said. He slipped from Midnight's back and reached up to help Maureen down. It seemed his hands gripped her about the waist several seconds longer than necessary.

"Inside the house?" she asked once her feet were planted firmly on solid ground. Ken led Midnight into the barn.

"You're half frozen. You need something warm."

She wanted to argue, tell him the car heater would chase away any chill, but the words never made it to her lips.

"Great idea," Karen said, "and while you're talking to my mom you might say a few words about letting people know where she's going."

"I might," Thom agreed, then whispered for Maureen's benefit, "but don't worry, I won't."

He led the way into the house. The coffee was already brewed, and he poured them each a cup. The girls had mysteriously disappeared.

"About Friday night," Thom said, bracing his lean hip against the kitchen counter. Maureen was sitting down, more shaken from the episode of being lost and found than she cared to admit.

"Friday night?"

"The telephone call from your ex-husband."

"What about it?" she asked defensively.

"I think we should talk about it."

"I don't." Maureen had no intention of rehashing the unpleasant encounter with Brian, especially not with Thom.

"Not what was said between you and your ex, but what happened to us after the call. We were just getting to the point where we could communicate, really communicate."

That wasn't the way Maureen remembered it. As she recalled, it wasn't talking they'd been involved in when the phone rang.

"Nothing happened, nor will it again," she announced in her firmest voice. She'd made a mistake by lowering her guard once with this man, and he'd taken quick advantage. She had no intention of repeating the error.

"You're wrong," Thom said gently. "Something did happen. Something very good. It's unfortunate that it ended when it did."

"Unfortunate" wasn't the word she'd use. Brian's call was a blatant reminder of her past mistakes. She would never allow another man to hurt her the way Brian had.

Thom set aside his mug, walked over to the table, and straddled a chair. He folded his arms over the back and smiled at her. "Don't look so worried, I'm a patient man. I've been waiting a long time for you. I can wait a little longer for you to trust me."

Waiting a long time for you. Maureen lowered her gaze, afraid of what he might read in her eyes. "Why me?"

It took him a moment to compose his thoughts. "That first afternoon when we talked on the phone, I realized you were as lonely as I was. We both had daughters about the same age. We'd both walked the floors, fretted, and worried if we were doing a good enough job as single parents." He flexed his hands as if searching for something just outside of his reach. "There was a sadness in you. I've known that, too. I realize you don't want to discuss your marriage. Not yet. I'm hoping that sometime in the future you'll change your mind. When you do, I'll be here, ready to listen."

"Stop," she pleaded in a ragged whisper. "Please."

"Dad," Paula called, and an instant later burst into the kitchen with Karen. The two girls smiled knowingly at each other.

"See, what did I tell you?" Karen said with a grin as broad as the Grand Canyon. "He's about to kiss her again, and my mom's going to let him."

Paul glanced around the dinner table at his two children and the mates they'd chosen. His son-in-law, Eric, was a fine young man. And the more Paul was around Annie, the more he liked the woman who would soon be his son's wife.

"Pass the potatoes," Joe said to his sister, who made it seem as if the bowl were much too heavy for her to lift. It was a game from their childhood days. Bethany loved to tease her brother about the amount of mashed potatoes he managed to consume.

"Dad, is that dinky little tree the only one you're going to put up this year?" The question came from his daughter.

"I'm too busy to deal with Christmas."

Paul noted the way his son and daughter exchanged glances. He didn't know what he'd said to give them pause, other than the truth. "I've got better things to do than fuss with a Christmas tree," he reiterated. "It surprises me the way you kids are making such a commotion about my decorating the house for the holidays."

"Mom—"

"It was different when your mother was alive," Paul agreed smoothly.

"But the house looks so drab," Bethany said. "What about the ceramic angels Mom used to set out?"

"And the snowmen I made in Boy Scouts years ago? Remember the ones made of huge balls of cotton?" Joe added.

Both his children were regarding him expectantly. "All the Christmas decorations are in the attic," Paul told them. He certainly had no intention of getting them down himself.

"Great. We'll decorate the house for you," Bethany said eagerly, sounding like a five-year-old all over again. "And after Christmas Eric and I will come back, take everything down, and put it away for you."

Paul wanted to tell his children not to bother, but it seemed so important to them. "All right," he agreed reluctantly. "If that's what you want."

"We do." Somehow it seemed to Paul that his son-in-law didn't look all that excited with the project—and Paul didn't blame him.

By the time they'd finished dragging down the boxes from the attic, Paul felt as if his world had been invaded by four monsters. Bethany and Eric strung lights around the living-room windows and set the three brightly colored angels on the windowsill, peering out into the dark night.

Joe and Annie set about decorating the fireplace just the way Barbara had. Four hand-knit stockings hung from the mantel the same way they had for more than twenty years.

Paul had wanted to remove Barbara's knit stocking the year before, but the kids had insisted they put it up. Their mother was as much a part of their family now as she had been before her death.

Paul hadn't had the strength to argue with them then, and he felt even less inclined to argue this year. It hurt to see the colorful red stocking hanging next to his own.

A swell of sadness all but paralyzed him.

"Where should we put the nativity scene?" Joe asked him.

The words came at Paul as if from a great distance and were barely discernible. He couldn't stop looking at the stocking and remembering all the happy Christmases he'd spent with Barbara at his side. How empty the holiday seemed now. How lonely his life was without her. Even with his children at his side, busily going about cheering him up, nothing felt right. He doubted that it ever would again.

Decorations wouldn't replace his wife.

Presents wouldn't lessen the ache in his heart.

A stocking, hung with loving hands on a fireplace mantel, wouldn't repair the giant hole left in his life with her passing.

"Dad?" Joe said, and this time his voice was more distinct.

"Sorry," Paul said, turning to look at his son. Joe and Annie held the figurines from the nativity scene that had been handed down to him from his mother many years earlier. "Yes?"

"Where do you want us to put these? Same place as before?"

Paul motioned toward the television. "Yes. On top of the television will be fine."

On the pretense of retrieving something from the attic, Paul left his children in the living room. He walked up the stairs, and the old wood creaked as he moved slowly from one step to the next.

For several moments he stood at the top of the stairs, not knowing which way to turn or why he was there. Leaning against the wall, he sagged downward until he sat on the top step. That was where Bethany found him a few minutes later.

"Dad," she said, frowning as she stood at the foot of the stairs. She stared up at him, and it seemed she didn't know what to say. "What are you doing there?"

He looked around, hoping to come up with an answer that would satisfy her. But he couldn't think of one. "I came up here for something and then forgot what I was here for. Have you ever done that?" He laughed to make light of his odd behavior.

"Joe and I wanted to talk to you."

"Talk to me," Paul repeated. He stood and walked down the stairs. "This sounds serious."

He discovered Joe and Annie sitting together on the sofa, holding hands. Eric stood beside the fireplace, and it seemed to Paul he looked uncomfortable. His son-in-law's gaze skittered away from his.

"Sit down," Bethany said, and gestured to his recliner.

Paul sat, and his daughter followed suit. Eric came and stood behind his wife.

"We're worried about you," Bethany began.

"Worried?" Paul laughed it off. "Whatever for?"

"You're not yourself," Joe said. "I noticed it right away."

Paul wanted to tell his son that springing the news of his engagement on him hadn't helped matters. But he bit back the words that would only do harm. "I'm fine," he insisted brightly.

"I think you might be suffering from depression," Bethany said, and her voice shook as she said the words. "Nothing's been the same since Mom died. Not with you. Not with anyone."

"Depression . . ." Paul said the word slowly, as if giving it his careful consideration. Then he shook his head. "I don't think so. I've been in the ministry for years, and I've done my share of counseling. I know the symptoms."

"But . . ."

Paul raised his hand to stop Joe from speaking. "If anything, I need a vacation. A few days away from the duties and responsibilities of the church. I may drive up the coast, visit an old friend or two."

Bethany and Joe exchanged glances. Paul smiled broadly at his children, looking to reassure them. "I'm perfectly all right," he said, making sure his voice was firm and confident.

"You're sure?" Bethany asked. She leaned back and stared up at her husband as if seeking his advice. Eric squeezed her hand, and that seemed to reassure her.

Joe looked to his older sister and seemed agreeable to accepting whatever she thought.

"I'm positive," Paul said, and then rubbed his palms together enthusiastically. "Now, did I hear someone mention popcorn earlier?"

"They don't believe him, do they?" Goodness cried, so flabbergasted that she wanted to stand up and argue with Bethany and Joe. Not that it would do any good. If she could appear in her full glory and splendor in front of Reverend Paul Morris and not have him so much as notice, then marching into his living room wouldn't help, either.

Resting on the banister, she viewed the scene taking place in the living room with a disparaging eye.

"It looks to me like Paul's two children swallowed his story hook, line, and sinker." Shirley sat on the top step, the very place Paul had been only a few moments earlier.

"How can they be so blind?" Mercy demanded. She cast Goodness a sympathetic look. "This case is by far the most difficult any of us have ever been assigned."

"I so desperately want to help Paul," Goodness said.

"What about your miracle idea?" Shirley asked.

"Scratch that." Goodness hoped her friends would leave the matter at that. She'd rarely felt more foolish.

"Scratch a miracle?"

Unfortunately, Goodness's response had only succeeded in rousing Mercy's interest.

"All right, Goodness, you'd better tell us what happened."

"Nothing much."

"You didn't think of a miracle for Pastor Paul?" Shirley asked.

Goodness's nod revealed her reluctance to discuss the subject. "It didn't work."

"The miracle?" the other two asked in astonishment.

"No. Oh, I might as well tell you what I did," she muttered. There wasn't any way she was going to salvage her pride in this. "I revealed myself to Reverend Morris, full of God's glory. Only . . ." Even now she could barely make herself say the words.

"Only . . . ," Shirley prompted.

"Only he didn't notice me."

"Didn't notice you?" This came in whispered disbelief from Mercy. "How is that possible?"

"I don't know," Goodness confessed.

Her friends gathered at her side. "While you two attended the basketball game, I was left to face"—she hesitated and swallowed—"indifference."

Shirley's arm went about her waist. "Apathy is the worst."

"Poor Goodness."

"Now you understand why I'm so completely frustrated with this assignment," Goodness managed. She wished now that she'd confessed her failure earlier. Her friends' support and encouragement were just the balm her injured pride needed.

"I'm disappointed in his children," Shirley said shortly. "I would think they'd recognize the signs. Both are intelligent adults with a good education. Their father's in deep emotional pain. He needs help."

"They do know," Goodness said, coming to Bethany and Joe's defense. "But they desperately want to believe everything is fine with their father. They wouldn't know what to do if it wasn't, so they ignore the obvious."

"How true," Mercy said thoughtfully. "Their father's always been emotionally strong. He's the one they turned to in times of trouble and need. The truth would upset them, so their father tells them what they secretly long to hear."

"Friends," Goodness said suddenly, and snapped her fingers. "That's what Paul Morris needs right now. The companionship of good friends." She smiled at her two compatriots. "Now all I need to do is round up a few."

When Ted arrived back from lunch, there was a message on his desk from Joy. It was brief and to the point. She had to break their dinner date. No explanation. No excuses. No date.

He tried phoning her and each time was assured she'd been given his message. Sometimes Ted was slow, real slow. Hit-him-over-the-head-with-a-billy-club slow.

Joy Palmer was avoiding him. What should have been obvious after two phone calls didn't hit him until he'd made four.

Ted was in sad shape. Real sad shape, not to have recognized that sooner. He'd kissed her, and it was as if his common sense had taken a flying leap out the proverbial window.

He'd liked Joy from the first. The woman enthralled him with her unabashed enthusiasm for life. The basketball game had cinched it. Even now he wasn't sure what had prompted him to tail her to her father's garage. From there the rest was history.

Unfortunately there was the small problem of Blythe. He needed to talk to her, but when he'd phoned she'd abruptly canceled their date without offering an explanation. He wondered if she'd heard about him and Joy but decided that was impossible. He would clear up matters with Blythe, but he'd wait for her to contact him. She would, he knew, and soon.

Ted left the office ten minutes late, trying to decide what he was going to do about Joy. From the office he headed directly to the Wilshire Grove Retirement Center. He smiled when he found Edith parked in her usual spot. On impulse he walked over and patted the Chevy's hood.

"There's no escaping me now," he told the vehicle, and was confident that if Joy did decide to leave, her car would be most uncooperative. After all, Edith had brought them together.

Ted went directly to Joy's office. He found her secretary in the outer office. "Joy Palmer, please," he said as if he had a long-standing appointment.

His method worked as the young woman, who looked like a volunteer or a trainee, flipped through the pages of the appointment book. "I'm sorry, but Joy isn't here."

"May I ask where she is?"

Once again the assistant sorted through a variety of pages and then looked up with an apologetic expression. "It says here she's meeting with the library committee, but—"

"Thanks." Ted didn't wait to hear the rest. It wasn't necessary. With his grandmother as president, he knew more than he ever cared to about her precious committee. No doubt they were meeting in the library.

He found the committee members gathered around a table there. Since his grandmother loved her work so much, he recognized each woman in her small group by name. There was Emily and Thelma, Vera and Lois, Mary Frances, Justine, Dorothy, Joyce, Rachel, and a couple of others who had their heads turned away from him so he couldn't see their faces.

Joy was one of those.

His grandmother was speaking—quite vehemently, he noted—when she saw him. Surprise caused her to falter, something he guessed didn't happen often.

"Ted," she said, recovering quickly.

Ted stepped into the compact room. "I'm sorry to interrupt you ladies," he said, and his gaze found and connected with Joy's. He loved the way the color rose up her neck and invaded her pale cheeks. "I need to speak with Joy Palmer, if that would be possible."

"I'm in the middle of a meeting," she protested, and looked to Catherine for support. She should have known better.

"It's all right, dear," Catherine said ever so sweetly. "We've already taken far more of your time than we intended. You go on and talk to your young man."

This part about the "young man" was said as if she hadn't a clue who Ted might be.

"Thanks, Grandma," he said, and winked.

Catherine returned the gesture.

Reluctantly, as if this were the last thing she wanted to do, Joy stood. It took her another couple of minutes to gather her notes and pencils.

By the time she joined him in the hallway outside the library, her face was fire-engine red. "Just exactly what are you doing here?"

"We have a dinner date, remember?"

"I broke it."

"I got your message. There're two things you need to know about me, Joy Palmer. Number one, I don't take 'no' easily, and number two, if you have something to tell me, I'd prefer you did it to my face."

"All right," she said, squaring her shoulders. "I can't go to dinner with you."

"Why can't you?" he pressed. He wouldn't make this easy for her, if that was what she assumed. He'd meant what he said about not taking "no" easily.

She stiffened and knotted her hands around the pad and pen she'd clenched against her chest. "Can't you just accept the fact I changed my mind?" she pleaded, her back pressed against the wall. "Take Blythe."

"I'm more interested in taking you," he told her simply. "I can't and won't accept the fact you've changed your mind."

Briefly she closed her eyes. She seemed to have gathered some inner strength, because when she opened them again, Ted saw something that hadn't been there earlier.

"I don't want to see you again, understand? That shouldn't be so difficult, should it?" Her voice was cool and unemotional, unlike everything he knew her to be.

"It wouldn't be so hard if I believed it."

"What do I have to do to convince you? My word should be enough."

"Not this time." He backed her against the wall and loomed above her. Her huge eyes followed his movements.

"Let me go," she insisted indignantly.

"In a minute," he promised. This wasn't what he'd planned, but then he didn't really have a plan. There was only one way he could think of to convince Joy she was lying to herself as much as him. And that was to kiss her.

"Ted."

"S-h-h," he whispered, lowering his mouth to hers. His kiss was gentle and lengthy and convincing.

He tasted her resistance but outlasted that patiently, outlining the shape of her lips with his tongue. He couldn't speak for her, but his own heart went into overdrive. Sweet heaven, she tasted good. Unlike anything he'd experienced in a lifetime.

By the time he eased his lips from hers, her eyes remained closed and she was breathing deep and hard. Her hands hung loosely at her sides, and the pen and pad would have fallen to the floor if he hadn't taken them from her unresisting fingers.

"Now, tell me again you don't want to see me."

She shook her head.

"You're going to dinner with me, Joy." This was a statement, and he wouldn't listen to any arguments.

"All right," she whispered, but she didn't sound pleased about it. "But only this one time."

"No." After he straightened matters out with Blythe, he intended this evening with Joy would be the first of many.

She seemed to find that same strength that had come to her earlier. "Then I won't go with you this evening."

"Why?" he asked, needing to know. "Am I so terrible?"

"No," she returned vehemently. "I . . . I've heard about this sort of thing happening."

"What sort of thing?"

"With men, right before they become engaged to one woman, they find themselves attracted to another. I don't want to be a passing fancy to you, Ted. Someone who will entertain and amuse you while you make up your mind about Blythe."

He laughed at how preposterous this sounded. He wanted to explain that it was over between him and Blythe, but she didn't give him the chance.

"She's the one you love, not me," Joy said. "She's the one you'll marry, not me." And then, as if it cost her dearly to say the words, she stiffened. "I can't allow you to use me, and that's what you'd do. If you insist on us dining this evening, then I'll go along, under the condition I stated. This will be last time I see you."

Joy could see that Ted was fast losing his patience with her. He'd told her that he wouldn't be seeing Blythe again, but frankly she didn't believe him.

"You're not a passing fancy," he said for what seemed the hundredth time. "I like you. I want to get to know you better."

"Then I suggest you get to know some other woman," she returned in completely reasonable tones. For now she intrigued him, but when the time came, Joy knew beyond a doubt that he'd go back to Blythe.

"All right," Ted said, ramming his fingers through his hair, "we'll do this your way. One date, but I'm not going to waste it on an ordinary dinner."

"Another basketball game," she suggested.

"No." He looked at his wristwatch. "Do you have time for coffee?"

"Coffee?"

"Yes. This is not a date, understand? I want the two of us to sit down together so I can ask you a series of questions."

"What kind of questions?" Joy didn't like the sound of this.

"Things that will help me know you better."

"Why?" she asked skeptically.

His look was filled with wide-eyed innocence. "So I can decide what we should do for our one and only date."

Joy didn't understand why he had to make this so difficult. "Can't we just go to dinner and be done with it?"

"No. If you'll only agree to go out with me once . . ." He let the rest fade, implying that her stubbornness had brought this on.

"Oh, all right," she said with a complete lack of graciousness. "There's coffee in the dining room. They're getting ready to serve dinner, so I suggest we take it into my office and talk there."

"Whatever you say."

Joy never could walk across the foyer without stopping to chat with the residents. Acting as advocate and ombudsman for the tenants, she felt it was important to know as much about each one as they were comfortable sharing.

Charles sat on the same chair he occupied most days and was staring sightlessly into the distance. Forgetting Ted was with her, Joy paused and sat down next to the old man.

"Hello, Charles," she said softly.

He smiled, or perhaps it was wishful thinking on her part. "I met with the library committee this afternoon, and I was wondering if you might consider doing a small job for us during the literary tea? We're going to need someone to collect donations. Do you think you might like that job?"

He said nothing, gave no indication he'd heard her question.

Joy leaned over and patted his hand. "You think about it, and we'll talk in the morning."

Ted was waiting for her just outside the double glass doors that led to the dining room.

"I'm sorry," she said. "I needed to ask Charles something before it slipped my mind."

"Did he hear you?"

"Of course," she answered, knowing she sounded defensive. "Just because he didn't clap his hands and sing 'Glory, hallelujah!' doesn't mean he didn't hear and understand me."

Ted's gaze narrowed as he studied her. "You really love these people, don't you?"

"'These people,' as you call them, are men and women like your grandmother. This isn't a nursing home, and the residents don't need extensive medical care. They're retired. They've lived productive lives and are determined to continue to do so. Charles is the exception. Sometimes his mind fades away into a time you and I will never know. Don't judge him for that."

"All right," Ted agreed, "I won't."

Joy expelled her breath forcefully, regretting her outburst. "I was more touchy than I should have been. I apologize."

"No problem."

She led him into the kitchen, which bustled with activity. The scent of fresh bread baking mingled with roast beef and vegetables. She handed Ted a cream-colored ceramic mug and led him to the huge coffee machine. When they'd both filled their mugs, she returned to her office and sat behind her desk.

"Okay," she said, forcing herself to relax, "what is it you want to know?"

Ted settled onto the chair as if it had been custom made for him. He crossed his long legs, propping his ankle against his knee, and held the mug with one hand. "Have you ever been in love?"

Hot coffee spilled out of the cup and burned Joy's chin. "What's that got to do with anything?"

"Quite a lot, as it happens."

In an effort to disguise her uneasiness, she sipped her coffee. "I fell in love three times when I was in high school. Unfortunately not a one of the boys knew my name." Now that she thought about it, it was clear that her pattern of worshiping from afar had began early in life.

"I mean really in love?" he pressed.

She set the coffee on her desk with a deliberate show of impatience. "If these are the kinds of questions you're going to ask, then the deal's off."

He grinned as if to suggest she'd have a much harder time getting rid of him than she suspected. "All right, there are a few other questions I can ask."

She relaxed and reached for her coffee once more. All this was for naught, and she knew it. It irritated her that she was forced into this silliness.

For now she was the brightest, most appealing woman he'd ever met. All that, of course, would change as soon as he got over the becoming-engaged jitters. Billy, one of her brothers, had shown identical symptoms. Her parents had been ready to pull their hair out.

"Did I tell you about my brother Billy?" she asked instead.

He frowned. "No."

"He dated Diana for two years. He bought her an engagement ring, and then the night before he was set to propose he met this cute girl in a bar. Overnight he was convinced he was in love. My mother didn't know what to think. My father took him out for a father/son talk, which ended up in a shouting match. To make a long story short, Bill and Diana are married and have three beautiful children."

"What happened to the girl he met in the bar?"

"I don't know," Joy cried. "No one does. That's my point. Are you or are you not going to marry Blythe?"

It took him two lifetimes to answer. "I sincerely doubt it."

"But you've considered marrying her?"

Another lifetime, then: "Yes."

Ted Griffin was both honest and fair, that much she'd say for him.

"I'm sure when Billy kissed—I think her name was Donna—he was convinced she was the best thing that had ever happened to him, that he'd found someone special."

"I'm not Billy."

"True, you're older and more sophisticated than my brother, but it holds true, don't you see? When a man is about to willingly surrender his freedom, something inside him resists. Something inside him fights against it. I've got two older brothers, and a dozen male cousins, and I've seen this phenomenon happen over and over again. So why don't we both save each other a lot of grief and just drop it now?"

"Sorry, no."

Joy should have known that would have been too easy. She threw her hands into the air. "All right, ask away. But kindly limit your questions to those less personal."

Ted smiled that devilish handsome smile of his and nodded. "You're a virgin, aren't you?"

Chapter

★ ✪ ★

10

Leta Johnson *looked up* from her desk when Paul walked into the church office. "Good morning," she said with her usual cheerfulness.

"Morning." He picked up the two pink message slips on the corner of her desk. One was from Steve Tenny and the other from Bernard Bartelli.

"How was your evening with Bethany and Joe?" Leta asked, and he was sure she was making idle conversation. It wasn't like her to beat around the bush. When she had something to say, she generally said it. He had often admired this trait in her. He didn't always like it, but he found himself in her debt enough to appreciate the woman she was.

"Our dinner was great," he answered absently. He was worried about the Bartellis. Madge remained hospitalized, and from what he understood, their children had been notified of her accident. It seemed heartless and unnecessary to make Madge suffer this way. Paul had been to visit her only once since she'd broken her hip. He would go again soon, he promised himself.

"I talked to Joe the other day and learned he's engaged."

"Yes," Paul said, looking up from the phone messages. "He brought Annie home for me to meet."

"He said the two of them would be heading to Oregon for Christmas so Annie's family could meet Joe."

"Yes." Again his answer came abstractedly. His thoughts centered on Madge and Bernard and their call and what he could possibly say to them.

"I was wondering," Leta continued, sounding unlike her confident self, "if you'd care to join me for dinner on Christmas?"

The invitation took Paul by surprise. He'd worked with Leta for years, and although she was a vital member of his congregation, they'd avoided, by mutual consent, any contact outside the office.

"It'll be just me this year as well," Leta explained quickly. "And seeing that you're going to be alone too, well, I thought we might keep each other company."

"I appreciate the invitation," Paul said, unsure of how to respond, "but . . ."

"I understand, Paul," she said, saving him from having to invent an excuse, if that was his intent. "Don't worry. It was just a thought." She returned to her typing, her nimble fingers bouncing over the keys.

To the best of his memory, it was the first time she'd ever called him by his given name.

Not having an answer for her, Paul walked into his office and gently closed the door. He needed to work on his sermon for Sunday. He'd put it off far too long already.

Sermon notes were tucked inside his study Bible. He stared at the text and experienced nothing. None of the passion. None of the energy. None of the urgency to spread the good news.

At last he closed the Bible and reached for the first pink slip. Steve Tenny answered the phone himself.

"Paul," Steve said enthusiastically, "it's good to hear from you."

One would think Paul had initiated the contact, when in reality he couldn't remember the last time he'd purposely telephoned Steve. He hadn't meant for it to have been so long. "I got the message you'd phoned."

"Yes," Steve said cheerily. "Are you sure I can't talk you into taking a few days off and going hiking with me?"

The offer was more tempting than ever, especially with Joe leaving soon with Annie. Then Paul thought about Madge Bartelli and knew he couldn't leave her now. "I can't," he said with real regret.

"Myrna and I understand Joe's going to be away Christmas Day," Steve began again. "It's hard for me to believe he's engaged. Time sure does fly, doesn't it?"

"It does," Paul agreed flatly.

"Anyway, Myrna and I were talking, and we want to invite you to spend Christmas Day with us. Myrna puts on quite a spread, and there's always plenty. We won't take no for an answer, Paul. Not this time."

Paul wasn't entirely sure what his plans were for the holiday. The idea of being alone, without responsibilities, without commitments, strongly appealed to him. He didn't want his friend to think he didn't appreciate the invitation, but at the moment he simply didn't know what he was going to do.

"Would it be all right if I got back to you?" he asked.

"Of course," Steve said.

Paul grinned. What he'd enjoyed most about his friend was his unabashed enthusiasm for life. Even a solid "no" wouldn't have discouraged Steve. "I want you to know how much I appreciate you and Myrna thinking of me," Paul said.

If he could have his own way, Paul mused, he'd go camping. Alone. He'd leave directly after the Christmas Eve services and head for the hills to a campsite he'd taken the family to many times over the years. Then he'd lie under the stars. Away from Barbara's red stocking over the fireplace. Away from the tattered cotton snowmen his son had made a dozen or so years earlier. Away from Christmas and church and friends, however good their intentions.

He'd stumble over the memories of Barbara while he was camping, too—Paul was wise enough to recognize that—but at least it wouldn't feel as if the heaviness of his grief were smothering him.

The phone rang, and line one lit up on his telephone. His line. Leta answered it for him, then buzzed him.

"Bernard Bartelli," she said through the intercom.

Paul ran a hand down his face. He had nothing to offer the old man. Resting his face in his hands, he tried to reason what he could possibly say to the grieving husband.

"Line one," Leta's voice said through the intercom.

The line continued to flash like a bright red beacon, and still Paul couldn't make himself reach for the receiver.

He couldn't listen to the other man's pain and not relive his own. He couldn't hear Bernard's frustration and anger without feeling it bubble up inside him all over again. Just when everything seemed to be getting better, he had to bear it all again, and he hadn't the strength. He hadn't the courage.

His hand trembled as he pushed the button to the intercom and steeled himself. "Please take a message."

Leta hesitated, then said, "I already told Mr. Bartelli you were in the office."

"I realize that," he answered, the words thick with regret. "Just take a message. I'll get back to him later." Although he released the intercom, it seemed an eternity before Leta picked up the receiver and the light on line one stopped flashing.

Paul covered his face with both hands and discovered he was trembling. His breath came fast and hard.

A knock sounded against his door, and with a guilty jerk of his shoulders he straightened. "Yes," he said, making his voice as unemotional and businesslike as he could.

Leta stepped just inside his office. "Mr. Bartelli wanted you to know that Madge is much worse. He's contacted the children, and they're coming. It doesn't look as though Madge will last until Christmas."

Paul's heart sank like a concrete block. "I see," he said.

"Bernard's spending most of his time at the hospital. You probably won't be able to catch him by phone there."

"You're right, of course. I'll stop in at the hospital soon." But he didn't say when. Didn't know when he'd work up the courage to lend comfort when he'd found none himself.

Leta didn't leave. She hedged as if she weren't sure what to say, then finally blurted out, "Do you want me to ask someone else to be with the Bartellis?"

"Someone else?" He was their pastor. But he wasn't there when they needed him.

"Steve Tenny or another one of the elders," she suggested.

Paul stared at her and realized how badly he'd failed the people he'd guided spiritually all these years. "Yes," he whispered, "perhaps that would be best."

Leta closed the door softly, and Paul pressed his elbows against his desk and hung his head as the shame and guilt pummeled him. Working on his sermon now was impossible. He felt bone-dry. He had nothing to say.

Some time later Paul found himself sitting in the back row of the sanctuary. The church was semidark. What light was available was muted by the stained glass. For a long time he did nothing but sit.

Two of the lambs he had vowed to shepherd had needed him, and he had turned his back on them. He'd surrendered his duties to another because he'd been unable to cope with all that was involved with Madge's illness.

It would have been easier, he mused, if the cancer that ate away at Madge Bartelli wasn't the same rare type that had claimed Barbara. One he knew so intimately himself. He recognized each stage, relived the agonies.

He couldn't do this anymore. Couldn't face Madge, knowing her pain. Couldn't console Bernard when he'd found no consolation himself.

He'd failed these two people he loved. Failed God. Failed himself.

The heaviness in his chest was almost unbearable.

He'd learned to live without Barbara, but he didn't know if he could live with the man that he'd become without her.

Catherine was absolutely delighted. She didn't know what was developing between Joy and her grandson, but whatever it was looked promising. The sparkle was back in his eyes, and when he'd winked at her, it was all she could do to keep from clapping her hands and laughing outright. That boy was up to something.

On the other hand, Joy looked thoroughly confused and more than a little flustered by the attention Ted was paying her. Her cheeks had glowed an unnatural shade of pink when she'd stood to leave the library.

Catherine might be an interfering old woman, but she'd certainly like to know what was happening between these two people she loved so dearly.

Someone tapped on her apartment door. She rarely kept it locked, and most people knew that. Ted stuck his head inside.

"Howdy, Grandma."

"Ted," she said, absolutely delighted to see him. "You're a sight for sore eyes."

"I don't suppose you have any of those chocolate chip cookies left over from the other day, do you?"

Catherine grinned. "I imagine I could dig up a couple, if you promise not to ruin your dinner."

"Promise," he said, coming inside the apartment and making himself at home.

Catherine moved into her tiny kitchen and brought out two cookies on a plate. Her head buzzed with questions about him and Joy, but she didn't want him to think she was prying.

"I see you've met our Joy," she said casually, and sat across from him.

Ted gobbled down both cookies before he answered. "She's about the stubbornest woman I've yet to meet."

"Joy Palmer?"

"You don't know her the way I do." His eyes flashed with humor. "I'd like to get to know her a whole lot better, but she's resisting me. Personally, I don't understand how she can continue to ignore my charm and good looks."

Catherine laughed. "Maybe she keeps stumbling over your humility."

Ted grinned and thoughtfully rubbed the side of his jaw. "Perhaps that's the problem."

"There isn't a man or woman here who isn't crazy about Joy," Catherine told him. "She's much more than the resident service director. She's our friend and our advocate. When I first moved to Wilshire Grove it wasn't an easy adjustment for me to make. I'm too independent. I like things my own way, but Joy was there to smooth away the rough edges, to make the transition as uncomplicated as possible."

"I'm taking her out."

Catherine tried not to show how pleased she was, but doubted that she succeeded. "That's wonderful."

Ted grew thoughtful. "You don't think my interest in her is a psychological male thing having to do with the fear of relinquishing my freedom, do you?"

Catherine wasn't sure she followed that entirely. "Ah, I don't think so."

He beamed her a wide smile. "Good. I didn't think so, either." He leaned back and relaxed once more. "I want my date with her to be special. Do you have any recommendations?"

Catherine thought about it for several moments, then nodded. "The antique car show. As you might have guessed, Joy has an appreciation for older things."

There was a knock at Catherine's front door. She waited for whomever it was to let themselves inside. A second knock followed, this one louder and more insistent.

Catherine stood and crossed the room. It was Blythe Holmes.

"Hello, Mrs. Goodwin," she said. She refused to meet Catherine's gaze as she surveyed the living room. "I'm looking for Ted."

"Blythe." Ted was on his feet. "What are you doing here?"

"Shucks," Paula said with a dramatic sigh, "I thought we might find them already kissing."

"It doesn't look like it's going to happen," Karen returned in a loud whisper. The two girls had their elbows wrapped around each other's necks.

"Would you two kindly stop talking about us like we can't hear you?" Maureen said crankily. It was mildly disconcerting to have two twelve-year-olds discussing her love life, as if she had one. A few innocent kisses shared with Thom Nichols hardly constituted a sexual relationship.

"Actually, I wanted to know if Karen could spend the night on Friday." Paula addressed herself to Maureen. "I already asked my dad, and he said I had to get your permission first, but he said it was fine with him."

Maureen didn't dare look at her daughter staring at her so hopefully. If she refused, it would crush Karen's heart. It wasn't as if she had other plans.

"I suppose it would be all right."

"I'll pick up Karen," Thom offered.

"But that means you'll need to drive into the city."

"No problem. I promised Paula I'd drive her around and show her the Christmas decorations. There's a list of addresses in the paper, and it's sort of a tradition we have."

"Karen would enjoy that."

"Wanna come?" The offer, uttered under his breath, was low and seductive.

"Ah, thanks, but no."

He laughed, but this too was for her ears alone. "I'll miss you. Don't worry, I'll show our girls a good time."

Maureen changed her mind a dozen times or more before Thom arrived to pick Karen up Friday evening. Viewing the Christmas lights was something she'd always wanted to do, and the temptation to join him and the girls was strong.

When she was with him, Maureen found it easy to forget her resolve. He was gentle and patient and a good father—everything that Brian had never been, except perhaps in the beginning and on rare occasions afterward. It irritated her how quickly she was pulled into the force of his personality.

Shortly after seven Thom and Paula called for Karen, who'd packed enough clothes for a two-week visit. The thought of spending an entire day at the ranch with her favorite twenty-five horses and newfound best friend was like being granted a weekend pass to paradise.

"Hello again," Maureen said, stepping aside to allow Thom into her home.

"Gone off on any long walks by yourself lately?" he asked, removing his Stetson. His presence seemed to fill the small house.

"A gentleman wouldn't remind me of that."

Thom's grin was off center. "I never claimed to be a gentleman."

Karen and Paula came out of the bedroom hauling Karen's three packed overnight bags.

"You'd think she was moving in," Maureen joked, then added, "No need to worry, there're some Barbie dolls and enough clothes to bankrupt Ken in there as well."

"You sure you won't change your mind and come with us?" Thom asked.

Maureen was tempted. More tempted than she cared to admit, even to herself. "No thanks. I've got a full evening planned."

"A hot date?" He actually looked worried. Maureen could have kissed him for that.

"Not exactly. I'm going to give my hair a hot oil treatment, change the polish on my nails, and read a murder mystery I've been saving. A woman murders her ex-husband and gets away with it," she said with a laugh.

"I'll give you a call in the morning," Thom promised, and then he did the most unexpected thing. He leaned forward and kissed her. It wasn't even a real kiss, more a peck on the cheek. A way of telling her he wanted her to enjoy her evening alone. A way of saying he was going to miss her. A way of saying he couldn't wait until he could see her again.

Maureen pressed her hand against her cheek for several minutes after they'd left. Then a smile touched her lips, one that grew until she was on the verge of giggling like a schoolgirl.

On her way into the bathroom to run a tub of hot, sudsy water, Maureen paused and reached for the phone. Her mother answered right away.

"Hello, Mom, it's me."

"Maureen. My goodness, I haven't heard from you in ages! I thought now that you lived closer we'd see more of you. I'm sorry we weren't able to take Karen out for her riding lesson the other day."

"It was no problem, everything worked out. But I did want to talk over something with you. I didn't say anything earlier because I was afraid you and I might have words over it."

"But, honey, what did I do?" Her mother sounded shocked and confused, and Maureen felt mildly guilty. Everything had turned out for the good, and Karen hadn't suffered from a nightmare in weeks.

"It's all right, Mom. Don't worry about it," Maureen hurried to reassure her mother. "But I really wish you hadn't phoned Thom Nichols and given him my name. I was going to call about the riding lessons for Karen, really I was, but before I could—"

"I didn't phone Thom Nichols," Beverly Shields insisted.

"You didn't?"

"No. How could I? You took the brochure, remember?"

"But then who did?"

*   *   *

"Shirley?" Mercy called sweetly. "You want to tell us all about a certain phone call to Nichols's Riding Stables? Goodness and I are all ears."

"I?" Shirley pressed a hand over her breast and wore a shocked look, as if she would never be caught doing anything so underhanded.

As far as Mercy was concerned, the older prayer ambassador did a poor job of feigning innocence.

"And after the lectures she's been giving us about keeping our feathers in a row."

"That's ducks in a row, and it's a valid point," Shirley insisted.

"Perhaps. But what do you think Gabriel will think once he learns about the stunt you pulled?" Mercy wagged her finger at her friend. "And so soon after our arrival on earth too."

"I had to do something drastic," Shirley insisted righteously. "It was apparent Maureen wasn't going to call the stables. Goodness slapped that brochure across her windshield, and the woman didn't even read it. She would have forgotten about the whole thing. That brochure could have stayed in the backseat of her car for months."

"One question." This came from Goodness, who looked rather peaked, Mercy thought. "Did you know Thom Nichols was a widower with a daughter the same age as Karen?"

"No. That came as a surprise. A pleasant one, I might add."

Goodness nodded. "Have you ever noticed how neatly everything seems to fall into place for Shirley?" she asked Mercy.

Shirley stiffened. "That's not necessarily true."

"Do you need a lecture on being good and staying away from the things of earth?" Mercy asked. This was remedial stuff, but exactly the kind of thing Shirley would ask her if their situations were reversed.

"Well, there is one small thing," Shirley admitted.

"Really?" Goodness and Mercy were all ears.

"In the last few weeks with Karen . . ."

"Yes?"

"I've felt a certain curiosity toward horses myself. Karen certainly does seem to enjoy her riding lessons, and, well . . ."

"Yes?"

"Well . . ."

"You want to ride?" Mercy couldn't believe what she was hearing. From Shirley, no less.

"That can be arranged, you know." Goodness was ever the optimist when it came to planning the impossible.

"Goodness," Mercy cried. Her friend had lost it. Angels, prayer ambassadors in particular, didn't gallop across the countryside on the backs of animals. She said so and was promptly reminded that they'd done far more improbable things in their tenure.

Before long the three were standing inside the corral with half a dozen beasts running circles around them. There was no shortage of animals from which to choose.

Taking her time, Shirley opted for a beautiful white mare.

"You're sure about this?" Mercy asked, uncertain even now that Shirley was doing the right thing. She'd hate to be called back to heaven for something so silly. If she was slated for trouble, it should be for something worth their while, like a visit to Hollywood. Mercy could get real interested in the movies.

Shirley gently rested her frame on the mare's back. "Hey," she said, smiling down at her two friends, "this isn't nearly as difficult as I assumed." With her hands holding on to the mane, she gently kicked her feet against the mare's sides until the feisty filly started to trot.

"Hey, look at me!" she cried, waving one arm in the air like a rodeo rider.

"Great," Goodness said.

"Say, do you two want to ride next?" Shirley asked.

"Ahh . . ."

"No thanks."

The horse started to gallop, and before anyone could do anything to stop her, the mare raced at breakneck speed for the fence. Shirley let out a wild scream of alarm.

The mare stopped abruptly just before she reached the wooden poles.

Shirley cried out as she went sliding ingloriously into the air, landing with a solid thump in a pile of hay. Goodness and Mercy carefully dug her out.

"Who would have believed it," Shirley said, brushing the straw from her arms. "Horses are vicious beasts. They're certainly not to be trusted."

Chapter

★ ✫ ★

11

"*I thought I'd find* you here," Blythe said to Ted, smiling broadly as if she'd been expected. She directed her attention to his grandmother. "It's good to see you again, Mrs. Goodwin."

"Catherine," his grandmother corrected graciously. "It's good to see you again, my dear."

Ted frowned, not knowing what to say. "Is something wrong at the office?"

Blythe cast him a look that said he was being ridiculous to suggest such a thing. "Nothing like that. It's just that I haven't seen hide nor hair of you in days."

Ted found that remark interesting since she'd broken their last date. Blythe sat on the chair Ted had vacated and picked up the empty cookie plate. "Ted," she said in a low, teasing voice, "you haven't been eating cookies again, have you?"

"Would you care for a cup of tea, dear?" Catherine offered, distracting her.

"That would be lovely."

"I was just leaving," Ted said, doing a poor job of disguising his frustration. It was true he needed to talk to Blythe, but he wasn't pleased at the way she'd popped in at his grandmother's unannounced. Nor did he want Joy to see him with the other woman. That would confirm everything she was thinking, which was ridiculous.

"Then I'll skip the tea, Mrs. Goodwin," Blythe said, and stood. "Ted, I hope you don't mind my tracking you down like this, but it's the night Bob and Carol asked us out for drinks. I was sure you'd forgotten. I meant to remind you, but by the time I got to your office you'd already left."

"Bob and Carol? Drinks?" Ted's mind was a blank. To the best of his memory he didn't know the couple.

"Wilson," Blythe supplied as if he shouldn't need to be reminded. "As in state senator Bob Wilson and his wife, Carol."

For the life of him, Ted couldn't remember meeting the man, let alone agreeing to having drinks with the couple. "Do I know these people?"

"Of course you do, and if you don't remember them, then you should," she returned. "Bob is one of the most influential men in Sacramento."

"Why would this senator and his wife invite me out for a drink?"

Blythe smiled rather smugly. "Bob phoned and suggested the four of us get together weeks ago. You don't remember? Honestly, Ted, what am I going to do with you?"

"I apologize. It must have completely slipped my mind," Ted hedged, looking for a tactful way to extract himself from the obligation. He'd never been keen on sitting around a crowded cocktail lounge and making small talk with people he barely knew.

"Senator Wilson's just the type of man who can help you," Blythe insisted. "He's powerful and influential and a decent guy. They're few and far between these days. This is the opportunity of a lifetime. Don't tell me you're going to back out at this late date." She cast him a pleading look. "It won't take long, I promise. An hour at the most, maybe two."

Her round eyes appealed to him until Ted gave in. It wouldn't hurt to meet the couple, he decided, especially since he'd supposedly agreed to this outing. Although, heaven help him, he didn't so much as recognize the couple's name.

"You'll come, won't you?"

"All right," he said reluctantly.

Blythe checked her watch. "We should probably leave right away."

"No problem," Ted said, and kissed his grandmother on the way to the door. Catherine wore a worried look, and he wondered if something were amiss with her. "I'll see you later," he promised.

"Go," she said, shooing him out the door, "and have fun."

With his back to Blythe, Ted met his grandmother's gaze and rolled his eyes, so she'd know what he really thought of this little get-together.

Blythe wrapped her arm around his and walked in a meandering crisscross pattern, with her head leaning against his shoulder. "I have the feeling you've been avoiding me lately," she said in a soft, sexy murmur.

"You're the one who broke our date," he reminded her.

"I know. I wasn't feeling well." Her arm tightened around his.

"So you said."

"I haven't talked to you in days," she purred, and rubbed against him like a warm, cuddly kitten.

"I've been busy." Now didn't seem the time to mention Joy.

"I hope you're not upset with me over that little mishap with the car. You were right, I was being silly. It's just that . . . well, you know what it's like when you have a new car, and mine was barely off the showroom floor."

Ted did know. "I might have overreacted myself," he said, willing to give her the benefit of the doubt. Now that she'd brought up the subject of the accident, he realized how much her attitude had troubled him. It was a side of her he'd never seen before, and frankly he hadn't liked it.

The elevator arrived, and they stepped inside. He did enjoy her company, and they certainly shared a great deal in common. For a time he'd actually considered proposing to Blythe.

Then how could he explain the powerful attraction he felt for Joy? He wondered if it was possible that what Joy claimed was true. Could his sudden interest in her be the same thing that happened to her brother Billy shortly before he became engaged?

Ted would rather not believe he was that fickle, but the evidence was standing next to him, her head on his shoulder. At one time he'd considered marrying Blythe, that much was true. Seriously considered it.

Until he'd met Joy. Until he'd sat next to this mechanic's daughter in a city park and kissed her. From that moment forward, everything had changed. Now all he had to do was convince her.

"You've gone quiet all of a sudden," Blythe said.

"Sorry."

"Is something on your mind?" Blythe traced her perfectly manicured nails down the length of his forearm. "Maybe you should spend the night and we can sort everything out," she whispered close to his ear.

"If I spend the night, we won't be talking, will we?"

Blythe laughed delightedly. "We could always talk afterward."

Ted smiled and squeezed her arm but discovered, to his chagrin, that he wasn't tempted by her invitation. In fact, the thought of making love to Blythe Holmes seemed very wrong. He couldn't account for that because he'd spent his share of evenings at her luxury condo.

It seemed to take the sluggish elevator ten minutes to reach the main floor, although in reality it was only a matter of seconds. The doors glided open slowly, and Blythe reached inside her purse for her car keys.

Ted started across the lobby, eager to make his escape, when the very thing he'd feared most happened. He saw Joy. She was sitting next to Charles, the elderly man she'd been talking to earlier. As before, it looked as if she were carrying on a lengthy one-sided conversation.

As luck would have it, she glanced up just then. Her eyes rounded with surprise and hurt when she saw him with Blythe. Her gaze held his for a moment, and then a sad, knowing look came over her and she looked away.

Ted wanted to stop, walk over, and explain, but he didn't know what he'd say, what excuse he'd offer. Of one thing he was sure: he'd never intended to hurt Joy. He couldn't bear knowing he had.

Just as Joy turned on the television and plopped down in front of it, the doorbell chimed. This was not the time for company. Joy had never felt less sociable in her life.

She walked over to the door and checked the peephole.

Ted Griffin.

Groaning, she twisted away from the door and closed her eyes. It would take a better woman than she was to deal with him just then.

She held her breath. He rang the bell again. Joy didn't dare move, or blink, or give any indication she was home. When she was calm and in control of her emotions, then and only then would she talk to the man who didn't seem to know his own mind.

Eventually he left, but Joy knew she hadn't fooled him. He'd been as aware of her on the other side of the door as she was of him.

Her reprieve didn't last long. The following morning when she arrived at the office, a dozen red roses awaited her. The card read simply "Ted." She kept them on the corner of her desk for the first hour, then decided she couldn't look at them and not think of him. Of course, she couldn't look at her pencil holder and not think of Ted, but that was beside the point.

She would have liked to make an excuse and disappear for the afternoon, but that was the coward's way out. The sooner she told him what had to be said, the better.

Joy was in the business office when he arrived. Through the plate-glass window, she saw him walk into the foyer. It would only be a matter of minutes before he tracked her down. Instead she followed him.

"Hello," she said evenly, in the long hallway leading to her office. "Were you looking for me?"

Ted whirled around, and it looked as if he were hard-pressed not to reach for her right then and there. Not that she would have allowed it. Not this time.

"I see you got my flowers," he said. He moved into her office and sat down as if this were his second home. For her part, Joy preferred to stand.

"I thought they looked very nice in the welcoming area," she said. "They weren't necessary."

"I wanted to explain about last night."

"No," she said firmly, and crossed her arms over her chest, "I'd rather you didn't." He seemed to want to object, but she stopped him by raising her index finger. "Please, it doesn't matter."

"It matters to me."

She ignored that, because what was important to her at that moment was breaking off a potentially devastating relationship. "Actually I'm pleased you stopped by. I wanted to talk to you."

"I want to talk to you, too. About our date, I was thinking—"

"There isn't going to be any date."

"That's not what you said earlier."

Joy smiled, but it was a rather sad smile. "A woman can change her mind. Please, Ted, just leave it at that."

He shook his head. "You keep forgetting. I don't take 'no' for an answer."

"This time you'll have to, because I won't be seeing you again." She met his gaze, her eyes cool, her voice calm and controlled. "I mean it, Ted. Kindly stay out of my life."

Maureen couldn't believe she slept so late. Ten o'clock on a Saturday morning. It had been years. Aeons. Longer than she could remember since she'd rested this well.

She might have lazed in bed even longer if the phone hadn't rung. "Hello," she answered on the tail end of a heady yawn.

"Mom? Is that you? You don't sound right. Are you sick or something?"

"No, my darling daughter, what you're hearing is the sound of your mother being exquisitely lazy."

"Lazy?"

"I'm still in bed."

A shocked silence followed. "Bed! Mom, you never stay in bed this long."

"I know," Maureen said dreamily, and yawned again. "I feel wonderful."

"Good," Karen said excitedly, "because we've got a surprise for you."

"A surprise?" The "we've" part of the conversation didn't escape her notice.

"A really fabulous surprise. You're coming to get me, aren't you?"

"Of course."

"Don't come until after four, understand? That's really important."

"After four. Why?"

"That's the surprise part. I don't want to ruin it so don't ask me a lot of questions because I really want to tell you and if I do Paula will be real disappointed and Thom too." She lowered her voice substantially. "But don't eat a big lunch, okay?"

"All right, all right." Maureen struggled to a sitting position. "Now before we hang up, tell me, did you have a good time last night?"

"Oh, Mom, the Christmas lights were so pretty and some people were serving hot apple cider and singing Christmas carols. One neighborhood was even collecting canned goods for food baskets. Thom brought bags and bags of things, and this stuff wasn't from the back of his cupboard, either. Thom let Paula and me go to the grocery store and shop with a cart and everything." Her voice dropped once again. "We were real careful and chose nutritious food, too. No candy or junk food."

Maureen heard a whisper in the background before Karen came back on the line. "There was one small bag of candy canes, but those were mainly for decorations."

"It sounds like you had a wonderful time." Meeting Paula and Thom had changed both their lives for the better.

"Paula and I decided to be friends for life."

"That's great."

"How's your hair with olive oil in it?"

"Olive oil?"

"I heard you tell Thom you were going to put oil in your hair. It sounded weird to me and Paula, but when she asked Thom he said it was a woman thing."

"That's hot oil, sweetheart, and we'll do it on your hair someday."

"Paula's, too?" she wanted to know right away.

"Paula's, too," Maureen promised.

"Okay, Mom, I'd better go because we've got a whole lot more to do before you get here. Don't be late, okay? And oh—no, I'd better not say anything more."

Smiling, Maureen replaced the receiver. A few moments later she climbed out of bed and dressed. She stood in the middle of her bedroom and wondered what those three had managed to cook up this time. A surprise. She could just imagine.

Saturdays were generally reserved for errands, and Maureen left the house shortly after talking to her daughter. She stopped off at the cleaners and the drugstore and did a quick bit of Christmas shopping before heading for Thom's ranch.

She arrived precisely at four. No sooner had she parked the car than Karen burst out of the house and raced toward her, her arms open wide as if it had been six months since they'd last seen each other.

Maureen caught her in her arms.

Thom and Paula followed Karen outside. Maureen's gaze met Thom's, and his eyes sparkled. "I understand you've got a surprise for me," she said, smiling at Thom. Keeping a cool facade with him had become much too difficult. It required more energy and effort than she could muster. Like Karen, she was happy, truly happy. Perhaps for the first time in years.

"Oh, Mom, it's so beautiful."

"What is?"

Both girls were looking at her as if they were about to burst wide open. Karen grabbed hold of her hand and led her toward the house. Maureen looked over her shoulder at Thom, who was grinning broadly.

"This is only part of the surprise," Karen explained as she opened the screen door and led Maureen into the formal living room. Maureen had been in Thom's home a number of times before, but she'd always gone in through the kitchen.

The living room was sunken, with a huge stone fireplace that dominated one entire wall. The naturally bright room was cheered by the extensive display of Christmas decorations. A massive flocked white Christmas tree, six feet tall or more, took up one corner where the ceiling slanted upward toward a skylight.

In all her life Maureen had never seen a more beautifully decorated Christmas tree. The limbs drooped downward, heavy with layers of white flocking. Blue glass bulbs of varying sizes glistened like the moon against a crystal-clear lake. Ribbons of gold delicately embraced the tree, woven between the branches.

"It's beautiful," Maureen whispered.

"We decorated the tree," Karen said, so excited she could barely speak. "First of all we went out and bought it. Thom let us pick it out and everything."

It seemed unbelievable to Maureen what an incredibly good job they'd done. The entire house looked as if it had been decorated by a professional. The contrast between her house and this one said a great deal about the two of them. It was as if all the joy had been taken out of Maureen's life by the divorce.

"A friend of Thom's put the snow on it for us."

"You couldn't have timed your arrival any better," Thom told her. "We just put the finishing touches on it about five minutes ago."

"This is only part of your surprise, though," Karen said, taking Maureen's hand once more and leading her into the dining room.

The polished mahogany table in the formal dining room was set with china dishes and linen napkins. A pair of sterling-silver candlesticks decorated with bayberry-scented candles and a bowl of fresh flowers sat proudly in the center.

"This is lovely," Maureen told them. "Did you girls do this as well?"

"No," Karen said quickly, "Thom bought that, for atmosphere."

Maureen leveled her gaze on the rancher, who looked entirely too pleased with himself. She was tempted to ask him exactly what he had up his sleeve, but she didn't.

"There're only two place settings," Maureen pointed out to her daughter.

"Mom," Karen said in that way of hers that made Maureen feel as if she'd suddenly lost a hundred points off her intelligence quotient.

"Take her into the kitchen, girls," Thom advised.

The party of four traipsed into the kitchen, and Maureen swore she'd seldom seen a bigger mess. It looked as if whoever was cooking had required every pot and kettle in the house. Tomato sauce was splattered across the stove top and the wall. Lettuce leaves trailed from the table to the refrigerator.

"What happened in here?" Maureen cried. Her instincts were to push up her sleeves and clean the mess before it got worse.

"I don't think this was such a good idea, Dad," Paula muttered.

"Take her back into the living room," Karen advised Thom, "and leave the rest to us."

Maureen felt as if she were trapped in a London fog. "What's going on here?"

"I believe what you just saw was our dinner," Thom explained.

He led her into the living room and sat her down. A bottle of wine was cooling in a bucket of ice, something Maureen had missed seeing earlier. Thom went to work removing the stubborn cork and pouring them each a generous glass.

"I hate to appear so dense," Maureen whispered, "but exactly what's happening?"

Thom smiled, and faced with the potency of his appeal, Maureen forced herself to look away. "The girls insisted on preparing us a romantic dinner," he explained. "They've taken care of everything themselves."

No sooner had he finished than Michael Bolton's low, sultry voice crooned over the stereo. From the corner of her eye, Maureen saw the two twelve-year-olds sticking their heads out from the kitchen door, studying Maureen and Thom. They appeared to be waiting for something to happen.

"We want you to talk and hold hands and whatever it is people do when they fall in love," Paula instructed. She held up a wooden spoon caked in red sauce. "Dinner will be ready in about . . ." She turned around, apparently needing Karen to supply the answer. "Twenty-two minutes," she informed them.

Maureen grew decidedly uncomfortable. She sipped her wine, and it seemed to go straight to her head.

"Don't look so worried," Thom said, leaning back and relaxing. "The girls just wanted to have some fun, and when I told them they could cook dinner, they concocted the idea of creating a romantic interlude for the two of us."

"Psst, Dad," Paula said from the kitchen doorway. "You're supposed to ask Maureen to dance now."

"I keep forgetting my cue," he whispered. Standing, he offered her his hand. "Shall we?"

"I . . . I'm not very good at this sort of thing."

"I'm not, either," he assured her.

Maureen decided she couldn't very well disappoint the girls, since they were looking on eagerly. She placed her hand in Thom's and stood. It amazed her how easily she slipped into his arms. It was as if she'd been doing it for half her life. As if this were exactly where she belonged. As if this were where she intended to stay for a very long time.

Thom pressed his cheek to hers. "This isn't so bad now, is it?"

"No," she admitted. She dared not close her eyes. Dared not allow herself to feel comfortable in a man's arms again. Rarely had she felt more awkward. She moved as if she had two left feet, as though dancing required far more talent than she possessed.

"Relax," Thom advised.

"I'm trying," she muttered. Her life was too good to tamper with now, she reminded herself. She'd need a team of psychologists to explain why she would willingly allow herself to be drawn into a second relationship. She refused to relinquish her freedom, refused to hand her heart to someone else who had the power to destroy her.

Thom's hold on her tightened perceptively. "Block out your ex-husband from your mind," he whispered close to her ear. "When I'm holding you, I'd prefer it if you thought about me."

Maureen felt a panic attack approaching. "This isn't going to work."

"Yes, it is," he said gently but insistently. "Close your eyes."

"I can't."

"Why not?"

"If I do—" She bit off the rest of what she was going to say when Thom's lips found her neck. Shivers of awareness scooted down her arms.

She could feel his smile against her cool skin. "That's better," he murmured seductively, "much better."

Almost against her will, Maureen's eyes drifted closed. Her head nestled closer to his, and any pretense of dancing became exactly that.

"He's going to kiss her now." Maureen recognized her daughter's voice.

"No, he isn't," Thom said in a stage whisper. "Not when he's got an audience."

The sound that followed sounded suspiciously like the closing of a door. Maureen waited a moment, but Thom seemed content to do nothing more than hold her.

"Are you going to kiss me?" she asked.

"Do you want me to?"

"I don't know." She knew exactly what she wanted, but she wasn't willing to ask for it.

She felt his shoulders move with a silent laugh. "I'm going to kiss you, and when I do, you're going to remember it for a good long while. When I do, you won't ever confuse me with another man again, understand?"

Maureen nodded.

"Now tell me true, Maureen Woods, do you or do you not want me to kiss you?"

She broke away just enough to look him in the eyes. Her gaze fell on the table with the polished silver and the two place settings. At some point when she hadn't noticed, the girls had come in and lit the candles. No man had ever wooed her this way. No man had ever taken such time and care to court her. Not even Brian.

"Do you?" Thom pressed, growing impatient.

Maureen's gaze was drawn back to him. She smiled shyly and nodded. She wanted his kiss. Wanted it desperately. "Please, oh, please."

* * *

"Dad's going to be all right," Joe told his sister confidently. "I feel a whole lot better about everything since we talked to him." He smiled at Annie, who sat on the other side of the living room, reading a magazine. He was making one final phone call to his sister before leaving town. Now that matters were straight with his father, there wasn't any need to stick around California any longer. Annie, understandably, was eager to see her family.

"You're sure about Dad?" Bethany pressed.

"Relatively sure."

"Eric seems to think we might be glossing over the facts here. Even when he tries to convince us otherwise, Dad doesn't seem like his old self."

"Will any of us ever be the same after losing Mom?" Joe asked. He didn't mean to sound impatient, but he'd talked to Annie and they'd decided that morning to head out early. He didn't want to change their plans again.

"No, I guess we won't," Bethany admitted reluctantly. "Have you told Dad you're leaving yet?"

"No. He's disappeared again. Mrs. Johnson said he left shortly after lunch and didn't say where he was going. He'll be back before dinner. Annie and I'll tell him then."

Paul hated the smell of a hospital. It was sickness and death and hopelessness and pain all mingled with disinfectant and medications. Even when Barbara was home for brief periods, the scent had never left her skin and hair.

It assaulted him when he walked into the Westside Medical Hospital like a wave of August heat. He stopped in the foyer, uncertain for a moment if he could continue.

By the sheer force of his guilt and shame, he made his way toward the elevator and Madge Bartelli's room. He expected to find Bernard either in the waiting room reserved for families or at Madge's bedside, but Madge's husband was neither place.

Madge must have heard him enter the room because her head rolled across the pillow toward Paul. Even in her agony she offered him a weak smile. "Hello, Pastor."

"Hello, Madge." At her bedside was the worn leather volume of Psalms he'd lent her. Barbara had read it often in those final weeks. When the pain was the worst, he'd read the words of comfort to her, but he'd found little solace himself.

"How nice of you to come."

He should have been to visit her much sooner and far more often. "Joe's home." That was the only excuse he could think to offer, weak as it was. He wanted to beg her to forgive his weakness, but he didn't come to burden her with his guilt.

"I understand he's marrying." Her words were so weak, they were barely audible.

"This summer, it seems."

"Ah," she said, and closed her eyes, "I'll miss the wedding."

After all his years of schooling, after all his years of counseling and training, Paul discovered he hadn't an answer to that.

"Give him and his bride-to-be my love."

"I will."

How frail she was, Paul noted, and sinking more each day. He wondered if her children would arrive in time and prayed they would.

Prayer.

He had done precious little of that in the last few weeks. He discovered he couldn't talk to God the way he had before Barbara's death. He had a chip on his shoulder, he guessed, although a pastor generally wasn't supposed to possess negative feelings. After all, what possible good would it do to be angry with almighty God?

"Where's Bernard?" Paul asked, afraid if he waited much longer she'd slip into a state of semiconsciousness.

"Chapel, I think. Talk to him, will you, Pastor? He's having a difficult time letting me go, and he must."

"Sleep now," Paul whispered. He claimed the fragile hand in his own and patted it. He couldn't tell this sweet, godly woman that he hadn't been able to relinquish his wife yet. Barbara was two years in the ground, and he clung to each memory of his wife until his life was so filled with stumbling blocks, he was no earthly good to anyone.

How long he sat at Madge's bedside he didn't know. Time lost meaning. He might even have slept some, he didn't know. But when he next looked up, Paul discovered Bernard standing across from him. The older man's shoulders were slumped forward as if standing upright were almost more than he could manage.

"She's resting comfortably now," Paul whispered.

Bernard nodded and sank onto the chair on the opposite side of the hospital bed.

Paul wondered when Bernard had last eaten. Or slept a full night through. *He* hadn't, Paul recalled. Not for weeks on end. He'd survived on bitter coffee out of a machine and stale sandwiches.

Paul came around to where Bernard was sitting. He didn't ask how the other man was holding up; he knew. He didn't ask about Madge's condition; he knew that, too.

"Let me buy you something to eat," he offered.

Bernard shook his head. "I'm not hungry."

Paul wrapped his arms around Bernard and gently pulled his head to his shoulder as if he were cradling a child.

A sob came from deep inside the older man's chest. It took some time to work its way up his parched throat, and when it was released it sounded like the cry of a wounded animal. One sob followed another and then another, until Bernard's shoulders heaved with emotion.

"I've loved Madge for nearly fifty years," he wailed.

"I know," Paul said soothingly.

"How will I ever live without her?"

"You'll learn," Paul assured him. His only hope was that his friend would learn better than he had.

"She's ready," Bernard said again, sobbing stronger now. "But I'm not. I can't let her go. God help me, I can't let her go."

"I know all about that, too," Paul whispered brokenly.

Chapter

★ ✦ ★

12

It wasn't supposed to be this way. Joy had made her decision about Ted and stuck to it in spite of his persuasive arguments.

After he'd left her, she'd expected a feeling of elation. A sense of well-being all the self-help books described when one responded with emotional maturity.

Joy had taken care of her inner child, seen to her own emotional needs without surrendering to the risky desires of her insecurities. It wasn't necessary for anyone to tell her Ted was the type who'd only hurt her in the end. That much was obvious from the moment she'd seen him walk out the door with Blythe Holmes on his arm.

What she hadn't anticipated was the down time. This feeling of loss and emptiness. It felt as if the whole world were in danger of swallowing her.

"Is something wrong, dear?" Catherine's voice broke Joy's musings. "You haven't seemed like yourself all day."

"I'm fine." Joy was supposed to be working on the invitations to the local writers' group for the literary tea, but Joy's mind had repeatedly gotten sidetracked. She tried not to think about Ted. She tried to make herself angry with him instead of feeling blue and dispirited about her life in general.

"Are you a little under the weather?" Catherine asked, and patted Joy's shoulder affectionately. "I understand the flu bug's making the rounds. You do look a bit peaked."

"I'm feeling just great," Joy insisted, forcing a smile. Physically she was, but emotionally she was searching for an excuse to burst into tears. A sentimental advertisement on television would do the trick.

"I understand you got Charles to agree to collect the donations for the library committee?"

"Yes." Joy was rather proud of that accomplishment. During one of his more lucid moments, she'd talked to him, and the retired soldier had been delighted at the prospect. He seemed less embroiled in his fantasy world of late, and Joy wanted to believe that was because the present one was gaining appeal.

"Everything is coming together so nicely."

"Yes, it is," Joy agreed. It felt as though her life were in shambles but everything else seemed to be going along smoothly.

"Ted's coming by this afternoon," Catherine announced, studying Joy carefully. "He called and invited me to dinner with him."

She said this softly as if testing the waters, looking for a response from Joy. Joy, however, was determined not to give her one. "I'll get these invitations in the mail this afternoon," she said, not being the least bit tactful about changing the subject.

Ever gracious, Catherine took the hint and followed Joy's lead. "Do you really think any of the writers will agree to attend our tea? It would mean so much to us, but it is rather late notice."

"We'll find out soon enough," Joy told her.

"I guess we will at that." Catherine hesitated in the doorway. "Why don't you stop at my apartment later," Ted's grandmother said unexpectedly. "We could have a cup of tea and a nice long chat."

"What about the other committee members?" Joy wasn't fooled. Catherine was hoping to detain her long enough so she'd be there when Ted arrived for their appointment.

"Ah, yes, the other committee members," Catherine hedged.

"Catherine," Joy said, shuffling through her emotions and planting both feet firmly on the floor. She needed to be grounded for this, because it was much too easy to let her romantic soul dominate what she knew was best.

"Yes, dear," the older woman said hopefully.

"I know what you're trying to do, and it won't work."

Catherine didn't make a pretense of pretending otherwise. Her cheeks flushed with bright color. "Forgive me, child, for being an interfering old woman. When I spoke with Ted earlier, he sounded utterly miserable. I was hoping . . ."

"I know exactly what you were hoping. Now listen, Catherine, I think you're one of the most delightful women I know, and your grandson isn't half bad."

"But," Catherine said, and her eyes twinkled as she said it. "There's always an exception amidst all that praise."

"But," Joy continued with a beleaguered sigh, "your matchmaking efforts won't work."

Catherine's small shoulders sagged a bit as she graciously accepted defeat. "Oh, dear, I'm just not very good at this sort of thing, am I? Can you forgive a meddling old woman?"

"Of course."

"It's just that it would do this old heart good if the two of you—" She stopped herself. "I'm doing it again, aren't I? When I promised myself I wouldn't." Apparently angry with herself, Catherine pressed her hands to her cheeks and shook her head sharply. "I'd best leave now before I say or do something else equally mindless."

Joy returned to the invitations. She wrote the address on one and paused when she noticed that Catherine continued to linger.

"Before I go," Catherine said quickly, as though it were important to get all the words out as fast as she could, "there's something I'd like to say. If I could handpick a wife for my grandson, I'd choose you."

Joy's heart gladdened with this compliment, but it didn't take away the ache of knowing it would never happen. "Thank you, Catherine." It was a sweet thing to say, and at the same time, although the older woman hadn't intended it to be that way, it was cruel.

Catherine left shortly afterward, and it seemed a sadness had settled over them both.

Joy had finished writing out the invitations and left her office when Lucille Thompson stopped her. Lucille had suffered a stroke a year earlier and had made incredible progress since. She managed with a walker these days, her steps slow and practiced.

"Joy," Lucille called, her eyes bright with the love of life. "Has the mail arrived?"

"I believe so." Generally it was delivered around noon and tucked into the individual mail slots shortly afterward.

"I'm waiting for a word from my daughter," Lucille said excitedly. "There's a possibility she might be able to join me for Christmas."

"That's wonderful, Lucille."

"I'm on my way up to my room now. Would you check my slot for me on the off chance Clarise has written? I'd so love it if we could be together."

"Of course." She watched as Lucille slowly made her way to the elevator. Although she'd almost completely recovered from the stroke, Lucille had worked diligently to learn to read and write all over again. The retired schoolteacher had looked tired just then.

Joy dropped off the envelopes and checked Lucille's mail slot. Sure enough, a fat letter was stuffed inside. Rather than sending someone else to Lucille's room with it, Joy decided to deliver it herself.

She waited for the elevator, which seemed to be getting slower all the time. Once she saw to Lucille's letter, Joy decided, she'd call it an afternoon. Not that there was any rush to hurry home.

The elevator arrived, and she stepped inside. The doors had started to close when out of the corner of her eye she saw someone rush across the foyer in an effort to catch it. She pushed the button to stop the elevator, and the doors yawned open reluctantly.

Ted Griffin stepped inside. He seemed even more surprised to see her than she did him.

"Hello, Joy," he said smoothly.

"Hello." Her voice was small and uneven. She focused her attention on the row of numbers above the door while her heart played a renegade game of hopscotch.

Casually, as if he'd planned their meeting, Ted punched the number to his grandmother's floor. The elevator started to move, but not fast enough to suit Joy. However, the speed of light wouldn't have suited her just then.

"It seems a bit odd that out of all the people living and working in this retirement center, I would walk into an elevator with you," he said as if there weren't the least bit of friction between them.

"Not really." Generally the fates were kinder than this, but she didn't say so.

"How have you been?"

Ted seemed determined to keep the conversation humming. "Fine," she said in the same cool tones.

"Yeah, me too."

A tense, thick silence filled the cubicle, until Joy found it nearly suffocating.

"This might not be the time or place," Ted said abruptly, and it sounded as though his patience were on a short fuse, "but I'd like to remind you that you owe me a date."

"That's not the way I remember it."

He took a moment to compose himself, she guessed, then started again on a different track. "I know you're upset because you saw me with Blythe."

"She has nothing to do with this," Joy insisted. She closed her eyes and snapped her mouth shut before she was drawn into an argument with him.

"Of course she does," Ted contested.

"Do you mind if we simply drop the subject?"

"I do mind. . . . I've missed you," he whispered, and his warm breath fanned her neck.

Shivers raced down Joy's arms, and she moved away from him. All at once the elevator came to a sudden, abrupt halt, jolting them both.

"What was that?" Joy asked. The lights dimmed and then faded completely, swallowing them in a dark void.

"Wonderful," he moaned. "Just wonderful."

"What?"

"It seems we just experienced a power outage," Ted explained, sounding as disgruntled as she felt.

"We might be stuck here for some time," he said next. "You might as well make yourself comfortable."

"I'm fine. Just kindly stay on your side of the elevator and I'll stay on mine."

He snickered softly, sounding amused. "Don't fret, you haven't got a thing to worry about."

Joe looked up from the television when Paul walked into the house. The visit with Madge Bartelli had left him mentally and physically exhausted. He probably wasn't good company now.

"Where have you been?" Joe asked, and reached for the remote control, silencing the television.

"Anyone looking for me?" Paul asked, setting the evening paper on the kitchen table. He rarely read more than the headlines these days. The news depressed him. Killings, hate, crime. It wore him down in ways it never had in years past.

"Mrs. Johnson called," Joe said. He stood and joined Paul in the kitchen.

Whatever Annie had fixed for dinner smelled delicious. Paul hoped his lack of an appetite wouldn't insult his future daughter-in-law. He couldn't visit the hospital and eat any time soon afterward. The institutional smells took away any desire for food. Leaving Madge and Bernard had left him emotionally bankrupt. He hadn't the energy to sit down and chat the way he would have any other night.

"Did she say what she wanted?"

"No, she was hoping I'd know where you'd gone."

Paul nodded.

"You know, Dad, it might not be a bad idea to inform Mrs. Johnson of your whereabouts."

"I suppose I should."

Annie stepped into the kitchen and smiled shyly in Paul's direction.

"Hello, Annie," he greeted her. He noted the way Joe's fiancée gravitated to his son's side as if she couldn't bear to be away from him for more than a few moments at a time.

"Hello."

"Dinner smells delicious," Paul said, "but unfortunately I've got someplace I need to be this evening, and—"

"You're leaving again?" Joe asked, sounding disappointed.

"I shouldn't be long."

"But you just got home."

"Yes, I know."

"But, Dad, I need to talk to you."

It was unusual for Joe to raise his voice. "All right, son." Paul pulled out a chair. "Let's both sit down and we'll talk."

Joe and Annie sat across the table from him. They joined their hands, and Paul noticed that his son's gaze couldn't seem to settle in any one place, as if the subject he wanted to discuss made him uncomfortable.

"Dad, Annie and I were thinking about heading to Oregon in the morning," Joe announced without preamble.

The news hit Paul like a rock square in the chest. Joe leaving, with Annie. So soon. It seemed he'd barely arrived. They'd barely had a chance to talk.

All the things he'd planned with his son had fallen by the way-side. The anticipation, the excitement and energy, had been for naught. Joe had his own life, and he didn't need his father messing it up.

"You don't mind, do you?" Annie asked in that velvety sweet voice of hers.

"Of course not. There's not that much to do around here, and I imagine you're anxious to see your family."

The young woman brightened immediately. "I swear my mother's been cooking all week. She can't wait for us to arrive so she can introduce Joe to all my relatives."

"But, Dad, we won't go if you'd rather we stayed here with you," Joe was quick to add. "Then . . ." He let the rest fade, apparently unsure what to say.

"Don't be silly," Paul said, making light of his disappointment. "There's nothing going on here." He imagined the two young people were bored.

Joe looked down at his hands as if he weren't sure he was doing the right thing. "The Christmas decorations are all up, and you'll be with Bethany and Eric, and—"

"It's fine, son, don't worry about me."

"Annie and I put a couple of presents to you under the tree," Joe said next.

Gifts. Sweet heaven, Paul hadn't purchased a thing for the two of them. Or anyone else, for that matter. He hadn't given a thought to buying Christmas gifts. Barbara had always seen to the task, and he'd been so plagued with his own troubles that it had slipped his mind. He felt like an utter fool.

"You didn't need to do that," he told his son and Annie. He really did wish that the two had saved their money. They needed it for college expenses, and if they were getting married the following summer, well, they should be saving what little funds they had for their wedding. But he said none of this.

The minute he could, Paul escaped the house and hurried over to the church office. He nearly stumbled over a chair on the way to his desk in his hurry to reach the phone.

Funny, he'd worked with Leta Johnson more years than he could remember, and he couldn't recall ever phoning her at home. Yet she was the first person he thought to contact.

She answered on the first ring. "Hello."

"Leta, it's Paul Morris. I'm sorry to call you unexpectedly like this, but I need a favor."

"Of course."

"Joe and Annie are leaving for Eugene in the morning. I seem to have put everything off until the last minute, and I don't have any gifts for them."

"What is it you want me to do?" Leta asked.

Paul swore the woman was dense. "I don't know about buying gifts, especially for a young woman. I'm asking that you go out and purchase whatever you think would be appropriate and wrap the presents for me."

His words were followed by a long silence.

"If you'd given me a bit more notice, I might have been able to help," Leta said without censure, "but I already have plans for this evening."

Paul sank onto the chair, thoroughly discouraged. He'd counted on Leta to come to his rescue the way she had a thousand times before. "Barbara was one who saw to gift buying," he murmured. "I wouldn't have a clue what to purchase for a young woman."

"I'm sure the sales clerks will be more than happy to help you."

Paul didn't share her confidence. "There isn't any way you could change your plans?" he asked hopefully.

If Barbara had been his right hand all those years, then Leta was of equal value when it came to church matters. In some ways she knew more about the inner workings of his church than he did himself. He had come to rely on her more and more of late, perhaps too much.

"I'm sorry, Paul," she said after a moment.

He heard the regret in her voice, and something else. Sadness? Paul couldn't be sure.

"I can't help you this time."

"I understand." He replaced the headpiece and leaned forward and propped his elbows against his desktop. Well, she'd certainly told him. He strongly suspected that he deserved it. Heaven help him, he'd do what he could to buy his children Christmas gifts. It would have been much easier if Leta had agreed to do it for him.

"Mercy, just exactly what are you doing?"

The prayer ambassador looked up from her perch on top of the elevator and examined the ends of her fingernails. "Doing?"

"Don't pretend you don't know what I'm talking about, either," Goodness cried.

"I'm not." Mercy checked the peephole. Joy and Ted still weren't talking to each other. The last ten minutes had been spent in complete silence.

"I need you to do something for me," Goodness said frantically. Mercy might have been swayed, but she knew her friend all too well, and dear, dear Goodness had a flair for drama. Her fellow prayer ambassador tended to exaggerate everything.

"What's happening now?"

"It's Pastor Morris. He went Christmas shopping, and it's turned into a disaster. I don't know what to do."

"What happened?" Goodness really did sound at her wit's end, but frankly Mercy had her hands full with the two stubborn humans she was dealing with at the moment. Stranding them together in the elevator had seemed like a stroke of genius earlier. Now she wasn't so certain.

Goodness wrung her hands. "Paul stopped off at a perfume counter in one of the big department stores," she began. "At first everything seemed to be going along just fine. The clerk was helping him make a selection, and he was sniffing a variety of scents. And then something went very wrong. The saleslady puffed a whiff of an old favorite into the air, and the pastor went stock-still. He left the store almost immediately without buying anything."

"But why?"

"That's what I don't understand," Goodness said with an air of defeat. "He sat in his car for the longest time and stared into space."

"Do you think it might have been the perfume his wife used?"

Goodness slumped into a sitting position beside Mercy. "Of course. Now why didn't I think of that? I happened to catch a look at the name, too. Heaven Scent."

"But it isn't heaven Pastor Morris is thinking about right now."

"No," Goodness agreed sadly. "Oh, Mercy, tell me what I can do to help him."

Unfortunately Mercy was having troubles of her own. "I don't know. I'm dealing with the two most obstinate humans I've yet to meet. They're perfect for each other, and neither one is willing to admit it."

"I'm afraid that we both need a few good miracles," Goodness said. "The problem is, I feel plumb dry."

Mercy looked down on Joy and Ted, sitting on the floor as far apart as they could get from each other, and shook her head. "I could do with a miracle or two myself," she mumbled.

"How long will you be gone this time?" Karen asked, dangling her legs over the edge of Maureen's mattress.

"Not long," she promised as she packed her suitcase.

"Do I have to go with Grandma when she drives you to the airport?"

A soft smile touched the edges of Maureen's mouth. "Not this time. Grandma isn't driving me."

"Then who is?"

"Thom."

Karen practically did a flip off the bed. "Really! Just the two of you together? Is it a date?"

"Karen, please, don't make more of this than what it is. Thom happened to have business in town this afternoon, and since he was headed in that direction himself, he offered to drop me off."

"Wow. Does Paula know about this?"

"I wouldn't know." She stopped and waved an empty hanger at her daughter. "I certainly hope you two haven't been talking to each other on the phone."

"Why not?"

The question was riddled with guilt. "Because, my darling daughter, it's long distance, and we can't afford for you to be chatting with Paula."

"Oh."

Maureen decided she'd prefer to know the worst now instead of being hit with the news when the phone bill arrived. "How many times have you called her?"

"Twice," came the squeaky reply, "maybe three times."

"Okay, just don't do it again."

"Maybe four times."

"Karen!"

"I won't do it again, I promise."

"Good." Maureen closed the lid of her suitcase and slipped it off the bed. The trip was only for overnight, and she really hated to go, especially this close to Christmas. "Speaking of bills, would you bring in the mail?"

"Sure." Karen took off like a rocket on the Fourth of July in her eagerness to comply with Maureen's request. Either this unaccustomed willingness had something to do with Christmas, or she was pleased as punch about Thom driving Maureen to the airport. Or maybe she was looking to intercept the phone bill.

Maureen liked Thom. All right, that was a mild understatement. He was gentle when she needed a man to be tender. He seemed to know what she needed without her having to say anything.

Breathless, Karen raced back into the house with a handful of mail. There were a couple of Christmas cards and the inevitable bill. The letter on printed stationery attracted her attention next.

Maureen read the letterhead, and her blood froze. The envelope listed the name of the law firm that had represented Brian in the divorce. When she hadn't heard from him following his phone call, she'd assumed he'd dropped the reason for his call. Apparently that wasn't the case.

"What's wrong, Mom?"

"Nothing, sweetheart."

"You don't look right all of a sudden, like you need to sit down or something."

Sitting down didn't seem to be such a bad idea. Maureen found a chair and slumped onto it. Her knees were shaking when she smiled over at Karen.

"Who's the letter from?" Karen asked next. "Dad?"

The kid was no dummy. "No, it seems to be from his attorney."

"You want me to open it for you?"

"No thanks," Maureen said. It took her a couple of moments to gather together the grit to tear open the envelope. She pulled out the folded sheet of paper and stopped when she found her daughter studying her intently.

"Don't look so worried," she said. "It's probably nothing."

"Probably," Karen agreed, but her gaze didn't waver from the letter.

Maureen read over the three brief paragraphs—twice, the second time slowly, absorbing each word carefully to be sure there was no misunderstanding.

"Well?" Karen prodded. "What's he want?"

"It says here that according to the terms of the divorce settlement, he has been assigned certain holidays for visitation."

"So? He's never wanted me for any of them before."

"I know, but apparently he's had a change of heart." Maureen didn't care to speculate what had brought all that about. "It says here that he's coming to pick you up on Christmas Eve and that he'll bring you back to the house early Christmas morning."

Karen's mouth formed into a small O. "Is that all?"

Maureen nodded. Her hand trembled as she folded the letter and returned it to the envelope.

"You don't care if I spend Christmas Eve with Dad, do you?"

"Of course I don't mind," Maureen said, lying through clenched teeth. Brian didn't deserve time with Karen. He'd contributed practically nothing to her upbringing, financially or emotionally. When it came to ranking him as a father, he didn't rate any higher than he had as a husband.

By the time Thom arrived Maureen felt as if she needed to talk to her attorney, Susan Gold, and find out what Karen's rights were in all this. She was on the phone on what seemed permanent hold when Karen let him into the house.

"I'll only be a minute," she said, cupping her hand over the mouthpiece.

Karen and Thom were talking, and her daughter was sending little glances her way as if she'd rather be listening to what Maureen was saying instead of entertaining Thom. Maureen tossed her a desperate plea for patience.

The receptionist came back on the line a minute later and informed Maureen that Susan was in court for the afternoon and would be tied up with this current case until after the holidays. She did promise to relay the message to Susan, however.

"Well, that's just Jim dandy," Maureen muttered, and replaced the telephone receiver. She placed her hands over her face and tried to calm her pounding heart. If there was any way she could get out of this trip, she'd do it. Karen's welfare was more important than anything, even her job.

"Maureen," Thom said gently, "you've had some distressing news?"

"Not really," she said, offering Karen a reassuring smile. She didn't want her daughter to overhear the conversation. "Could you get my suitcase for me, sweetheart?"

"It's too heavy for me, remember?" Karen looked guilelessly from Thom to her and back again.

"Not this time. It's only an overnight case."

"Oh." Karen sounded terribly disappointed.

"I got a letter from my husband's attorney," Maureen whispered as soon as Karen was out of earshot. "He wants Karen to spend Christmas Eve with him."

"And you object to that?"

"No . . . yes," she revised heatedly. "You'd have to know Brian to understand why this distresses me so much. He's going to hurt Karen the same way he hurt me. He'll build up her hopes, ply her with promises he has no intention of keeping. I can see it all happening, and I refuse to sit by and do nothing."

"Do you have any legal grounds on which to refuse him?"

Maureen shook her head. "But the moral grounds should be enough." She felt vehement about that.

"How does Karen feel about seeing her father?"

As if by magic, Karen appeared carrying Maureen's suitcase. "Here you go, Mom," she said brightly. She plopped down on the sofa and folded her arms over her chest. "I was just thinking, Mom, about going to Dad's for Christmas Eve."

"Yes, sweetheart?"

"Should I take his new wife and baby a Christmas gift?"

Chapter

★ ☆ ★

13

"*Sit down and* we'll have a cup of coffee before your flight boards," Thom suggested. He scooted into the booth across from her. "You're as wound up as a tight spring."

"I can't help it." Maureen had been in turmoil from the moment the letter arrived from Brian's attorney.

"It seems to me Karen isn't nearly as upset as you are."

"Of course she isn't," Maureen said, irritated that he didn't appreciate her circumstances. He couldn't. His marriage had been a loving, healthy relationship. He couldn't possibly understand what she and Karen had endured because of Brian.

"Then it seems to me you should let Karen go and enjoy herself."

"You don't understand," she said, shaking her head.

A waitress arrived with plastic menus tucked under her arm. She carried the coffeepot with her.

"Just coffee," Thom told her.

"Brian will only hurt Karen," she insisted under her breath once the waitress had filled the mugs and left. "Never having gone through a divorce, you can't appreciate what all this means. Brian left us. He turned his back and walked away." What she didn't say was that he'd emptied their bank account on his way out the door.

"Tell me about Brian," Thom suggested. "Then maybe I will understand."

"I don't want to talk about him. Every time I do my blood pressure soars and I overdose on antacid tablets."

Thom grinned. "It seems to me you're all riled up as it is."

That was true enough. "All right," she said. She owed him that much for the way he'd helped Karen. For the way he'd helped her.

Maureen drew in a deep breath as she sorted through the memories.

Many of them had been tainted by her bitterness over the years, and she wanted to be as fair as possible. Although heaven knew Brian didn't deserve that.

"We met in college. I was shy and didn't have a lot of friends. Brian and I were in a math class together. I've always been good with numbers, and Brian was in way over his head and failing badly. He went to the teacher for help, and she suggested he talk to me."

"You tutored him."

"Yes."

"Did he pass the class?"

Maureen nodded. "Yes, but just barely. He was so pleased, he asked me out to dinner. I hadn't dated very much in high school, and Brian was outgoing and popular. I felt like the luckiest girl in the world to have him pay attention to me."

"How long did you date before you were married?"

"Three years. What upsets me now, as I look back, is that I knew the kind of person Brian was from the beginning. He changed his major five times. Even then he fluttered from one interest to another. He couldn't seem to hold a job more than a couple of months.

"There was always a good reason he had to quit, you understand. No matter where he worked, there was someone who had it in for him. Another favorite excuse was an incompetent co-worker he couldn't bear to be around.

"Once, I was away for a week. . . . I don't remember what, a family obligation, I think." She paused and cupped her hand around the mug. It hurt even now to confess this. "When I came back a friend told me she'd seen Brian with some other girl. I didn't believe her. I thought she was jealous and trying to break us up so she could have Brian for herself."

"He had affairs?" The question was asked in the gentlest of voices as if carefully peeling back the bandage from a half-healed wound.

"Affairs?" Maureen laughed. "Where do you want me to start?" She didn't give him a chance to answer. "Six months after we were married a burly truck driver stopped me in the parking lot outside our apartment building. He asked me to give a message to my husband. I was to tell Brian to stay away from his wife, and if he didn't, the trucker claimed he'd kill Brian."

"You told Brian?"

"Of course. I was scared out of my wits. This guy was serious. Brian convinced me he had the wrong guy, and like a gullible fool"— she paused and raised her eyes to the ceiling—"I believed him." It astonished her how dense she'd been, how long it had taken her to wake up and accept reality. Denial was sometimes underrated as far as she was concerned.

"When did you realize the truth?" This too came in the same gentle, caring voice, almost as if Thom were afraid of hurting her by asking.

"It took far longer than it should have. I saw him with another woman. I don't think I would have believed it otherwise. Later, after I'd dried my eyes and composed myself, I confronted him." She stopped, remembering that scene and how naive she'd been.

"He admitted he was involved with the other woman, but claimed she was older and had set out to seduce him. He cried and told me how sorry he was, and then he begged me not to divorce him."

"Were you planning to leave him?" he asked.

"I don't know what I would have done. It was shortly afterward that we decided to have Karen. He was attentive and loving for a while, but that soon changed. This time I was a little smarter, a little wiser."

"The affairs continued?"

Maureen nodded. "After a while I began to pick up cues when he was going into another relationship. All at once his appearance would be important, and he'd spend more time in front of a mirror."

"Did you confront him?"

"Naturally. He denied everything. He claimed I was imagining things, that I'd become obsessively jealous. We had some real humdinger fights. Dear God, I can't believe I stayed in that sick marriage as long as I did. The love was gone long before the marriage ended."

"How was he with Karen?"

Maureen stiffened. "The same way he is with every other woman in his life. He used her. He'd build up her hopes with promises he had no intention of keeping."

"He left you."

"Yes." It was the one thing that plagued Maureen the most about her divorce. Brian had walked out on her. After years of infidelity, years of mental abuse, he'd had the unmitigated gall to empty the savings account she'd struggled so hard to build and leave her. It rankled still.

Thom didn't say anything for a brief moment, then asked, "The divorce was messy?"

"As messy as I could make it." Maureen had turned the other cheek with Brian far too often. In the beginning, revenge was what gave her the incentive to get out bed each morning. It motivated her now.

By the time the divorce was final, Maureen was relatively confident it would take Brian and his live-in lover the better part of the next ten years to pay off the attorney's fees. She wanted him to be miserable, as miserable as he'd made her.

Thom frowned. "How did Karen stand up through all of this?"

"As well as could be expected." Maureen had done her best to shield her daughter from the worst of the divorce. If she had any regrets, it was that Karen had been hurt in all this. She soothed her conscience by blaming Brian.

However, as Maureen looked back over her life since the divorce, she was forced to admit how much better off she and Karen were without her ex-husband.

"And since the divorce?"

Karen's nightmares had been much better since she'd started the horseback riding. But Maureen was well aware that a few lessons weren't the cure-all to Karen's troubles. It was just that she couldn't afford counseling on top of everything else.

"And since," Maureen repeated, "she's doing all right."

"All right?"

"She needs counseling. For that matter, so do I."

"It helped me tremendously after Pam died."

"You had counseling?"

Thom's hands gripped the mug. "I'm not ashamed to admit I needed it."

Maureen knew from previous conversations that Thom had been deeply in love with his wife. From what he'd told her about his marriage, it had sounded ideal, almost too good to be true.

"The counseling helped."

"I'm sure it did." She stared into the murky depths of her own coffee.

"As strange as it may seem, I had to work hard at forgiving Pam for dying."

"Forgiving her?"

"I know that must sound unreasonable. At the time I couldn't justify my feelings. One night shortly after the funeral, I was cooking dinner and the potatoes boiled onto the stove. It was a little thing, but I was so angry I damn near put my fist through the wall."

"Angry? But why?"

"If Pam had been there, it never would have happened. I wouldn't be coming in from the barn and left to deal with dinner for Paula and me. It'd be on the table." His smile was filled with a wry sadness. "In my heart I know Pam didn't want to die any more than we wanted her to, but I still had to learn to forgive her." Thom raised the coffee mug to his lips and hesitated. "It might help you."

"What might?"

"Forgiving Brian."

Maureen stared at him, hardly able to believe what he'd said. "Forgive Brian? You've got to be kidding."

It might have been Joy's imagination, but even the air seemed to chill between her and Ted, trapped as they were in the elevator.

He hadn't spoken in ten minutes or longer. Those minutes were probably the most intense of Joy's life. Her legs were growing tired, and she wondered just how much longer it would take for the electricity to return so she could escape these uncomfortable circumstances. She wondered what had happened to cause the outage; her fears mounted.

"You can sit on my jacket if you like," Ted suggested, breaking the quiet.

"I'm fine," she returned, and then, because it had been a generous thing to do, she added, "Thanks for the offer, though."

A silence, then, "You're welcome."

Joy smiled into the darkness, and she had the distinct impression that Ted was grinning, too, although she had no way of knowing if that were so.

The elevator car remained pitch-black. It amazed her how much she could feel in the dark. How alive her senses were, sharing this compact space with him. Ted was as far removed from her as was humanly possible. She could feel his breath on the back of her neck, feel the heavy thud of his heartbeat.

"I wish I had a match," she said, thinking out loud. The lack of light was dangerous to her emotional well-being. Already she was moving closer to him, mentally, if not physically. After fifteen minutes alone with him, she was thinking that her steadfast rule about dating a man involved with someone else should be more of a guideline.

"Matches," Ted repeated. "Don't tell me you're afraid of the bogeyman?"

"No. Well, maybe a little," she conceded.

It grew tiresome to stand after a while, and her feet were beginning to hurt. "If you don't mind, I'll take you up on that offer," she said.

"The coat or the date?"

"The coat."

"Damn," he muttered.

Joy could hear the laughter in his voice. She wished she didn't find it so easy to smile when she was with him. A rustling sound followed as he removed his suit coat and spread it on the floor.

"It seems a shame to dirty your jacket."

"There's nothing here the dry cleaners can't remove."

Fumbling with her hands to find her way, Joy lowered herself onto his suit jacket. She sat with her legs scooted to one side and her weight leveled onto one arm.

Sitting, she soon discovered, meant being close was unavoidable. She didn't need their shoulders to touch to feel his presence. He was there, bigger than life.

"I apologize for snapping at you," she said, regretting her earlier behavior. It wasn't his fault the electricity had gone out, although she would have been happy to blame him.

"My temperament wasn't any better," he admitted, and then with regret added, "What's happened to us, Joy? We used to be friends, remember? Good friends. I've never enjoyed an evening more than the one I spent at the Lakers game with you."

"Yes, well—"

"When I'm with you," he said, cutting her off, "I feel everything more intensely. Hell, I don't even know what I did that was so terrible. Okay, okay, I know it has to do with Blythe—"

"I don't think it's a good idea for us to talk."

"Not talk?" He sounded incredulous.

"About us," she clarified. "I can't see beating the subject into the ground, can you?" Any further discussion would lead to more hurt, and she'd been miserable enough the last few days. In her heart of hearts she'd accepted that he was going to marry Blythe Holmes.

"I see." His words were pensive. "If you'd give me an opportunity, I'd like to tell you about Blythe and me."

"Please, no," she said quickly before he had a chance to drag the other woman between them. Not that Blythe wasn't already there, as bold as could be. She had been since the beginning: suave, sophisticated, reminding Joy of everything she would never be.

Other than being strikingly beautiful, Blythe Holmes was sober faced and serious minded. One couldn't look at the woman and not speculate at her importance. She was the perfect wife and professional for an up-and-coming engineer. Ted's future was bright. Catherine had bragged about her grandson's achievements often enough for Joy to know he was considered brilliant.

"All right, we won't talk about us," Ted agreed reluctantly.

Joy wasn't sure if it was by accident or design, but they seemed to be moving closer to each other. Sitting side by side as they were, their shoulders touched. Then, without her being sure how he managed it, Ted positioned himself behind her.

It was difficult to keep her back straight, and then gradually, almost without conscious effort, she found herself using his broad chest for support.

His hands cupped her shoulders and eased her back even more. Joy closed her eyes and against her better judgment allowed herself to be drawn into the warm, welcome circle of his arms. His nose nuzzled the side of her neck, and his hot breath fanned her cool skin.

Unable to raise so much as a token resistance, Joy decided she was weak, much weaker than she ever realized. For the first time in days she felt warm and content. It was cold outside Ted's arms, cold and lonely. She knew his attention was temporary, fleeting at best, but she needed his touch and his tenderness.

Joy, a willing participant, maneuvered their positions so they faced each other. His hands framed her face, and his thumb skidded across her lips. She knew he intended to kiss her long before he brought his mouth to hers. Knew it and welcomed it.

His mouth was warm and moist when it settled over hers. Joy sighed at the simple pleasure his touch produced. They'd kissed before. This keen sense of satisfaction shouldn't have come as a surprise, yet it did.

He wove his fingers into her hair, bunching it up in his hands as his mouth glided over hers. He molded the shape of her lips with his, with a heat and a need that seared her senses.

A frightening kind of excitement took hold of Joy, and she opened her mouth to him. Ted's tongue went in search of hers, and she moaned aloud at this new level of intimacy.

Joy wasn't sure where they would have progressed from there if the lights hadn't suddenly gone back on and the elevator hadn't abruptly jolted them back into the real world.

Ted muttered something under his breath that she couldn't fully decipher. What she did manage to hear, she agreed with entirely.

"I have a dinner engagement with my grandmother," he told her. He continued to hold her, although the elevator had started to move. "Can I come see you afterward?"

"Ah." It shouldn't be this difficult to decide.

He kissed her again with a hunger that sent her world spinning off its orbit. "Okay," she agreed, sounding weak and unsure. At the moment she was both.

"Joy," he said, helping her to her feet, "you've got to trust me. I'm not going to hurt you, I promise. Trust me, all right? That's all I ask."

The elevator arrived, and Ted stepped off reluctantly. He backed out of the elevator and raised his fingers to his lips in a gesture of farewell.

"Said the spider to the fly," Joy murmured.

Trust him. That was all he'd asked. Her heart told her she should, and her head, her know-it-all head, insisted otherwise. Joy grinned and decided to believe her heart.

"What happened?" she asked the first person she saw when she stepped off the elevator.

"Happened?" questioned Justine, a library committee member.

"With the electricity."

Justine stared at her blankly. "I don't know."

"We didn't lose power?"

"No," Justine said. "What makes you ask?"

Joy barely had time to get home, shower, and change her clothes before Ted showed up outside her door.

"That was fast," she said, but in truth she was pleased. The timer on the oven dinged and she padded barefoot back into her kitchen.

Ted caught her by the hand and brought her into his embrace. She wasn't given the opportunity to protest, although she wasn't certain she would have, before he kissed her.

She was breathless and witless by the time he finished.

"That was about the fastest dinner on record," he told her. "As soon as Grandma learned I was meeting you, she insisted she wasn't hungry."

"You didn't believe her, did you?"

"Not on your life."

"Good."

"But that doesn't mean I didn't take her to her favorite fast-food place, order her the works, and drive her back to the Wilshire Grove in record time."

"Ted, you didn't!"

"Yes, I did. I'm not wasting a minute more without you. I'm crazy about you, Joy."

She shut her eyes and turned her head away from him. "Don't say that, please. It's difficult enough."

He gripped her by the shoulders and turned her so that it was impossible to hide from him. "You don't want to hear how I feel about you?"

"No." He was sincere now, but all that would change. Soon he'd have a change of heart. Soon he'd discover the same way Billy had what was most attractive about her: simply that she didn't represent any threat to his freedom.

The sermon was one Paul had given before, and he sincerely hoped no one remembered it. He stood at the pulpit and looked out over the congregation of believers he'd been a shepherd to for almost twenty years. His gaze drifted from one face to another, and he experienced an achy kind of sadness.

"Let us pray," he said after a moment, and bowed his head. He said the words by rote, but they had lost their meaning for him. At one time they'd come from his heart, but no more. He didn't feel as if he had one any longer—at least none to speak of.

When he'd finished praying, he closed the Bible, turned, and sat down. The choir in their shiny blue robes stood, and organ music crescendoed through the building. Soon the melody of male and female voices blended in song. It was a favorite Christmas carol from his childhood.

Paul didn't sing. He didn't think it was possible to do so with a heavy heart.

Joe and Annie were gone. Joe had phoned to say they'd arrived at Annie's family home safely. He joked with his dad that meeting her parents was like falling into a jar of honey. Annie must have been listening because Joe claimed her family was so pleased he'd agreed to marry her, they were throwing a party in his honor.

Paul had laughed. The happiness in his son's voice lifted his spirits. He didn't blame Joe for wanting to head out early. There wasn't anything in Los Angeles to hold him down.

When the singing was over, Paul stood and offered the benediction. The congregation filed out of the wide double doors at the back of the church. As was his habit, Paul stood in the doorway and shook hands.

"Merry Christmas, Pastor," said Steve Tenny's wife, gripping his hand in both of hers. "We're looking forward to having you spend Christmas with us."

"I don't believe I've gotten back to Steve about that. I will soon," Paul promised. He'd always liked Myrna. Barbara had enjoyed her friendship for a good many years.

Bernard Bartelli stood back, waiting for the bulk of the crowd to file past. His shoulders were hunched and his eyes weary with fatigue that reached far deeper than the physical.

Paul clasped the older man's hand firmly in his own. They didn't speak, didn't exchange pleasantries. Bernard kept his gaze lowered and shuffled past with his head low; if he'd wanted to say anything, he had changed his mind.

Paul watched as the old man ambled toward the parking lot. It was in his mind to follow after him and ask about Madge's condition. But he already knew the answer. She was failing more each hour.

It wouldn't be long now, and then Bernard would be as alone as Paul was. It wouldn't be long, and Bernard would sit in this same church and feel God had not only turned his back on him, but shoved the door closed in his face.

The white-hot anger that seared through his blood surprised Paul. He'd never been an angry man. Rarely had he clenched his fist or raised his voice. Rarely had he voiced his discontent. And never to God.

He could feel the heat work its way through him, yet it seemed not like the poison he dreaded, but like an energy that invigorated him.

He waited until the church was empty, then marched up the center aisle and stood in the middle of the church. His chest swelled as his lungs filled with oxygen. He held his breath until he chest ached, then slowly, purposely, expelled it little by little.

"You promised healing," Paul said out loud. The sound of his voice echoed eerily in the vacant room. His eyes rested on the closed Bible propped up in the middle of the altar.

He was a crazy man, standing in church and talking out loud to a God who refused to listen.

"You promised!" he shouted at the top of his voice. His mind rattled off all the Bible verses he'd claimed in Barbara's behalf. One by one they marched through his mind like soldiers, shoulders squared at attention. But these promises Paul had put such faith in were like miniature toy soldiers, ineffective and worthless. All his prayers, all his pleadings, had been returned to him empty.

Now the pain, the heartache, was repeating itself with Madge. Once more Paul had to sit by and watch someone he cared for suffer. He discovered, with heartfelt regret, that it wasn't any easier the second go-around.

He looked at Bernard and saw a reflection of himself, broken, beaten, battered. Hanging on by a thread, and that thread was tattered.

After a while, Paul felt foolish standing alone in the middle of the church. Alone he knew well. The church part was what made him so uncomfortable. Funny, he'd spent the better part of his life in church; now he felt as out of place as a Sunday morning golfer.

He turned around and was about to leave when he saw Leta Johnson waiting for him at the back of the church. He certainly hoped she hadn't been standing there long.

"Did you forget something?" he asked defensively, embarrassed that she'd found him this way. He reached into a pew and placed a hymn book into the proper slot.

"No. I just wanted to see if Joe and Annie made it to Eugene all right."

"He phoned last night. They're fine."

"I'm glad to hear it."

Leta wasn't one to make small talk. Generally she got right to the crux of the matter, but she seemed to be hedging now. It wasn't the first time, and he wondered what was troubling her. He stopped and waited, giving her ample time to say what she wanted.

"It's about Madge Bartelli."

"I saw Bernard," Paul told her.

"Two of her children have arrived, and a couple of the women from the church are delivering meals."

"That's a good idea." One he should have thought of himself. This was exactly the type of thing Barbara had been so good at organizing.

"I hope you don't mind."

For reasons beyond Paul's meager comprehension, Leta seemed nervous about having done this. She'd seen a need and filled it. He was grateful.

He might have thought of it himself, if he hadn't been in the middle of a mental breakdown. Imagine standing alone in church and shouting at God! Anyone, even Leta, might suggest he visit a mental health clinic. Not a bad idea in light of his actions.

"Paul." Leta's voice drifted through the fog of his murky thoughts. "Are you feeling all right?"

"I'm great," he said enthusiastically. "Really."

She looked as if she doubted him, as well she should. "I'll see you Monday morning," she said, and walked a couple of steps in reverse.

"Monday," he repeated.

Paul waited until she'd turned and left the building before he strolled out of the sanctuary and into his office. He sat on his chair and stared at the row upon row of hardback books that lined his office wall. Theology, commentaries, concordances, all able and ready to help him understand God.

It came to him, sadly, that he had no interest in divine matters. No interest in anything related to a god who allowed good women to suffer. A god who allowed husbands to stand by and watch them die, helpless to do anything but pray. Paul knew exactly where prayer had gotten him. It had carried him all the way to the cemetery.

Someone once told him that he had a choice when he buried his wife. He could either accept her death and grow and mature in his faith or turn bitter and angry toward God.

Better or bitter.

He'd tried to be better. Tried to find the good in every situation. Unfortunately he wasn't as spiritually strong as he'd assumed.

Paul rolled a clean sheet of stationery into the typewriter on his desk. The younger generation were more comfortable with computers, but he preferred an old-fashioned typewriter.

He stared at the blank page, then drew in a deep breath and wrote out his letter of resignation.

"No," Goodness cried, hovering over the bookcases above Paul Morris's head. "You can't quit. Not now."

Angels rarely wept, but Goodness had the overwhelming urge to break into heart-wrenching sobs. She'd failed him. She should never have accepted this assignment, never have agreed to help. Everything she'd done thus far had been ineffectual.

"Goodness."

The celestial call came directly from Gabriel. She was being called back. Goodness didn't blame him; she'd blown this assignment. From the moment she'd pleaded with Gabriel to let her help Paul Morris, she'd been sucked deeper into the quicksand of his problems.

Immediately following his summons, Goodness was ushered into the prayer room in the glory of heaven. She kept her head lowered, her chin tucked in. Her wings drooped so far down, the tips scraped the surface of the floor.

"I understand matters aren't going very well with Paul Morris," Gabriel said.

It seemed to Goodness that his voice boomed louder than thunder. "He wrote out his letter of resignation," she told him in a small voice. "He's leaving the church, walking away from all those people who care about him. He assumes he hasn't got anything to say that will help, but he's wrong."

"I see." Gabriel clasped his hands behind his back and walked around Goodness. "What efforts have you made to help him?"

"Ah . . ."

"I already know that you put the binder filled with his study notes back on the bookshelf. It's something I would generally frown upon, but in this case, I believe it was the best thing to do."

"You do?" Encouraged, Goodness raised her head an inch.

"I also know about your so-called miracle."

Her head went back down.

"It didn't work, did it?"

"No," she admitted miserably. "I shone with the love of God so brightly, anyone else would have been blinded. Reverend Morris didn't notice."

"What have you done since?"

Goodness bit into her lower lip, afraid she'd disappointed Gabriel, destroyed his faith in her. "Nothing."

"Nothing?"

"I've walked with him," she explained, thinking how weak and useless that sounded. She waited for a chastisement, but when none came, she elaborated. "When he sat in the car alone and miserable, I sat with him. When he stood outside and waved good-bye to Joe and Annie, I waved with him."

"And just now?"

"Just now," she whispered, "I stood beside him in the middle of the church and held him upright." Naturally Paul didn't know that. If he wasn't aware of her presence when she was full of the glory of the Lord, then he wouldn't sense it when she stood silently at his side.

"You held him upright?"

"Yes." Goodness was afraid she'd broken some rule she knew nothing about.

"That's all he needs, Goodness. No tricks. No miracles. No shenanigans. You're doing everything exactly right."

"But he's resigning from the church."

Gabriel cocked one thick eyebrow. "Is he? Why don't you go back and find that out for yourself?"

Chapter

★ ✯ ★

14

"*Here, what do* you think?" Joy asked, holding up a frilly pink dress that didn't look big enough to fit a doll, let alone a child. The skirt had a white apron trimmed with a lacy ruffle. Just the sort of thing women, no matter what age, enjoyed dressing in.

"It's pretty, but it's not my color," Ted teased.

"It's not for you! The dress is perfect for my niece, Ellen Joy." She added it to the stack of items in Ted's arms.

They were Christmas shopping, and like every other man Ted knew, he wasn't keen on crowds and malls. But he discovered that anything, even plowing his way through cranky last-minute shoppers, was fun with Joy.

"You're not buying anything?" she commented.

"How can I, when you're buying out the store?"

"Oh, dear, you're right. I've been thoughtless, haven't I? I dragged you into the children's section and didn't give you a chance to look for anything you wanted. I've been completely selfish."

He stopped her by pressing a hand to her forearm. "I finished my shopping weeks ago."

She looked at him and blinked as if she weren't sure she'd heard him correctly. "You did?"

"You seem to forget I'm an engineer. I like my life neat and orderly . . . most of the time," he amended. What he didn't tell her was that a few years back he'd left everything until Christmas Eve. The only store open had been a corner grocery. No one could say his gifts hadn't been creative. His boss had enjoyed the standing rib roast, and his grandmother had gotten a real kick out of the twelve pairs of multicolored panty hose. This year he'd ordered almost everything through a fancy mail-order catalog Blythe had recommended. It had been expensive, but hassle free.

"I love Christmas," Joy said, and her eyes brightened.

Ted discovered he couldn't be with Joy for any length of time and not want to kiss her. He couldn't look at her and not be affected. He'd never felt this way about a woman, never been this keen for one's company. It was as if he were incomplete when they were apart.

For the last few months he'd assumed he was in love with Blythe. She was smart and energetic. He'd realized one day that thirty was fast approaching and had decided it was time he started thinking about settling down. He'd admired Blythe for her beauty and her brains. Not a bad start. It wasn't until he'd spent time with Joy that he'd realized what the other woman was missing.

Heart.

Joy possessed a generosity of spirit that drew others to her the way a child is attracted to something bright and fun. Ted discovered that, like everyone else, he was no exception.

Every time he was with Joy, he came away feeling better about himself in some small way. This was her gift, her God-given talent: to draw out the best in others.

It didn't surprise him that the residents at Wilshire Grove talked about her as if she were the greatest thing since the invention of the juicer.

"Uncle," he muttered, shifting the load of goodies in his arms.

"You want to buy something for your uncle?" Joy asked.

"No, 'uncle' as in I need a break," Ted said as if he'd already endured more than should be asked of any one male. "A man can only take so much of this shopping business."

Ted didn't know who it was who'd claimed women were the weaker sex, but apparently they'd never ventured into a shopping mall with one.

Joy laughed, and Ted realized this was something else he loved about her. The sound of her laughter had an almost musical chime to it, as if it were magical.

"We can leave any time," she assured him. "You've been a good sport. I'll pay for these things, and we can find some place to sit down. I'd hate to have you poop out on me so early."

"This is early?" Ted asked, feigning astonishment. "We've been here for hours."

"One hour," she corrected.

"You're joking."

"It was only an hour," she told him. "Maybe a cup of coffee will revive you."

Actually Ted wasn't half as bushed as he was letting on.

They left the mall and found a quaint Italian restaurant on a side street. The hostess seated them at a table with a red-checkered table-cloth by a corner. Since it was nearly noon, they decided to order lunch.

"Everything looks wonderful," Joy said, scanning the menu.

Ted offered a couple of suggestions.

"I'll try the veal scallopini," she said, and sighed as if the decision had been an exhausting one. She closed her eyes momentarily. "I can't believe this is happening."

"What?" he teased. "That you're eating Italian?"

"No, that I'm with you!"

"I know I'm quite the catch, but—"

"You know what I mean. It's like this is all unreal. I feel like I'm going to wake up and discover this is a dream. You're still planning to come tomorrow night, aren't you?" she asked, changing the subject. "And please, oh, please, promise me you won't believe a single word my brothers tell you about me."

"How could I doubt your very own brothers?" Ted asked innocently.

"Ted!"

He laughed, enjoying her discomfort. He loved the way . . . he realized a good portion of the morning he'd been telling himself all the things he loved about Joy. Her enthusiasm and optimism for life, her laughter and appreciation of the little things. It hadn't occurred to him that he might be in love with her.

Ted wasn't a man who gave his heart easily. But from the moment Edith had crankily decided to ease out of her parking space and smash into Blythe's car, he felt as if he'd been smacked over the head by fate.

"My brothers take delight in embarrassing me," she told him, waving a bread stick at him, "especially Billy. They're both married now, and they seem to think I should be, too, so be prepared for that."

"They're going to marry us? Tomorrow evening?"

"No." She giggled. "But they're going to make hints along those lines. Usually I say something silly, but the last time I upset my mother, and then—"

Curiosity got the better of him. "You upset your mother? What did you say?"

"I was joking. I said something about not being able to marry Jack until he got approval from the parole board."

Ted did a poor job of smothering a laugh. "And just who's this Jack?"

"A friend . . . former friend," she amended.

"How good a friend?"

Joy wove the bread stick between her fingers with amazing dexterity. "You sound jealous."

"I am. Now tell me about Jack."

"We dated a couple of times, is all. He'd been married before, and, well, I didn't like the kind of father he was. I figured if he ignored his children, then he wouldn't treat a woman any differently, so I broke it off before it ever got started."

"Smart woman."

"You're only saying that because you'd rather I wasn't dating Jack," she said, cocking her head to one side.

"True." He wasn't going to lie about it. He'd be damn uncomfortable if she were involved in a relationship now. Of all her concerns, it was the one about Blythe he understood best. Ironically, she refused to discuss the other woman, although he'd broached the subject a number of times. Joy wouldn't let him explain what was going on between him and his fellow engineer.

Two hours later, after leaving Joy, he discovered he was still smiling. After their busy morning, he decided to spend a lazy afternoon in front of the television. He kicked off his shoes and flopped down on the sofa, contemplating a nap. Although the college football game was supposed to be between the top-rated national teams, he found his attention wandering.

Was he in love with Joy? Hell if he knew. But he felt like standing up on the coffee table and pounding his chest and letting loose with a yell that would rival Tarzan's.

When the doorbell chimed, he leaped up, hoping it might be Joy. It was impossible, but damn it all, he wanted it to be Joy. It didn't seem right that the two of them were apart.

When he opened his door, the last person he expected to see was Blythe. Well, all the better. It was time they sat down and talked. Not that he hadn't tried. One would think it would be a simple matter to clear the air, but she'd put him off a number of times.

"Hello, Blythe."

"Ted." Her hands were buried in the pockets of her jacket. "I'm sorry to drop in unannounced this way. Do you have a few moments?"

"Of course." He stepped aside to let her into the apartment. Something was wrong. She was pale and quiet, and her eyes were red and blotchy as if she'd been crying.

"Thanks," she said. She sat on the edge of the sofa, and Ted sat next to her. He reached for his remote control and turned off the television.

"Is something wrong?" he asked. He'd never seen Blythe like this.

"I haven't seen much of you lately, so I'm not sure how you're going to feel about this."

"It's true we need to talk," he said, not yet registering the second part of her statement. Then it hit him. "How I'm going to feel about what?" he asked.

She pulled a ragged tissue from inside her pocket and blew her nose. "I went to the doctor recently. As you know, I haven't been feeling well."

"What's wrong?" Ted asked, growing concerned.

She covered her face with both hands. "I can't believe I was so stupid." Slowly she lowered her hands and with effort composed herself. She started to speak once and then stopped, briefly closed her eyes, and began again.

"Blythe?"

"I'm pregnant, Ted, and you're the baby's father."

"Do you want me to leave the night-light on for you?" Karen's grandmother asked.

Karen hesitated. "No, that's for little kids. I don't need a night-light."

"How about the nightmares?" Beverly Shields sat on the edge of the mattress and carefully tucked the blankets around Karen's shoulders.

"I haven't had one in a while," Karen told her. She didn't mention the one the evening her dad had phoned. It was the first time Paula had spent the night. She'd awakened everyone with her crying and felt terrible afterward, wondering what Paula would think of her. But Paula had told her about the nightmares she'd had after her mother had died. That made Karen feel better. She'd liked Paula even better afterward. There wasn't anything she couldn't tell her new friend, she decided. Paula understood.

"Your mother will be back before you know it."

Karen nodded. "Dad wants me to spend Christmas Eve with him," she said in an effort to detain her grandma. She really did want the night-light on and regretted flippantly saying she should turn it off.

"Your dad called?"

"No, his attorney wrote Mom a letter."

Her grandmother's shoulders made a funny little up-and-down movement. "I imagine your mother's upset about that."

"Big time," Karen assured her. "Luckily Thom was there. He's a calming influence."

Beverly's pencil-thin eyebrows arched expressively. "A calming influence?"

"Yes. He drove her to the airport. You know what, Grandma? I hope Thom Nichols sweeps my mom right off her feet. That's what she really needs, a man who loves her. Not someone like my dad, who only knows how to love for a little while. Thom's the kind of man who loves for a long time."

"How wise you sound, child," her grandmother said softly.

Karen sat up in bed and arranged the covers around her hips. "Paula and I've got it all figured out," she said, speaking fast because she was excited and happy. "Paula's mom died and my dad left us, and she likes my mom and I think her dad's really cool. So we decided the four of us would make a really, really great family."

"You think that, do you?"

"Yup. Now all we need to do is convince everyone else involved. Did Mom tell you about the romantic dinner Paula and I cooked for her and Thom?" Karen was proud of that.

"I can't say that she did."

"She didn't tell you?" Karen was appalled, and after all the work she'd gone to, too. "The spaghetti sauce was a little too thick, and the noodles overcooked, but only a little. Mom and Thom did a good job of making it sound like everything was perfect, though. They were great about it."

"So how'd everything go?"

Karen covered her mouth and giggled. "They kissed, and they weren't even standing under the mistletoe." She lowered her voice so her grandpa wouldn't overhear her. "It wasn't the first time I saw them kissing, either."

Karen noticed how her grandmother's interest piqued when she started talking about the two of them kissing.

"I see," Beverly Shields said. "Well, that does sound promising."

"We think so."

"We?" Beverly questioned.

"Paula and me. You know, Grandma, when we first moved to this neighborhood I didn't think I'd ever make friends again. Then I met Paula, and it was like God wanted the two of us to be together. Already we've decided to be friends for life."

"That's wonderful, sweetheart."

"I just wish . . ." She lowered her lashes, because it did hurt to think about her mom and her dad and the way they continued to hate each other.

"What do you wish?"

"Nothing." She didn't want to talk about it, not even with family.

Beverly stood. "You'll call me if you need anything."

"I'm not a kid anymore."

"Sometimes I forget that, Karen," Beverly said softly. "You'll need to forgive me."

"That's okay." She rolled onto one side and pulled the covers over her shoulder.

"Sleep well."

Her grandmother stood in the doorway, her hand on the door-knob. She hesitated, and Karen liked to think that maybe her grandma was saying a prayer over her the way she had that one night. She hoped that she was.

"I'll sleep good," Karen promised, but she wasn't so sure about that. It never felt right when she wasn't in her own bed with her own pillow that she could beat up and bend just the way she liked.

The room went dark when the door closed, and Karen kept her eyes wide open for a couple of minutes until they adjusted to the lack of light. She'd rather she was home. Not that she was afraid.

It was the dream that worried her. The last time she'd spent the night at her grandparents' house, the nightmare had come. She didn't want it to return.

It was a long time before Karen felt herself relax enough to fall asleep.

It happened then the way it always did. She was in a bedroom in a home she didn't recognize when she heard her mom and her dad arguing. She was younger than she was now, probably only five, because she was sitting on the floor, playing with baby dolls. Doll clothes were scattered all over the carpet, and she was afraid her parents were angry because she'd made such a big mess.

The fighting grew louder and louder, and Karen covered her ears. But even that didn't help. The words were cruel and ugly and seemed so sharp that they cut at her skin even though they weren't directed at her.

Karen moved into the kitchen, where her mother and father were shouting, only now they were speaking in a foreign language. She couldn't understand what they were saying any longer. But the words were just as ugly and spiked, so that each one hurt the other. Not just Karen, but each other. Her father's face was bloody from all the words. Her mother's, too.

Desperately Karen tried to get Maureen's attention, thinking she could distract her mother easier than she could her father. But when she walked over and tugged at Maureen's blouse, her mother ignored her and gestured for her to move away. Her hands, Karen noticed, had blood on them from all the ugly words.

Frantic now, Karen went to her father next and pleaded with him to stop and listen to her. But he was embroiled in the intense argument and ignored her.

Distraught by this point, Karen stood on a chair and screamed for them to notice her. But it did no good. She held out her arms to them, but they were always just out of reach.

Then there was a knife, a big one that looked like the kind hunters used. It appeared as if by magic. It was polished and gleamed in the light. Sometimes her mother was the one holding the knife, and at other times it was her father.

This time it was her father.

He raised his arm and pulled the knife back, all the while talking to her mother in the language Karen couldn't understand.

Maureen's eyes were round and terrified as she backed away. The knife grew bigger and sharper. Her mother's voice pleaded with him. Karen still couldn't understand the words, but she knew that her mother was afraid. Karen was afraid for her. Maureen ran and hid in the bathroom and locked the door.

This was the part that always confused Karen, because she could see through the bathroom wall as if it weren't there. Her mother had a phone with her, and she dialed the police and was screaming that her husband was about to kill her.

But she had the wrong number, and the people on the other line didn't care.

Karen was weeping by then, crying for her mother to dial 911. She pleaded with her daddy not to hurt her mother. Her dad didn't listen, and neither did anyone else.

It was at this point that the bathroom door opened, and the stranger who had been her father walked in. Maureen stood inside the bathtub, her back flattened against the wall.

Karen tried to stop him. She threw herself in front of him and held on to his legs, but he moved forward, dragging her with him. Karen tried so hard to get him to stop, but he wouldn't.

Her mother screamed, and Karen watched as her father lowered the knife, plunging it into her mother's heart. When he drew out the blade, it was coated red with blood.

Karen screamed. Her mother was dead. Her father had killed her mother.

She screamed and screamed and screamed.

"Karen . . . Karen!"

Bright lights blinded her. Karen's heart beat like a race car piston. Her skin felt cold and clammy, and her forehead was damp with sweat.

"Sweetheart."

The soothing, gentle voice belonged to her grandmother. Karen clung to her, holding on as tight as she could as the image of her mother's bloody body faded from her memory.

"It's all right. It was a dream."

Karen started to sob. She hated it when she cried, but she couldn't make herself stop. "Sometimes I don't think it's a dream," she whispered. "Sometimes I think it all really happened."

"What happened, honey? Can you tell me about it?"

"No," she said emphatically, and shook her head. She didn't want to talk about it. Didn't want to tell her grandmother about the knife and the blood and the hate.

Her grandma's arms were wrapped around her, and she swayed gently back and forth.

Maureen stared at the television screen in the hotel room. It was like a thousand other hotel rooms she'd stayed in for these business trips. She was restless and not the least bit tired, although she'd been on the go since early that morning. By all rights she should be exhausted.

She decided to take a long, hot shower and soothe her aching muscles. In addition, she wanted to think over the things that Thom had said to her.

Forgive Brian?

Clearly the man didn't know what he was talking about. His wife had died. Forgiving her for dying couldn't be compared to the craziness she'd been subjected to in the years she was married to Brian.

Thom didn't know the half of it. She told him about the infidelities and troubles her ex-husband had holding a job. What she hadn't gone into were the brushes with the law, the get-rich-quick schemes. The stealing.

Only what he'd taken hadn't been from strangers. He'd robbed his own wife and daughter.

Maureen's blood pressure rose just thinking about it. Shaking her head, wanting to throw off the ugly thoughts, she undressed and turned on the shower. The water pressure left a lot to be desired, so she cut the shower short.

Dressed in her robe, a towel wrapped around her hair, she moved back into the room. And froze.

The pad by the telephone had moved and was on the bed.

Had someone been in the room? She checked the door and found the chain securely in place.

She picked up the pad and found CALL KAREN scribbled on it. It was the most bizarre thing she'd ever seen.

Generally Maureen didn't call her parents when she was out of town. They had a number where she could be reached, and if there was an emergency, they could phone her.

It was late, after ten, and her parents were sure to be in bed. Their sleep habits had changed now that they were older, and they retired earlier.

CALL KAREN.

Maureen didn't know who had left the message or how it had gotten into her room, but she wasn't messing with fate. She sat on the edge of the bed and reached for the telephone.

"Maureen, is that you? I can't believed you called." Her mother's voice greeted her, sounding worried and distraught. "I was just trying to decide if I should phone you."

"Mom, what's wrong?" Maureen's heart constricted with fear.

"It's Karen. She's had another one of those dreams."

"Oh, dear."

"It would help if you talked to her."

"Of course."

A moment passed before her daughter got on the line. "Mom?"

Maureen could tell that Karen had been sobbing; she also knew how much the twelve-year-old hated to cry. "Hi, sweetheart."

"Are you okay?"

The kid was scared out of her mind and worried about Maureen. "I'm fine. How about you?"

"Mom?" Karen asked, and sniffled. "Do you hate my dad enough to kill him?"

*   *   *

Paul felt as free as the breeze. The letter of resignation was typed, copied, and ready to be mailed to the list of church elders. And to think he'd managed all that without Leta's help. Amazing.

The one thing he didn't know how to run was the postage meter, so he left everything on Leta's desk with a note that explained he had resigned. He asked that she mail out the letters first thing the following morning.

Now that the decision had been made to leave the ministry, Paul experienced a sensation of freedom so potent, he felt drunk. For a man who avoided anything remotely related to alcohol, the sensation was heady.

On the way back to his house, Paul wandered into the garage and rooted through his camping equipment. Having sorted through most everything recently, he easily found the camp stove, sleeping bag, tent, and other supplies he needed. And since the car was conveniently parked there, he loaded up the gear in the trunk.

When he was finished he walked into the house. For the first time in recent memory, he was hungry. He paused in an attempt to remember when he'd last sat down to a meal. Probably one Annie had cooked, and they'd left, what? . . . two days ago—no, three.

He rummaged through the refrigerator, brought out eggs and cheese—a little dry and dark around the edges, but still edible. An omelet. He used to be famous for his omelets. Family famous.

He cracked the eggs into a bowl and whipped them with a fork and had the silliest urge to sing. Only an hour or so earlier he couldn't force himself to utter a single note of a well-loved Christmas carol; now he bellowed it out as if performing in an Italian opera.

The meal was delicious, the best he'd had in weeks. Nothing against Annie, but Joe's wife-to-be had a thing or two to learn about cooking. He remembered Barbara's first attempts at creating meals. Once again he smiled.

He stacked the dishes in the sink, filled it with soapy water, and left to pack his clothes. He intended on packing light. A sweater and an extra set of clothes plus a few changes of underwear were all he needed, he decided.

He checked the house one last time before he headed for the car. On second thought, he went back to the church. He didn't stay long, anxious as he was to be on his way.

He remembered what Joe had said about letting someone know where he was. Bethany might phone, and when she learned he'd resigned and no one knew where he was . . . well, she'd worry about him and he didn't want to spoil her Christmas.

It was only fair, too, that he let Leta know that she'd been a good secretary over the years. She deserved that much. He didn't worry about the elders finding a replacement for him. As far as he was concerned, he hadn't done the church much good the last several months anyway.

Sitting back down at his desk, his favorite fishing hat perched atop his head, Paul typed out a minor list of instructions for Leta. He listed the name of the campground where he was headed and wished everyone a Merry Christmas. For the first time that season, he meant it.

Eager to be on his way, Paul got into the car and was ready to leave when he remembered the dirty dishes soaking in the sink. He sat for a moment, then decided to leave them. He'd wash them when he returned.

The drive to the campground took him nearly two hours. It was a peaceful drive, with only his thoughts to keep him company. But this time they weren't weighted down with regrets about what a poor job he was doing seeing to the spiritual needs of his congregation.

If he had any regrets, they all fell in the area of Madge Bartelli. He loved the old woman. But she was the straw that had broken him.

God had asked too much of him. It had been difficult enough to watch Barbara die, but to ask him to go through the ordeal a second time was unfair.

"Unfair," he said aloud, and felt better for having said it.

He paid his fee at the private campground and located the very campsite he and Joe had stayed at a few years earlier, or one he assumed was the same. Pitching the tent on his own was no problem, although it took him longer without Joe there to lend a hand.

He set up the camp stove and lantern and stored the food he'd bought on his way out of town.

Dusk came with perfect timing. Paul was sitting on a log, his tent pitched, his dinner cooking, humming softly to himself. He hadn't felt this content in years.

When he'd finished his meal, he sat and watched the stars appear one by one against a backdrop of black velvet.

Barbara had never been keen on camping, but she'd been a good sport, especially in the early years of their marriage. Later, after the kids were born, Barbara had stayed home and Paul had taken the kids with him.

Now it was just him, sitting alone in the night. No responsibilities. No obligations. No clock to punch.

How he missed his wife in those bittersweet moments. How he wished she were at his side. How he longed to tuck his arm around her shoulders and to have her head rest against his chest.

His arms were empty. As empty as the night. As empty as his heart.

The freedom he'd experienced earlier was replaced with a crushing pain. For the first time since Barbara's death, he could identify his feeling.

Betrayal. God had betrayed him.

He found he was standing, his face turned to the sky. His back was as straight as a flagpole and his arms as stiff. They dangled at his sides, and his hands were clenched into tight fists. He'd wanted to run away. Escape. But his misery had followed him.

"Damn you!" Paul shouted into the silence. His words echoed back to him, bouncing off the hillside again and again, until gradually they faded.

Damn you. Damn you. Damn you.

Sadly, Paul realized he was the one damned.

Chapter

★ ✯ ★

15

"*I imagine you're* wondering why I've called you all here," Gabriel said to his three charges.

Shirley, Goodness, and Mercy glanced nervously at one another. Gabriel could see that they were anxious about this meeting, especially Goodness, whom he'd talked to briefly only recently. They stood straight and tall, their wings folded neatly behind them. Each one wore a worried, if not mildly curious, look.

"I'll admit we're a bit inquisitive," Shirley was brave enough to acknowledge.

Mercy stepped forward eagerly. "I want you to know, Gabriel, I haven't been up to any of my old tricks. None of that kid stuff for me!"

"You mean other than what happened with Edith?" he asked evenly.

"Oh. That was quite a while ago now."

Gabriel rubbed his chin thoughtfully. "And as I recall, there's the small matter of sitting in an elevator shaft recently. Would you care to explain to me how that happened?"

"Ah, no," she answered in a small voice.

"That's what I thought. Now tell me how Catherine Goodwin's prayer request is being handled."

Mercy's head drooped, and her eyes avoided his.

"I believe there've been circumstances out of Mercy's control," Goodness intervened on her friend's behalf.

"Would you care to explain what's happening, Mercy?" Gabriel linked his hands behind his back and paced in front of the three prayer ambassadors.

"Well," she faltered, as if unsure where to start. "Catherine asked that Ted marry the woman God intended."

"That's correct."

"I wish she'd been more specific," Mercy muttered. "It's clear to me Joy and Ted are ideally suited. They care deeply for each other."

"That's wonderful," Gabriel said. "Then matters are progressing smoothly. I couldn't be more pleased." He gave her a wide smile. "I had my doubts, Mercy, but you've done an excellent job."

"Ah." Mercy cleared her throat and raised her index finger. "Everything's not going quite as well as it appears," she said miserably.

"Oh? Are there complications?"

Mercy nodded. "Just when it looked as if everything were about to fall into place the way it should . . ."

"Just a minute." Goodness raised her hand and frowned. "Did you consider that perhaps Blythe and Ted were supposed to be married?" she asked her friend.

"Not until recently," Mercy admitted with reluctance, cringing at the idea of the two together. A dejected, unhappy look came into her eyes. "It doesn't matter anymore."

"Why's that?" Gabriel asked.

"Ted's asked Blythe to marry him."

The announcement was followed by a short, stunned silence.

"I see," Gabriel said, and then focused his attention on Shirley. "How's everything progressing with Karen?"

The oldest of the three angels brightened. "Fabulous. She's taking riding lessons and has made a new friend, and you wouldn't believe the changes in her mother. Maureen's been dating Thom Nichols, the owner of the riding stable. The two have a lot in common." She offered him a Little Mary Sunshine smile and added, "A romance seems to be brewing there."

"I'm pleased to hear this," Gabriel said. "You've proven yourself once more. How about Karen's nightmares?"

The light in Shirley's eyes faded. "She woke with one recently, and it took her grandmother almost an hour to calm her back down."

"From what I understand, her mother was away on a business trip that night, and out of the blue, Maureen happened to phone her parents' home."

Shirley had a small coughing seizure. "Yes, as luck would have it . . ."

"Luck?"

"Karen needed to talk to her mother," Shirley insisted with a righteous tinge. "It was such a little thing to leave a message for Maureen on the bed."

"We'll talk more about that later," he said severely, and moved down the line. He faced Goodness, the last of the trio. "How's Paul?"

Goodness looked more discouraged than ever. "As you already know, he's resigned as pastor."

Shirley and Mercy gasped.

"In all fairness, I believe you've made a mistake, Gabriel, in assigning me this prayer request. I don't know how to help Pastor Morris. He's camped somewhere in the tules, roasting chocolate squares and marshmallows between graham crackers and singing silly songs."

"I see. Are you asking to be relieved from this assignment?" Gabriel asked. He'd known from the first what a difficult case this would be for the young Goodness, but no one had appreciated his insight.

"No," Goodness said firmly, surprising him. It looked as if she were even more shocked at herself. "I refuse to give up on Paul Morris. He's given up on himself, but I won't do it. There's got to be a way for him to overcome this depression."

"Perhaps," Gabriel suggested, "what he needs is a little help from his friends."

"Friends?" Goodness questioned. "You mean like Shirley, Mercy, and me?"

"Perhaps a few human friends might be persuaded to help," Gabriel suggested. It didn't escape his notice how easily the three of them were willing to fall back on their old tricks.

Goodness and Mercy exchanged a look, one Gabriel preferred not to question. He looked over the three prayer ambassadors standing before him. They'd surprised him by how well they'd managed thus far. Better than he'd anticipated.

"You may go now," he said.

Three pairs of eyes widened. "Go?" Shirley questioned. "You mean back to earth?"

"Yes. As far as I can see, the requests you're working on are progressing without major difficulties. I'll expect all three of you back here early on Christmas Eve."

"Did he say everything's progressing without major difficulties?" Mercy asked under her breath.

"I think so," Goodness responded.

"I don't understand," Shirley said in the same muted tones.

"Let's not question it," Mercy suggested, and was gone. Goodness and Shirley followed, and Gabriel returned to the giant Book of Prayer, doing his best to hide a grin.

*   *   *

The beautiful red dress was new and by far the most expensive one she'd ever owned. Joy hung it on the outside of her closet door, folded her arms, and stepped back to admire it.

When she first caught sight of the silk party dress on a mannequin in a store window, she had no intention of buying it. She must have stared at it for a full five minutes before she found the nerve to walk inside the store and ask the price. She flinched when the sales clerk told her it was $350.

The clerk was very good at her job, and before Joy was quite sure how it had happened, she was in the dressing room staring at herself in the mirror in the same silk dress. It fit as if it had been made for her.

After some weighty decision making regarding finances, Joy bought it for the sheer pleasure of watching Ted's face when he saw her wearing it. She could just imagine him looking up and having his jaw drop open as if someone had unscrewed its hinges. Then he'd try to speak, and after a few unsuccessful attempts, he'd simply take her in his arms and kiss her.

Three hundred and fifty bucks. It was cheap at half that price just thinking about Ted's reaction to her in it.

With reluctance, she left her bedroom and the red dress and drove over to her parents' house to help her mother prepare for the huge family party.

With her brothers married, it became almost impossible for everyone to be together on Christmas Day proper. Several years back, her mother had decided they would celebrate a family Christmas the weekend before.

"What can I do to help?" Joy said as she came into the kitchen. She reached for a radish from the relish tray and munched noisily on it.

"You can keep your hands out of that," Erlene Palmer said teasingly. Her mother was busy cutting fresh fruit for a gelatin salad, one of her brother's favorites, as Joy recalled. "You can tell me about the young man you're bringing with you. You said his name was Ted."

"Yes."

"I don't suppose this is the same Ted your father mentioned not long ago?"

"Yes."

"He's tall and good-looking. An engineer, right?"

"Yes."

"Your father spoke highly of him."

Joy figured her mother knew everything there was to know already, so she kept her mouth closed. Shuffling around inside the open refrigerator, she created enough space to hide the relish tray before it tempted anyone else.

"Well?" her mother said when she reappeared. "I'm waiting."

Joy sat on the stool on the other side of the counter from her mother. "It seems to me you know everything already."

"Details, maybe." Erlene's fingers agilely cut bananas into even slices as she spoke. "What I want to know is how you feel about him. Are you in love with him?"

"Mom! I barely know him."

Her mother's faint smile was comment enough. "I don't think I've ever seen you act this way toward a man."

"And just how am I acting?"

"Dreamy-eyed. You don't think your mother notices these things?" she asked, and laughed softly. "Every time you say his name your eyes go soft and this look comes over you. It reminds me of the way I felt when I first met your father."

"This is different."

"Oh?"

"Mom, I don't know. Yes, I like him, and that's a weak word. It doesn't even begin to describe the way I feel about Ted. But I'm afraid."

"Afraid?" Her mother raised quizzical eyes to her.

"You know what it's like when something wonderful happens. Like the time Joe won the full-ride football scholarship, and when we learned Diana was pregnant with twins. An excitement comes over me, but I'm afraid to believe it's really true. That's the way I feel about Ted."

"Time will fix that."

"But sometimes it's better to be cautious. Remember, Diana miscarried the twins."

"But she and Bill have three beautiful children now."

"Yes, I know." Joy laughed softly. "I'm so crazy about this guy, I bought myself a dress that cost three hundred and fifty dollars."

She had her mother's attention now.

"I'm planning to wear it tonight. You know why I bought that dress?"

"Of course I do. You wanted to see Ted's reaction when he first saw you wearing it. Why does any woman spend that much money on anything?"

It seemed her mother understood her better than she realized.

Joy stayed and helped prepare for the big dinner and the family festivities that followed. She was humming Christmas music when she let herself back into her apartment.

After putting her purse away, she walked into the bathroom and turned on the water for a long, leisurely soak in the tub.

A faint sound in the distance distracted her, and she realized it was her phone. She turned off the water and grabbed the bedroom telephone.

"Merry Christmas," she greeted cheerfully.

A silence.

"Hello?" she tried again.

"Joy, it's Ted."

"Well, hello there," she said, pleased to hear from him, especially when she'd be seeing him in less than two hours.

"Joy, listen, something's come up and I won't be able to make the dinner with your family." His words were flat, devoid of emotion.

"I see." She waited for an explanation, but none was forthcoming.

"I tried to phone earlier."

"I was shopping, and then I was over at my parents' house."

There was another short silence. She tensed, waiting. Somehow she knew he was going to say something that would hurt her. Some inner defense mechanism prepared her for the worst.

"Blythe stopped by my place yesterday," he began, "and I've had to do some heavy-duty thinking since. There's no easy way to say this. No easy way—"

"Then don't," she interrupted him, making sure her words betrayed none of the pain she was experiencing. "You don't need to say another word. I understand."

"I'm sure you don't."

"But what does it matter, right?" She pressed her hand to her forehead and sat down on the edge of her bed, uncertain that her legs would continue to support her.

"You're right," he said miserably, "what does it matter?"

"It was fun while it lasted, and I can still take the dress back, so there's nothing to worry about."

"Still take the dress back?"

She laughed once, shortly, and feared it was more sob than any display of mirth. "As you so eloquently put it, what does it matter. Good-bye, Ted Griffin. Have a wonderful life."

"You, too, my beautiful Joy."

She replaced the receiver, but her hand held firmly on to it, knowing this was her one last connection with Ted.

It was as if she'd been waiting for this moment from the first.

Her gaze fell on the beautiful party dress. She wanted very much to wear that someday, but not if she couldn't wear it for Ted.

*   *   *

Catherine Goodwin was delighted. Everything was going far better with her grandson than she dared hope. It seemed Ted had all but given up seeing Blythe Holmes. Catherine wished the young woman the very best, but frankly she was absolutely thrilled that Ted was dating Joy Palmer.

Although Catherine tried hard not to meddle in Ted's life, it was difficult not to voice her opinion. But the boy had a decent head on his shoulders, and she trusted him to make the right decision.

With Christmas less than a week away now, she was busier than ever. The literary tea was scheduled in the first half of the week, and there was much work left that needed to be done on that.

The knock on her door was followed almost immediately by the sound of it opening.

"Grandma, are you here?"

"Ted." Catherine was elated to have him drop by unexpectedly. Her smile faltered a little when she noticed that Blythe was with him. The two held hands, and it seemed to Catherine that the other woman was much subdued from their previous meetings.

"What a pleasant surprise. Sit down, please."

"We're only here for a few minutes," Ted explained as he led Blythe to the davenport. The two sat down together.

"Let me put on a pot of tea. Or would you rather have coffee?"

"Nothing for me," Blythe told her.

"Nothing, thanks," Ted added.

"Well, what are you two up to this fine evening?" Catherine asked, and sat across from them. She folded her hands when she noticed the look in her grandson's eyes. Whatever was on his mind was serious.

"We wanted you to be the first to know," Ted said.

The enthusiasm was forced, Catherine realized, but she said nothing.

"Blythe and I have decided to marry. The wedding will take place right after the first of the year."

"So soon?" Catherine couldn't keep the shock out of her voice. It was disappointment enough that Ted had chosen the woman she felt least suited him, but to hold the wedding in less than two weeks was an even greater surprise.

Blythe and Ted glanced at each other. His fiancée's lips formed a shaky smile. "There's a reason we've decided to go ahead with the wedding right away, Mrs. Goodwin."

"A reason?"

"Yes, Grandma. We're going to have a baby."

The two left shortly after their announcement, but Catherine stayed seated right where she was. The shock vibrated through her like the blast of sound waves from a bullhorn.

Ted and Blythe married. A baby.

Catherine closed her eyes. Her prayer for her grandson had been a simple one. She had asked that God guide Ted to the woman of his choice.

She had her answer. Only she didn't like it.

But that was all right; she'd often disagreed with God's decisions. After plenty of disappointments and heartache over the years, Catherine had learned something far more important.

To trust.

Maureen looked over to her boss's desk and made sure he was occupied before she reached for the telephone receiver and punched out the familiar number of the law firm that had represented her in the divorce. Although her attorney was away, Maureen felt she needed legal advice.

"Beckman, Crest, and Gold. How may I direct your call?" The receptionist rattled off the words in a monotone.

"Hello, this is Maureen Woods," she said, keeping her voice low. "I understand Susan Gold is in court, but I need to speak to an attorney. It's very important. Can you tell me who's available to take my call?"

"Would you rather have an appointment?"

"No," was Maureen's automatic response. She couldn't afford the time off work or the additional attorney's fees. Not once had she been in the law firm's office when it hadn't cost her two hundred dollars or more. "It's just a quick question having to do with the divorce settlement."

"Hold, please."

Maureen was left to twiddle her thumbs for several elongated seconds before the receptionist returned. "Glenn Crest can speak to you now."

"Thank you," she said, and waited for the senior partner to pick up the receiver. It seemed to her that she remembered meeting Glenn early on in her divorce proceedings. He was older, well established, and knowledgeable. She trusted him.

"Hello, Ms. Woods, it's good to hear from you again," he greeted her in a smooth voice. "How may I help you?"

"It has to do with Karen, my daughter."

"Yes."

Maureen could hear him shuffling papers and hoped he had her file in front of him and was quickly reviewing the case. Since she owed her soul to legal fees, she sincerely hoped Glenn could help her. "My ex-husband's attorney sent me a letter. Brian wants Karen to spend Christmas Eve with him."

"According to the terms of your agreement—"

"I know all about the terms," she said, cutting him off. "But he owes me months of back child support."

"I'm afraid there aren't any stipulations regarding late child support and visitation rights."

Maureen already knew that, but she still hoped. "You don't understand," she said, the frustration getting the better of her. "I'm afraid . . . I'm afraid." The words skidded to a halt in her mind as she stepped directly in front of her worst fear.

"Yes, Ms. Woods?"

"I'm afraid," she repeated shakily, "that Brian's going to ask for full custody of Karen."

Paul woke to the sound of birds chirping. It amazed him how beautiful a morning could be and that he could be a part of that beauty.

He dressed, climbed out of the tent, and brewed coffee in a blue enamel pot. Cradling the mug of steaming coffee in his hands, he sat on the edge of the picnic table and made plans for his day.

After breakfast he'd go on a hike, the same one he'd taken with Joe several years back. The five-mile trek was sure to tire him out, so when he returned to his campsite, he'd take a leisurely nap and soak in the sun.

He'd worry later on about what he'd pack for the hike. Breakfast had never excited him, and he was satisfied with a granola bar.

His plans made, Paul rinsed out the coffeepot and changed into his hiking boots. He was about to start on the hike when he heard the sound of another camper stirring.

Paul could see the tent, which was several spaces down from his own. The privately owned grounds didn't get much business in the winter months, he knew. As far as he could tell, he and his neighbor were the only two campers on the grounds. Of course, with Christmas less than a week away, business was probably off. Not many folks were thinking about the great outdoors this time of the year.

Paul loaded his backpack, settled it in the middle of his back, and reached for his walking stick. He started down the dirt road past the occupied campsite, just as the tent flap opened and a burly man stepped out. The man stretched his arms high above his head and yawned loudly.

Paul hesitated.

It couldn't be. If he hadn't known better, he'd think the camper was none other than Steve Tenny.

The two men eyed each other suspiciously.

"Paul?"

"Steve?"

"What are you doing here?" Paul demanded. He wanted to accuse Steve of finding his letter of resignation and following him out of town, but that was ridiculous.

"Camping," Steve answered.

"By yourself?"

Steve nodded. "The city gets to me every now and again, and I need to escape for a few days. It seems to me I've invited you along a number of times."

Paul nodded. "I'm here for the fresh air," he said, unwilling to tell his friend the whole truth. Although he wasn't entirely sure what the whole truth was.

"We're going to have to go a lot farther than this for some fresh air," Steve commented dryly.

Paul couldn't agree with him more. The Los Angeles smog was better in the winter months, but it had followed him a hundred miles or more.

"Actually, I came here to clear my head," Paul announced to his friend.

"Clear your head?"

Paul's hand tightened around the walking stick. "I wrote out my letter of resignation," he announced. Folks would find out soon enough. Steve would discover the envelope waiting for him when he arrived home anyway. There wasn't any need to keep it a secret.

"Resigned?" Steve echoed, the word low and stunned. "You?" He wandered around the campsite as if he'd lost his sense of direction. He looked at Paul and shook his head slowly, as if he were having trouble taking it in. "This is going to take some getting used to, I'm afraid. Sit down a minute, will you? I need a cup of coffee."

Paul had half a mind to say he was just leaving for a favorite hiking trail, but it was clear the church elder was shaken by his news. It didn't seem fair to announce his intentions and then casually walk away.

As it turned out, Paul brewed the coffee while Steve ambled around, paused, and scratched his head every now and again.

"You're sure about this?" he asked at one point.

"Sure I made the right decision?" Paul asked, rephrasing his friend's question. "Yes."

"Do you mind if I ask why?"

Actually Paul did. He didn't want anyone to talk him out of it. The decision was made, and he felt strongly that he'd done the right thing.

"I'd prefer not to talk about it, Steve. No offense."

"None taken," Steve assured him. He sat on a folding chair and clung to the cup of coffee as if it were all that stood between him and ruin.

"It's time I moved on," Paul offered, wanting to break the stilted silence.

"Have you decided upon another church?"

"No," Paul admitted. "I need a break."

"What are you going to do?"

Other than take a few days for camping and a little hiking, he hadn't given the matter much thought. He probably should start thinking about it soon. He'd need a way to support himself and help pay the last of Joe's college expenses. Funny, the thought of what he'd do for money had never occurred to him until this moment.

"I don't know what I'll do with myself," he admitted. He took a drink of coffee and set the mug aside, eager to be on his way.

"Where you headed?" Steve asked next.

Paul told him about the hiking trail.

"I don't suppose you'd like company?" Steve asked hopefully. "Listen, if you'd rather not have me along, just say the word. I know I can be a real nuisance at times."

"What makes you say that?" Paul asked, genuinely surprised.

"We used to spend quite a bit of time together, don't you remember? Then Barbara got sick and, I don't know, everything changed."

Paul didn't feel any comment was necessary. "You're welcome to come along if you like," he told his old friend. He wasn't seeking company, but he didn't have the heart to turn Steve down.

Paul's generosity was rewarded with a big smile from Steve. He'd forgotten how much he enjoyed Steve's companionship. As Steve had said, the two had grown apart following Barbara's illness and death. The fault was his own, Paul realized with regret.

As if he understood that Paul had been seeking solitude, Steve didn't seem inclined to talk on the hike, which took all of the morning and a small part of the afternoon.

Steve strolled back to his campsite and dropped onto the folding chair. "Guess I'm not in as good a shape as I thought," he muttered. "I think I'll rest up and then find a phone and call Myrna. She tends to worry if she doesn't hear from me."

"I'll talk to you later, then," Paul said.

Steve hesitated. "I'm not going to say anything to Myrna about what you told me, about you resigning from the church."

"It's fine, Steve. Everyone will learn about it sooner or later."

"I suppose you're right," he agreed with some reluctance, "but I was thinking that if you were to change your mind, then the fewer people who know about it the better."

"I'm not going to change my mind," Paul said with confidence.

Paul decided to rest himself. He cushioned a rock with his sleeping bag and leaned against it to soak up the sun. He heard Steve drive off and smiled softly to himself. His friend didn't realize how fortunate he was to have a wife, even if that meant he had to leave a campground to phone her.

He was half dozing when he heard a car approach. At first he assumed it was Steve returning, but the engine sound didn't match the clunker his friend drove.

Paul opened one eye to find a familiar-looking car slowly making its way down the dirt road. It took him a moment or two to realize the vehicle belonged to Leta Johnson, his secretary. Former secretary, he reminded himself.

Paul stood when Leta parked and climbed out of the car. She glared at him, fairly sizzling with righteous indignation.

"If you want to resign, that's fine with me," she snapped, slapping down the sealed envelopes on the top of the picnic table. "But you can damn well mail your own letters. As a matter of interest, Bernard Bartelli phoned. Madge hasn't much longer to live. He asked for you. Just exactly what am I supposed to tell that dear man? Tell me, Paul."

Her voice broke, and Paul realized he'd been a fool to think he could run away from his responsibilities.

"Tell him I'm on my way to the hospital right now," Paul said, and started to gather up his equipment.

Chapter

★ ✬ ★

16

Karen was on the phone when Maureen walked in the door that evening after work. She was tired and frustrated and in no mood to cook dinner. The Christmas tree wasn't up yet, and she had a stack of cards left to write, and if she didn't mail them the following morning, it was doubtful they'd arrive before Christmas.

She set down her briefcase and her purse and saw her daughter give her a look rife with guilt. Without being obvious, Maureen listened in to half of the conversation. She walked into the kitchen and opened the refrigerator, removed the chicken breasts she intended to roast, and set them on the counter.

"Sure, that will be fine." Karen's gaze followed Maureen around the kitchen.

"Okay," Karen added, and nodded. Her face lit up with a bright smile. "Don't worry, okay? I'll tell Mom."

Brian.

It could only be her ex-husband, Maureen decided. He'd gone behind her back and telephoned Karen when he knew Maureen wouldn't be there to act as a buffer. The man had sunk to new levels of deceit.

"I'm looking forward to it, too."

Maureen wasn't going to scold Karen for speaking to Brian, but she wanted to make sure this sort of thing didn't happen again.

All contact with their daughter was to be arranged with Maureen in advance. It wasn't Karen's fault that Brian had gone against the provisions stated in the divorce settlement. He knew the terms as well as she did. The next time her ex-husband called when Karen was home alone, Karen would be instructed to phone him back.

Brian could talk to Karen only when Maureen was present, and he damn well knew it.

"I can't wait," Karen whispered excitedly into the mouthpiece.

So Brian was up to his old tricks, Maureen mused. No doubt he was making promises he had no intention of keeping. Then again . . . Her stomach tightened as she considered the alternative. Perhaps he would make his promises good. If he intended on fighting her for custody of Karen, then he'd need their daughter's cooperation. What better way than to give her the things Maureen couldn't? He was married with a baby, and Karen loved babies. It would be just like him to plot to steal their daughter away from her. How he'd love to collect child support payments from her!

A moment or so later, Karen hung up the phone. She didn't say anything right away. Then: "That was Dad."

Although Maureen was so tense she felt as if she were about to be sick, she managed a smile. "What did he have to say?"

Karen avoided meeting Maureen's eyes. "Not much. He said he'd be by about six on Christmas Eve to pick me up. We're going to his house for dinner, and then we're going to open gifts."

"I'd rather you hadn't talked to him, Karen," Maureen said in gentle tones, wanting to be sure her daughter understood that she wasn't upset with her. The wrongdoing was all Brian's.

Karen sat at the kitchen table and propped her face in her hands. "I'd figured you'd say that. Dad thought you would, too."

Already Brian was trying to pit her daughter against her.

"All he wanted to do was tell me what time he was picking me up. You don't need to make a federal case out of it."

"I don't mean to sound petty," Maureen said stiffly, "but the terms of the divorce were set this way for a reason."

"Yes, so you could make Dad's life miserable." Karen leaped out of the chair with enough force to send it toppling backward. "You want to keep me away from him. You want to punish him because he's got a good life and you don't."

"Karen." Maureen couldn't believe what she was hearing. "That's not true."

"Did you ever stop to think," Karen said, her eyes bright with tears, "that you were punishing me, too? I love Dad. I miss him sometimes. I know he wasn't a very good husband, and he may not be a very good father, but you seem to forget something, Mom. He's the only dad I've got."

"But—"

"Do you have to spoil what little time I have with him? Do you?"

"I didn't mean—"

"Why do you think Dad hasn't seen me in over a year? I know why . . . because you make it as difficult as you can for him to have visitation rights."

"Did he tell you that?" Maureen demanded.

"No. He didn't have to, I've seen it myself." Karen's face was tinged red. "I don't want to talk to you anymore," she insisted, and raced from the kitchen.

The silence was like that after an atomic blast. Maureen braced her hands against the counter and waited for the feelings of guilt and anger to pass. An odd combination of emotions warred with each other, battling for dominance. What Karen said was basically true. She had made it as difficult as she could for Karen to visit her father, but it was for Karen's own protection. She couldn't expect a twelve-year-old to understand or appreciate that.

Maureen set the two chicken breasts in the oven and then sank onto the chair. The conversation with Karen played itself back in her mind. Her daughter was almost a teenager, certainly old enough to form her own opinions.

Karen had admitted Brian hadn't been a very good husband. That was putting it mildly. She seemed to know where he ranked in the father department, too. Nevertheless, she looked forward to spending time with him. It went without saying that she was anxious to meet her half brother.

It hurt to think of Brian with another child. The fact that he still had the power to wound her amazed Maureen. In some way she felt cheated; Karen was right about that, too. For to all outward appearances Brian, the liar, the cheat, the thief, had a better life than she had.

Maureen waited until her nerves had settled down before she approached her daughter. She knocked politely on Karen's bedroom door and waited.

"Who is it?"

Maureen played along. "Mom. Can we talk a moment?" She opened the door and looked inside the room.

Her daughter was sprawled across her mattress with the portable phone pressed to her ear. She wore another one of those guilty looks, and Maureen guessed that she was talking long distance to Paula.

"When you're finished speaking to Paula, I'd like a word with you myself."

"All right."

No more than a couple of minutes later, Karen reappeared in the kitchen. Her face was marked with red smudges, and she held herself stiffly.

"How's Paula?"

"Fine."

"Did she offer you any pearls of wisdom you care to pass along?" Maureen asked next. She was sinking lower than she thought. Here she was, well over thirty, seeking counsel from a pair of twelve-year-olds.

"Not really."

Maureen sucked in her breath and decided the only way to get this over with was to say what needed to be said. "I'm sorry, sweetheart."

Karen regarded her suspiciously. "Then I can go to Dad's on Christmas Eve without you making a big deal over it?"

"Yes," Maureen said, and added generously, "And I want you to enjoy yourself and to spoil your half brother with lots and lots of attention."

"You do?"

Maureen discovered it was true. Karen deserved this time with her father and his new family. She'd been cheated enough already.

Maureen's feelings toward Brian hadn't changed and wouldn't. Her ex-husband was a two-timing bastard. It was the reason they were divorced.

"What about you, Mom? Will you be all right by yourself?"

"Of course," Maureen said automatically. It was then that she realized what Karen being with Brian and his family meant.

She was going to be alone on Christmas Eve.

Catherine checked her compact living room a second time to be sure everything was in its proper place. She hadn't done much decorating for Christmas. A tiny artificial tree with shiny red bulbs served as a centerpiece on her small table. The Christmas cards she'd received, she'd hung on the wall in a festive display. She tried to look at the apartment through Blythe's young eyes and hoped it passed muster.

Catherine had phoned Ted's fiancée that morning to ask her to tea. Blythe had seemed surprised, first to hear from Catherine and then by the invitation. She'd been a tad hesitant but eventually had agreed to come.

Catherine was grateful. Since this was to be her grandson's wife, it was important that the two of them understand and appreciate each other.

They'd started off on the wrong foot. Catherine blamed herself for that. She'd been extra critical. The woman who'd sat next to Ted when he'd announced their engagement was even more subdued from the one she'd first met. Catherine imagined the pregnancy had something to do with that.

A baby.

So she was to be a great-grandmother. The thought excited her, although she already was a grandmother and great-grandmother many times over. But this unborn child shared part of her love for Earl.

Blythe arrived right on time.

"Welcome," Catherine greeted the young woman with a wide grin. "Please come in. I've already got the tea brewing."

Blythe stepped into the small apartment and looked around as if she expected someone else would be there as well. It seemed to Catherine that she looked mildly relieved to find it was just the two of them.

They sat next to each other, and Catherine poured the tea and handed Blythe the delicate china cup, her finest. "I imagine you're curious why I asked you here on such short notice."

"Frankly, I am," Blythe admitted.

Catherine noted that the other woman seemed a bit peaked. Apparently Blythe wasn't having an easy time with the pregnancy. First ones were often difficult. Her own, so many years in the past, certainly had been.

"I have a gift for you." Catherine reached for the small wrapped package on the corner of the end table. "I've cherished this for over fifty years. To be honest, I never intended to part with it, but after giving the matter some thought, I've decided I want you to have it."

Blythe frowned as she tore away the bow and the ribbon. She lifted the lid and stared into the bed of black velvet. "This is the cameo you wore the day we first met."

"Yes." Catherine was pleased she remembered it.

"It's lovely," Blythe whispered, and raised wide questioning eyes to Catherine.

"It was a gift from my first husband, Earl Standish." She settled back on the sofa and relaxed, holding the teacup and saucer in her hands. "We met shortly after the attack on Pearl Harbor and were married several months later. That was many years ago now."

"You said Earl Standish was your first husband? I didn't realize . . . Ted told me you were married for forty years to Frank Goodwin."

"Forty-three very good years," she elaborated. "Frank was a dear, sweet man and he loved me, and I loved him. I bore Frank two sons, and we had a wonderful life together, but all those years, Frank knew that I never stopped loving Earl. I couldn't stop loving him."

"But why were you married to Frank . . ." Blythe hesitated, clearly confused.

"Earl died in the war." Even now, fifty years after having received that horrible telegram from the War Department, Catherine could barely speak the words without her heart twisting with pain.

"I'm sorry."

Catherine nodded instead of speaking. She needed a few moments to compose herself before explaining. "He was an Airborne Ranger. He parachuted into France on June 6, 1944. You probably don't know the significance of that day, do you?"

Blythe shook her head.

"It was D-Day, the day the Allied troops invaded France—the turning point of the Second World War. A little less than a year later, and the Axis powers surrendered. The war was over." Except for Catherine. A war waged within her for years following the news of Earl's death. It was as if her very heart had been ripped from her that fateful morning in June. As if her own life were over as a single bullet stole her beloved husband from her.

"I thought Ted was related to you through his mother."

"Emma was Earl's and my daughter," Catherine explained. Emma was the reason Catherine had gone on living. The reason she'd gotten out of bed in the morning and struggled through each new day. In the beginning she'd dragged the pain of the last one with her until the load became so heavy, the grief so burdensome, she couldn't continue. That was when she'd made her peace, such as it was.

"I don't know to this day if I ever recovered emotionally from losing Earl. I think sometimes we love so deeply, so profoundly, that anything else pales by comparison. It was that way with Earl and me."

"Do you still think about him, after all this time?" Blythe asked with surprise.

"Fifty years later and not a day passes that some memory of Earl doesn't come to mind. We were together so short a time. Too short."

"It must have been so difficult for you alone with Emma."

"The difficult part was that Earl was no longer with us. Anything else I could deal with or reason out, but not that Earl should die.

"He never knew the beautiful daughter we created, and I ached for Emma to remember her father. He would have been so proud of her, as proud as she is of him. Unfortunately she has no memory of him."

"But you got on with your life, you married again."

"Yes, in time," Catherine admitted, but it had taken nearly five years. She might never have remarried if it hadn't been for Frank's gentle persistence. He'd wooed her for three of those years.

Like Earl, he'd been a soldier, but the fates had been kinder to him, and he'd returned home from the campaign in the South Pacific to a hero's welcome. He'd been gentle with her, cajoling her for weeks before she'd agreed to go out with him.

Catherine never fully understood why Frank fell in love with her. She wasn't interested in remarrying, wasn't even interested in another relationship. Yet there he was, loving, gentle, eager to be a part of her and Emma's life.

By then she'd accepted Earl's death and made her peace with God. The battle had been hard won. Catherine had told God that if this was the way he treated his friends, it was little wonder he had so few.

She smiled at the memory.

"I loved Frank," she said, "not with the same intensity that I did Earl, but I did love him. A woman doesn't spend forty-three years married to a man without strong feelings."

"I don't understand why you're giving me this pin," Blythe whispered brokenly. "You said yourself you never intended to part with it."

"That's because it's the only piece of jewelry I have that Earl gave me, other than a plain gold wedding band. To this day, whenever I put on that cameo, I can feel Earl's love for me, as strong now as it was all those years ago."

Blythe tensed, and her shoulders went stiff. "I'm sorry, I can't accept this gift."

"Of course you can, child. I want you to have it. It's fitting that Ted's wife would wear it. You see, Ted was an Airborne Ranger himself for a time, like his grandfather."

"Yes, I know, but I still can't accept it." She tried to push the box into Catherine's hands.

"Blythe, it would do me a great honor if you were to take the cameo. Please. Accept it with my love and with Earl's. You're soon to be a part of this family, a very important part. This baby is Earl's first great-grandchild."

Blythe stilled, as if she weren't sure what to do.

"Recently I asked God to send the woman of his choice into Ted's life," Catherine went on to say, "and Ted chose to ask you to be his wife."

"That's because of the baby."

"I know, dear, but the baby is his responsibility."

Blythe didn't say anything for a long time and seemed to be struggling within herself. "He's in love with someone else," she admitted candidly. Her face hardened, her features went sharp and tight. "He didn't think I knew, but I'm not as stupid as everyone seems to believe."

"No one thinks anything of the sort," Catherine said sternly.

Blythe folded her hands and briefly closed her eyes. "I asked him about her. Joy, isn't it?"

Catherine nodded.

"You know what he said? He said that it didn't matter, that I was the woman he was going to marry. You know the crazy part—he's actually excited about the baby."

That didn't surprise Catherine. Ted was a wonderful uncle. Many times she'd watched him with his cousins and marveled at his patience with small children.

"This baby may not have been planned," Catherine said evenly, "but that doesn't mean he or she isn't loved or welcome. Emma wasn't planned, either. I didn't intend to get pregnant on our honeymoon, but these things happen."

Blythe lowered her gaze. "I think you should know something. In the beginning, I didn't want this baby. When I first learned I was pregnant, I seriously considered an abortion. It was so tempting, an easy way out, but when I went to make the appointment, I couldn't do it. I just couldn't make myself do it."

Catherine was forever grateful that Blythe hadn't resorted to anything so drastic. "But you didn't, and that's the important thing. That took courage, Blythe."

"Not really." She briefly covered her face with her hands. "I can't believe I did anything so stupid as to get pregnant. I know better than to let something like this happen. My stupidity isn't the baby's fault."

Catherine wished she could say or do something to ease Blythe's discomfort. Blythe was restless and seemed to be on the verge of tears.

"I'm really sorry, but I can't accept your beautiful pin," Blythe said finally, and set the box back on the end table.

Catherine winced at the sharp edge of her words. "If you won't accept it for yourself, then take it for the child. Someday when he is older you can tell the child about his great-grandfather who died in the Second World War, and perhaps you could put in a kind word about me."

"Ah." Blythe shook her head from side to side in a wild motion. "No, I'm afraid I can't do that, either."

"Blythe, my dear, what is it?"

"He's in love with Joy."

"Yes, I know, but Ted's committed to you."

"You don't understand."

"What is it?" Catherine asked softly. "Tell me." Gently she took the younger woman in her arms. Blythe buried her face in her shoulder and broke into huge sobs.

"Whatever it is will take care of itself," Catherine whispered soothingly. "Now, now, it can't be so bad."

"But it is," Blythe insisted, rubbing the moisture from her face. "I can't take the cameo. I can't give it to this baby."

"Of course you can."

"No," she cried with such strength, she startled Catherine. "I can't." She stiffened as if she expected to be struck or attacked. "Ted isn't the baby's father. He's married, you see, and he doesn't want anything to do with me."

Paul drove directly from the campground to the hospital. On the two-hour drive back into the city, he tried to compose his thoughts, decide what he could possibly say that would help the Bartelli family deal with Madge's impending death.

Paul knew Bernard and the Bartelli children were emotionally prepared. As emotionally prepared as one could expect.

By the time Barbara had reached the point of death, Paul was of two minds. He'd wanted more than anything that her suffering end. Yet at the same time, he'd mentally clung to her, unwilling and unable to release her from life. He hadn't thought he could go on without her. In retrospect, his fears had been well founded.

Paul had forever changed the day Barbara died. He'd nursed the pain of that wound for so long, he didn't remember what it was like to feel anything other than a pressing sadness.

He didn't want the Bartelli family to make the same mistakes he had, so he mulled over what he could say, what he might do, that would make a difference.

As he reviewed his own response to death, Paul recognized how angry he'd been. Still was. For two long years he'd submerged the anger, unaware of what it was doing to him. Only recently, when he'd stood in the middle of the church and screamed out at the unfairness of death, had he touched upon his fury. Only when he'd cried out in frustration and from a deep well of pain had Paul become aware of how outrage had subtly impacted both his life and his ministry.

He'd tried to deal with his anger intellectually, reason it out. He'd tried to convince himself that as a man of the cloth he wasn't like everyone else. Why he should feel exempt from the most crushing of life's disappointments, he didn't know.

What he'd failed to do was deal with Barbara's loss in his heart. In his gut.

His faith should have been strong enough to carry his doubts, strong enough to answer the unanswerable. He was a man of God. He was a man who'd dedicated his life to the ministry. A man who eased others' pain, but not his own.

The conflict came when his mind declared war on his emotions. Faith merged with doubt, and, like water and oil, the two refused to blend, and soon Paul couldn't tell the difference between hope and despair. Both felt the same to him.

Once, a long time before, someone had told Paul that the greatest beauty was watered by tears. He'd shed his tears, mourned the loss of his wife, and had yet to find any beauty in her death.

The hospital parking lot was full. If Paul had been looking for a reason to turn away, one was presented to him on a tarnished platter.

"I'm sorry, Bernard, I would have been there in your hour of need, but there wasn't a parking space available." How ludicrous that sounded.

Paul circled the lot once more and mumbled under his breath when he didn't see a single available spot. Not even someone walking through, someone he could follow in order to claim their spot.

Paul eased his eyes heavenward. "If you want me here, you'll provide the space."

The words had barely escaped his lips when a car unexpectedly jerked out of a parking space directly in front of him. Paul's mouth fell open.

"All right, all right," he muttered, "so you want me here."

Once he parked, Paul walked into the hospital and took the elevator to the appropriate floor. He stepped onto the floor and walked toward the waiting area. There he found two of the three Bartelli children. He knew them from years past, but they stared at him as though he were a stranger.

"Hello," he said, walking into the waiting area. He introduced himself.

"I'm Rod," said the older of the Bartelli sons, exchanging handshakes with Paul.

"Luke." The middle son shook his hand next.

"Anna and my dad are in with Mom," Rod explained. He lowered his voice. "I don't think it will be much longer. She held on until we could all get here. She seems to be waiting for you."

Paul swallowed uncomfortably with that bit of information. "How's your father holding up?" He directed the question to the older of the two men.

Rod looked him directly in the eye. "Not good. His heart isn't good. I don't know how much more of this he can take."

"I'll see what I can do," Paul promised, although he feared it wouldn't be nearly enough.

He found Bernard and Anna sitting at Madge's bedside. Madge was as pale as the sheets. Her eyes were closed, and Paul wondered if she'd slipped into a coma. It would be merciful if she had.

"Pastor." Bernard stood when he noticed Paul standing in the doorway. "Mrs. Johnson said she wasn't sure if she'd be able to reach you or not."

"I came as soon as I heard."

Madge's eyes fluttered open. "Pastor," she said in a voice so weak, Paul had to strain to hear. "Good. Good," she repeated weakly. "I've been waiting for you."

"You want to talk to me?" Paul asked.

She moistened her dry lips. Again her voice was low, and she closed her eyes as though the effort drained her of what little strength she possessed. "Yes."

"She's been repeatedly asking for you," Anna explained softly.

"Alone."

The request came from Madge.

"Mom wants us to leave her with Pastor Morris," Anna said to her father. The two left the room.

When they were gone, Madge opened her eyes. They were dull with pain and drugs. "It won't be long now," she whispered.

"No," Paul agreed. "Are you afraid, Madge?" Perhaps that was the reason she wanted to talk to him privately, he thought.

She smiled, and Paul swore it was one of the most beautiful smiles he'd ever seen. "No. I'm thinking about when we adopted Anna," she said. "How eager we were for our little girl. Bernard and the boys had a room all prepared for her. Waiting to love her." She paused, and Paul suspected she needed to renew her strength before she continued. "God is waiting to welcome me with the same love we had for Anna."

"Yes." Paul had never doubted that Barbara was in heaven or the warm welcome she received.

"I'll be healed at last," Madge whispered.

"Healed?" The word tightened around his vocal cords. He'd pleaded with God, begged, implored, bargained. He would have sold his very soul to have seen Barbara healed.

Faith. His faith hadn't been a tiny mustard seed. When they'd first learned Barbara had cancer, and the odds given her, Paul had been confident, even cocky. His faith was the size of an avocado seed.

Through it all, his wife had remained committed to God's will. It came to the point that Paul couldn't bear to hear the words.

God had willed his wife to this terrible disease.

God had willed her to suffer.

God had willed her death.

Dying himself would have been easier to bear.

Now he stood at the bedside of yet another woman of faith. A woman who had loved and served God faithfully. And she too was about to cross the bridge that led from one life to another.

She too talked of healing.

"There will be no cancer in heaven," Madge whispered.

"Would you like me to read to you from Psalms?" Paul asked. He didn't know what to say to her.

"Barbara is healed."

Paul felt as if the softly whispered words reached up and slapped him hard across the face. Jolted, he stepped back involuntarily.

His wife was free of cancer. Free of pain. Free of earth's restrictions. He was the one who was bound, tied up in doubts, choking on skepticism, gagging on all the trite phrases good people of God had force-fed him.

If one more person told him that all things worked together for good for those who loved God, Paul swore he was going to vomit. If another well-meaning church-attending zealot dared to approach him with trite words, he didn't know if he'd act responsibly.

Faith and despair.

Despair and faith.

So alike he couldn't tell them apart any longer. They'd merged in his mind and his heart until he wasn't able to distinguish one from the other.

"Call them," Madge whispered. "I waited so you'd know."

He frowned. Know?

Unwilling to question Madge, he returned to the waiting area and called the Bartelli children and Bernard. The four gathered quietly around Madge's bedside.

Paul opened the book of Psalms, the very one he'd read at Barbara's deathbed. As he whispered the words, he realized that for the first time since Barbara's death, he found solace in the verses.

Faith and despair. For the first time in two long years, he was beginning to understand the difference.

There is no cancer in heaven, Madge had told him.

Barbara was healed.

Chapter

★ ✦ ★

17

There wasn't one logical reason that Joy could name for keeping the red dress. Three hundred and fifty dollars was a lot of money to pay for something to hang in her closet.

Even if she dragged it out and admired it once or twice a week, it would take a long time to justify that much money for one silly dress.

Ted hadn't even seen her wearing it. That was what distressed her the most. It would have been much better if he'd come to see her, to explain what was happening between him and Blythe. She could have put on the red dress just so he'd know what he was leaving behind. That was ridiculous, of course. One didn't wear a party dress for a big brush-off.

As it happened, Ted had phoned. The coward. It had all been very polite. He'd stiffly announced that he'd asked Blythe to marry him. By then it hadn't come as any big shock. Joy knew something was up when he'd canceled dinner with her family. His message had come through loud and clear.

It was over. Nice knowing ya, kid. See you around sometime.

Joy was a big girl. She accepted his decision, dealt with the pain and disappointment as best she could. Nevertheless, she was downright sorry about the red dress.

After placing the plastic wrap over it, she pinned the sales receipt to the front and hung it on the back of the closet door. She stepped away to admire it one last time before heading for the department store.

"Keep it."

The voice came as distinctly as if she'd left the radio playing.

"Keep the dress," the same voice repeated.

Joy whirled around to be sure someone wasn't standing behind her. She shook her head as if she had water in her ears. Obviously she was hearing things. Sure, she'd been under a lot of pressure lately, but she didn't think it was bad enough for her to be hearing strange voices.

The dress.

Her gaze softened as she studied the bright, gay color and remembered how special and beautiful she'd felt wearing it.

"All right," she said aloud. If she had taken to hallucinating, then she wasn't above answering. "I'll keep the dress. There, are you satisfied?"

Silence.

Joy was worse off than she realized; she was actually waiting for a response. She'd keep the dress. Now all she needed was an occasion to wear it. More important, a man who would appreciate seeing her in it.

But it wasn't just any man who interested Joy Palmer. She wanted Ted. Why was it the unattainable was always the most appealing? Well, he was marrying Blythe.

With the decision made not to return the dress, Joy flopped down in front of her television set. She folded her arms and stared at the blank screen.

This had to be one of the most depressing Christmases on record. Her spirits were so low, they were scraping bottom. It wasn't fair that one male, who apparently didn't know his own heart or his own mind, should level her to staring at a blank television screen.

There was always something to be grateful for, she reminded herself, but at the moment she was hard-pressed to decide what.

Old Charles, she mused and smiled softly. He was ready, willing, and able to collect donations for the literary tea. He seemed to be more like himself these last few days, and it was a pleasure to watch him slowly come out of his shell.

Catherine Goodwin seemed to be having her share of problems lately. If it wasn't for the older woman's connection to Ted, Joy would have sought her out that afternoon following Ted's fiancée's visit.

Joy had seen Blythe walk through the lobby, stiff and elegant as ever. It was difficult in her frame of mind to be charitable toward the other woman. Joy didn't need anyone to tell her she was being unfair.

Afterward, Joy had seen Catherine slip into the chapel. She hadn't come out for a long time, and she'd seemed burdened and sad. Perhaps later Catherine would be willing to tell Joy what was causing her such concern.

Joy's doorbell chimed, and she sprang off the sofa. A beleaguered postal worker stood on the other side, ready for her to sign a clip-board.

"I didn't know you people worked this late," she commented when he handed her a pen.

"We try not to, but this time of year it's crazy."

"Merry Christmas," Joy told him when he handed her the small package.

She examined the box, but there wasn't any name on the return address. Nor did she recognize the street name. It must have been valuable if her signature was required. Her heart started to pound, and she opened the door and raced after the mailman.

She found him waiting for the elevator. "Who's this package from?" she asked hurriedly.

He checked the clipboard. "Eastman Jewelry."

"I didn't order anything from them."

"You'll have to take that up with Eastman. All I do is deliver, some-one else covers complaints."

"I know, but if someone sent it, wouldn't their name be on the package?"

"Not necessarily." He studied the numbers above the elevator.

"I mean—"

"You might want to open it up and check inside. There could be something in there."

"Oh, right." Joy hadn't thought of that.

The elevator arrived and he stepped inside, looking grateful to make an escape before she hounded him with more questions.

Joy returned to her apartment and set the package on the table. She gingerly peeled away the paper, being sure to keep the address and return labels intact. Once the brown wrapping paper was removed, she discovered a white box. Inside was a black velvet case.

Joy held her breath as she carefully pried open the lid. Inside was a wide, textured gold bangle. She gave an involuntary gasp. Whoever had ordered this had spent a fortune. Gold bangles didn't come cheap.

She lifted it from its bed of plush velvet and saw that it was engraved. TO JOY, WITH LOVE, FROM EDITH AND FRIENDS.

Edith. And friends? In other words, Edith and Ted Griffin. For the first time since their stilted telephone conversation, Joy felt tears brim in her eyes.

Damn it all, why did he have to go and do something sweet like this? It would have been much easier to forget him if he hadn't used the word *love*.

*   *   *

Ted sat on the edge of his chair his elbows braced against his knees. Within a few weeks he'd be married to Blythe. Soon he'd be both a husband and a father.

The question that plagued him most was how long it would take him to stop thinking about Joy. An hour didn't pass without some thought of her waltzing through his mind, bringing a deluge of regrets.

That very afternoon, when he was supposed to have been working on an important project, his boss had found him gazing out the window like a lovelorn adolescent. In some ways that was how he felt.

Engaged to one woman, in love with another. How the hell had he gotten himself into this mess? No matter what his feelings now, he was determined to make the best of this situation. Blythe and their child deserved that much.

He stood, reached for his jacket, and headed out the door. Perhaps by the time he reached Blythe's apartment he'd have dredged up some enthusiasm for this dinner party.

When he arrived at his fiancée's, he was surprised to find that she hadn't changed out of the business suit she'd worn to the office that afternoon.

He was even more surprised when she lit a cigarette and blew a stream of smoke at the ceiling. It was all he could do not to ask her not to smoke when she was pregnant. Apparently she experienced a pang of guilt herself because she put out the cigarette after a single puff.

"I thought you'd given up smoking," he said dryly.

"I had. After these last couple of weeks I might take it up again."

"I hope you don't mean that."

She ignored the comment. "I had tea with your grandmother this afternoon." She waited as if she expected him to make some statement.

"That's nice." A rather dull remark, but he hadn't a clue what she wanted him to say.

"I take it your grandmother hasn't spoken to you?"

"No," he admitted, "should she?"

Blythe gave a cold, short laugh. Ted disliked the cynical, pessimistic moods she sometimes slipped into.

"If it had been me, I'd have been on the phone so fast it'd make your head spin."

Ted was lost. He'd come to escort Blythe to a dinner party, and she was speaking in riddles. "I'm afraid I don't understand."

"I don't expect you to," she said, and slipped the diamond engagement ring from her finger. It came off with some difficulty. She stared at it a moment and then deposited it in his hand.

"Blythe?"

She sobbed once. It could have been a laugh, but with Blythe it was sometimes difficult to tell.

Ted stared at the diamond in the palm of his hand and frowned. "If this is because of—"

"You can have your precious Joy now," she said bitterly.

"Blythe," Ted said gently, not wanting to distress her, "we've already been through this once."

She turned her back to him. "The baby isn't yours."

Ted reeled backward and sank onto the end of the sofa, sitting on the arm. "What do you mean?"

"Do you need me to spell it out for you?" She whirled around to face him. "You're not the father of this child."

"But—"

"I assumed it wouldn't matter." She brushed the hair from her face. "I thought that I could make you believe that a couple of weeks one way or the other in a pregnancy doesn't mean anything. But I can't marry you, Ted. I know that now."

"What about you and the baby?"

"What about us? The way I figure it, this kid is stuck with me as a mother. Who knows? I might even enjoy this parenting business."

Madge was gone. She'd died peacefully, surrounded by those who loved her. With the grace and composure that had marked her time on earth, the gentle old woman had slipped silently, serenely from one world to the next.

Paul looked to Bernard and knew the older man suffered from an overwhelming sense of unreality and profound loss. If it had been in his power, Bernard would have reached for his wife and pulled her back, and clung to her.

It was what Paul had wanted in Barbara's final moments.

Desperately tired and emotionally exhausted, Paul returned to the house. He walked in the back door, to be greeted by dirty dishes soaking in the sink. They reminded him of the urgency with which he'd left.

He heated a single cup of coffee in the microwave and carried it into his office with him. He wanted to sit a spell and sort through the emotions Madge's death had resurrected.

He knew that his own grief had been all-encompassing and severe for several months now. Only recently had it occurred to him that his capacity for pain was indicative of his capability to experience joy. He was ready for the pendulum to swing in that direction.

Other matters plagued him as well. Bernard had asked Paul to give the eulogy at Madge's funeral. Paul had reluctantly agreed. Now wasn't the time to tell the grieving man that he'd resigned from his ministerial duties at the church. Now wasn't the time to inform the bereaved husband that Paul had turned his back on his congregation.

Paul stood in the doorway of his small den and stared at the book-lined shelves. Several volumes were spread about in a haphazard fashion. In times past, he had been fastidious about his library. Never a book out of place. Never an unfiled paper or an unanswered letter.

He hadn't noticed that the room had gotten quite so disorganized and regretted that he'd neglected some of the most beloved volumes in his wide collection.

After tucking his books back in their proper places, he sat down at his desk. The surface was reasonably neat. Either Joe or Annie had made an effort to straighten up for him. Stacks of sermon notes and other slips of paper were piled onto one corner, held down by a white binder.

The binder resembled the one he'd kept for his notes on John's Gospel, the one he planned to write a book from someday, but it couldn't possibly be his notes. He'd tossed them in the garbage himself and then later made sure it was emptied into the Dumpster.

He regretted the action now, but it was done, and nothing could undo it.

He sat on the old mahogany chair, which moaned in protest. Curiosity made him reach for the tattered white binder. He flipped it open and read the first line.

He gasped and wheeled back from his desk as if burned. It was his sermon notes from the Gospel of John. It simply wasn't possible.

With his very own eyes Paul had seen the sanitation worker empty the Dumpster no more than two or three minutes after he'd emptied his garbage.

Leta Johnson.

Somehow she must have discovered what he'd done and gone after the sanitation truck and convinced them to let her have the binder.

As far as he was concerned, his secretary had overstepped the boundaries of what he considered her duties. She'd stretched the limits of her job description to the breaking point.

Furious in a way he rarely was, he marched across the yard and into the church, past the sanctuary and directly into his office.

Leta looked up from her computer screen when he entered the room.

"You're fired," he announced heatedly.

To his utter amazement she didn't so much as blink. "As I recall, you've resigned. In other words, you don't work here any longer. You can't fire me." Without missing a beat, she returned to her typing.

"You got into that Dumpster and—"

She glared at him above the rim of her bifocals. "I beg your pardon?"

"My sermon notes on John's Gospel."

"What about them?"

"I threw them out."

Her eyes widened momentarily with what looked like dismay, but she met his gaze straight on. "You're saying I did what?"

"Dug them out of the garbage."

"Oh, puhleese."

He'd worked with Leta for a lot of years, and never once had she used that tone of voice with him.

"Do you honestly believe I have the time or inclination to follow you around and check every bit of paper you toss? I can tell you I don't. As for your sermon notes, well, you're barking up the wrong tree."

All at once Paul felt incredibly foolish. His indignation had carried him this far but had quickly deserted him. He rubbed a hand down his face. Instead of chastising Leta, he should be thanking her for driving into the hills and finding him. Thanking her for serving faithfully as his secretary for these many years.

"I appreciate what you did this morning," he told her. "Driving to the campground was above and beyond the call of duty."

"Does this mean I can have my job back?" Leta asked with a soft smile.

Paul grinned and nodded. "Sure thing, but as you said, I don't have any right to be firing or hiring you."

Leta held up the envelopes, addressed to the church elders, that contained his letter of registration. "If anything mysteriously disappears into the garbage, it's going to be these."

Paul stared at the envelopes for a long time before moving into his own office. He sat behind his desk and looked about the room. It was as familiar and as comfortable as a favorite pair of old shoes.

He leaned back on the chair and closed his eyes. The last twenty-four hours had certainly been full. He'd written out his letter of resignation. Then he'd escaped into the hills and been called back to be with Madge Bartelli when she died.

When he opened his eyes, he found Leta standing in the doorway. "Madge?" she asked softly.

"Gone," he told her, unable to disguise his regret.

She nodded and swallowed once. Paul knew it was an effort for her not to break into tears. "I'm going to miss her," Leta whispered.

"We all will."

"Bethany phoned." She walked over and placed the pink message slip on his desk. "I wasn't sure what you wanted me to tell her."

His daughter was a dear, but she tended to overreact now and again. Her response, had Leta mentioned his resignation, didn't bear thinking about.

"What did you tell her?" he asked.

"That you'd been called out of town, but that I expected you back any time."

"Did she press you for details?"

"Is Bethany your daughter?"

"She worries too much."

Leta didn't say anything for the longest time. The silence between them was uncomfortable, almost as if it were anticipating something happening.

"You're feeling better, aren't you, Paul?"

He needed a moment to think about that. "Yes, I think I am. Being with Madge in the end helped. Good friends helped," he said, thinking of Steve Tenny.

"Prayer helped," Leta offered.

"I'm sure I've been on many a prayer list."

"I can't speak for anyone else, Pastor, but you've been on mine."

"Thank you, Leta." He opened his desk drawer and reached for a pen. "Two things," he said. "First off, is that invitation for Christmas dinner still open?"

Leta looked as if she were about to faint. She literally fell onto the chair. "Ah, I'm afraid the Tennys asked me to join them, and I've accepted."

"That's not a problem, they invited me as well. I'll phone Steve later and ask if he minds adding one more plate to the dinner table."

"There was something more?"

"Yes," Paul said, leaning back on his chair, relaxed now. Confident he'd made the right decision. "I've decided to submit my resignation after all. We'll need a replacement for me, effective next Sunday."

*   *   *

If Maureen kept worrying about Brian wanting custody of Karen, she was going to make herself sick. His sudden desire to spend time with his daughter, talking to Karen behind Maureen's back, making plans with her, all seemed to add up to one thing. He would soon apply for custody of Karen.

Maureen didn't know what to do.

She didn't want to plague her parents with her problems, but she couldn't go on like this much longer. Brian always could jerk her chain. Always could make her miserable.

Maureen waited until Karen was asleep and hoped her mother was awake when she punched out the button that predialed her parents' home phone.

It rang three times before a male voice answered. "Nichols's Riding Stables."

"Thom?" Dumbfounded, Maureen stared down at the telephone. She'd been avoiding him since their last conversation. He talked about forgiveness while all she could think about was revenge. Being with Thom made her feel petty and vindictive.

"Maureen? This is a pleasant surprise."

"But I didn't dial your number," she insisted.

He chuckled. "It seems we've had this telephone conversation before. You did dial it. Otherwise why would I have answered the phone?"

"But—"

"You've got me now."

She smiled. The sound of his voice worked wonders on her tired, achy muscles, especially her neck.

"Something's on your mind?"

How well this man knew her.

"It's Brian. I'm convinced he's going to fight me for custody of Karen."

Thom was silent long enough for her to know he'd taken her concerns seriously. "Are you sure you're not making a mountain out of a molehill?" he asked.

"I wish I were. The more I think about it, the more sense it makes. Brian hasn't seen Karen in over a year. All at once he's willing to pay attorney fees and fight like a bullmoose to have his daughter spend Christmas with him."

"Perhaps he's had a change of heart."

"If that's the case, one would think he'd pay me the back child support payments he owes me."

"Perhaps," Thom agreed. "Go on."

"He phoned Karen when he knew I wouldn't be home." She drew in a deep, steadying breath at the fresh wave of anger and frustration. "According to the terms of our settlement, all contact with Karen is to have prior approval from me."

"That seems pretty severe."

"He agreed to those terms," Maureen said, and knew she sounded defensive.

"All right, let's look past that. Brian contacted Karen without prior notice or approval from you."

"Yes." She could hear the panic level rise in her voice. "I don't know what he said to her. I could only hear what Karen said, but it sounded like, oh, I don't know, like he planned on showing her a wonderful Christmas."

Thom was silent for a time. "This worries you?"

"Of course it does. Don't you see? Brian's the type of man who only thinks about one person, and that's himself. If he's being good to Karen, there's a reason."

"People change, Maureen."

"Not Brian. The man is—" She bit off saying a choice word. "He's going to take Karen away from me. The more I analyze what's happening, the more I realize what he's doing. If he's looking to get back at me, there's no better way than through Karen."

"Why don't you ask him?" Thom suggested. "If you're that worried, and clearly you are, then call him right now and ask. Wouldn't you rather deal with the truth than suffer with speculation?"

"Ask Brian?" she repeated. It was probably the most dangerous thing she could do. "I can't do that. If he isn't already thinking along those lines, why give him the idea? You don't know my ex-husband. If he even suspects something would worry me, he'd play up on it and make me as miserable as possible."

"Maureen, you've been divorced a long time."

"What's that got to do with anything?"

"Brian's remarried."

"Yes, and he has a son, too, but that doesn't mean anything."

"I think it must. He's supporting a wife and his son and supposedly Karen."

"I sincerely doubt he's supporting anyone. Wanna bet he's home with the baby while wife number two brings in the paycheck?" She sounded cynical and bitter, but with damn good reason.

"Maureen," Thom said, dragging out her name in that thoughtful way of his, "have you given any more thought to what I said the other night?"

"About what?" She was stalling, not wanting to admit his words had hounded her ever since.

"Forgiveness."

"I don't believe it's possible, Thom. I have thought about it, almost constantly. But you have no way of realizing how much Brian hurt me and Karen."

"But I do," he countered. "I see it in your eyes when you speak of him. I look at Karen and wonder how any man could turn his back on his own daughter."

Maureen felt tears stinging the backs of her eyes.

"Where does it stop, Maureen?"

"What do you mean?"

"You phone the attorney about him with a list of wrongdoings. He contacts his attorney about you. Who suffers in all this?"

Maureen already knew the answer to this. She'd faced it that evening. "Karen," she said in a small, weak voice.

"You're hurting, too, but you need to realize that most of that pain is self-inflicted. Don't forgive Brian because he deserves it. Don't do it because he's asking you to pardon him for all the ugly, hurtful wrongs."

Maureen wouldn't live to see that day. "Don't worry, it'd never happen."

"Do it for you," Thom advised softly. "And for Karen."

"I'll try," she promised. He made it sound so easy, as if all she had to do was let nearly fifteen years of accumulated resentments roll off her back like rainwater off a mallard.

"Now if Karen's going to be with her dad, what are you doing Christmas Eve?" Thom asked.

"Nothing much." For a time she'd thought she'd join her parents, but they had already made plans with longtime family friends. They'd invited Maureen to join them, but she didn't want to intrude. She'd made an excuse, and they'd accepted it.

"Would you like to come out to the ranch?" Thom asked. "Paula and I would love to have you."

The offer was by far the most tempting one she'd had. "I'd like to, but . . ."

"What's holding you back?"

"I'd rather be close by in case Karen phones." Maureen didn't anticipate any trouble between father and daughter, but she wasn't taking any chances.

"You're sure?"

"Yes," she told him reluctantly, "but thanks for the invitation." The way it looked, she'd have a peaceful evening home by herself. That was fine. She could bake sugar cookies and decorate them for Christmas Day. If she got really ambitious, she just might whip up a batch of fudge.

They spoke for a few moments longer, and when Maureen hung up, she thanked whatever it was that had caused her to dial Thom's phone number instead of her mother's.

She knew she'd live through the horrors of the damned the minute her daughter drove off with her ex-husband if she didn't have some peace of mind on the subject. She reached for the phone book and looked up Brian's number. A woman answered. Maureen hadn't met Brian's new wife. The fact was, she pitied the poor woman.

"This is Maureen Woods," she said stiffly.

An awkward silence followed.

"Just a moment, please, and I'll get Brian."

A polite little thing, Maureen mused. She only hoped Brian didn't overly abuse her.

Her ex-husband came on the line almost immediately. "Maureen?" he demanded crossly.

"Yes."

"What do you want now? More money? Lawyers' fees? Or wasn't fifteen years of making my life hell good enough for you?"

Maureen nearly bit her tongue in half to keep from rising to the bait. "None of that," she said without emotion. "Just a question." However, getting the words out of her mouth proved to be damn near impossible.

"What?"

She closed her eyes and drew in a deep breath. "Do you or do you not intend to seek custody of Karen?"

Her words were followed by a short, static-filled silence. "Got you worried, do I?"

How he'd love to see her crawl on her knees and beg. Maureen was convinced he'd sell his soul just to see her squirm. At the moment she was prepared to do all three.

"Yes," she admitted, hoping none of the emotion bled into her voice. "I'm worried."

He hesitated, seeming to enjoy her discomfort, and then he said, "Don't be. We both know Karen's better off with you than me. I'll raise her if you want, but I doubt that you do."

With that he hung up the phone.

Chapter

★ ✱ ★

18

Catherine couldn't remember a time the Wilshire Grove Retirement Center looked more festive. Swags of evergreen were draped about the room and festooned with huge red bows of velvet. Several long tables were connected and covered with a lace tablecloth, the center's finest. A series of silver platters filled with a variety of homemade cookies graced the tables. The sterling-silver punch bowl was at one end and the matching coffee and tea service at the other.

Emily and Thelma, two of the most hardworking members of the library committee, stepped back and admired their handiwork.

"It's lovely," Emily said.

Catherine couldn't agree with her more. "I couldn't have done it without you two, and Joy."

Joy had seen to most of the wall decorations and had been at the center until all hours of the night. Catherine didn't know what time the resident service director had finally gone home. All she knew was that she'd gone up to her apartment close to eleven and Joy had assured Catherine that she was nearly finished. She'd promised to leave for home soon. But from the lush display of decorations, Catherine realized Joy must have been there half the night or longer.

The subject of her thoughts strolled in the door, wearing a bright smile. Of all that she admired about Joy Palmer, Catherine was most in awe of her inner strength. This business with Ted must have been painful and terribly disappointing, but each day, despite her own unhappiness, Joy had come to work with a smile on her face and in her heart.

"The decorations are beautiful," Catherine said enthusiastically, wanting Joy to know how much she appreciated the extra work the other woman put into the literary tea.

"I thought you promised to leave when we all went up to bed," Thelma reminded her.

"I did," Joy said, "but I just couldn't leave them alone." She scanned the room. "Has anyone seen Charles this morning?"

"He's been ready for the tea since before six," Emily told her.

"I'll drop my jacket and purse off in my office and be right back." She disappeared, and Catherine walked over to the table and fanned out the paper napkins.

"Are we going to start soon?" Charles strolled up beside her and asked impatiently. "I've been eyeing those chocolate chip cookies of yours all morning. Seems to me the man who's going to collect the donations might need a bit of nourishment beforehand."

"Are you asking me to sneak you a cookie, Charles?"

"You bet I am," he said, and winked at her.

Catherine pursed her lips together to keep from laughing. "I can't get over the change in you in the last couple of weeks."

"I got the very heaven scared out of me," he explained as he inched his hand toward the silver platter.

Catherine swiped at his arm. "Kindly keep out of the cookies. Now what do you mean, you had the very heaven scared out of you?"

"It's true. I'd say I got the hell scared out of me, only it was an angel who sat down next to me as plain as I'm standing here talking to you. Now I know what you're thinking, but I'm telling you right now, Catherine Goodwin, I saw an angel."

"A real angel?" Catherine had heard of angelic visitations, but she'd never experienced the phenomenon herself. "When?"

"It was one of those days when I was thinking about the war and all the good men we lost in battle. Some days I can't get the looks of those fighting men out of my mind."

It was difficult for Catherine to hear such words, but she nodded to encourage him to continue.

"Joy came and sat down next to me and took my hand, and there was something so gentle and sweet in the way she talked to me. It was the day your grandson . . . Jed, Fred . . . what is it now?"

"Ted."

"Right, Ted. He was with her, and he was watching her talk to me, and it seemed to me that he was sweet on her. Can't say that I blame him. If I was fifty years younger, I'd be wanting her myself."

"You said something about an angel?"

"Right." He reached for the chocolate chip cookie then and grabbed hold of it before Catherine could stop him.

"Sh-h," he said under his breath as he quickly placed the cookie inside his pocket. "No one saw." He straightened and looked around as if he suspected his actions had garnered attention. "Now back to the angel part. Joy left with your grandson, and I started to slip back into myself the way I do, when an angel sat down right where Joy had been."

"An angel? How'd you know it was an angel?"

"She. The angel was a she. Prettiest blue eyes I've ever seen. As blue as turquoise. Blond hair and wings, too, just the way I've always seen in pictures. I knew immediately she was an angel."

"Did she speak to you?"

"Ah, now that's the funny part. I think she did, but then I'm not right sure."

"What did she say?"

"First off she told me that life here in Wilshire Grove was a whole lot better than burying myself in the past, particularly if it had been so miserable. Then she said—"

"Now, Charles, I'm sure you thought—"

"Hush now," he muttered, cutting her off. "I don't know what you're thinking. I wouldn't have told you this much if the angel didn't mention you by name."

"Me?" Catherine flattened her hand over her breast.

"I swear it's true. The angel told me she didn't have a lot of time to be talking to me because she was on assignment."

"On assignment?"

"Yes, she claimed she was here because of you!" Having said that, Charles turned and walked away.

Catherine stood still for several moments while Charles's words sank in. The angel was there, on assignment, and because of her. Well, Catherine didn't want to be accused of disbelief, but if the angel had been there on her account, she hoped the poor dear knew what a terrible mess Ted had gotten himself involved in.

Catherine hadn't seen or heard from her grandson in several days and suspected that he was trying to avoid Joy.

"One of the authors has arrived," Lucille announced, her eyes alive with delight. "Shall I seat her in the dining room?"

"That would be perfect."

"It looks like your grandson is coming as well," Lucille told her.

"Ted?" Catherine turned around to discover him walking in through the double-wide glass doors.

He smiled warmly when he saw Catherine and hurried to her side. Gripping her gently by the shoulder, he kissed her cheek with a loud smack. "Say, what's going on around here?"

"We're having our literary tea." She didn't want to ask him what he was doing there in the middle of the day, but by the same token she was curious.

"Where's Joy?" he wanted to know, looking past Catherine. Without waiting for permission, he reached for a chocolate chip cookie.

"Ted!" she chastised.

"Wasn't that for me?"

"It most certainly was not."

"Sorry." But he sounded anything but. Catherine had rarely seen him in a more cheerful frame of mind.

"Do you know where I can find Joy?" he asked a second time.

"Why?"

"Because I need to talk to her. I'll explain everything to you later, I promise."

Catherine was of two minds. She didn't want Ted abusing Joy's heart, but she wasn't willing to lie to him, either. "Joy arrived a few moments ago. She's probably still in her office. But Ted, please, be good to her."

"I plan on doing that for a very long while. Thanks, Grandma," he said, and kissed her again. When her back was turned, he reached around her and grabbed a second cookie.

Joy yawned as she locked her purse in the bottom desk drawer. She couldn't remember the last time she'd been this tired. After the literary tea, she could relax. She straightened, and her gaze collided with that of Ted Griffin. He stood in her doorway, taking up nearly the entire space. He crossed his arms and his ankles and was smiling at her with a wide, cocky grin.

"Ted?" She resisted the effort to rub her eyes. First she was hearing voices, now she feared she might be seeing visions as well.

"Yup, it's me." He moved into the room and sat on the chair across from her. She had a new calendar ready for the upcoming year on the corner of her desk, and he reached for that. After flipping several pages, he looked up at her. "What are you doing April twenty-seventh?"

"April twenty-seventh?" she echoed. "I don't know. Why? Stop. Before you say another word, you'd better tell me what you're doing here." Standing required some effort. He had the most curious weakening effect upon her.

"First answer my question."

The man frustrated her to no end. She felt like tossing her hands in the air. "April. Nothing. I'm doing nothing."

"Great. How would you like to get married that day?"

"Sure, do you have anyone in mind? Or are you going to pull some poor, unsuspecting stranger off the street and ask if he'd be interested in marrying me?"

"I wasn't planning on anything that drastic. The fact is I was counting on you marrying me."

Joy had no trouble finding the chair. She toppled straight onto it. "You?"

"The way I figure it, April should give you plenty of time to get together everything you need for a fancy wedding. Talk to your mother, and if you need more time, let me know."

Joy couldn't have managed an entire sentence had her life depended on it. "Blythe?"

"Ah, yes, Blythe. I suppose we'd best clear up that subject once and for all. She came to me, explained that she was pregnant."

Joy sucked in her breath.

"Not to worry, I'm not the father."

"But . . ."

"I know. She was desperate enough to lie about it and then had a change of heart. For all her faults, Blythe isn't a bad person. She's made a few mistakes, but then we've all done that."

Joy nodded repeatedly.

"She knew I was in love with you."

"You love me?" The question was barely above a whisper.

"I generally don't propose to women I don't love, with the one exception of Blythe. Now may I go on?"

"Please."

"To her credit, Blythe realized she couldn't continue with the lie. It took a tremendous amount of courage for her to break matters off when she did."

"How's she doing?" Joy asked.

Ted's gaze grew sober. "She's decided to have the baby. I went with her to a couple of local adoption agencies yesterday. She isn't sure what she wants to do yet. I was pleased that neither agency pressured her. She's agreed to counseling, which will help. I told her we'd help her any way we could."

"We'd help her?"

"Do you mind?"

"No." Joy smiled, more than willing to be generous to the other woman in spite of the problems she'd caused.

"So," Ted said, and heaved a sigh, "what's the verdict? Are you willing to put up with my irritating habits, love me for the next fifty to seventy years, and bear my children?"

Joy had the most incredible urge to cry. Nodding enthusiastically, she reached for a tissue. "I love you so damn much," she choked out between sobs, and then noisily blew her nose.

Ted's grin was slow and sensual. "Yes, I know."

She waved her hand at him, and he laughed.

Joy didn't know who got up first, but soon they were in each other's arms. Their kiss was deep and heady. By the time they broke apart, Joy was convinced April wouldn't be soon enough to suit either of them.

"You're wearing the bangle," he said, his chin resting on the crown of her head.

"I wondered if you'd notice. And of course I'm wearing it. Not only is it the most beautiful piece of jewelry I own, but it was the only thing I had of you."

"You had my heart."

"I . . . but I didn't know that."

"Do you know it now?"

"Oh, yes." She had the distinct impression that it would take the rest of their lives for her to fully appreciate this man she loved.

Bells rang in the distance, but with such enthusiasm they sounded through the building like a fire alarm. Several of the office staff stood in the doorways and looked into the foyer.

"What in the name of heaven is that?" Ted asked, frowning.

Joy laughed and linked her arms around his waist. "That must be Charles. Someone just made a donation to the library fund."

"Are you sure you'll be all right here by yourself?" Karen asked Maureen. She stood in front of the living-room window with the draperies pushed aside, waiting for her father.

"I'll be perfectly fine."

"What are you having for dinner?" Karen asked, as if this were of major importance.

"I don't know yet, but don't you worry, whatever I eat will be fabulous."

"Cordon bleu," Karen suggested.

Maureen laughed. "Just where did you hear about that?"

"From Paula. That's what she and her dad have every Christmas Eve. You take chicken breast and pound it out real thin and then you add a slice of ham, but it has to be a really thin slice, and then you add the cheese and you roll it all up and bread it."

The kid was amazing. "And when did Paula give you the recipe?"

"Ah . . ."

"You've been talking long distance again."

"Mom, we haven't seen each other in . . . forever. We're friends. You can't separate us like this and not expect us to talk. But don't worry, we've been taking turns calling each other, and we only discuss the things that are most important."

"Like sharing recipes?"

"Right," Karen answered.

"You don't happen to have Paula's number on speed dial, do you?"

"Yes, why?"

So that explained how she happened to reach Thom when she'd dialed her mother. "Never mind."

The draperies flew back into place. "Dad's here," Karen said, grabbed her overnight bag, and flew toward the door. Her hand was on the knob when Maureen stopped her.

"I'll go out with you. I want to talk to him," she said, and reached for her sweater.

Karen cast her mother a wide-eyed appeal. She bit into her lower lip, then said, "Mom, please don't do this."

"All I want to do is talk," Maureen assured her.

Karen groaned.

Maureen ignored her and stepped outside. Brian had parked at the curb and was standing next to his car.

He eyed her wearily. "Maureen."

"Brian." She buried her hands deep inside the sweater pockets.

"I suppose you're wondering what time I'll have Karen back to you in the morning?"

"Yeah." That was as good a place to start their conversation as any.

"Is ten too late?" he wanted to know.

"That'll be fine."

"Can we go now?" Karen asked, apparently eager to be on her way. Maureen couldn't blame her, given the situation.

"In a minute," she said.

"You can get in the car if you want." Brian looked at Maureen as if he half expected her to challenge him.

"I won't keep you, but—"

"I appreciate it." His hand was on the car, and he was ready to turn away.

"Brian," she said quickly. The rest of the words were so thick in her throat, she didn't know if she could ever get them out.

"What now?" he demanded impatiently. "Isn't it bad enough that you pester me at all hours of the night?"

"I have something to tell you," she said. "Something important."

"What? That you've hired a new attorney? I suppose you're going to ask for a raise in your child support payments?"

"No."

"Then just say it, will you? I haven't got all night."

"All right." She gathered her composure. "Basically, I want you to know that I'm sorry."

Even in what little light the moon afforded, Maureen could read her ex-husband's confusion. "Sorry? What the hell for?"

Actually, she wasn't sure where to start. "Everything, I guess. I made the divorce more difficult and painful than it needed to be. And since then I've done whatever I could to make you miserable."

"Yeah," he agreed, leaning his weight onto one leg, "you might say that."

"The problem was, in the process I made everyone else miserable, too, including Karen and myself. I got so bogged down in hating you that I forgot about living my own life. I want you to know I regret that."

"You don't hate me anymore?" he asked as though he weren't sure he should believe her.

"No. I can't afford the luxury."

He laughed as though amazed. "You know, Maureen, you were always a beautiful woman."

"Thank you. I fell in love with you once. You're Karen's father, and if for nothing else, I'll always be grateful to you for fathering her."

"You know, I'm not half bad. Oh, sure, I have a little trouble keeping a job now and again, but there are a hell of a lot worse men in this world."

"That's true. Now shall we call a truce?" she asked.

"A truce?"

She held out her hand to him. He shook it once, then stepped back almost as though he were afraid it was all a trick and something would soon explode in his face.

"Since we can't be married, let's make the best of being good parents to Karen," Maureen suggested. "And maybe someday you and I might even discover we can be civil to each other again."

"Not a bad idea. Can I go now?"

"Sure."

He placed his hand on the car door, then paused. "Did your attorney put you up to this?"

"My attorney?"

"Yeah. Did she tell you to bury the hatchet and let bygones be bygones?"

"No."

Karen rolled down the car window and folded her arms in the opening. "No, her new boyfriend did," she explained, leaning the upper half of her body out the window.

"Boyfriend? You mean to tell me you've got yourself a boyfriend? I'd say it's about time, Maureen. You should have let me know you were ready to date. I could have set you up with one of my friends."

Maureen smiled. "Thanks, Brian, I'll keep that in mind."

He opened the door, and Karen scrambled out of the way. "Bye, Mom!" she yelled, stretching over the backseat in order to wave.

Maureen returned the gesture. It hadn't been easy. She'd nearly choked on the apology. It wasn't forgiveness. Not even close to that. Forgiving Brian would take time and effort, but she'd taken the first ministep in that direction.

With a bounce in her gait, she returned to the house. It seemed bright and cheerful, even with a Christmas tree that was only half decorated.

A string of lights were wound from top to bottom, and Karen had gotten the first couple of boxes of ornaments on the lower branches, but the rest was up to her. She'd never let it go so long before, but it was a perfect task for Christmas Eve.

She had put on some Christmas music and brought out the rest of the decorations when the doorbell chimed. Tinsel was draped around her neck and a box of wrapping paper was tucked under her arm.

"Merry Christmas," Thom and Paula shouted simultaneously when she opened the door.

"You couldn't join us for Christmas Eve, so we came to you," Thom explained. He carried a serving dish, his hands buried deep inside thick pot holders. Paula had a large bowl.

"Chicken cordon bleu," Paula explained as they stepped into the house. "I gave Karen the recipe. And my special garden salad, minus tomatoes."

"Here, put it in the kitchen," Maureen instructed them, clearing a path.

"Oh, great, you haven't decorated your tree yet," Paula said after setting the salad on the table. "Can I help? I'm really good at this sort of thing." She didn't wait for Maureen to answer but raced back into the living room.

Thom set the hot dish down in the center of the table, and before he had a chance to remove the pot holders, she was in his arms. Standing on the tips of her toes, she kissed him, using her mouth and tongue in ways that made her regret they weren't alone.

Thom's arms were tight about her. His words were little more than a breathless murmur. "I'll cook your dinner every night if you promise to reward me like that."

Maureen smiled and raised her lips back to his. "You've got yourself a deal."

Paul straightened the trio of angel figurines that adorned his living-room window. Christmas Eve. He looked out into the darkness and felt a renewed sense of happiness. It was the season, yes, but more. He felt as though a heaviness had been lifted from his heart, from his life.

His hand held back the curtain, and a pair of headlights cut through the night in the distance. He suspected it was Bethany and Eric. They'd phoned to say they'd be over for Christmas Eve with some important news. Eric had been waiting better than a year for his promotion, and Paul guessed this was what they were about to celebrate.

He'd set the table himself and brought out Barbara's finest lace tablecloth and the china dishes. Three years of accumulated dust had made it necessary for him to wash them before he placed the delicate plates at the dinner table. He couldn't remember if he was supposed to run the fancy tableware through the dishwasher or not, so to be on the safe side he'd washed each one by hand.

The task reminded him of all the nights he'd dried dishes for Barbara. The happy times they'd shared as a couple had been many. Unfortunately he'd allowed his memories of her to be connected with her illness.

All he remembered was her pain.

All he could think about was his ongoing frustration and the intense feeling of helplessness.

All he could think about was his loss.

Like Madge, she was free of cancer now. Healed by the glorious hand of God. Not as he'd expected. Not as he'd wished. But healed.

Sure enough, the headlights slowed as they neared the house. Eric parked the car at the curb, and Paul watched as his son-in-law walked around the car and helped his wife out the passenger door. Eric took her hand, and some unspoken message passed between the two.

Not knowing they were being watched, Eric and Bethany kissed. Paul smiled, knowing well how it was to be deeply in love. His daughter and son-in-law were a good match.

He held open the door and greeted Bethany with a big hug. The two men exchanged hearty handshakes.

"I can't believe it's Christmas Eve already," Bethany said.

"I can," Eric muttered. "You would too if you'd gone out to do any Christmas shopping this morning."

"That's what you get for saving everything for the last moment," Bethany chastised, but without any real conviction. She sniffed the air. "What smells so good?"

Paul wiggled his eyebrows. "Your favorite fast-food chicken."

"Daddy, you didn't." Just the way she said it indicated that she hoped he had.

"Since the cook refused to name those eleven herbs and spices, I had no choice but to buy us a big bucket of the original recipe. I figured I might as well pick up all the fixings while I was at it."

"But I was going to cook for us," she protested, although she didn't look the least bit disappointed.

"You still can if you want." But if Paul were a wagering man, he'd have bet his daughter would be content with chicken, mashed potatoes and gravy, and the other goodies he'd bought.

"Who set the table?" Bethany asked, looking into the dining room.

"Me," Paul answered. "There isn't anyone else, is there?"

"No," Bethany agreed, but she seemed surprised. "The house looks great."

"We decorated it together, remember?" She really shouldn't need to be reminded. Paul couldn't understand why she studied him with such amazement.

"What?" he asked when he could bear her scrutiny no longer.

"Something's different," she said. "You're different. I don't know. It's as if you're really listening now, really seeing."

"I didn't before?" He stuck his index finger in his ear and jerked it back and forth a few times. "Maybe I should have my hearing tested."

"Are you two going to jabber all night?" Eric asked, carrying the bucket of chicken into the dining room. "I don't know about the rest of you, but I've developed an appetite."

"I'm starved," Bethany said.

"Come to think of it," Paul added, "so am I."

The three carried the varied cardboard serving dishes to the table. They sat down, joined hands, and said grace. It didn't take them long to load up their plates.

"You bought enough food to feed a family of eight," Bethany commented, a chicken leg poised in front of her mouth.

"One never knows when feeding Eric," Paul teased, and winked at his son-in-law.

Eric was good-natured enough not to retaliate.

"As I recall, there was something important you wanted to tell me," Paul reminded them.

Eric and Bethany exchanged happy glances. "Do you want to tell him?" Bethany asked her husband.

Eric grinned broadly and gestured toward his wife. "You go right ahead."

Bethany reached for a paper napkin and wiped her fingers free of grease. "Well, Dad," she said, and the happiness seemed to bubble up inside her like fizz in a soda can. She reached for Eric's hand and gripped it hard. "We're going to have a baby." Having said that, she started to cry, but these were happy tears, and her eyes were quickly dry. "We couldn't be more pleased."

"Bethany, Eric," Paul said, amazed he hadn't guessed sooner, "that's wonderful news."

"The baby's due on August tenth."

Paul's gaze found his daughter's.

"Yes, Daddy, I know. That was Mom's birthday. It's like God is returning to me a small part of Mom. I know that sounds silly, but I believe the baby's a girl. I've already chosen her name. Bobbi Jo. The baby name book explained that Bobbi is another name for Barbara."

"And the Jo is for Bethany Jo," Eric added.

"It's a beautiful name. Your mother would have been so pleased." Paul was pleased himself. Although his daughter and Eric had been married four years, he hadn't thought much about grandchildren. Frankly, he rather liked the idea.

"And on the off chance we happen to have a son," Eric said, "we've decided on Anthony Paul."

"Anthony Paul," Paul repeated. He was so proud, his shirt buttons were in danger of popping open. "That has a nice sound to it."

Bethany shared a smile with her husband. "We thought you two proud grandpas would think so."

The front door opened. "Are you expecting anyone?" Bethany asked.

"No." Paul pushed his chair away from the table and stood.

"Where is everyone?" a familiar voice called from the entryway.

"Joe." Paul hurried into the other room.

His son hugged him as if it had been weeks instead of days since their last meeting.

"I thought you were spending Christmas with Annie and her family?"

"We'll be together every Christmas for the rest of our lives. Her parents are great, but you know, it just didn't seem right not to be with you."

Paul slapped his son across the back. "Come and join us," he urged. "We were just sitting down to a four-course dinner."

"I'm so hungry I could eat an elephant."

"I suspect," Eric said under his breath to Paul, "that a chicken will do just as well."

Chapter

★☆★

19

Goodness *stood next* to the church organist and watched as the woman's fingers gracefully played out an often sung Christmas carol. Mercy and Shirley would be joining her soon. Then the three of them together would meet Gabriel.

The prayer ambassador's gaze rested on Reverend Paul Morris, and a renewed sense of love filled her for this special man who'd been through so much. He'd walked through the valley of the shadow of death and had struggled to find a path to the other side.

Paul's children—Bethany with her husband, Eric, and Joe—were in the front pew. They watched their father with a deep sense of love and appreciation.

When the singing was finished, Paul stepped to the pulpit and smiled at his audience. The message was short and simple, yet it packed a powerful punch. Goodness doubted that anyone could sit and listen to this humble man and not be deeply affected. She mused about the great preachers through the ages and wanted to believe that someday Paul Morris's name would be counted among them.

It didn't seem likely, however. Following instructions, Leta Johnson had arranged for a speaker for Sunday morning worship service. Paul had rewritten his letter of resignation and mailed it out himself.

As far as Goodness knew, this was the last time Paul Morris would be preaching. To anyone. Frankly, she wondered what Gabriel had to say about that. The archangel had seemed to believe Paul would change his mind. Personally, Goodness didn't want to be around when Gariel discovered the truth.

Goodness looked around the crowded church and saw several familiar faces. Steve Tenny sat with his wife, Myrna. The two smiled at each other as if sharing a private joke. Although Goodness had no way of reading their thoughts, she guessed at what they were thinking. Paul was his old self again, and they marveled at the changes they saw in him.

Leta Johnson sat on a side pew, her Bible spread open in her lap. She stared up at Paul with a look of almost pure adoration.

Goodness's gaze narrowed, and she studied the church secretary a second time. Then she slowly shook her head. "Naw," she said, unwilling to believe what she was seeing.

"What are you shaking your head about?" Gabriel's voice was powerful enough to move them both outside the church building. Goodness landed on her feet in front of the church steps.

"Gabriel?" Goodness said quickly, in an effort to disguise her distress. "Aren't you early?"

"No, Mercy and Shirley are late. What are those two up to now?"

"Ah . . ."

"Never mind. I can see you've got plenty of questions regarding Paul."

"Well, yes, but they can wait until another time, if you prefer."

The archangel studied her closely. "Why the glum look?" he asked, frowning.

Goodness knew it would do no good to hide anything from Gabriel; he found out everything sooner or later anyway. She'd rather get this over with now and be done with it. "He mailed out his letter of resignation," she announced flatly.

"I know." He said this as if it were of no concern.

"But . . ." She was dumbfounded, not knowing what to say. "I thought . . . assumed that he would continue preaching."

"He does, magnificently, too, for many years to come."

Goodness sat down on the top step. "You've completely lost me. I failed, Gabriel. Reverend Paul Morris has decided to give up the ministry," she announced miserably.

"Is that a fact?"

Goodness noted that Gabriel didn't seem all that distressed by the news.

"You didn't fail, Goodness. I'm very pleased with how hard you worked."

"I didn't fail?" She lifted her head.

"No. Paul's going to take a year's sabbatical. During this time he's going to write a book."

"On the Gospel of John," Goodness said enthusiastically. She should have guessed as much, should have realized old Gabe had something up his sleeve. No wonder he hadn't complained overly much when she'd rescued Paul's sermon notes from the garbage truck. She'd actually saved the day. He was probably thinking of ways to reward her.

"No." The archangel dashed her hopes with a solitary word. "Paul's book will touch many lives, influence great thinkers of his time, and become a national best-seller."

"He isn't writing about John?"

"No, but the subject is near and dear to his heart. Death."

Frankly, Goodness was disappointed. "Wow, what a downer."

"Trust me, his book will give those grieving such hope that the sting of death will have lost some of its power."

"I suppose that's all right, but I do think he should think about good ol' John. I don't know about you, but I was impressed with his notes."

"Perhaps someday," Gabriel said noncommittally.

Goodness did feel better. She cared deeply about Paul Morris, although she'd never quite forgiven him for missing her one glorious miracle.

"What about Bethany's baby?" Only archangels and a few chosen others were allowed to look into the future, but it seemed to Goodness that they were notoriously selfish with the information.

Gabriel hesitated. "A baby girl."

"Yes." Goodness tightened her fist and then shoved back her elbow in a gesture of elation.

"You were hoping for a girl?"

"Yes." She folded her hands and pleaded with him. "I hope Bobbi Jo's born August tenth."

The beginning of a smile touched the archangel's mouth. "She'll make her arrival a week early, which works out very well because of Joe's wedding."

"Oh, yes, I nearly forgot about Joe and Annie."

"They'll live a long, happy married life, and so will Paul and Leta."

Goodness's eyes grew round. "Get outta here. Leta and Paul Morris?"

"Yes. You accurately read that look. Leta's been sweet on Paul for over a year now. It'll take him another year to work through his grief, write the book I mentioned, and then return to his full ministerial duties at Applegate Christian. Then and only then will he be ready to love again. Leta, as you're well aware, is a patient woman."

Goodness's low spirits shifted. "This really hasn't worked out so poorly then after all."

"No, Goodness, I'm pleased with your efforts with Paul, and other than a few minor shenanigans, you behaved maturely."

"Do you think I might be sent out routinely on prayer requests?" she asked excitedly. "I've learned my lesson, really I have."

"So I can see. But that decision isn't mine to make."

She would have pressed him further if Mercy and Shirley hadn't arrived just then, both breathless, their wings fluttering.

Mercy pressed her hand over her breast. "You wouldn't believe the day I've had. The next time someone mentions the words *love* and *marriage,* I'm headed for the nearest storm cloud. You can't begin to imagine what I've had to deal with in the last few days."

"No one promised you a rose garden," Gabriel reminded the prayer ambassador. "From what I understand, matters became quite involved."

"Involved? Is the pope Catholic? First off, Blythe tricked Catherine's grandson into a marriage proposal."

"They know all that," Shirley interrupted impatiently. "Tell us what happened this evening."

"You want me to skip over the very best parts?" Mercy asked, her eyes wide with disbelief. "Do you have a clue of what it took to convince Blythe to admit the truth?"

"You convinced her to tell Catherine the baby wasn't Ted's?" The question came from Gabriel and had the ring of challenge in it.

"Not entirely on my own, mind you," Mercy was quick to add, her eyes avoiding Gabriel's.

"But Blythe did confess the truth?" Goodness wanted to know.

"Yes, and soon afterward Ted proposed to Joy."

"Wonderful." Shirley clapped her hands together.

"Where are they now?"

"The two are spending Christmas Eve with Catherine."

"How sweet," Shirley said with a romantic sigh.

"Perhaps you'd care to explain what old Charles said about a certain angel visiting him," Gabriel said sternly.

"Ah . . . well . . ."

"I seemed to hear something about you speaking to Joy Palmer and instructing her to keep a party dress. What was that all about?"

Once again Mercy cast a flustered, helpless look at Gabriel. "I think I might have helped Charles."

"Were you assigned to him?"

"No." Mercy swallowed tightly.

"That's what I thought. Now about the dress?"

"It's the most perfectly beautiful dress you've ever seen. Joy looked absolutely spectacular in it. She was going to return it to the department store, and I knew she was going to regret that," Mercy explained, talking so fast the words blended together. "I was working hard on Blythe, and I knew she was close to confessing the truth. It didn't make sense for Joy to take back a party dress when she was going to need it so soon."

"Soon?"

"New Year's Eve party at Ted's company," Mercy said, in the know. "He got the invitation last week."

"So you've taken to reading his mail?" Gabriel asked in a deep, rich voice that spoke of disapproval.

"Not always," Mercy admitted. "Just sometimes."

"I see." The archangel didn't look any too pleased.

"They're going to marry, aren't they?" Mercy wanted to know.

Once more Gabriel hesitated before revealing the future. "Ted and Joy. Yes."

"Children?"

"Three. Two boys and a girl, in rapid succession. They name their daughter Catherine."

"What about Blythe and her baby?" The question came from Shirley, which made sense. As a former guardian angel, Shirley was often concerned about children's welfare.

"Blythe will deliver a healthy baby boy this coming summer. After counseling and a good deal of soul-searching, she'll decide to give the child up for adoption. Blythe will personally choose his parents, and the two will exchange letters for the first year. Giving her son a good home was probably the most unselfish act of her life. It helps mature her."

"Does she marry?" Goodness asked. It seemed only right that Blythe find happiness.

"Yes, to a friend of Ted and Joy's. They'll introduce them two years from now, and the couple will marry after a whirlwind courtship. Blythe and her husband will have two children."

"So everything turned out well in the end."

"It wasn't the end," Gabriel corrected, "but the beginning."

"That's so romantic," Mercy said, and sighed. She rested her cheek on the back of her hands and floated several feet off the ground.

"I can't get over how good we are," Shirley said, and buffed her nails against her chest. "I mean, when we first started out, who would have believed we'd meet with such unabashed success?"

"Not I," Gabriel was the first to agree. "I was sure each one of these assignments was far more complicated than any of you were capable of handling."

"The key to our success," Shirley informed him primly, "is that we work so well together."

"That's it," Mercy agreed, crossing her arms and wearing a smug look. "We're willing to help each other."

"Is that right," Goodness said, her arms folded over her chest as well. She tapped her foot just so they'd remember exactly how little help she had gotten from her two best friends. "I seem to recall that the two of you were at the Forum while I was stuck with Paul, who completely ignored me."

"Of course, Goodness had a more difficult assignment," Shirley said, rushing to get all the words out.

"That she did," Mercy agreed.

"Tell me about Karen and her mother," Gabriel asked, apparently looking to sidetrack the three before they broke into an argument.

"Well, Karen's spending the night with her dad."

"Is she enjoying herself?"

"Yes. Brian's new wife is a gentle creature, and Karen's half brother is as cute as a bug's ear. Karen's crazy about him. I overheard Brian suggesting that once Karen is a little older, she can baby-sit for them."

"Sure, he thinks he doesn't need to pay his own daughter." The cynical remark came from Mercy.

"You might be right about that," Shirley added in a whisper.

"What about Maureen, Thom, and Paula?" Gabriel asked next.

"They're having a good time. After dinner, they finish decorating the tree, then Thom convinces Maureen to take a ride with him and Paula. He drives around to the parade of homes decorated for Christmas. The same route he took with the girls that Friday night."

"What I want to know is how Maureen met a man as perfect for her as Thom?" Goodness asked.

Shirley clasped her hands behind her back and whistled. "Don't look at me," she said when Goodness focused her attention on her. "Really. All I did was place the brochure at Maureen's disposal."

"Rather pointedly, as I recall," Goodness reminded her.

Gabriel frowned. "There was a little something about mixed-up phone calls, as I remember."

"Yes, well, that was just a little thing, don't you think?"

Gabriel ignored the question. "Go on," he instructed, gesturing toward Shirley. "I'm curious as to what's happening between Thom and Maureen."

"I am, too, but what I still want to know is how, out of all the stables in the world, Shirley found Thom's. He's helped her through every hurdle. I can't believe that the Maureen Woods we first met is the same woman who stood before her ex-husband this evening and apologized."

"I was rather proud of her myself," Shirley admitted. "It took real courage to face Brian and admit she was wrong."

"Raw courage," Goodness amended. "She couldn't have done it without Thom's encouragement."

Gabriel cleared his throat. "Moving on, let's discuss—"

"Moving on?" Mercy looked up at the archangel. Slowly her gaze met Goodness's, and then Goodness's wide gaze traveled to Shirley.

"Could it be?" Goodness whispered to her friends, "that our very own Gabriel, the renowned archangel, isn't beneath a little manipulation of his own?"

"How else do we explain Thom and Maureen meeting?" Mercy wanted to know.

"How else do we explain a whole lot of other matters?" Shirley raised the question suspiciously.

"Thom and Maureen will marry this summer," Gabriel said, ignoring them. Goodness noted that he didn't need to be prodded to explain the future this time. She guessed he was grateful to turn the subject away from himself.

So Gabriel had arranged for Thom and Maureen to meet, Goodness mused. Would wonders never cease? Apparently not.

"Maureen will give up her job with the bank and take over the bookkeeping duties for Thom," he told them. "When she sees the mess his ledgers are in, she'll think he married her just because she knows how to balance a checkbook."

"What about Paula and Karen?" Shirley asked.

"They remain the best of friends even as stepsisters. They'll have some loud fights in their teenage years, but nothing will ever stand between them. Not other friends, not boys, not school.

"When Karen said they'd decided to be friends for life, she wasn't joking. The two were able to help each other in ways their parents couldn't."

"That's wonderful," Shirley said.

"What about Thom and Maureen?"

"They have two more children. Two little boys, a year apart. Thom loves his daughters, but the afternoon his first son is born, Thom Nichols will shed tears of joy."

"Does Maureen ever learn to ride?" Mercy asked.

"Not really. She leaves the horseback riding to Thom and the girls."

"I can't say that I blame her," Shirley said, and it was clear to

Goodness that her dignity had taken a beating on her one venture atop a horse.

"We did good, don't you think?" Goodness asked Gabriel. She felt worlds better knowing that Paul hadn't turned his back on the ministry.

"You three amaze me."

"Can we do it again?" Shirley asked eagerly.

"New York City," Mercy suggested. "Now *there's* a city that could use a few more angels."

"You're getting ahead of yourself," Gabriel cautioned. "Let's take one Christmas at a time."

They started to rise skyward, the four of them together, drifting effortlessly upward toward the realm of glory. Heavenly music floated down to greet them. Songs unlike anything sung on earth. Thick white clouds parted, ushering them home. It was a night to celebrate.

Touched by Angels

To Gaylynn Hoffman
My very own personal angel

Chapter

★ ✦ ★

1

The young man wore a staple in one ear. Brynn Cassidy tried not to stare as he paraded past her and slouched down in the desk in the farthest corner of the classroom. His nose was decorated with a safety pin. The fact that his hair was cut in a Mohawk style and dyed orange shouldn't faze her. She'd been told what to expect.

Manhattan High School wasn't St. Mary Academy, the parochial girls' high school where she'd taught for the last two years. But teaching here was an opportunity she couldn't let pass her by. She'd accepted this position to test her theories and gain experience in dealing with students from a disadvantaged neighborhood.

Next, a young lady entered the room in a miniskirt, blouse and no bra. Her hair, pitch-black and stringy, covered her far better than her choice of outfits. She glanced around, shrugged, and claimed the seat closest to the door as if it were important to make a fast getaway.

The room filled quickly. The school building itself was said to be dilapidated and run-down, but that didn't trouble Brynn. St. Mary Academy was a turn-of-the-century structure with high ceilings and lovely polished wood floors that smelled of lemon oil.

When Brynn learned Manhattan High in the Washington Heights area had been constructed in the early 1950s, she'd expected it to be an improvement, but she was wrong. Like so many other schools, Manhattan High had been forced to make some difficult budget choices. Thanks to three failed school bond levies, modernizing the classrooms was on the low end of the priority list.

"Will everyone kindly take a seat," Brynn instructed nervously. She stood in front of the class and was ignored, which wasn't surprising since the bell had yet to ring.

Looking for something constructive to do, she walked over to the badly chipped blackboard and wrote out her name.

The bell rang, and several of the kids stopped talking long enough to indicate their irritation at being interrupted. The level of conversation increased once the bell finished.

Brynn returned to the front center of the room and waited. She'd learned early in her teaching career never to outshout her students. It only made her look foolish, and it didn't work. After five full minutes of being ignored, she went to the wall and flipped the light switch a couple of times. This technique had worked elsewhere but had only a mild effect upon this class. The level of talking decreased momentarily while several glanced her way, then quickly continued their ongoing conversations.

Brynn decided she had no option but to wait them out. It demanded the longest fifteen minutes of her life to stand in front of that classroom until thirty people voluntarily gave her their attention.

It might have taken longer if the boy, Hispanic from the look of him, hadn't raised his right hand and snapped his fingers. Ten or so other Hispanics stopped talking and turned around on their seats. An African American followed suit, and several of the others clustered together went silent.

The class had divided itself along ethnic lines, Brynn noted. The Hispanics sat in the front, the African Americans chose the back.

Once silence reigned, Brynn stepped forward. "Good morning," she said with her brightest smile. "My name's Miss Cassidy."

"Why ain't you married?"

"Because I'm not," she answered simply, preferring not to get trapped in a conversation about herself. "I'm your teacher, and—"

"You're new, ain't you?"

"Yes," Brynn answered politely. "As you already know, we're involved in an experimental program called Interdisciplinary Learning."

"That doesn't sound like something a nice girl like you should be teaching," one of the boys called out.

Despite herself, Brynn smiled. "We'll be spending three hours together each afternoon, exploring senior English, world history, and social science. You'll notice how the classes are grouped along parallel lines."

"Is she speaking English?" one girl whispered loudly, leaning toward another.

Brynn decided it would be best to explain the concept in simpler terms. "The classes we'll be studying are connected by subject. We'll read *The Diary of Anne Frank* for the English portion, the history section will involve the study of World War II, and in the last part of the session I'd like to discuss the justification for war and other value clarification."

"All three hours will be spent with you?"

"That's right," Brynn said. "You'll know me better than any other teacher, and by the same token, I'll know you. I'd like it if we could work together as a team."

"If we're going to be spending this much time with one teacher, then it only seems right that you tell us something about yourself first," the Hispanic boy who'd quieted the class said. Since she owed him a favor, she agreed.

"What do you want to know?"

"How long you been teaching?"

"This is my third year."

"If she lasts the first week," someone suggested under his breath.

"I'll last," Brynn assured them. "I'm too young to retire and too stubborn to quit."

"Where'd you come from?"

"Rhode Island."

"Why'd you decide to teach here?"

"She's a fool, that's why," someone answered for her.

"That's not true," Brynn countered. "As I explained earlier, we're involved in an experimental program that's being sponsored by the federal government. I was asked to participate."

"Why'd you do it?"

The questions were making her decidedly uncomfortable. "Part of the agreement would be that a portion of my student loan would be forgiven."

"Forgiven?"

"That's the word the government used."

"Where'd you teach before?" a Chinese girl asked, her gaze shyly meeting Brynn's.

"St. Mary Academy. It's a private school for girls near Rochester."

"La de da," one of the boys said in a high-pitched voice. He stood, dropped his wrists, and pranced around his desk.

"Hey, could you set me up with one of those nice Catholic girls?"

Brynn didn't bother to answer.

"Do you color your hair or is it naturally red?"

"It's auburn," Brynn corrected, "and it's as natural as it comes."

"What do you think, dummy, with a name like Cassidy? She's Irish, can't you tell?"

"Dummy?" Brynn repeated, and then added in a *Home Alone* voice, "I don't think so. If he were dumb, he wouldn't be a high school senior. This brings up something I consider vital to this class. Respect. I won't tolerate any name calling, racial slurs, or put-downs."

"You been in girls' school too long, Teach. That's just the way we talk. If Malcolm here wants to call Denzil a nigger, he's got a right 'cause he's a nigger himself."

"Not in this classroom he won't. The only thing I'll ask of you in the way of deportment is mutual respect."

"I don't even know you, how am I supposed to respect you?"

It was a good question and one Brynn couldn't slough off.

"Especially if the only reason you decided to take this job was so you could be forgiven for something you did to the government."

"That's not the only reason I took the job," Brynn pressed, "I want to teach you to dream."

"Excuse me?" A girl with her hair woven into tiny braids all over her head sat upright. "You're making us sound like babies."

"I'm not suggesting naps," Brynn explained. "How many of you know what you're going to do after you graduate from high school?"

One hand went up, from the same Hispanic youth who'd helped her earlier.

"Your name is?"

"Emilio Alcantara."

"Hello, Emilio. Tell me what your dreams are."

"I got plenty of those. I dream about Michelle and Nikki and . . ." His friends made several catcalls, and Brynn smiled and shook her head.

"I'm talking about the future. After high school, five years down the road. We all need a dream, something to pin our hopes on, something that gives us a reason to wake up in the morning."

"You mean a dream like Martin Luther King?"

"Yes," she said enthusiastically. "An ambition to do something, travel somewhere, or be something."

"Why?" The boy who asked had caught her attention earlier. He seemed indifferent to everything that was going on around him. A couple of the kids had said something to him, but he'd ignored them as if they weren't there or, more appropriately, as if he weren't entirely there himself. Briefly she wondered if he were on drugs.

"Why?" Brynn repeated. "Because dreaming is a necessary part of life, like eating or sleeping. Sometimes we just forget about it, is all. We'll be exploring more about this later, but I guarantee you one thing, by the end of this quarter, there'll be plenty for you to think and dream about."

"You know," said the girl who'd claimed the desk closest to the door, "you might be all right, but it's going to take some doing, getting used to a teacher who doesn't look any older than one of us."

"She isn't married, either. Say, Teach, do you want me to set you up?" Emilio asked. "I got an older brother who could use a chick like you."

"Thanks, but no thanks," Brynn answered, reaching for her attendance book. "Now that you know about me, it's time for me to learn something about each one of you."

"But we don't know you!" two or three protested in turn.

Brynn held the book against her breast and sighed. "What other information do you need?"

Questions were tossed at her in every which direction. She put a stop to them with a wave of her hand. "Listen, I'll give you the basics and then we'll have to get started. My first name is Brynn."

"How many kids in your family?"

"Eight."

"Eight!"

"She's Irish and Catholic, ain't she?"

Brynn ignored the comment. "I'm the fourth oldest and the first girl. My oldest brother is thirty-three and my youngest sister is sixteen." She lowered the grade book and called out, "Yolanda Aguilar."

"Here." The Hispanic girl raised her hand and waved enthusiastically.

Brynn looked at Yolanda and made a notation next to the girl's name. "Emilio Alcantara is here," she said, making a second notation.

"What are you writing down about me?" Emilio demanded. He sat up on his chair and craned his neck toward her as if that would be enough to read what she'd written.

"I said you sat in the front row and revealed leadership characteristics."

"I do?" He sounded surprised.

"What'd you say about me?" Yolanda asked.

"That you're energetic and personable."

"How'd you know that?"

"Yeah, how'd you figure that about Yolanda?" another boy demanded, then leaned over to the student at the desk next to him. "What's personable mean?"

"Sh-h, I'm next and I want to know what she's gonna say about me."

"Modesto Diaz," Brynn called out, looking at the youth above the grade book.

He curled his upper lip and snarled at her. "Yo."

Brynn added her comment to the book.

"What'd ya say?" Modesto insisted, straightening. He was halfway out of his seat. "I gotta right to know since you told the others."

"I wrote down that you have a flair for the dramatic."

"What's that mean?" Modesto asked Emilio under his breath.

"The hell if I know," Emilio complained. "She's gonna be one weird teacher."

By lunchtime Brynn was convinced Emilio was right. She was completely out of touch with their world. Her vocabulary, which she'd never thought of as especially advanced, served to confuse her students. Half the morning was spent repeating in simpler terms what she'd said previously.

She'd no more than handed out *The Diary of Anne Frank* and briefly described to them Anne's story when the bell rang for their first break. The classroom emptied so fast, one would think the school was on fire.

Brynn sat down at her desk and exhaled sharply, weary to the bone. This was her first day in an inner-city high school, and she was going to need help—lots of help, and she didn't expect it to come in the form of the PTA.

Bowing her head, she murmured a simple prayer, asking for patience and guidance. She yearned to teach her students to dream, to look to the future with enthusiasm. She hungered for them to see beyond the troubles they faced day in and day out and reach for the stars, and she wanted to be the one to show them the way.

Brynn's whispered prayer fluttered past the chipped blackboard, echoed silently through the scarred halls, as it winged its way toward heaven. The request soared, swiftly spanning the distance between man and God. Carried on the brisk winds of faith, guided by devotion, navigated by love, it arrived fresh and bright at the very feet of the Archangel Gabriel.

"Brynn Cassidy," Gabriel repeated slowly as he flipped through the cumbersome book, marking the entry. He was writing when he glanced up to find Shirley, Goodness, and Mercy standing directly across the desk from him. He'd never seen the three look more—he hated the term—angelic. Their wings were neatly folded in place and they smiled serenely as if the world were at their feet.

"It's that time of year again," Goodness reminded him, grinning broadly.

Gabriel's hand tightened around the quill pen. Heaven help him, he was going to be left to deal with these three lovable troublemakers once more.

"Time of year for what?" he asked. Gabriel was playing dumb in a stalling effort. For the past two years this trio of prayer ambassadors had visited earth, working their own unique brand of miracles. A sort of divine intervention run amuck.

"We'd like to try our hand in the Big Apple," Mercy explained with limited patience. It was apparent she was eager to get her assignment and be on her way. "We've been looking forward to working together again," she reminded him primly. "One would assume that with the success of the past two years we'd have proven ourselves beyond question."

"We don't mean to be impertinent," Goodness inserted, glaring at her fellow prayer ambassador, "but I find myself agreeing with Mercy."

"Brynn Cassidy," Shirley repeated softly, reading over Gabriel's shoulder.

Gabriel deliberately closed the huge book, cutting off Shirley's view. The last thing he needed was for the former guardian angel to take a hankering for this particular assignment.

The students of Manhattan High would require a far more experienced angel than Shirley. Why, her tender heart would be mush by the end of a week, working with this group of adolescents. Frankly, Gabriel didn't expect Brynn Cassidy to last long herself.

Gabriel knew all about the young teacher. Her mother and grandfather had been praying for her for several years. As far as Gabriel was concerned, Brynn Cassidy was far more suited to teaching the proper young ladies of St. Mary Academy. Manhattan High was a graveyard of lost souls. An unseen storm cloud had settled over the school, feeding on tears yet to be shed and broken promises. Brynn's humble faith was like a newborn lamb placed in the midst of ravenous wolves. She'd quickly be devoured. Naturally Gabriel would do what he could to aid her, but one ill-equipped prayer ambassador would hardly be sufficient.

"Brynn needs me," Shirley said, looking him squarely in the eye.

"She needs an army. I don't mean to discourage you," Gabriel said, feeling mildly guilty, "I'm sure we'll find a more appropriate assignment for you. A less complicated request," he muttered more to himself than to Shirley.

As he recalled, a prayer request had come in that morning from a teenage girl in Boston who needed a date for prom night. Surely Shirley could scrounge up a decent young man. As for Goodness and Mercy, why, there were any number of less demanding requests with which to occupy them.

"Give me a minute," he said, flipping through the unwieldy book, finding a page, and running his index finger down the large number of entries. "I'm sure I'll come up with something appropriate for each of you."

"No arguments?" Goodness asked, her eyes wide with surprise.

"Wow, maybe we have proven ourselves."

"I want to talk to Goodness about Hannah Morganstern," Gabriel said, his brow creased with contemplation.

"Yes," Goodness answered excitedly.

"Her family owns one of the most popular delis in all of New York," the archangel went on to explain.

Goodness and Mercy looked at each other and squealed with delight. The two joined hands and danced a happy jig around his desk, kicking up their heels.

"What about me?" Mercy asked, breathless with excitement.

"Jenny Lancaster," Gabriel said decisively. "She moved to New York from Custer, Montana, three years ago, hoping to make a name for herself on Broadway."

"Has she?"

"No," Gabriel said with a sigh of regret. "It's time to go home, only she can't bear to face that. You see, she doesn't want to disappoint her family, and I'm afraid she's stretched the truth and told them things that weren't altogether true. You're going to have to help her make the decision."

"I can do it."

"Without moving the Statue of Liberty?" Gabriel demanded.

"That's kid stuff," Goodness muttered.

"Maybe so, but is Rockefeller Center safe?"

The two found little humor in his question. It was then that Gabriel noticed that Shirley had disappeared.

"Where's Shirley?"

Goodness and Mercy glanced over their shoulders. "I haven't a clue."

"I didn't see her leave."

Gabriel had a sneaking suspicion he already knew where the prayer ambassador had disappeared to. "Wait here," he instructed impatiently. He raised his massive arms and with one wide, sweeping motion parted the clouds of heaven and descended from paradise to the mundane world.

He found Shirley right where he suspected: in an inner-city class-room, keeping a close watch on a young, inexperienced school-teacher.

Brynn finished her lunch and poured herself a cup of coffee. Stand-ing at the window, she looked out over the concrete jungle that made up the city.

St. Philip's, the cathedral located across the street, had once been the pride of the diocese. The stained-glass windows, depicting the Stations of the Cross, had aged badly over the years. A flight of con-crete steps led to the eight-foot-tall double doors. The church was a magnificent piece of Gothic architecture, but like Manhattan High, it had fallen upon harsh economic times.

When Brynn had first been approached about this assignment, she'd visited New York City and loved it. There was a rhythm to the city, a musical beat that had set her heart to racing.

In her mind's eye came a picture of prosperity and abundance. Not of wealth or riches in the monetary sense, but of purpose. The feeling had stayed with her in the days that followed, and when she'd penned her name to the contract, Brynn had felt instinctively that she was doing the right thing.

Following the break, Brynn headed down the crowded hallway. Several students leaned against their lockers in passionate embraces. This was a foreign element to Brynn, since she'd attended a parochial girls' high school as well as taught in one. It was a bit of a shock to discover how friendly students were allowed to get in the school hall-way.

A ruckus broke out at the end of the corridor, and several heated words in Spanish flew at her like fiery darts. Brynn's knowledge of the language was limited, but she was well aware the two boys weren't exchanging pleasantries.

After making her way to the problem, she found Emilio Alcantara and an African American she didn't know staring each other down. A crowd had circled around the two.

"Is there a problem here?" Brynn asked, maneuvering into the tight circle.

"If you know what's good for you, Teach, you'd better leave," Emilio advised.

"I can't do that, and now I suggest you two boys give it up and go about your business. Fighting isn't going to solve anything."

The black boy looked at her with such unadulterated hatred that for a wild second Brynn was caught speechless. She'd never had a student, or anyone else, look at her in quite that way.

A shiver ran up her spine when she noticed both boys had knives. She grabbed Suzie Chang, the shy girl from her class, by the shoulder. "Get help immediately," she ordered, her heart in her throat.

Suzie took off running.

By then the Hispanic youths had lined one side of the hallway and the blacks dominated the second half. The two ethnic groups glared at one another, waiting for an excuse, any excuse, to fight. The atmosphere was explosive, the tension as tightly strung as a fiddle.

Without thinking, Brynn positioned herself between the two boys. Her head was spinning and she felt lightheaded with fear. "Stop," she ordered in her most authoritative voice, but the request sounded hollow even to her own ears.

The sound of footsteps running toward her was so welcome, Brynn nearly collapsed with relief. A male teacher and a janitor exploded onto the scene, and the knives disappeared as if by magic. Emilio and the other youth looked as if they were the best of friends. Emilio wrapped his arm around the black youth.

"What's happening, bro?"

"What's going on here?" Doug Keast, the teacher, demanded, looking to Brynn.

"Emilio and this young man were involved in an exchange of words. Everything's under control now. Thanks for your help."

"Knives?"

Brynn hesitated, not wanting to rat on Emilio but at the same time unwilling to lie. "They both drew out knives, but—"

"I don't need to know anything more than that," Doug barked, escorting both youths to the principal's office. "I'll need you to make a statement."

"What's going to happen?" Brynn asked, scurrying behind Doug and Emilio. A second male teacher appeared to escort the other boy.

"I'm gonna be suspended," Emilio said, glaring at her as if she'd turned traitor on him. "I thought you were different," he spat out. "You ain't no different than any of the other teachers." His dark eyes, leveled at her, were filled with animosity.

"Listen here, Emilio, it wasn't me who got involved in an altercation."

"A what? You know, if you're going to teach English, the least you could do is learn to speak it first."

"A fight," she said, losing her patience. She was half trotting in order to keep up with Doug's long-legged stride. Her fellow teacher was making haste for Mr. Whalen's office.

"You know the rules about knives on school property," Doug told Emilio.

"What knife?" the youth demanded. "She was seeing things. I didn't have any knife, and neither did Grover, ain't that right, bro?"

"The new teach needs glasses," Grover claimed, sounding as if they'd been strolling through a bed of wildflowers.

"Tell him, Miss Cassidy," Emilio said, staring at her. "There wasn't any sign of knives, now, was there?"

"If you expect me to lie on your behalf, I won't do it," Brynn told him in no uncertain terms. "And if you're both expelled, then—"

"They'll be suspended for three days," Doug interrupted.

"Then you have no one to blame but yourselves," she finished.

"I ain't coming back," Grover announced in chilling tones. "School ain't gonna help me or my homies. I'm outta here, understand?" He jerked his elbow free from the teacher and strolled out the door, letting it slam in his wake.

"Good riddance," the man murmured.

"I'll talk to him," Brynn said, going after Grover.

She hadn't taken two steps when Doug Keast stopped her. "Let him go."

"But—"

"He's right. Grover's nothing but bad news." Doug looked to Emilio as if to suggest the Hispanic boy fell into the same category.

"Emilio's different," Brynn insisted. "Grover's choosing to give up, to fail. Emilio's got a future."

"Yeah," Emilio muttered, pulling himself free of Doug's hold. "Some future. First you tell me what a great leader I am and then you get me kicked out of school." Having made that little speech, he slumped down on the worn vinyl sofa outside Mr. Whalen's office.

"Did you see the knives?" Gabriel asked Shirley gently. "They were real, and the risk to Brynn is equally grave. She could have been seriously hurt."

"The woman's in profound need of heavenly intervention," Shirley said forcefully. "In other words, this teacher needs me."

"Ah . . ." Gabriel hated to be the one to break the news, but Shirley was out of her league. He'd hoped the prayer ambassador would see it for herself, but now he wasn't so sure.

"I know what you're thinking," Shirley said, eager to prove herself. "You think I'm in way over my head."

"My thoughts were running along those lines," Gabriel admitted.

"I believe I could help Brynn," Shirley insisted, and then stiffened her shoulders. "You're the one in charge of handling the prayer assignments, and I have no option but to accept your decision, but I want to help Brynn Cassidy teach her students to dream. I want to stand at her side when their eyes light up with discovery, and I especially long to be there when she tells them about faith in God."

"There are other teachers who need you," Gabriel assured her. "And they aren't trapped in a poor neighborhood school."

"I see," Shirley whispered, hanging her head in defeat.

"Perhaps another year," Gabriel suggested.

"Perhaps." The word was so low, it dragged against the floor.

Gently patting the discouraged angel on her shoulder, Gabriel escorted her back to heaven, where Goodness and Mercy awaited their return.

"I'll find another assignment for Shirley in a moment," he promised, "but first, I want to introduce Goodness to Hannah Morganstern."

Chapter

★ ☆ ★

2

"Hannah who?" Goodness asked, looking puzzled.

"Morganstern," Gabriel supplied. "The prayer request came in from Hannah's mother and grandmother. They want her to make a good marriage." He opened the cumbersome book that listed the incoming prayer requests and smoothly folded back the page. Running his index finger down a list of names, he paused when he located Hannah's.

Gabriel smiled, pleased with himself. This request would be a simple matter and would quickly appease the novice prayer ambassador. The sooner Goodness was back where she belonged, the better for all concerned.

As it happened, Hannah was close to becoming engaged to Carl Rabinsky, the rabbi's son. Carl was a fine, upstanding young man with a bright future.

Hannah's family was delighted that their daughter had chosen such an outstanding marriage candidate. A professional matchmaker couldn't have come up with a better choice. Goodness would soon recognize how advantageous such a marriage would be for Hannah. Naturally the prayer ambassador would accept full credit for the match, which was fine with Gabriel as long as she left well enough alone.

By his best estimate, Gabriel would have Goodness out of harm's way within a day or two. Heaven knew he wouldn't rest until all three were back where they belonged. There was no telling the trouble they could rouse in the Big Apple. Gabriel cringed involuntarily at the thought of Shirley, Goodness, and Mercy loose on the unsuspecting souls of New York City.

They did try. He'd give them that much. The three angels were dear hearts, but frankly they were trouble with a capital T. There was no end to the mischief they managed to muster each Christmas. The season was hectic enough without having to deal with those three.

"When can I see Hannah?" Goodness asked eagerly.

"When are you going to tell me more about Jenny Lancaster?" Mercy asked, crowding her way between him and Goodness. The smallest of the three juggled her elbows until she'd jockeyed herself into position. "I'm looking forward to meeting Jenny."

"It's my turn," Goodness reminded her friend sternly.

"Be patient," Gabriel advised the two. At times he felt like a referee at a hockey match. "Goodness, let me take you down to meet Hannah."

"I want to come," Mercy insisted.

"Me, too." Shirley was determined not to be left behind.

Gabriel hadn't planned on making an expedition out of this. He'd thought it would be a simple matter to point out Hannah to Goodness, then introduce her to Carl. They'd be back before either of Goodness's friends had time to miss her. He was about to reassure Mercy and Shirley of this when he noticed that the three had looped their arms together. They stood before him with a determination that would have shook Moses before that unfortunate incident on Mt. Sinai.

"All right, all right," he grumbled under his breath. These particular prayer ambassadors had a way about them that foiled him at every turn. Only this year, he was simplifying matters. Their assignments were all straightforward requests that would bring them back to heaven in record time. Nothing complicated. Nothing involved. Assignments each one should be able to arrange in record time. This Christmas, Gabriel promised himself, wouldn't be like the past two.

Stepping away from the others, the archangel raised his massive arms and with one sure movement parted the massive clouds of heaven. A thin layer of mist remained, and gradually he was able to make out the earth below. Soon the four of them narrowed in on the big city. Skyscrapers punctured the sky. The top floors of the twin towers of the World Trade Center came clearly into focus. Then he viewed the landmark Brooklyn Bridge, followed by Times Square.

"This is New York City?" Goodness breathed in awe.

"My heavens, what's that?" Mercy asked, pointing to the street below.

Gabriel grinned. His timing couldn't have been better. They'd arrived in time to witness Macy's Thanksgiving Day parade. A giant balloon replica of a popular comic-strip dog floated far above the street, steered by several silly-looking adults dressed in elf costumes.

"It looks like some kind of parade," Shirley answered before he had a chance to explain.

A marching band, the trombone players with their instruments aiming skyward, blared a lively rendition of an easily recognizable Christmas ditty. A fierce pounding of drums added to the excitement of the music.

"This is wonderful," Goodness said, and spread-eagled herself across the top of a blossom-laden float. Six men dressed as toy soldiers stood guard over an open treasure chest filled with a variety of brightly wrapped gifts in gold and silver paper.

"You wanted to meet Hannah," Gabriel reminded her, hiding a smile. Goodness's eyes were as round as a two-year-old child's.

"In a minute," Goodness told him. It was apparent she was more interested in watching the parade than in meeting her young charge.

With a stiff-kneed walk, one of the toy soldiers marched to the end of the float. A fairy princess appeared, with dainty wings strapped to her back, and scooped up handfuls of candy. Smiling, she tossed them into the cheering crowd.

"You call those wings?" Mercy asked on a disdainful note.

"We're here to meet Hannah Morganstern," Gabriel felt obligated to remind the three.

"I'm ready," Goodness announced, reluctantly tearing herself away from the dazzling scene.

"If we must," Mercy added with a decided lack of enthusiasm.

"Do you think Brynn Cassidy's here?" Shirley's gaze scanned the thick crowds that crammed the cement sidewalks. "What about the kids from the school? They'd come, wouldn't they?"

"We're supposed to meet Hannah, remember?" Gabriel reminded Shirley. He should have known it would be a mistake to bring the others. "There's Hannah now," he said in an effort to divert their attention. He motioned toward a group of parade watchers standing along Central Park West.

"Hannah's the petite woman with the blue angel scarf tied around her neck." Gabriel had a soft spot in his heart when it came to the gentle Jewish woman. She reminded him of Rebecca, the young woman God had chosen for Abraham's only son.

"She's lovely."

Gabriel agreed. "Hannah's the only child, born later in life to a devoted couple. Ruth Morganstern prayed faithfully for many years for a daughter."

"Leah Lundberg did the same," Mercy reminded Gabriel. "I don't understand why God makes some couples wait."

"It's not for us to question."

"I know," Mercy agreed, "His timing is always perfect."

"Getting back to Hannah," Gabriel tried again. "The Morgansterns have raised their daughter well. They couldn't be more proud of her, and rightly so. Hannah is well loved by many."

"Do you mind if Shirley and I entertain ourselves for a few moments?" Mercy asked, and her eyes twinkled with mischief. Gabriel noticed the angel was staring at the reader board above Times Square.

"You can go on without us," Shirley insisted.

"No way. Listen, you two. Shirley . . . Mercy," Gabriel stuttered, wanting to stop them before they vanished. Unfortunately he was too late. He clenched his jaw and turned to Goodness.

"You don't have a thing to worry about," Goodness assured him. "They can take care of themselves."

That was what Gabriel was afraid of.

He was about to go after Mercy and Shirley himself when Goodness tugged at his sleeve. "Tell me what you know about Hannah Morganstern. You said her mother and grandmother are looking for Hannah to make a good marriage."

"Yes," he muttered. He would need his wits to make this assignment sound more difficult than it was.

"Well, if that's the case," Goodness muttered, her shoulders heaving with a deliberate sigh, "I certainly hope she isn't interested in the young man she's with. It's perfectly obvious they aren't the least bit suited."

Gabriel's attention went back to the street corner where he'd last seen Hannah.

"What's wrong with Carl Rabinsky?" he demanded.

"Just look."

"Carl, couldn't we please stay a bit longer?" Hannah asked. She pleaded with him with her eyes, hoping she could find a way to change his mind. Carl had agreed to attend the Thanksgiving Day parade with her, but they'd barely arrived and already he was anxious to leave. She knew he was having trouble with the headmaster at the Hebrew academy where he taught and had been preoccupied most of the day.

"Ten minutes more, then," Carl conceded indulgently. His gloved hand squeezed hers. "I'm sorry, but I told you earlier that this just isn't my thing."

"I know." Hannah was grateful he'd consented to come. She only wished he could enjoy the festivities as much as she did. Hannah found the merrymaking contagious—the children, the excitement, the wonderful silliness that surrounded this time of year.

"Oh, Carl, look," she said, pointing toward the huge float making its way down the wide street. "It's a scene from the *Nutcracker Suite*."

Carl smiled tolerantly and pointedly glanced at his watch. "Five more minutes," he announced under his breath. "If you want to see more of the parade, you can watch it on television."

Television. Never. Hannah refused to allow his stick-in-the-mud attitude to spoil her fun. Standing on the tips of her toes, she peered down the bustling street, hoping to catch a glimpse of what was coming next. The distinct tones of an approaching band floated toward her.

Unable to see, she edged her way into the crowd until she was wedged against the waist-high barrier to the street. She stayed there until the marching musicians passed, applauding their efforts. The tall, distinguished-looking man standing next to her whistled boister-ously. Hannah looked up at him and smiled warmly. Their eyes met, and he returned the friendly gesture.

The man looked vaguely familiar, but then it wasn't uncommon for Hannah to see someone she thought she knew. Working in the family-owned, kosher-style deli, she met literally hundreds of people on a daily basis.

His eyes were a deep, rich shade of coffee brown. They sparkled with delight as he looked down on her. He had a kind face, appeal-ing but not particularly handsome. His hair needed to be trimmed, but that gave him a rumble-tumble look that she found endearing. It was apparent he was some kind of businessman; she could tell that much from the way he dressed and the way he stood. Besides, if he frequented her parents' deli, then chances were he worked in one of the office buildings close by.

"Do I know you?" he asked, frowning slightly.

"I'm Hannah Morganstern," she said. "Most people recognize me from my parents' deli."

"Of course. Your father serves the best pastrami in town." He held out his hand to her. "I'm Joshua Shadduck."

"Hello, Joshua." The noise level made it difficult to carry on a con-versation.

They shook hands, and Hannah glanced over her shoulder, look-ing for Carl. He wasn't there. She scanned the crowd once more, cer-tain he wouldn't have left her intentionally. Carl would never do that, yet he was nowhere in sight. Anxious now, she stood on her tiptoes and looked around.

"Oh, dear," she whispered, and bit into her lower lip.

"Is something wrong?" Joshua lowered his head close to her so she could hear him.

"My friend. I'm afraid we've gotten separated."

"That happens in crowds like these."

"I know, but . . ." She continued to study the huge throng. The crowd was moving, milling about. "I didn't mean to leave him behind." Carl would be worried and flustered. If she ever hoped to talk him into attending another parade, he'd be sure to remind her of this.

"I'll help you look," Joshua offered.

"You don't need to do that." She was the one to blame. If she hadn't been so impatient to see what was ahead, she wouldn't have lost Carl.

"Tell me what he looks like," Joshua suggested. Since he was head and shoulders taller than she, his chances of finding Carl were far better than her own.

"Let me think," she mumbled. She went with the most obvious: his clothing. "He had on a black wool overcoat."

Joshua leveled his eyes on her, amusement bracketing the sides of his mouth. "Hannah, every man here has on a black wool overcoat."

"Yes . . . I know. He's five ten or so, and . . . he's probably frowning. He only came because I wanted to see the parade, and he's probably annoyed with me for disappearing like this."

"A frowning man, five ten, in a black wool overcoat."

Their eyes met once more, and for no reason Hannah could explain, they both started laughing.

"He's probably given up on me and left," she conceded, and glanced longingly over her shoulder, not wanting to miss the rest of the parade. "I should probably go back myself," she said with regret.

"Why? Your friend can find his own way home, can't he?"

"Yes, but . . ."

"Stay," he urged. His hand cupped her elbow, his touch light and encouraging. His eyes smiled with warmth and pleasure, something she'd found sadly lacking in Carl. Her friend had only tolerated the merriment. Macy's parade was one more thing Carl considered frivolous and impractical. He often mentioned the overwhelming cost of such a production. To Carl's way of thinking, this money would be better spent feeding the hungry or aiding the homeless.

Hannah had no argument to offer. The parade would go on no

matter how wasteful Carl found it to be, and she could see no reason not to enjoy it.

"Oh, look," she said, pointing down the street at the oncoming float. She glanced at Joshua and discovered that he viewed the winter festival creation with the same keen enjoyment and wonder that she did.

One lazy snowflake drifted down from the lead gray sky. Another soon followed.

"Snow!" Delighted, Hannah held up her hand to catch a fluffy flake. It melted in the palm of her hand.

"It's a perfect conclusion to the parade, don't you think?" Joshua asked. Pressed against him as she was, Hannah couldn't help noticing how warm and close he was.

"Is it over? Already?" She didn't want it to be.

"Do you have to hurry back?" Joshua asked. "We could take a short stroll in Central Park and enjoy the snow."

It went without saying that she shouldn't. Her family would be waiting for her. They assumed she was with Carl, not some strange man she barely recognized. Her father had always been protective of her. She was his jewel. Hannah remembered how pleased her parents had been when she'd first started dating Carl. The fact that he was a rabbi's son added to their endorsement of the young man.

"A stroll in Central Park," she repeated, and then before she could change her mind, she nodded. Her willingness to spend time with him, a man who was little more than a stranger, would be frowned upon by everyone concerned.

"Goodness," Gabriel warned, "don't even think about it."

"About what?" The fact that the archangel was traveling with her had cramped her style considerably.

"I know what you've got up your sleeve."

"What?" Archangels knew so little about romance; what else was she to do? Gabriel thought Carl Rabinsky was the perfect husband for Hannah. Anyone with half a brain could see how ill suited the young couple was. Carl was a determined man, sincere in his faith. Unfortunately he'd fallen into a common trap. He was big on religion and weak on faith.

"I can see what you're thinking and I'm telling you right now, it isn't going to work," Gabriel continued, disapproval beaming from his piercing eyes. "Joshua Shadduck is an important attorney. The two have nothing in common."

"Joshua is Jewish, isn't he?"

"Yes, but that has nothing to do with the issues here. Goodness, listen to me. You're stirring up a hornets' nest if you continue in this vein. I absolutely forbid it, do you understand?"

"Yes, but—"

"There're no buts about it." Gabriel's brow was knit with a thick frown. He opened his mouth and Goodness was convinced he was about to argue further with her when a breathless, but elated, Shirley arrived.

"I found Brynn Cassidy," the other angel announced gleefully. "She's with Suzie Chang, one of the girls from her class."

"We're discussing something important here," Goodness said. She refused to let Shirley interrupt her now. Not when she was about to make an important point. She glared at the archangel. "Didn't you notice Joshua and Hannah together? It's as plain as the wings on your back that they're right for each other." Anyone with eyes would recognize how lonely Joshua was. Success wasn't all it was cracked up to be. It seemed to her that he'd come to this realization himself recently. As far as Goodness could tell, Hannah Morganstern complemented his life, and she wasn't about to let Gabriel tell her otherwise.

"What I'm saying," Gabriel insisted, "is that you must leave well enough alone. You think I didn't notice the way you manipulated Hannah and Joshua? I'm not blind. You practically steered her right into him."

Goodness released a pent-up sigh. Dealing with Gabriel often required persistence. "I realize you find this difficult to believe, but I'm something of an expert in matters involving the heart. Remember last year?"

"I'm not likely to forget it," the archangel muttered. "I was nearly sent back to singing with the choir because of you three."

Goodness ignored his comment, which she was sure was a gross exaggeration.

"Promise me you'll keep your hands off of Hannah and Joshua," Gabriel warned, "otherwise I'll have you restringing harps for the rest of your days."

The threat was an empty one, and Goodness knew it.

"Did anyone hear me?" Shirley asked excitedly. "I actually located Brynn Cassidy. Don't you realize what a miracle that was in this crowd?"

"I heard you," Gabriel told her with a sour look. "Miracle or not, you won't be working with Brynn Cassidy. The schoolteacher needs far more help than you can offer. You can't work with Brynn and those kids from the high school. I have another assignment waiting for you," Gabriel insisted with a hard edge to his voice.

"But—"

"It's a take-it-or-leave-it situation."

Goodness feared that Shirley was about to blow it. She was relieved when the other angel snapped her mouth closed. At times, Shirley could be downright argumentative. If Shirley made the mistake of debating this Brynn Cassidy issue, the archangel just might pull all three of them out of New York City. Goodness didn't want that to happen just when matters were beginning to look promising.

Without being obvious, she scanned the dispersing crowds, hoping to catch a glimpse of Hannah and Joshua. She found them strolling through Central Park, deep in conversation. The two were oblivious of everything around them. They made a striking couple, she mused, immeasurably pleased with herself. Archangels might be high-and-mighty creatures, but they knew little of dealing with humans and love. When it came to affairs of the heart, Goodness was far more knowledgeable than Gabriel. The problem, and admittedly it was a big one, was convincing him of that.

Joshua wasn't sure what had happened to him. He'd suggested this walk in the park with Hannah for purely selfish reasons. The Thanksgiving Day parade had been enjoyable, but it hadn't been nearly as much fun until Hannah had joined him.

He remembered her with a clarity that surprised him. She was the daughter of the deli owner. When he'd claimed her father made the best pastrami in town, he hadn't been exaggerating. Over the last few years he'd visited the deli a number of times, but generally he had his lunch delivered. Hannah might well have been to his office.

Hannah was a delicate creature, beautiful in ways that struck a man's soul. She wasn't like the crisp, business professionals he knew and worked with on a daily basis. She inspired him with her gentle goodness. Although he'd never met the man she was with—Carl, if he remembered his name correctly—already he found he didn't much like him. If Joshua had become separated from Hannah in a crowd, it would have taken a lot more than a little congestion for him to stop searching for her. Hannah hadn't said a lot, but it was obvious Carl didn't enjoy parades.

Joshua had taken Hannah's hand while strolling through the park. The snow had long since stopped, but the afternoon remained crisp and cold. A perfect winter day.

The moment their hands linked, Joshua experienced a faint stirring of emotion. Faint stirring, nothing, he mused with a bleak smile. It felt as if someone had punched him in the stomach with a pipe iron.

He wondered if this was the woman he'd been searching for all these months. He certainly hadn't expected her to be the daughter of a deli owner. It didn't matter, he decided. Who was he to question fate? They'd met, and being with her, laughing, joking, talking, had felt instinctively right. Never had he been more comfortable with anyone.

It embarrassed him, the way he couldn't stop staring at her. She had such beautiful eyes, but then everything about Hannah was beautiful. She was guileless and genuine, and when she looked up and blinked, Josh swore he could see all the way to her soul.

"We've been talking all this time and I never asked where you work," Hannah commented.

"I'm an attorney." He would have mentioned the name of the law firm, one of the most prestigious in Manhattan, but he didn't want to sound as though he were bragging. Knowing Hannah, he doubted that it would impress her. More than likely she wouldn't recognize the name of the firm.

"A lawyer." She said this as if the information distressed her.

"You don't like attorneys?"

"No, it's not that. I think there are some wonderful attorneys, only . . ."

"Yes," he prodded.

"My parents were recently involved in a frivolous lawsuit, and my dad's convinced the real culprits in the case were the lawyers. I'm afraid he's developed something of a prejudice, but I don't think that will last long."

"Good. I'd hate to get off on the wrong foot with your family."

At the mention of her parents, Hannah looked at her watch. "Oh, dear," she said anxiously. "I didn't realize how late it was." She took several steps backward. "Thank you for a wonderful time. I'm sorry to rush off like this."

She'd turned and was speed-walking away from him before he'd had time to react. "Hannah," he called.

She spun around.

"I'd like to see you again."

Her eyes were wide, and she seemed to hesitate. Joshua decided it was best not to press her.

"Don't worry," he said. "I'll stop in at the deli and we can talk about it then."

She nodded abruptly, and it was plain she was in a hurry to get away.

"If it'll reassure you, I'll avoid mentioning I'm an attorney."

Her beautiful eyes brightened with a soft smile before she hurried out of the park. Joshua buried his hands in his pockets and ambled along the walkway toward Cherry Hill Fountain. He kicked lazily at burnt orange-colored leaves.

Joshua found himself smiling broadly. His patience had paid off. For nearly thirty years he'd been waiting to meet a woman like Hannah Morganstern. To think all this time she'd been right under his nose. He threw back his head and laughed. The sound of his delight echoed through the park.

Hannah hurried into the apartment on top of the family deli, stripping the blue scarf from her neck.

"I'm home."

"Thank heaven you're home; I was worried, you're so late," her mother said, planting her hand over her heart as she stepped out of the kitchen. "Your father and I didn't know what to think when Carl phoned and asked if you'd returned safely."

"The parade was wonderful," Hannah said.

"What happened with Carl?" Her father stood with the morning paper clenched in his hands. He studied her over the top of his spectacles.

"I don't know," Hannah told them, walking into the kitchen. The smells of turkey and sage, pumpkin pie and applesauce, that greeted her caused her to pause and inhale deeply. Her stomach growled, reminding her how hungry she was.

"Carl claims you disappeared into the crowd."

"I wanted to get a closer look at the floats," Hannah explained as she lifted the lid off a cast-iron kettle. Broth simmered with a mixture of savory herbs floated on the slowly churning surface.

"There's nothing to worry about now that you're back safe and sound," her father muttered, studying his daughter as though he expected something of her. Hannah knew exactly what her family was hoping. They wanted Carl to ask for her hand in marriage.

"Carl said he'd be by later," Ruth Morganstern said, and shared a secret look with her husband of many years. The exchange confirmed Hannah's suspicions.

"We both think the world of Carl," her father told Hannah unnecessarily. "He's a good man."

478 ★ Debbie Macomber

"Dependable," her mother added.

"Honorable."

"A righteous man." Her mother nodded for emphasis.

Hannah offered them both a shaky smile and headed toward her bedroom. She didn't want to discuss Carl, not when her head was spinning from her time with another man. "I'm going to change my shoes and then I'll be back to help you with dinner."

Her father looped his arms around Ruth's shoulders. "Take your time," her mother called out after her. "Dinner won't be ready for some time yet."

Inside her bedroom, Hannah slumped on the edge of her mattress. It would be impossible to tell them about meeting Joshua now. He was the man who caused her heart to sing. She couldn't disappoint them. Not with her family extolling Carl's virtues.

Hannah had only briefly discussed marriage with Carl. Their parents had been the ones who frequently spoke of the two entering into an agreement. As far as Carl's family was concerned, the marriage was a foregone conclusion. Her parents seemed to feel the same way.

Hannah lay back and stared up at the bedroom ceiling. Carl was a wonderful man. He was everything her parents had said and much more. Someday she probably would marry Carl.

She closed her eyes and thought about what their lives would be like together. She liked Carl, enjoyed his company. When he kissed her it was something sweet and gentle. But try as she might, Hannah couldn't imagine Carl ever being passionate. A smile cracked her lips, and she chided herself silently.

In her mind's eye she thought about the children she might have with Carl. But instead of conjuring up babies, her mind filled with Joshua Shadduck.

She shook her head in an effort to dispel the image. If only he wasn't an attorney. If only she'd met him last year at this time. If only . . .

"Hannah."

Guiltily she bolted off the bed. "Yes, Mama."

"Carl's on the phone. He wants to know what took you so long. He's been worried. You should have phoned him first thing."

Hurriedly Hannah reached for her shoes. "Tell him I'll be right there."

"Hannah will marry Carl," Gabriel said, as if he needed to convince himself.

Goodness was wise enough to say nothing. She'd learned the hard way that it was often more advantageous to hold one's tongue with the archangel.

"You understand this, don't you?" Gabriel asked pointedly.

"I'm sure you're right," the prayer ambassador answered without emotion. It demanded everything she had to hide her true feelings.

Gabriel studied her with a weary look. "You're sure you can handle this case?"

"Positive." She beamed him her brightest, most innocent smile.

"No monkey business."

Goodness's eyes rounded with indignation. "I wouldn't dream of it."

"Just remember that promise."

"Can I please meet Jenny Lancaster now?" Mercy asked.

Goodness wanted to kiss her friend for distracting Gabriel. She didn't know how much longer she would have been able to hide her feelings.

"Ah, yes. Jenny." Gabriel turned his attention away from Goodness and exhaled sharply. "I'd almost forgotten. Now there's a sorry case. Let me take you to her now."

Chapter

★ ☆ ★

3

"Jenny, wake up." Michelle Jordan burst into the bedroom and pulled open the thick drapes. Brilliant sunlight spilled into the room as Jenny Lancaster struggled to an upright position.

"What time is it?" she asked, yawning loudly. It couldn't be morning. Not yet. Not so soon. Her eyes burned and it felt as though she hadn't slept more than an hour or two.

"It's party time." Michelle dramatically threw her arms into the air.

Jenny collapsed against her pillow. "Not for me."

"For both of us, girl." Michelle curled up at the foot of Jenny's bed. "John Peterman's sent out a casting call for a new Lehman musical. He's going to need twenty singers and dancers. I don't know about you, but I intend to be one of those who ends up on stage opening night. Now you can come along and audition with me, or you can sleep the rest of your life away."

Jenny closed her eyes. The choice shouldn't be this difficult. There was a time when she would have leapt out of bed, bright-eyed and bushy-tailed, grabbed her dancing shoes, and headed out the front door. Not so these days. At twenty-three Jenny Lancaster felt like a has-been. Or, more appropriate, a never-was.

"Are you coming or not?"

Another cattle call. Jenny had given up counting the number of times she'd set her heart on getting a bit part on Broadway. Off Broadway, near Broadway. She didn't care. This was her dream. Her goal. Her ambition.

She'd left Custer, Montana, blessedly naive about the cutthroat world of the stage. Three years later she felt washed-out, washed-up, and ready for the wringer.

Three years was a long time to subsist on one's dreams. Jenny would have thrown in the towel a long time before now if it hadn't been for one thing. Her family and friends back home believed in her. She was the bright, shining star the community had pinned its hopes upon. Back home she could outsing, outdance, and outact anyone in town. But in New York she was just another pretty face with talent.

"Twenty singers and dancers," Jenny repeated, still trying to decide if another audition was worth all the pain involved. She wasn't sure her heart could stand another rejection. "Does twenty singers and twenty dancers mean Peterman needs forty people?"

"I don't know," Michelle said with her characteristic boundless energy. "It doesn't matter, does it?"

It did. Jenny sat upright and rubbed a hand down her face. "I don't know if I'm up to this. Rejection hurts. Frankly I'm not sure this is what I really want anymore," she whispered. Admitting this to her best friend was hard, but it needed to be said. She loved New York, but at heart she would always be a country girl.

"You can't think of it like that. Rejections are simply the rungs to the ladder of success," Michelle announced, ever positive, ever confident.

Jenny sighed audibly. "You've been listening to motivational tapes again, haven't you?"

Michelle nodded. "It shows that much?"

"Yes." Almost against her will, Jenny tossed aside the bedding and climbed off the mattress. "All right, I'll go, but I'll need a few minutes to put myself together."

"Good girl." Michelle pulled open her bottom drawer and took out a pair of black leotards. "You don't want to spend the rest of your life waitressing at Arnold's, do you? Sure you get to sing, but it isn't anywhere close to Broadway."

Jenny sincerely hoped her roommate didn't let anyone back in Custer know that. The entire town firmly believed in her talent. Firmly believed in her.

After so much time, she couldn't continue to make up excuses why her name didn't light up a marquee. So she'd stretched the truth. All right, she'd elasticized it to the point where it was no longer recognizable. Performing in an Off Broadway musical was a long shot from her job as a singing waitress. Her friends and family believed she was well on the road to becoming a star. Little could be further from the truth. The light of ambition in Jenny's eyes had dimmed considerably in the past three years. Not so long ago she would have jumped at the chance to audition for John Peterman.

These days it was difficult to find the energy to drag herself out of bed.

"I don't know if all this trouble is worth the effort," she confessed as she reached for her beige dancing shoes.

"Don't talk like that, Jenny. This is your dream." She hugged her clenched fists to her breast. "Don't let go now. Not when you're so close to making it all come true."

Jenny wished she shared her friend's limitless enthusiasm. Michelle had been spurned as many times as Jenny. Yet her roommate continued to bounce back with renewed optimism, ever hopeful, ever cheerful, ever certain their big break was just around the next corner.

Part of Jenny's reluctance had to do with the season. Christmastime away from her family had always been difficult, but it seemed even more so this year. Not only could she not afford the trip home, but once she was with her family and friends, Jenny realized, she'd never be able to continue with the lie. One look and her parents would guess the truth.

Then there was Trey, their neighbor and longtime family friend. The boy next door, only anyone who met the cattle rancher would be hard-pressed to refer to him as a boy. Whenever Jenny became disheartened, she closed her eyes and remembered Trey.

Trey sitting atop his roan, his Stetson dipped low enough to disguise his eyes. He did that on purpose, she believed, just so she couldn't read his expression. His ranch bordered her father's spread, so Trey had been around for as long as Jenny could remember.

While in school, Jenny had never given much thought to her handsome neighbor. In the years since she'd been away, all that had changed. Whenever Jenny thought about home, it was Trey LaRue who popped into her mind. Trey riding the open range. Trey gentling a startled filly. Trey carrying a sick calf.

Of course he might be married by now, although she doubted it. Surely her mother would have said something if he'd tied the knot. He was at the age—past it, really—when most ranchers married. Three years was a long time to be away from home. Although she remembered him, there was nothing to say he thought about her. A lot of things changed over time.

"Are you ready?" Michelle asked. Her roommate's eagerness was a burr under Jenny's saddle. By all that was right, she should be in bed. Her feet hadn't stopped hurting, nor had her back ceased to ache. Yet when she'd finished dancing her heart out, singing until her vocal cords were strained, she'd be due back at Arnold's.

"I'm as ready as I'll ever be." Even as she said the words, Jenny felt a sinking sensation in the pit of her stomach. Auditioning seemed a waste of effort. A waste of time. A waste of her heart.

"That's Jenny?" Mercy asked Gabriel, standing in the corner of the tiny apartment.

"That's her."

"Who's been praying for her?" This question came from Goodness.

Mercy glared at her friend as if to say she was the one who would be asking the questions. After all, this was her assignment. Goodness had already met her charge, and as always, her friend was looking to meddle. Mercy knew that look and sincerely hoped Gabriel didn't.

"The prayer originated from her neighbor in Montana," Gabriel answered. He frowned as he said it, as if plowing through his memory to put a name to the request. "Trey LaRue, I believe," he said decisively. "Trey's known Jenny most of his life."

"What has he asked?"

"Trey wants Jenny to come home for the holidays. It seems Jenny's father has been feeling poorly. Dillon Lancaster won't ask his daughter to come home, and neither will Jenny's mother. But both miss her terribly."

"Why don't they visit New York?" The solution seemed obvious to Mercy. She could easily manipulate the couple into heading for the wonders of the big city. Naturally Goodness and Shirley would be willing to lend her a hand. Already she was formulating a plan.

Why, the three of them had gotten so good at this sort of thing that it wouldn't surprise her if the Lancasters never guessed how they'd gotten to New York. A little celestial manipulation never hurt anyone.

"Jenny has discouraged them from coming," Gabriel explained.

"But why . . ." Mercy stopped herself. She already knew the answer. Jenny didn't want her family to know that she'd lied. She wasn't starring in an Off Broadway production of *Guys and Dolls*. She was a waitress who quite literally sang for her supper. The line of success she'd fed her family was gagging the young woman now. Jenny couldn't allow her parents to see where she worked. Being forced to admit the truth would humiliate her, so she continued to sabotage herself.

Lies were like that, Mercy realized, and wondered why humans so readily fell into that trap. She'd seen for herself how lies tainted human lives. Would they never learn?

What had started out as a slight exaggeration on Jenny's part had turned into a monster that separated her from those she loved most. All because she hadn't wanted to disappoint her family. Instead she'd disappointed herself.

"This shouldn't be so hard, should it?" Goodness said, looping her arm through Mercy's. "From what we've seen, Jenny's ready to give it up and head back to Montana all on her own. Not just for Christmas, either. After all the disappointment she's suffered, she's more than ready for the green, green pastures of home. I can't say that I blame her. The time has come for her to face up to a few home truths."

Gabriel's brow rose as if Goodness's insight surprised him, and Mercy's friend beamed. "Is that a fact?"

"I wouldn't be so fast to form an opinion about Jenny," Gabriel warned. "She's very talented. I shouldn't need to remind you what God says about the desires of one's heart."

"You mean she isn't ready to relinquish her dream?" Mercy asked. She'd read the situation the same as Goodness. It seemed all Jenny needed was one good excuse to pack her bags and head home to Montana. And to Trey, the young man who cared enough to pray for her return.

"I'm not here to answer those questions," Gabriel said, "but I don't think you should underestimate the power of a dream. Jenny has lived and breathed little else for three long years. It's true she's discouraged, but that doesn't mean she's willing to give up. You might be surprised to discover just how close she really is to seeing her name in lights. Don't forget," Gabriel warned, "that the darkest hour is just before dawn. She could be on the brink of something big."

"Do you really think so?" Mercy felt the excitement churning inside her. But that enthusiasm slowly ground to a halt as she studied the archangel. "Is there something you know that we don't?" Gabriel occasionally withheld information in a blatant effort to teach them a lesson. Mercy had long suspected it to be so.

"No," the archangel assured them. "Just don't be so quick to assume the obvious."

"My oh my, she is talented," Mercy admitted, watching her young charge's agile leap across the stage.

It was at times like this that Jenny realized how badly she hungered for this dream. Once she stood on stage with the other dancers, her adrenaline started flowing, pumping her deflated hopes until they soared higher and higher.

This was where she belonged, where she longed to be. Her heart hummed with excitement, waiting for the opportunity to prove herself.

"Jenny Lancaster." Her name was called by a man sitting in the theater seating. Since the lights blocked her view, the casting director was no more than a hoarse, detached voice. From her best guess, she figured he was somewhere in the first five or six rows.

Jenny stepped forward and handed the piano man her sheet music.

"What will you be singing?" asked the same uninterested voice.

She moved one step and peered into the dark. "'Don't Cry for Me, Argentina.'"

"Fine. Give us your best eight bars."

It was always the same. Rarely did it vary. Jenny suspected she could have sung a tune from a *Sesame Street* production and no one would have known the difference, least of all the casting director. He'd made up his mind even before her turn had come, even before she'd been given a chance to prove what she could do.

Argentina might not weep for her, but Jenny felt the tears welling up inside her. Tears of disappointment. Tears of struggle. Tears of a dream that refused to die.

The first chords from the piano filled the silence. Jenny hung her head and closed her eyes, allowing the music to transport her to another world. She drew in a deep breath and slowly lifted her head. No longer was Jenny Lancaster auditioning for a bit part; she was playing the role of her life. Within the magic of a few notes, she was transformed from a disillusioned waitress into the ambitious wife of a South American dictator.

"Wow." Mercy was set back on her wings. "That girl can sing."

"She is talented," Shirley was quick to agree.

"Incredible." Goodness seemed to be at a loss for words, which was completely unlike her.

Mercy knew she could accept no credit for Jenny's skill; nevertheless she experienced a deep sense of pride that she should be assigned to this amazing young woman.

"Her voice, why, it's almost . . . "

"Angelic," Gabriel supplied, grinning broadly. It was a rare treat to find the archangel in such good spirits.

"Yes," Mercy agreed. "Angelic."

"You believe you can handle this request?" he questioned.

Mercy was sure she could. "Yes," she assured him confidently.

"Leave everything to me." Somehow, some way, Mercy would come up with the means of helping Jenny fulfill her dreams. With a little help from her friends.

Anyone with this much talent, this much heart, deserved a break. A bit of intercession from the heavenly realm never hurt. Naturally Mercy wasn't about to let Gabriel know her plans, but then what he didn't know couldn't hurt him.

And while she had her hand in Jenny's life, Mercy decided, she might as well do what she could about getting the talented singer home for the holidays.

"No funny stuff," Gabriel warned.

Mercy managed to look offended. "Gabriel, please, you insult me."

"I won't have you hot-wiring cars and sending them where you will."

Mercy's shoulders went back in a display of outrage. "I'd never resort to anything that underhanded."

Gabriel didn't say anything for several moments. Then, scratching his head, he studied the three prayer ambassadors. "Can anyone tell me why I don't believe you?"

Chapter

★ ☆ ★

4

"*I'd like everyone to take out* a clean piece of paper," Brynn instructed, standing in front of the classroom. It sounded like a simple enough request, one would think. But from the moaning and groaning, it was as if she'd sprung a surprise quiz on them.

"You aren't going to make us write again, are you?" Emilio Alcantara groaned aloud, voicing, Brynn suspected, the thoughts of half the class.

"Yes, I am," she said, unwilling to let her students' lack of enthusiasm dampen her spirits.

Yolanda leaned so far out of her desk toward Denzil Johnson that she nearly toppled onto the floor.

"Yolanda," Brynn said, "is there a problem?"

"I don't have any paper. I wanted to borrow a piece from Denzil."

"Get your own paper, woman," the black youth protested. "What do I look like, a friggin' Wal-Mart?"

"I loaned you paper last week." Yolanda's dark eyes snapped with outrage.

"That's because you were lucky enough to have me sit next to you. I never said nothin' about paying you back."

Yolanda's mouth thinned, and it looked as if she were about to explode when Suzie Chang saved the day.

"I have an extra sheet she can use," the Chinese girl volunteered shyly, tearing off a clean page from her tablet and passing it across the aisle to Yolanda. The Hispanic girl grabbed it and glared at Denzil as if to say it would be a cold day in hell before he got anything from her again.

"Thank you, Suzie," Brynn said, eager to return to the writing assignment.

"What are you going to have us write about this time?" Emilio asked. "Not something stupid, I hope."

Teaching the value clarification portion of the class had proved to be the most difficult for Brynn. She wanted to make this as interesting and as much fun as she could, but she often found herself on a completely different wavelength from her students.

The incident with Emilio in the hallway was a prime example. The teenager had actually expected her to lie on his behalf. Emilio didn't understand why she'd told the truth about the knife. He'd missed three days of school and consequently blamed her. He saw nothing wrong with his own behavior but seemed to feel that she'd been the one to betray his trust.

It had taken the better part of another week for his sullen mood in class to disappear. She wasn't sure even now what she'd done to get back into his good graces. Whatever it was, she was grateful. Emilio was a natural leader, so his attitude was quickly picked up by the others in class.

Ever since the incident with Emilio she'd been subjected to an attitude of mistrust. It was as if she'd fallen from grace in the eyes of her students.

"First off, don't put your name on the top of the page."

"You don't want our names?" This clearly came as a surprise since she'd so often instructed them to remember just that.

"No names," she reiterated. "Now I'd like each of you to write one hundred and fifty words."

"We gotta count them?"

"That's about a page and a half," Brynn explained. "The subject of your paper is this: If I could kiss anyone in this classroom, who would it be, and why."

For a moment the entire class looked at her as if they couldn't believe what she'd said. Someone smothered a giggle and catcalls echoed across the room.

It didn't take anyone long to get involved in the project. Soon heads were bowed over the paper, and her students wrote feverishly. Brynn liked to involve her students in some type of writing assignment, often on a daily basis. She did this for a number of reasons, but first and foremost was an effort to require them to clarify their thoughts on certain subjects. She attempted to balance a serious topic one day, followed by a lighter one the next.

Although she'd been teaching the class for a number of weeks now, whenever they were asked to write, her students put up a royal stink. Often they bombarded her with silly questions or employed other delay tactics in an effort to forestall the assignment.

Not this time. Looking at them now, writing as fast as their hands would allow, one would think the first student finished would be excused for what remained of the quarter.

"When you're done writing, please bring the papers to my desk." The class was both cooperative and silent. The cooperation part was a welcome relief. Brynn was beginning to feel like a salmon swimming upstream. Every inch was a struggle, every day a challenge.

One by one, her class delivered their papers to her desk. Before long Brynn had accumulated a tidy stack.

Curious whispers followed.

"Aren't you going to read them?" someone asked.

"I will later," she promised, as if this were a normal assignment.

"Wait a minute," Emilio said, slouching down on his seat. "I gotta right to know how many women want me."

Several of the girls booed, suggesting he wasn't the one on their list.

Emilio planted his hand over his heart and looked deeply grieved by their lack of appreciation for his obvious charms.

"Did anyone put me down?" Modesto demanded. "Emilio's got a point, you know."

"One thing's for sure, no one picked Mike," taunted a boy in the back of class.

Mike was a loner and rarely contributed to class discussions. He suffered from a bad case of acne and kept his distance from the others. Brynn had never seen him talk to any of the other students. In many ways her heart went out to Mike, and she struggled to reach him. To have someone taunt him now was cruel and unnecessary. For the first time Brynn wondered about the wisdom of her assignment. It had sounded like such fun when she'd planned it.

"Don't be so sure," Brynn said, and reached for the stack of papers. Her relief was great when she saw that one of the first papers mentioned Mike's name. "Here's a paper for Mike."

"You gotta be kidding." This came from Modesto. The youth sat up and turned around to stare at Mike.

Brynn walked down the aisle and handed Mike the paper.

"How come he gets to read his and I can't have mine?" This came from Emilio.

The corners of Mike's mouth turned up and revealed a brief smile when she laid the sheet down on his desk.

"I'll get to you soon enough," Brynn promised.

"If anyone chose him," Yolanda joked.

"Do bears shit in the woods?"

"Emilio," Brynn admonished. "I won't have that language in my class."

"Sorry, Miss Cassidy."

"Careful," Brynn heard someone say under their breath. "She might get you suspended again."

The next paper listed Emilio's name. She handed it to him and he let out a triumphant cry and punctured the air with his fist. "What did I tell you?" he shouted. "Women are crazy about me." Excited and pleased, he was halfway out of his desk. "I got charisma, you know. Real charisma."

Brynn walked up and down the aisles, delivering the papers. It flustered her a bit when she found her own name toward the top of the page. Emilio's handwriting was immediately recognizable, and she flushed. She'd never intended for anyone to put down her name.

"You aren't going to want these back, are you?" Yolanda pleaded.

"No. Keep them."

"Miss Cassidy." Denzil's hand waved frantically. "There must be some mistake. I didn't get any papers."

"That's because you're greedy," Yolanda took delight in informing him. "Besides, why would anyone want to kiss you?"

"Hey, you didn't have any problem the other night."

"I'd had too much to drink and you know it."

"That's not what you said earlier."

The bell rang just then, and Brynn was saved from having to break off a spat between the two for the second time that day. Whatever was taking place between Yolanda and Denzil was best settled outside the classroom.

"For your assignment," Brynn said, raising her hand to capture their attention before the room emptied, "read the next chapter of *The Diary of Anne Frank.*"

Her words were followed by a loud moan.

"I'll see everyone tomorrow afternoon. Have a good evening."

It never ceased to amaze Brynn how fast her classroom emptied. It was as though her students stampeded toward the door in an effort to escape a nuclear holocaust.

As was her habit at the end of the day, Brynn sat at her desk and graded assignments, but today she didn't have much time because of a dental appointment near her apartment in New Jersey. After a half hour, she tucked what she hadn't finished into her briefcase and headed toward the staff parking lot.

"Yo, Miss Cassidy!" Emilio raced toward her.

"Hello, Emilio."

His steps soon matched hers. "You probably guessed it was me who wrote down your name, right?"

Brynn could feel her face growing warm.

"Listen, I thought I should explain," he said quickly, looking slightly embarrassed himself. "I gotta be careful paying too much attention to any one chick. You see, there are three or four in the class who've got the hots for me. I was trying to be diplomic about it."

"Diplomatic."

"Yeah, that."

"I understand, Emilio, and applaud your efforts."

"Good, 'cause I don't need chick trouble."

"I figured it was something like that," she assured him.

"Great."

"I'll see you tomorrow," she said, doing her best to disguise her amusement. One thing was certain: she didn't want to be the cause of "chick problems" for Emilio Alcantara.

Emilio turned and hurried across the parking lot toward the basketball hoop where his friends were busy playing two on two.

Brynn climbed inside her car and turned the key. It flickered to life, sputtered, and then quickly died. Surprised, she tried again, with the same results. She hadn't left her lights on that morning, she was sure of that. Her vehicle had recently been serviced. She tried once more, and this time the engine did nothing more than cough and choke.

"No, please, no," Brynn murmured, and pressed her forehead against the steering wheel. Trouble with her car was the last thing she needed.

Hannah shouldn't be this eager to see Joshua again, but she was. Again and again her gaze drifted toward the deli's front door as she waited impatiently for the man she'd met at Macy's Thanksgiving Day parade.

Her heart pounded like a race car piston every time she thought about Joshua. He'd been so gentle and caring. So considerate.

Although they'd only just met, they hadn't lacked for conversation. Joshua was the kind of man she could talk to for hours on end. Generally Hannah found herself tongue-tied and uneasy around men, but not with Joshua. It was as if they'd been friends for a long time.

Friends.

The word comforted her and eased her conscience.

Carl had joined her family for Thanksgiving dinner, and afterward he'd sat in the living room with her father. The two men had talked far into the evening, debating political issues and other matters. Before he'd left, Hannah's parents had discreetly left the room, affording her time alone with her beau. At first Carl and Hannah had seemed awkward with each other, Carl as much as she.

In an effort to ease the discomfort, she apologized for having lost him while at the parade. Carl reminded her that he felt responsible for her safety and suggested that in the years to come they'd watch the parade on television.

Hannah had lowered her head to hide her disappointment. Then, almost as if it were expected of him, Carl had leaned forward and gently pressed his lips to hers.

It was a sweet kiss, undemanding and totally lacking in passion.

Standing in the deli, Hannah closed her eyes and tried to dredge up some emotion, some deep feelings for Carl. But try as she might, she felt nothing. Surely not desire. Definitely no compelling yearning for his company. He was Carl, the rabbi's son. The man her parents felt would make her the perfect husband.

"Hannah," her mother admonished, coming out of the kitchen. Her arms were loaded with a tray of sliced bread. "Are you ill?"

"No, Mama."

"Then why do you stand there with your eyes closed? We have customers."

"I'm sorry." And Hannah was. She didn't know what was wrong with her to dawdle when there was work to be done.

Her mother peeled off a list of lunch orders from the fax machine, smoothed them out on the counter, and went about assembling sandwiches with a skill and dexterity that spoke of many years' experience.

Hannah lent a hand, packing the orders into plain brown bags and marking each one. The scent of freshly baked bread spilled out of the kitchen and into the front of the deli, mingling with those of sliced pastrami and knishes, her father's specialties.

After a few minutes, Hannah tried again. "Mama, tell me how you met Dad."

Ruth Morganstern slowly lifted her eyes to Hannah. She appeared surprised by the question. "I don't have time for such foolishness now."

Disappointed, Hannah said nothing.

"We have orders and you're asking me about your father and me?" She laughed lightly. "It was so many years ago now. For over forty years I've loved this man. I don't remember when we met."

"You don't remember?" David shouted from the far side of the deli. "Forty-three years and you don't remember? What kind of wife forgets the day she met the man who would be her husband?"

Ruth laughed and dismissed him with a wave. "I remember some things."

"I should hope to God you do."

"He was handsome," Hannah's mother said out of the corner of her mouth.

"I'm still handsome."

"More so then," Ruth added, her eyes crinkling with amusement.

"Your mother was even more beautiful than she is now," Hannah's father called back. "I'd look at her and forget all about slicing meat. The time I courted her I nearly lost two fingers."

Hannah laughed, delighted at the exchange between her parents. It seemed the lunch crowd, pressed against the glass display case, lost their impatience, and there were shared smiles all around.

Her father handed a thick pastrami sandwich on a paper plate to a young businessman. "You'll have to excuse my daughter," he said under his breath, but loudly enough for Hannah to hear. "She's in love."

In love? This was news to Hannah. But then, if she were to marry Carl, it was implied that they cared deeply for each other. Hannah liked Carl, respected him. He was a good, honorable man and, according to her parents, a fine catch.

Her mother couldn't have been more pleased when Hannah first started dating Carl. A rabbi's son. In Ruth's eyes, Carl was a better catch than a doctor or even an attorney.

An attorney. Automatically Hannah's thoughts drifted back to Joshua, although he'd never been far from her mind since they'd met.

"Here," Ruth said, handing Hannah the bag loaded with faxed orders. "With your head full of romance, can I trust you not to confuse these orders?" she teased affectionately.

"Of course," Hannah answered, and blushed.

"Your head's some place else these days." Her mother leveled her gaze on Hannah. "Your head and your heart." Hannah reached for her hand-knit scarf and wool coat. The deli employed a number of runners, but she was often needed to fill in during the lunch-hour rush.

"I won't be long," she promised before heading out into the cold.

Both her parents stared after her, and Hannah had the distinct impression that they would soon be bragging to their customers about her imminent engagement to Carl.

The wind nipped at her face as she hurried along Front Street in the bustling financial district. Taxis honked with impatience and a bus roared past, leaving her to choke on its exhaust.

Hannah's steps were filled with purpose as she wove her way in and around the foot traffic. She hadn't gone more than a block when she heard someone call her name. After a moment's hesitation, she looked over her shoulder. She didn't see anyone she knew.

"Hannah, wait."

The voice was recognizable now. Joshua.

She scanned the crowd but couldn't see him. Then she found him, standing on the other side of the street. He raised his arm high above his head and waved to attract her attention.

Standing on her tiptoes, Hannah smiled and waved back.

Joshua gestured for her to wait, and as soon as the traffic passed, he jogged across the street.

"Hello again," he said, smiling down on her.

"Hello."

There didn't seem to be anything more to say, but her pulse quickened and she felt as if her heart were trying to escape from inside her chest.

"I was on my way to the deli when I saw you."

"I'm delivering orders," she told him. She didn't have time to talk, not when hungry customers were waiting for their lunches. "I can't visit now." Regret settled over her. All day she'd waited for the opportunity to see Joshua again, and now, when she did happen upon him, she was forced to leave.

"I'll come with you," he suggested.

"But . . ."

"Do you have to get back right away?"

She should. She knew she should. Her parents might need her to make a second run and possibly a third. She hedged, not sure what to do.

"Five minutes," Joshua suggested. "Ten. Listen, I'll help you deliver these orders and you won't be away any time at all. Don't say no, Hannah."

Hannah knew she shouldn't, but she found it even more difficult to turn him down, to deny herself the pleasure of this one short encounter. She gave him a barely discernible nod, praying she was doing the right thing.

Even before she had a chance to think the matter through, Joshua reached inside her carrying bag and grabbed three lunch orders. Not giving her time to protest, he rattled off the address to his office and instructed her to meet him there in ten minutes.

Feeling slightly guilty, she hurried to deliver what remained of the orders. Hannah often took a couple of minutes to chat with her customers, many of whom she considered friends, but not this afternoon. She was in and out as fast as she could manage it.

As soon as she could, she made her way to Joshua's office building. Crammed inside an elevator, she headed for the twenty-sixth floor. The elevator doors slid open and she stepped into an office complex lavishly decorated in mauves and grays. The names of the law firm partners were elegantly sprawled in large gold letters across one fabric-covered wall.

Hannah had been inside this complex a number of times and knew it to be one of the most prestigious law firms in Manhattan. She'd had no idea Joshua was a part of this firm.

Law clerks bustled about, and the phone jingled. Clients lingered in the waiting room.

"May I help you?" the receptionist asked. If she recognized Hannah as the girl from the deli, she didn't say anything.

"I'm Hannah Morganstern," she said.

The woman's face relaxed into a smile. "Ah yes, Mr. Shadduck said you'd be here soon. I'll have someone take you right back." She motioned toward one of the law clerks.

Hannah was escorted down a wide hallway. The law clerk gestured toward Joshua's door, which was open. Joshua stood on the far side of the office. He must have sensed her arrival because he turned around and his face brightened with a warm, welcoming smile.

She knew it was impolite to stare, but she couldn't take her eyes off the framed list of achievements that lined his walls. This was no ordinary man. He was rich and powerful.

"What's wrong?"

She pulled her gaze away from the wall, surprised he had read her so easily. "I've never been inside your office before." She'd delivered his lunch any number of times but had never been past the foyer and the receptionist. She recognized Joshua from the times he'd come into the deli himself.

"Sit down. I'll ring Mary for something hot. Which do you prefer? Coffee or tea?"

"I . . . I really can't stay." To think that she'd allowed this important attorney to deliver lunches on her behalf. Hannah was mortified to the very marrow of her bones.

"You can't stay? Why not? I thought we had this all settled." He walked toward her and reached for her hand. Hannah didn't know if it was from the cold or the shock of seeing Joshua in this environment, but her fingers were icy cold.

"You're freezing." He rubbed her right hand between his own two hands. "You should be wearing gloves."

She felt completely out of her element. Pride prevented her from making up some excuse and rushing away. "I . . . I didn't know," she whispered.

Josh led her to a comfortable brown leather sofa and sat her down. "Didn't know what?"

Hannah held her tongue rather than blurt out the truth. When they'd met at the parade he was a familiar face, someone she recognized. In this office, he was the epitome of the man her father distrusted.

"I've been thinking about you all weekend," he said. "How was your Thanksgiving?"

Now was the perfect opportunity to tell him how close she was to becoming engaged to Carl. She could bring Carl's name up naturally and explain the situation. She could tell him how Carl had joined her family for dinner. How Carl and her father had talked. How Carl had kissed her good night. How they'd met on the Sabbath, after services in the synagogue.

"It was very nice," she said instead, wanting to kick herself. "How about you?"

"I ate with my mother and grandmother."

That started it. Within a matter of minutes he had her laughing over something his grandmother said, and they were immersed in conversation.

Twenty minutes slipped by, and it seemed like only five. "I have to get back," she said, unable to disguise her regret. "Thank you for the tea . . . for everything." She wouldn't indulge herself again. Not with Joshua.

Whatever made her so bold, Hannah would never know. She stood, prepared to walk away, and before she left, she pressed the palm of her hand to Joshua's clean-shaven face.

"Good-bye, Joshua," she said, and not giving him time to answer, she hurried from his office.

Her mother eyed her wearily when Hannah arrived back at the deli. "What took you?" she asked.

"I got sidetracked," Hannah admitted.

"Next time don't visit so long," her father warned her. "We needed you here."

"I'm sorry I'm late. Do you need me to make another run?"

"Don't worry, Louise was able to do it." Her mother rattled off a list of tasks. Hannah was grateful to work in the kitchen the rest of the afternoon.

"Hannah," her father called two hours later. "A package's been delivered for you."

"For me?" Drying her hands on a linen towel, Hannah stepped out to the front of the deli. A freckle-faced delivery boy held out a small, flat box. "Hannah Morganstern?"

"That's me."

"Sign here." He thrust a clipboard at her.

Hannah penned her name and then, with her parents watching, unwrapped the flat, oblong box.

Inside were a pair of expensive leather gloves and a note from Joshua.

"I've never heard you sing better," Michelle said as she and Jenny returned to their shared apartment. "Oh, Jenny, this is the break we've been waiting for. We're going to sing and dance on Broadway. I can feel it in my bones. We're really going to make it."

They often built each other up after an audition. Casting directors weren't known for lavishing potential stars with positive feedback, so they gave it to each other.

"Your voice . . ." Michelle hesitated as though she had trouble finding the words. "It's different now. There's a depth and maturity that wasn't there six months ago." Michelle set the mail on the kitchen table. "Don't misunderstand me, you've always been good, but this afternoon you were nothing short of brilliant."

Jenny rolled her eyes.

"I'm not blowing smoke out my ears, either." Michelle sounded slightly offended. "I mean it, Jenny. I really think you're going to get a part, maybe even one of the leads."

Jenny knew otherwise. She sang out her heart the way she did for every audition. Nothing was going to change. She refused to build up her hopes again.

"This looks interesting," Michelle said, holding up an envelope and tossing it to her. "It's addressed to you. It might even be a Christmas card. Already? Good grief, it's not even December yet."

Jenny examined the envelope, her gaze scanning the return address. She recognized it immediately, and her breath jammed in her throat.

"Jenny? What is it?"

"It's from Trey," she whispered.

"Trey who?"

She stood and walked around the table while motioning with

her hands, unable to formulate the words. "Trey LaRue . . . my neighbor, or rather my parents' neighbor."

"You've never mentioned him before," Michelle said.

"I haven't?" That seemed impossible. He was an integral part of what she considered home and family.

"Well, open it and find out what he has to say," Michelle encouraged.

That seemed the most logical thing to do. Jenny's hand trembled as she peeled back the flap and withdrew a card. A colorful turkey decorated the front, its plumage fanned out across the top. She opened the card and found Trey had written only one short sentence: "I'm eager to see you this Christmas." His name was listed below in smooth, even strokes of the fountain pen.

Jenny's heart sank to the pit of her stomach. She handed the card to Michelle.

"You're going home for the holidays?"

Jenny shook her head. "You know I can't. Not with money so tight." Not after she'd let everyone believe she had a starring role in an Off Broadway production.

"I like his signature," Michelle said, studying the card. "You can tell a lot about a man by the way he signs his name." Her look was thoughtful. "But," she continued, grinning at Jenny, "I'd rather have you tell me all about him yourself."

"What can I say?" Jenny murmured, surprised to discover she didn't want to discuss Trey with her best friend.

She'd never missed home more than she did right at that moment. She longed to gaze into a night sky where the stars weren't obliterated by city lights. She wanted to close her eyes and smell the scent of fresh hay. Home was cattle and mud and frustration. Home was love. Home was Trey.

"He hasn't written you before, has he?" Michelle pressed.

"No."

"Why now?"

Jenny shrugged. "I don't know. He owns the spread next to ours," she volunteered, hoping her friend would help her reason it out. A smile touched the edges of her mouth. "He's a cowboy from head to foot. Full of grit and mettle. Stubborn and determined, with skin as tan as leather and a constitution of iron."

"Did you date him?"

"No . . . he's older than me by several years." Eight years had made a world of difference when she was in high school, but it didn't seem all that important now. "He's probably one of the most decent, hardworking men I've ever known."

"It's obvious he's wants you to come home."

Jenny set aside the card and exhaled a long, slow breath. "Well, I can't, so there's no use sitting around here stewing about it."

"It seems a shame, after him writing and all."

"I can't go home," Jenny said forcefully. "You can't, either, because the both of us are going to have plum roles in the new Lehman musical, and we'll be in the thick of rehearsals."

"You're right," Michelle said as if this were something she hadn't considered.

"We'll be stars."

"Stars," Michelle repeated. "Our names will light up the marquee."

"Bright lights, and bright futures." But even as she said the words, they rang false in her ears.

"Goodness." Gabriel was furious. Shirley, Goodness, and Mercy had ignored him at every turn, and he wasn't putting up with it this year. His schedule was busy enough without those three meddling in matters that were none of their concern.

"You called?" The three shot up to heaven, looking as innocent as newborn lambs. Their feathery wings were tucked firmly in place, and their expressions were filled with guileless innocence.

"Shirley," he roared. "Did I or did I not tell you to stay away from Brynn Cassidy?" He didn't give her a chance to reply. "Might I ask what you were doing in her classroom this afternoon? This is your assignment," he said, handing her a slip of paper. "Now I expect you to help Craig Houle. If I see you anywhere close to Manhattan High School again, it will be cause for disciplinary action."

The three gasped.

Gabriel refused to allow these prayer ambassadors to manipulate him any further.

"Goodness, what did I tell you about Hannah? You don't think I know that you had a hand in Joshua Shadduck running into her this afternoon? Well, I'm on to your games. You will keep your fingers out of her life, is that understood?"

Goodness nodded.

"As for you, Mercy . . ." He looked down over his notes and, flustered, ran a hand over his face. He glanced up at the third angel. "Oh my, you're going to need all the help you can get."

Chapter

★ ✭ ★

5

"Gabriel handed you an assignment on a piece of paper." Goodness was offended on Shirley's behalf, and rightly so. Never in their two-year history of working the Christmas holiday prayer rush had they been treated so shabbily. It was downright degrading.

"It might not be so bad," Mercy suggested, gathering close to her friend's side. The third angel was the peacemaker of the group. "The least we can do is give Gabriel the benefit of the doubt."

Shirley peeled open the folded sheet. Goodness and Mercy crowded close in an effort to read over her shoulder.

"The prayer request is from Craig Houle," the angel told them. "He's ten and has asked God for a chess set for Christmas."

"You've got to be kidding." Mercy flapped her wings in a display of disgust. "A chess set for a ten-year-old boy. Why, that's an insult to our good names."

"We have a tradition to uphold."

Goodness couldn't stay in one spot, not when she was this angry. "It's a matter of pride. If anyone could help Brynn Cassidy with those high schoolers, it's Shirley. This other stuff is child's play."

"Exactly!" Shirley declared. "We have something to prove, so let's do it."

Indignant, the three returned to earth, their feathers in a dither, swirling down on the unsuspecting city like the Horsemen due from the Apocalypse.

"Exactly where does this Craig Houle live?" Goodness demanded as the three hovered over the Queensboro Bridge. Gabriel should count his blessings. There was a time, not so long past, when Goodness would have taken delight in dallying with streetlights and rerouting New York City traffic.

"According to this, Craig lives on Roosevelt Island," Shirley answered, reading over the request form. "At this time of day, he's most likely in school."

"Yes, but it's his parents we need to influence, right?" Mercy asked, thinking on her feet—er, wings.

"Right," the other two agreed.

"Then all we need do is convince his mother or father to do a little pre-Christmas shopping."

Goodness made a tsk-tsk sound. "I think it's time we taught Gabriel a lesson on just how good we are."

"I don't believe I've ever been more offended," Shirley said as the three briskly headed toward Roosevelt Island.

Peggy Houle walked down the quiet hospital corridor and sat at the nurses' station. Her rubber soles barely made a sound on the polished tile floor.

She started to make a notation in one of her patient's charts when she noticed a newspaper spread open across the top of the counter.

"That's odd," she mumbled to herself, and scooted the paper aside.

She looked around, wondering who'd left it. One thing was certain: none of the nurses were accorded the luxury of sitting down and reading. Not while on duty, at any rate. The hospital was short staffed as it was, and breaks, even the ones allotted them in the terms of their contract, were often few and far between.

"My dogs are barking." Ellen Freeman, another nurse, joined Peggy. She slipped off her shoe and rubbed her sore toes. "This is what I get for not breaking in these new shoes first." She reached for the newspaper. "Who left this?"

"I don't know. It wasn't here five minutes ago."

"Look," Ellen said, pointing to the printed page. "There's a gigantic toy sale going on for the next couple of days. I haven't even started my Christmas shopping."

"I was finished last week," Peggy said, feeling almost smug. She'd hit the stores her first day off following Thanksgiving and finished it all in one fell swoop—wrapping paper, new decorations, tinsel, the whole nine yards.

There wasn't a reason on this earth good enough for her to voluntarily step inside a store again in the whole month of December. Not when it seemed the entire city had gone crazy. At the end of her shift all Peggy wanted to do was head home.

"I've been thinking I'd buy the kids educational gifts this year,"

Ellen murmured. "Something that will stir their minds instead of those brainless television games. I can't tell you how sick I am of them sitting like zombies holding on to their joysticks."

"A chess set?" Peggy said, and snapped her head back, startled.

"A chess set," Ellen repeated, oblivious of her friend's chagrin. "Now that I think about it, you're right. A chess set is an excellent idea."

"What did I just say?"

"A chess set." Ellen looked up, surprised. "Is something wrong?"

"No . . . the funniest thing just happened." Peggy slapped the side of her head, hoping that would help.

"What?" Ellen was curious now.

"The words *a chess set* echoed in my ear. Three times, and each time I swear I was hearing a different voice."

"I still think it's an excellent idea," Ellen said, and replaced her shoe. "Are you sure you won't come to the toy store with me?"

"Ah . . ." Peggy hesitated, then found herself agreeing. "Sure," she mumbled, "why not?" For the life of her, she couldn't imagine why she was doing such a thing. "Who knows, maybe Craig would be interested in learning how to play chess himself," she said to justify her actions. After all, it was a good idea. Her son would enjoy learning the game.

Peggy leaned back on her chair. Abruptly she shook her head, then repeatedly slapped her hand against her ear. "It happened again," she said incredulously.

"You heard the words *a chess set*?"

"No," Peggy said, and shook her head like a dog fresh out of the water. "It was the same three voices, only this time they said . . . "

"Yes," Ellen prodded.

"You aren't going to believe this." Peggy wasn't entirely sure she believed it herself. "*Piece of cake,*" she mumbled, and shrugged, completely baffled.

"Oh, my," Shirley said, pointing into the distance. "Brynn Cassidy's in trouble." It was just what she'd expected would happen.

"Trouble?" Mercy repeated. "What's wrong?"

Cocky with their success, Goodness brushed the grit from her hands. "Trouble's our middle name. Brynn doesn't have a thing to worry about."

"Brynn might not, but we do," Mercy said, looking skeptical. "Gabriel isn't going to like this one bit. Not after the warning he gave us to stay away from her."

"Brynn's car won't start," Shirley informed her friends, her voice growing more concerned. "And I don't like the looks of those men either." Clad in black leather jackets, two men stood on the other side of the chain-link fence, watching her.

Brynn climbed out of her car and opened the hood. She cast a wary eye toward the men.

"If ever I've seen anyone with evil intentions, it's those two," Shirley informed her friends.

"They've got knives," Mercy said, tugging on Goodness's sleeve.

"We've got to do something," Shirley cried, hoping to hide her panic.

"You don't dare," Goodness insisted, gripping Shirley by the arm and stopping her. "Mercy's right. If Gabriel finds out, it'd be just the excuse he's looking for to stick us with guard duty."

"Then I'll take matters into my own hands," Shirley insisted.

"Talk to Gabriel," Mercy suggested. "Goodness and I can keep those two thugs occupied while you reason this out with him."

"Did I hear someone mention my name?" Gabriel appeared just then, startling the three angels.

"Gabriel," Shirley said boldly, "we need to talk."

"Indeed we do. What's this I hear about Peggy Houle experiencing hearing problems?"

Shirley, Goodness, and Mercy clammed up so fast their teeth made clicking sounds when their jaws closed.

"I strongly suspect a bit of . . . intercession."

"I have a question of my own." Shirley stepped forward and bravely confronted the archangel. "Exactly whom have you assigned to work with Brynn Cassidy?"

Gabriel hesitated. "As a matter of course, I hadn't gotten around to choosing anyone just yet."

This was all Shirley needed to hear. "It's exactly as I suspected," she turned to inform her two friends with an indignant huff. "In the meantime Brynn Cassidy flounders, while heaven looks on unconcerned."

When she dared, Shirley chanced a look in his direction. "I want in," she informed Gabriel, her hand braced against her hip.

"What makes you think you can handle this case?" Gabriel's intense eyes burned holes straight into her.

"I can't," Shirley admitted. "At least not alone, but I have two friends who can help. In addition to . . . "

"Yes," Gabriel prodded.

"In addition to my friends, there's you."

"Me?"

"And a host of heavenly assistance that's always on call."

Gabriel sighed. "You just might need it."

Shirley opened her mouth to further her argument, then realized what the archangel had said. "You mean to say you're willing to give me the assignment?" The winds of indignity that had ruffled her sails fell slack. "Really?"

From the tight set of his mouth, the archangel looked as if he already regretted this. "One condition. You must agree to call for help when you need it."

"I promise," Shirley said solemnly, and smiled at her two friends.

"Just remember we can accomplish all things with the power of God."

"All things," Shirley, Goodness, and Mercy repeated.

"We'll start right now," Gabriel suggested. "I'll let you take care of the problem of those two malcontents."

"Sure thing," Shirley said, eager to get started on the assignment now that it was officially hers. She eyed the two men watching Brynn, and almost felt sorry for them. It seemed to her they were prime candidates for a bit of intervention. Perhaps they should meet up with an old friend, one they weren't eager to see. Like their parole officer. Angel Shirley in disguise.

"I sincerely hope you know a good mechanic." Gabriel cast his gaze over to the disabled vehicle; then without a sound, without a clue, he disappeared.

"We do know a good mechanic, don't we?" Shirley asked, looking to her friends.

Goodness and Mercy stared back blankly.

"No," said Mercy to Shirley. "We thought *you* did."

It was barely after four and already the sky was growing dark. Within a half hour night would settle over the city like a black velvet quilt.

Brynn Cassidy had long since given up the idea of seeing her dentist. Missing the appointment to have her teeth cleaned was a minor inconvenience compared to the hassles of dealing with car troubles.

She couldn't leave her Ford Escort here overnight, that much she knew. In this high-crime area, she'd be fortunate to find the shell of her vehicle left by morning. Nor did she know of a good garage, especially one close by. She cast a look across the street, surprised and grateful that the two men lingering there moments earlier had disappeared.

"Are you having trouble, Miss Cassidy?" Emilio walked up to her, a basketball tucked under one arm.

Brynn was so grateful that someone had asked that it was all she could do to keep from blurting out her troubles. "It won't start, and I haven't got a clue what could be wrong."

Emilio walked around her vehicle as though inspecting it. "I know a little bit about engines."

"Do you think you might look at it?"

"Sure thing." Emilio slid halfway inside the driver's seat. One foot remained on the asphalt parking lot while he turned the ignition key. He pumped the gas pedal a couple of times while her car made a sick grinding sound.

"Do you know what's wrong?" Brynn asked expectantly.

"You sure it isn't your battery?" Emilio asked.

"Good grief, I wouldn't know."

The teenager seemed to find her answer amusing. "You know all them fancy words, Teach, but you aren't so smart when it comes to cars, are you?"

Brynn was more than willing to admit it. "Is it serious?" she asked.

Emilio shrugged. "I haven't got a clue."

"I thought you said you knew something about cars."

"I do, but I ain't no Mr. Goodwrench."

"Thanks anyway, Emilio. I appreciate your help." He'd done a lot more than her fellow teachers. Most had walked right past her.

Brynn closed the hood and locked up the car. She didn't want to leave it, but she didn't have any choice. Its hood shut with a bang that echoed through the darkening afternoon. She swung the strap of her purse over her shoulder, and with her back stiff, not knowing where to turn, she started out of the parking lot.

"Where you going?" Emilio asked, bouncing the basketball and weaving it in and out of his legs as he walked alongside her.

"I'd better get a tow truck."

"My brother can do that."

Brynn paused. "Your brother?"

"Roberto. He's owns a mechanic shop. If you want, I'll take you there. He'll know what to do."

Frankly, Brynn wished Emilio had said something about his brother sooner. "That would be great."

"Yeah, well, remember how much I helped you the next time you're tempted to have me suspended."

The three-block walk took only a matter of minutes. Brynn spied Roberto's shop when they turned the corner. It looked as if the garage had once been a neighborhood gas station. The corners of the cement building were chipped and the entire structure was badly in need of a fresh coat of paint.

Emilio opened the glass front door and walked inside. "Roberto!" he shouted.

His brother's reply was muffled.

"He's in the garage," Emilio said, gesturing to the narrow doorway that led to a large open area that served as the repair shop. Brynn followed her student inside.

"I drummed up some business for you," Emilio announced proudly, and motioned toward Brynn.

Roberto Alcantara slowly unfolded from a quarter panel of the blue Metro and reached for the pink rag tucked inside his coveralls pocket.

"Hello, Mr. Alcantara."

"Call him Roberto," Emilio insisted. "This is Miss Cassidy," he continued, looking well pleased with himself. "She's the teacher I was telling you about."

"Hello."

Roberto nodded and wiped his hands. His face remained emotionless.

"Miss Cassidy's having car troubles."

"My car won't start," she elaborated. "I doubt that it's the battery. It ran perfectly fine this morning . . . at least I thought it had."

"She doesn't know anything about cars," Emilio inserted. "Her specialty is dangling particles."

"Participles," Brynn corrected.

Emilio chuckled. "See what I mean?"

"I'm pleased to meet you, Miss Cassidy," Roberto said coolly, and tossed the rag onto his tool bench.

"I left my car in the school parking lot." She twisted her arm around and pointed in the direction of the school, which was completely unnecessary. Roberto Alcantara knew very well where the high school was.

Roberto said something to Emilio in Spanish. Emilio nodded quickly, then turned abruptly and hurried out of the garage. Within a matter of a minute she heard the youth talking on the phone, again in Spanish. Before he left, he collected her car keys.

"I've had Emilio call for a tow truck," Roberto informed her. "He'll meet the driver over at the school."

"Thank you. I can't tell you how much I appreciate your help."

Roberto said nothing.

Without being obvious, Brynn studied Emilio's brother. Roberto was tall and lean. His skin was the color of warm honey, his eyes and hair as dark a shade of brown as she'd ever seen. She guessed him to be around her own age, perhaps a year or two older. He wasn't openly hostile, but he did nothing to put her at ease. Every attempt at conversation was dead-ended.

As the minutes passed, the silence became more and more strained. Brynn wondered what she could have done to earn his disapproval, then realized it must be the incident with Emilio in the hall the first day she was at the school.

"I imagine you're upset with me because I was the one responsible for Emilio's suspension," she tried again. She wouldn't apologize, but she was prepared to state her side of the case. If he was willing to listen, that was.

"I'm not the least bit upset," he surprised her by answering. "Emilio knows the rules. He deserved what he got." He returned to working on the Metro and ignored her.

The next time he straightened, Brynn asked, "You don't like me, do you?" Normally she wouldn't be so confrontational, but it had been one of those days. If she'd done something to offend him, she wanted to know about it.

"That's right," he concurred.

"Do you mind telling me why?"

Apparently this was just the doorway he'd been waiting to walk through. Roberto met her look brazenly and continued. "Because you're filling my brother's head with nonsense."

"How do you mean?" Brynn struggled not to sound defensive and doubted that she'd succeeded.

He flung his arm in the air. "All your talk about the importance of an education. A high school diploma isn't going to help Emilio any more than it did me. Tell me, Miss Cassidy, exactly how is the history of World War II going to feed a family? Will reading about Anne Frank get him a decent job?"

"Yes . . . well, not directly," she faltered. "Education is the answer for Emilio." She couldn't believe Roberto would say such a thing.

"Emilio would be better off if he dropped out of school now and learned a trade." He turned his back on her and appeared to be looking for something on his tool bench. He carelessly tossed aside a wrench and reached for another.

"I soundly disagree," Brynn said.

"That's your right."

In all her years, Brynn had never heard anyone discourage someone from an education. "Don't tell me you actually want your brother to quit school. Surely your parents object to that."

"I'm the only family Emilio's got," Roberto announced.

"I'm sorry to hear that, especially if you think he shouldn't complete his education."

"I nearly had him convinced to come work with me here in the garage, but then you arrived and all of a sudden he's talking about goals and dreams and other such nonsense."

"It isn't nonsense," she argued.

Roberto threw down a rag and shook his head. "No matter what happens, my brother and I will live and die in this neighborhood. All your talk isn't going to change one damn thing."

Hannah knew it was coming. The minute Carl arrived with his parents, following synagogue, she knew. He'd come to ask her to be his wife. Come to stake his claim. She didn't know why he'd chosen now; then again, perhaps she did. Hannah knew that Carl had experienced pressure from his own family. They had dated several months now, and it was time to make a decision. He taught at the local Hebrew academy, and his position there was secure, despite his differences with the headmaster.

Together with her mother and father, Hannah led Carl's family into the compact living room. An expectant silence settled over the group as the two sets of parents exchanged happy glances.

Carl looked to Hannah, and she read the apology in his eyes. He hadn't wanted it to be like this, either. He would have preferred for them to speak privately first, but like her, he was caught in the trap of obligation and family tradition.

"Carl." The rabbi looked to his son.

Carl cleared his throat. "Hannah and I have been seeing each other exclusively now for several months," he began. His hands were clasped in his lap, and he seemed to be as uncomfortable with this as Hannah was. "It should come as no surprise that I have deep feelings for your daughter."

David and Ruth smiled and nodded.

Hannah read the delight in their eyes. This was their dream for her, what they'd been anxiously waiting to happen for weeks. If anything, they seemed surprised it had taken this long.

"Our Hannah has deep feelings for Carl as well," her father assured the rabbi and his wife. He looked to his daughter for confirmation.

Hannah had no option but to agree, and really, it wasn't a stretch of the truth. She did care for Carl. He had been both generous and considerate.

"I have a good job and make a respectable income," Carl said.

Her father nodded.

"I can afford to care for Hannah."

Again her father confirmed his approval with a quick nod.

The room went silent as everyone waited with breathless anticipation for what was to come next.

"With your permission, David and Ruth," Carl continued, his voice low and firm, "I would like to ask Hannah to be my wife."

Hannah watched as her sensible mother dissolved into tears of happiness and, perhaps, relief. Her father's face beamed with love and pride.

David cleared his throat as if to say his words were those of importance. "We couldn't ask for a better man for our only child. You have our permission and our heartfelt approval. May God deeply bless you both."

"Hannah?" Carl turned his attention to her.

Five people looked to her. She held their dreams in the palm of her hand. With everything in her she wanted to ask Carl to give her time before she decided. But to do so now would embarrass him and deeply disappoint their families.

"Hannah?" her mother asked softly.

Hannah glanced toward her parents. All her life she'd done as they wanted. She'd been a good daughter, an obedient child.

"Oh, Carl," she whispered.

Her mother dabbed at her eyes. Carl's mother sniffled.

"I couldn't be more honored than to be your wife."

The tension in the room evaporated as Carl's and her parents leapt to their feet and hugged each other. The only two not embracing were Carl and Hannah.

Carl moved to her side and knelt on the floor next to her chair. His eyes held hers captive. "I'll make you a good husband, Hannah."

She lowered her gaze. "And I'll be a good wife."

Joshua glanced at his watch and was surprised at the time. He'd been held up in court earlier that morning and been playing catch-up the rest of the day. Earlier he'd decided to stop off at the deli and be sure Hannah had received his gift. Frankly he'd been surprised not to hear from her before now.

It came as something of a surprise the way Hannah had filled his mind and his heart. For too many years he'd been whizzing down the fast lane of life, building his career and making a name for himself.

Then one morning, out of the blue, he'd woken with a hollow feeling in the pit of his stomach. This feeling, this emptiness, was something his grandmother's cooking wasn't going to satisfy.

It was then Joshua realized that what he was missing was a wife and family. He knew his mother had been wanting him to marry for a good long while. Only he had a certain type of woman in mind, and he didn't know if such a woman existed in this modern age.

First and foremost he sought a woman who shared his faith. One who would stand devotedly at his side through the years. A woman who would make his dreams hers and allow him to be part of hers. One who was kind and gentle. Loving and tender. Sensible.

He'd searched for months for this paragon of virtue, until he was convinced a woman such as this no longer existed.

Then he'd met Hannah.

After their first afternoon together, he'd realized she was exactly the type of woman he'd been longing to meet. To think all this time she'd been right under his nose. The local deli owner's daughter.

Joshua reached for his coat, and after telling his secretary where he'd be, he headed toward what many in New York considered to be the best deli in town.

When he was less than a block away from the deli, Joshua spied Hannah. She was walking with an older woman, whom he assumed must be her mother. It was hard not to raise his arm and attract her attention the way he had at their previous meeting. But since she was advancing toward him, there didn't seem to be much point.

Joshua frowned when he noticed Hannah wasn't wearing the gloves he'd had delivered. Then he noticed her eyes. How easy she was to read. Whatever she was doing didn't please her. Even from this distance he felt her resistance.

Just then she looked up, and he caught her gaze. Briefly her eyes widened with alarm and she gnawed on her lower lip as though she weren't sure what to do.

Without her saying a word, Joshua received her message. She didn't want him to greet her. Silently she pleaded with him to walk on past. It offended him, but he didn't question her request.

Without a word they strolled past each other like total strangers. Three steps on the other side of Hannah, Joshua turned, hoping for some telltale sign that would clue him to what was wrong.

She glanced over her shoulder, and in that briefest of seconds,

Joshua read her eyes. She was grateful. Later, when she could, she promised silently, she would explain everything.

It probably had something to do with what she'd told him the day of the parade. Her parents had been involved in a frivolous lawsuit. The fact that her family didn't take kindly to attorneys wouldn't dissuade him. He was very much interested in knowing Hannah better. Once her family had an opportunity to know him, they'd be willing to overlook the fact that he was an attorney. Joshua smiled to himself.

He would be patient, because Hannah Morganstern was well worth the effort. After all, he'd been looking for her most of his adult life.

"This must be old home week," Michelle said as she walked into the apartment and tossed the mail on the kitchen table. "There's another letter with a postmark from Custer, Montana."

"There is?" Dressed in her slip and standing in front of the ironing board, Jenny set aside the iron and walked over to the table. She reached for the envelope and read the return address. "It's from my mother."

"At least you hear from your mother," Michelle complained as she shucked off her coat and scarf. "It's been three months since my mother last wrote me."

"But she calls once a week."

"True."

But Jenny understood what her friend was saying. It was a relief to get something in the mail other than bills.

She opened the envelope and withdrew the letter. It was exactly what she expected. Her mother had broken her silence and joined Trey to ask her to come home for the holidays.

It hurt more than words could voice having to explain that she couldn't leave New York. Jenny had long since run out of money, out of excuses, and, worse yet, out of ideas.

"What'd she say?" Michelle asked. Her roommate stood in front of the open refrigerator and stared at its meager contents. Rather than explain, Jenny handed the single sheet of stationery to her friend. Michelle scanned the page, then raised her eyes to Jenny.

"Your mother wants you to come home for Christmas."

Jenny sank onto the sofa and tucked her feet beneath her. "Christmas has always been so special with our family. I don't think I've met anyone who could put on a spread the way Mom does. She makes this incredible sage dressing for the turkey, and the scent of it fills the house." She closed her eyes, and the memory was so powerful, she could almost smell the pungent herbs right then.

"Maybe there's a way you could manage to make it home," Michelle said sympathetically.

"There isn't," Jenny said, unwilling even to listen to suggestions. No one needed to tell her that she'd done this to herself.

Christmas with her mom and dad and little brother. A lump formed in her throat.

Christmas on the range. Snow glistening in the moonlight, sleigh rides every December. Decorating the tree together had long been a family tradition. Her father would set a pot of wassail to warm over the fireplace, and they'd sing carols while they strung the lights and added the tinsel. The ranch hands and neighbors would stop over for a cup of her father's special brew. Trey came every year.

"Jenny?"

Her eyes popped open. "Sorry. I guess I got carried away there for a moment."

"Why hasn't your family come to see you?"

"Mom and Dad?" Jenny supposed she should have considered that a long time ago, but try as she might she couldn't picture her parents in New York. To the best of her knowledge they'd never been more than three hundred miles away from the ranch. Their lives revolved around the care and feeding of a thousand head of cattle. It would be unheard of for her father to leave the ranch unattended.

There'd been a time when Jenny hated the mere mention of the word *beef*. How eager she'd been to escape to the big city and find her way in the world. How eager she'd been to disassociate herself from the Flying L Ranch.

"Did you hear anything from Peterman?" she asked Michelle, needing to change the subject before she became downright maudlin.

"Not a word. Rumor has it he's looking for a particular kind of girl."

"Oh?" Jenny feigned interest. It went without saying that whatever character type the famous director sought wasn't likely to be Jenny. She had lost count of the number of times she'd auditioned for John Peterman. He hadn't chosen her yet, and she doubted he would this time.

She didn't know when she'd started all this stinking thinking. About the time she'd told the first lie to her parents. Negative thoughts had crowded her mind ever since.

"I can't shake the feeling you're going to be offered one of the major roles," Michelle said. "Mark my words, Jenny Lancaster. We're both headed for Broadway."

"This is the saddest thing I've ever seen," Mercy told her two friends. "Jenny wants nothing more than to go home for the holidays, and can't."

"Surely there's a way we can help her."

"I'm convinced there is." Goodness spoke with utter confidence. "All we may need to do is pull a few strings. That shouldn't be so difficult."

Mercy smiled. "We've been doing that for years, haven't we?"

"Maybe we should make it impossible for Jenny to refuse her mother."

Mercy looked to the former guardian angel. "What do you mean?"

Shirley pointed to the Thanksgiving card tucked in Jenny's bedroom mirror. "Perhaps all we really need to do is give her a good enough excuse to head home."

Chapter

★ ✰ ★

6

Jenny didn't want to do it. Her heart ached every time she thought about refusing her mother's plea. The list of fabricated excuses was as long as her arm.

She waited until she had the apartment to herself and then sat down at the table. She bolstered herself with a cup of hot chocolate and a plate of butter cookies. With pen in hand, she wrote:

> *Dearest Mom and Dad,*
>   *You don't know how it pains me to tell you I won't make it home for the holidays. I love you both more than words can say. I think of you every day. Know that my heart will be with you, but this is the price of success. . . .*

Jenny wadded up the letter and unceremoniously tossed it into the garbage. She tried again, and after six or seven lines the second sheet followed the path of the first.

A half hour later, the table was nearly obliterated with discarded attempts. It hadn't been this difficult to answer Trey's card. Her brief note to her former neighbor had been cheerful and witty when she'd sent along her regrets.

Anyone who knew her well might have been able to read between the lines of her lighthearted message. But not Trey, she decided. Her witty note would amuse him.

In the end, Jenny penned three short lines to her parents and left it at that. She couldn't come. She was sorry, and she'd miss them terribly.

Not once did she mention the Off Broadway production she'd told them she was in. Jenny refused to perpetrate the lie any further than she had already.

By the time Michelle returned from her errands, Jenny was in a real funk. Depressed and miserable, she battled off a case of the blues, determined not to get caught in the trap of feeling sorry for herself.

"You know what we need?" her friend said.

"What?"

"A little fun. It's the season of joy, and yet here we are, moping around waiting for the phone to ring." Their agent hadn't called, and Jenny didn't care what people said. No news was not good news. No news was no news. And this time the waiting had never seemed more interminable.

"What if we had a party?" Michelle asked.

"A Christmas party," Jenny added, warming to the idea. "That's perfect." Then reality set in. "But how would we possibly feed all our friends?" It was difficult enough to scrounge up meals for the two of them.

"We'll make it a potluck," Michelle suggested. "All we need supply are the drinks, plus plates and silverware. Between us we could manage that, couldn't we?"

"Sure we could." Jenny's nod was eager. Her spirits lifted just thinking about the celebration. She needed this, needed something to take her mind off how much she would miss Montana. "We can make the invitations ourselves."

"Let's hand them out. That way we could save on postage," Michelle said, offering another money-saving idea.

"Who should we invite?"

"Bill and Susan," Michelle suggested.

The couple had meet in drama school and had married that summer. Jenny and Michelle had been bridesmaids. Jenny had joked about how the two of them always seemed to end up as bridesmaids.

"What about Cliff?" Jenny asked.

"Abby, too."

The list continued until they were afraid they'd forget, so they decided to write them all down.

Michelle sat at the table and reached for a pen. "Good grief, what happened here? It looks like a paper massacre."

The tightness gripped Jenny's throat. "I finally wrote my parents and told them I wouldn't be home." Just saying the words aloud increased the ache.

"Next year you'll be with your family," Michelle said with confidence.

"You're right," Jenny said, forcing herself to think positive

516 ★ *Debbie Macomber*

thoughts. Surely living in the same city in which Norman Vincent Peale had preached his philosophy of positive thinking should teach her something. Yet here she was doing it again: stinking thinking.

"Bill and Susan," Michelle mumbled as she repeated the names of their mutual friends. "Abby. Cliff. John."

The phone pealed and they froze.

Michelle looked to Jenny.

Jenny to Michelle.

"You answer it," her roommate instructed.

"You," Jenny insisted, shaking her head. It had been like this all week. The instant the phone jingled they hoped, prayed, it was Irene, their agent. If it wasn't Irene, then perhaps it was the casting director and maybe even the great and mighty John Peterman himself. It wasn't likely, but they could dream.

"It's probably some schmuck wanting to sell us aluminum siding," Michelle joked.

"Or someone doing a survey on cat food."

But Jenny noticed that neither one of them took their eyes away from the kitchen telephone.

Michelle edged herself from the chair on the third ring and reached the phone. "Hello, this is Jenny and Michelle's place," she said cheerfully in a perfect rendition of the efficient secretary.

Jenny studied her friend. Afraid to hope. Afraid to care.

"It's for you," Michelle stated, and handed her the receiver. Then she mouthed, "It's a man."

Jenny pointed her finger at her heart, wondering if she'd misunderstood. "For me?"

Michelle nodded.

She took the phone and said in a friendly but professional-sounding voice, "This is Jenny Lancaster."

"Hello, Jenny."

Trey.

Jenny couldn't have been more shocked if it'd been Andrew Lloyd Webber himself, wanting her to star in his next musical.

"Trey!" she said, barely managing to hide her shock.

"I got your note," he announced.

"It was a surprise to get your Thanksgiving card," she said, holding the receiver with both hands. She felt lightheaded and wasn't sure if it was the shock of Trey's call or the fact that she hadn't eaten all day.

"You aren't coming home for the holidays."

Trey, her family. Everyone seemed to be pressuring her. It felt as if the walls were closing in around her. "I can't come," she told him, unable to disguise her own bitter disappointment. "I want to be there. More than anything, but I can't."

"That's what your note said. So the bright lights of the city have blinded you?"

"No." She longed to tell him how she hungered for the peace and solitude of Montana. New York City held its own excitement, its own energy. So often she'd walked down the crowded avenues and felt a rhythm, a cadence, that all but sang up from the asphalt. For three years she'd marched to that beat and hummed its special brand of music.

Yet the lone cry in the barren hills of home played longingly to her soul, its melody haunting her.

"Your family misses you," Trey said, tightening the screws of her regrets.

Jenny bit into her lower lip.

"I miss you," Trey added.

Jenny's eyes flew open. Trey, the man who'd invaded her dreams for weeks, admitted to missing her. He'd as much as said he wanted her home.

Regrets clamored against her chest, their fists sharp and pain filled. "I can't come," she whispered miserably.

Her words were met with silence.

"Can't or won't?" he asked starkly.

Brynn Cassidy crossed the street in front of Manhattan High and St. Philip's Cathedral. She found Father Grady, the gray-haired priest who'd become her friend, in the vestibule.

"Hello, Father," she said.

"Brynn, it's good to see you, my girl." His green Irish eyes lit up with warm delight.

"I got your message. You wanted to see me?"

"Yes. Come over to the rectory and I'll have Mrs. Houghton brew us a pot of tea."

Brynn glanced at her watch. She enjoyed visiting with Father Grady, but the older priest liked to talk and she didn't have time that afternoon.

Father Grady's eyes followed hers. "Do you have an appointment?"

"I have to stop off at Roberto Alcantara's this afternoon and pick up my car."

"I know Roberto well," Father Grady said, and motioned for her to precede him out of the church. "He's a fine young man." He paused to glance her way, and it seemed to Brynn that the priest was looking for her to elaborate. She didn't.

"Emilio's in my class."

"Ah, yes, Emilio. Roberto's done his best to keep his brother out of trouble. There haven't been problems with Emilio, have there?"

"No, no," Brynn was quick to tell him.

Father Grady's face relaxed.

Brynn lowered her gaze. It wasn't Emilio she'd clashed with, but Roberto. "I'm afraid Roberto doesn't think much of me."

Father Grady opened the door to the rectory. "I'm sure you're mistaken."

Brynn followed him inside. She preferred not to tell him about their brief confrontation. It rankled still. Roberto Alcantara had been both rude and unreasonable. But more than that, he'd been wrong.

"I'm not sure I have time for tea," she reiterated when she realized that Father Grady fully intended for her to stay and chat anyway.

"Nonsense." He escorted Brynn into the parlor and left her while he went in search of Mrs. Houghton, the elderly housekeeper who cared for Father Grady and the bishop when he was in residence.

Father Grady returned shortly with a tray and two cups. "I was hoping you'd be able to stop over this afternoon," he said as he set the tray on the coffee table. He handed Brynn a delicate china cup and took one himself before sitting across from her on the velvet settee. "The church is sponsoring a dance this Friday evening for the youth group."

Brynn had seen the posters. "I've heard several of the kids mention it."

"We generally have a good turnout."

Brynn was sure that was true.

"I was wondering," Father Grady said, studying her above the china cup, "if you'd agree to be one of the chaperones."

The request took Brynn by surprise, although in retrospect she supposed it shouldn't.

"The children are quite fond of you," he added as if he felt flattering her would be necessary. "Modesto Diaz mentioned your name the other day. He said . . ." Father Grady paused, and his eyes sparkled with humor.

"Yes?" Brynn prodded.

"Well, Modesto did say you were a little weird, but that he liked you anyway."

Brynn was sure her students didn't quite know what to make of her teaching methods.

"I realize it's an imposition asking you at this late date," Father

Grady continued. "I'd consider it a personal favor if you could come."

"I'll be happy to chaperone the dance," Brynn murmured.

"Now," Father Grady said, and set down his teacup. "Tell me what happened between you and Roberto Alcantara."

"It's nothing," she said, preferring to make light of their differences. "Actually Roberto's been most helpful. My car broke down and he's fixing it for me."

Father Grady said nothing.

"I was on my way to pick it up now."

"Roberto's been through some difficult times," the priest told her. "I'm not at liberty to tell you all the circumstances, but . . . "

"Oh, please, no. I wouldn't want you to break a confidence. It's nothing, really."

"If Roberto offended you . . . "

"He didn't. We had a difference of opinion."

Father Grady seemed relieved. "I'm glad to hear that. If you do find him disagreeable, all I ask is that you give him a bit of slack. He's a good man. I'd vouch for him any day."

"I'm sure what you say is true." Brynn stood and set the teacup back on the tray. "Now I really must be going."

Father Grady escorted her to the front door. "I'll see you Friday evening, then, around seven?"

Brynn nodded. "I'll be here."

The priest's eyes brightened with a smile. "Thank you, Brynn, I promise you won't regret this."

Brynn briskly walked the few blocks to Roberto Alcantara's garage. Earlier that afternoon, Emilio had personally delivered the message that her car was ready for her. The youth made sure the entire class heard him, as though the two of them had a personal business arrangement. Brynn had been forced to conceal her irritation.

As the afternoon progressed, she discovered she wasn't looking forward to another encounter with Emilio's older brother. The man was way off base. It was impossible to reason with anyone who regarded education as a waste of time. The fact that he'd actually urged his younger brother to drop out of school was nothing short of criminal.

"Yo, Miss Cassidy." Emilio, Modesto, and a few more of the boys from her class drove past her slowly and waved.

Brynn returned the gesture automatically. It wasn't until they'd turned the corner that she realized the boys were joyriding in her car.

Brynn bristled and hurried the last block to Roberto's. When she reached the garage, she stormed in the door. "Emilio's driving around in my car."

Roberto, who was working on another car, straightened. "Yes, I know."

She blinked. "You know."

"Yes, I gave him the keys myself."

The man had a way of flustering her unlike anyone she'd ever encountered. "Well, I want it back."

"You'll get it." He returned to the truck he was working on, disappearing behind the hood.

"Do you generally allow Emilio to ride around in your customer's cars?"

"No." His answer was clipped and didn't invite further inquiries.

His attitude—in fact, everything about Roberto—irritated Brynn. "I want my car returned," she insisted, her voice raised and tight. No matter what Father Grady claimed, it was plain to her that this man didn't have one shred of responsibility.

"And you'll have it."

Brynn crossed her arms and started to pace. Twice she made a show of looking at her watch.

"Emilio will be back any moment," Roberto said, continuing to work on another vehicle.

Bent over the engine as he was, Brynn couldn't see his face, but she had the distinct impression the mechanic was smiling. Her irritation amused him. That infuriated Brynn all the more.

"I want you to know that I don't appreciate being kept waiting."

Roberto straightened and reached for an oil rag; his dark, intense eyes meshed with hers. "I'm not one of your students, Miss Cassidy, so there's no need to yell."

"I was not yelling." She realized she was and lowered her voice immediately.

Roberto grinned broadly. "I suppose you'd like to send me to the principal."

"Ah-ha!" Her arm flew out and she pointed at him with her index finger, wagging it while she gathered her thoughts. "I thought as much. You blame me because your brother was suspended."

"On the contrary. Emilio knows not to fight on school grounds. What is it the law enforcement people are so fond of quoting? Do the crime, pay the time. My brother deserved what he got."

"But you blame me?"

"No, I just wish you'd quit filling my brother's head with garbage." Brynn clenched her jaw in an effort not to argue. This was the same mine-riddled ground they'd covered earlier. Brynn had no desire to do battle with Roberto a second time.

From the corner of her eye, she saw her car pull into an empty parking slot in front of the garage.

"Yo, Miss Cassidy," Emilio called out. "Your car's running like a dream."

Despite her misgivings, Brynn managed a smile. "If I could please have my bill," she said with stiff politeness.

Roberto gestured toward his brother. "Emilio will take care of that."

Brynn hesitated before leaving the garage for the small outer office where Emilio stood. Although Roberto had been deliberately rude, she felt obligated to him. "I want you to know I appreciate your help."

Involved once again with another vehicle, Roberto didn't bother to answer. It was almost as if he were ignoring her. His lack of a response to her peace offering offended her pride. Swallowing the small hurt, Brynn brushed the hair from her face.

"Your car runs like new," Emilio told her as he stepped behind the cash register. "Roberto asked me to test-drive it around the block. I hope you don't mind that I let a couple of my posse join me."

"Four is more than a couple," she informed him primly.

"I know," the youth said with a flash of pearly white teeth. "But it isn't every day that we can say we rode in a teacher's car."

Brynn decided it was best to not comment.

Emilio located the work order for her vehicle and scanned its contents. Brynn had been waiting for this moment, praying that the expense wouldn't wipe out the meager remainder of her budget for the month. The Escort had well over two hundred thousand miles on it and thus far had been relatively problem free. With the dread building up inside her, she opened her purse and took out her checkbook.

Something didn't appear to be right, because Emilio looked up from the bill. "I need to ask Roberto something," he said, and walked around from behind the counter. In the other room, the two brothers talked in hushed tones.

Emilio returned, wearing a wide grin. "It's on the house," he announced.

Brynn wasn't sure she understood. "What do you mean?"

Pride gleamed in the youth's dark eyes. "You don't owe us anything."

"But I can't let you do that. . . ."

"Roberto insists."

Still Brynn argued. "That wouldn't be right."

"It's a gift, Miss Cassidy," Emilio said with a deep sigh of frustration. "Didn't you ever learn you're not supposed to question someone when they give you a gift? Some lady with manners wrote it up in a book. You read all the time . . . you must have read that."

Brynn was uncertain. "Let me at least pay for any parts."

"No way." The teenager held up both hands as though she were holding him up.

"But carburetors can be expensive." She didn't want Roberto absorbing the cost of this.

"Roberto says he found another carburetor at the junkyard and got it for next to nothing. Besides, he let me do most of the work myself." His dark eyes pleaded with her to accept this small gift.

"Emilio, I don't know how to thank you."

His face erupted in a wide smile. "I'll think of something."

Roberto shouted from the other room, and Emilio's smart smile disappeared. "Think nothing of it, Miss Cassidy."

"Thank you both again." Brynn felt like a fool for having made such an issue of Emilio driving her vehicle. She glanced toward the garage, but Roberto was bent over the side of the truck, busy at work. "Tell your brother that I'm grateful."

"I will." Emilio followed her outside and held open her car door for her.

When she couldn't find her car keys, she eyed the youth. A desperate look came over him, and he slapped his hands over his shirt and pants pockets, then laughed and withdrew them from his hip pocket. "I had you worried there, didn't I?"

Brynn rolled her eyes, then started the engine. As Emilio had said earlier, it purred like new. Her car sounded better than it had in years. She backed out of the driveway. It was as she started down the street that she noticed Roberto Alcantara watching her from inside the building.

He owed her an apology, Roberto reasoned. He'd been angry and frustrated the day they'd met, and he'd taken his irritation out on her. True, he believed the things he'd said, but generally he kept his opinions to himself. It had helped relieve his irritation to sound off at Emilio's teacher; but it hadn't been fair.

An hour before he'd met Brynn, Roberto had learned his offer to lease a building in another neighborhood had been rejected. It hadn't been the first time a landlord had refused to rent to him. Naturally he'd been given some flimsy excuse, but Roberto had learned long ago the real reason. No one wanted a Hispanic taking up residence nearby.

Brynn Cassidy was everything Emilio had said. Bright. Intelligent. Pretty. Roberto feared his younger brother was half in love with her himself. But this spunky teacher was off-limits to the both of them, and Roberto knew it. It would be best if he never saw her again.

Funny how a woman could be so dangerous; but Roberto had recognized it from the first moment they'd met. Brynn Cassidy just might teach him to dream, too.

Friday evening Brynn arrived at the gymnasium behind St. Philip's. She walked in the gaily decorated room and stopped to admire the decorations. Red and green streamers were looped across the ceiling from one end of the room to the other. A refreshment table was set up alongside the folded bleachers.

"Hello, Miss Cassidy." The first one to greet her was Suzie Chang, who looked exceptionally pretty in a dark blue silk pants suit.

"Oh, Suzie, you look so nice."

The Chinese girl lowered her head and blushed. "So do you."

Brynn hadn't been exactly sure what to wear and had opted for a blouse and skirt and patent-leather flats. Although she'd attended a number of school dances at St. Mary's, she'd never actually served as a chaperone. Generally the girls' school relied on parents and members of the PTA.

"Miss Cassidy," Emilio called. He helped himself to a handful of cookies. "What are you doing here?"

"I'm a chaperone."

"Hey, that's cool. So's my brother."

Brynn hadn't recognized Roberto without his coveralls. She hadn't given Roberto much notice before, but now . . . caught by his piercing dark eyes, Brynn found it difficult to look away.

"Hello, Roberto."

"Miss Cassidy." He nodded politely in her direction.

The music started. It came from a sound system with large speakers that blared from the front of the stage. No one seemed to want to be the first one on the dance floor.

"Hey, you two," Emilio said. "Shouldn't you start the dancing or something?"

*   *   *

Hannah needed to talk to Joshua. It was important that she return the gloves as soon as possible. It was wrong of her to have kept them this long. Then to walk past him on the street and pretend that she didn't know him was a terrible insult. She'd witnessed for herself the surprise and confusion in his gaze. Yet she was forever grateful that he'd read her silent message and hadn't greeted her. Hannah didn't know how she would explain knowing him to her mother.

For herself, Hannah was both bewildered and guilty, and she felt like a coward. It was unfair to Joshua to lead him to believe that she was free to care for him. Unfair to Carl, who'd courted her faithfully these many months. She'd juggled with her conscience until she couldn't think straight any longer.

"I do wish we weren't doing this," Hannah said to her mother.

"Doing what?" Ruth questioned. "Buying my daughter a trousseau? Don't be ridiculous."

"We haven't set the wedding date yet."

"You will soon enough." In the eyes of her parents she was all but married to Carl Rabinsky.

"Your father and I have patiently waited all these years for a man who was worthy of you."

A lifetime of accepting what her parents felt was right was what helped Hannah hold her tongue.

"Such a wedding you'll have," Ruth promised, her eyes alight with excitement.

Hannah found she couldn't look at her mother.

"Your father's already talking about the food for the reception. I promise you it will be one that people will talk about for years to come. You are our only child. God's gift to us. Our joy."

"Mama, what if I don't love Carl?"

Her mother hesitated, but for only a moment. "Nonsense. I know you, Hannah, you wouldn't have agreed to be his wife if you didn't love him. Carl will make you a good husband. Every girl has doubts when it comes time to pledge her heart to one man."

"What if I'd met another man?"

"Who?" her mother demanded as if this were impossible.

"Someone I liked very much and would like to know better."

Her mother frowned and shook her head. "You won't. But if you do, then talk to Carl. Tell him your thoughts."

"I will," Hannah promised, but she had the feeling that it would be even more difficult to discuss this matter with Carl than with her mother.

"Now come along, we have lots to buy."

Hannah shuffled along beside her mother. Never had she dreamed that she would dread a shopping expedition the way she did this one.

It was in Saks Fifth Avenue that her mother stopped. "Shall we look at wedding dresses?" Ruth asked, her eyes warm and gentle.

"Don't you think that would be premature?" Already Hannah's arms were burdened with packages. "I'm tired, Mama, can we go home?"

Ruth released a low sigh. "Yes, perhaps that would be for the best."

Outside once more, Hannah felt invigorated as the cold hit against her cheeks. She matched her steps with those of her mother, who walked along, humming softly to herself. It took Hannah a moment to realize where the melody was coming from.

"You're singing," Hannah commented.

Ruth laughed and nodded. "So I am. I do when I'm especially happy." As they stopped for traffic, Ruth placed her hands against Hannah's pink cheeks. "You're going to be the most beautiful bride in all of New York. Mark my words, Hannah Morganstern. I get excited every time I think about planning your wedding."

Once they were back at the deli, Hannah escaped to her room. As soon as she could, she made an excuse to go out. Almost always she told her parents where she was going, but not this time.

When she arrived at Joshua's office the receptionist recognized her.

"Is Mr. Shadduck available?" she asked.

The woman looked down at the schedule. "He left no more than a minute ago."

"Oh." She wasn't able to hide her frustration.

"You might be able to catch him."

"Thank you." Hannah rushed out of the office and hurried into the first available elevator. Her heart felt as though it would explode as she made her way to the front of the office building. On the sidewalk, she looked both ways and sighed with relief when she spied Joshua walking away from her, carrying a briefcase.

"Joshua," she called.

He turned at the sound of her voice, and his face lit up with pleasure. "Hannah." He started toward her.

"I'm so sorry," she said in a breathless rush. She planted her hand over her heart in an effort to regain her breath.

Joshua wrapped his arm around her shoulders and steered her out of the heavy foot traffic. "Don't worry about it," he said gently.

"But . . ." She'd been unforgivably rude.

"Let's sit down a minute and talk this out," he suggested.

Hannah knew his idea was much better than her handing him back his gift in the middle of a New York sidewalk. At the same time, she feared that spending time with Joshua, even a short amount, would make it all the more difficult to do what she knew she must.

They strolled until Joshua pointed across the street to a five-star hotel famous for its afternoon teas.

Hannah wanted to protest that a cafe would serve just as well, but she wasn't given the opportunity. Before she could suggest someplace else, Joshua had taken her by the arm. Together they raced across the street.

The hotel lobby was filled with polished crystal. Enormous chandeliers gleamed from above, their glittering lights transforming the entire area.

Huge floral wreaths decorated in gold lamé bows hung from marble columns. The registration desk was checkered with poinsettias. Light music swirled about them like a cool autumn mist. Before Hannah had a chance to comment, she was led into a private dining room.

Before Joshua could give the man instructions, the waiter handed them a gold-tasseled menu. Joshua ordered the tea, and the other man quietly slipped away.

Joshua smiled at her. "You said there was something you wanted to tell me?"

Chapter

★ ✬ ★

7

This meeting with Joshua was so much more difficult than Hannah thought it would be. But there was no help for it. She had to tell him she was engaged to Carl. To delay any longer would be a grave disservice to them both. As they sat in the elegant hotel restaurant waiting for the tea to be served, Hannah struggled to find the words.

"Joshua," she said, dragging a deep breath through her lungs, her heart heavy.

"You received the gloves?"

"Yes, thank you, but I can't accept—"

"Joshua Shadduck?"

Hannah was cut off midsentence by a well-dressed middle-aged woman who stopped at their table. Her gaze drifted from Joshua to Hannah, and her eyes were marked with warm approval.

"Gloria." Joshua stood and enthusiastically hugged the white-haired woman. He turned to Hannah. "Hannah Morganstern, meet Judge Fowler."

Impressed to meet a judge, Hannah smiled and said, "I'm honored."

"I've been meaning to get in touch with you all week," Gloria said. Her gaze connected briefly with Hannah's once again. "But I can see that now isn't a good time. I promise I'll call you soon."

"I'll look forward to hearing from you," Joshua returned. Before he could reseat himself, the judge whispered something in his ear, then turned away.

Joshua grinned broadly, then explained to Hannah. "She approves."

"Approves?"

"Of you. She told me it was high time I . . . well, never mind."

"Joshua." A stout figure of a man approached their table next. "By George, it's good to see you," he said, sounding genuinely pleased.

"Hello, Tom." Although Hannah didn't know Joshua well, she could hear the frustration in his voice.

The other man studied Hannah with barely disguised admiration. His blue eyes twinkled. Before Joshua could introduce him properly, he stretched his hand across the table. "Tom Colfax," he said.

"Hannah Morganstern," she replied, and they exchanged brief handshakes.

Tom's admiration was straightforward. "I know this sounds like a worn-out line, but have we met?"

"I don't think so," Hannah replied.

Tom rubbed the side of his jaw, then shook his head as if to say he was certain he'd seen her someplace before.

The two men exchanged information, then Tom drifted away. He continued to wear a puzzled look and glanced over his shoulder once.

Joshua exhaled sharply. "This isn't going to work," he muttered.

That was what Hannah had been struggling to tell him since they'd met, but she hadn't been able to put it into words.

Joshua set the linen napkin on the table. "Come on, let's get out of here."

Hannah's first instinct was to argue, but she wasn't given the chance as she followed Joshua through the elegantly decorated lobby to the street outside. "Where are we going?" she asked, a little breathless.

He turned as though he hadn't given the matter a second thought. "I don't know. My apartment is a short walk from here."

"I can't," she said, her heart in her throat. "I have to be back shortly."

Joshua's gaze narrowed as if to suggest he didn't believe her. "Already?"

"Yes." She should have told him earlier and been done with it, but each time she shared his company it became more difficult. Now she found herself frantic to say what she must.

"Joshua, please listen to me." She hardly sounded like herself. Her voice was tight with emotion as she brushed the hair from her cheek. She opened her purse and handed him the soft deerskin gloves. "I can't keep these. They're a lovely, thoughtful gift, but I can't accept them."

He took the gloves, but his eyes revealed his disappointment. "Why not?"

People wove their way around them, and her throat tightened with regret. "I'm so sorry, Joshua, so very sorry, but I'm . . . There's someone else." That sounded much better than announcing she was engaged.

Joshua's face revealed nothing. "The man you were with at the parade?"

"Yes."

"The one who abandoned you?" His feelings for Carl were more than clear.

"Carl didn't abandon me, we simply lost each other." Carl hadn't deserted her, not on purpose, and she found it important that Joshua know that. Carl might have his faults, but nearly everyone was flawed in one way or another. He'd gotten separated from her on Thanksgiving Day, and with so many people crowding the sidewalks, watching the parade, it had been impossible for him to find her again.

For a long time Joshua said nothing. Then, "Are you going to marry him?"

A definitive answer was her only recourse. Joshua deserved the truth. To hedge now might give him reason to believe there was a chance for them.

"We're engaged."

"That wasn't my question. I asked if you were going to marry him."

"Yes . . . of course." But she sounded unsure even to her own ears.

He hesitated, but only for a moment. "I see."

Now was the time to turn away. To end any kind of relationship before it began. One thing was certain: she shouldn't have paused. But she did. "I like you, Joshua." More than she should. More than she wanted to. "I misled you, and I regret that."

"Carl isn't right for you." His words were stark and cool, his gaze intense.

"You don't know that," she argued. "You've never even met Carl."

"I know you."

She lowered her eyes because meeting his gaze had become impossible. Her throat felt as if it were about to close up on her. "I have to go."

"Not yet," he said, stopping her. He backed her into the shadows until her shoulders butted against the side of the brick structure. Instinctively she clenched the lapels of his overcoat. Even when she realized he intended to kiss her, she couldn't find the words to object. Being inherently honest, Hannah realized this was exactly what she'd wanted for a long time.

Slowly, as though he expected her to protest, Joshua lowered his mouth to hers. She assumed his kiss would be hard and demanding, a penance required for having misled him. A penalty to be paid.

But she was wrong.

He pressed his lips gently over hers in the lightest, the tenderest, of contacts. So sweet. So smooth. The pressure increased, so gradual at first that she didn't notice. His lips worked over hers, sliding, then deepening, encouraging her to open to him.

With him as her tutor, Hannah eased open her mouth and moaned. This was nothing like the quick pecks and almost apologetic exchanges she'd experienced with Carl. Nothing like anything she'd experienced with anyone. Her nails dug into his coat, and she responded with a lifetime of pent-up longings.

It seemed to require a great deal of effort for Joshua to break off the kiss. Even then he seemed to ease himself away from her with a series of short but equally potent kisses.

He held her against him, and she stayed, the ragged edge of his breathing echoing in her ear. Her own breathing was just as unstable. Wrapped in the warm cocoon of his arms, Hannah never wanted to leave.

"Please . . . my family is waiting. They don't know where I am." It was pointless to continue. Pointless to torture themselves.

His arms tightened before he released her. "Meet me," he whispered against her cheek. "Monday evening at eight at the skating rink at Rockefeller Center."

"I can't. You know I can't."

"Be there, Hannah," he pleaded. "I need time to think. We both do. You don't love Carl."

"Joshua . . . "

"You don't love him," he returned with conviction, "otherwise you'd never have allowed me to kiss you like that." With that he turned away.

Hannah wanted to run after him and explain that she wouldn't show. She had no intention of continuing this charade. That was why she'd told him about Carl. It was too late for them. Much too late.

"Joshua," she called.

He ignored her, and because she was forced into it, she raced after him. She was out of breath by the time she reached him.

"I won't be there," she cried. "I won't."

He turned, and for the first time since she'd told him about her commitment to Carl, he smiled, saying without words that he believed otherwise.

"You'll be wasting your time," she argued heatedly.

Joshua said nothing, then wrapped his arm around her waist and dragged her to him. His kiss was short but thorough. When he finished, he exhaled slowly. "You'll be there," he said with supreme confidence. "You won't be able to stay away."

"Will Hannah meet Joshua?" Shirley asked Goodness. The two had parked themselves atop a light fixture in the Morgansterns' deli. Hannah's father was locking the doors while her mother was upstairs preparing the evening meal.

"What do you think?" Goodness was downright gleeful.

"What do I think?" Shirley repeated. "I think you're headed for serious trouble with Gabriel, that's what I think."

Goodness couldn't have disagreed more. "Gabriel knew exactly what was going to happen," she insisted. "He might think Carl Rabinsky is the cat's meow, but you and I both know he isn't the right man for Hannah."

Shirley's look was skeptical. "Why isn't he?"

"It's clear to me that Carl's as confused about all this as Hannah. The poor boy's parents had more to do with the engagement than he did. They pushed him into it."

"How do you know that?"

"I don't," Goodness confessed reluctantly, "but I'd wager a good deal that was the case."

"What you're wagering," Shirley seemed to feel obliged to tell her, "is our futures. You've done this before, you know. My heaven," she continued, wringing her hands. "I can't get involved in your prayer request, not when I've got troubles of my own."

"Oh?"

"It's Brynn and Roberto. This is simply not the time for her to walk around with her head in the clouds. She needs her wits about her. I'm afraid something serious is about to happen, and I can't be constantly fretting about what you're getting into."

"Me?" If she didn't know better, Goodness would be insulted.

"Yes, you. I beg of you, Goodness, kindly leave matters be with Carl and Hannah."

Goodness considered it seriously, but not for long. She didn't mean to be a rabble-rouser, but there were some matters that one couldn't ignore. Unfortunately this was one of those times.

"I can't."

Shirley groaned, and her head slumped forward. "Why did I know you were going to say that?"

532 ★ *Debbie Macomber*

"I'm sorry, really I am. But I asked myself exactly why Gabriel would assign this particular prayer request to me."

"What do you mean?"

"Think about it," Goodness said, crossing her arms. "Ruth Morganstern prayed that Hannah would make a good marriage."

"Yes," Shirley agreed impatiently.

"It was as clear as the feathers in our wings that Carl was about to ask for Hannah's hand in marriage. Both Hannah's parents are nuts about Carl, and his family about her."

"So?"

Goodness had a hard time believing that her fellow prayer ambassador could be so thickheaded. "Don't you see?"

"Obviously not."

"Well," Goodness said with a sorry lack of patience, "Gabriel assumed the assignment would be a snap. An engagement to Carl was in the cards already. Really all that was required was for me to stand back and let it happen. Once Hannah was formally engaged to Carl I was supposed to pretend it was all my doing and promptly return to heaven, the assignment complete."

"Hannah is formally engaged to Carl," Shirley reminded her.

Shirley was missing her point entirely. "That's true, but Gabriel doesn't know that."

"In other words," Shirley said, walking circles around Goodness as she mulled over the situation, "you think this job is another one of Gabriel's little token assignments."

Goodness folded her arms and nodded with a good deal of ceremony. "I do indeed, and frankly I'm insulted."

"You mean like the chess set for Craig?"

Goodness nodded. "Exactly."

This information seemed to fluster her friend. "My oh my, I don't know what to think."

"Well, I do," Goodness returned with a hint of self-righteousness. "It was clear to me from the first that Carl Rabinsky isn't the right husband for Hannah. In good conscience I can't idly stand by and let her marry the wrong man."

"What are you going to do?" Shirley asked, and then crunched up her face as if she were afraid of the answer.

Goodness relaxed and smiled. "I'm not sure yet, but I do know one thing."

"What's that?"

"She's not going to marry Carl."

*   *   *

Sunday morning Brynn quietly slipped inside the pew at St. Philip's, crossed herself, and knelt on the padded kneeler. She closed her eyes and bowed her head, fully intending to pray. But it wasn't thoughts of God that filled her mind. Instead she found herself mulling over the night before with the church youth group and Roberto Alcantara.

Every time Brynn remembered the dance in which they'd shared the duty as chaperones, a warm, expectant feeling stole over her. It had all started innocently enough when they'd first danced together. No one seemed to want to be the first couple on the floor, so Roberto, stiffly, had asked her. She knew from the way his lips tightened that he wasn't keen on being her partner. Taking it personally, she'd glared back at him, letting it be known that she didn't relish his company, either.

Yet from that shaky beginning, something fragile and exciting had blossomed. As the music started, Roberto had held her awkwardly in his arms, his body rigid, as if to avoid touching her.

Then gradually, as they'd warmed to the rhythm of the music, he'd relaxed. Because he had, she had too. Slowly, almost without being aware of what was happening, she'd found herself tucked securely in Roberto's arms. It amazed her how well they performed together, how easy his steps were to follow. Anyone looking at them would have assumed they were longtime partners. Halfway through the dance Roberto had smiled, and she'd shyly returned the gesture. Then he'd tucked his head close to hers, and they'd continued to sway gracefully across the polished gym floor.

From that point forward in the evening, Brynn had looked for an excuse to dance with Roberto a second time. Unfortunately their duties had prevented them from spending any more time together. The teenage dance had gone on until almost midnight, and the high schoolers couldn't have kept them apart more had they plotted to do so.

From the silent messages Roberto had sent her way, from the quick exchanges of eye contact, she'd realized that he was as eager to be with her as she was with him.

After the dance, Roberto had walked her to her car. At first they'd been shy with each other, not knowing what to say. But gradually that had changed, and they'd chatted freely. Brynn was certain Roberto had meant to ask her for a date, but before he'd had a chance, a fight had broken out between two boys. In his frustration, Roberto had closed his eyes and forcefully released his breath. Brynn had felt the regret in him as he'd turned away and hurried toward the scuffle.

Long after she was home, Brynn had found it impossible to sleep. Again and again her mind had reviewed the one dance she'd shared with Roberto. The memory had left her hungering to learn what would have happened had they been free to enjoy each other's company.

The more she thought about Roberto, the more she admired his accomplishments. He worked hard and seemed determined to make his business a successful enterprise. He genuinely cared about his brother's welfare and took an active role in the community. Father Grady, whom Brynn considered to be an excellent judge of character, couldn't say enough good about Roberto.

True, they'd started off on the wrong foot, but Brynn was eager to make up for that and start again. If she did have God's attention, then what she sought was for Roberto to be at church this morning.

Giving up the pretense of praying, Brynn opened her eyes and sat on the hard wooden pew. She didn't see Roberto and couldn't swivel around to look without being obvious.

Triumphant organ music announced the beginning of mass, which Father Grady celebrated. Not until Brynn stood to follow the others to the altar for communion did she spy Roberto. Instantly her heart gladdened.

He saw her too, because she watched as a brief smile touched his eyes.

After mass Roberto was waiting on the top of the church steps for her. Following the throng of the faithful out of the large double-wide doors, Brynn saw Roberto almost immediately and waved.

"So we meet again," she said. She hated the breathless quality to her voice, but she couldn't hide how pleased she was to see him.

He acknowledged her with a short nod.

"Did the boys give you any trouble last night?" she asked, wanting to learn the outcome of the fight.

He shrugged as though to say it wasn't anything serious. "I separated them and had Emilio take Modesto with him."

"I'm glad."

Once again Brynn noted what a fine figure of a man Roberto made. She didn't know what had blinded her earlier.

"So it was Modesto," she murmured. That didn't surprise her.

"Mike and Modesto were going at it until—"

"Mike?" Brynn interrupted. "Not Mike Glasser?"

"That's the name."

Brynn hadn't seen the morose young man all evening. But then it would be characteristic of Mike to conceal himself in the shadows. If he had come to the dance, then perhaps some girl had caught his eye. Brynn hoped that was the case. She genuinely liked Mike and wished she knew how to reach him.

"It surprises me that Mike would fight anyone, especially Modesto." Although she said the words aloud, she didn't expect Roberto to comment. Mike wasn't a fighter. Modesto was much more savvy when it came to such matters. The Hispanic youth would have dropped Mike in record time.

"Whatever plagued him was a hot issue," Roberto commented. "From what the others told me, Mike went after Modesto without provocation. The funny thing is, I don't think Modesto really wanted to fight him."

"But you were able to break it up before anyone was hurt?" she asked, unable to hide her concern.

Roberto nodded, and a hint of a smile turned up the edges of his mouth. "No problem."

Brynn relaxed.

Roberto was about to say something when Emilio strolled past casually and stopped as though surprised to find his older brother spending time with his teacher. "Mornin', Miss Cassidy."

"Morning, Emilio."

The teenager turned to his brother. "Have you asked her yet?"

Roberto answered in Spanish, his voice low and threatening.

Emilio ignored him. "He's going to invite you over to the apartment for breakfast. I'm supposed to make myself scarce." He grinned boyishly and added in a low voice, "I'd be careful if I were you, 'cause it looks to me like my big brother intends to put the make on you."

Brynn couldn't keep from laughing, but Roberto wasn't amused. He spoke again, and his tone was clear. He wanted his brother to shut up and leave them alone.

If Emilio felt the least bit threatened by his brother, he didn't let it show. If anything, the younger Alcantara couldn't have looked more pleased.

"You should have seen Roberto this morning," he continued undaunted. His smile was full and cocky. "He was up at the crack of dawn, shaving and splashing on that fancy cologne he likes so well."

"Emilio." Again Roberto threatened him.

"He likes you, Teach, big time."

Brynn knew smiling was probably the worst thing she could do, but she couldn't make herself stop. Emilio was telling her everything she wanted to hear.

Disgruntled, Roberto pulled his wallet from his hip pocket and jerked out a twenty-dollar bill. "Get lost for a couple of hours," he instructed.

A wide grin split Emilio's face. "I'm outta here." He looked to Brynn and winked. "Have fun, you two." With that he was gone.

"I apologize for my brother," Roberto said flatly.

Brynn arched one brow. "Was what Emilio said true? Do you intend to put the make on me?"

His intensely dark eyes didn't waver from hers. "That depends."

"On what?"

"Several matters," he said, and cleared his throat. "Mostly on if you feel the same way about me as I do you." He reached for her hand and laced his fingers with hers. "I'd be honored if you'd join me for breakfast."

"Does that mean you're volunteering to cook?"

He didn't hesitate. "Yes."

"Then I accept."

Hand in hand they strolled down the sidewalk.

"We have nothing in common." It was as though he felt obligated to remind her of that.

"I certainly don't agree with your views on education," she added. If he was looking for reasons they shouldn't see each other, she had a list of her own.

Roberto's chest deflated as he released a pent-up breath. "You're Irish, I'm Hispanic. I have no business bringing you home with me."

"But you are, aren't you?"

"Yes," he said, as though admitting to a fault.

"Why?" Perhaps she should leave matters as they are and not ask.

"Because I had to know." His voice was gruff with impatience, but Brynn understood. She was equally curious. Equally fascinated with him.

"I needed to know, too," she admitted softly.

Roberto's hand squeezed hers, and when she looked up, he smiled.

He brought her to the apartment he shared with his brother. The compact unit was decorated with large overstuffed pieces of furniture. The royal blue material had several crocheted doilies flattened across the back.

"My mother made those," Roberto explained when Brynn ran her finger over the delicately crafted cotton threads.

"They're lovely."

"So are you."

Before Brynn could comment, Roberto turned her in his arms. She came willingly, without a qualm, eager for his kiss. He didn't disappoint her. Soon his mouth settled firmly over hers. His kiss was both hot and compelling. Brynn's breath caught in her throat as he wrapped her securely in his arms. She buried her face in the hollow of his neck and breathed in the warm, spicy rum scent of him. The bay cologne reminded her of what Emilio had said, and she smiled softly and pressed her lips against his smoothly shaven skin.

"I meant to wait to kiss you," he confessed, his lips in her hair. "At least until after breakfast."

"I didn't want to wait."

He continued to caress her back. "We shouldn't be doing this."

"You're right," she agreed, and stepped up onto the tips of her toes to kiss him again. The world dissolved, melting away any resistance that might have remained. "We're both crazy."

"The world is crazy," Roberto agreed, "but I haven't the strength to resist you."

Brynn closed her eyes and pressed her head against the solid strength of his shoulder. She was content to stay as they were, but she wasn't blind to their differences. What Roberto said was true. They had little in common other than the fact that they were crazy about each other.

Jenny was convinced she was coming down with a cold. Her throat ached, and she alternated between hot flashes and the chills. And she swore every bone in her body ached. A cold complicated by the flu.

She managed to sing her way through the two production numbers she was involved in from *South Pacific*. She smiled as if she hadn't a care in the world, delivered the dinners to her customers, and counted the minutes until she'd finished her shift.

When she returned to the apartment the first thing she did was take a long, hot shower. Even with the comfort of warm water raining down on her, she developed a hacking cough.

"You don't sound so good," Michelle called from the other side of the bathroom.

"I'm miserable."

"Do you want me to get you some aspirin?" her roommate offered.

"No thanks," Jenny said as she opened the door. "I took some when I got home." Dressed in a thick terry-cloth robe, she ambled into the living room and buried herself under the wool afghan her mother had mailed her last Christmas.

"I bet a nice hot bowl of chicken soup would help you to feel better."

"I'm fine, Nurse Michelle," Jenny teased.

"You need something," her roommate insisted.

What she needed, Jenny realized, wasn't to be easily found. More than at any other time since her arrival in New York, Jenny needed her family.

Jenny could feel a sneeze coming on, and she reached for a tissue and nearly blew a hole through it with the force of her misery.

"My goodness." Michelle laughed.

"What about the Christmas party?" Jenny asked, wanting to take her mind off her woes. She needed to divert Michelle before she whipped out a thermometer and dispensed massive doses of TLC. Struggling as she was against bouts of self-pity, Jenny preferred to suffer alone.

"Oh, my goodness, the party! I nearly forgot." Michelle walked over to her purse and took out a list. "I talked to Paul. You remember Paul Fredricks, don't you?"

Jenny nodded, although she hadn't a clue who Paul was. She'd figure it out in a moment.

"Anyway, Paul says the fifth would work out great."

"The fifth is fine with me." For the life of her, Jenny couldn't figure out why they would need to clear the date with Paul Fredricks, but again that was something she would leave to reason out later.

"Do you agree?"

"Sure." One day was as good as any other as far as she was concerned. "I'll make sure I have the fifth off."

"Good. I added Paul's name to the list while I was at it. You don't object, do you?"

"Of course he can come. The more the merrier." Paul Fredricks, of course. He was the actor who'd captured Michelle's attention and her heart after one short meeting. Her roommate seemed to think no one had noticed. Perhaps no one else had, but Jenny wasn't as easily fooled.

"Look," Michelle said, standing inside the kitchen. "The message machine is blinking."

"I forgot to check," Jenny admitted. The first order of business when she'd returned home was aspirin and a hot shower. "Who called?"

"I don't know." Michelle pushed down the button and reached for a pad and pen.

"It's Irene," Michelle cried.

It would be just like their agent to leave the most important news of their careers on the answering machine.

"I don't know where you girls are," Irene's elevated voice said, "but I sincerely hope you'll be home soon. Now listen up! I talked to John Peterman this afternoon, and he wants you both back for a second audition first thing in the morning. I repeat, he wants to see you both again."

Michelle looked to Jenny.

Jenny looked to Michelle.

Michelle threw open her arms and screamed.

Her cold forgotten, Jenny tossed aside the quilt and raced over to her friend's open arms. Together they danced around the living room, screaming at the top of their lungs.

Then Jenny started to cough again.

Chapter

★ ☆ ★

8

"Suzie, can I see you after class?" Brynn asked the Chinese girl. Of all her students, Brynn found real encouragement in watching this particular teenager's progress. Suzie's written essays revealed a quick, analytical mind and a thirst for knowledge. Brynn hadn't said anything to Suzie, but she'd taken it upon herself to inquire about the possibility of a full-ride scholarship for the girl.

Suzie glanced up from her desk and blinked. "Did I do something wrong?"

"No, not at all," Brynn quickly assured her. She patted Suzie's shoulder, and the girl returned to her writing assignment.

"Do you want to see me, too?" Malcolm called from the back of the classroom, disrupting the calm. That was Malcolm's specialty.

"Not today," she said.

Malcolm folded his muscular arms and leaned back on his desk chair until his shoulders were braced against the wall. His eyes were round with irritation. "I heard you stopped by my place yesterday and asked to speak to my mother. If you got something to say to her, you can say it to me first." He lifted his chin an inch in open defiance.

It was clear Malcolm didn't trust her. Brynn doubted that many of her students did, although she'd worked hard to gain their confidence. Again and again she butted her head against the thick walls of doubt and suspicion. To the best of her knowledge she hadn't gone against her word once, yet her students acted as if they were waiting for her to knife them in the back. Certainly the incident with Emilio that first day hadn't helped matters any.

"My stepdad said you stopped by my place, too." This was from Yolanda.

"Are you looking to make trouble for us?" It was Malcolm again. "What'd you want with my mom?"

"Yeah. You ain't got no right to talk about me behind my back."

Brynn could see that she'd best explain the purpose of those after-school visits. She'd hoped meeting her students' families would be a positive experience; instead she'd incurred the mistrust and ire of her class.

Emilio sat up and looked over his shoulder. "Miss Cassidy comes to my apartment most every afternoon, and I ain't making no fuss about it."

His remark was followed by several boos and hisses. Emilio just smiled. He reveled in the fact that Brynn had been seeing a good deal of Roberto. What he said, however, wasn't true.

"All right, all right," Brynn said, holding up her hands. "It looks like I owe you an explanation."

"You're damn right you do."

Brynn looked into a sea of angry faces. "Malcolm, you're right. I did stop off at your place yesterday afternoon. I wanted to tell your mother it was a pleasure to have you in my class and report to her that your progress in the last few weeks has been nothing short of amazing."

Malcolm's mouth snapped closed. He looked confused, then relieved. "You wanted to tell her good things about me?"

"Is that why you came to my house?" Yolanda asked.

"Yes. I'd hoped to visit everyone's family by the end of the quarter. Yolanda, I couldn't be more pleased with how well you're doing. You've maintained a B average, and I wanted your family to know how hard you've been working."

"You won't be able to say that about me."

Denzil was right about that. His grades had been dismal, and he gave little if any thought or effort to his assignments. His contributions to the class were limited to disruptions and arguments.

"Well," she said, thinking on her feet. "I thought I'd tell your parents how I've noticed your ability to argue an issue from any point. That's the quality of a good attorney. If you were the least bit interested, you could make a career learning the law."

"An attorney?" Denzil sat up straighter on his chair. "Me, an attorney?" He laughed under his breath. "I've had lots of experience with the law, and I've met some of those fast-talkin' lawyers, too. Only they were looking to toss my butt in jail."

"There are other kinds of attorneys," Brynn told him.

"I could wear one of those fancy silk suits, couldn't I?"

"Of course. Listen, Denzil," she said, her convictions causing her voice to grow strong and sure, "this is exactly what I've been telling you all quarter. You can be anything you want. The power is right here inside you." She held her clenched fist against her breast. "All you've got to do is want it bad enough."

"I ain't never had anyone tell my mother good things about me," Yolanda said. "The only time a teacher ever came to my house was because she thought I took something out of her stinking purse." Looking away, she sighed loudly. "I did it, too, because that teacher was a real jerk. She wasn't even fair."

"You got any good things to tell Roberto about me?" Emilio asked, and draped his elbows over the back of his seat. He was sitting proud.

"I have plenty to tell Roberto about you," Brynn teased as she rubbed the chalk dust from the palms of her hands.

The class laughed, just as Brynn intended they should.

"Now that I've answered your questions, please return to your writing assignment." Generally, when she directed her students' attention back to a written task, a grumble of discontent would spread across the room. Not this time.

After the bell rang, dismissing the class, Suzie Chang made her way to Brynn's desk. The shy girl clenched her books tightly. "You wanted to talk to me, Miss Cassidy?"

"Yes," Brynn said, scooting the chair back. "Suzie, you're an excellent student. This last paper you wrote about Anne Frank is as good as anything I've read on the subject. You revealed both insight and sensitivity to the Jewish girl's plight."

Uncomfortable with the praise, the teenager lowered her gaze. "Thank you."

"I'd like to know if you plan on attending college next year."

"College." The girl's eyes lit up briefly, then she sobered and slowly shook her head. "I can't."

"But Suzie, you're exactly the kind of student who should continue their education. I can feel the hunger in you, the desire to learn. There's a way, I promise you. I can help you if you want."

The girl shifted her weight from one foot to the other. She kept her head lowered and refused to meet Brynn's eyes. "I can't, Miss Cassidy."

"Suzie, didn't you hear what I said to Denzil earlier? Where there's a will, there's a way. Now if you're worried about the money, there are scholarships. I'll help you fill out the applications, and . . . "

Suzie's head snapped up, and Brynn noticed that the teenager's face was streaked with tears. "A scholarship isn't going to help me, Miss Cassidy. Nothing will." Having said that, Suzie turned and raced out of the classroom.

Stunned, Brynn sat at her desk for several moments, pondering Suzie's words. Nothing would help her? That made no sense.

Feeling as though she'd somehow failed her brightest student, Brynn left the building, determined to try again to meet Denzil's and Malcolm's parents. Perhaps she'd have more success now that the word was out that she wanted to compliment the teens instead of complain.

A block away from the school the streets were dirty, filled with litter and broken glass. A discarded davenport was turned upside down and garbage dumped in the ripped undercarriage. The smells of rotting food were potent enough to cause Brynn to turn her head away.

Dusk settled over the city. The streetlights that weren't broken blinked on, casting a clouded yellow glow to the filth on the sidewalk.

From the distance, Brynn watched as a man approached her. She stiffened, then reminded herself she had nothing to fear. This was a violent neighborhood, but like Father Grady, Brynn had faith in the goodwill of those who occupied the tenements.

As the figure of the man grew near, Brynn recognized Roberto. When he realized it was she, his steps became quick and filled with purpose. The tension drained from her, and Brynn relaxed. They'd met twice in the last week, swift snatches of time they'd stolen in an effort to be together. Five minutes. Ten. Just long enough to convey that they wished it could be longer.

"Roberto." She didn't bother to disguise her happiness.

Roberto was frowning. "It's true, then," he said, sounding none too pleased.

"What is?" she asked, surprised by his attitude.

"Emilio stopped off at the garage to tell me you were parading around these streets after school visiting families."

"I wanted—"

"Don't you realize it's dark now by four-thirty?" he barked. He jerked off his baseball cap and slapped it against his knee in a display of disgust.

"Roberto, what's wrong?"

"Are you crazy, woman?" He said something in Spanish, and from his tone, it was just as well she didn't understand. "You're inviting trouble. I thought you had more sense than this."

"Roberto, if you'd only listen."

"To what? Don't you realize this is New York City? You're targeting yourself to be the next crime victim. You're inviting trouble. I can't follow you around and protect you."

She didn't appreciate his attitude, but she didn't want to argue, not when they'd come so far. She stiffened her shoulders and glared right back at him. The cold wind whipped about her face as she struggled with her composure. "I know what I'm doing."

"You haven't got a clue," Roberto snapped. "What could possibly be so important for you to risk your life?"

She tried to tell herself that he was so angry because he cared, but his attitude stung. The people in this neighborhood knew her. She couldn't go more than a few houses before she met someone she recognized from either the school or the church.

"Don't you understand?" Roberto said, gripping her by the shoulders. "You can't change the world on your own."

"But I can help these kids."

"Brynn, oh, my darling fool." Briefly he closed his eyes, struggling to hold on to his temper. "You can do nothing. You can change nothing. Denzil, Malcolm, and all the rest will live and die in this neighborhood the same way Emilio and I will."

"That's not true," she argued. She could make a difference. She believed that with all her heart. That was the reason she was here.

"Grow up," he said, his fingers biting deep into her coat. "You've got to step out of this dreamworld you're living in. Look around you. Can't you see?"

Brynn refused to believe what he said. "We have a difference of opinion, Roberto, but that's no reason to treat me like a child."

He seemed to be struggling within himself. After a moment, he dropped his hands and his features hardened. "Go home, Brynn. For the love of God, go home where you belong. You don't fit in here. Just go!" he shouted, and gave her a light push.

She blanched. "You don't mean that."

"I've never been more serious in my life. Pack your bags and head back to Rhode Island or wherever it was you came from before you get yourself killed. Please, Brynn." This last part came on a rush of emotion.

The pain his words produced sucked the breath from her lungs. At first she could barely think, and when she spoke her voice betrayed her pain. "You want me to leave?"

He held himself stiffly away from her and didn't answer for several moments. Then something broke within him, and he expelled his breath forcefully. Before her heart beat again, before she could take another breath, Roberto brought her into his arms. "No, I don't want you to go."

Her arms circled his waist, and he relaxed. Nothing had ever felt more right than to be in Roberto's arms.

"Promise me, if you're so anxious to go out nights, you'll let either me or Emilio accompany you."

She remembered his words about not having the time to be her bodyguard and knew he'd said those hurtful things only because he was worried for her.

"Promise?" he demanded.

She nodded, and he kissed the top of her head.

Beneath the warm, golden glow of the streetlight, the man who'd shouted at her only moments earlier now bent his head to kiss her. "What am I going to do with you?" he said.

Brynn smiled to herself, content in his arms. In time he'd realize she could make a difference. If it was only to be in one life, then so be it, but she wouldn't walk away from her students, nor would she leave this neighborhood, no matter what Roberto thought.

Jenny stood on stage, dressed in her tights and dancing shoes. Five others stood with her, including Michelle. All triple threats. Each one accomplished in singing, dancing, and acting. Each one eager to be John Peterman's latest Broadway discovery. Each one pleading silently to be chosen for this role. Any role. A chance.

Bright lights blinded her, but Jenny was accustomed to not being able to view her audience. Her throat was raw and her head throbbed, but she ignored the cold and flu symptoms as best she could.

"Miss Lancaster."

The man with the booming voice called her name. Jenny stepped forward and shaded her eyes with her hand. "Yes."

"You sang 'Don't Cry for Me, Argentina' in the first audition, is that correct?"

"Yes." Her voice quivered with the strain of answering his questions.

"Did you bring your sheet music with you?"

"Yes." She looked to the man sitting at the piano.

"What will you be singing this time?"

With her cold and her throat feeling the way it did, Jenny knew her voice wouldn't carry any musical number with more than a two-octave range. Normally her voice was able to scale four octaves, something that had amazed and thrilled her music teachers in Custer, Montana. But such versatility wasn't uncommon here in New York.

"I'll be singing 'Rainy Days and Mondays,'" Jenny told the faceless voice. The first piano notes broke into the silence. She was forced to clear her throat, which had tightened up on her to where she could barely speak, let alone sing.

The piano player looked at her when she didn't come in on cue and played the introduction a second time. She opened her mouth and nothing came out. She tried again, and what sound did escape wasn't anywhere close to being considered musical.

Miserable, Jenny raised her hand and stopped the piano player. There was no use continuing. Not now. She couldn't do it.

"I'm sorry," she mumbled, wavered, and reached out blindly, afraid she was about to collapse.

Michelle gripped her hand. "Jenny's sick . . . she shouldn't even be here."

Her roommate placed her arm around Jenny's shoulders, and she slumped against Michelle, needing her friend's support to remain upright.

"She has a fever of a hundred and two," Michelle informed the casting director.

"And you are?" the loud voice boomed.

Michelle stiffened. "Her roommate. I realize this is none of my business, but I'm afraid Jenny's sick. If you want to hear her sing, our agent can supply you with any number of tapes. Come on, Jenny," Michelle said, steering her off the stage. "I'm taking you home."

"No," Jenny protested. It was bad enough that her best chance of ever appearing on Broadway was being taken away, but she wouldn't allow her own misfortune to ruin Michelle's chances, too. "You stay here."

"But—"

"I insist. Don't argue with me. This is your chance."

"But, Jenny—"

"Michelle Jordan!" the voice shouted.

Michelle wavered and looked over her shoulder.

"Are you staying or going?" the voice asked.

"Staying," Jenny answered for her. She'd meant to shout. She'd put all her effort into making herself heard, but what remained of her voice was shockingly weak.

"Oh, Jenny, are you sure you'll be all right?"

"Of course. All I need is a little rest." She managed to put on a bright smile, which depleted what little energy remained. "I'll get a taxi," she promised a second time. A real luxury, considering her finances.

"You promise?"

"Yes. Now break a leg, kid," she said in her best Humphrey Bogart imitation. "You'll have to make it for both of us." She felt like weeping but managed to keep the tears at bay until she was outside the theater.

It was snowing. Wouldn't you know it? Every man, woman, and child in New York would be looking for a cab. Jenny stepped halfway out into the street and raised her arm in an effort to hail a taxi. The cold snow was a welcome coolant as it drifted onto her upturned face.

"You're going to help her, aren't you?" Goodness asked Mercy. "That poor girl's sick and miserable."

"Of course I'm going to help her." Mercy was indignant that her friend would believe otherwise. "It's just that this is the worst time imaginable for her to find an empty taxi."

"Well, do something."

"What would you suggest?" Mercy snapped, impatient herself.

"Stop traffic."

Mercy grinned. Why hadn't she thought of that herself? It wouldn't be so difficult to create a distraction. Not with Goodness there to help her. Naturally it would work; she just hoped Gabriel didn't find out about this.

"Come on," she said, sharing a gleeful smile with her friend.

"Where are we going?"

"Times Square," Mercy answered.

"Yes, but . . . "

Even Goodness looked surprised, and Mercy grinned sheepishly. "Don't worry, Gabriel will never hear of it." Well, at least she hoped that was the case.

"Look." Someone near Jenny stretched out their arm and pointed toward the huge electronic billboard above Times Square. "What in heaven's name is going on?"

Jenny looked up and did a double take. The sign that had flashed a huge Santa drinking a bottle of Coca-Cola only minutes earlier had disappeared. In its stead stood a picture of her own face, with the words flashing "Jenny needs a cab. Help Jenny."

She blinked, certain she was seeing things. Her fever must be higher than she realized for her to hallucinate this way. Obviously she'd stepped over the edge of reality.

Cars slowed to a crawl. Any number of people paused and pointed to the sign.

"Are you Jenny?" a bag lady who was nearly bent in half asked her. She wore a ragged wool coat. A worn shopping bag was draped over her forearm.

"Yes," Jenny whispered.

"I'm here to help you," the old woman proclaimed. "I'll get you that cab, now don't you worry none."

"I'm sick," Jenny whispered.

"Yes, I know, dear, now don't you fret. You'll be home soon enough." Holding Jenny by the arm, the old woman marched her out into the middle of midtown traffic and stood in front of the first yellow cab she spied.

The cabdriver stuck his head out the window and shouted angrily. Apparently he hadn't been in the country long, because his accent was so thick that it was nearly impossible to understand him.

"This is Jenny." The bag lady opened the cab door and stuck her head inside. "She's sick and needs to get home."

"I don't care if she's the president," the man inside the cab muttered, clenching his briefcase as if he expected the woman to snatch it from him. "I'm not giving up this cab. Driver," he instructed, "do something."

The driver twisted around and placed his hands over his ears. "Only been in America one day."

The passenger said something under his breath.

Undeterred, the bag lady tried a second time. "That sign up there says this woman needs help. Now get out."

The dignified-looking businessman bristled. "What sign?"

"Look at the billboard!" she shouted. "Now do as I say."

Jenny remained in a daze, barely able to decipher what was happening around her. Horns blared. People stopped and stared. Traffic snarled even worse than it normally did. No one moved.

"You're Jenny?" the businessman leaned halfway out of the cab to ask her.

"Yes," she whispered.

"Oh, all right," he muttered, and with that he hopped out of the cab.

Jenny turned to thank the bag lady who'd helped her, but she'd disappeared into the crowd. Safe and warm, Jenny climbed inside the cab, laid back her head, and closed her eyes. The next thing she knew the driver pulled up in front of her apartment complex. She couldn't remember giving him her address.

"How'd you know where I lived?" she asked as she pulled out her limited cash reserve to pay him.

"The old lady told me."

"But . . ." Jenny shook her head, hoping to clear her thoughts. She'd never seen that woman before in her life. How could the bag lady have known where she lived?

"Good job," Goodness said, standing under the blinking lights of Times Square.

Mercy was downright proud of herself. She'd pulled off the role of the bag lady with the finesse that had done all angels proud. "Jenny never even guessed she was dealing with an angel," she bragged to her friend.

"I see you had a bit of a problem with that businessman, though. He didn't seem willing to give up his seat."

"A nonbeliever," Mercy explained. "He prefers to take care of matters himself. Poor fellow. He doesn't know what he's missing."

"It looks to me like he's missing his cab." Goodness chuckled and pointed to the street below. The man stood with his shoulders hunched against the cold, his arm raised in a desperate effort to hail a taxi.

Joshua was about to give up hope that Hannah would show. He'd waited a half hour and was tempted to admit he'd been wrong. His face stung with cold and his fingers were numb. He might have left if it hadn't been for the skaters gliding over the ice and all the bright lights on the fifty-foot-tall Christmas tree. Both held his attention and kept him from dwelling on his disappointment.

This was the first day of Hanukkah, the Jewish holiday that observed the freedom of religion. These few days in December celebrated the hope for peace. This night Jewish families around the world lit the first candle of the menorah, commemorating the Jewish recapture of the Temple in Jerusalem from the Hellenic Syrians in 164 B.C. It was the holiday honoring "the miracle of the oil."

If Joshua remembered his history correctly, only one small jar of undefiled oil could be found for the Temple's menorah. It should have been enough for only one day, but the jar lasted eight days, until a fresh supply could be delivered.

Joshua had never considered himself a particularly religious man. He preferred to think of himself as a man of faith. In the darkness of winter, his people celebrated the return of light.

That was the way Joshua thought of Hannah. She was a ray of sunshine in a world that had been filled with dark ambition. A ray of hope. He hated placing Hannah in the awkward position of having to choose between him and Carl, but he was confident she didn't love the other man. He would have staked his career on that.

This evening would be telling. What he'd said to Hannah earlier about her not being able to stay away was true. If she truly cared for him the way he suspected, she'd find a means of meeting him.

Rockefeller Center was big, but somehow, some way, they'd connect. Joshua checked his watch one last time: 8:40.

His disappointment was keen. He'd wanted her to come. Willed her there. But it was apparent now that he'd been wrong. He had no option but to release her; she'd made her choice. He'd found her too late.

He'd turned away from the ice-skating rink when out of the blue he saw her. In that moment, it was as though the weight of the world lifted from his shoulders and his heart sang.

Hannah saw him, too, but her beautiful blue eyes were devoid of emotion. She hurried toward him, and he held out his hands to greet her.

By the time she'd gripped his fingers with her own, she was breathless and barely able to talk. Her eyes were bright with questions. With doubts and confusion. Without speaking, she told him everything he needed to know. She hadn't wanted to come. Had decided to stay away . . . and found she couldn't.

"You were right," she said with a sadness that was nearly his undoing. "I had to come. A hundred times I told myself the best thing for both of us was if I stayed away. What have you done to me, Joshua? What have you done?"

It was difficult not to pull her into his arms and comfort her. It was what he wanted. His heart was full, spilling over. The fact that his love brought her unhappiness wasn't lost on him. In time he'd make up for the unpleasantness he'd caused her. If only she would be patient, he'd prove to her she'd made the right decision.

"I think we should talk this out," she suggested. She seemed to harbor the hope that they could sit across from each other and reason away their mutual attraction. It wasn't as simple as that, but she'd need to reach that realization herself.

"All right." He sought nothing more than to be with her. It

wouldn't have mattered what they did. In many ways, he felt he was already fully acquainted with Hannah. He knew he loved her. He knew he wanted her to be his wife and the mother of his children.

How or when he'd come to realize all this, he couldn't answer. He was a man who dealt with facts, who argued cases. A man who generally was uncomfortable defining feelings. But when it came to Hannah Morganstern, Joshua found he was an expert on identifying his emotions.

"Come on," he said, tucking her hand in the crook of his arm. "I'll buy us a cup of hot chocolate."

A fragile, tentative smile touched her mouth. Her beautiful, kissable mouth.

"I'm beginning to think we're both a little nuts," she said.

"I couldn't agree with you more, but it's a good kind of crazy. Being with you makes me happy, Hannah. You're beautiful and generous and loving."

She lowered her head, uneasy with compliments.

Joshua found a table, and after she was seated, he walked over to the refreshment booth and bought two steaming cups of hot chocolate.

When he returned, she glanced up at him shyly. "The most amazing thing happened this evening."

"Oh?" He sipped from the edge of the paper cup, the steam wafting upward.

"When I told you I couldn't meet you, it wasn't because I didn't want to. Carl had asked me to attend the candle-lighting ceremony with him. It's the first day of Hanukkah," she told him unnecessarily.

"I know."

"I knew there wasn't any way I could possibly break our date. Then at the last minute Carl phoned. He came down with the flu."

That explained why Hannah was late. She'd been at the synagogue with her family and then rushed from there to Rockefeller Center.

"When I left in such a hurry, I'm sure my parents thought I was going to see Carl . . . instead I'm meeting another man." Sadness coated her words. It was clear she hated deceiving those she loved.

"I'm sure that given time, your family will learn to like me as much as they do Carl," he assured her gently. He regretted bringing the other man into the conversation. It seemed they spent half their precious time together discussing the rabbi's son.

Hannah's gaze drifted to the ice-skaters and then back to him. "I hardly know you myself."

"Ask me anything you like," he invited her.

"You've never married?"

"No. I've been waiting for you, Hannah Morganstern." By the way the color drained from her face, Joshua realized he'd said the wrong thing. He didn't mean to rush Hannah. Because he was confident didn't mean he had to get cocky.

"I'm engaged to Carl," she whispered. "Doesn't that matter to you?"

"It matters a great deal." He wasn't going to lie. When she'd told him, he'd been both frustrated and angry. Later he'd realized just how fortunate it was that they'd met before the wedding. "I figure I found you just in time."

He didn't ask her if she felt the same way. Didn't bombard her with questions. That wasn't necessary. He already knew. She felt everything he did, only for her, it wasn't so simple. Tied up with her feelings for him was a lifetime of adhering to her parents' wishes.

"I'll go to your family," Joshua offered, "and explain."

"Explain what?" she asked miserably. "There's nothing to tell them, Joshua. I haven't changed my mind about anything."

Chapter

Hannah *had no intention of staying* with Joshua. Her only purpose in meeting him was to explain once and for all that a relationship between them was impossible. It was too late for them. She was engaged to Carl now, and they'd soon be planning their wedding.

That had been the reason she'd decided to meet Joshua: so he'd know. Yet the moment she'd found him, her heart had been filled with a yearning, a wonder, that she couldn't reason away.

She couldn't look at him, she feared, and not reveal what was in her heart, so she focused her attention on the ice-skaters. As a child she'd loved it when her mother had taken her to this very rink. Although she'd struggled to remain upright, Hannah had enjoyed the simple pleasure of gliding freely over the ice. When she'd tired, she'd sat and watched others, admiring the skillful athletes as they'd leapt and spun their way across the rink. In her child's mind, she'd dreamed about someday being as graceful and talented.

"Come," Joshua said, and reached for her hand. He'd been silent since she'd announced that she fully intended to marry Carl. Hannah hoped he would accept her decision graciously and let matters drop between them. It was as difficult for him as it was for her, but she couldn't tell him that. She willed him to leave because she hadn't the strength to do it herself.

"Where are we going?"

His eyes revealed nothing, then he smiled in that gentle way of his. "Ice-skating."

"But, Joshua, it's been years. I'm not sure I even remember how."

"It's been years for me, too."

"I can't," she insisted. "Really. I should get back before Mama asks questions. I can't lie."

554 ★ Debbie Macomber

Joshua stiffened. Surely he understood that she'd intended never to see him again. Surely he realized that she'd come this evening only because Carl had canceled at the last moment. Even now that surprised her.

"I'm not asking you to lie," Joshua explained, his hand clasping hers firmly. "All I want is for you to skate with me."

Hannah gazed longingly toward the ice. She was tempted. Oh, heaven, she was tempted. It wasn't so much to ask, she decided, not when she wanted this so badly herself.

"All right," she agreed. "But for only a short time."

"Agreed."

Joshua left her briefly, after checking her shoe size, and returned a few moments later with two pairs of ice skates. After lacing up his own, he knelt in front of her to be sure her skates were tied properly.

"You may well regret this," she said, linking her arm through his. Her legs wobbled when they stepped onto the ice, but Joshua's grip about her waist was firm.

Her first few steps were tentative and awkward. If not for Joshua, she was sure she would have fallen. "I can't believe I let you talk me into doing this," she said, concentrating on staying on her feet.

"You're doing just fine."

He was being kind, and she said so. Their first whirl around the rink was marked with her clumsy attempts to remain upright. Even with Joshua holding on to her, Hannah's arms flailed out in front of her a number of times in an effort to maintain her balance.

Before long she found a certain rhythm and glided over the smooth surface. Gaining confidence, she relaxed her grip on Joshua's arm, and he gradually released her. Skating backward in front of her, he smiled and praised her skill.

"Do you think anyone from the Ice Capades is watching?" she joked.

Joshua chuckled.

Thinking herself clever, Hannah decided to speed past Joshua. Unfortunately, in her effort to impress him, she lost her footing. Her feet slipped out from under her so quickly that she didn't have time to react. Arms flailing, she landed butt first on the hard, cold ice.

Joshua nearly fell on top of her, trying to keep her from losing her balance. By some minor miracle he managed to remain on his feet. Smiling broadly, he skated wide circles around her.

"You think this is funny, do you?" she asked, her dignity sadly bruised.

"Hilarious."

Hannah's rear end was getting wet and cold from the ice. She stretched out her arm, silently seeking his assistance. Joshua ignored her hand. Bracing his fists against his hips, his skates perpendicular to each other, he circled her.

"Joshua," she pleaded.

Chuckling, he helped her to her feet.

They skated for more than an hour, and then afterward, because she was unbelievably hungry, they ate huge hot dogs. Mustard dripped onto Hannah's forearm, and Joshua dabbed it away with a paper napkin, teasing her about being so messy.

Time seemed to drift away from them. Never could Hannah remember enjoying anyone's company more. It had been like this from the first moment they'd met.

"I have to go," she said sadly when she noticed the time. It seemed she was always saying that to him.

He hailed a taxi and sat next to her on the seat. When they arrived outside her parents' deli, Joshua paid the driver and climbed out of the cab with her.

On the abandoned sidewalk, Hannah stood with her head bowed, her heart thudding hard and heavy with dread against her chest.

"I can't see you again." The best way was to say it flat out and leave no room for speculation. It was difficult, but necessary.

"Hannah . . ."

"I'm engaged to another man," she said as firmly as she could manage, afraid her voice would catch with emotion. "I can't string you along. It isn't fair to you. Please, Joshua, try to understand."

"Can't do this to me?" he repeated, and it seemed to her that he found encouragement in her words.

She didn't want to argue with him. She glanced longingly toward the door, wanting this last farewell to be over as quickly as possible. Not wanting to dwell on the unpleasantness of hurting him.

"Good-bye, Joshua."

He caught her by the shoulders and brought her into his arms. She didn't resist him. Hadn't the strength. His kiss was more potent than Irish whiskey. More heady than fine wine.

"Don't you think you should be more worried about hurting Carl than me?" he asked, his lips against her hair. "You said you couldn't do this to *me*."

"I can't do this to Carl, either," she said in a rush, her words dwindling to a mere whisper. She squeezed her eyes closed, realizing her mistake. Her first thought had been of Joshua, not Carl.

"You don't love him," Joshua insisted.

Hannah backed away from him. "Please accept this, Joshua. I can't . . . I won't see you again."

He opened his mouth, then snapped it closed as if biting off an argument. "It isn't in me to make you miserable, Hannah. Nor can I force you into a relationship against your will. I'm here night or day, whenever you need me." He pulled a business card from his wallet, then wrote something on the back of it. "Here's my address and phone number. You can reach me twenty-four hours a day. Call me when you're ready."

"I won't call."

"Take the card anyway."

He opened her hand and planted it in her palm, then folded her fingers over it.

Having done that, he kissed her again until her knees felt as though they would give out on her. She could barely manage to breathe when he lifted his head from hers. He reached up and tenderly slid his index finger down the side of her face.

"Call me," he whispered, his voice low and seductive.

Pride demanded that she tell him she wouldn't be making that phone call, but his kiss had stolen her breath away. By the time her lungs had recovered, he'd turned and walked away.

Realizing she was still clutching the business card, she buried it in her coat pocket and as silently as possible unlocked the door to the deli.

Soundlessly she made her way up the backstairs to the family apartment. All the lights were out, and Hannah sighed with relief. Her parents had gone to bed.

Guided by what little moonlight was available, she crept toward her bedroom. Just when she thought she was home free, her father spoke from behind her.

"Hannah?"

She swallowed tightly.

"For the love of heaven, where have you been? Don't you have a clue what time it is? Your mother and I have been half sick worrying about you."

All through the afternoon, Brynn noticed that Suzie Chang's eyes avoided hers. Although the teenager didn't contribute freely to class discussions, if Brynn called upon her, Suzie would willingly share her thoughts.

Often Brynn had been grateful for Suzie's contributions. Her other students tended to get sidetracked easily. Brynn had come to rely on Suzie to subtly steer the topic back on course. Reading the teenager generally wasn't difficult, and Brynn knew from the way Suzie's eyes brightened when she had something she wanted to say.

It wasn't that way this afternoon, however. Suzie seemed to be trapped in a world all her own. Knowing the girl was miserable nearly broke Brynn's heart.

Brynn blamed herself. It had been wrong for her to look into scholarship possibilities without first discussing the idea with Suzie. Her intentions had been good, but in the process she'd somehow managed to hurt the girl.

The bell rang, and Brynn stopped Suzie on her way out the door.

"Could I speak to you for a few moments?" Brynn asked, hoping her voice didn't betray her worries.

"I can't this afternoon, Miss Cassidy," the teenager mumbled, her head bowed.

"It'll only take a moment, Suzie."

The room emptied, and Suzie stood just inside the classroom, her gaze fastened to the floor. She trembled like a frightened rabbit.

"It's about our discussion from the other day," Brynn began. "Remember I asked you if you had any plans for higher education."

"I can't go to college, Miss Cassidy."

"Suzie, if I said something to offend you, then I'm truly sorry."

The teenager bit into her lower lip, then slowly lifted her head. She offered Brynn a weak smile. "You didn't offend me. I was honored that you felt I . . ." She paused, and her dark eyes filled with tears.

"Suzie?"

The girl turned away and would have rushed from the room, Brynn suspected, if she hadn't stopped her.

"Can you tell me what's wrong?" Brynn asked gently.

Suzie trembled as she ran the back of her hand under each eye. "I don't want to trouble you with my problems."

"It's no trouble," Brynn assured her gently. "I'll do anything I can to help you."

"You can't help me, Miss Cassidy. No one can."

"I can try." With her arm around Suzie's shoulder, Brynn steered the girl to her desk and handed her a tissue.

Suzie's thin shoulders shook with repressed sobs. "Oh, Miss Cassidy, I don't know what I'm going to do."

"The first thing is to dry your eyes. There isn't anything so terrible that you can't tell me."

Suzie looked up and studied Brynn as though to gauge her sincerity. Brynn met her look without flinching. She hadn't a clue why Suzie was so unhappy. Naturally she had her suspicions, but she hoped it wasn't as traumatic as the girl seemed to feel.

"I can't go to college," Suzie announced on a wobbly, emotion-laden breath. "I don't even know if I'll be able to graduate from high school."

Brynn waited, giving the teenager the freedom to continue without the interruption of questions.

Suzie stiffened and looked away, as if meeting her eyes were more than she could manage. "I haven't told anyone." The words were low and filled with trepidation.

Brynn gripped the younger girl's hand, and Suzie squeezed her fingers hard enough to cause her pain.

"I'm pregnant," she whispered.

The news shouldn't have surprised Brynn, but it did. Suzie didn't have a boyfriend at school—in fact, to the best of Brynn's knowledge, the only social activity Suzie had ever participated in had been the dance at the church.

"How far along are you?"

"Almost six months."

"Six months!" Brynn couldn't disguise her surprise.

"I realize I barely show. . . . I've lost weight because I didn't want anyone to know. I was afraid if my father found out, he'd make me have an abortion," she said in a rush, her voice barely audible. "I don't want to kill my baby."

"Of course you don't."

"I want this baby, Miss Cassidy. I love him so much already. When I first realized I was pregnant, I thought I would die; then later, after I felt him move . . . it was such an incredible feeling."

"The father?" Brynn didn't want to pry, but surely the baby's father should be helping Suzie with some of these difficult decisions. Surely he could stand with her when she told her parents.

"I . . . haven't told him either." This was admitted with the same downcast look Suzie had worn earlier.

"But, Suzie . . . "

"He's got his own troubles, and I don't want to burden him with my news."

"Burden him?" Brynn couldn't keep the irritation out of her voice. "Suzie, this child is his responsibility, too. You shouldn't have to deal with this alone. There are decisions to be made. For one thing, you won't be able to hide your condition much longer."

"I know, but I don't want him to worry about me. He can't help, and . . . and if I told him about the baby, it would only make him feel worse. He loves me. I know he does." She buried her face in her hands, and her shoulders shook with silent tears.

Brynn patted Suzie's back gently.

"I don't know what I'm going to do, Miss Cassidy. I don't know what will happen when my family learns about the baby."

"You're going to have to tell your parents."

Suzie wiped the tears from her face. "I'm afraid my father will make me leave home, and I won't have anywhere to live. I want to finish high school, and what you said about me getting a scholarship for college, well, I never thought I could do anything like that."

"But of course you can. Your grades are excellent, but more than that, you have a clear desire to learn. Have you taken the SAT test?"

Suzie shook her head.

"But before you consider college, you're going to need to make a decision about your future, yours and the baby's. I can't help you with that, but I do know that the school counselor can help guide you. Will you talk with her?"

Suzie hesitated, then nodded. "I like Mrs. Christian."

Brynn walked down to the office with her and waited while Suzie made an appointment with the school counselor for the next day.

"If there's anything more I can do, let me know, okay?" Brynn asked when Suzie had finished.

The teenage girl started to cry once more, and Brynn hugged her close and whispered reassurances. "Everything will work out, Suzie, don't worry."

The teenager sniffled and left the school. Silently Brynn returned to her classroom and sagged onto her seat, her heart heavy with Suzie's news.

Suzie was pregnant. The girl was little more than a child herself. So tiny and delicate, it was a wonder she'd been able to disguise her pregnancy this long. The fact that she'd gone without prenatal care hadn't escaped Brynn's notice, either.

The desire to wrap her arms around the teenage girl and protect her from the harsh reality of being a single mother nearly overwhelmed Brynn. More than one of her students was a mother. Brynn had been surprised to learn Yolanda had a two-year-old son. The boy stayed with Yolanda's mother while Yolanda attended classes to complete her education. Denzil had bragged to her about fathering three children. He'd done so in an effort to shock her. The fact that he was sexually active didn't astound her, but his attitude toward the number of children he'd fathered with different girls did.

By the time Brynn left the school, she felt as though she carried the weight of the world on her shoulders. It seemed only natural to seek out Father Grady, but the parish priest was gone for the afternoon.

Mrs. Houghton, his housekeeper, seemed to sense Brynn had come for more than their usual friendly chat. "Do you want me to try to reach Father Grady?" the kindly older woman asked.

Brynn stood outside on the rectory steps. She shook her head. "No, that won't be necessary. I'll talk to him later."

"Are you all right, dearie?"

"I'm fine," Brynn assured her, but she wasn't.

Blindly she made her way toward the subway station, but as she neared the entrance, she hesitated. The thought of returning to an empty apartment held no appeal. With no clear destination in mind, she turned back, her shoulders slumped and her steps slow.

Roberto. She needed him. Although she trusted Roberto, she couldn't tell him about Suzie's condition. That would be breaking the teenager's confidence.

By the time she arrived at his garage, her eyes burned with unshed tears. The tight knot in her throat made it difficult to speak.

Roberto was bent over the hood of a car, and when she walked into the shop, he glanced up. He knew immediately that something wasn't right.

"Brynn, what's wrong?"

"Nothing," she lied. "Would you mind holding me for a little bit?" she asked, and her voice cracked.

He didn't hesitate, didn't question her, but simply did as she requested. Gently he laid aside his tools and brought her into the wide circle of his arms. "I'm greasy," he advised with regret, his touch light and tender.

Brynn burrowed deeper, needing his comfort. "I don't care."

His arms came fully around her then as he brought her against his solid strength. The hurt and fear, the disappointment and doubt, produced a hard, bitter tightness in her chest, and she clung to him.

"Brynn," Roberto whispered against her hair, stroking it away from her face, "can you tell me what's upset you so?"

She shook her head. The dream she'd had for her students seemed to have crumbled at her feet. Suzie had shown such promise, and Brynn had wanted so much for her. An unplanned pregnancy wasn't the end of the world, but Brynn didn't want Suzie caught in the trap like so many others. The teenager loved and wanted this child, enough to hide her pregnancy past the time she could have had an abortion. Enough to stand up against the wrath of her family.

As best she could, Brynn swallowed the emotion. "It was just one of those days," she said, drawing in a quick, stabilizing breath.

"It was more than that." He led her to a stool next to his workbench, and when she was seated, he paced the floor in front of her. "It's this neighborhood, isn't it?" His voice was gruff with anger. "You don't belong here. I told you that before and you refused to listen." He continued muttering in Spanish, knowing full well she couldn't understand him.

"Roberto." She reached out to him, but he ignored her. "Stop talking like that. Nothing you say is going to convince me to leave."

He rubbed his hands clean on a pink flannel rag and then burrowed his splayed fingers through his thick hair, leaving deep indentations.

"If I'd known this would upset you, I wouldn't have come." Brynn felt bad about that now. "I'm fine, really. There's nothing you can do except . . ."

Yes?" he prodded.

She hesitated and held her arms open to him. "Could you please kiss me?" The world felt right when Roberto held her and loved her.

The beginnings of a smile edged up the fringes of his mouth. He walked over to where she sat and captured her upturned face between his callused hands. Her own hands found the curves of his shoulders. He felt stable and strong, and she needed that security. Someone to hold on to while trapped in one of life's storms.

"Roberto." His name came as soft as mist across a Scottish moor.

He closed his eyes as if struggling against her. She felt his breath against her face and touched his lip with the pad of her index finger. His mouth was moist and warm.

The simple action was all he seemed to need. Roberto bent forward and claimed her mouth in a long, leisurely kiss. Since the night of the dance, he'd kissed her any number of times. Each episode taught her something more about this man. He'd enthralled her from the first. He felt strongly about his younger brother, accepting responsibility for Emilio's welfare. At the same time, Roberto cared deeply about the neighborhood, confronting injustice, prejudice, and hatred. Every time she met Father Grady, the priest sang Roberto's praises. Already she was half in love with him herself.

She knew a part of Roberto wanted her to quit teaching at Manhattan High. He didn't want her to deal with the squalor and misery he confronted day in and day out. He'd rather she returned to teaching at the prim and proper girls' school. Yet at the same time, he was learning, just as she was, that they had a good deal in common. The barriers that had kept them apart seemed to shrink a bit more each time they were together.

"I hope you'll listen to reason this time." His lips were less than an inch from her own.

Brynn linked her arms around his neck and bounced her mouth against his. "Just being with you makes everything seem better. Thank you."

His face tightened. "Brynn, for the love of—"

She stopped him cold with a long, lingering kiss. When she regained her voice, she whispered, "I'm falling in love with you, Roberto Alcantara."

He reacted as if she'd pulled out a gun and fired at him. He groaned and rubbed his hand down his face. "That's the last thing I wanted to happen." He edged away from her until his backside collided with the side panel of the car on which he'd been working moments earlier.

"Roberto . . ."

"Don't you know not to tell a man that?" he asked gruffly. Then he whirled around and walked out of the shop as if she'd deeply insulted him.

The fever felt as if it were about to take the top of her head off as Jenny struggled out of her clothes and into her pajamas. The fever or the bitter pill of disappointment, she didn't know which.

Someone knocked against the apartment door.

"Michelle, can you get that?" Jenny called out before she remembered that her roommate was still at the audition with John Peterman and company.

Struggling out of bed, Jenny reached for her robe. She'd never looked or felt worse in her life and was in no mood to deal with a door-to-door salesman.

The knock came a second time, sharp and impatient.

Grumbling under her breath, she tied the sash loosely around her waist and then unlatched the door lock without checking the peephole first. "Whatever you're selling, I'm not interested."

The words left her mouth and collided with a solid male chest. Jenny frowned and slowly looked up.

If she hadn't been feeling lightheaded earlier, she felt that way now.

"Trey," she whispered, so shocked there was no sound in her voice. He stood bold as life directly in front of her, all six feet four of him.

With his Stetson adding another couple of inches to his height, he made for an intimidating figure.

"Jenny?"

Another woman might have fainted then and there, but by this point Jenny had endured so much that another shock barely fazed her.

"I've been sick."

"It certainly looks that way. Can I come inside?"

She nodded, too numb and too confused to find an excuse to refuse him. Not that she wanted to. He was a hundred times more compelling than she remembered. A hundred times more devastating. He didn't seem to realize that in New York a man this good-looking generally appeared in fashion magazines.

"You should be in bed," he commented as he walked inside the tiny apartment. He glanced around, and his gaze narrowed as if to say he found it impossible to understand why anyone would choose to live in a place this small. A man who rode the wide-open range would have to feel claustrophobic in New York City, Jenny reflected.

Despite her shock at seeing him, she maintained her wits. It would serve him right if she told him that she *had* been in bed and had been forced out of it in order to answer the door.

"What are you doing in town?" she asked. She gestured toward the sofa.

Gingerly he sat on the edge of the thin cushion and held on to his cowboy hat with both hands between his parted knees. "What am I doing in New York?" he said. "What else would someone like me come to this crazy town for? I came to see you, Jenny Lancaster."

"See me?" Now that the excitement had started to fade, Jenny felt the dread take over.

"You wrote and said you wouldn't be home for Christmas, remember? I thought about that, then decided if you wouldn't come to me, there was no option but for me to visit you."

She lowered her head, and her hair, stringy and damp from the snow, fell forward. "I can't go home, Trey, I just can't." The dread was replaced with a heavy sadness.

He didn't say anything for several tense minutes. "Your parents were terribly disappointed."

The pain tightened her chest. "I know."

"I was disappointed, too."

Slowly she lifted her gaze until their eyes met and held. A woman could get lost and wish never to be found in eyes that dark. Funny she'd never noticed that when she was growing up.

He continued to hold her look for several breathless moments. "I've missed you, Jenny."

She bit into her lower lip.

Trey had never been a man for a lot of words. And the years apart hadn't improved the situation, Jenny noticed. He rotated the brim of his hat in his hands.

"When you first left Custer I thought you'd come to New York and get this singing and dancing craze out of your head. Then when you became so successful, it seemed this was your destiny. But I always counted on seeing you again."

She couldn't bear to listen to him repeat the lies she'd fed her family and friends. She bent forward and buried her face in her hands.

"Jenny?" he asked gently, his tender concern ripping at her heart. "Do you need a doctor?"

She shook her head. What she really needed was a priest. Someone who could absolve her from the guilt. Someone who could help her repair the damage she'd done to herself and her family. Someone to show her what to do now.

He moved from the sofa and knelt on the thin carpet in front of her. As though he weren't sure what to do next, he placed his hand on her back. "Jenny, are you crying?"

She didn't answer him, although there wasn't any use trying to hide it.

He hesitated, stood, and then reached down and gathered her in his arms. Then, as if she weighed next to nothing, he lifted her from the chair. One moment she was doubled over, struggling to hold back the giant sobs, and the next thing she knew she was being carried.

"Trey, what are you doing?" she demanded.

"Taking care of you." He sat back down on the sofa, holding her in his lap, his arms around her. "I never was much good at dealing with a woman's tears. Holding you just seemed the right thing to do."

She wrapped her arms around his neck and buried her face in his shoulder. For the longest time he did nothing but hold her, and she did nothing but let him.

"Tell me about Charlie," she begged, wanting to hear everything he could say about her family. Her brother wrote the least of anyone.

Trey chuckled and rubbed his hand down the side of his lean jaw. "I suspect you've heard he's sweet on Mary Lou."

Jenny's head came off Trey's chest. "Mary Lou Perkins?" That seemed impossible. First off, Mary Lou had been engaged to Brad Harper when Jenny had left Custer. Then she'd learned that the wedding had been called off at the last minute—word was Brad had gotten cold feet. But Jenny had assumed that the two would eventually marry.

Trey grinned. "Charlie's right sweet on her, and after three years Brad may just have lost his girl."

"It serves Brad Harper right. He had his chance," she said, siding with her brother.

She felt Trey's smile against her hair. "Last I heard, Charlie and Mary Lou had decided to announce their engagement to the community on Christmas Day."

"Oh." She wouldn't be there. One more nail in the coffin of her guilt.

"If you won't be there for Christmas, Jenny, will you come home for your brother's wedding?"

Chapter

★ ✶ ★

10

"Aren't you going to help Jenny?" Goodness asked. The three crowded in the corner of the tiny living room, hovering over Trey and Jenny.

Mercy knew that her friend had a soft heart. In fact, it was Goodness's tender nature plus her weakness for electronic devices that had been the main source of their difficulties over the last couple of years. To be fair, Goodness had matured. Either that or she'd become accustomed to such things as fifty-two-inch television screens. Not once in the past two Christmases had Goodness appeared on pay-per-view. Mercy was downright proud of her friend's progress.

"Mercy," Goodness snapped. "I asked you something important."

The warm thoughts Mercy had entertained about her fellow prayer ambassador vanished. "I brought Trey LaRue to New York, didn't I?"

"You did that?" Shirley joined them and sounded downright impressed. Mercy's evaluation of the third angel rose by several degrees.

Mercy was proud of her efforts and grateful someone had noticed. She tucked her thumbs in her waistband and rocked back on her heels. "You're darn tootin' I brought Trey LaRue to town."

"She's been hanging around cowpokes again," Goodness whispered out of the side of her mouth. "She's starting to talk just like one of 'em. The next thing we know she'll be wearing a buckle as big as a chastity belt and bragging about her rat-chasing dog."

"Not me," Mercy contradicted. "I've been too busy arranging Trey's trip east. I found he isn't as susceptible to suggestion as some humans are, especially schoolteachers and young Jewish women—if you catch my drift. I had my work cut out just getting him to New York. Must've taken three or four people suggesting he visit Jenny for him to take the hint."

Goodness frowned and apparently didn't take Mercy's words kindly.

"But look what happened to Jenny while you were away," Shirley commented glumly. "She's sick. My goodness, the poor girl looks wretched."

"That couldn't be helped." There was only so much one angel could do, and no one seemed to appreciate Mercy's efforts on this assignment. Least of all her two best friends.

"Has Jenny told him the truth yet?" Goodness asked, making herself comfortable. She usually preferred to dangle from light fixtures, but not in these tight quarters. "She isn't going to be able to keep it from him, is she?"

"Not now," Mercy agreed. It wouldn't do any good to remind her companions that she could lead a horse to water, but she couldn't make him saddle himself. She paused. Was that how the saying went? She'd heard some smart-talkin' fellow in Montana say something along those lines, and at the time it had made perfect sense.

"What's this I heard about Jenny's brother?" Shirley asked impatiently. "Is he really getting engaged?"

"That's another thing." Mercy flung herself across the back of a living room chair and supported her head with the palm of her hand. "Does anyone here understand what I had to go through to arrange this last-minute romance between Charles Lancaster and Mary Lou Perkins?"

"You did that?" Shirley asked, amazed.

"Well, not entirely," Mercy admitted with some reluctance, although she'd be willing to accept a certain amount of credit. "All Charlie really needed was a little encouragement."

"And you supplied that?"

Mercy shrugged. "Some."

Goodness beamed her approval. "Good thinking."

"What about poor Jenny?" Shirley asked, studying the down-and-out actress.

"I don't know," Mercy admitted. "What she does and doesn't tell Trey is up to her."

"How long will Trey be in town?"

Mercy didn't have the answer to that, either. "Your guess is as good as mine."

"He'll be here for the party, won't he?" Goodness wanted to know.

It took Mercy a moment to remember the Christmas potluck Jenny and Michelle were holding. She hadn't a clue where the two young actresses intended on putting everyone, but they seemed to think they could manage.

"I don't know what Trey's plans are," she muttered. It seemed her friends insisted upon asking her questions she couldn't answer. "All I know is that however long he stays, it'll be long enough."

Her words were followed by a short silence. "Are you saying you know something we don't?" Shirley inquired.

Mercy's smug smile was all the answer she intended to give them.

Brynn stood in front of her class, and her gaze rested on Suzie Chang's empty desk in the middle of the room. It seemed as if the space were magnified until it appeared to crowd everyone against the walls.

The lessons that day involved the history of the Second World War, and although Brynn was prepared to discuss the Battle of the Bulge, her mind was elsewhere.

All she could think about was Suzie.

"This afternoon," Brynn said, forcing her attention back to the history lesson, "we are going to be talking about . . . sex." The word raced out of her mouth before she could stop herself.

Modesto cheered and sat up straighter on his desk chair. "Hey, Miss Cassidy, I bet I could teach you more than you could teach me." He laughed, thinking himself downright comical.

"Not if my brother hears about it," Emilio warned, his eyes narrowing. "Miss Cassidy is his woman."

"I'm no one's woman," Brynn corrected evenly.

"No one owns another person," Pearl Washington insisted righteously. To the best of Brynn's knowledge, this was the first time the young black girl had freely contributed to any class discussion. "A woman's body is her own, just the way a boy's body is his own."

"You're right, sister."

"I didn't plan this talk," Brynn admitted, wondering if she was treading over a minefield. "But this is a subject that's been on my mind lately, and I'd like us to have an open discussion. I'll share my thoughts with you, and you can share your feelings with me."

"Ask me anything you want," Emilio said proudly.

"In other words, you've got all the answers?"

"Sure." Emilio glanced over his shoulder to be sure he had his friends' support. "Most of us in class do. Come on, Miss Cassidy, we been around, you know?"

"Yeah, I do know. But making love isn't like sampling chocolates. It's much more involved than that. There are responsibilities and consequences."

"Yeah. I'm raising one of those consequences right now," Yolanda volunteered, "and it ain't easy."

"Hey, sister, don't look at me. I wasn't the one who got you knocked up." Denzil raised both hands in a gesture of innocence.

"Shut up, Denzil."

"I want to talk about accountability," Brynn said, ignoring the two. "About being mature enough to accept the responsibility for our actions."

"Are you going to lecture us, Teach?"

"No. I'm going to share with you at least fifteen different ways of making love without doing it."

Several of the boys glanced back and forth at each other as if she'd suddenly turned into someone they didn't know.

"I have the feeling I'm not going to like any of those ways," Malcolm muttered.

Pearl stood at her desk and pointed a finger at her chest. "Why is it a guy thinks that because he spends a little money on me, it entitles him to a piece of my soul?"

"Some girls expect it," Malcolm argued just as heatedly. "Half the time the girls are all over me asking for it."

"Yeah," Emilio agreed. "There are plenty of times I'd prefer not to . . . you know, and if I don't ask, then the girl's feelings are all hurt. It ain't just us men, you know."

"Men?" Yolanda challenged. "I notice you call us girls, but you're men. Why doesn't the *man* who fathered Jason kindly step forward?" With her fists braced against her sides, Yolanda looked around slowly, then released a sigh of disgust. "That's what I thought."

"Enough," Brynn said, putting an end to the argument before it escalated into a shouting match. She could talk until she was ready to faint, and she doubted it would do any good, but she had to try. One thing was clear: her students were as opinionated over the topic as she was herself.

While she had their attention, she spoke from the heart, listing the reasons she felt it was important to wait to experiment with lovemaking until after marriage. The intensity of her feelings must have reached her class because there was a respectful silence when she finished.

"Miss Cassidy," Emilio said when she'd concluded, "I don't mean to be discourteous or anything, but you're living in a dreamworld if you believe a man's going to wait to make love to his woman."

"Don't be so sure, Emilio. Teenagers across the world are making pledges to keep themselves pure."

"There ain't nothing pure in this neighborhood," someone else told her. "Not even the water."

"But it has to start somewhere," Brynn said, and walked over to the chipped blackboard. In large bold-faced letters, she wrote I WILL ABSTAIN FROM PREMARITAL SEX. "I say let it start with me." She signed her name below.

Holding up the piece of chalk, she asked, "Anyone else?"

A tense moment passed before Yolanda slid from her seat. With her head held high, the teenager walked up and took the chalk out of Brynn's hand. She wrote her name in huge letters below Brynn's.

Turning around to face the class, she said, "A *boy* will tell you anything you want to hear until you give him what he wants. Then he'll forget he ever knew you. A *man* will make you his wife first."

Pearl Washington walked up and wrote her name down next. She turned around and glared at Denzil. Then, one hand braced against her hip, Pearl returned to her desk. On the walk back to the end of the row, she continued to glare at Denzil.

"I think you just got cut off, man," Malcolm whispered loudly enough for everyone in the class to hear.

"You keep saying how much you love me," Pearl mocked him. "If you love me so much, prove it."

"I ain't adding my name to that list," Denzil shouted angrily.

Pearl blinked several times but said nothing.

"Don't you worry, Pearl, Denzil is nothing but a *boy*," Yolanda said to comfort the other girl.

When she least expected it, Mike rose from his seat and walked forward. With a bit of flare he added his name to the list, the first boy in class to do so.

"Oh sure, Mike," Malcolm called sarcastically. "You should be so lucky to get laid."

Why the others chose to taunt Mike, Brynn didn't understand. She liked Mike and appreciated the courage it had taken for him to step forward. The desire to defend him was strong, but she realized that would only make matters worse for the youth.

"Mike's more of a man than you are," Pearl insisted. "A hell of a lot more than Denzil will ever be."

Emilio sat on his seat, frowning. After a couple of moments he stood and trekked the short distance to the blackboard.

"Emilio, are you nuts, man?" Modesto asked.

Emilio turned around and faced his friends. "You know what? Miss Cassidy is right. My brother's always talking about what it means to be responsible, and really that's all Miss Cassidy is saying, too. I ain't no priest, but the way I figure it, women will respect me if they know I ain't after nothing."

After Emilio listed his name, three other male students added their promise.

When they'd finished, Brynn took the chalk, stepped to the blackboard, and wrote I WILL PRACTICE SAFE SEX. Then she drew a line beneath the words and waited.

"Next we're going to discuss protection," she said.

Later that afternoon, after her class had been dismissed for the day, Brynn felt good about the spontaneous way in which they'd discussed the subject of sex. It might have gone differently had she planned it. Instead the students themselves had contributed their feelings and insights, and because she'd listened to them, they had been willing to hear her out as well.

She studied each name on the two lists and prayed that their talk would make a difference in how they chose to live their lives.

"Miss Cassidy."

Brynn looked up to find Suzie standing in the doorway. "Am I disturbing you?"

"No, of course not." Brynn stood. "How did your session go with Mrs. Christian?"

"All right, I guess. She made an appointment for me at the health clinic."

"That's good, isn't it?"

"My baby's healthy," Suzie said with a shy smile. "I feel him kick and move all the time now." The teenager's gaze moved to the blackboard. "I . . . I heard about what you did. It's all over the school. You talked about birth control and responsible sex because of me, didn't you?"

Brynn couldn't very well deny it. "I didn't break your confidence, Suzie. No one knows what you told me." She felt it was important to assure Suzie of that.

"I knew you wouldn't say anything." Suzie studied the list. "Emilio signed his name." Although it was a statement, the surprise in her voice made it a question.

"Several of the young men in class did."

"Do you think I could add my name?" she asked, diverting her eyes from Brynn's. "Or is it too late?"

"I'd be proud if you did," Brynn told her.

Suzie walked up and added her name to the first list. "I'm going to talk to my mother this afternoon. She'll be angry with me and she'll want me to tell her who the father is, but I won't."

"You can't protect him forever," Brynn said gently.

"I know. Mom will be angry, but not nearly as much as my father."

"Do you want me to come with you?" Brynn asked.

Suzie considered the offer, then shook her head. "No, but thank you for volunteering."

No sooner had Suzie left than Brynn was asked to come down to the office. It was the first time she'd received such a request. She wasn't left to wonder at the reason.

She knew.

If what Suzie said was true, then Mr. Whalen, the principal, had heard what she'd done.

Allen Whalen invited her into his office, and after she'd stepped inside, he closed the door firmly. The sound of it clicking alerted her to the fact that this wasn't going to be a friendly chat.

Brynn respected Allen Whalen. He was a big, no-nonsense man and a fair disciplinarian. He had zero tolerance for drugs and alcohol and didn't shy away from confrontations, often suspending students for fighting or other disruptions. Emilio could testify to that.

"Sit down, Brynn," Allen said, and motioned for her to take a seat on the other side of his desk. More than likely this was the identical chair in which Emilio had sat the first day of the quarter following his fight with Grover.

"First off," Allen said, leaning forward, "I want you to know I've heard good things about you. The kids seem to feel kindly toward you, and that's a plus. I understand you've made a point to visit the families of your students."

"Yes, I—"

"While your efforts are commendable," Allen interrupted, "I don't feel it's a good idea for you to become emotionally involved with your students."

Brynn opened her mouth to explain her purpose, but once again she wasn't allowed to continue.

"You're young, and idealistic. Perhaps a little too young to deal with the reality of our situation here."

"Mr. Whalen, if you'd allow me to explain . . ."

He gestured with his hand, indicating that he wasn't finished. "I had my doubts about this government project. As far as I'm concerned, the less the federal government has to do with the school system, the better. I would never have agreed to this program had I realized . . ." He paused and leaned forward, pressing his elbows against the top of his cluttered desk. "I don't want to get sidetracked here. The reason I asked you to my office has nothing to do with the government or why you're at Manhattan High."

"Yes?" She sat straight, her back as stiff as a steel pipe.

"I received a phone call from two mothers this afternoon," he prefaced, his face growing tight with displeasure. "Don't tell me, Miss Cassidy, that you actually discussed birth control methods with your history class."

Rather than hedge, Brynn answered him in a straightforward manner. "As a matter of fact, I did."

Allen Whalen's eyes drifted closed momentarily. "In your history class, Miss Cassidy?"

"It needed to be said."

"And you felt you were the most qualified to advise a classroom full of young adults? I take it you've attended the course the district requires before teaching sex education?"

"No. The discussion was spontaneous. I certainly didn't plan to spend the afternoon discussing the benefits of condoms."

"In other words, you just decided this needed to be said and you were the one to do it?"

"If you put it like that, then I have no option but to say yes." She had no defense and didn't think it would help her case if she had.

Mr. Whalen mulled over her answers. "In case you weren't aware of it, this community is largely Catholic."

Brynn folded her hands on her lap. "I'm Catholic myself."

"That is no excuse," he said, then stopped abruptly. "You're Catholic?"

"My name is Cassidy and my hair is red." She didn't mean to be sarcastic, but it should have been obvious.

"Then you must be aware of the church's standing on the subject of birth control."

"I am indeed." She didn't blink. Didn't hesitate. Didn't doubt for an instant that he was furious with her.

"I'm afraid, Miss Cassidy, that in light of this admission, I have no choice but to place a letter of reprimand in your file."

Brynn swallowed tightly. "I've always known you to be a fair man. If you feel I deserve to be formally reprimanded for my actions, then I can only assume that you're right."

"You're a history and English teacher. In the future please remember that." He reached for a piece of paper and started writing.

Brynn sat where she was for several awkward moments.

After a while, he glanced up. "You may leave."

When Brynn walked out of the office, she found three secretaries staring at her. Their looks were sympathetic as she whisked past. The whispers started the moment she was around the corner.

*   *   *

"Hello, Hannah."

Hannah looked up from the novel she was reading. "Carl," she said, unable to hide her surprise and her guilt. No one had told her he planned to stop by that evening. "How are you feeling?" She hadn't spoken to him since his bout with the flu.

Her fiancé claimed the recliner across from her. "Much better, thank you."

Hannah noted that her heart didn't leap with excitement the way it did whenever she saw Joshua. Nor did she experience a twinge of pleasure just because they were together. Carl was Carl. Dedicated, devout, determined. But soon, if everything went as their mothers had planned, he would be more than an unexpected guest. He would be her husband.

"My mother stopped by to talk to your mother," he explained with a wry grin. "They're discussing the details of the wedding."

Hannah's gaze fell back to the pages of the novel. "My mother wants to hire a wedding coordinator," she told him. "I heard her discussing the matter over the phone."

"She must have been talking to my mother, because I heard her say something about it as well."

Hannah smiled and looked away. She noticed with regret that they didn't seem to have a whole lot to say to each other.

"I thought we should set a time to shop for the engagement ring," Carl suggested, almost as if he were grateful for something to discuss.

"That would be nice."

"How about after the first of the year?" he proposed.

"Great." The further into the future, the better.

A disjointed silence followed, as though there were nothing left to say.

"Carl." Her father's face lit up with delight as he walked into the living room. "Ruth didn't mention that you were coming."

Carl stood, and the two men exchanged hearty handshakes. David Morganstern slapped Hannah's fiancé across the back. "By heaven, it's good to see you. You've been making yourself scarce around here these last few days."

"I've been busy."

"Ruth said you'd come down with a twenty-four-hour bug the other night."

"I'm fine now."

Hannah watched as the transformation took place in the man who was to be her husband. It seemed his face brightened as soon as her father walked into the room.

Soon the two entered into a lively debate over some political matter that didn't interest Hannah. While they chatted, Hannah went into the kitchen, brewed tea, and served that along with freshly baked sugar cookies.

Helen Rabinsky and Hannah's mother were engrossed in their own conversation and seemed unaware of her. As she expected, the women were debating the pros and cons of hiring a wedding coordinator.

After a time, Hannah escaped to her bedroom and closed the door. She doubted anyone would miss her.

Sitting on top of her bed, her knees bent, Hannah closed her eyes and remembered her time with Joshua at the skating rink. It wasn't right that she should be thinking of another man. Not with Carl on the other side of the door.

Joshua's business card remained inside her coat pocket, but she didn't need to retrieve it to find the number. In the last two days, she'd stared at that card so often, she'd committed the phone number to memory.

When she feared she might be missed, Hannah returned to the living room. Carl glanced her way and smiled affectionately.

"Carl," she said, "would you like to go for a walk, or something?"

"A walk?" he repeated with a decided lack of enthusiasm. "It's below freezing."

"How about if we went ice-skating?" she suggested next.

"Tonight?"

"I don't know what's gotten into that daughter of mine," her father commented, and chuckled. "Two nights ago she walks over to Rockefeller Center and goes ice-skating."

"I don't skate," Carl said with a touch of sadness.

"I could teach you," she offered expectantly. "It isn't difficult, and we could have a lot of fun."

Carl looked from Hannah to her father and then back again. "Would you mind if we stayed here?"

"Remember your young man's just getting over the flu, Hannah," her father reminded her gently. "Carl will take you ice-skating another time."

She tried to hide her disappointment and must have succeeded. An hour later, Helen Rabinsky announced it was time to leave. Carl stood, and for no reason Hannah could fathom the two of them were left alone. It didn't take her long to realize her family was giving her and Carl a private moment together.

"Thanks for stopping by, Carl," she said.

"It was good to see you again, Hannah." He leaned forward and pressed his mouth to hers. It was a gentle kiss, but passionless. It was unfair to compare the kisses she'd shared with Joshua to the quick exchanges between her and Carl. But Hannah couldn't help it.

Joshua's kisses made her feel as though she'd been hit by a freight train. The emotional impact left her reeling long afterward. She knew that her kisses affected him in the same magical, exciting way. Joshua made her feel like a sensual, alluring woman.

"I'll be calling you soon," Carl promised.

Hannah nodded, afraid to speak for fear of what she'd say. Intuitively she realized she couldn't marry Carl. He didn't love her any more than she loved him. He was as miserable about this arrangement as she was, but they were both caught in the trap. One of them had to break it.

As soon as Hannah and her parents were alone, her mother turned and clapped her hands gleefully. "Helen agrees that we should hire a wedding coordinator. I couldn't be more pleased. She suggested we talk to Wanda Thorndike." She hugged Hannah briefly. "I'll make an appointment with Wanda first thing in the morning."

Hannah wanted to object, to explain that she felt they were rushing matters, but she wasn't given the opportunity.

"I overheard Carl suggest that he and Hannah pick out engagement rings right after the first of the year."

"David," her mother said, sighing, "you can't imagine everything we need to consider for a large wedding."

"We haven't picked a date yet," Hannah reminded her family, dread weighing down her words.

"My dear, you're as naive as Helen and I were about all this. The wedding coordinator will be the one to choose that. She'll know what's available and when. Personally I'd prefer a June wedding. You should be a traditional June bride, but that's barely six months away, and I don't know if we could manage it in that time. One thing I'm going to have to insist we do right away, and that's shop for your dress."

"Mom—"

"Helen was telling me it sometimes takes as long as six months to have a dress made and delivered."

"But—"

"I know, darling, we're throwing a lot at you. Just be patient." Humming happily to herself, Ruth Morganstern returned to the kitchen and the wedding brochures she'd pored over only moments earlier.

Hannah's father chuckled. "I don't know when I've last seen your mother so pleased. This wedding has given her a renewed lease on life."

Hannah couldn't find it in her heart to disappoint them. Not then. Later, she promised herself. She'd sit down with them both and explain that she didn't love Carl.

By noon the following day the deli was filled with the usual lunch crowd. Her father hand sliced pastrami into thick wedges while Hannah and her mother assembled the sandwiches.

Runners delivered orders as fast as they could be packed.

The routine was one in which Hannah had worked most of her life. She never questioned that she would help in the deli; it was assumed.

Around two, the heavy lunch crowd had begun to thin out. Her mother returned to the kitchen to make up a fresh batch of potato salad. Her father was preoccupied with ordering supplies when Hannah looked up to discover Joshua standing on the other side of the counter.

"Joshua," she whispered in a low rush of air. Just seeing him again had knocked the breath out of her. She couldn't disguise her delight. Her heart went into second gear as she glanced over her shoulder to be sure no one was paying them any mind. "What are you doing here?" she asked in a whisper.

"I came for lunch."

Of course. She reached for a pencil, prepared to take his order.

He read the printed menu that hung on the wall behind her. "I'll have a pastrami on rye and a cup of coffee."

She wrote down his order with trembling hands.

"Are you going to make it for me yourself?"

She nodded, avoiding eye contact. She wouldn't be able to hide how pleased she was to see him again if she looked up.

"You didn't phone," he whispered just loudly enough for her to hear.

"Potato is the soup of the day," she said.

"Hannah, look at me."

"I can't."

"Why can't you?"

She closed her eyes and braced herself. "You shouldn't have come here."

"You don't want my business?"

He was making this difficult.

"You've thought about contacting me, haven't you?"

Again she didn't answer. "Would you care for a bowl of soup with your sandwich?"

He didn't respond for a number of seconds, and then, "The only thing I want is you, Hannah."

"If you'll take a number, I'll have your lunch delivered."

"Will you bring it?" he asked.

Her nod was nearly imperceptible. She saw the tension leave him and couldn't keep from glancing up and offering him a quick smile. It took only a moment or more to finish compiling his sandwich. She carried that and a cup of coffee to his table and was pleased to note he sat as far away from the counter as possible.

"Thank you, Hannah," he said when she placed the plate on the table. "Would you care to join me?"

"I can't." Her hands folded over the back of the chair across from him. She glanced over her shoulder, fearing her father would notice the two of them together.

"Is that your father?" Joshua asked, looking around her.

"Yes. Mom's in the kitchen."

"He doesn't look like the kind of man who would force his daughter into a loveless marriage."

"Joshua, please."

He picked up the sandwich, and once again, Hannah looked back to make sure no one was watching her. "I sometimes walk by the pond in Central Park," she whispered.

Joshua went still. "When?"

"I was thinking of taking a stroll there this afternoon."

"In an hour?"

"Yes."

Joshua's handsome face broke into a wide grin. "I've always favored walking as an excellent form of exercise."

Chapter

★ ✪ ★

11

"*Are you sure you're up to this?*" Trey asked Jenny for the third time since they'd boarded the ferry headed for Ellis Island.

"I wouldn't have suggested sight-seeing if I wasn't feeling better," Jenny insisted. They stood and watched as the New York skyline began to fade into the distance. "I want you to visit Ellis Island," she continued. "It's an emotional experience, at least it was for me the first time I made the trip. I found my great-grandfather's name there."

"Your great-grandfather? How?"

"I looked his name up on the computer. It showed me the year he arrived from Germany and his age at the time. I felt as though I'd stumbled upon an open treasure chest, only this one contained a part of my heritage."

"This was your mother's grandfather?"

Jenny answered him with a quick nod. "Can you imagine packing everything you own in this world in a single suitcase?" she asked, awed by the raw courage and grit her great-grandfather had shown when he was little more than a teenager. "He came to America with nothing but his dreams and the desire for a new life."

"Is that so unusual?" Trey asked.

"Of course it is," she answered, feeling slightly offended that Trey didn't recognize the fortitude and faith her great-grandfather had demonstrated. "He didn't have an easy life here, you know. First off he didn't speak the language, and although he was well educated he was forced into taking a menial job. For years he and my grandmother struggled to make a decent life for themselves and their family. I can't tell you how much I admire them for that."

"What you did, leaving Montana for a chance on Broadway, wasn't all that different."

"Me?" Jenny didn't see the correlation. Of course there was the obvious one, but her great-grandfather had come to America friendless and without the loving support of his family.

"As I recall, when you left Custer you went with a solitary suitcase. You came to the Big Apple without a job, with little money, and with only your dreams to feed you."

"True," she admitted reluctantly, not wanting Trey to continue comparing her with her great-grandfather. Not when she fell so far short.

Trey placed his hand on her shoulder. "It hasn't been easy for you, has it?" he asked gently.

He didn't know the half of it. Jenny turned her face into the wind and let the breeze off the Hudson River buffet against her. The thickness in her throat tightened to painful proportions, and she knew she dared not try to talk. Trey had tried to paint her as some kind of heroine, seeking her way in a new world. In retrospect, Jenny wasn't sure she'd done the right thing to leave Montana. She wasn't sure she was cut out for life in the city. In three years she'd never managed to feel at home in New York.

Jenny didn't see herself as any modern-day champion.

"Jenny?"

Trey's face had knit into a worried frown.

"I'm doing great," she told him quickly, perhaps too quickly, because she felt his close scrutiny. Smiling, just then, would have been impossible.

Trey moved closer to her by the railing. The wind hit against him. His arm came loosely around her shoulder, and, needing him, she pressed her head against his solid strength.

"There's something you should know," she said after dragging a deep breath through her lungs. She closed her eyes, unwilling to continue the pretense any longer. "I'm not what you think."

"Jenny—"

"No, please, let me finish." This was so much more difficult than she'd thought it would be. Trey had come all this way from Montana thinking she was a Broadway star. Either she told him herself or he'd learn it on his own.

A dozen times since his arrival she'd been tempted to blurt out the truth. It had held her prisoner, tortured her, and she couldn't stand the pressure any longer.

"I'm not starring in an Off Broadway production of *South Pacific*. I'm a waitress, a singing waitress. I lied, and I want you to know how very sorry I am." Her voice pitched and heaved with emotion as she hurried to get all the words out at once for fear she'd break down and weep.

The pressure of his arm around her increased slightly. "I realized that right away."

He knew and hadn't said anything.

"The first place I headed when I arrived in New York was the theater. I wanted to see you perform."

Jenny's throat constricted. "I'm so ashamed to have lied, but I had to tell my family something. It's been so long, and . . . you've got to believe I gave it my best shot, and now, well, now it seems I'm buried neck deep in the lie. Mom and Dad are so proud of me, and they've told everyone, and—"

"Come home, Jenny."

"No." Her response was automatic and sharp.

The brightness in Trey's eyes dimmed, and she turned away, unable to meet his gaze. It sounded as if he were eager to hear she'd failed. Glad of it. Well, she wasn't through yet. She was close, so close she could taste it. If John Peterman didn't want her for this play, then there were other parts, other producers. She wouldn't give up. She refused to turn her back when she was this close. Not even Trey could convince her to do that.

"I may not be the star I led everyone to believe," she told him stiffly, "but I'm an actress, and a damn talented one. I realize I've probably disappointed you, and I'm sorry for that, but I'm not willing to throw in the towel yet."

Trey didn't answer her, and the air between them was strained and tight.

"I shouldn't have asked it of you," he said as the boat neared Ellis Island.

It was as close to an apology as she was likely to get from Trey. She stepped away from him, letting the breeze whip against her face while she mulled over his words.

Trey stepped back, and she noticed the attention he generated with his tall, lean good looks. He was obviously out of place with his scuffed snakeskin boots and weatherbeaten Stetson, yet he'd dressed in the height of fashion. Jenny knew more than one male model who would have given anything for that rawboned, natural look.

"Jenny," Trey said, coming to stand next to her, "I don't really think what you did was so terrible. Sure you stretched the truth a bit, but under the circumstances that's understandable."

"But hardly commendable."

Trey didn't agree or disagree. "What you did was burden yourself. It seems to me these New York theater people must have holes in their heads not to realize how talented you are."

This was what Jenny loved about home the most. When it came to talent, the good folks in Custer believed none had more than Jenny Lancaster.

"Those responsible for the theater in New York meet lots of talented men and women with big dreams and a lot of ambition. That was a difficult lesson for me to learn, and I suspect that in some ways I haven't completely accepted it. I'm good, Trey, and I know it, but there are any number of equally talented people just waiting for their big break, the same way as me."

The ferry docked and the passengers disembarked onto the island. Most everyone headed directly for the Ellis Island Immigration Museum.

"There's something I want you to see first," Jenny said, leading Trey toward the flagpole. A brass railinglike border ran the circumference of the island. Embossed in the polished metal were hundreds of names, a small representation of the thousands of immigrants who'd made their way to America between 1892 and 1924. The first time Jenny had visited, she'd walked around the entire island until she'd found what she was looking for.

"My great-grandfather's name is listed here," she told him excitedly. Her fingertips ran over the raised letters. Anton Hellmich. A sense of pride moved her to know that this man's blood ran through her veins. "You can't imagine how excited I was when I discovered this. I called my mother that very night." She doubted that Trey understood what a rare thing it was for her to phone home. With her finances so tight, Jenny usually wrote letters and made up excuses why it was difficult for her to phone. Talking to her mother, hearing her father's gruff, loving voice, increased her longing for home and her family all the more.

"Anton Hellmich," Trey repeated slowly. He placed his callused hand on top of hers and laced their fingers together. His skin was rough and hard from the long hours he worked his spread. Her skin was silky smooth.

Once again Trey ran the thick pad of his index finger over the raised letters with her. His touch, so warm and caring, so gentle, was like a healing balm to her wounded pride.

Barely realizing what she was doing, Jenny turned so that she faced him. Before another moment passed, before her heart could beat again, Trey's arms were clasped around her as he brought her into his arms.

She watched the transformation come over him, as if he were

caught in some winless battle. The muscles in his jaw clenched. Then, moving slowly, as though hypnotized, he lowered his mouth to hers. His lips over hers, moist and warm, were as gentle as lambskin.

Jenny closed her eyes as tightly as she could, seeking to blot out the world and everything around them. Everything but Trey. For the first time since her arrival she didn't want to be subjected to the sights and sounds of the New York waterfront. She didn't want to hear the buzz of aircraft overhead. For this one moment she wanted to be as far away from other people as she could get.

Trey's kiss was everything Jenny had ever dreamed, everything she could have anticipated. She trembled in his arms, needing his strength, his comfort, more than she'd ever needed anything in her life. She clung to him, not wanting him to let her go. Not ever.

Snuggling closer, she stood on the tips of her toes. Her breasts nuzzled his chest, and a new brand of sensations shot through her. Trey recognized the difference, and his tongue went in search of hers as the kiss deepened. By the time they broke apart, Jenny's knees were weak. It didn't seem possible that anything would feel this wonderful.

Jenny had been kissed before, plenty of times. She wasn't a novice to the art, but with Trey all things became new. Everything changed.

When they broke apart, Jenny could feel the heat invade her cheeks. She was actually blushing, which was something that hadn't happened since she was in junior high.

"Trey?" she whispered, pleading with him to explain what was happening to them. She was at a loss to understand, let alone explain.

He answered by kissing her again, this time deeper and with such intensity that her senses spun out of control. When he'd finished, he held her close and whispered, but his words were low and filled with emotion.

"I've waited so long to hold you like this."

"Oh, Trey, I've missed you so much."

His fingers were in her hair, and he angled her head to kiss her again and again. His breathing was harsh with excitement and need.

"Come home, Jenny," he pleaded. "For the love of God, give up on this madness and come back home where you belong."

The pond near Cherry Hill fountain had always been one of Hannah's favorite spots in Central Park. Because she was late, she feared Joshua would have given up waiting for her. Barely taking time to look both ways, she raced across Fifty-ninth Street. Her heart pounded in her throat as she approached the pond. Excitement filled her when she spied Joshua standing along the edge of the water, feeding the goldfish. Hannah half ran to meet him.

"I'm so sorry I'm late," she said breathlessly when she joined him. "It took me much longer to get away than I thought it would."

Joshua glanced at her and enfolded her with a warm smile of welcome. "I was feeding the fish, and didn't notice." He handed her a fistful of stale bread crumbs for her to toss onto the water's still surface. Huge goldfish, some marked with black-and-white blotches, battled for the crumbs, stirring up the water's smooth surface.

"This has always been one of my favorite places," Joshua said.

"Mine too," she admitted. It didn't surprise her that Joshua felt the same way about this place as she did. They appreciated many of the same things.

They stood side by side, content without speaking, satisfied simply to be in each other's company.

"There's something I need to tell you," Hannah said once she'd regained her breath and her equilibrium. Being with Joshua always seemed to pull her off center.

Joshua hesitated, and his eyes sparkled. "Am I going to need to sit down to hear it?"

"No. At least I don't think so." She thought about what she had to say and realized he was the last person she should be telling instead of the first. "I've decided not to marry Carl."

"I know." Joshua tossed the last of the bread crumbs into the pond with a flourish.

Of all the reactions Hannah had expected from Joshua, she'd never anticipated this calm acceptance. She frowned. "What did you say?"

"I said, I knew you weren't going to marry Carl."

"And how could you be so confident of that?" she asked. She hadn't realized it herself until the night before. Once she'd admitted that she couldn't go through with the wedding, she'd felt as though a great weight had been lifted from her heart. It hadn't been an easy decision, and she didn't want him to think she'd made it flippantly.

"I knew you weren't going to be marrying Carl, my sweet, adorable Hannah, for one simple reason. I fully intend for you to marry me."

Hannah blinked back her surprise.

"And yes, if you're wondering, that's a marriage proposal."

"But I'm already engaged to Carl," she argued, saying the first thing that came to mind. He'd shocked her so thoroughly that she wasn't sure how to respond. The second thing that came to mind was that she would have liked nothing better than to be Joshua's wife. She was forced into biting her lips to keep from blurting it out.

He warmed her with another of his bone-melting smiles. "You see, I realized something the very first time we met."

"You did?"

"It's simple, really," he said with the calm reasoning of an attorney. "I realized you and I were meant to be together."

"But what about Carl?" she pleaded. "I was already engaged to him when we met." While that wasn't technically true, for all intents and purposes she might as well have been betrothed to the rabbi's son. In the eyes of both families, all that needed to be decided was if they should or shouldn't hire a wedding coordinator.

"I suppose I sound overly confident of myself," Joshua said, and reached inside his coat pocket for his leather gloves. "I wasn't sure about any of this until recently, though. The night at Rockefeller Center, to be exact. I gave you my business card, remember?"

"I didn't phone you."

"True," he was gracious enough to agree, "and I'll admit I haven't been sleeping well because I fully expected you to contact me long before now." He reached for her hand and raised it to his lips, brushing her knuckles with his mouth. "You and I share something very special, Hannah. I don't know what I would have done had you decided to go ahead with the wedding with Carl."

Hannah dipped her head. "I haven't said anything to him yet." It was far easier to tell Joshua of her decision first. She realized she was behaving like a coward, but she sincerely felt that Carl would experience a deep sense of relief once she asked him to release her from the engagement. She was certain he shared her feelings. They were both eager to please their parents and had allowed themselves unwittingly to be drawn into a self-made trap.

Joshua loved her. The knowledge shook her because she didn't understand how anyone as powerful and intelligent as Joshua could care for someone like her. "I've treated you terribly. I've ignored you, pretended I didn't know you, and shunned you."

"When something is of high value, then it's worth a few inconveniences," Joshua said, and gently bounced his mouth over hers. "In many ways I'm grateful to you."

"Me?"

"I'd almost given up thinking about God until I met you. My life was full and busy, but I felt an aching loneliness. I prayed, but I felt as if my prayers floated away to nothingness. Until the morning of the Thanksgiving Day parade, I was convinced God didn't listen to prayers any longer."

"But he does," Hannah insisted.

"I know. He sent you into my life." Joshua ran his finger down the side of her face. "You'll be talking to Carl soon?"

She nodded. It wasn't a task she relished, but it was one she couldn't delay. To wait for the right moment would only make it more difficult. "I thought I'd discuss it with him first, and then the two of us could explain it to our parents together."

Joshua's gaze narrowed briefly, and she knew he wasn't keen on this part of her plan.

"Carl and I need to present a united front," she explained. "Otherwise I'm afraid they'll manipulate us individually to change our minds."

Joshua considered her words, then asked, "Could they change your mind, Hannah?"

His question fell into a weighted silence. Hannah considered her answer for several thought-provoking moments. "Carl's a good man, and he'll make some woman an excellent husband, but that woman won't be me," she admitted, then added, "Nothing's going to change the way I feel about you, Joshua. Nothing."

"You'll tell him soon, then?"

She nodded. "The sooner the better." She didn't relish this task, but she couldn't put it off, either.

"Do you want me to come with you?" Joshua volunteered.

"No." That would only make matters worse, Hannah realized. Her news would be difficult enough for Carl without adding the complication of her feelings for another man.

Joshua looked at his watch. "I have to get back to the office."

It was easy to forget that Joshua was an important man. If she ever doubted his feelings for her, all she'd need to do was remember the time he took out of his busy schedule to be with her.

"One thing before you go?" she asked, reaching out and gripping hold of his forearm.

"Anything."

She felt foolish asking this of him. "Would you mind very much if we kissed again?"

The warm light that invaded his eyes was all the answer she needed. Joshua wrapped her in his embrace and drugged her with a number of long, slow kisses.

"Is that enough?" he asked.

She couldn't manage anything more than a slight groan.

Joshua closed his eyes and inhaled deeply. "Unfortunately I feel the same way myself. I promise you the day will come when we won't stop with the kissing, Hannah. Frankly the sooner that day arrives, the better."

Joshua left her to return to his office. The warm glow of his kisses carried Hannah all the way to Carl's apartment building. He should be home, seeing that school had been out for several hours. Hannah had been to his place only twice. Carl was an orderly man who kept his quarters meticulously clean. Hannah had never known anyone more gifted in the area of organization than Carl Rabinsky.

Not once on the long walk did Hannah doubt that she was doing the right thing. Only when she arrived at his building did she hesitate. Gathering her courage about her, she squared her shoulders and pressed the doorbell.

Carl's low voice came over the intercom. "Who is it?"

"Hannah," she said, standing on her tiptoes and speaking directly into the intercom to make sure he could hear her.

"Hannah? My goodness, what are you doing here?"

"I came to talk to you. Could I come up?"

"Of course."

A couple of seconds later a buzzer rang and the lock on the front door released, allowing Hannah inside the building. More nervous now than ever, she took the elevator up to Carl's apartment. By the time she arrived outside his door, she was convinced her heart was ready to pound straight through her chest.

"This is a surprise," Carl said, leading her into the living room. The area was nothing like she remembered. Books and papers littered the table. Unopened mail was scattered across the coffee table. This wasn't like Carl. Not once in all the time she'd known him had he displayed any signs of sloppiness.

"Is something wrong?" Hannah asked, watching him.

"I don't think there's any reason to try to hide it any longer," he said, sinking into the chair and covering his face with both hands. "I should have told you sooner."

Hannah didn't know what to think. "Told me what?" she asked gently. She'd never seen Carl like this.

He raised his head slowly, his look tortured. "But then I haven't found the courage to tell anyone."

Hannah waited, knowing Carl would get around to explaining himself eventually. He shifted uncomfortably in his chair and refused to look at her.

"I lost my position with the school," he blurted out, then squeezed his eyes closed. "I couldn't take it any longer, and I got into an argument with Hiram. Since he's the headmaster and I'm nothing more than a teacher, he fired me." Carl raised his head and squared his shoulders. "If you want to call off the wedding, I'll understand. I don't deserve a good woman like you."

Brynn didn't tell anyone about the formal reprimand that Mr. Whalen had placed inside her employment file. There didn't seem to be any need. Everything he'd said was true. She had stepped over the line, but try as she would, Brynn couldn't make herself regret the impromptu discussion with her students. If she'd managed to reach just one member of her class, then it had been worth the trouble.

Her thoughts were heavy as she made her way home that afternoon. Dinner was simmering on top of the stove when her telephone rang. She reached for it automatically.

"Hello," she said.

"It's Roberto."

Brynn closed her eyes. The sound of his voice, with his soft, lilting accent, was like sinking neck deep into a warm bath in the dead of winter.

"I heard you're teaching sex education now, too." He sounded more amused than angry with her, which was a welcome change.

"I really stuck my foot in it this time," she told him.

"Although he probably wouldn't come out and say as much, I think Emilio was grateful to have someone talk frankly about the subject. Girls can be pushy these days. As pushy as the boys."

"I'm sure that's true." After some of the things she'd seen in the last few weeks, there was little that would shock Brynn anymore.

"Although if you cared to get pushy with me, we might strike some agreement."

Brynn laughed. "Keep dreaming, Roberto."

The mechanic's chuckle slowly faded. "You do that to me," he said, his voice low and serious. "You make me want to dream, but then I wonder . . . Never mind. I didn't call you to talk about dreams."

"Oh?"

"I want to take you to dinner." His voice grew so serious that she wondered if there were some hidden significance behind his request.

"When?" she asked, not that it would have mattered to her. He could have suggested next June and she would have agreed readily.

"Is Friday all right?"

"Yes," she said automatically.

"I'll pick you up at six-thirty." How formal he sounded, as though he were unsure of himself.

"That'll be fine," she assured him. "I'll look forward to it."

"Me too." The smile was back in his voice, as if to say now that the awkward part was over, he could go back to being himself. "Thank you, Brynn."

"Whatever for?" She was thinking his appreciation had something to do with what Emilio had told her about the class discussion.

"For agreeing to be my date."

Not until Brynn was talking to Father Grady did she realize the significance in Roberto's having asked her to dinner.

She met the parish priest after school, responding to a message he'd sent asking to speak with her. She guessed correctly that Father Grady had heard about her talk with her students.

"Are you going to lecture me about the error of my ways?" she asked him directly. They were walking toward the rectory. Father Grady's hands were folded behind his back, and he avoided meeting her eyes.

"No," he said slowly, "although I fully suspect you know the church's teachings in the area of birth control."

"I know, I just don't happen to agree."

Father Grady released a long, slow breath. "I'm not going to say anything about this again, but I'm disappointed in you, Brynn. I don't know what happened for you to decide it was your duty to discuss this particular subject with your class, but my guess is this entire matter was spontaneous on your part.

"I strongly suspect one of the girls is pregnant. Well, it isn't the first time, nor will it be the last. These things happen."

"Birth control—"

"Promotes promiscuity," the priest argued.

"It would be better if we agreed to disagree," Brynn said evenly. She didn't want to get into a verbal battle with the one person she considered her friend.

They didn't speak for several moments.

"Roberto asked me to dinner Friday night," Brynn said, wanting to break the tension between them.

Father Grady's face broke into a wide smile. "He asked you, did he?"

"Is there something important about this dinner date I don't know about?"

"Not particularly," the priest informed her, "only that it's probably the first time Roberto's dated in the last four or five years."

"You're joking!"

"No. While he was in high school, he held down two part-time jobs in an effort to earn enough money for his mother to travel to the United States. Every penny went toward that goal. There wasn't time for dances or anything else a normal teenager enjoys."

"But he's an excellent dancer." Being in his arms had seemed as right as rain, as the saying went.

"He comes by that talent naturally," Father Grady explained. "But he's never taken the opportunity to indulge in the small pleasures in life. He sacrificed his youth for the sake of his mother."

"I've never met her."

"You won't," Father Grady said sadly. "She died before Roberto had saved enough money."

Brynn felt Roberto's frustration. "I'm so sorry."

"Roberto blamed himself."

"But how could he?" She hated the thought of his taking on blame when he'd already sacrificed so much.

"He seemed to think that he'd failed her."

"Surely he understands that isn't the case."

"Intellectually I believe he does, but not emotionally, although I have hope now that he's taken such a keen interest in you." Father looked well pleased with himself, as though he were the one responsible for bringing her and Roberto together. "You've been good for that young man, but by the same token Roberto has been good for you."

"I like him so much," she whispered. Sometimes it frightened her how deeply she cared for Roberto. He wasn't like any other man she'd dated. He was deep and intense, intelligent and generous.

"I suspected you did."

"Not at first," she countered. "Roberto and I rubbed each other the wrong way in the beginning." Even now they were at different poles on the subject of education. No matter how hard she tried to persuade him, Roberto refused to listen to reason.

Then it dawned on her why Roberto was so opinionated. Father Grady had unraveled the mystery. Roberto had stayed in school and worked, saving his money in order to bring his mother from Mexico. She'd died before he had been able to save enough. If Roberto had been working full-time instead of trying to balance two part-time jobs with his schooling, he might have been able to help his mother. Because he'd stayed in high school the help he had to offer her had come too late.

Chapter

★ ✖ ★

12

Emilio followed Roberto around the apartment like a lost puppy, offering him unwanted advice for his dinner date with Brynn.

"First you've got to tell Miss Cassidy how beautiful she looks," Emilio instructed, "then gently take her in your arms and kiss her, but only lightly. Remember that, because it's important. You don't want to start something too soon. Women don't like a guy coming on heavy first thing. They want to be wined and dined first."

"Emilio," Roberto warned under his breath as he tightened the knot in his tie in front of the bedroom mirror, "I can handle this on my own."

"But I know Miss Cassidy better than you do. Don't forget I see her practically every day."

But his brother didn't view her as Roberto did. To Emilio she was his teacher, the first one he'd liked well enough to mention. To Roberto Brynn was a warm, desirable, generous woman. When they kissed the electricity between them was as powerful as Hoover Dam.

In the beginning he'd attempted to ignore the way the air sizzled every time they were together. A touch of antagonism had proved to be his best defense, and it had worked until Father Grady had manipulated them into chaperoning the dance at the church hall. Before he knew what had happened to him, Brynn was in his arms and life hadn't been the same since.

"Where are you taking her to dinner?" Emilio asked, following him across the bedroom.

Roberto splashed on a touch of spice-scented cologne. "I haven't decided yet." Actually he had, but he didn't want his brother dropping by unexpectedly with some phony excuse.

Emilio frowned with disapproval. "That's not going to work, bro, you've got to plan these things well in advance. You should have made reservations for a classy woman like Miss Cassidy."

If the truth be known, Emilio's attitude toward Brynn amused him. The way Emilio talked about her, one would think his brother was half in love with her himself.

"You can't just walk into any restaurant and expect a decent table to be waiting for you."

Roberto reached for his wool jacket. He hoped Brynn didn't recognize it as the same one from the dance. He owned only one suit, and he wasn't about to go out and purchase another just because of a silly dinner date.

"How do you know all this?" Roberto probed.

"I been around," Emilio answered with a hint of defiance.

That might be true, but Roberto didn't think Emilio had ever taken a girl out on a fancy dinner date.

"You got her flowers, didn't you?"

Roberto hadn't thought of that. "No."

"Oh, man," he said, shaking his head, "you're going to blow this."

"I'll pick some up on the way."

Emilio's face relaxed. "Good idea."

Roberto headed for the door, then stopped for his overcoat and gloves. The leather gloves were new and necessary to hide the car grease he couldn't remove from around his nails.

Once more Emilio followed him. "I know the perfect restaurant," he said excitedly, and snapped his fingers. "It's perfect. Call Mama Celeste's and make a reservation. The food's great and they think you walk on water ever since you repaired their van."

"Good idea." Unfortunately that was exactly where Roberto had already planned to take Brynn. He turned and met his brother, eye to eye. He couldn't remember when Emilio had grown so tall. Nearly ten years separated them, and Roberto had become accustomed to being the older, wiser, bigger brother. He wasn't taller by much, and that surprised him.

"I've already made arrangements to take Brynn to Mama Celeste's," he admitted. "And I don't want you making any excuses to stop by there this evening. Do I make myself clear?"

One corner of Emilio's mouth lifted with a cocky half smile. "What's it worth to you?"

Roberto's eyes narrowed into a dark scowl, and Emilio laughed. "Hey, I was just kidding, bro."

Roberto opened the front door. "Don't wait up for me."

"Are you kidding, man? This is one night I'm going to want to hear about."

Brynn had been less nervous for her first high school prom. She checked her appearance a dozen or more times before the doorbell rang. Her inclination was to rush across the room and throw open the door, but she forced herself to remain calm and collected.

Roberto stood on the other side of the door, so handsome her breath locked in her lungs. It reminded her of the night of the church dance. He'd knocked her senses for a loop then, too.

Looking away, she stepped aside to allow him into her apartment. "Hello, Roberto."

He inclined his head slightly. "You look lovely." Smiling, he stepped into her apartment and tenderly pressed his lips to her cheek.

Surprised and delighted, Brynn raised her hand to her face, her fingers investigating the spot where he'd kissed her.

Next he presented her with a small bouquet of flowers.

"Roberto, how sweet. Thank you." She led the way into the kitchen, where she placed the bouquet of pink carnations and minia-ture purple irises in a tall crystal vase.

"I didn't think to buy any wine," she said, regretting now that she hadn't thought of that beforehand.

"We'll have wine later," he said.

"I'll only be a minute," she said, and gestured self-consciously toward the bedroom. "I need to get my coat."

The ride to the restaurant, an Italian one from the looks of it, took several minutes. Roberto, the perfect gentleman, helped her out of the car and then escorted her inside.

The moment she walked through the door, Brynn was greeted with the scents of basil and simmering tomato. Garlic permeated the air, and she inhaled deeply, the smell alone enough to make her hun-gry. No one needed to tell her how good the food would be.

Roberto apparently knew the owners, and standing with his arm tucked around her waist, he introduced her.

"Brynn Cassidy, meet Stefano and Celeste Seti."

She shook hands with the white-haired gentleman who was smil-ing broadly. His wife, Mama Celeste herself, planted her hands on her face and mumbled something in Italian to her husband. Brynn couldn't understand a word. Whatever it was appeared to please the grandmotherly woman. With a wide smile she kissed Roberto on both cheeks and promised them, in heavily accented English, the best dinner of their lives.

Soon they were seated at a table. Before Brynn had a chance to smooth the linen napkin on her lap, she was served red wine, thick slices of bread, and a large block of cheese.

The food never seemed to stop coming. Brynn sampled one fabulous dish after another. There must have been three or four different appetizers—shrimp, eggplant, tiny meatballs—before a huge Caesar salad arrived. When Brynn was convinced she couldn't eat another bite, the pasta was brought to their table by Stefano, who insisted she would break Celeste's heart if she didn't take a large portion of the specialty of the house. From the envious looks being sent her way, Brynn had the feeling if she couldn't finish the clam spaghetti, any number of volunteers would gladly step in for her.

"More wine, more wine," Stefano insisted, replenishing their glasses when she'd finished the best pasta she'd ever tasted. Brynn wasn't given a chance to refuse the wine. Stefano filled her glass and carried away their empty plates.

"I've never had such good food in my life," she murmured, and scooted back her chair. She planted her hands on her stomach. "But if I don't stop eating now, I won't be able to walk."

"No dessert?" Roberto teased.

They finished with a cup of dark coffee. Stefano and Celeste visited their table before they left, and this time it was Brynn who was hugged and kissed. Mama's eyes watered, and she dabbed at their corners with the hem of her apron.

Once they were outside, Roberto headed for the car.

"Would you mind very much if we walked awhile?" Brynn asked. Physical movement would help ease the stuffed feeling. Besides, she didn't want the evening to end so soon.

"By all means, let's walk," Roberto agreed. He reached for her hand and set a slow, easy pace. The night was crisp and cold.

"It looks like it might snow."

Roberto glanced skyward. "Wishful thinking on your part," he murmured. "There's barely a cloud in the sky."

He was right. The image of them walking together, hand in hand through lightly falling snow, appealed to her.

Although she'd enjoyed their dinner, her one regret was that with all the food being served, and Stefano checking to be sure everything was to their liking, there hadn't been much of a chance for the two of them to talk.

"Thank you, Roberto, for a wonderful meal."

He released her hand and slipped his arm around her waist. "Thank you for coming with me."

Brynn pressed her head against his shoulder. "What made you decide to ask me out?" She wasn't sure what prompted the question, but she was curious.

"I wanted everything to be right for you."

"Be right?"

He exhaled slowly as though he weren't sure how to explain himself. "You aren't like other women I've known."

Brynn smiled to herself. "Is that a compliment?"

Roberto was taken aback by her question. "I meant it to be. Have I insulted you?"

"No," she assured him.

"You're special, Brynn. Not only to me, but to Emilio and his friends, too. They think a lot of you. I've heard the teens talk about you, and when they do, well, it's with respect. It takes a lot to impress kids these days."

"And how do *you* feel about me?" she asked. It would be far easier for her if Roberto came right out and told her. She'd never been so bold with a man, but this wasn't a normal relationship.

"Me?" He hesitated, taking some time to formulate his thoughts. "You're stubborn and strong-willed."

Brynn wouldn't deny it. "If you think I'm stubborn, you should meet my mother." She bit down on her lip when she realized what she'd said. Reminding him of the mother he'd lost was the last thing she wanted.

"So you inherited the trait." He sounded amused, and Brynn was relieved.

"I care for you, Roberto," she told him softly. "More than I care for anyone other than my family." If he wasn't willing to acknowledge his feelings for her, then she'd be the first one to say it. "Knowing you has blessed my life. When I have a problem, you're the person I want to share it with. When something good happens, you're the one I want to tell. I find myself thinking about you a lot, probably more than I should."

His arm tightened around her middle. "I feel the same way about you. I want very much to kiss you, Brynn," he said with a deep sigh that revealed his longing for her, "but I don't want to do it in public. Not again. I'll wait until we get back to your apartment."

Brynn's heart swelled with emotion as she looked to him. "We could leave now, don't you think?"

Roberto chuckled, and together they raced across the street and back to Mama Celeste's, where Roberto's car was parked.

As they neared Brynn's apartment their amusement ebbed, replaced with a growing anticipation. Brynn's hand shook slightly as she unlocked the front door, knowing that soon she would be in Roberto's arms.

Together they walked into her apartment. Brynn didn't bother to turn on the lights. Once the door was closed, she lifted her arms and reached for Roberto.

With a deep-seated groan, he backed her against the door and kissed her.

The kiss was like fire, a spontaneous combustion of desire and need. Once wasn't near enough to satisfy either of them, and Roberto kissed her again and again. He surprised her with his tongue, and she gasped as he thrust it deep inside her mouth, stroking and teasing her. Gradually her gasp became a whimper that trembled from her lips.

When she was sure they were both about to faint with the intensity of their lovemaking, Roberto pulled away. She noted that his chest was heaving; hers was, too. In the dim light he looked down on her, and she met his look recklessly, unafraid for him to see all the love and longing in her eyes. Her fingers clung to the lapels of his suit as she studied him.

She waited, needing to know he'd experienced the same wonder she had. He closed his eyes momentarily, his breath deep and harsh, as though he needed to separate himself from her, if not physically, then emotionally.

Brynn might have been offended if he hadn't continued to hold her close and with such tender care. She pressed her head to his chest and listened to the strong, fast-paced beat of his heart.

"I don't dare touch you again," he whispered thickly.

"Why not?"

"You make me lose my head."

"That's bad?" she asked.

She felt his smile against her cheek. "Not exactly. It would be very easy to take you into that bedroom and make love to you, but I won't."

"You won't?" She couldn't believe she was asking him this.

"I can't allow that to happen. Once would never be enough with you. I would want you again and again, and that would only lead to—"

A loud knock sounded against the door, startling them both. Roberto's eyes met hers in the faded light. "You're expecting someone?"

She shook her head.

"Who is it?" she asked, struggling to make her voice strong enough to be heard.

Roberto turned on the light switch.

"Emilio," Roberto's brother shouted from the other side.

Roberto stiffened with irritation and opened the front door.

"It's Modesto," Emilio cried as he stumbled into the apartment. His eyes were wide with panic and fear. The teenager slumped onto the sofa and covered his face with both hands. "Modesto's been shot."

Jammed inside Jenny and Michelle's dinky apartment for the potluck Christmas party, everyone seemed to be talking at once. Trey felt as out of place as a bull moose at one of those fancy dog shows, the ones with dolled-up poodles with painted toenails.

Jenny's acting friends were certainly a mixed breed. There were everyday people, the kind he would have been hard-pressed to guess were show people, and then there were the others. The others, he noted, tended to be flamboyant attention seekers.

It made for an interesting evening, he would admit that much. Holding his drink, he found a quiet corner and played the role of casual observer.

A couple of times Jenny drifted his way, but she wasn't able to stay for long. Trey understood. Since she shared hostessing duties with her roommate, she couldn't very well give him all her attention. Though to be honest, that was what Trey would have preferred.

He sipped the wine, a fruity-flavored one he wouldn't normally drink, but all the market had offered. He found himself watching Jenny, mesmerized by her. She was as beautiful as he remembered, more so. Yet he couldn't look at her without his gut twisting up in a knot. This had been his lot when she was growing up. Loving her from afar.

Next to burying his parents, the most difficult thing Trey had ever done was to let Jenny Lancaster leave Custer, Montana, without telling her how much he loved her. He hadn't felt particularly self-sacrificing and noble at the time. He didn't feel that way now. It was just that he had some decisions to make, damned important ones, and they involved Jenny.

He loved her, and although he'd tried to forget her in the last three years, he couldn't. Countless times he'd attempted to convince himself to look for greener pastures.

It hadn't worked.

He'd spent the better part of ten years in love with Jenny, and it didn't appear that time or distance was going to change the way he felt.

She'd been little more than fifteen when he'd first recognized her as a woman. Until then she'd been a pesky kid. Living next door, so to speak, Trey had dealt mostly with Dillon, Jenny's father.

He remembered the day he'd realized she was a woman. He'd driven over to talk to her father about one thing or another and gone into the barn. Jenny had been there, grooming her filly and practicing her lines for a school play, when he'd stumbled upon her by accident. Without missing a beat, she'd continued with a flawless delivery. She'd ended her soliloquy by dramatically throwing herself into his arms, then leaning back and planting the back of her hand against her forehead. Less than a second passed before she'd recovered from her death, leaped upright, and asked him what he'd thought of her performance.

What he'd saw, Trey realized now, was the most beautiful woman he'd ever laid eyes on. Until that moment Trey had thought of Jenny as a kid. But it hadn't been a child he'd held in those few moments.

Trey had scowled and muttered something about needing to talk to Dillon. Then for the next several years he'd waited impatiently for Jenny to grow up so he could court her. Three long, torturous years. It hadn't been easy watching her date one young buck after another. Nor had he liked her riding over to tell him about her dates and seeking his advice.

Trey suspected Jenny's parents knew how he felt about their daughter. But if they did, neither one said anything to him, and for that he was grateful.

By the time Jenny entered community college, she was dating one particular young man, and it looked for a time as if the two of them might be growing serious. More than once Trey had thought to go to her with his heart on his sleeve and tell her the way he felt.

This happened shortly after his parents had died, one after the other, within a nine-month period, and he was struggling financially. Dealing with his family's estate had drained his ready cash. Unfortunately this was about the same time that beef prices had plummeted. While he was fighting off the banks and barely holding his head above water financially wasn't the time to be asking a woman to be his wife.

By the time he felt he had something to offer Jenny, she'd made the decision to leave Montana for New York.

Trey remembered that Jenny's family had thrown a big going-away party for her. Trey couldn't force himself to attend. He knew if he let her leave, there was a good chance he'd never see her again, at least not the Jenny he knew. New York would change her. New York would make her into one of those sophisticated women who carried their dogs under their arms while they went clothes shopping.

Letting Jenny leave Montana was a testament of how much he loved her. His love couldn't compete with her dreams. The bright lights of Broadway was her destiny. He was a cattle rancher with damn little to offer someone as talented as Jenny Lancaster.

At the last minute, Trey had stopped by the ranch and managed to wish her his very best. He remembered he'd said something corny about her breaking her leg in New York. Then he'd stood with her family and waved good-bye.

She'd driven off with her friends and taken his heart with her.

Afterward, Trey had gone home and gotten soundly drunk.

The first year after she'd left had been the worst. He'd made a dozen or more excuses to visit the Lancasters and ask about her. He'd been tempted to write her but had promised himself he wouldn't. She was out of his life now and would soon be a big shot on Broadway.

Only it hadn't happened quite like that. By the second Christmas she was away, he'd been semisuccessful in pushing the memory of her to the back of his mind. He still asked about her occasionally and was surprised to learn that her name wasn't lighting up any marquees. It was then that he'd begun to hope Jenny would throw in the towel and move home to lick her wounds.

It was the small quiver in her voice when he'd phoned that had first alerted Trey to the fact that something was wrong. He hadn't been able to put his finger on it. After all this time, he didn't expect Jenny to be the same person she'd been when she'd left Custer. He wasn't sure now what he had expected. Instead of sounding happy, she'd seemed sad, and he'd sensed in her a deep pain she couldn't hide.

He'd mulled that over for a number of days, and then it seemed everyone he knew on God's green earth started talking about New York. Before he could question the wisdom of his actions, he'd booked the flight to New York and subsequently learned the truth. He wasn't relieved or glad at her lack of success. His first reaction had been anger that those fancy, worldly men had been blind to her talents.

Trey wanted to take Jenny back to Montana. He wanted to love her, comfort her, and take care of her. More than that, he wanted to wipe away the frustration and disappointment.

He hadn't meant to ask her to come home so abruptly, but the words had refused to remain unsaid. The first time he'd asked, her response had been quick and sharp.

No.

That had been before he'd kissed her. When he'd asked a second time, she hadn't answered.

Someone slipped a tape inside the cassette player, and a fresh batch of Christmas music filled the room. Several started to sing, and soon Trey heard three distinct parts, blending in perfect harmony.

Within a few moments everyone had stopped chatting to sing along. Jenny drifted over to Trey's side. He'd never tire of hearing her sing. This, he decided, was what angels must sound like. Her voice conjured up that image for him.

The old Christmas carols were his personal favorites, and when the first introductory notes of "Silent Night" played, Trey sang along himself. It surprised him how well his deep voice blended with Jenny's.

Pleasure lit up her eyes when she turned to smile at him.

He returned the gesture and draped his arm around her shoulder. A couple of the men in the group glanced his way and frowned. Trey didn't blame them for being jealous. He had battled down the affliction every time Jenny so much as glanced at another man. In the beginning it had damn near eaten him alive, but time and effort had helped him master his feelings.

Soon the music faded, taken over with small talk. The crowd was beginning to get to him, so he decided to step outside for some fresh air. To his surprise, Jenny grabbed her coat and followed him.

"Come with me," she said, and led him to the fire escape. She sat down and patted the space next to her. "I used to sit out here in the hottest nights of summer," she said. Her breath produced clouded puffs in the cold night air. "Out here with the sky bright with stars was as close as I could get to feeling like I was in Montana again," she admitted.

It was hard for Trey to hold his tongue. He'd already asked her twice to come back to Custer with him. He wouldn't do it again.

"I wondered if you ever thought about home," he said.

"Every day."

"Did you think about me, Jenny?" He braced himself, fearing he wouldn't like her answer. He had never said a solitary word about his feelings for her.

When she looked up at him, Trey noticed that her eyes were bright with unshed tears. "I thought about you a lot, Trey. I don't know why, but in the last six months it seemed you were on my mind nearly every day."

"You never wrote me," he reminded her.

Her smile was weak at best. "You didn't write me, either."

That he couldn't argue with.

"Did you . . . did you think about me, Trey?"

"Every damn minute of every damn day you've been away," he admitted huskily. He kissed her then, simply because he needed her so badly. He'd loved her for so long, he didn't know what it was not to love her.

Her ready response left him lightheaded. The kiss went on and on until they were both desperate to breathe.

"Oh, Trey," she whispered, and buried her face against his neck.

It was heaven to hold her and the purest form of torture he had ever experienced. Heaven and hell.

The door abruptly opened behind them, and a couple stumbled out, giggling.

"Sorry!" the male voice charged. "We haven't interrupted anything, have we?"

"Modesto's been shot." Shirley landed on the fire escape with such an urgency that she nearly unseated Mercy.

"My goodness," Mercy said, gasping.

"Did someone call for me?" Goodness asked, joining her two friends.

"Modesto's in the hospital," Shirley blurted out in a dither. "It was a gang shooting . . . someone he didn't even know. We've got to get there."

"What about Brynn?" Mercy asked, following her friend.

"She's already at New York General with Roberto and his brother. Emilio's in a bad way."

"Oh my."

Together the three of them left Jenny and headed across town. They soon descended into the hospital waiting room, where the situation was tense.

Emilio sat in the corner of the room, bent forward, his elbows braced against his knees. Shirley couldn't remember ever seeing the teenager look more stricken. Roberto sat next to his brother, and Brynn couldn't seem to hold still. She paced from one side of the room to the other.

Modesto's mother was weeping softly. His older sister had her arm around their mother, but she looked as though she were about to break into tears herself.

"They've been waiting two hours," Shirley informed her friends.

"What's taking so long?"

"Modesto's in surgery."

"How did something like this happen?" Mercy asked. In all the time they'd been working together, they'd never been a part of this kind of tragedy.

"I don't know what to do for them." Shirley turned to face her two friends. Always before she'd been the one with the most experience and the one the other two had looked up to for help. She looked desperately to Goodness for help.

"This is just terrible," Mercy murmured, wringing her hands. "Just terrible. Poor Modesto."

"Poor Brynn." Shirley stood near the young teacher and watched her pace. "She's nearly beside herself with worry."

"Stand with her," Goodness urged. "Give her your strength."

"Mine?" Shirley was beside herself. Never had she felt more inadequate. "Gabriel was right. I don't have nearly enough experience to help Brynn the way I should. She needs me and I've failed her."

Brynn collapsed into a chair, and Shirley sat next to her and folded her wing protectively over the young woman.

"Stay with her," Goodness suggested. "I'm going to find out what I can about Modesto's condition."

"I'll go with you," Mercy said, joining Goodness. "Don't you worry about a thing," she said, looking back at Shirley. "I'm sure everything's under control."

The last thing Shirley wanted was to be left alone. She ached the same way Brynn did, worried the same way Brynn did. She shared her charge's feelings of inadequacy. If ever Gabriel was right, it was now.

"Shirley."

Just thinking about him seemed to have conjured up the archangel.

"Gabriel," she said, leaping to attention.

"How are things going?" His presence seemed to fill up the hospital waiting room.

Shirley thought briefly of bluffing her way out of this, then figured Gabriel would be able to see through her in less time than it took for a heart to beat.

"It's about Modesto," she explained, distraught and near tears herself.

"I know all about the boy."

"Can you tell me what's going to happen to him?"

Gabriel inclined his head slightly. "He'll recover in time."

Shirley sighed with heartfelt relief. "Thank God."

"I'll mention it the next time we talk," Gabriel assured her.

Sheepishly Shirley looked to the mighty archangel. "You were right," she admitted sadly.

"That's always nice to know, but exactly what am I right about this time?"

"Me helping Brynn. She's falling in love with Roberto."

"So I understand."

Shirley waited for Gabriel to voice his disapproval, but he didn't.

"Mr. Whalen placed a formal reprimand in her file."

"I heard about that as well."

"Suzie's pregnant."

"Yes."

"Everything's one giant mess, and it's all my fault." She hung her head, not wanting to view the disappointment in Gabriel's eyes.

"Your fault?" Gabriel echoed, then chuckled softly. "You've got it all wrong." Gently he placed his wings around Shirley's burdened shoulders. "I couldn't be more proud had I trained you myself." He paused and sighed deeply. "Come to think of it, I have."

Chapter

★ ☆ ★

13

Hannah returned home from an errand her mother had sent her on, and hurried up the stairs to her family's living quarters. She hadn't taken more than a few steps into their apartment when aunts, uncles, cousins, and her beloved grandmother shouted, "Surprise!"

Hannah blinked back her shock. She stared at the sea of faces and noticed Carl's parents were present as well. Ruth rushed forward and hugged Hannah enthusiastically.

"It's an engagement party," her mother announced when Hannah stared at her, unable to disguise her anxiety.

Hannah looked at Carl, who was thrust into the middle of the room with her. She hadn't seen him since he'd confessed that he'd been fired.

Admitting to his family that he'd lost his job would have mortified Carl. Hannah might never have learned the truth had she not arrived unexpectedly on his doorstep the afternoon she'd met Joshua.

When she recognized how troubled Carl was over the loss of his job, she knew she couldn't deliver even more depressing news. So she'd been forced to bide her time.

"Apparently this party is in our honor," Carl explained.

Somehow Hannah managed to return a smile, but she didn't know how she would possibly make it through this party.

To be fair, Carl didn't look any more pleased than she did with the unexpectedness of their engagement party. He had told her earlier that since he was no longer employed, they would need to postpone the wedding. The next step was to announce this to their families. Carl had wanted time to tell his parents first, and Hannah had agreed. Now they were being forced to pretend all was well when they were keenly aware that it wasn't.

Once the pressure was off to set a wedding date, Hannah would be free to tell Carl about having met Joshua. He would understand. She was sure of that.

Hannah glanced around the room. It was filled to capacity with family, aunts, uncles, cousins, and longtime friends who'd come to wish her and Carl happiness.

Because it was expected of her, Hannah took Carl around and introduced him to her relatives.

Her grandmother gazed at her fondly from a position of honor, the recliner. Hannah had always felt close to Sylvia Morganstern. Surely she would know something was wrong. Surely her grandmother would recognize that she wasn't in love with Carl. Hannah realized she wouldn't be able to hide her feelings from the one who'd known and loved her all her life.

"Come and say hello to your aunt Edith," Ruth said, placing her arm around Hannah's waist and leading her across the room.

Carl traipsed behind obediently. Hannah didn't know how anyone could look at the two of them and believe they were in love. Nor did she know how she could continue to pretend to be an eager bride when she intended to break their engagement at the earliest possible moment.

Briefly she closed her eyes and hoped Joshua would never learn of this engagement party. Thus far he'd been wonderfully patient with her, but she didn't know how long that would last, especially when he learned she hadn't broken off the engagement with Carl the way she'd promised.

"Hannah, my dear," her grandmother said, and patted the empty seat beside her. "First introduce me to your young man and then sit down. I'm going to be greedy and hog you all to myself for a few moments."

"Carl, this is my grandma Morganstern."

"I'm so pleased to meet you," Carl said formally and with deep respect.

Her grandmother asked him a number of gentle questions, which he answered, although it was clear to Hannah that he was eager to escape. Before he left, he was kind enough to bring Hannah and Sylvia each a cup of punch. Then as quickly as he could, he wandered away.

Her grandmother reached for Hannah's hand and squeezed her slim fingers affectionately. "Now tell me all about you and Carl. How long have you been dating? How'd you meet?"

It demanded all the fortitude Hannah possessed to keep from

blurting out the truth. If anyone would understand about her loving Joshua, it would be her grandmother.

"He looks like a good man."

Hannah smiled and agreed. "He'll be a good husband." But not to her. She glanced in Carl's direction and found she could barely look at him and not experience a crushing sense of guilt.

"Hannah?"

Her gaze continued to follow the man she'd promised to marry. It astonished her that she could ever have agreed to be Carl's wife, especially when it was so painfully obvious they were mismatched.

"Carl is a wonderful man. He's loyal and dedicated." Hannah lowered her gaze, hoping her grandmother wouldn't guess the love she nurtured in her heart was for another man.

Everyone seemed to be having a wonderful time. Together Hannah's parents brought one food tray after another out from the kitchen. The buffet-style meal was set on the dining room table. Because her parents were in the food business, this had been a labor of love, and the spread was something to behold.

"I've taken enough of your time," Sylvia insisted, patting Hannah's hand. "It looks like your mother's ready for you and Carl."

It didn't escape Hannah's notice that her grandmother didn't comment on what a nice couple Hannah and Carl made. She was deeply relieved Sylvia hadn't pressed her with more questions. It was difficult enough to deceive her mother and father, but nearly impossible to maintain the pretense in front of her grandmother.

Hannah joined Carl, and it seemed everyone was staring at them, waiting for something to happen.

Carl reached for her hand and whispered, "I spoke to my father."

A sense of relief nearly swallowed her whole, and she turned to face him. "You did?"

Carl's gaze shifted about the room. "He's going to talk to the school board as soon as possible and see what can be done. I'm confident he'll be able to straighten everything out."

"That's wonderful, Carl."

His fingers tightened over hers. "I can't tell you how worried I've been over this."

Hannah had been concerned as well, but not for the reasons Carl assumed.

"Everything's going to work out, Hannah, I promise you that."

"Of course it will." And as soon as Carl's misunderstanding with the headmaster was cleared up, she'd be free to break the engagement.

Hannah's father asked Carl's father, Rabbi Rabinsky, to say a short prayer before they ate. The rabbi stepped forward and placed one hand on his son's shoulder and the other on Hannah's. He closed his eyes, and the room went still.

The prayer was short and potent, asking God to shower His love upon the two of them and to fill their lives with good things.

When he raised his head, there was a murmur of agreement. Her family loved her, Hannah realized, and they wished her and Carl much happiness.

Soon her relatives and other guests were busy filling their plates. Hannah wasn't the least bit hungry, but to not eat might have alerted her mother that something was wrong, so she dished up with the others.

Hannah and Carl were ushered to the seats of honor, and she noticed that he didn't seem to have much of an appetite himself.

The party sat in a large circle, their plates resting on their laps. It was Aunt Edith who asked the question first.

"Well, you two, don't keep me in suspense any longer. When's the wedding date?"

Everyone seemed to wait for Hannah to answer. The room filled with an expectant silence. Hannah looked first to her mother for help and then to Carl. Neither seemed inclined to respond.

"I believe Mother and Helen felt that the wedding coordinator should be the one to decide that," Hannah explained when no one came to her rescue.

"Nonsense," Edith said, dismissing the idea with a wave of her hand. "It's up to the two of you to set the date. Let the wedding coordinator work around the one you've chosen."

"But—" Hannah wasn't allowed to finish.

"I agree," Cousin Hariette intoned. "If you're going to have an outsider make all the arrangements, then it's vital they know from the first who's in change. A wedding's no small thing, and it's best to get started on the right foot."

"I've wondered about this," Hannah's father murmured, looking to Ruth.

"Springtime," Edith suggested next. "When the flowers are starting to bloom. There's nothing like fresh flowers for a wedding."

"Oh no," Hannah said quickly. "We can't possibly have the wedding so soon . . . there wouldn't be near enough time, would there?" She looked to Carl for support.

"I'm afraid Hannah's right," her mother concurred. "We were thinking June."

"June," Edith repeated. "June would be perfect."

Cousin Hariette brought out a new calendar and flipped through the pages until she located the month.

"I don't think Carl and I are in any rush," Hannah offered, but it seemed no one was listening to her. Both her own mother and Carl's crowded around, peering over Hariette's shoulder, scanning the June page on the pocket calendar.

"The sixteenth sounds perfectly lovely."

"The closer to the middle of the month the better, from what I hear," another aunt offered.

"I don't think we need to choose a date right now, do you?" Hannah tried once more.

Her grandma Morganstern studied her closely, and Hannah realized she'd best not say anything more. Not then, at least.

"What do you think of June sixteenth?" The question was directed to Carl, who had his fork poised in front of his mouth.

"Give the young man a chance to eat," her father said, coming to Carl's rescue.

With his mouth full of food, Carl nodded enthusiastically. Hannah felt he was silently commenting on what her father had said. Unfortunately everyone else in the room seemed to think he was agreeing to the wedding date.

"That settles that," Ruth said cheerfully. "The wedding is set for June sixteenth."

The news of Modesto Diaz's injury spread quickly, and soon a number of Brynn's students had gathered at the hospital. Again and again Emilio was forced to repeat the grisly details of what had happened—first to the police who came to question him, then to the curious and the fearful.

Father Grady arrived, and Brynn was grateful. She felt at a loss as to how to help Modesto's mother and sister deal with the tragedy. After what seemed a lifetime, the surgeon appeared. His look was grave as he announced that the surgery had been a success. Modesto wasn't completely out of danger, and his condition was guarded. But the teen was doing as well as could be expected.

Following a translation of the physician's words, Modesto's mother clenched her hands together, turned her face toward heaven, and wept loudly. His sister cried silently with relief. For the first time since he'd appeared at her apartment door, some color started to return to Emilio's face.

Roberto looked to Brynn and she to him. His relief was evident. Hers, too, she guessed, as she battled down the urge to weep.

While they'd sat through those interminable hours, Roberto had remained beside his brother, offering Emilio his support and love. The younger Alcantara had needed his brother.

Brynn, however, had found sitting impossible, so she'd done what she always did when she was nervous: she'd paced. Back and forth, until she'd feared her path would leave permanent creases in the thin carpet.

Now she felt the need to be close to Roberto. He apparently shared her sudden desire, because he crossed the area. Without a word, he took her into his arms and held her firmly against him. She drank in his strength, absorbed his calm. His hold was tight, almost punishing, as if he planned on never letting her go.

Brynn knew that the two of them had attracted the attention of the others, but she didn't care who saw them together. Gradually Roberto did release her, but not before she felt his muscles tighten. His relief turned to anger as he faced Father Grady.

"It's this neighborhood," Roberto said between clenched teeth. "It could have been Emilio who was shot, or you, or Brynn." His face was tight and fierce. His brother was all the family he had left.

"I know, I know," Father Grady said gently.

Roberto stalked to the far side of the room, his back to Brynn.

She wasn't entirely certain what was happening. Now wasn't the time for explanations, but she knew Father Grady would explain everything to her later.

"I'll take you home now," Roberto announced starkly to Brynn.

She followed him through the crowded hospital corridor outside. The cold night air hit her like an unexpected slap. The wind stung her face and eyes as she hurried to keep pace with Roberto.

For Brynn's sake, Roberto tried to control his anger, but he couldn't think of his younger brother and Modesto facing a nameless gunman on the same streets where children had played only hours earlier. His anger went deep and bordered on rage.

He focused his resentment on the neighborhood and the frustration he felt each time he'd tried to make a better life for himself and Emilio.

It could have been his brother lying in that hospital bed. He could have lost Emilio. The thought terrified him. He'd promised his mother that he would watch after his brother, raise him right. He had failed her in other ways, but not this time. By heaven, not this time.

Roberto glanced over at Brynn, who sat next to him stiffly. She'd never seen this side of him. She didn't know he could be an angry, frustrated brute. This was what happened when those he loved were threatened.

Love.

Just mentally saying the word made him squirm. He was dangerously close to falling for the pretty Irish teacher. He didn't need anyone to tell him what a mistake that would be. It went without saying that a college-educated beauty like Brynn Cassidy had nothing in common with the likes of him. She should be dating a stockbroker or an attorney, not someone who had trouble getting the grease from beneath his fingernails.

He was living in a dreamworld if he thought anything could develop between them. God had delivered that message loud and clear. Roberto knew what he had to do next.

First off, he had to stop thinking about Brynn as a friend. They'd never been that. As for making her his lover, however much he would like to entertain the notion, she was off-limits. He'd make excuses not to see her again, and soon enough she'd get the message. Their relationship would be over before it ever started. Whatever it might have been was gone now.

Having made that decision, Roberto felt some of the hard ball of anger dissipate. He was in control again. His life was back in order.

One thing he vowed. Somehow, some way, with God's help, he was going to find his way out of this neighborhood.

Brynn's class was quiet and subdued on Monday. Normally her students tested her patience by chattering like monkeys long after the bell rang. Not this day. They filed into the room and sat at their desks and stared at her as though they anticipated some great revelation from her.

"By now most of you have heard about what happened to Modesto," she said.

"It ain't fair, Miss Cassidy," Yolanda said.

"Life isn't fair," Denzil answered.

"Modesto wasn't doing anything."

"He isn't bad, you know."

"Of course he isn't." Brynn felt at a loss as to how to answer their fears, nor did it seem right to dig into her lessons when it was obvious her students needed to talk about what had happened to their friend.

"I went to see him at the hospital," Emilio announced, his voice void of emotion. "They wouldn't let me in."

"Modesto's in intensive care. I know because I called," someone else claimed.

"He's going to live, isn't he?"

Brynn couldn't answer that, so she repeated as best she could what the physician had said. "His chances are very good, but there's always the possibility of complications."

"We weren't doing nothin'," Emilio said to no one in particular. "The police tried to make it sound like we were on the prowl looking for trouble. Man, if I was looking for action, I'd take my posse with me."

There were murmurs of agreement.

Emilio leaned forward and placed his hands over his face. He looked both vulnerable and afraid. Wanting to comfort him, Brynn walked over to his side and placed her hand gently on his shoulder.

He shrugged it off viciously and glared up at her. "Don't touch me," he snapped.

Such behavior wasn't like Emilio. If she considered any one student an ally, it would be Roberto's brother.

She stepped back, but not before Emilio slid out of his seat and stormed out of the room. The glass panel in the door rattled as he slammed it closed.

"Emilio." She started after him. If he was caught in the hall without a pass, he'd be sent to the principal's office. If he mouthed off to Mr. Whalen, he was likely to be suspended a second time, and if that happened, it was doubtful he'd be back.

Brynn stopped at the door. "Suzie," she called, "would you take over for me for a few moments?"

The teenager's eyes widened with apprehension before she nodded.

"Thank you," Brynn whispered, and left the classroom. She was breaking another cardinal rule by doing so. If she was discovered, she would receive another formal reprimand. She weighed the decision carefully before stepping into the hallway. Something was very wrong with Emilio, and she had to find out what.

She found him crouched on the floor next to a dented beige locker at the end of the hall. His head hung between his knees.

"Emilio." She said his name gently.

He didn't look up.

"It wasn't your fault."

"Leave me alone," he said, his voice uncharacteristically hard and cold.

"You can't blame yourself for what happened to Modesto," she offered.

This time he hissed something in Spanish, and for once Brynn was grateful for her limited language skills. One thing was certain: he wasn't inviting her to talk matters out.

"You can't stay here," she said, looking both ways down the hall. "Please, Emilio, come back into the class."

He shook his head.

"If they find you—"

"Yeah, yeah, I know. I'll get suspended. Do you really think I care, Miss Cassidy? I don't."

"I care."

"Am I supposed to appreciate that?"

"Yes."

He looked away, and it seemed that he was wishing her back into the classroom. "Leave me alone."

"You're hurting, Emilio. I want to help."

He lifted his head and stared at the ceiling. "Modesto's the one who's in pain, not me."

"Do you think Modesto wouldn't be in as much pain if you'd been shot, too?"

"Yes," he shouted, and slammed his fist into the locker directly beside him. The noise exploded in the silent hallway like a cannon shot, echoing off the sides.

For sure they'd be found now. Brynn closed her eyes and inhaled a deep, calming breath. Emilio didn't want her help, didn't need her.

"I'm sorry this happened to you, Emilio," she said softly. "So very sorry." Knowing he wouldn't accept her help, she turned and started back to her classroom.

"I ran."

She paused. So that was what this was all about. Emilio thought himself a coward because he'd deserted his friend and saved his own life.

Brynn turned back and squatted next to him. Her legs ached before she spoke. "I would have run, too. It was probably what saved you from being shot as well."

Emilio said nothing.

"Do you think Modesto wouldn't have tried to escape had you been the one hit first?"

Again Emilio didn't respond.

"You acted instinctively," Brynn tried again. "You had nothing with which to defend yourself. The option had been taken away from you."

A parched cry worked its way through his throat, and he buried his face in his arms with a muffled sob.

Brynn longed to touch him, but she was afraid that her comfort was the last thing he sought. Because her muscles were cramping, she placed her knees on the cold floor.

"There's no shame in what you did," she whispered.

His shoulders shook, and unable to watch him and do nothing, Brynn braced her hand against the curve of his shoulder.

The pain, the doubt, the fears and self-recriminations, broke like a fire hydrant inside him. His shoulders shook violently with uncontrollable sobs. One after another tumbled from his lips until his cries became those of an injured animal.

Kneeling at his side, Brynn gently tucked his head against her breast and held him. Gently she rocked back and forth, fighting emotion while the pain poured from Emilio Alcantara's heart.

"Will you be seeing Trey this afternoon?" Michelle asked Jenny.

"I don't know." They hadn't made plans to get together, and she had to work later in the day. She'd told him her schedule and had expected to hear from him. Thus far she'd been disappointed.

Michelle wandered into their living room, a plastic trash bag in hand. She picked up an empty wine bottle and tossed it inside. "Your friend certainly generated a lot of interest."

Jenny had noticed that much herself.

"I had to tell Julia Leonard to wipe the drool off her chin."

Jenny smiled.

"That guy's a hunk, girl. How come you never mentioned how handsome he is? It's like he walked in directly from the range. Someone asked me if he'd left his horse parked outside." Michelle ditched a paper plate in the trash bag. "There was something else I noticed."

"What's that?" Jenny asked, tossing a beer can into the accumulated garbage.

"He only had eyes for you."

"I've known Trey LaRue nearly all my life," Jenny explained.

Michelle straightened and studied Jenny for a couple of moments. "By the way, what kind of name is Trey, anyway? It sounds like it's French or something."

"His real name's Mark."

"Mark? How'd his family get Trey out of that?"

"His grandfather's name was Mark and his father's name was Mark, and when he was born the story goes that there were so many Marks floating around, they decided to call him Trey."

"Oh, I get it now. Trey for the third Mark," Michelle murmured.

"Right." Jenny returned to picking up the clutter left over from the party.

"Are you going to marry him?" her roommate shocked her by asking next.

"Marry him?"

"Why not?" Michelle asked flippantly. "It's as clear as melted snow the guy's in love with you. When I first met him I thought it was rather sweet of him to travel all this way to see you. It's a definite boost to a woman's ego to have a man from her past idolize her. I could certainly do with a couple of men like Trey myself."

"He's never once mentioned marriage to me, nor will he." Jenny's reply was defensive, and she knew it.

Michelle's eyebrows flirted with her hairline. "You'd be tempted to accept his proposal if he did, wouldn't you?"

"Don't be ridiculous." But she wasn't nearly as confident as she sounded. She didn't know what she'd say if Trey proposed. One thing was certain: she didn't like the turn their conversation had taken. It hadn't bothered her when Michelle mentioned the open curiosity of their friends toward Trey. It hadn't hurt her pride any to have Trey fend off the friendly advances made by the more aggressive of her peers. Frankly, Jenny didn't blame her friends. Trey had the same overwhelming effect upon her senses.

The few kisses they'd shared before being interrupted had haunted her. She wanted him to kiss and touch her again just so she'd know what they'd shared had been as good as she remembered.

"Can you honestly picture someone like Trey living in New York?" she asked Michelle heatedly. "Within a month he'd go stark, raving mad. Trey's the type of man who needs plenty of wide-open space."

"If he loved you . . . "

"No." Jenny wouldn't consider it. Besides, it was a moot point. The very idea that he'd propose was ludicrous. He was in town only a few days, exactly how many he had yet to tell her. When he left she'd ride out to the airport with him and see him off. But the mere thought of Trey heading back to Montana produced an emptiness she couldn't shake.

"Jenny?" Michelle broke into her musings.

She smiled weakly and resumed her task, but her mind wasn't on it.

"Of course if you married Trey, you wouldn't necessarily need to live in New York. There are—"

"Are you suggesting I return to Montana?" Jenny demanded. "What are you trying to tell me, Michelle? That it's time I admitted the truth, that I'm a no-talent wannabe and that I'll never make it on Broadway or, for that matter, anyplace else?" She was desperate to breathe by the time she'd finished.

Visibly shocked by Jenny's outburst, Michelle stood frozen and stared at her.

Jenny sagged into the chair. "I didn't mean that."

"I didn't either," Michelle whispered. "I believe in you as strongly as I do in myself."

"I know." They'd been each other's cheering squad for too long for Jenny to doubt her friend now. Over the last three years they'd been through so much together. Jenny knew Michelle wished her nothing but unbridled success. Anything else would have been completely out of character.

The phone rang just then.

The last few days had been a tense time for them both. Michelle was due to hear the results of her second audition with John Peterman. If it were in her power, Jenny would award her friend the role, but it wasn't.

"You want me to get it?" she asked Michelle.

"No, I will," Michelle answered, and walked over to the wall phone. She reached for it and paused, her hand inches from the receiver. "You get it, all right?" she asked, and moved away.

It pealed a third time before Jenny could reach it.

"I should be the one to answer," Michelle said abruptly and ripped the receiver off the hook. "This is Michelle Jordan," she greeted cheerfully, as if she had been sitting idly by the phone without a care in the world. She listened for a moment, then, "Well, hello," she said seductively, eyeing Jenny. "And how are you?"

A second pause while Jenny was left to wonder who was at the other end of the line.

"Of course. . . . No, it's no problem whatsoever." She pressed the mouthpiece against her shoulder. "It's Trey. He wants to talk to you. Do you want me to tell him you're here, or would you rather I make up some excuse and tell him you are out for the day?"

Chapter

★ ✭ ★

14

Emilio was absent from school the following afternoon. Brynn's heart sank. She couldn't very well cancel the most important test this term because one student hadn't bothered to show.

Emilio had left school the day before without returning to class, but when Brynn had tried to reach him later, the phone had gone unanswered. With her own commitments, she hadn't been able to seek out Roberto, nor had she been able to talk to him.

Her day felt incomplete without some form of contact with Roberto. Little by little she'd opened her heart to Emilio's older brother. There was such passion in Roberto, such intensity. The other men she'd dated had been neither hot nor cold. Nothing excited them. Not injustice. Not good fortune. Not tickets to a play-off football game. Brynn had been left wondering what would happen if any of them ever won the lottery.

There was no doubt in her mind, however, where Roberto stood on any number of subjects. He rarely hesitated to make his opinions known. Although she often disagreed with him, she appreciated the fact that he was willing to take a stand. He cared deeply for those he loved. That was what had attracted her to him in the beginning.

Every time he kissed her the experience left her shaken. One thing was certain: Roberto Alcantara would never be a lukewarm lover.

"Is everyone ready for their midterms?" she asked the class. Standing in front of the room, she cradled the test papers against her chest.

A low rumble of responses came from her students. As the papers were being handed out, Brynn noted that Emilio wasn't the only student absent that day. Modesto's desk was conspicuously empty. His condition remained listed as serious, but from what she'd heard he would soon be upgraded to satisfactory.

Mike Glasser was gone as well. That disappointed her. She'd tried hard to bring the loner out of his shell, but nothing had worked. His attitude baffled her. When she looked directly at him, she assumed his mind was a thousand miles away, yet when she quizzed him, he knew the answers. The boy was keenly intelligent, but he refused to apply himself.

Brynn walked around the room while her class took the exam. This was by far the most important test she'd given, and she'd worked long hours composing the essay questions. Her students' responses were the best way she had of gauging how well she'd done her job.

The class discussions were thought-provoking and often heated. Brynn was thrilled that she could make her students care about what had happened in the world fifty years earlier. She felt it was important for them to do more than memorize dates and names.

Her goal was for them to look back at history and learn from the past. She wanted them to gain insight and perspective from a journal written by a teenage Jewish girl, who, despite the years separating their worlds, wasn't unlike them. It excited Brynn when her students recognized that they shared the same dreams, the same aspirations, as Anne Frank.

More important, Brynn wanted her students to reason through this material and willingly share their feelings with her. A number of the test questions had no right or wrong answers. All she wanted was for each of her students to reflect on this time period in American and European history and then express their thoughts.

When Brynn strolled past Suzie's desk, she was surprised to discover that the girl's paper was blank.

Unwilling to break the concentration of any of the others, Brynn resisted the urge to ask Suzie if something was wrong. She noticed that the girl wore a maternity top and wondered if anyone else recognized Suzie was pregnant.

Pen in hand, Suzie briefly acknowledged Brynn, then bent forward and started to write.

As Brynn walked past Emilio's empty desk, she couldn't help wondering what had kept him from class. It wasn't as if he hadn't known about this test or realized its significance. Brynn had been talking about it for several days, reviewing the material so it would be fresh in their minds. Now and again she'd purposely screw up the dates and would take pride when someone, often a student she wouldn't expect to know the difference, would correct her.

After class had been dismissed, Brynn quickly reviewed the test results and was pleased with what she read. Because she was anxious to talk to Emilio, she left school as soon as she could without checking for messages. She rarely received anything more than the dittoed sheets the school printed for all staff members. With the advent of Christmas, and most all the classes winding down, she didn't expect anything of real importance.

Eager to see Roberto, Brynn walked to his garage first. The sky was dark with thick gray clouds the color of tempered steel, and the wind added an extra chill to the late afternoon. Nevertheless, Brynn was happy. She'd had her first real date with Roberto, and even though their evening had ended abruptly, their time together had proved what she'd long suspected. Roberto cared about her the same way she did about him.

Brynn's parents were anxious for her to come home for Christmas, but she'd already decided against making the trip. She hadn't told her mother, and wouldn't, but she preferred to stay right here in New York with Roberto. She'd mentioned him in passing several times, and in the last telephone conversation, she'd confessed she was strongly attracted to him.

The bell chimed over the doorway when she entered his garage. She rubbed her hands together to chase away the chill. No one greeted her.

"Is anyone here?" she called out, thinking it odd that Roberto hadn't locked up the garage.

A minute later Roberto appeared, dressed in greasy overalls. He wiped his hands clean on a rag, his face devoid of emotion. He nodded once and greeted her without revealing any pleasure in seeing her. "Hello, Brynn."

None of the warmth or welcome she'd felt on their dinner date was apparent. Puzzled by his attitude, Brynn felt like walking out the door and coming back to try this all over again.

"Is something wrong?" she asked.

He shook his head. "You tell me."

"Well . . ." Baffled, she wasn't sure what had happened. "Emilio wasn't in class this afternoon."

"Yes, I know."

"There was an important test."

He shrugged as though to say that was of no importance to him.

"Is Emilio ill?"

"No."

"Then where was he?"

"Running errands for me," Roberto informed her briskly.

"You mean to say you knew he was purposely skipping classes and you let him?" Anger swelled inside her, but she did a good job of maintaining her composure.

"Yes. Emilio announced this morning that he didn't feel like going to school, and I told him the choice was his."

This was a discussion they'd had in the past, and they'd always ended up arguing about the importance of education. Nothing she said would change Roberto's opinion, and certainly nothing he said would alter her feelings.

"I want to talk to Emilio," she said, unwilling to be drawn into a verbal battle neither one of them could win.

"He isn't here," Roberto continued stoically.

"When do you expect him back?"

He didn't hesitate. "I don't know."

Brynn could see that discussing Emilio would be a losing proposition. She looked past Roberto, hoping to gain perspective on what was happening between them.

"How was your day?" she asked in an effort to put the conversation back on an even keel.

"Busy." He glanced over his shoulder as though to say there was plenty left for him to do and her silly questions were keeping him from his chores.

Brynn wasn't sure what to do or say. She could play cute word games and dance around the issue, but that would solve nothing. They'd done all that before.

"If you've got something to say to me, Roberto, I'd appreciate it if you came out and said it." She stiffened, knowing instinctively what was on his mind.

A flicker of surprise flashed in and out of his eyes. He hadn't anticipated her being this direct, she guessed. Normally she wasn't. Whenever it was possible she avoided confrontation, but she'd learned that in dealing with Roberto, she was better off taking the offensive.

From the first time since she'd arrived, he hesitated.

"Let me say it for you, then," she offered. "You've come to some monumental decision about us."

"Brynn—"

"Let me finish," she insisted, forcing herself to sound light and airy, as though his attitude didn't affect her one way or the other. "You've decided that it'd probably be best for us not to see each other again. Am I right?"

His jaw had gone white. "Something along those lines, but I don't think now is the time to discuss it."

"It seems to me this is as good a time as any," she responded with a flippant air. "You know what they say about there being no time like the present."

"Perhaps, but—"

"Why, Roberto?" she asked simply. Her chest tightened, and this time she couldn't hide the pain in her voice. "Did I do something unforgivable? Something so terrible that you can't find it in your heart to forgive me?"

"No," he said harshly, and briefly closed his eyes. "For what it's worth . . ." He stopped himself, then started again, his eyes as gentle as she'd ever seen them. He didn't want to hurt her, that much was evident.

"Whatever it is," she whispered forcefully, "we can work it out."

He shook his head. "I never intended to become emotionally involved with you. We're both intelligent enough to realize we're all wrong together." He clenched the muscles along the side of his jaw, and when he spoke his voice was filled with regret. "I blame myself. Matters should never have gone this far."

"What am I supposed to do? Forget I ever met you? When I bump into you on the street, do you want me to turn and walk the other way?"

"No . . . "

"I've never been the type of person who can turn my feelings on and off at will. Tell me what it is you want from me. Just tell me and I promise I'll walk out that door and it'll be as though we'd never met."

For a long time he didn't answer her.

"I'm waiting," she told him. "I'm not a difficult person to talk to, Roberto. At least others don't seem to have a problem. Tell me," she said again, more emphatically this time, "what is it you want."

His hands clenched into fists. "I want you to leave New York," he said, his voice strained. "You don't belong here. You and all this non-sense about teaching these kids to wish for the impossible. Try filling Modesto's head with that garbage now, why don't you? He's fighting for his life. We're light-years away from anything more than survival. You're beating your head against a stone wall, only you haven't learned that yet. Personally I don't want to be the one who's left to pick up the pieces when you do."

His words ripped open her heart, and just then she found it impossible to reply.

"There'll be someone else for you soon enough," he continued.

"Someone else?" She couldn't believe he would suggest she was the type to leap from one relationship to the next in some crazy form of emotional hopscotch.

"Who you date is your own business. All I ask is that you leave me out of it."

It, she reasoned, meant her life. He wanted nothing more to do with her.

Had she possessed a sliver of pride, Brynn would have turned and walked out. Instead she forced herself to stay, even when she knew that it meant more pain.

Her emotions battled with each other. She wanted to strike back at him, hurt him the same way he'd hurt her. And in the next millisecond she longed to throw herself in his arms and beg him to change his mind.

In the end she did neither. From some reserve of strength she knew nothing about, she scrounged up a genuine, heartfelt smile. "You're right," she told him, "there will be someone else." In time. Then, because she couldn't make herself leave without touching him, Brynn gently placed her hand against his cheek.

A muscle leapt in his face as he steeled himself against her.

"Good-bye, Roberto. Godspeed."

She dropped her hand and was about to turn away when he reached out and grabbed hold of her shoulder and whirled her around. Crushed against him as she was, Brynn buried her face in his chest and clung. His kiss was hard and urgent, and she knew the moment he released her that he regretted ever having touched her.

"Good-bye, Brynn Cassidy. Have a good life."

She nearly sobbed aloud, but she managed to hold the emotion inside. "You too, Roberto Alcantara."

"How can you stand there and do nothing?" Goodness demanded of Shirley. "Roberto should have his head examined."

"Personally, I agree, but unfortunately he has a free will to decide whatever he wants."

"Free will? I'm telling you right now that's the crux of the problem with humans. They can do anything they want, and they've let it go to their heads."

"That's the whole tamale in a nutshell," Shirley concurred, then scratched her head, wondering why that sounded wrong.

"I have half a mind to shake up this city."

Shirley wished Mercy were with her. She'd seen Goodness in this mood before, and it was downright frightening. The last time had been in Bremerton, Washington, when Goodness had gotten her hand on an aircraft carrier. The naval command was still trying to figure that one out.

"Goodness, are you thinking what I think you're thinking?"

"Someone needs to shake up this town."

"Personally," Shirley said, trying to be as diplomatic as possible, "I wouldn't advise you to mess with New York."

Goodness appeared unconvinced. "Texas frightens the wings off me, but I can handle New York."

"I still don't think this is a good idea."

"You don't even know what I'm going to do."

Shirley didn't want to know. Oh my, where was Mercy when she really needed her? When Goodness was in this frame of mind, she was more than Shirley could handle alone.

Shirley glanced around her, searching for help.

"Staten Island."

"No," Shirley cried in a panic, leaping in front of her friend, "not the Statue of Liberty!"

Goodness pretended not to notice her, which frightened Shirley all the more. "Let me see," Goodness mumbled, "what could I do to jar a few folks into realizing the error of their ways?"

"Don't you think we should talk this out first?" Shirley asked hopefully. "I mean, just because matters are going poorly with my assignment, there's no reason to take it out on the entire city. There're plenty of good things happening, too."

Goodness hesitated, and hope surged through Shirley that she might be able to reason her friend out of pulling some disastrous stunt.

"I'm sure everything must be going well with Hannah and Joshua." As soon as she spoke, Shirley recognized the error of her ways.

"As a matter of fact, they're not going well at all."

"Oh, I'm sorry to hear that."

"Hannah and Carl have set their wedding date for June sixteenth."

"But I thought . . . didn't you say that Hannah had fallen in love with Joshua Shadduck?"

"She has, and he's head over heels crazy about her."

Shirley assumed this would be good news. "I thought that was what you wanted."

"It is."

Shirley remained puzzled. "The last thing you told me was that Hannah had agreed to break off her engagement with Carl."

"That's what I thought, too," Goodness said with a disgruntled sigh, "only it didn't happen that way. Instead her family pressured her into setting a wedding date, and before she knew what to do, it was all decided for her. She's scheduled to marry Carl Rabinsky in June."

"Oh, poor, poor Hannah."

"Hannah nothing," Goodness cried. "What about Joshua? He trusted her. She's supposed to be in love with him, remember? The fact is, I don't trust Hannah to do the right thing by Joshua."

"There's plenty of time yet," Shirley said in an effort to placate her friend. "Just because Hannah and Joshua's relationship has gone slightly off course doesn't mean you should do anything so drastic as disrupt the best-known New York landmark."

Goodness didn't agree or disagree with her. "I'm so frustrated with these humans, I could scream."

Shirley was about to suggest just that when to her great relief Mercy arrived, looking serene and happy.

"What's happenin'?" Mercy asked as though she hadn't a care in the world.

While Goodness went into a short explanation about Hannah and Joshua, Shirley studied the other angel. Then it came to her in a flash. Mercy had been up to something herself.

"Mercy, I'm shocked at you," Shirley cried. Oh my, what would Gabriel do if he learned about this?

"What?" Mercy asked, but wasn't able to hide a guilty look.

"Tell me where you've been!" Shirley asked, her eyes narrowing.

"Me?" Mercy had perfected that look of innocence. She might even be able to fool Gabriel.

Although she asked, Shirley knew. "Don't tell me, please don't tell me you've been riding the escalators again?"

Mercy shifted her gaze away. "Just for a little while."

"Mercy." Shirley was outraged. One of them had to show a little responsibility. Why, oh why did it have to be her?

"I can't believe you'd jeopardize our entire mission by doing any-thing so silly." She closed her eyes and shook her head.

"Actually, I'm in the mood for a little fun myself," Goodness said.

"Goodness, no," Shirley cried.

"You wanna have some fun?" Goodness asked Mercy.

"Oh, I have been, but after what happened this afternoon, I'm game for just about anything."

Shirley opened and closed her mouth. At this point her protests would fall upon deaf ears, and she knew it.

A twinkle sparked from Goodness's eyes as she smiled over at Shirley. "Are you coming along or not?"

"You're headed for trouble."

Goodness laughed. "So what else is new? There's only so much of this being on my best behavior that I can take."

Mercy released an exaggerated sigh. "Boy oh boy, do I identify with that. I can't remember the last time I slid down an escalator railing. By golly, it felt good."

"If you want the truth, I would have thought you'd have discovered the Holland Tunnel before now."

The corners of Mercy's mouth started to quiver.

"What did you do?" Shirley asked suspiciously.

Mercy gave an innocent shrug. "Remember that traffic jam all the newspapers reported not long ago?"

"You caused that?"

Mercy grasped her hands behind her back and shook her head. "Not me. I didn't have a thing to do with it. "

Goodness's eyes lit up brighter than a Fourth of July sparkler. "If Mercy can mess around with the Holland Tunnel, then no one's going to mind if Lady Liberty takes a short stroll."

"Goodness, no."

"Oh, come on, Shirley, let your feathers dangle a little. Gabriel isn't going to hear about this."

"I don't think we should risk it," she said cautiously. "Really. Shouldn't we talk this out?"

Goodness shook her head. "Are you in or out, Shirley? It's time to separate the wheat from the chaff."

"Ah . . ."

Goodness and Mercy started to pull away. "I'm in," Shirley said hastily. "I just hope I don't end up playing a harp for all eternity."

The talk filled the deli all day, until Hannah was sick of hearing about it. Some people, obviously tourists, claimed that the Statue of Liberty had done a 360-degree turn. It was by far the most ridiculous thing Hannah had ever heard.

Someone from the financial district claimed he'd watched the grand lady make the complete rotation. There were said to be news tapes of it as well.

Hannah remained skeptical. Years earlier, some magician claimed to have made the Statue of Liberty disappear. All this talk now didn't impress Hannah. Besides, she had other matters on her mind.

She needed to see Joshua and had been unable to reach him all afternoon. Making phone calls during business hours was difficult for her. Privacy was always at a premium in the kitchen, and she didn't dare risk someone listening in on her conversation.

When she had a free moment, a rare commodity this busy time of the year, she raced upstairs and phoned Joshua's office. Unfortunately he was out, but his secretary promised to give him the message as soon as he returned.

But Joshua couldn't return her call, and they both knew it, so Hannah was left to fret. When she did see him, she wasn't sure she could tell him about what happened.

December was the busiest month for the deli. Her father's meat and cheese trays had a reputation that was citywide. After the normal lunchtime rush, Hannah was left to deal with people who stopped by to order the trays.

She was busy with a customer when she saw Joshua. Although she was desperate to talk to him, this was the worst possible place.

"I think I'll change that from slices of cheddar cheese to Monterey Jack," Mrs. Synder, a longtime customer, was saying.

Hannah bit into her lower lip and watched as Joshua made his way to the counter where her father was making thick pastrami sandwiches.

"Monterey Jack," the woman repeated, louder this time.

"Oh, sorry," Hannah said, and quickly made the notation.

"Do you have Greek olives?"

"Yes. No," she said quickly, correcting herself.

"Do you or don't you?" came the impatient question.

"No, I'm sorry." Hannah forced herself to concentrate on completing the order form.

"How much will that be?"

Grateful that she was close to finishing, Hannah quickly tallied the figures.

"Really? I expected it to be much more than that," Mrs. Synder said, looking pleased.

Hannah immediately refigured the total. She was prime for making a mistake.

"Do you still serve that fantastic cheesecake?" the woman asked.

A male voice answered the question for her. "It's the best in New York."

Joshua.

Hannah's head snapped up. "Thank you," she said, her gaze connecting with his. "My mother makes it herself."

"Throw one in for me, then," Mrs. Synder said, grinning broadly.

"I'll be happy to." Hannah added the cheesecake to the tally. "Everything will be ready for you the afternoon of the twenty-second."

"Thank you for your help."

Hannah's gaze moved past Mrs. Synder to Joshua. His eyes were warm and tender as they met hers.

"Can I help you?" she asked, turning the page on her ordering pad. She could feel the color creep up her neck. Anyone who knew her well would realize that Joshua wasn't just any customer.

"Hello, beautiful."

"Joshua," she mumbled under her breath, "be careful, someone might hear you."

"That doesn't bother me. You are beautiful."

"Thank you. I think you are, too."

He laughed then, but not loudly enough to attract attention. "You phoned me?"

She nodded and chanced a look in her father's direction. She was grateful to see that he was otherwise occupied. Her mother was busy in the kitchen but could appear at any moment.

"You talked to Carl?"

She hesitated, then nodded. "But I wasn't able to break the engagement."

Even from her side of the counter, Hannah could sense Joshua's frustration.

"I couldn't tell him, not then," she hurried to explain. "When I arrived, I learned that he'd been fired from his job. He got in an argument with the headmaster. Carl was depressed and miserable. I couldn't add to his distress."

"What do you plan to do, marry him and make him feel better?"

"Of course not."

"That's what it sounds like, Hannah." His voice was gentle, but she knew he was disappointed.

"I'd never marry Carl. I promise you that. Please, you've got to believe me."

He said nothing, as if placing his faith in her were something he wasn't certain he should do. Hannah fought to keep from blurting how much she loved him.

"Young man, is my daughter helping you?"

It was her father. Hannah tensed, and her eyes pleaded with Joshua's not to reveal their secret. It would only be for a while longer, she promised him silently.

He pulled his gaze away from her. "She's been very helpful," he answered.

"Are you ordering a meat tray?"

"I thought I might give it a try." He reached for a brochure and began to leaf through it. "You're Mr. Morganstern, aren't you?" he said just when it seemed her father was about to turn away. Hannah didn't understand why Joshua didn't let him leave. Certainly he felt as awkward about all this as she did.

"Yes." Her father's warm smile came through on the lone word.

"Joshua Shadduck," Joshua said, extending his hand across the counter.

Her father hesitated before peeling off the protective plastic glove from his fingers and exchanging handshakes.

"This is my daughter, Hannah."

"Actually, I've met Hannah before," Joshua said, his gaze resting on her.

Hannah tensed, afraid Joshua had completely lost his patience with her and was about to reveal the truth.

"She's delivered lunches to my office a number of times. Hannah's a wonderful young woman."

"Thank you. Naturally her mother and I share your opinion." Her father placed his arm affectionately around her shoulder. "Where's your office?"

Joshua told him.

"So you're an attorney."

Hannah noticed that her father's voice had gone a shade cooler and wondered if Joshua had sensed the difference himself.

"I was recently made a partner in the firm," Joshua explained proudly.

"Congratulations."

"I'm rather pleased myself." Joshua's gaze returned to Hannah.

It must have been the warm way in which he regarded her that prompted her father to continue the conversation. Generally he didn't spend a lot of time chatting with customers.

"We have reason to celebrate as well," he said, gently squeezing Hannah's shoulder. "Our daughter was recently engaged."

Joshua's smile dimmed somewhat. "Then congratulations are in order."

"Thank you," she said without emotion.

"My wife and I feel truly blessed to have our daughter. She's our greatest joy."

"Dad, please, I'm sure Mr. Shadduck doesn't want to hear all this."

"Nonsense. You do my heart proud. The world is a better place because of you."

Hannah was embarrassed, and she was certain Joshua found all this amusing.

"She's a lovely girl," Joshua told her father.

"She'll make a beautiful bride, don't you agree?"

"Oh yes," Joshua was quick to concur.

"I'm sure my wife and I will be sending out wedding invitations to a select few of our most valued customers. Now that the date's been set we can start making up the guest list."

Joshua said nothing, but his eyes narrowed fractionally.

"Daddy, I don't think—"

"The wedding date for your daughter has been set?" Joshua interrupted.

"Yes, we decided that only last night, isn't that right, sweetheart?"

Hannah nodded miserably.

"June sixteenth," her father informed him.

Joshua's gaze didn't leave hers. "Congratulations, Hannah," he said. "I'm sure you and your young man will be very happy." Having said that, he turned and walked out the door.

Chapter

★ ✷ ★

15

Trey didn't dislike New York. If anything, he was pleasantly surprised. He'd expected it to be the concrete jungle he'd read about, with treeless, crime-ridden streets. He was confident there was plenty of crime, but he hadn't seen any. And even in the heart of Manhattan he'd noticed an abundance of trees.

If he had any complaints, it was the noise. He wondered how a man was supposed to sleep through all that racket. The traffic outside his hotel never ceased—horns honking, brakes screeching. And he was bombarded by an array of sounds he could never hope to identify; he heard them all, even twenty stories up in his hotel room.

The city had its own clamor, nothing like the sounds in the country: the cry of a lone wolf, the hoot of an owl as it flew with the moonlight bouncing off its wing . . . Trey imagined that given the opportunity, he'd become accustomed to city noises. But there was a snowball's chance in hell of his ever living in New York City. No, he was a country boy, and like John Denver, he thanked God for that. Too much more of life here and he'd have men with nets chasing him through Central Park.

An early riser by nature, Trey was up and out the door just after dawn, heading for the hole-in-the-wall doughnut shop across the street from the hotel. The hotel served a decent cup of coffee, but there was no way he was going to pay a buck fifty for a two-bit cup of coffee. The doughnut shop was more to his liking, although he couldn't say that anyone had been all that friendly. He'd been coming in for coffee and a doughnut every morning since he'd arrived, and no one had said much of anything to him.

The same people were there every morning, too. Some businessman who drank his coffee and shared his company with the financial section of the newspaper. A lady who came in wearing tennis shoes and walked out in high heels.

Trey sat at the counter, sipping his coffee and watching the short-order cook, a rotund fellow with a prickly disposition, fry an order of hash browns. A waitress who looked to be in her forties bustled around refilling coffee.

Actually, Trey realized, he wasn't in the mood for company this morning. He had some heavy-duty thinking to do.

Twice he'd asked Jenny to leave New York and come back to Montana with him. Twice she'd told him no. The time had come for him to play his trump card, give her some incentive to return to Custer.

He planned to ask her to be his wife.

Generally when a man proposed to a woman he was fairly confident of her response. Trey figured his chances with Jenny were less than fifty-fifty. Although he'd worked hard to build up his herd, he didn't have a whole lot in the way of material wealth to offer her. A few hundred head of cattle, a run-down house that badly needed a woman's touch. And a heart so full of love that he nearly burst wide open every time he thought of Jenny and himself raising a family together.

Trey was a realist, and he was well aware that he couldn't compete with the bright lights of Broadway. He didn't have any diamond ring to offer her, either. Not yet.

The fact was, he hadn't thought about asking Jenny to marry him until after they'd kissed that first time. He'd always dreamed it would be like that with them, but the reality had knocked him for a loop. Jenny's kisses gave him hope that she might harbor some tenderness for him.

Never having proposed to a woman before, Trey had no idea how to go about it. Did a man of the nineties get down on one knee? Should he remove his hat and place it over his heart? None of those things sounded right to him. But since he was asking Jenny the most important question of his life, he didn't figure he should do it without showing some semblance of respect.

On impulse, Trey slipped off the stool and looked around the doughnut shop. The place held the same five or six people who frequented the place every morning.

"Can I have your attention, please," he said in a loud voice.

The businessman lowered the newspaper. The cook turned around, the spatula raised in one hand.

"My name's Trey LaRue," he said. "I've been having coffee here every morning since I arrived in this city, and it seems time I introduced myself. I take it you folks all know each other."

The five other customers stared back blankly.

"You don't know each other?"

"No." It was the woman with one high heel and one tennis shoe.

"Well then, don't you think it's time you introduced yourselves to one another? I'm Trey, and I'm visiting from Montana."

"Hello, Trey," the waitress responded. "I'm Trixie."

"I'm Bob, and I'm in advertising."

"I'm Mary Lou, and I'm an assistant editor at a publishing house." She waved one shoe in greeting.

The others went around the compact space and introduced themselves and told what they did for a living. Trey acknowledged each one with a brisk nod.

"What brings you to New York?" The question came from the cook, whose name was Steve.

"I came to ask a special woman to be my wife."

"Has she agreed?" This came from his editor friend.

"Not yet." He splayed his fingers through his hair, feeling less confident about his decision. "The fact is, I haven't asked her yet. I'm not exactly sure how to go about it."

"Just come right out and ask her," Bob advised.

"But wine and dine her," was Trixie's advice.

"Yeah," Bob teased, "get her good and soused first."

Mary Lou shook her head slowly. "Don't you listen to any of that. You tell that young woman what's in your heart. That's all you need to do, and if she feels as strongly about you as you do about her, nothing else will be necessary."

"I shouldn't take her to a fancy dinner, then?" Trey asked. His new-found friends confused him more than they helped.

"Dinner and champagne won't hurt," Trixie assured him, "but Mary Lou's right. Just tell this special lady what's in your heart and go from there."

That sounded like a lot less trouble than getting down on one knee, Trey decided.

"You might try singing to her."

Everyone turned to stare at Steve, Trey included. As far as Trey was concerned, there were certain things a man didn't do, and break into song was one of them. One of Jenny's male friends might consider that, but not him.

"Women like romance, and there ain't nothing more romantic than to sing. You don't even have to have that great a voice," Steve added, a cigarette hanging from the side of his mouth.

"I won't be doing any singing," Trey said emphatically.

"You love her, don't you?" Steve smashed the cigarette into an ash-tray.

"Yeah."

"Then romance her."

"He's right about that," the assistant editor acknowledged. "There isn't a woman alive who doesn't want to be courted by the man she loves."

Singing was out of the question, but there were other ways to prove he was as tenderhearted as the men she'd dated in the big city. "What about flowers and chocolates?"

Only the day before, Trey had walked into one of those fancy sweet shops by accident. He'd been blown away at the prices. Why, a man could feed a horse for a month on what they wanted for a box of chocolates! French ones.

Mary Lou shook her head. "Be more imaginative than that."

"Jenny loves those fat bagels vendors sell on the street corners here," he said, thinking out loud.

"You can't woo a woman with bagels," the guy in advertising insisted. He folded the newspaper and tucked it under his arm. "I've got to get to the office. You'll let us know what happens, won't you?"

"Sure thing," Trey promised. He checked his watch. It was early yet. Jenny would still be sleeping, but he'd told her he'd be by to pick her up this morning. She wanted to take him up to the top of the World Trade Center.

Trey left some change on the counter. "I appreciate the advice," he told his newfound friends.

"Good luck," Trixie said with a smile.

"If he's getting married, he'll need it," the short-order cook teased, then laughed when Trixie swatted him across the backside with a dishrag.

An hour later Trey stood outside Jenny's apartment complex. He paced the sidewalk in front of her building, rehearsing in his mind what he wanted to say. It took another ten minutes before he'd gathered up enough gumption to go inside.

He'd no sooner knocked than the door flew open and there was Jenny, standing on the other side. When she saw him, her face lit up with a smile as bright as a July sun. As long as he lived, he'd never grow weary of seeing Jenny smile.

"Mornin'," he greeted her, touching the edge of his hat in a genteel salute.

"Oh, Trey, you'll never guess what."

Before he could prepare himself, she leapt into his arms. Whatever it was that brought Jenny this close must be good, he thought.

"Irene phoned this morning!"

"Irene's your agent, right?"

"Right." Then, not giving him an opportunity to ask anything more, she blurted out, "John Peterman phoned and asked if she had an audio of me."

Trey didn't know who this John Peterman was, but he was fairly certain he wasn't going to like the other man.

As soon as she could, Hannah left the deli to find Joshua. If she explained how she'd been pressured into setting a wedding date, surely he'd understand. Surely he'd be sympathetic and willing to listen to reason.

The angry, pained look in his eyes haunted her, especially knowing that she was responsible for putting it there. Joshua didn't deserve to be treated as if she were ashamed of loving him. Yet she could find no fair way out of this dilemma.

Her first stop was at Joshua's office. When he wasn't there, she didn't know what to do. Depressed and miserable, she started walking, barely aware of her destination. She was unconscious of the street sounds, the people who moved crisply past her; all she could think to do was walk.

She appreciated Joshua's feelings. If the situation were reversed, she'd feel the same way. Joshua was an honorable man, and it went against his grain to be involved with a woman engaged to another man. Nor was he comfortable meeting her without her parents' knowledge.

Hannah didn't like that aspect of their relationship, either, but for now it couldn't be helped. She didn't want to break the engagement with Carl until this matter with the school had been cleared up.

Suddenly aware of her surroundings, Hannah realized she was close to her grandmother's apartment.

Sylvia's tired eyes brightened when she opened the door. "Hannah, my dear, this is a pleasant surprise!"

Hannah kissed her grandmother's cheek.

"I just brewed myself a pot of tea. Join me, please."

"I'd love some tea." Hannah followed her grandmother into the kitchen, then carried the tray with two dainty china cups into the living room.

Hannah loved this room, with its personal touches. An end table with a small clock that had been in the family for close to a hundred years. Antique photographs. Hand-crocheted doilies. An array of family photos lining the fireplace mantel.

Hannah's favorite picture was one of her grandfather taken when he was a young man recently emigrated to America. Another favorite was of her father as a youngster, less than ten years of age.

"Sit," Sylvia instructed after settling herself in the oak rocker she loved. She took a sip of tea, then held the delicate china cup with both hands. "Actually, I wondered when you'd come. I've been waiting, you know."

"Waiting for me?" Hannah turned from the familiar photographs and met her grandmother's keen eyes.

"I know you far too well not to recognize when something is bothering you."

Hannah lowered her gaze. She didn't bother to deny that she was troubled. Nor was she surprised that her grandmother had guessed. She suspected Sylvia had known her true feelings from the moment she'd introduced Carl.

"You look tired, Hannah."

She was unbelievably so. But the bone weariness that drained her energy had little to do with the long hours she worked at the deli or the number of customers she served. It was a fatigue of the heart, of pretending to love Carl, of giving the impression that she was happy.

"You don't need to tell me anything you don't feel comfortable sharing." Her grandmother's tone was loving and tender. "Just sit with me a spell and soak in the silence. I don't know how a person can sort everything out unless they can hear themselves think."

Sylvia swayed gently in the oak rocker and sipped her tea. A soft creaking noise eked up from the hardwood floor beneath the braided rug.

"It's about Carl and me," Hannah said after a long while. She stood and walked over to the fireplace, where a gentle flame flickered over the logs. After running her hand against the top of the mantel, she turned and faced her grandmother.

"I guessed all this involved Carl."

Hannah smiled to herself, appreciating Sylvia's insight. She sat on the braided rug next to her grandmother. Sylvia's hand stroked the top of Hannah's head.

"I've been praying for you for a good many years, Hannah. Long before you were born, I asked God if he would see fit to give my son a child, and he gave us you."

It was a story Hannah had heard often. Her childless parents had longed desperately for a baby. The doctors had told them it would take a miracle.

Like Hannah in the story of Samuel, a familiar one in the Bible, her mother and family had prayed diligently for a child. Samuel's mother, like her own, had wept and pleaded with God in the temple with such anguish that Eli, the priest, had assumed she was drunk. When she spoke of her longing for a son, Eli had assured her that God had heard her prayer and that in a year's time she would have a son.

After nearly twenty years of marriage, Ruth had conceived, and the Morganstern family had rejoiced. When David learned his wife was pregnant, he'd been the one to decide on his daughter's name. Hannah had been named after Elkanah's wife, whose faith had been richly rewarded.

All her life Hannah had been loved and cherished. That was what made disappointing her family so difficult.

"Through the years, I have continued to pray for you," Sylvia went on. "As you entered your teen years, I added your husband to my list."

"My husband?"

"The man you would marry. It seemed to me that God in his almighty wisdom would choose an extraordinary man for you. A man of character, a man of wisdom and discernment. A man who would love you with all his heart."

Her grandmother's gentle words caused Hannah's throat to thicken with tears. "I don't love Carl," she whispered brokenly.

Sylvia's hand didn't pause as she continued to stroke Hannah's crown. "I realized that almost immediately. You've met someone else, haven't you?"

"Yes, and Grandma, he's a good man, just the way you say. I can't tell you how fortunate I feel to even know him. I love him so much that it frightens me. . . . I'm so afraid I'm going to lose him."

"He loves you?"

Hannah nodded. The knowledge should have filled her with an incredible sense of wonder that a man as wonderful as Joshua would care for her.

"Then why would you lose him?" her grandmother questioned.

"Because of Carl."

It was as if Sylvia had forgotten Hannah were engaged to the other man. "Ah yes, Carl."

"Carl's a good man," Hannah whispered. She didn't want to hurt him, either.

"Carl's a fine young man, but he's not the one for you."

"Joshua is." There was no doubt in Hannah's mind about that.

"Joshua," Sylvia repeated slowly, as if testing the name on her tongue. She shook her head once and said decisively, "If you love him the way you claim, then you have nothing to fear."

"But everyone expects me to marry Carl. You saw what happened, how we were pressured into setting a date for the wedding."

Her grandmother said nothing, which increased Hannah's guilt.

"I wanted to break the engagement," Hannah said all at once, running the words together. She didn't think it was fair to tell her grandmother that Carl had recently lost his job; the fewer who knew, the better. The best way to handle it was to be diplomatic, she decided.

"This is a bad time for Carl," she offered. "He's under a lot of pressure right now. I wanted to tell him about meeting Joshua. I've tried—honest, I have—but something always happens. For a long time I figured that it was too late for Joshua and me. I even tried not to see him again."

"That wouldn't have worked."

Hannah glanced up at her grandmother, wondering at the strength and conviction in the older woman's words.

"You and Joshua were meant to be together," Sylvia elaborated.

Hannah rested her head against her grandmother's knee. "Joshua came into the deli this afternoon."

"David knows him?"

"He's a frequent customer."

"Then he knows good food when he tastes it."

Hannah smiled.

"Tell me what happened," Sylvia encouraged.

"Joshua wanted to talk to me, but it was impossible there. I'm sure he was about to suggest that we meet elsewhere—we've done it before—but he didn't get the chance.

"Somehow Joshua and Dad got involved in a conversation, and then Dad told him that Carl and I had set the wedding date. He actually invited Joshua to the wedding."

Her grandmother sighed heavily. "I don't imagine Joshua was pleased."

"He looked so hurt." That was the only way she could think to describe the anguish she'd witnessed in Joshua's eyes. "He congratulated me, and before I had a chance to explain, he left the deli. I got away as soon as I could and hurried to his office, but he wasn't there and his secretary couldn't tell me when he'd be back. I've got to talk to him." She squeezed her eyes shut, berating herself silently.

"What would you have said if he had been at his office?" her grandmother questioned.

"I longed to explain how Carl and I had been coerced into picking a date for the wedding."

"Do you think that was what he wanted to hear?"

"No," Hannah murmured miserably. "He wants to hear that I've told Carl about us. He needs to know that I've broken off the engagement, and that my family's been told that I won't be marrying Carl."

"My guess is that he'd be willing to speak to your parents with you."

Hannah dreaded telling her parents most. She'd never considered having Joshua stand with her and immediately knew that he would want to be there. He'd never ask her to confront her family alone.

With an energy that had escaped her earlier, she leapt to her feet. "I've got to talk to him."

"Joshua?" her grandmother asked.

"No, Carl. I can't worry about his feelings any longer. He doesn't need me to hold his hand."

"Good girl." Her grandmother's face beamed with pride.

"Joshua is the man I love, he deserves my loyalty. As soon as I've talked to Carl, I'll speak to Joshua."

Sylvia looked well pleased. "That, my dear, sounds like a plan."

The anger inside Roberto simmered just below the exploding point. His patience was gone, his temper unreasonable, his mood black. He'd probably offended every customer he'd dealt with in the last couple of days. Matters would improve drastically, he realized, if he could stop thinking about Brynn. But that seemed impossible.

He wished to hell she'd leave. Pack her bags, hand in her resignation, and go back where she belonged. Because she sure as hell didn't fit in this neighborhood. A delicate, beautiful rosebud among thistles.

The only way to convince her he wanted nothing more to do with her was to shove her out of his life. His chest ached with a crippling tightness for all that he'd lost. He hadn't meant to do it then and there, but she'd forced his actions, coming to him the way she had.

Modesto's injuries had convinced him of the terrible risk Brynn was taking working in this neighborhood. She was an easy target. Too easy. She refused to listen to reason and defied him at every turn. Fine. She could do as she damn well pleased, but he would have no part of it. Or her.

If she wanted to sacrifice herself over a bunch of screwy, idealistic goals, so be it. But he wasn't standing by idly to watch her fall on her face. Nor would he be there to pick up the pieces.

For her own good, she had to leave this neighborhood, and she wouldn't as long as he encouraged her to remain. That was exactly what their relationship was doing.

It was over, and nothing would change his mind. Not this time. Not with Modesto in the hospital, a bullet hole in his chest, and his brother screaming with nightmares.

Roberto heard a movement behind him and glanced over his shoulder to find Emilio standing just inside the garage.

"You gonna bite my head off?" Emilio asked.

"That depends on what you want."

"Nothing."

"Then what are you doing here?" Roberto threw a wrench toward the workbench. It landed with a discordant clanking sound. He never abused his tools, but then there was a first time for everything. A first time to fall in love. A first time to turn his back and run from what he wanted most.

"I'm bored," Emilio confessed. "I thought it'd be fun to stay home."

"Then go back to school," Roberto said without emotion. He hadn't changed his mind about education, but he was willing to agree that Brynn might have a point. For a long time he'd thought Emilio would work with him at the garage. He could teach his brother, and the two of them could be partners. But Emilio didn't have the knack for working on cars. He liked people, liked being around them.

"I don't want to go to school," his brother confessed, walking all the way into the garage. He planted the tips of his fingers in his jeans pockets. This was the stance he chose when he had something to hide. His brother tended to be transparent about such things, and frankly, Roberto was grateful.

Unwilling to reveal he knew something was amiss, Roberto continued to work on the car, removing the carburetor from an engine. "I thought you liked your classes."

Emilio shrugged. "The best are the ones Miss Cassidy teaches. She makes learning fun, but she isn't an easy teacher. Sometimes after school me and the others talk about her."

Roberto stiffened, then asked nonchalantly, "What do you have to say?" Emilio and the other boys in the class weren't blind. Brynn was as beautiful as she was naive.

"She talks about things that make a person think, about war and prejudice, and stuff like that. Just about every day she gives us a writing assignment and then has us read what we wrote and talk about it."

"Like what?"

Emilio's eyes brightened as he spoke. "We're reading this book about Anne Frank. She was this Jewish girl, who—"

"I know who Anne Frank is."

"You do?" This appeared to impress Emilio. "Well, Miss Cassidy asked us to pretend we were the ones in hiding. To share this compact space with another family, to live in constant fear of discovery."

"And?"

"And we did, and then she had some of us read what we'd written, and I was surprised, you know, by how she tied it in to what's going on in our world today. Social issues and that sort of thing. The guys and me sometimes talk about the same things we did in class. I don't do that with any of my other subjects."

"She's a good teacher, then."

"The best I've ever had."

That did and didn't surprise Roberto. He knew Brynn was popular with the kids, but that didn't say much about her ability to teach a class.

"Then go back," Roberto said as though it should be an easy decision. He never did understand Emilio's sudden desire to quit. The teenager certainly wasn't any help here at the garage, mooning around, looking miserable. Everything he'd asked Emilio to do thus far, with the exception of errands, he'd had to do over.

"I can't."

His brother's low, trembling voice caused Roberto to look up. "Why can't you?"

Emilio shrugged.

"If you like school, then go."

"I'm not going back," Emilio insisted with a ring of rebellion.

Roberto frowned and gave Emilio his full attention. Something was very wrong. "First you said you can't go back, and now you're telling me you won't? Which is it?"

Emilio looked decidedly uncomfortable. "Both."

Leaning against the work bench, Roberto crossed his arms. "You'd better explain that."

Emilio took a short stroll around the garage. "I can't go back because . . ." He hesitated.

"Because why?" Roberto pressed.

Emilio whirled around, his eyes flashing with open defiance. "Because I'm embarrassed, that's why."

"Embarrassed about what?" He hadn't a clue what his brother could possibly have done that would cause this reaction.

"I made a fool of myself in front of Miss Cassidy." He admitted this between clenched teeth, as if to say that was all he was willing to admit.

Roberto snickered and shook his head. Emilio wasn't the only one to play the fool when it came to dealing with the beautiful redhead. All at once it dawned on him that Emilio might have fallen in love with her, too.

His brother seemed to read Roberto's thoughts. "It's not what you think," he snapped. "She's your woman, not mine."

Roberto returned to the carburetor rather than look his brother in the eye. "She's not mine, either," he said forcefully, "and that's the way I want it. The less you say about it the better. Understand?"

Emilio didn't say anything, but Roberto felt his brother's scrutiny. He regretted having said this much, but Emilio would have figured it out sooner or later.

"Now get your butt over to school."

Emilio didn't budge. "Why is it so hellfire important for me to get an education? I thought you said it was a waste of time. What changed your mind?"

The last thing Roberto wanted was to be dragged into an argument over the pros and cons of education. "You changed my mind. I gained nothing in high school, least of all a decent education. But it's different for you. Now don't make me embarrass you further by dragging you back."

Emilio hesitated, as though he didn't know what to do. "You'd do it, too."

Roberto grinned. "Don't doubt it. Now get your sorry ass over there."

"I'm going to tell Miss Cassidy you forced me to come."

"Fine, tell her." He'd rather Emilio didn't mention his name, but he wouldn't give his brother something to hold over him, either. Swallowing his pride was a small gift he could give the two people he loved most in this world. His brother would have his education, and Brynn would have the pleasure of knowing that he'd changed his mind about school.

The decision made, Emilio disappeared.

Roberto heard the door slam and paused long enough to look out the window to see Emilio racing down the street, kicking up his heels in his eagerness to get back to school.

It didn't seem an hour had passed before Emilio was back. He looked more like his usual self than he had over the last couple of days, loitering around the shop, disgruntled and miserable.

"I thought you went back to school," Roberto said with a scowl.

"I did go back. School's over."

Roberto glanced at the clock above the door. Emilio was right.

"A couple of the guys are waiting for me. We're going to visit Modesto. He can have company now, and we thought we'd see if we could find any good-looking nurses."

"Then what are you doing here?"

"I got a message for you from Miss Cassidy."

Roberto steeled himself. He didn't want to play any games, notes back and forth, that sort of thing. It was over, and the sooner she accepted it, the better.

"I don't want it," he said forcefully.

"It?"

"The note or whatever it is she gave you."

"She didn't give me anything. She just wanted me to tell you something."

"Fine," he said stiffly, "tell me."

"She said thank you."

"For what?"

Emilio's look told him the answer to that should have been obvious. "For me coming back to school. I told her you were the one who insisted I did, and she got all teary eyed and asked me to tell you she appreciated that."

The pain in Roberto's chest tightened. "You've told me, now get out of here. I've got work to do."

Chapter

* 🌟 *

16

Jenny didn't know what to think about Trey. He hadn't been himself for nearly two days. She'd spent as much time with him as her schedule would allow, but that was only an hour or two each day. Perhaps he was disappointed in her.

She'd taken him to all the tourist spots. Only recently they'd been up to the top of the World Trade Center and to the United Nations building.

By nature Trey was a man of few words, but he'd been less communicative than usual the last couple of days. That worried her.

"Are there any other sights you want to see?" Jenny asked as they strolled lazily through Central Park, feeding the birds.

"I can't say that there are," Trey said, tossing birdseed to a flock of people-friendly pigeons. Others flew over instantly from a variety of directions, looking for a handout. Their wings made a ruffling sound that carried with the wind.

Jenny tossed a fistful of seeds and laughed at the way the silver birds battled over the goodies.

"I was thinking maybe we could go to dinner this evening," Trey said unexpectedly.

"Dinner," Jenny repeated. She'd promised Michelle they would have their own small Christmas that evening, since her friend would soon be heading home for the holidays. Jenny's schedule at the restaurant had changed a number of times with other girls needing time away. She'd worked all the extra hours she could. The only night she'd been free in nearly two weeks had been the evening of the Christmas potluck. Surely Michelle would understand.

"I'll need to check with Michelle first." She didn't tell Trey the reason, because another, more intrusive thought immediately came to mind.

Trey was going back to Montana.

Dinner would be his way of telling her good-bye. An empty feeling, one that chilled her heart, came so swiftly it felt as if someone had slapped her viciously across the back.

"When's your flight?" she asked point-blank.

Trey didn't answer her right away, and she thought he might not have heard her. "Two days' time."

So she was right.

"I can't stay any longer, Jenny. I'd like to, but I've got a herd of cattle to worry about, and I can't leave Pete alone much longer."

"I understand." If anyone could appreciate his need to return, it was she. After all, she was a rancher's daughter. That Trey had stayed in New York this long was something of a surprise. Just when she was growing accustomed to having him with her. Just when her heart felt whole again. He was going to leave her. "Maybe you'll be able to visit again soon," she said, fighting to disguise the ache in her heart. Next time. The only way she could deal with his leaving was to look into the future and the promise of his return.

The birdseed gone, Jenny experienced the need to sit down. She walked over and sank onto a park bench.

Trey joined her. "When will you be able to talk to Michelle?"

For a moment Jenny didn't know what he was talking about. "Soon," she said, and then remembered Trey had asked her to dinner. A fond farewell dinner. A "gee, but it's been swell" good-bye dinner.

Her stomach clenched, then tied itself into a knot that tightened with each breath. As the ache intensified, Jenny realized how much she wanted Trey to stay. How much she needed him in her life.

Sitting on the edge of the park bench, her hands buried deep in her coat pockets, Jenny tried to compose herself, fearing she'd embarrass them both by breaking into tears.

"Jenny—"

"Michelle's at the apartment now. We can go ask her," she suggested cheerfully. That she could fool Trey into thinking nothing was amiss was a testament to how truly talented an actress she was.

"Michelle's there now?"

Jenny checked her watch. "If not, she will be any minute. Why don't we go back to the apartment? It's about lunchtime anyway. I can fix you a sandwich. I make an excellent peanut butter and jelly."

He didn't answer her right away. "If that's what you want."

"Sure," she said, rushing to her feet as though tickled pink to return to her small, cramped apartment and slap together two pieces of bread.

It didn't escape Jenny's notice that Trey didn't speak a single word on the way home. Perhaps it was the subway, which she knew confused him; it had her in the beginning, too, but now she was a pro when it came to finding her way around the city. Of course she didn't take it at night, and never when she was alone.

She unlocked the apartment door and stepped inside.

"It doesn't look like Michelle's back," Trey murmured.

"She'll be here any time," Jenny said confidently. Now that she was home, in familiar surroundings, she didn't know how much longer she'd be able to keep up the pretense. The tightening, empty feeling in the pit of her stomach had spread to her heart and her throat. Tears threatened to spill down her cheeks.

"Make yourself comfortable and I'll get you a sandwich," she said, eager for an excuse to leave him. She needed this time to compose herself, to figure out how she was going to see him off and do it with a smile. No one was that good an actress.

"I'm not hungry."

"You will be soon enough," she said, hoping she sounded enthusiastic. "If you don't want it, I'll eat it later." She walked into the kitchen and braced her hands against the kitchen sink and closed her eyes. Inhaling deep breaths didn't seem to help.

Trey was going back to Montana, where he belonged—where she belonged, too. Only she was too proud to admit it, too stubborn to throw in the towel. For three years she'd given all that she had, looking for a chance to prove herself. All that effort, all her talent, had gotten her was a job as a singing waitress in a two-star restaurant.

Leaning forward, she propped her elbows on the kitchen counter and pushed the hair away from her forehead. She tried taking in short breaths, followed by deep ones. Nothing seemed to help.

Damn it all, she was going to cry. Trey would see, and then he'd want to know what was wrong. She didn't know what she would tell him.

If Michelle came home, perhaps her friend could distract him until Jenny had collected herself.

She felt the first tears slip from the corners of her eyes. She'd held them back for so long that it was as if a dam had burst inside her. The tears marked more than Trey's return home. They represented the frustration, the disappointment, of three hard years of her life. Three long, fruitless years.

"Jenny, is something wrong?" Trey stood directly behind her. She could feel the warmth of his body so close to her own.

"I'm fine," she answered in a strained voice. She straightened, wiped the telltale moisture from her face, and reached toward the bread box.

"You don't sound fine. Turn around." His hand fell gently on her shoulder.

She might have been able to pull it off if he hadn't been so tender with her. The moment he touched her, she knew she was lost. The sob was a painful tightening in her chest that worked its way up to her throat.

She turned in his arms and let his torso muffle her cry. Her shoulders shook as he wrapped her in his embrace.

"Jenny, my heaven, what is it?"

She didn't answer him; she couldn't.

His hand stroked her hair, and Jenny was confident he had no idea what to do with her. She feared her tears embarrassed him as much as they did her.

"Oh my," she said, breaking away from him. She smeared the traces of tears away from her cheeks and from some hidden reserve of strength offered him an apologetic smile. "I wonder what that was all about."

Trey didn't respond. Instead he tucked his finger beneath her chin and lowered his mouth to hers. They'd kissed before, and the hot sensation between them had shocked Jenny. He kissed her again and again, each kiss gaining in intensity and momentum until she was struggling for control.

"Jenny, sweet Jenny," he whispered, his voice husky and low. "I don't think you know what kissing you does to me."

"I do know, because you do the same thing to me." She ran her tongue along the underside of his jaw and felt his body tense against hers. She'd never experienced such a powerful sense of control over a man.

He cupped her face between his hands for another deep, breath-stealing kiss.

"Tell me why you were crying," he whispered.

Jenny closed her eyes. Her hands bit into the material of his shirt, her hold so tight that her fingers lost feeling. "I . . . I'm going to miss you, Trey."

He stiffened, and she wondered if she'd said something wrong. "You don't need to worry," she hurried to assure him. "I'm a big girl, really."

He led her into the living room and sat her down in the chair, then he started moving around as though he needed to sit himself but couldn't find an available seat.

"Trey?"

He held out his hand. "I've got something to ask you. I was going to wait until tonight at dinner, but now seems as good a time as any."

"Ask me what?"

He looked decidedly uncomfortable. "I'm not sure how to do this. I've never done it before, and hell"—he paused and dragged a deep breath through his lungs—"I damn well never plan to do it again."

"You've never done what?"

"Propose," he snapped, then seemed to realize what he'd said. He ceased his roaming and stood directly in front of her. "I love you, Jenny Lancaster. I've loved you from the time you were fifteen years old. . . ."

"Fifteen? But you never let on . . . you never told me."

He frowned. "If I'd said anything, your father would have had me arrested, as well he should have. I never wanted you to leave Montana, but you deserved your chance. You've had it, and now it's time to come home. With me, with the promise you'll be my wife." His eyes grew dark and serious as he got down on one knee in front of her. "Come home with me, Jenny. Marry me, and mother my children. I don't have a lot to offer you, except a heart that will always be yours."

Jenny was too stunned to respond. She pressed her hand over her mouth and battled down a fresh batch of emotion.

The front door opened and Trey stood up abruptly and, irritated, glanced over his shoulder.

"Hello, everyone," Michelle greeted as she whirled into the room like a prairie dust storm. She hesitated and looked from Trey and Jenny. "I'm not disrupting anything, am I?"

"Yes," Trey answered before Jenny could.

"Oh, sorry. Do you want me to discreetly disappear for a few moments?"

"That would be much appreciated." Again it was Trey who responded.

Michelle had just started to tiptoe from the room when the telephone rang. "I'll get it," she said, and then tossed Trey an apologetic look. "I've been waiting for a call all week."

Trey rubbed his hand along the back of his neck and gave her an impatient nod.

Michelle answered on the second ring, and her gaze swiveled automatically toward Jenny. She placed her hand over the mouthpiece. "It's for you."

"Me?" Jenny asked.

"It's Irene."

Jenny leapt off the sofa and hurried to the phone. "Irene," she said eagerly, unable to hide her delight. When her agent phoned it was generally with good news.

"Jenny." Irene sounded excited. "I just got off the phone with John Peterman. He's wants you for the second lead in his new play. This is it, kiddo. All your hard work has finally paid off. We couldn't ask for better money or better terms. You're on your way now."

Dumbstruck, Jenny listened while Irene relayed the details of her contract. When her agent had finished, Jenny replaced the receiver and turned to Michelle, who stood beside her expectantly.

"I got the second lead," she whispered, her voice revealing the extent of her shock. "John Peterman wants me."

Michelle let out a wild scream and hugged her enthusiastically. Then the two of them did a dance about the room, laughing, crying, their joy spilling over like champagne poured too fast from the bottle.

A good five minutes passed before Jenny remembered Trey, and then she couldn't find him.

"Where'd he go?" Jenny asked her roommate.

Michelle gave her a blank look. "I don't know. He must have left."

The minute Brynn walked into the school she knew something was very wrong. One of the secretaries sat at her desk, weeping silently. A handful of teachers stood in the corner of the office, talking in whispers. The tension in the room was thick enough to slice and butter.

Not knowing what was wrong, Brynn walked over to her cubicle and cleared out the space. As she suspected, there were a number of printed sheets detailing information about the winter break. The teachers' Christmas party was scheduled for that evening. Since her surname began with a C, she was responsible for supplying a main dish. Another paper detailed the period schedule for the last day.

Brynn slipped the papers into her bag. A white envelope fluttered from her space and landed on the floor. It was addressed to her personally, and she wondered who had put it there. On closer inspection, she realized the handwriting was familiar. It took a moment to recognize it was from Mike Glasser.

"Did you hear?" Doug Keast asked as he reached for his own papers.

"Hear about what?" Brynn had never been particularly fond of Doug. Not since the day he'd been so eager to have Emilio hauled off to the office. She had no problem with the school's policy regarding fighting, but she questioned the other teacher's attitude. It seemed Doug had welcomed the opportunity to see Emilio expelled.

"Mike Glasser."

"What about him?" she asked.

"He blew his brains out." Doug pointed his finger to his temple and pulled an imaginary trigger. "His mother found him late yesterday afternoon." Doug hesitated. "Say, isn't he one of the kids in your program?"

Mike, dead? A suicide? It was as if Doug had pulled the floor out from under her. The information came at her like a fist in the dark.

Brynn gasped and slumped against the wall. It demanded every ounce of strength she possessed to remain upright. Involuntarily she started to hyperventilate, and she reached out and grabbed hold of the back of a chair.

"Brynn?" Doug's arm came around her. "Here, sit down. Do you need something?"

"Water. Could you please get me a glass of water?" A shocking, total numbness shrouded her.

"Of course. Listen, I'm sorry." Doug steered her to a table and sat her down. "I guess I shouldn't have told you like that." His voice was full of apology.

Brynn was too numb to respond.

Dead. Mike, the young man she'd tried so hard to reach, was dead. There would be no more tomorrows. No dreams for Mike. No future.

The letter. Mike had written her a letter. A suicide note. No. No, please, please no. Had he written it to her as a desperate cry for help? Dear God, please no. She hadn't collected her messages in two days.

Her hands shook so badly that Brynn was barely able to retrieve the long white envelope from inside her bag. She ripped it open and pulled out a single sheet.

Miss Cassidy,

By the time you read this, I'll be dead. I'm not going to go into the reasons why I'm doing this because that wouldn't solve anything. For me death is the only solution. This is what I want. Life is simply too fucking painful.

I imagine you're wondering why I'm writing you. There's someone I care about, and she's going to take this hard. I don't know anyone who can help Suzie through this, except maybe you.

Suzie's the best thing that ever happened to me, and I love her. She tried to help me, but she couldn't. No one could.

My dad killed himself when I was a kid. I used to get upset about it, but now I understand why he did it. Dying is easier than living.

Unable to continue because her eyes had blurred with tears, Brynn paused long enough to search for a tissue, then returned to Mike's letter.

> *You don't owe me any favors, but I know you like Suzie.*
> *Talk to her for me, would you? Tell her I'm sorry. Tell her . . . Shit, you'll know what to say. It isn't her fault. It's no one's fault. Not Suzie's. Not yours. Not mine. It's better this way for everyone.*
> *I know I don't have any right to lay this on you, but there's no one else I trust. If you would, I'd appreciate it if you said something to my mother, too. You're good with words and you'll know what to tell her.*
> *Since this is the last thing I'll ever write, there's something I'd like to know. I wish I could have traded places with Anne Frank. She wanted to live, when all I could think about was dying. You're a good teacher, Miss Cassidy. You made me care.*
>
> *Mike*

Doug Keast returned with a paper cup filled with water. Brynn thanked him with a brisk nod as she folded the letter and placed it back inside the envelope.

"Are you sure you're all right?" he asked.

Brynn nodded. She wanted nothing more to do with Doug Keast and was grateful when the first bell rang.

"Brynn," her fellow teacher pressed, "do you want me to call someone? You don't look so good."

"I'll be fine." But she wouldn't be. It would be a long while before she would feel right again. Brynn couldn't keep from thinking that she should have known something was wrong. She should have been able to reach Mike. Should have realized the depth of his despair.

And Suzie. Poor Suzie. Brynn was certain the teenager had never told Mike she was pregnant. Suzie had loved him and tried to protect him. Mike had loved her enough to ask Brynn to help her through her grief. Brynn didn't know what she could possibly say that would comfort Suzie and Mike's mother.

By some miracle, she made it through the morning, teaching by rote. Not everyone had heard about Mike's death, but then only a handful of her morning students knew him.

At lunchtime, still numb, still in shock, Brynn returned to the office to ask about Suzie Chang. As she suspected, Suzie was absent.

She wrote down Suzie's home address, tucked it inside her pocket, and returned to her classroom.

Her heart ached. Her body ached, and she wondered if she would emotionally survive this day. The burden of explaining and comforting seemed beyond her.

When it was time for her afternoon class, Brynn sat at her desk. One by one, her students paraded single file past her. Mike's desk in the center of the room sat empty. Brynn found she couldn't look at it without experiencing a tremendous sense of loss.

Everyone appeared to be watching her, waiting for her to say something. Brynn walked to the front of the room. The silence was deafening.

"By now I'm sure you've all heard about Mike," she said, and was shocked at how thin her voice had become. She struggled with her composure. "Talking about it might do us all some good. Perhaps you can help me understand why Mike would take his own life?"

"It's stupid," Pearl Washington said.

"But Mike wasn't stupid," Brynn insisted. "When I could get him to express his feelings, I found his essays to be full of insight." She realized as she spoke how dark his writing was, how bleakly he saw the world. Then and now. Guilt swamped her senses. She should have seen it coming, should have realized how much pain he was in.

"He should have told someone," Emilio suggested.

"Who?" Brynn asked. "Told them what?"

"We weren't exactly his friends," Yolanda reminded everyone sadly.

"He didn't want no friends," Denzil insisted.

"Okay, so he wasn't Mr. Personality, but he wasn't so bad, you know."

"Are you sorry he's dead?" Brynn asked.

A chorus of regrets chimed back, and Brynn knew that the class was suffering just as she was. Mike had asked her to talk to Suzie, to help Suzie. What he hadn't realized was that they were all going to need help dealing with his death.

"He never let on, you know?" someone complained.

"I don't think he knew how to share his pain," Brynn suggested.

Yolanda started to cry. "It makes me mad."

"What does?" Brynn questioned, struggling not to weep herself.

"That he didn't give any of us a chance to tell him good-bye. When Modesto was shot it was bad, but this is worse because I feel like there was something I should have done, something I should have said. Maybe if I'd been friendlier, it would have helped."

"I don't think any of us had a clue how much emotional pain Mike was in," Brynn told them solemnly. "Death was obviously something Mike had been entertaining for a long time. It was wrong, and now each one of us is left with recriminations."

Brynn paused at the sharp pain in her chest. "I can't blame Mike, but I wish I'd known how much he was hurting. I might have been able to help him. Like Yolanda said, we never got a chance to say good-bye."

"I want to get in his face and make him listen to reason," one of the girls shouted. "He's hurt so many people."

"He was in pain himself."

"I wish I could talk to him."

"You can," Brynn whispered.

"But how?" Denzil asked. "It isn't like we can write him a letter."

"Why can't we?" Brynn asked, remembering how much writing had helped her deal with the death of her beloved grandmother five years earlier. "It's true Mike won't be reading it, but writing Mike might help each of us deal with the shock of what he did."

"Miss Cassidy's right."

Binders opened and spiral notebooks appeared as her students automatically reached for a fresh piece of paper. They did this without Brynn so much as asking.

The remainder of the time was spent writing Mike. Brynn wrote her own letter and found herself struggling to hold in the emotion as she placed feelings of doubt on the page. When she glanced up, she found several of her students were weeping.

Afterward, those who were willing read their letters aloud.

Emilio volunteered first. Looking shaken but determined, he faced the class. "Mike, don't do it, man. Don't do it." Then he slid back onto his seat.

Pearl stood beside her desk. "Why do I hurt so bad? I barely knew you, and yet I feel some responsibility for your death. You sat three desks away from me. Three desks and you couldn't reach that far? Three desks and I couldn't see your pain? I'm sorry, Mike. Forgive me."

Yolanda, tears streaming down her face, volunteered next. "Thank you, Mike, for what you taught me. I wasn't your friend, but I wish I had been. I never took the time to talk to you. But you touched my life. Never again will I sit in a classroom and not look around me. I wish I'd known how much pain you were in. I'd like to think you would have told me had I asked. Only I never asked. Next time will be different. Next time I'm going to look."

When the bell rang her class filed out of the room with little of the enthusiasm they generally showed at the end of a day.

652   ★   *Debbie Macomber*

"Will you find out about Mike's funeral?" Emilio asked.

The other kids stopped and waited for Brynn to respond.

"We want to know," Yolanda said.

"I think it would help if we went."

There was a chorus of agreement.

"You were the only friends Mike had," Brynn said.

"It's too bad we didn't do a better job of it," Yolanda said just loudly enough for Brynn to hear.

Brynn left the school as soon as she could. She had Suzie's address with her and walked over to the teenager's apartment. The girl's mother greeted her at the door and was painfully polite as she ushered Brynn into the living room.

"Is Suzie home?" Brynn asked.

"No. She with Mike's mother."

Brynn studied the delicate Chinese woman who struggled with English. "My daughter has torn heart."

Brynn placed her hand over her own heart. It did indeed feel as if it had been torn. "Please tell Suzie that I'm looking for her."

"Yes. Thank you very much to coming." Her English was heavily accented and barely understandable.

Before she left, Brynn placed her hand on the other woman's shoulder. "Suzie is a wonderful girl. I feel honored to have been the teacher of such a fine student."

The delicate woman's eyes avoided Brynn's, but she thought she might have detected a smile.

When Brynn arrived at Mike's, his mother was at the funeral home, making the arrangements for her son's burial. Brynn left feeling as if she'd failed everyone. Mike. Suzie. His mother. Her students. Herself.

Her apartment was cold and bleak. She walked inside and stood in the dark, feeling as though she carried the burden of the world on her shoulders. With a heavy heart, she turned on the light switch and walked over to her desk.

It might have helped her had she been able to cry, but there were no tears left inside her. With a steady, sure hand, she wrote out her letter of resignation to give to Mr. Whalen in the morning. When school resumed after the first of the year, she wouldn't be there.

Roberto was right, and had been from the first, she realized. She didn't belong here. She'd failed Mike, but most of all she'd failed herself.

*   *   *

"She isn't actually going to quit, is she?" Mercy asked.

Shirley stood with her hand planted protectively over Brynn's shoulder. Mercy knew that her friend had been with her charge from the moment Brynn had learned about Mike's suicide.

"What happened with Mike wasn't her fault." Mercy wished there was something she could do. Poor Shirley was at a loss as to know how to help.

"I know."

Brynn leaned forward and pressed her forehead against her folded arms.

"Isn't there something we can do for you?" Mercy asked.

Shirley shook her head.

It was then that Mercy realized her friend was weeping. "Oh, Shirley."

"I'm sorry," the other angel said softly. "It's just that I can't bear to see Brynn feeling this defeated."

"What's going to happen?"

Shirley rubbed her hand under her nose. "I don't know. Gabriel's the one who can tell us that. But . . . "

"Yes?" Mercy prodded.

"I think it might be best if Brynn returned to Rhode Island."

Mercy was shocked. "But why?"

"She cares too much. If she'd had a more experienced angel assigned to help her . . . "

"You can't blame yourself," Mercy cried, outraged at the suggestion.

"She needs Roberto," Shirley added.

"Then let's get him," Mercy suggested. There were ways of dealing with stubborn men, and she wasn't opposed to using them. If Roberto Alcantara thought that he could trample over this sweet young woman's heart, well, there was a thing or two Mercy could teach that man. She'd take a great deal of pleasure in doing it, too.

"No," Shirley said with surprising strength. "Leave Roberto out of this."

"But—"

"He has what he wants."

"You're sure of that?" the strong male voice spoke from behind them.

"Gabriel." Mercy was quick to jump to attention.

"How's Jenny?" the archangel asked her.

Mercy brightened. "Great. At least she was the last time I checked.

She was chosen for a major role in a new musical. It's the chance of a lifetime. She couldn't be more thrilled."

"What makes you think that?"

Mercy hesitated. This sounded like one of those trick questions. "I . . . I . . ."

"What happened to Trey? The last I heard he'd disappeared, and Jenny was looking for him. He'd checked out of the hotel by the time she arrived."

"Trey, well, that is a bit unfortunate." Mercy did feel bad about the young man who'd set his heart on loving Jenny all these years. "I'm afraid he's gone."

"Gone?" Gabriel frowned, and when he did, he was something fierce to behold.

Mercy edged closer to her friend. "Yes, he left New York. He had a little trouble changing his airplane ticket, but managed to catch an earlier flight."

Brynn's doorbell chimed, and she straightened and wiped the tears from her face.

"Who's coming?" Shirley directed the question to Gabriel.

"Suzie Chang," he answered. "Apparently there is a letter Brynn needs to share with the girl."

Chapter

★ ✯ ★

17

Talking to Carl proved to be so much more difficult than Hannah had thought it would be. She'd waited all day for him, practiced in her mind how to break the news as gently as possible.

She'd left her grandmother's filled with conviction. In the time since, her clear purpose had become clouded with the time-honored traditions of duty and honor.

"I know you're wondering why I asked to see you," Hannah said as she brought Carl a cup of tea and set it on the table in the family kitchen. She was nervous, and the hot liquid sloshed over the edges of the cup.

Hannah didn't worry that her parents would interrupt them. Her family seemed to think it was important that Hannah and Carl have time together alone, and for once Hannah was grateful.

"I've been wanting to talk to you, too," Carl said, smiling broadly. He looked happy, more so than she could remember in a long while. She suspected the situation with the school had been cleared up, and she was pleased for his sake.

"My father had a go-around with the school headmaster himself," Carl said, gloating a little.

So she was right.

"I have my job back, Hannah, and if anyone's position is in jeopardy, it's Hiram Stienfield's."

"I couldn't be more pleased," she said, but before she could relay her own, less welcome news, Carl continued.

"As you might guess, my mind is greatly relieved."

"Of course, and now . . . "

"We can seriously start planning for our wedding," he finished for her.

"As a matter of fact, that was what I wanted to talk to you about. . . ."

"Now I agree June is an excellent time of year, but personally I'd prefer May." Once again Carl wouldn't allow her to continue.

"Carl, would you please listen to me?"

"In a minute. There are a number of reasons I prefer May."

"Carl!"

"My mother's birthday is in May, and then there's Mother's Day. I've always found it convenient to cluster certain dates together whenever possible. It helps to keep track, and if we're going to need to buy . . ." He stopped abruptly when Hannah stood up.

She walked over to the stove. Now she understood what it was about Carl that had always disturbed her. He refused to listen.

"Hannah?" he asked gently. "You're upset, aren't you?"

"Yes," she said between gritted teeth, unwilling to hide it.

"Your heart's set on June, isn't it?"

"No," she said forcefully, and whirled around. "I'm not going to marry you." There, she'd said it, but in far less diplomatic terms than she'd wanted.

A stunned, disbelieving silence followed. At last she'd found a way to capture his attention.

"You're honestly breaking our engagement?"

He seemed to need confirmation. "Yes," she said firmly.

He scratched the side of his head. "Don't you think that's a bit drastic, considering that I'm willing to give up the May date? I'd like to think I'm a reasonable man. If you don't want the wedding in May, why don't you just say so?"

"I don't want the wedding in May or June or any other month of the year." She folded her arms and released a deep sigh of frustration. "This is the crux of the problem between us. You don't hear me. I'm trying to tell you something important, and either you don't care or you've already got your mind made up."

He stiffened. "I don't see it that way."

Hannah had never intended for them to discuss their basic personality differences. "I want to break the engagement, Carl. I deeply regret hurting you, but I'm fairly certain you aren't in love with me."

"Don't be ridiculous," he snapped. "Of course I love you. I think you're wonderful. You'll make me a good wife, you're supportive and—"

"You're doing it again," she cried, clenching her fists at her sides. Hannah so seldom raised her voice that it shocked even her.

Carl looked genuinely baffled. "I don't understand. Hannah, listen, tell me whatever it is that you find offensive. I can change."

"It doesn't matter."

"But of course it matters. I realize that marriage is an important step and you're bound to have second thoughts, every woman does. Now it's true," he said, and raised his right hand with a dismissive gesture, "that I've been wrapped up in my own problems of late. I haven't paid you nearly enough attention, have I? Naturally you're feeling shortchanged in the romance department, and frankly I don't blame you."

"Carl," she whispered, "you don't love me."

"Nonsense. I asked you to marry me, didn't I?"

"Okay," she whispered, her patience wearing paper thin. "Let's try this from a different angle. I can't marry you, Carl, because I don't love *you*."

He laughed. The man had the nerve to actually laugh aloud.

Dumbfounded, all Hannah could do was stare at him.

"Of course you love me," he countered, sounding relieved. He placed his hand on his chest as if to restrain the bubbling amusement welling up inside him. "Hannah, these doubts of yours are only natural. I had them, too."

"And now you don't?"

"Occasionally," he was willing to admit. "But I've worked through those feelings, and given time, you will, too."

Hannah had hoped that she could talk to Carl without telling him about Joshua. It was one thing to break the engagement and something else entirely to mention she'd fallen in love with another man. She'd hoped to spare Carl that.

"The problem as I see it," Carl said, talking to her as he would one of his students, "is that people are rarely willing to see through their difficulties. Our society is caught up in fast-food restaurants, 'pay' later mentality, and instant gratification. My dear Hannah, what you're feeling isn't so difficult to understand. But we've made a commitment to each other, and we can't treat it lightly."

"Carl, I'm terminating our engagement." She couldn't say it any plainer than that.

"It's times such as these that we need to hold on to each other instead of letting go of the most important relationship of our lives."

Hannah's heart was pounding so hard and fast, it felt as though her ribs were about to break. "I've met someone else," she said forcefully.

Her words stopped Carl cold. His eyes narrowed. "Who?"

"You don't know him."

"Don't be so sure. Tell me his name."

"What does it matter what his name is?" she demanded. "I love him and he loves me."

Looking completely taken aback, Carl pulled out a kitchen chair and slumped onto it.

"To be honest, Carl, I didn't think you'd care."

"Not care?" he cried as though her comment had outraged him. "Of course I care. Some man, some stranger, has stolen my bride, and you seem to think that it really shouldn't matter."

Hannah knew it was his ego speaking and was sorrier than she could say. "If you're looking to blame anyone, blame me," she told him gently. "I never intended to tell you about him, but then I couldn't make you listen, and—"

His head jerked up. "You weren't going to tell me?"

"All I wanted to do was break the engagement, but you refused to believe me . . . you weren't hearing me."

"Don't be ridiculous. I heard every word you said."

Hannah wasn't going to get into an argument with him, but this was too much. "You keep discounting me, offering excuses and reasons for my wanting to call off the engagement. You've given me no option but to tell you about Joshua."

"Joshua . . ." He repeated the name as if he were reading it off a post office poster.

"I'm genuinely sorry."

"You're serious? This isn't some stupid joke?"

"I can't marry you, Carl, nor can I go on pretending I love you."

The silence that followed fell like a butcher's cleaver into the middle of the room.

Carl reached for his jacket, swinging it over his shoulders like a shawl in his rush to get away from her. "Do your parents know?"

Hannah hesitated. "They will soon enough."

He walked toward the stairway, his steps abrupt and urgent. "If this other man is who you love, then all I can say is you're welcome to him. Just don't come crying to me when you've regained your senses."

"Joshua isn't going to break my heart," she assured him softly. "I realize this is painful, Carl, but I'd like it if we could be friends."

"Friends?" he echoed as though it were a ridiculous suggestion. "You've got to be kidding. Frankly, Hannah, I doubt that I'll ever want to see you again." Having said that, he stormed out of the apartment, slamming the door behind him. The pictures on the walls shook with the force of his exit.

"Hannah?" A moment later her father called from the bottom of the stairs.

"Yes," she said, hoping she sounded calm and assured.

"Is everything all right between you and Carl?"

She didn't hesitate, and the relief in her voice was evident. "Don't worry, Dad, everything's the way it should be."

There came a time in every man's life when he had to admit he'd made a mistake, learn from it, and move forward. Joshua had reached that point the afternoon he'd heard Hannah's father invite him to his daughter's wedding to another man.

Even now he couldn't find it in his heart to be angry with Hannah. Her inability to break her engagement highlighted what had attracted her to him. She was loyal to a fault, caring, and tenderhearted. Family took priority.

A part of him would always love her, he realized. Knowing her for this short period had blessed his life, but now it was time to own up to a few home truths.

First off, his love was hurting her. Because of the tenderness he held for Hannah, he couldn't continue to make her miserable. The truth was, he'd found her too late.

His decision made, Joshua had hoped to experience some sort of emotional release, but he didn't. If anything, he felt considerably worse. He'd stewed and fretted, doubted and reasoned, until he was blue with the effort. Nothing would ever change. Hannah loved him, but it went against the very grain of her being to defy and disappoint her family.

The snowstorm that had been predicted for that afternoon had already darkened the sky. Another night of sitting home alone, thinking about Hannah, would solve nothing.

Unfortunately all his favorite escapes had been ruined. He couldn't walk past Rockefeller Center now and not remember the time he and Hannah had skated together. Nor could he forget how good she'd felt in his arms.

This was the real problem: he couldn't forget.

The time had come to seek greener pastures, and he had just the woman in mind. He reached for the phone and dialed Carol's number.

"Hannah," her mother called to her from the hallway. "Your father and I need to talk to you."

Hannah opened her bedroom door, her coat draped over her arm. Ruth's eyes widened with distress. "You're not going out, are you?"

"Yes."

Ruth hesitated and looked to her husband.

"Did you need me to get you something?" Hannah asked, then added, "I don't know when I'll be home."

"No. . . . I just received a call from Carl's mother. Is it true, honey, have you broken the engagement with Carl?"

Hannah should have realized something like this would happen. Carl had gone directly to his family and listed her sins. Hannah regretted that she hadn't prepared her parents for the news, but she'd been hoping to confront them with Joshua at her side.

"I don't love Carl," she told her mother gently. "I'm sorry, Mom, I know how much you and Dad like him, but I don't feel the same way."

"There's someone else?" her mother questioned, her voice revealing the depth of her disbelief. "Helen seems to think you've been seeing another man on the sly, without any of us knowing. I assured her that couldn't possibly be true."

David Morganstern stood behind his wife, his hand on Ruth's shoulder. His eyes, dark and inquisitive, rested on his daughter.

"His name's Joshua Shadduck," she admitted. "He's an attorney."

Her mother gasped softly and covered her mouth with her hand. Hannah wasn't sure if this was because she'd admitted to dating someone while engaged to Carl or because Joshua was an attorney.

Her father frowned. "Didn't I recently meet this young man?"

Ashamed that she'd deceived them both, Hannah lowered her gaze. "Yes. He was in the deli."

"How could you have fallen in love with him?" her mother asked, her voice raised with disbelief. "How could you hurt Carl like this? He's such a good man. We couldn't ask for a better husband for you."

"Joshua will make me a good husband, too."

"I forbid you from seeing this Joshua again," her father said sternly.

"Daddy, I've never defied you. I've always done what you've asked, but I love Joshua with all my heart. I need to see him. I need to be with him."

Her parents stared back at her, too shocked to respond right away.

"How did you meet him?" The question came from her mother a moment later.

"We met at the Thanksgiving Day parade. Then, before I had a chance to analyze how I felt about him, Carl asked me to marry him. I didn't want to agree, but at the time it seemed like the best thing to do. You and Dad were so pleased, and you both like Carl."

"He's been like a son to me," her father admitted sadly.

"I'm sorry, Dad," Hannah whispered. "I didn't mean to disappoint you." Before either one could say anything more, she rushed out of the apartment.

"Hannah, please, don't go," her mother shouted from the top of the stairway, but Hannah pretended not to hear. Never in all her life had she ignored her mother and father.

Hannah caught a taxi outside the deli and read the driver the Riverside Drive address Joshua had written down on the back of his business card.

"It looks like it might snow," she said, glancing toward the darkening sky. The sooner she reached Joshua, the better. She needed him now as never before. When she told him what had happened, he'd come with her and together they'd talk to her family and make everything right.

The driver mumbled something in return that she didn't understand.

Several minutes later the cabdriver pulled over to the curb and flipped off the meter. Hannah gazed out the car window at the high-rise apartment building and experienced a sense of relief. The man she loved, the man she'd defied her family to marry, lived in this building.

"Lady, are you going to stare out the window all day?"

"No, sorry." She returned her attention to her purse and pulled out her wallet. From the corner of her eye, she caught sight of a familiar figure. Looking up, she saw Joshua coming out of the building. She raised her hand and was about to call him when, suddenly, she stopped. The happy shout died in her throat.

Joshua wasn't alone.

Standing beside him was the most beautiful, elegant-looking woman Hannah had ever seen. Joshua slipped his arm around the other woman's waist, bent down, and kissed her gently on the lips.

Her heart pounding like a locomotive chugging uphill, Hannah hurled herself back against the seat, not wanting him to see her.

"Lady, are you going to pay me or not?" the cabbie asked a second time with far less patience.

"Yes, yes, of course." Hannah leaned forward just far enough to peek at Joshua. It was apparent the two were long-term acquaintances. The woman with him gazed up adoringly, as though this were the happiest day of her life.

"Please," Hannah whispered. "Take me home."

"You got the money or don't you?" the taxi driver asked.

She handed him a twenty-dollar bill for security. "Now take me back," she pleaded. She'd go home because she had nowhere else to go. With her tail between her legs, her heart heavy with pain, she'd return to her family, who would love and support her despite the fact that she'd deeply embarrassed and disappointed them.

"All right, if you want to go back, then fine, I'll take you." The driver hesitated, and Hannah met his gaze in the rearview mirror. "Is everything all right?" he asked gently.

"No," Hannah whispered.

She was too late. Joshua had found someone else.

Mike Glasser was buried two days later. Father Grady was scheduled to say the funeral mass and had spent considerable time counseling Mike's mother, Louise.

Brynn was one of the first to arrive at the church. She slipped into the pew and knelt down on the padded kneeler. It might have helped if she'd been able to release her grief, but she held on to it with both hands, clenching it to her breast, fearing what would happen if she ever let go.

Mike's death was a constant, painful reminder of how badly she'd failed him and her other students. How badly she'd failed herself.

Emilio walked into church and sat in the pew directly across from her. Yolanda and Pearl arrived together and sat in front of Brynn.

The huge church was nearly half full with a number of other students and faculty members from Manhattan High. Mike's suicide had had a powerful impact on those who'd known him.

Organ music, deep and somber, filled the church. Mike's mother and a handful of other relatives arrived. Together they walked down the center aisle. Louise Glasser's shoulders were bent under the weight of her grief. She appeared to be leaning heavily on the girl walking beside her. The two clung to each other. It didn't take Brynn long to realize the one with Mike's mother was Suzie Chang. They needed each other.

Brynn had met with them both, separately. They'd come together as strangers with a common bond. Both had loved Mike. Both deeply grieved his death.

Organ music surged through the church as a man's voice, hauntingly melodic, rang loud and clear from the choir loft. The voice, a baritone, reached out and consoled with music those who'd gathered to mourn Mike's death. Brynn recognized the singer's voice immediately.

Roberto.

Even from this distance his voice filled her with a bitter sadness. It settled in the pit of her stomach, and a chill came over her as she closed her eyes and soaked in the comfort of the song. She pretended it was Roberto's arms around her.

Since her last meeting with Roberto, Brynn had tried to push all thoughts of him from her mind. By the sheer force of her determination, she'd partially succeeded. Despite her efforts to purge him from her thoughts, she couldn't keep from feeling that something important, something vital, was missing.

Once, a year or so before, Brynn had lost her purse. A knot had formed in her stomach that refused to go away until she was able to replace everything that had been lost. A similar sensation had been with her since her last meeting with Roberto. She was lost, and the way she felt just then, nothing would ever be right again. She supposed her thinking was melodramatic. In time she'd be able to put these weeks in New York behind her.

As Roberto had encouraged her from the beginning, she would return to where she belonged. But she wouldn't go back to Rhode Island the same as when she'd left. No, when she headed home, she'd be bringing a lot of emotional baggage with her.

Father Grady said the mass. A wake was scheduled in the parish hall immediately following the service. Brynn knew she was expected to show. It was as good a time as any to tell her students that she wouldn't be back in class following winter vacation. Already they'd been assigned another teacher, one with more experience than she.

Most of Brynn's apartment was packed. Depending on road conditions, she should be ready to leave in another day, two at the most.

When the service was over, Mike's family filed out first, then each row followed in turn.

Brynn stayed behind. She wanted a few moments alone before she headed over to the parish hall. With her head bowed, she tried to pray. Lately it had been a losing battle. Every concern she gave to God had claw marks all over it.

Not only had her abilities as a teacher been questioned, but her faith, once so stable and sure, had been badly shaken. She recognized that in time it would right itself again, but just then even that looked doubtful.

Footsteps sounded on the tile floor behind her. Brynn kept her head lowered, resenting the intrusion. She needed this time alone. She wasn't ready to join the others.

To her surprise it was Roberto who slipped into the pew and sat next to her. He didn't say anything, simply sat at her side, his head bowed in prayer.

After a while he touched her forearm. "The others are waiting."

"I know," she whispered back. "Tell them I'll be there in a few minutes."

He didn't leave.

"I'm fine, Roberto. I appreciate your concern, but there's nothing to worry about." She hoped her weak smile would convince him she was telling the truth.

He didn't budge. "I know you too well to believe that."

She stiffened. His words set fire under her. "You don't know me at all, you never did."

Seeing that he wasn't going to leave her, she stood abruptly and made her way out of the pew and down the side aisle. Her crisp steps echoed in the empty church.

She must have risen too quickly, because she hadn't gone more than a few feet when her head started to swim and the room began to spin. Reaching out to the end of the wooden row, she caught herself in time to keep from collapsing.

Roberto was at her side in an instant. He murmured something impatient in Spanish and led her to the back of the church.

"Stay here," he insisted, and disappeared. No more than a minute passed before he returned with a glass of water.

"There's nothing wrong with me," she insisted. She didn't want him to touch her. Didn't want him close to her. He was the one who wanted her out of his life. She'd go. Kicking and screaming, she'd abided by his wishes. However difficult, however painful. He had no reason to complain.

"When was the last time you had anything to eat?"

Brynn couldn't remember, but she wasn't about to let Roberto know that. "I'm fine," she insisted stiffly. "I'd appreciate it if you'd kindly leave me alone."

"Brynn, please listen."

"If I understood you correctly, you don't want anything more to do with me. All I ask is that you respect my wishes, as I have yours."

He hesitated, and Brynn felt a small sense of satisfaction, knowing her words had hit their mark.

"Allow me to escort you to the wake. Please." She knew that the "please" had cost him a great deal.

"Why?" She didn't understand the necessity of this.

"It's a little thing, isn't it?"

It would be petty to refuse him, so she agreed. His arm came around her shoulder. She meant to shake it off, but the moment he brought her close to his side, the tears that had refused to come broke free in a surging dam of grief.

Brynn sank into the pew at the back of the vestibule and wept as though her very soul had been ripped from her body.

"It's all right," Roberto whispered, cradling her in his arms, pressing her head to his chest.

She didn't mean to cling to him, but her pride be damned, she needed him as she'd never needed anyone.

He spoke again in Spanish, his voice low and soothing. Tucking her head against his shoulder, he rocked back and forth gently.

"You were right," she admitted when the shoulder-shaking sobs had abated. "You tried to tell me, but I wouldn't listen. Now Mike's dead and—"

"You can't blame yourself."

On a conscious level Brynn agreed with him, but deep inside she felt she carried a portion of the blame. Mike had trusted her enough to write her. She was the one person in all the world to whom he felt comfortable enough communicating his last wishes. Yet she'd been oblivious of his pain, deaf to his needs. The boy had been desperate, and she had been blind.

In retrospect Brynn realized that Mike had been trying to tell her in subtle ways of the hopelessness he experienced. His essays had been full of it. The dark side. Despondent words from a despondent youth.

Abruptly, Brynn pulled away from Roberto. In addition to his comfort, his embrace was a painful reminder that he wanted nothing more to do with her. If this was a contest, she was declaring him the winner.

"I won't be coming back," she announced firmly, surprised at the strength of her voice. "I've already given Mr. Whalen my letter of resignation. In January the kids will have a new teacher."

"Do Emilio and the others know?" Roberto asked.

"Not yet."

"When do you plan to tell them?"

"Now."

Something flashed in his eyes. "It's for the best."

She noticed that Roberto didn't try to talk her out of leaving. She realized that was what she wanted, what she longed with all her being for him to do.

She stood. "I'll do it now," she said, and boldly walked out the door.

* * *

"What are we going to tell Gabriel?" Shirley demanded of her two friends. The three had gathered in the choir loft following Mike's funeral, at a loss as to how to report their progress to the archangel.

"This is the first time we've failed. He'll understand," Mercy offered.

"He might accept one failure, but all three of us?"

"What happened this year?" Goodness threw her arms into the air, thoroughly disgusted by this unexpected turn of events.

Shirley cast them a disgruntled look. "It might have helped matters if you two hadn't been playing on escalators and writing on billboards in Times Square."

"Blaming each other isn't going to help."

"But it's nearly Christmas Eve," Mercy protested. "I can't possibly see us turning everything around at this late point."

"Maybe there's a chance if we work together."

Shirley shook her head slowly. "It seems to me working together is what got us into this mess."

"All right, let's each report what's happening with our charges," Goodness suggested, and gestured for Shirley to go first.

"Well, as you can see," Shirley said, pointing to Brynn, who sat in the corner of the parish hall, "Brynn has said good-bye to her class. She's miserable, and blames herself for Mike's death."

"What's going to happen to her?"

"I haven't a clue," Shirley said, and sounded thoroughly miserable. "Gabriel was right, this assignment was too much for me. I'll leave him to pick up the pieces. It's going to take an archangel to bring about some good from this tragedy."

"Roberto loves her," Goodness said, studying Emilio's brother.

"Yes, I know," Shirley said sadly. "Letting her leave is a sign of how much he cares for her."

"There's nothing more you can do?" Mercy asked. "Perhaps what Brynn needs is a little talking to from the three of us."

"I'm afraid that would send her packing faster than anything."

"Okay, okay," Goodness said, looking to Mercy. "What's happening with Jenny?"

"I thought she'd be overjoyed to get this chance to star on Broadway. It's been her dream."

"And she isn't happy?"

Mercy shrugged, apparently unable to come up with an explanation of her charge's behavior. "She's moped around the apartment for two days now. I'm afraid she wants Trey with her *and* a chance to star on Broadway, but she can't have both."

"Oh boy," Shirley muttered. "And what is Gabriel going to say about that?"

"I don't know, but I have the distinct notion he's going to think I was responsible for getting the play's director to notice her. I wasn't, truly I wasn't."

"I believe you," Shirley murmured, but her opinion wasn't the one that mattered, and all three knew it.

"That leaves me to tell you about Hannah," Goodness said, and her disappointment was keen. "She broke off the engagement with Carl."

"Good." Both Shirley and Mercy brightened.

"But it was too late." Goodness told them that Joshua was dating Carol seriously now.

"Joshua found someone else?" Shirley asked. "I don't believe it."

Mercy crossed her arms and pursed her lips. "Men can be so fickle."

"In my opinion he still loves Hannah."

"But he doesn't know that Hannah broke her engagement with Carl, does he?"

"It might have made a difference," Shirley insisted.

"It's too late," Goodness informed them sadly. "Hannah saw him with the other woman."

"We can fix that," Mercy said confidently. "This sort of thing is right up our alley."

"It won't work. Not this time."

"Why not?" Shirley insisted.

"Because Joshua has decided to cut his losses and look elsewhere for a wife."

"And Hannah?"

"Hannah will live with her parents the rest of her life and never marry."

"Just a minute," Mercy said, and rolled up her sleeves. "We can fix that, and while we're at it, there are ways to deal with men as stubborn as Roberto."

"What about you and Jenny?" Goodness asked.

Some of Mercy's brightness dimmed. "I don't know what we can do about Jenny and Trey."

Shirley rubbed her chin. "I have an idea. All isn't lost yet."

Chapter

★ ✦ ★

18

From inside his office Joshua heard the raised voices of the reception-ist and an angry man. He stepped into the hallway and heard David Morganstern, Hannah's father, demanding to see him.

"It's all right, Julie," Joshua said, coming forward, "I'll see Mr. Morganstern."

David shot the receptionist a look of triumph and straightened the cuffs of his coat sleeves. "I told you Mr. Shadduck would see me."

"He doesn't have an appointment," Julie told Joshua, "and he refused to make one."

"It's all right, Julie."

Joshua escorted David into his office. The older man paused in the doorway and looked around. He didn't seem overly impressed. "Mighty fancy digs you have here."

"Thank you." Giving the impression of nonchalance, Joshua sat down at his desk and invited Hannah's father to make himself com-fortable. "What can I do for you, Mr. Morganstern?"

David sat on the cushion as if he expected it to jump up and bite him at any moment. "I've come to ask you a few questions, young man. I recently learned, through no fault of my daughter's, that you've been sneaking around with Hannah. I want you to know I don't like it one bit."

Joshua folded his hands on top of the desk and waited.

"I wanted to meet the man face-to-face who played havoc with my daughter's life." It was clear David's feelings ran strong and fervent. The older gentleman bolted out of the chair and stood directly in front of Joshua's desk.

Joshua wondered exactly how much David knew about the two of them and feared saying more than he should.

"Your silence tells me everything I need to know," David said, spitting out the words, revealing his distaste. "I find you to be the most despicable kind of man."

Joshua didn't blame Morganstern. His behavior had been less than honorable. He'd never been comfortable meeting Hannah on the sly, kissing her, urging her to continue their relationship while she was engaged to another man. He wasn't comfortable now, offering excuses.

"How is she?" Joshua couldn't keep himself from asking.

"How do you think?" David demanded.

"You have my apology," Joshua said, hoping the other man understood the full extent of his regret.

"What about Carl? Are you willing to apologize to him, too? What about Hannah? My daughter gave you her heart, and it meant nothing to the mighty, powerful attorney. You people seem to think you have the right to disrupt lives. It's time someone made you accountable for your actions."

"You want me to apologize to Carl?" Joshua asked, willing to do whatever he could to appease Hannah's family and make matters easier for her. Personally he thought the less Carl knew about him, the better.

David considered his offer, then shrugged. "No. Carl and our family aren't exactly on speaking terms."

Joshua leaned forward slightly, wondering if he'd heard him correctly. "Why aren't you?"

David sat back down and eyed Joshua suspiciously. "You mean to say you honestly don't know?"

"I wouldn't ask if I did."

"Hannah loves you."

The confirmation of her feelings should have brought him joy; instead he was filled with a deep, painful sense of loss. "I love her, too."

"Not in my book," David fumed. "You leave her to face Carl alone, and when she breaks the engagement, you dump her."

It was Joshua's turn to bolt upright. "Hannah broke off the engagement?"

David frowned and nodded. "You mean to say you didn't know?"

Joshua came out from behind his desk. "No."

"She defied both her mother and me when we insisted she not see you again. Then less than a half hour after she leaves, she returns, tells us how sorry she is for having upset us, and goes to her bedroom. She hasn't been herself since. She won't talk about you or Carl, but it's plain as the nose on my face that she's miserable."

"She never told me. I knew how difficult all this was for her. She didn't want to hurt anyone, least of all her family and especially not Carl. Every time she promised to break the engagement something more would happen to prevent it. I felt the only thing I could do was step aside."

It was clear David wasn't interested in hearing explanations. "Do you or don't you love my daughter?"

"I love her," Joshua said with conviction.

"Then what are your intentions?"

He didn't hesitate. "I want to marry her."

David glanced around the office once more, this time with a less critical eye. "Talk to Hannah first, and then you and I might strike some kind of agreement. We could do with a lawyer in the family." He started toward the door, then stopped abruptly and turned around. "Are you coming or not, young man?"

Joshua laughed and reached for his coat. "Coming."

David nodded once, profoundly. "Good, that's exactly what I wanted to hear."

Hannah was working the counter when Joshua walked inside the deli, her father at his side.

"Hannah," David shouted, "you've got company. Take him upstairs and serve him a piece of your mother's cheesecake."

Hannah ignored her father and directed her question to Joshua. "What are you doing here?"

"I came to talk to you. I suggest we go upstairs as your father advised." They'd already attracted more than enough attention.

"Go," Ruth Morganstern insisted to Hannah. "This way, young man," she said, and directed Joshua around the counter, pointing the way to their private quarters.

Joshua followed Hannah up the stairs. She paused halfway up and turned to face him. From her position on the stairway they were at eye level. It required more discipline than he'd needed in quite some time not to kiss her right then and there.

"What did my father say to you?" she demanded. Her eyes were full of fire. "I don't need your pity, Joshua Shadduck."

"My pity?" This came at him out of the blue. "If anyone is asking questions, it should be me. The last thing I heard was your father inviting me to your wedding to another man."

Hannah's shoulders went stiff. "The last time I saw you, you were kissing another woman."

He frowned. "Who?"

"How should I know?" she flared.

The door at the bottom of the stairs opened. "Upstairs, Hannah. The entire deli is listening in on your conversation."

If ever Hannah needed an incentive, this appeared to be it. She raced up the remainder of the stairs.

Joshua was left with no choice but to follow her, which he did gladly. He found her standing in front of a window, looking out, her back to him, her arms folded around her middle.

"Her name's Carol," he said gently, wanting to clear the air as soon as he could so they could move on to the more important matters. "I've known her for a number of years."

"You should marry her," she suggested, turning to face him.

"I can't. She's a wonderful woman, but she isn't you. You're the one who owns my heart. You have from nearly the first moment we met. I had to let you go, Hannah, surely you understand that. My love was hurting you. The family pressures on you to marry Carl were over-whelming. Stepping aside was the only decent thing to do."

"It didn't take you long to recover, did it?"

She was jealous of Carol, and Joshua thrilled at the realization. "I see it's done a bit of good for you to know how I've felt these last few weeks. It wasn't easy on me when you were spending time with Carl. It was probably the most difficult thing I've ever done."

"I always loved you, and you knew it. You never had a single rea-son to be jealous."

Joshua longed to hold and kiss her too much to argue the point. "Are you going to marry me or not, Hannah Morganstern?"

Her eyes searched his as if she questioned the sincerity of his proposal.

"I love you," he added tenderly, and held open his arms to her.

It didn't take her long to find her way into his embrace. When she slipped her arms around his middle, Joshua sighed with a sense of peace, of homecoming. He'd been waiting all his life for this woman, and now that she was his, he didn't intend to lose her.

Tunneling his fingers through her hair, Joshua positioned his mouth to kiss her.

"I've been so unhappy," she admitted on the tail end of a soft moan.

"Me, too." He kissed her again.

"But you weren't lonely," she accused. "I was miserable and lonely."

"I love you, Hannah," he said, laying his heart at her feet. "You're going to marry me, aren't you?"

"Oh yes."

"Good." He held her against him protectively. "It's the oddest thing," he mumbled, nuzzling his face close to hers.

"What is?" she said, thrilling him with small kisses along the underside of his jaw.

"Your father claims I gave him my business card. I never did. I haven't a clue where he got it."

"Me either," Hannah said. "Does it matter?"

Joshua chuckled. "Not in the least."

The last thing Brynn anticipated when she was ready to leave New York was car problems. Ever since Roberto had worked on her carburetor, her Escort had been running like a dream. Now, however, the engine wouldn't so much as crank.

The first thing she did was contact her family and tell them. Her parents were concerned about her, and they weren't happy to have her traveling home alone, but she couldn't very well desert her vehicle.

Sitting inside her apartment, she thumbed through the telephone directory, looking for a garage listing, knowing full well her chances of finding someone willing to work on her car on Christmas Eve were damn near impossible.

Her doorbell chimed, and disheartened, Brynn slipped off the stool. When she checked her peephole the first person she saw was Emilio, but there were a number of others she recognized with him.

After flipping open the latch, she found herself facing a throng of her students and their parents.

"What's going on here?" she asked. There must have been close to fifty people jam-packed into her hallway.

"We don't want you to leave, Miss Cassidy," Emilio said, serving as spokesperson for the group. "After Mike's funeral a number of us went and talked to Mr. Whalen. We asked that the school refuse to accept your letter of resignation."

"I don't know how much we were able to influence him," Yolanda said, laughing nervously. "I think our parents had a far greater impact."

Suzie Chang's delicate mother pressed forward and in halting English said, "You say it honor to have Suzie in class. We say it greater honor to have you for teacher."

A cry of agreement followed the Chinese woman's words.

"We love you, Miss Cassidy."

Brynn couldn't speak for the lump in her throat. Never in all her dreams had she expected anything like this.

"Mr. Whalen says you can have your job back, if you want it,"

Denzil's mother told her. "For the first time in his life, my son's doing well in school. He's talking about something other than video games."

"What do you say, Miss Cassidy?"

Frankly, Brynn was left speechless.

"Say something," Emilio urged.

"I don't know . . . I just don't know."

"Give the girl some room to breathe." Parents and teens parted so Father Grady could make his way to the front.

"Father Grady!"

"You didn't know I was here? My dear, I was the one who drove the bus."

"You brought the church bus?" Brynn placed both hands over her mouth to keep from laughing out loud.

"Roberto's driving it around the block, looking for a place to park now."

"Roberto," Brynn whispered his name.

"I'm telling you right now, Teach," Emilio advised from the corner of his mouth, "you have to be patient with my brother, but once he learns something, you'll never have to teach him again."

She caught sight of Roberto just then, hurrying down the corridor, breathing hard. He slowed his pace when he saw her.

"Will you stay, Miss Cassidy?"

Brynn reached out and touched Yolanda's face. Then, because it seemed to be so important to everyone else, she nodded.

A loud cheer went up, and Brynn's next-door neighbor opened the door and stuck out her head. "Ralph, I told you there was a party going on in the hallway. Come and look."

"Hello, Mrs. Camden," Brynn called, and waved.

"Is everyone invited?" her neighbor asked.

"Of course," Father Grady answered. "Come with us. We got what we came for." One by one they filed down the hallway. Lorraine Camden and her husband joined the line, chattering as they went.

"Where are we going?" Brynn heard the older woman ask.

"To the bus," someone answered.

"Ralph, they have a bus."

"Yes, Lorraine, I heard."

Soon only Brynn and Roberto were left. She led him inside her apartment and closed the door. With her back pressed against it, she studied him.

Finally, when she couldn't stand not to know any longer, she asked, "You want me to stay, too?"

He avoided eye contact. "It's a dangerous neighborhood."

"You didn't answer my question."

"Yes!" he shouted as if it made him mad to have to say it. "I want you to stay."

"Why?" She wasn't going to make it easy for him.

"Because you're a damn good teacher and there isn't a student in your class who didn't protest when they learned you were leaving."

She took two steps away from the door. "I'm not talking about my students. I'm asking why you don't want me to leave."

"Me?" He swallowed uncomfortably, then pointed to the door. "Father Grady might have a problem driving the bus. It would be better if we continued this conversation some other time."

She laughed softly. "Not on your life, buster."

To her amazement, Roberto broke out laughing. "Buster. That's exactly why I love you so damn much, Brynn Cassidy. The worst you can think to call me is Buster." He whispered something in Spanish.

"If you love me, then why were you so eager to be rid of me?"

He channeled his fingers through his hair and sighed audibly. "Because I love you. This neighborhood has a way of dragging people down. Eventually it would happen to you, and I couldn't bear to sit by and watch that."

"As long as you're with me that's not going to happen. We can help each other."

He buried both hands deep in his pockets. "I'd like to be self-sacrificing and send you back to that fancy girls' school, but I can't. The problem is I need you as much as Emilio and his friends."

"That's a start," she said, smiling through her tears. She held her arms out to him.

Roberto reached for her and kissed her gently.

"I need you, too, Roberto . . . so much," she whispered, kissing him freely and fully.

Roberto groaned and forced her lips to part beneath his. His tongue probed hers in a silken dance, then plunged forward, unleashing a fiery passion.

At last, groaning, he broke away. "Come with me."

"Where?"

"Onto the bus. Father Grady can't drive worth beans."

"Where are we headed?"

"Church," he told her. "Do you mind?"

She laughed. "No, I don't mind. It seems like the perfect place for us to be on Christmas Eve."

* * *

The weather was perfect for such a night. Trey glanced at the clear, bright sky as he made his way from the house to the barn. When he'd finished feeding the horses and settling them down for the evening, he planned on stopping off at the Lancasters' for some of Dillon's wassail. It had become tradition that he join Jenny's family for the Christmas Eve celebration.

He'd eat dinner with them, and then they'd attend church services together. The last couple of years the family had invited him to stay for the gift opening, but Trey had refused.

He'd often spent time with the Lancasters on the off chance they could tell him something about Jenny. This year he knew everything there was to know. He'd come for dinner and attend the evening church service, and then, as always, he'd head home. Alone.

Jenny hadn't contacted him since he'd left New York, not that he'd expected she would.

Pausing in the hallway, Trey picked up the box of fancy chocolates he'd bought for Jenny's mother. He figured every woman deserved a box of expensive French candies one time in her life. Besides, he owed Paula.

The Lancaster house was bright with outside lights. Trey never could pull into their yard and not think of Jenny. The tightness around his heart felt almost physical as he climbed down from his truck and headed inside.

His timing was perfect. Charlie, Jenny's brother, and his fiancée, Mary Lou, were carrying serving dishes to the dining room table.

"Hello, Trey. Welcome." Paula kissed him on the cheek. Trey tucked the chocolates under the tree and shook Dillon's hand.

"Think it'll snow?" Dillon asked. It was the same question his friend proposed every Christmas Eve.

"Not this year," Trey told him, knowing it would disappoint Dillon.

The smells coming from the kitchen were tantalizing enough to convince a confirmed bachelor to find a wife.

Dillon offered him a glass of hot wassail, but Trey declined. He didn't figure there was enough time to finish it before dinner was served.

"Mom, are these the linen napkins you were looking for earlier?" a soft voice asked from the vicinity of the hallway.

It was a good thing Trey hadn't been holding a drink. Sure as hell, he would have dropped it. The voice he heard belonged to Jenny. She paused momentarily when she walked into the room. "Hello, Trey. Merry Christmas."

Trey felt as if someone had knocked him behind the knees with a baseball bat. He stared at Dillon. "What's Jenny doing home?"

Dillon looked well pleased. "You'll have to ask her that yourself."

Trey intended on doing exactly that. He followed her into the kitchen and stood behind her while she dished up a mound of steaming mashed potatoes.

"When did you arrive?" he asked.

"This morning." She answered him as though there were a hundred other more important items occupying her mind at that moment. "I do need to talk to you, however. I didn't take kindly to your leaving New York without saying good-bye."

"Trey, would you mind putting the relish plate on the table?" Paula asked.

"In a minute." He wasn't budging until he had the answer he wanted.

"The potatoes are ready," Jenny announced, and handed the bowl to her brother, who promptly delivered them to the table.

"What about the play?" Trey insisted.

"What about it?"

"I thought you said the rehearsals started before Christmas."

"They did." Jenny dipped her finger inside the gravy boat and licked it clean. "Mom, this is your best ever."

"Thank you, darling."

Charlie returned, and Trey handed Jenny's brother the relish dish. He followed Jenny to the other side of the kitchen. "Shouldn't you be there?" he asked.

"Where?"

He figured she was being deliberately obtuse, and it irritated him to no end. "Practicing," he said louder than he intended.

"Not really," she mumbled, then said to her mother, "As far as I can see, everything's on the table."

"Great. Call your father and we'll sit down."

"Dinner," Jenny called, and the family started to gather around the dining room table.

"Jenny." Trey's hand on her arm stopped her. Silently he pleaded with her to tell him what was going on. "Why aren't you in New York?"

"You honestly don't know?"

Baffled, he shook his head.

"I'm marrying you, Trey. We've got the next fifty years to discuss all this, but right now dinner is getting cold." She left him standing in the middle of her mother's kitchen with his mouth sagging open so far, it damn near bounced against the floor.

By the time he'd recovered enough to walk into the dining room, everyone was seated and waiting for him.

"Trey, would you care to say grace?"

Everyone looked to him, but for the life of him Trey couldn't take his eyes off Jenny long enough to do as her mother requested.

"It seems Trey's otherwise occupied," Dillon said, chuckling. "I'll be happy to say the blessing."

The Lancaster family bowed their heads while Dillon offered up a short prayer of thanksgiving. When he'd finished, he looked to Trey. "Sit down, Trey. Your place is directly across from Jenny. Once you're seated, would you kindly pass the mashed potatoes?"

Trey was certain he gave them all a good laugh. The first thing he did was pour gravy over the sweet potatoes. He couldn't help it. Nothing could make him stop staring at Jenny. He doubted he ate two bites of the entire dinner.

Twice she looked up and smiled, and it was damn near all he could do not to reach for her right there.

"I'd appreciate a few minutes alone with Jenny after dinner," he said, looking to her parents.

"You don't need our permission," Dillon responded. "Jenny makes her own decisions."

An eternity passed before the meal was over. Jenny tormented him during dessert by licking the whipped cream off the back of her fork—her eyes locked on him the entire time.

When she announced she was too full to take another bite, Trey nearly picked her up out of the chair in his eagerness to get her alone.

"How about a stroll to the barn," she suggested.

"Fine." He didn't care if she suggested New Zealand; he wasn't waiting another minute for her to explain her earlier statement.

The night was clear and crisp. Trey led her by the hand into the barn. "All right," he demanded without turning on any of the lights. "Did you mean what you said earlier?"

"I said a number of things. Which one do you mean?"

"Jenny, for the love of heaven." He jerked her into his arms, and it wasn't until she slammed against his chest that he realized how willingly she'd come.

"You big oaf," she said, solidly planting her lips over his before he had a chance to kiss her. Wanting her as badly as he did, for as long as he had, Trey nearly crumpled to the floor under the weight of his joy. The kiss was slow and deep and moist.

"Oaf?" he repeated, holding her head so he could kiss her

again and again. Fifty years wouldn't be nearly enough to satisfy him.

"You didn't stick around long enough for me to answer. If you're going to propose to a woman, the least you can do is wait for the response."

He kissed her just long enough to cut off her tirade. "Answer me now."

She threw back her head and laughed. "First I think I'll make you suffer."

She hadn't a clue to how much he'd already been suffering. His breath came fast and heavy as she brought his mouth down to hers once more.

"Jenny, I love you."

"Yes, I know. We're going to be very happy, Trey. First we're going to get married, then we're going to start our family. I want a house full of children. I've been so hungry for family."

His throat went thick. "That sounds perfectly fine with me." He kissed her a dozen times, and even the gentleness between them, the love and tenderness, were far from being sated. "What about New York?" He had to know.

"Michelle got the part."

"But I heard . . . Irene asked to talk to you."

"It's true they offered it to me first, but when I declined, the role went to Michelle."

"But this was your big dream."

"I loved New York, but I love you more. Montana is where I belong, right here with you. I knew it a long time ago, but was too stubborn to admit it. I'm home now."

The back porch light went on, and Dillon appeared on the top step, although there wasn't any chance he could see them. "Hey, you two, it's about time for church. Are you ready or not?"

Trey's hand squeezed Jenny's. "We'll be inside in a minute."

"Is there going to be a wedding?"

"Yes, sir," Trey shouted back. "Soon, too, the sooner the better."

Dillon laughed. "Welcome to the family."

Trey kissed Jenny one last time, and with their arms wrapped around each other, they headed for the house.

They hadn't gone more than a few steps when thick, flat flakes of snow drifted down from the sky.

"I thought you said it wasn't going to snow," Dillon challenged, waiting for them on the back porch.

Trey looked up to the bright, clear sky. "I don't know where it's coming from," he mumbled, puzzled.

"Maybe someone up there is telling us how pleased they are to hear we're going to be married," Jenny suggested.

Trey kept his eyes trained on the cloudless sky. "Maybe you're right."

"It seems to me we've met in a similar spot before," Gabriel said to Shirley, Goodness, and Mercy as they sat in the choir loft of St. Philip's. The congregation crowded into the church for the Christmas Eve ceremonies. Candles brightened the interior, and pure red poinsettias decorated the altar.

"Hello again," Shirley said, leaning over the loft to get a better view of Brynn and Roberto. The two sat together, holding hands and singing. They appeared to have eyes only for each other.

"Brynn's decided to stay," Shirley told Gabriel, although it was unnecessary. The archangel was well aware of Brynn's future plans.

"You outdid yourself, Shirley. You all did. I'm proud of you."

All three prayer ambassadors blushed with pleasure. "Thank you," Shirley said.

"There is that one small matter involving Brynn's car, however."

Shirley glanced guiltily toward her two friends, whose attention seemed to be conveniently occupied elsewhere. "I had to do something, and fast," she rushed to explain. "She was about to leave, and the church bus was due any time."

"Don't worry about it," Gabriel said benevolently. "Tampering with a car engine is small potatoes compared to horsing around with the Statue of Liberty."

That captured Goodness's and Mercy's attention.

"What does the future hold for Brynn?" Shirley asked in a diversionary tactic.

"Ah yes, Brynn."

"Will she marry Roberto?" Shirley asked.

"Yes, next year at this time, to be exact. Eventually Roberto will find a way out of this neighborhood, too. His shop will inspire other Hispanics to start their own businesses."

"What about Emilio, Suzie, and the baby?"

"Emilio will go on to college and become a teacher himself. The day will come when he'll be at Manhattan High once more, but not as a student."

"Emilio?" Shirley didn't bother to disguise her amazement.

"He's an intelligent young man."

"What about Suzie and Modesto?"

"Suzie will have a baby girl in the spring. She'll decide to raise the child herself, and with the help of Mike's mother and her own family she'll be able to attend college. Suzie is going to major in medicine and do great work in the study of depression and its treatment."

"And Modesto?"

Gabriel frowned and shook his head sadly. "Not long after he recovers from the gunshot he'll become heavily involved in drugs and waste his life."

"Oh, dear."

"What about Trey and Jenny?" Mercy asked.

"Ah yes, Jenny." Gabriel turned his attention to Mercy. "Isn't it amazing that snow would fall from a cloudless sky?" He watched his favorite prayer ambassadors squirm and had a difficult time not chuckling.

"They'll marry on Valentine's Day," he informed her.

Mercy clapped her hands together. "That's perfect."

"In the next six years they'll add two girls and two boys to their family. The girls will be as talented as their mother, and the three will form a singing group and frequently perform at church functions. The boys won't be able to carry a tune to save their lives."

"That's sweet. Will Jenny have any regrets about giving up her chance to perform on Broadway?"

"Not a one," Gabriel assured Mercy.

"Hannah and Joshua?"

"Ah yes . . ." Gabriel scratched the side of his face. "They'll marry this June, and Hannah's mother will fight with the wedding coordinator from the first moment they meet. The wedding will be one of the most talked-about affairs in New York. It'll be lovely." Gabriel smiled to himself. "Ten years from now, when their son and daughter are still young, Joshua will run for state senator and win. Joshua realizes that Hannah is not only his wife and partner for life, she's his greatest political asset as well.

"Are you ready?" Gabriel asked, gesturing skyward.

The three nodded. In the distance the archangel could hear music from the harps of heaven. It was a night wrapped in glory and time for them to head home.